See what others have said about Peter A Hubbard's 'Tears' trilogy

The US Review of Books "The result is a masterclass of investigative acumen, psychological insight, and global coordination."

HOLLYWOOD Book Reviews "The writing style has a literary structure that crafts poignant visuals drawing you into the intensity of the moment, such as a mushroom cloud described with sooty gray contrails against the blue sky and compared to a canvas from Dante's Inferno."

Pacific Book Review "The action and intensity of the plot balanced out the depth of relationship building that occurred with this cast of characters, from the protagonist's own traumatic past that brought her into the field and into a life of government and military service, to the tragedies which befell the children who would become the faces behind the movement which these terrorists fuel their campaign with."

Christina Avina-Professional Book Reviewer "As a fan of this genre, I was enthralled with the author's writing and was even more moved by the rich themes developed in this book, including the heavy look at the morality behind those who are radicalized or brainwashed into committing such heinous actions after having witnessed or experiencing their own brand of injustice early on in life. The cycle of violence and destruction plays a major role in this thriller."

Look for The Tears of Hope
The Tears of Wonder
The Tears of Joy

And the best 'How to' book ever written, 'The Handbook of Personal Power'.
Find them at https//: pahubbardbooks.com, or
https://linktr.ee/peterahubbard

the island of tears

BOOK 4 OF THE *TEARS* STORIES

PETER A. HUBBARD

Published in the United States of America

Brilliant Books Literary
137 Forest Park Lane Thomasville
North Carolina 27360 USA

ISBN:
Paperback: 979-8-88945-394-9
Ebook: 979-8-88945-395-6
Hardback: 979-8-88945-396-3

Mollydookers
ADVERTISING I DESIGN I DIGITAL I PRINT

CHAPTER ONE

The room was lit in part by the strident sun, cutting through the early morning haze to blaze away at the adobe structure. Outside, the desert sand fluttered uncomfortably, uncertain whether or not to fly away in the light wind or just sink back to the ground exhausted. Outside, it was over one hundred and twenty degrees, the sky a deep blue without a single blemish. Inside, it was a cool seventy-two degrees, maintained by heat sinks and clever engineering that nanotechnology had made possible. That part of the room that escaped the sun was illuminated by soft incandescent bulbs shaped like airy balloons, floating just below the rough wooded ceiling, which had been shaped out of planks from a recovered sunken galleon.

The ocean respected the desert, and the tiny waves that broke on the foreshore were so small as to only move single grains of sand. The light woosh the lazy sea made was the only sound that could be heard unless you entered that room and suddenly your body would vibrate with the stirring melody from an ancient wind-up record player, on which an even older record, warped from years of abuse, bobbed up and down as it rotated, its scratchy sound making the billowing explosion of the orchestration all the more potent for the added reality of scratches and hisses.

To her ear, the 1812 overture had never sounded better with its booming, thudding conclusion. A lone woman, slender of build, long jet black hair falling evenly to her waist, her sun brown skin radiating both health and inner strength, stood slowly and looked at the majesty of the natural elements fighting each other for time and place, in their endless dance that had been billions of years in the making. Wearing a loose-fitting tropical-colored caftan with bright blue painted toenails peeking out of a ruffled hemline, she looked like a runway model on holiday.

Well, her little evolution had only been three decades in the making, and her role in it was just eight years long. But she liked to think that what she and others like her had achieved in that short time would surpass or at least equal the most potent natural disasters the planet had ever experienced. And in a strange way, bring balance back into a fractured world. Her partner, just one year younger but by far decades smarter, lay sleeping guilelessly on the multicolored couch. They had worked for the last thirty hours nonstop to put the finishing touches on the work they judged to be their finest.

The vast laboratory that sat under their feet, cheerfully hidden by bohemian rugs and throws, ancient furniture turned black with age, and casually placed bric-à-brac, was still humming. She could feel it through her long, bare feet. Machines that hadn't existed just a year ago had been left rumbling and singing to themselves in the way well-behaved machines do as they completed their computer-directed and monitored tasks. While she didn't question what they were doing, she was sad that their campaign to free abandoned refugee children around the world had come to such a sudden stop, due to anticipated political greed, the never-ending lust for power, and the ubiquitous human need for homeostasis.

And politics.

Her sisters had launched the most devastating attacks on an unwary world just months ago, initially succeeding in their primary objective - to get thousands of young parentless children out of festering refugee camps and placed in loving homes. Three locations had gone 'live', one at a smallish town in the mid-west of America called Helena; one in the famous historical city of Roanoke; and one in faraway New Zealand, in the small township of Dargaville.

Their brilliant plan to have young, parentless refugees placed in loving homes had worked, and over four thousand bright young girls now had adoptive parents dedicated to their care and nurture. And the homes they were living in were the most magnificent example of advanced technology ever conceived.

Then a converted cruise liner carrying five thousand displaced children under the age of ten on its way to America had been sunk in the Atlantic Ocean. How and by whom was not known. But what was known was that one of her sisters, captaining a converted gunboat on its way to place undetectable nuclear shells in strategic locations around America to force the hand of the American government, had been unceremoniously blown out of the water by the navy.

That, and the fact that Interpol had managed to take some thirty other nuclear shells out of circulation, preventing the planned blackmail the women had been relying on to achieve their aim, had effectively killed their 'Plan B.' But, as her feet vibrated to the silent music of her underground machines and her body resonated to the finale of the booming and scratchy orchestration, she smiled.

They had a 'Plan C', and she and her companion would once again engage a careless world in their endeavor to free every young, desperate, abandoned refugee child and provide them loving homes and a chance to live with hope in their hearts all around the world.

After all, their mentor had set up sufficient funds years ago, in nineteen countries, to guarantee the success of their quest. Billions of euros and dollars had been salted away in trust funds specifically for just this one purpose.

Advanced technology machinery had been provided following the devastating attacks to allow the world to move on again, albeit in a more natural, ecologically responsible manner, and all the world had to do was pay attention as they peeled back layers of the technology onion, adjust their thinking, and start caring for the planet and the refugee children as much as they cared about their wallets.

The one thing that they had all learned from their experience of changing the world forever by killing off all sources of fuel, oil, gas, and coal, killing the internet, crashing almost every computer on the planet, and attacking strategic targets with drones and automated weapons, setting the religious world on fire, is that they could not trust mercenaries to do their job properly. While in the main, the mercenaries had executed their tasks, their natural greed and lack of a moral compass and conscience had ensured their destruction by both Interpol and the armies and navies of the world.

Now the women would have to rely on another type of warrior - a homegrown one, an invisible one, one who had been liberated from the horror and certain death in the refugee camps, placed in loving homes, and educated to the fullest extent of their innate talent. Experience told them that they would not recruit one hundred percent of those refugees who now owed their lives to their mentor and his incredible plan to change the world, but they only needed a precious few, and they would succeed.

Nothing was surer in her mind. She turned to her companion and lovingly tapped her on the shoulder.

"Crissy, time to wake and shine. We have things to do, places to go, people to see. It's our turn in the sun!"

CHAPTER TWO

The problem with numbers is that once they get too large, most people don't relate them to their actual impact. Ask a person working in a factory if what they do every day can remediate a large corporate loss in the millions, and most will say 'no.'

So how would you react to these numbers?

Over fifty million people were killed, millions more were injured, and a billion or more people were displaced from their homes, now migrating across whatever border was handy.

Tens of millions of cars and vehicles of all types were abandoned and stranded where they had stopped, blocking roads and freeways with their rusting carcasses, looking like a massive encrustation on the bottom of a boat gone wrong.

No fuel—gas, oil, or coal—other than heavily protected strategic reserves which were the sole province of governments, and diminishing by the day.

No internet-no world-wide media-no computers, except for a very few lucky people working outside the chaos of what was the 'new' world. Old-style analogue phone lines still existed, unreliable undersea cables still linked parts of the world, and the most precious possession a person could have was an old-style phone handset and a fax machine. Or if you had a very, very old valve-powered short-wave radio, and knew how to use it, you were king of your narrow world.

No internet. None at all, and children deprived of their digital drugs ran around like demented souls until it sunk in.

And the real problem with the internet had been that the 'three clicks', 'three-second' attention span had made everyone immune to the reality of what was happening around the world in real-time, measured in weeks, days, hours, and minutes. Broadcast news had degenerated into soundbites, talking heads, and journalists making the news instead of reporting it. The so-called news cycle had gained a life of its own, fulfilling its own prophecy. Fake news!

Then it had all stopped in what had seemed to be a single heartbeat, and the previously overburdened airwaves sighed with relief and into the ensuing vacuum created by no information, no manufactured opinions, no talking heads to tell us all what to do and how to think, and the end of fake news, flowed panic. Unmitigated people power at its very worst.

Corporate and government distrust was at an all-time high when the terrorists struck, and the reaction of ordinary people was immediate and devastating.

But predictable.

Roaming gangs of cutthroat individuals out for lust and savagery, killing and pillaging as and where they wished. No reason why, other than the very fabric of civil order had completely collapsed in many countries, allowing the most base of human instincts to surface and uncontrolled, cut loose like a huge farm machine scything through a wheat field.

Corrupted, festering, bloated, rotting bodies littered the streets, creating all manner of disease, and from the outside, the world truly felt as if it had come to the edge of a precipitous, momentous decision, where the only choice besides immediate death and starvation was run and hide, and pretend.

Pretend it would get better, pretend it would all go away, pretend that someone would come and save you from the dark.

Lawmakers in every country fled from their seats of once presumed power, hiding out from their constituents, pretending to be just 'ordinary' people, fearful for their lives. But they died just the same as everyone else did and suddenly found that there was such rage in the world that all the money, all the possessions, all the wealth, all the knowledge and skill they might have acquired was worth less than nothing and actually put a target on their back, and on the backs of their families.

There were pockets of sanity, mostly in small towns in rural areas, which, after the initial shock of the worldwide attacks wore off, became prime destinations for fleeing families focused purely on survival.

It was personal. How can I feed my family and keep them alive?

Food and water shortages were legion. Neighbors bashed and attacked neighbors for a loaf of bread or a tin of baked beans. All the social capital that had been accumulated during the recent pandemic and the global consolidation created by Russia's insane attack on Ukraine and other European countries had been destroyed by wanton greed, or the strong will to survive.

With no oil, gas, or coal, no internet, very little commerce, almost no computers or electronics, and total chaos dominating most landscapes, the world was in a serious amount of hurt and looked to stay that way for the foreseeable future.

Interpol Section Five's involvement had started in earnest with the interrogation of a young woman, who came to be the pivot in the hunt for the female refugee terrorists who had authored the greatest selective destruction and terror ever experienced. However, the damage from the terror attacks had started days before the interrogation and would continue for the next three months or longer, if we didn't slap them down. Unfortunately, we were decades late to the party, and played catch-up for the first two months, until the terrorist agenda became clear, and some of the terrorists had been successfully removed from the game board. But the threat was still very much real, as we were learning from a bitter and tragic experience.

On the day that Amira (no last name at this time) was taken out of the refugee camp at Baalbek, Lebanon, sometime around or just after the turn of the century, one hundred and six children under the age of ten died, to be added to the pile of dead bodies in the fire pit reserved for this gruesome daily task. The average was one hundred and forty dead every day, so, in many ways, this was a good day for the camp.

It was a very good day for Amira, around five or six years old, orphaned by a senseless war, and still alive only due to happenstance in that she had been collected up while still essentially a baby with a hoard of other distressed and abandoned children and taken to the camp by nurses from the Red Crescent.

With no one to claim her, she was literally dumped in a large tent that already held some two hundred children and just two adults – women who had taken on the task of trying to keep their young and mostly compliant changes alive for another day. They did their very best, replaced by other loving women from time to time when the task proved too much, and in spite of the odds, kept many of their charges alive. As fast as some died, their beds were filled with the next collection of abandoned children.

The fact that these conditions existed, that the UNHCR and other Aid Agencies visited these camps at least annually, and that the death rate was so high and so consistent, yet the continual wars and skirmishes forced more and more desperate people into these camps, was a global tragedy that the whole of the modern world should have taken responsibility for.

And do something about it.

It didn't, and as the crisis in the camps got worse throughout the Middle East, Europe and Northern Africa—if you can imagine worse—an Iman who was teaching in a camp next to a Jesuit priest in a cobbled-together school decided to take matters into his own hands and rescue the smartest and the brightest of the starving children and have them fostered by caring families around the world.

Everything in Amira's testimony had been set in motion by a single Iman pissed off at his family, for reasons unknown, but easily guessable. A man with untold wealth, because by chance he had the money, being seventh in line for the Throne of Arabia, and one of the many signatories of the Pan Arabia Wealth Fund. He started setting up seemingly legitimate funds in multiple countries, and as we found out—once we had taken down the lead mercenary, a stunningly professional killer known as 'Shetani', and analyzed his communications with Al Hemish al-bin Mohammad Karesish, or Mohammad bin Azaria as he had changed his name to — billions and billions of dollars had been secreted in some thirty countries that had fueled the attacks that had crippled the world

Of course, there was a lot more to this story, as we all found out around twenty years after he had taken the first of the refugee children, when in a series of stunning attacks by unmanned aircraft and other vehicles the Vatican was bombed at the time of the Conclave to elect a new Pope, chopping off the head of the Catholic Church in one foul blow; sixty percent of the Dome of the Rock was destroyed, causing both Christians and Muslims to rise up in arms; sections of the Grand Mosque were blown up, further driving nails into the sides of Muslins all over the world; West Point was carpet bombed, killing thousands of cadets as well as the Chief of Staff, causing Americans all over the world to arc up; the Internet was destroyed, creating havoc in the world's communications, and some said, took everyone back to the nineteen seventies in terms of capability and capacity; the Space Station was destroyed, and by a fluke of timing, with no loss of life, as the astronauts were practicing an evacuation maneuver at the time of the attack; ninety five percent of the world's oil, gas and coal supplies were destroyed or blocked, some of them for thousands of years, and Lloyds of London, the oldest and most respected insurer and reinsurer had been crippled by the permanent destruction of their three major data hubs.

The world, literally, was in chaos. Civil war broke out in most countries, with hundreds of thousands killed or displaced. Commerce at any level, local, national, or international, stopped dead in its tracks. Survivors foraged in garbage dumps or simply killed their neighbors for whatever food they had tucked away. Anarchy reigned supreme, and in some countries, the situation was so bad it was impossible to see how they could ever recover. The worldwide pandemic of just five years previous had taught a strong lesson about the strength of community, which had promptly been discarded as household fought household, neighbor fought neighbor, and ultimately, county fought country.

And people fled the big cities in their thousands, heading to the smaller towns and villages where the disruption was seen to be less brutal, and the possibility of retaining some sort of humanity a little higher.

And in the post-terrorist attack analysis that I was currently working through, all seven hundred pages of it, the likelihood was it had been masterminded by one man and carried out by less than ten women ex-refugees, and a bunch of around three hundred mercenary terrorists. And an ex-Stasi agent. If I hadn't lived through it all attack by attack and been so closely involved from day one as an investigator for Interpol, I would have not believed it possible that so few people could do so much damage on a global scale.

And in such a short amount of time.

It was, undoubtedly, the most sophisticated, technologically orientated attack since the atomic bomb was dropped on Japan.

Less than twenty-three days from the first attack until the mercenary terrorists had been wiped off the face of the earth by a series of coordinated military actions in sixteen countries instigated by intelligence provided by Interpol.

Interpol had been able to have observers at two of these attacks, up close and personal, thanks to a cadre of military specialists attached to our unit.

Due to the sheer scale of the attacks and their aftermath, we had been forced to consider the possibility that the investigation would have to be conducted in two or three phases — as we had been directly involved in the forceful elimination of the mercenary terrorists in the middle of our investigation into the banker and his refugees after they physically attacked one of our working locations.

The small problem of discovering that every area of interest to investigators worldwide suffered from some type of electronic masking was just the icing on the cake. We knew exactly where some of the terrorists had been hiding — but all movement in and out of those areas was invisible to us, even before they crashed the internet.. There was some very sophisticated technology being used against us, and it seemed that it had been developed, at least initially, by some of the refugees once they reached the University level of their education. And by people embedded in our systems for perhaps thirty or forty years.

How did we come to this conclusion?

Well, Amira's interrogation pointed to the major highlights but left a lot unanswered.

Her sponsor, a woman called 'Helen'-and ex Stasi field agent named Natasha Trotsky-had offered Amira a role going forward in the planning and execution of the worldwide attack, but Amira had stalled, hidden, then done a runner and remained invisible to the world for five years. Subsequently, all her work was stolen by her partner, a Chinese master hacker, and her sponsor, who had effectively mentored her through the various schools and colleges, mostly as a means of keeping an eye on her and her work, until the field trial of her breakthrough nano work in Nova Scotia.

Amira's principal work had been in nanotechnology, both of the oil-eating variety and the kill-the-image type — we had experienced the bitter end of both developments and struggled to make headway against their impact. She had also worked on computer code, and her work had led directly to the terrorists being able to conceal areas of interest from prying eyes for some years.

But through diligent police work, the expert assistance of special forces from our member countries, and a lot of grit and determination we had rid the world of the main plotters, planners, and facilitators of these gruesome attacks on humanity. Or so we had thought.

We had a large number of prisoners, all locked away in concrete holes for the rest of their natural lives, the prime agents removed from the playing field, and now at the just-past-three-month mark, a sullen quiet had descended on the world, as leaders everywhere looked to the sky for hope, in the form of incredibly efficient solar panels and power packs, a product of the genius that had been the refugee women, designed and created by them as part of their 'Plan B' to reestablish order in a broken world. And give hope. And force the acceptance of thousands of young, smart girls being moved out of the refugee camps into private homes.

What a brilliant plan it was!

Their geniuses had designed ecological factories that, using nanotechnology, produced seriously super-efficient panels and power supplies and had created whole communities that they had sent these to, having seeded the sites with six billion euros some five or six years previously in order to create ecologically responsible homes and communities, homes which they sold at a heavy discount to displaced families who had fled the major cities at the peak of the civil unrest.

The kicker in the contract was that to be able to purchase a four-bedroom home in a magnificent neighborhood for $150,000 or less, they had to accept a young refugee child. If they did so, they not only got the home but also an annual stipend of $50,000 to support the refugee child, and all their education and medical bills were taken care of. And if they had their own children, they were provided with free education all the way through college.

It was a seriously good offer and one that the family of John Vernon, Special Agent FBI, had taken up in Helena, the hub of the first detected refugee project. He had collected his children just two weeks ago and was already enamored with the bright young girls, who exhibited all the hallmarks of high intelligence and quick wit. He and his wife were working as hard as they could to weave the newest members of their family into their daily lives and they were both challenged and heartened by the experience.

They both were still having issues with the way their little girls hoarded their food, hiding at least half of every meal in a small tin hidden under one bed. The psychologist who was supporting them believed it would only be a matter of time before this behavior changed, as the girls became convinced that the food would not suddenly disappear.

Nearly a thousand other families were sharing the same experience, as the new township of "Hope", as it had been labeled by the Helena city council, grew organically as more and more homes went up. There were two other cities springing up at a similar rate, one in Roanoke, the other in faraway New Zealand, in a little town called Dargaville. The only blight on the terrorists' plans was that one of their own—Maribelle Assiano, a woman terrorist who had fled from her bolt hole in Ireland just before the local Garda arrived to arrest her—sank a ship on its way to America full of refugee children, with the loss of everyone on board.

No one understood why she had done that to her own cause.

Like the converted luxury passenger liner, she and her modified gunboat were now just a collection of radiated particles, some deep in the mud of the ocean bottom and some still being carried around the Atlantic by the wind, her crew and boat having been comprehensively blown out of the water—literally—by American submarines.

The nuclear material she had stolen and had planned to utilize in undetectable nuclear bombs had imploded during the attack, creating a tsunami so large it bashed itself to the death against the shores of every country that had exposure to the Atlantic Ocean; it had rolled an American destroyer, and nearly sunk two submarines, and thrown the aircraft carrier I was on up and around like a toy!

It was an experience I never wanted to have again.

I had Agent Vernon's report on my chipped desk, right next to a report from the geeks confirming that we still had at least 36 more women refugees to find and deal with that we knew of, out of some 700 who had been placed in homes all over the world. At some point, I would have to determine how the adoptive families had been found and the children placed. For now, finding the remaining women had to be my focus, so I turned my attention to Indigo, the head of our Italian office and the king of the geeks. Unlike my two partners, he was dressed smartly in his office attire, a stunning blue/black uniform with red stripes running up his legs, making him look taller than he really was. One side of his chest was decorated with colorful ribbons, attesting to the deadly combat he had been exposed to and survived during his legitimate and storied military career.

We didn't give out medals; if we had, the other side of his chest would be flooded with them as well.

"Indigo, how certain are we that this is the number?" In his usual fashion, he delicately placed a massive mug of steaming coffee on my desk, then with a flourish, handed mugs to Sandra and Fay, both of whom were sprawling on the ancient leather couch someone had dragged into the dark corner that served as my office. Sandra was, for her, dressed down, wearing a bright blue tracksuit split open to her waist, revealing an even brighter green t-shirt with frogs jumping all over it. Thankfully, Fay has dressed more appropriately, in neutral cargo pants and a jacket, but her booted feet were up on a metal chair that had been reversed for the purpose.

I had given the entire team a day off, and I was now paying for it as the tempo in the office was at zero. No geeks beavering away, no screens shouting rude things at us—even the usual Italian guard was noticeable by their absence. We weren't back on the clock for another two hours, so I had no choice but to accept the somewhat relaxed and out-of-character behavior of my team, who had simply turned up once they found out I was at my desk.

"Jessica, we have run the data through several times, and Shami, Luigi, Stefarino, and Malcolm have gone through all the intelligence we took from Trotsky, and they agree on the number of women who now have no information or families in the system. The FBI, as you can imagine, are being very thorough, as are most of the other security agencies. The magic number is 36." I looked at my Italian head; dressed as he was, he looked sleek and sharp, unlike my two female companions, who looked like they had just rolled out of their beds. Or someone else's. Then I looked at my drab apparel, which under the circumstances made me queen of the fashion stakes, and decided to celebrate the fact that they had turned up and let everything else go.

Besides, even if they had arrived in hessian sacks, they would still have made me look bland, no matter what I had on.

"Okay, is anyone interested in an early breakfast?" Two pairs of sleepy eyes turned to look at me, and Indigo bobbed his head. I stood up, pulled a windcheater over my shoulders, and headed out the massive stone archway that led to the canals. I felt rather than saw Fay and Sandra behind me, and as we exited the ancient church we used as our headquarters in Italy, we were swarmed by uniformed troops, who formed up around us protectively.

"*Stai giù, per favore, stiamo solo facendo una breve passeggiata.*" They ignored me, so I gave Indigo a hard look; he got the message and waved to the guards, who retreated back into the walls. I walked on, heading down the narrow walkway around an old building now covered with moss and slime, half in and half out of the canal, then past the entrance to a museum, across a small bridge, and then to an even smaller trattoria, where we snagged an outside table. Indigo hurried over to the owner, someone we had gotten to know over the weeks we had been in our new headquarters, placed our order, then sat down next to me, facing the canal. Sandra has zipped up her tracksuit and was now visibly vibrating with energy, bouncing up and down on her seat, an ancient stained wicker chair that was probably six times as old as she was. Fay had managed to sit on the other side of me, so in effect, I was surrounded again, with no choice in the matter.

Buggar the Boss and his directives!

My dark thoughts were shredded by the aroma of excellent coffee, which a busboy dressed in a starched white shirt and red waistcoat set in front of us, followed by huge pastries filled with egg, cheese, salami, and green herbs, which leaked out the sides like an amoeba trying to escape an attack by a squid.

I drank and attacked the breakfast as if it would be the last one I would have for some time. Which had been my experience over the past few months. Suddenly, Sandra tensed up, knocking my knee with hers, and I saw her weapon appear from out of her tracksuit top. What had caught her attention was a magnificent canal boat, which was just sliding to a stop twenty meters from our office. Indigo was speaking rapidly into a small handheld, and I saw the flash of his guards disappearing into the entrance.

All hell broke loose, the side of our office blew out, rocks and bricks streaking up into the sky followed by dark smoke, only to come crashing back down into the canal, leaving thin wisps of bright gray contrails trailing behind them. Then the percussion reached us, just as Indigo and Sandra pulled me to the ground and behind the table that Fay had upended. We were showered and pelted by brick matter, dirt, dust, and smelly bits of the canal, and we could just hear the boat returning the way it had come. Sandra was reaching around the table to take a shot, but I pulled her hand back in and shook my head.

"No. Let them go. Indigo, get the locals on it, please." Sandra gave me a look that was full of anger, but I forgave her, they knew where our office was but obviously didn't have assets close to us on the ground, or they would have taken us out at the trattoria. We waited for the debris to subside, then slowly stood up, our breakfast now just a dim memory. The owner ran out, all apologetic. Indigo calmed him down, paid him, and then we slowly and very carefully, walked back. Our office was now at least one layer thinner, and we could see the exposed red brick that made up the middle sandwich of the immense stone wall that had stood for centuries. The guard and a posse of soldiers had come from somewhere and were busily throwing rock and brick into the canal, clearing the doorway, which because of its clever design snaked through a big 'S' bend, which had effectively prevented whatever the terrorist had fired at us from penetrating the office.

However, the blast wave had done considerable damage, and Indigo had tears in his eyes as we surveyed the smashed screens, battered espresso machines, workstations, and library walls. Even my dark corner was now just a pile of rubble. I rolled my shoulders, and Sandra flicked her blond hair back from her face as she placed her hands on her hips.

"Well, we were going to redecorate; maybe this is a sign?" Her bubbly expression belied her anger, but at least the lights were on, and her green eyes sparkled with contained fury. Fay was more reserved and tilted her head to one side as if looking for something.

"So, if this is normal, maybe I'll consider going back to the relative safety and calm of the FBI!" We all laughed, Indigo came in and looked at me with tears in his eyes, the office was his, after all, and he rubbed his gritty hands together as if washing something off.

By my count, this was the eighth time the terrorists had tried to kill me, or my team, including being shot down over the Atlantic, blown out of the air in two different helicopters, being shirtfronted by militia in Montana, thugs in Chicago, and trained terrorists in Israel.

"Ladies, my apologies, we need to move. A police boat has just been sunk, and the perpetrators are now busy getting away, but unless they head out to sea, they will find themselves in a trap somewhere. I've warned Tom, my brother, and have guards picking up the geeks. Where to?" His plaintive look warmed my heart; it was me they were after, not the team or even the office; a sadistic bastard had placed a fatwa on my head; the last news I had was thirty million euros; it was supposed to have been canceled, but maybe the message hadn't got to everyone yet.

Or maybe they just wanted me dead. Where to go? Then I had an inspiration.

"Indigo, get us all to the ship we commandeered; the US Navy has it parked somewhere. Get all our electronics on it. I will ask the admiral for a small crew." As I had already had a conversation with the admiral earlier today, I knew where he was and I knew his mood. I flicked open my mini, dialed him up, and watched his chiseled face swim into focus again.

"I thought I had got rid of you."

"No such luck, although someone just tried to blast us out of our headquarters, which is why I'm calling again." His face scrunched up in anger, his eyes went to tiny pinpricks, and he leaned so far forward that his face went out of focus.

"Who was it this time?" I shook my head and rolled my shoulders, an angry admiral wasn't going to hear me, so I tried to calm him down.

"Admiral, the second time they have tried for our office, the local police are on it; only superficial damage done to the building, although we will now move the geeks and our administrative team for a short time. I want to use that ship we took off the terrorists. Can you lend me a small crew? I'll have Tom stand up his team, and Indigo will provide his team, so we'll be well covered, but it would help to have a helicopter and some weapons if you can manage it."

"Where will you operate?"

"Probably in the Med, we need to do some deep diving into the data, and that will take some days, then we'll move back on land somewhere, once we get a handle on who attacked us." He pulled back, revealing that he too was dressed casually, but at least he had on a collared shirt.

"Give me an hour or two, and I'll see what I can set up. But for Christ's sake, don't get yourself killed!"

"No, sir. Thank you." And I hung up.

Luckily, Tom and his team with Indigo were used to moving us all around Europe, so we had it down pat. I thought the geeks might enjoy the novelty of working on a ship, then saw Indigo moving towards me with a serious look on his face.

"Comandante, i fanatici sono stati informati delle sue intenzioni e hanno un altro suggerimento."

"What's their suggestion?"

"They want to move in with Stefarino and his team." I thought about that. It was, in fact, an excellent idea, so I nodded.

"Make it so. A lot easier for us without all their gear in any case. We will need a solid link to them. The minis won't be powerful enough to handle all the data." He nodded, moved off to make the arrangements, and I looked around at my trashed corner, rescued some of the debris, then headed off to pack a bag. Before I could walk out of the room, my mini buzzed against my leg.

"Jessica, I'm nixing your move to the ship. There's a military facility the Italians will let us use; it's near Milan. Leave the geeks with the monks. I'll send you the location and details soonest." I looked at the Boss's face and wondered who had called him and why he didn't want us on the ship. But if the military base was well set up, or if we could set it up the way that suited us best, then that was a far better option. The directions and details came through, and I saw the three thousand-meter strip and buildings, and noticed that it nestled against the small hills of Comazzo. I flicked it to Tom and Indigo. Sandra looked over my shoulder and nodded.

"Much better idea." I looked at her, wondered how she kept up her bubby energy levels and snapped the mini shut.

"Just for that, you can manage the move." And I left her gaping behind me as I went to my room. Then to cap a perfect day so far, my mini buzzed at me again.

"Jessica, I just got a message from General Anthony, you're going to a land base, but that's not why I'm calling. We've just had a delayed report from the USS Indiana, the destroyer that we had in the Mediterranean. The one we pulled out to shadow the gun boat. It seems they picked up a trace of one of your shells on the way up the Irish Sea before they were rolled."

"Where?" My blood ran cold, the hair stood up on the back of my neck, and Sandra plowed into my back because I froze on the spot.

"A small town called Dundalk, on the east coast. The report was delayed because of the damage has been done to the ship by the tsunami, and the time it took us to get a salvage crew onboard." I nodded, understanding, I shook my head in disbelief at the trouble these women terrorists were causing us.

"Thank you, admiral, can you send us the tape, please?"

"It's on its way. Will you need our help?" I thought about that, thought about everything that had happened in the last two weeks, mentally positioned my teams to solve this new problem, and slowly nodded my head.

"Yes. Maybe. You still have your factory ship and her escorts in the Med?"

"Yes."

"Okay, leave them there for now. If we need backup, you'll be the first to know." I turned to look at Fay.

"Get yourself and Tom and the quick reaction team out to the airport. Once we're organized, Indigo will have to move us in absentia." She nodded and pulled her mini out. I dialed my favorite grandfather substitute.

"Arie, hi, sorry to bug you again, I need your C-17 and the 104 commando on standby again, fast jet, we've turned up another shell." His face showed his composure, but his eyes tightened noticeably, and he leaned forward slightly.

"Where?"

"Ireland." He visibly relaxed, having had two nuclear shells recovered from his doorstep in northern Gaza, then survived a nuclear explosion in south Gaza. One that has taken some seventeen hundred Israeli lives so far, with some still dying from radiation poisoning. And it was only the grace of God that there hadn't been more dead, because the wind was blowing out to sea and away from Israel at the time Amir Abbas had made his fatal mistake and turned himself and his cohorts into a bloody atomic mist.

"What do you plan to do?"

"Get Fay and the C-17 to confirm location, then the 104 can pick me up on their way to Ireland, and we'll sort it out from there." He nodded, obviously thinking all the options through.

"How did you not detect them the first time you swept the area?" I shrugged my shoulders. I could only think of one reason.

"Timing. We were too early." He nodded. Waved his hand in a circular motion, bobbed his head, and said.

"Stay safe, Jessica." And he disappeared from my screen.

So, we had more shells out there. I remembered the data the geeks had pulled from the Irish website, and it had listed target sites, all of which we had checked out with no result. Maybe timing again? Fay would have to find out once she pinpointed the location of the shell in Ireland.

Once the tape from the admiral arrived, I threw the data up on the big screen, one of only two to have survived the blast damage, tried to pinpoint the location, but the angle was too extreme, so all I could see was a positive signal in a ten-square-kilometer area. Fay would refine that. I thought about what we would need to do next, then looked at the map of Europe.

The original web page our geeks had pulled the data from was over a year old, but if a shell turned up in one location that had been mentioned, maybe it was wise to assume there would be others. I framed a target list in my head, transferred it to a message, and fired it off to Fay.

We were on the hunt again, and it felt good, but I still had an unanswered question bugging me. Then I started thinking again, shook my head in disgust, and tapped Fay on the shoulder to get her attention.

"Who do you have that can command the C-17 and the search?" She looked at me, her deep green eyes mirroring her confusion. One minute ago I had sent her off, and now I was stepping her down, and I cursed my current inability to just sit down and think calmly, and do something once, well.

"Ito, the navigator, is more than competent, and I can talk to him from wherever I am if he needs it."

"Good. Set it up. I want you back in Israel. I need you to question the girls who did the programming of the games, and the smart-arse psychologist, Rena Niele. I need to know where this nuclear threat strategy fits into their game plan. And yes, I should have asked them earlier, I just forgot to." She gave me a smile that suggested she wasn't upset at being sent off, which made me feel a little better. As a highly trained ex-FBI Supervisory Special Agent, her interrogation skills were possibly the best we had. I threw one more thing at her.

"Have Indigo send four of his boys and girls with you. They are not to let you out of their sight." She gave me a wan smile and disappeared off down the corridor to find Indigo. I knew how she felt. I had been shadowed by someone for the last month and a half, ever since the terrorists put a fatwa on my head. It cramped my style, and worse, to my way of thinking, it wasted valuable resources of which we only had a few in the first place.

Then I put my head back into the immediate game and thought through how the terrorists had managed to move shells under our noses, given the broad reach the use of the US Navy had given us, and concluded that one of only two options was relevant: the terrorists had yet another electronic method of camouflaging their equipment, or the timing had favored them in the first place.

My vote was on the timing because we had been very fast off the mark and very thorough in our scanning with ships, drones, helicopters, and planes.

In the end it really didn't matter. One had turned up in Ireland, and while we had found it by accident, I was always happy to have Lady Luck work for me.

"The 104 will be at DaVinci in fifty minutes. The C-17 is airborne and headed for the Irish coast, ETA is five hours from now. You need to get dressed." Sandra's voice worked its way into my brain, and I snapped back into the 'now'.

"Thanks. Get Tom and Bob to stand up a quick reaction team each, get Indigo to provide fast jet transport, and have them ready to fly at a moment's notice. If we missed one shell, we might have missed more. If I remember the original target list from the Irish website Paris and London were on it. Have we got detectors on our aircraft?"

"Yes, transmission and receptors, Indigo had three fast jets fitted just as a backup." I looked at Sandra, bouncing up and down like someone coming off a meth high, obviously excited about going after the terrorists again, and shook my head.

What it was to be young and fearless!

CHAPTER THREE

Moriah O'Sullivan sat in her apartment, overlooking the waterfront at Dundalk Bay, which at this time of the day was mostly mud and a weeping dredged boat channel, not totally unattractive but not one that would necessarily draw the tourists.

If there were any.

She turned from her desk and looked at the large wooden container perched up against her wall, the yellow stripe making it look both imposing and important. She did not know what was in it, and truth be told, she didn't want to. She had a detailed set of written instructions sitting on her desk. She only knew that four other young women, refugees like her, sat in their rooms in Dublin, Glasgow, London, and Paris, probably thinking the same thoughts as she was. The box had been delivered just weeks ago, with strict instructions to keep it safe, not try to open the military-specification coded locks, and to stand by for further instructions.

It was explained that she played a pivotal role in an operation to free more refugee children, and in all honesty, once she thought about her own history, she had little doubt that it was both her duty and her honor to help the women who had approached her. She had also been promised ten thousand euros, which would offset her lack of income in the last three months due to the chaos caused by the terrorist attacks.

She had been just ten when her parents were killed during the Russian invasion of Syria. They were left for dead alongside their burning handcart, on which the family's entire belongings lay smoldering. Ten was a very impressionable age in Moriah's short life. She took in her surroundings and the circumstances in which she now found herself in. She managed to survive long enough to be picked up by a woman with a red cross on her arm due to her innate intelligence. She had been taken to a refugee camp just across the border, where the conditions were simply atrocious, and as she huddled up inside her dirty, tattered, and patched dress, she swore she would get out somehow.

A burning pyre of little bodies was a constant reminder that she had to somehow escape from the stifling and corrosive environment she found herself in. It may well be seen as a haven from the atrocities outside, but to her it was a living hell.

It took her nearly six months before she finally drew the attention of a visiting nurse from Red Crescent, who was intrigued by her language skills. Sensing she had a wunderkind on her hands and aware of an old man's mission to save smart young girls, she took the little girl to a way station, where she was transferred to a dowl and sailed to her new home.

She didn't know where it was, and she didn't understand the language (old Gaelic), but she instinctively understood the open and unreserved welcome her new parents provided to her. They gave her their name and christened her 'Moriah,' after the family's maternal grandmother. She excelled in school, going off to the university in Belfast at fifteen on a full scholarship, where she majored in Social Psychology, International Politics and Law, and learned how to be a teacher.

She was regarded as one of the best to ever grace the campus of the little Catholic school just outside Dundalk, where she did her teaching apprenticeship, then was moved back to the university to work with Ph.D. students and lecture, where again, she thrived. Then, just six weeks ago, she was approached by one of her very senior law advisers. She was asked if she would, in memory of refugee children everywhere, store a box in her little flat. The professor had been very gentle, brushing her silken black hair back from her chiseled face, her bright brown eyes never leaving those of her protegee. The university had been shuttered since the attacks on the Vatican and the Dome of the Rock due to the immediate uprising of religious factions all over the country.

The conversation had occurred in her flat, and it had never occurred to her to ask how her tutor had managed to get to her amid the civil unrest that still surged up and down the country like an ocean wave gone rogue.

The same conversation was happening in four other cities, she was told, and the boxes would be collected sometime in the next two to three months.

She expected someone to turn up any week now to take it away from her, relieving her of her duty. A duty she would happily complete if only to see the smile on her tutor's face. But first she had to receive an encrypted radio signal, giving her the security code against which she could check the credentials of whoever came for the box.

She stared at the little burst transmitter that had been left with her, sitting on her desk with the thin black aerial wire running out her open window. A chilled wind whistled through the open gap, and not for the first time, she thanked her mother for providing her with the wonderful snow coat she had received for Christmas. Its fur-lined collar turned up; half of it hid her face, and her colored watch cap tried to hide the rest. Her creamy cheeks were still pink from the bitter cold, but she was used to small inconveniences, moving as she did daily between the university and her flat, some sixty miles apart, a commute she made in a very old and drafty Austin Morris that was new back in the nineteen sixties.

But beggars couldn't be choosers, and her stipend only went so far, and with her brother able to fix anything mechanical her car, though old in every single bit of it, ran like clockwork, albeit one with rusty springs and pushrods!

Except for the heater. And perhaps the driver's window on occasions stuck either open or half closed. But it was hers, free and clear, and she loved it as every bit as she did of her somewhat eclectic life.

She had defined listening times, ninety minutes apart, and so far, she had not missed even one of the transmission windows in nearly a month. But the only thing she had heard was silence, or if she turned the volume up on her set, atmospheric static. She had a small, portable, but very old valve tape recorder set up alongside the radio for those times she was asleep.

She was as prepared as she could be, so she waited with a calm and focused disposition as she read the undergraduate paper from one of her students. Reaching for her red editing pen, she sighed. The younger generation, energetic as they were, could not spell to save their lives!

"Moriah, come with me now, I can't wait any longer!" The sultry voice of her sister, always impatient and always full of energy, broke through her concentration. She slipped her thin reading glasses off her nose and looked at her sister with her iridescent green, pixie-like eyes and a wan smile. Today she had hidden her unruly yellow locks under a red and blue striped knitted beanie, reminiscent of something a passionate football fan might wear.

"And where would you be wanting to drag me off to now?" Her university remained shuttered because of the civil unrest, and the corrections she was now making were to three- or four-month-old papers she had rescued from her small room at the college before it had been closed down. By rights, she should have done her assessments much sooner, but to be truthful, she lacked the energy as the community around her shredded and tore itself apart. Against the backdrop of violence and bloodshed, marking exam papers seemed like a trivial task.

Her sister had become an expert at scrounging food and supplies with the help of her friends from the dance club. They had formed a strong, vibrant gang, even defending the apartment block from marauders.

"O'Malley has found an old wind-up record player, so we're going to have a dance and party in the old basketball court. We need you and your famous keys to make it all happen!"

The keys she was referring to were the building manager's that she had taken off his dead body after a brutal and vicious attack on the building two months before that had been fought off by the local Garda, but not without severe loss on both sides. Since then, everyone they could contact has been brought into the apartment block, housed, and looked after as best they could.

But she had kept the keys close and parts of the building locked away from curious eyes. She was not the eldest; she was just a young woman now with a new purpose in life, but with her sister's friends by her side, she managed to control the comings and goings in and out of the building in a sensible and, so far, safe manner. And many of her elders had recognized the steel in her spine and the unfailing intent in her eyes and added both their moral and physical support to her assuming the position of temporary building manager.

So she would give up her marking and accompany her sister to the basement, which had been converted into temporary housing for over a hundred homeless people as well as the core meeting area for any event. And next to it was a huge abandoned basketball court, locked away for times such as this. Old concrete pilings, barbed wire, and building refuse were piled in different corners, and the concrete floor bore a huge crack across the middle, almost as deep as a person. But the young gang members had cleared an area about the size of a half-court, swept away the debris, and claimed it as their own play area, albeit only accessible with the building manager's keys. Three tired and bent orange and white-striped road warning beacons provided the only barrier to the crack, and as in all things unnatural, they had taken on a life of their own in terms of reputation.

It was haunted. It had been made by the fairies, who were mad at humans for fighting each other. It was the work of evil spirits who cracked the earth in their anger. The truth was less glamorous—the foundations had been washed away over the years by unrelenting rain, and the concrete had simply collapsed.

They walked through the temporary cots and sleeping bags and maneuvered around the piles of personal belongings, the smell of cooking cabbage and boiled vegetables heavy in the air. During the day, the majority of the temporary residents used the common areas on the third floor, where a small gym, a larger TV room, and an even larger library offered a welcome break from the confining space of the basement. Women and children had claimed the library, and the men had claimed the TV room, where sports videos at least a year old were played over and over again. Strangely, some were still losing money betting on the prerecorded results!

Very few of the displaced people use the gym, something the occupants of the building were grateful for, as this gave them the illusion of their own space in spite of the crushing circumstances.

It was only two days after the first attacks on the Vatican, the Dome of the Rock, the Grand Mosque, and West Point that the civil insurrection started in Ireland. Mostly, it was Catholics arcing up over the deaths of the majority of Cardinals and the heads of the church protesting in the streets. Then the Muslim community, though small, took to the streets to add their fury to the mix. Then the rumors started about the lack of fuel and oil, crowding the streets with panicked people and providing a physical, visceral signal of exactly what had happened and what was at stake.

Then the internet stopped—computers went dark right across the world, and mass communication that had been taken for granted simply disappeared—and was never explained by any authoritative source.

Initially, people fled back to their homes, fearful of what might happen next. Then roaming gangs of disenchanted youths and thugs started to rule the streets, and the killing started.

The Garda—in this case—did their best, and the smarter citizens in Belfast and the other major cities in Ireland took to the hills, literally packing their belongings in cars and trucks and heading for the rural and remote areas of Ireland. Their pilgrimage was evidenced by the thousands of abandoned vehicles along every roadside, lane, and track, and in the case of places like Dundalk Bay, while many just passed through heading further south, some stayed, and the lucky ones were taken in as temporary residents in apartment buildings like Moriah's. This gruesome picture was replicated all over Ireland, in towns and villages big and small.

The death and destruction had moved through the country like a huge wave, finally dissipating when the military was authorized to shoot at their fellow citizens, something that had not happened in Ireland since the end of the Troubles decades ago.

There were still roving gangs, but they were now smaller and more discrete, choosing to work the remote farmhouses and smaller villages to the west. There was still great uncertainty, with food supply chains in tatters, and normal commerce non-existent. Bartering was the order of the day, and rural farmers and croppers were providing where modern industry could not.

It was not lost on those who still held the trembling and uncertain reins of power that Ireland had reverted back to what it did best—grow, harvest, farm, herd, and work the land still rich in potential, and survive by being cut off from the rest of the world as if swallowed by an abyss.

The biggest export Ireland was famous for was its people, who were smart, educated, bright, and agile. While exit immigration had slowed down a little since Brexit, it was a fact that the young still deserted Ireland in their droves.

Which had given the original female refugee planners an idea.

The country was fertile—surrounded by oceans on every side and rich in minerals and nutrients. At the time of the first attack three months ago, over 30% of the available housing was vacant, either left by families migrating to another country or just abandoned months or years before as their occupants tired of the daily struggle. The population of Ireland was less than three million, which was down some two and a half million from the highest figure recorded in 2022.

Their idea was simple: select women and children as blended families and set them up in the available accommodations while building energy-efficient, ecologically sound new dwellings, schools, universities, hospitals, and everything else needed for a new, modern civilization. Not one that would take over the lore, history, and culture of the country, but one that would drive a new narrative on the shoulders of the natural wonder that was Ireland.

Four massive trust accounts had been set up six years ago, and only one had been detected by Interpol and shut down after the terrorists built a special-purpose ship designed to rain down terror all over the Mediterranean. Once again, the mercenary terrorists had failed the women's cause, and in the end, even one of their own had turned against them, sinking one of the refugee ships with over five thousand young lives lost.

Add to that was the fact that Interpol had shut down their manufacturing facility in Toyoko, impounded all the ship sets that were known, and incarcerated the majority of the planners and women responsible for the first and second trajectories of terrorist attacks.

But now they were back on track.

They had five nuclear-capable shells hidden in Ireland, Scotland, England, and France that they had to hide at any cost. And they had their new nano weapon, which was more in the field of economics than atomics—the likes of which the world had never seen or even imagined before. And if their inspired solar panels and batteries had made their mark, then their new technology would dominate the world.

For a price. The freedom of every refugee child they could find.

Based on their success in getting the migration of young female children established in two locations, the United States and New Zealand, they had secured destinations for at least another two hundred thousand refugee girls. And that was before they opened up Canada, Greenland, Chile, Portugal, Denmark, Norway, Finland, Estonia, Sri Lanka, the Solomon Islands, Japan, and Iceland. Each of those countries could absorb at least thirty to fifty thousand refugees with ease; all they had to do was convince Interpol to remove the Red Notices they had placed on the accounting firms that held the funds.

Free up the manufacturing facility in Toyoko and use the engineers from the American Army who have successfully built two additional plants at Point Roberts.

Then an ecological plant could be fabricated in each country from the boxed ship sets that sat on their docks gathering dust, and the new towns and cities could be erected using the panels and power supplies. Commerce would grow organically around each development and become self-sustaining within years.

And that, generally, came down to what the Americans would allow to happen. They now had access to the technology the women had created, and they had two living models to duplicate. With Roanoke and Helena leading the way, they had the skills to replicate the model anywhere in the world where a plant could be established. And over twenty-five ship sets required to create a fully functioning plant were already in place, just waiting to be unpacked, erected, and put into production.

And what Moriah didn't know as she stepped into the dark, abandoned court, was that she had been selected to manage the first new village in Ireland, built as an extension of Dundalk Bay, using the new technology perfected by Kathryn and Crissy in the faraway Arabian Sea. A new village that would become the poster child for the women refugees and their plan to free every child they could, and as fast as they could. And a precursor to a million home plan.

She looked around at the crushed infrastructure and shook her head in sorrow at the wanton waste. She rubbed her sister on the shoulders, causing her long red hair to fly around her pretty face, and smiled wistfully.

"Make sure you stay away from that hole. I wouldn't want to be trying to fish you out of there anytime soon." Her sister mealy giggled as befitted someone only thirteen and full of life. A whole swag of young people came out of the basement in a noisy mess, and Moriah took her leave. She nodded politely to the few adults who stood at the edge of the court and made her way back up the fire stairs to her flat. They only had power for two hours a day, and that was used exclusively for cooking breakfast and dinner.

They were relying on masses of solar panels on the rooftop to charge scavenged ancient car batteries and, so far, were managing, supported by wind turbines that ran along the gutter on all sides. It wasn't what they were all used to, but it was what they had, so no good complaining. And now that everyone was eating fresh vegetables and meat straight off the farms surrounding the seaside town, the need for refrigeration had been minimized. The daily foraging by the gang of young people linked to her sister kept the building supplied, and bartering had become the new currency.

That was how they built the solar panels and wind farm.

As she entered her little flat, the gray, dull light from the overcast filtering between her hand-made curtains, she heard a shrill whistle and raced to the receiver. She saw her recorder working, so she relaxed and waited until the high-pitched noise stopped. She rewound the tape, drew in a deep breath, then pressed 'play' with one shaking finger.

"You will ask when, and they will reply 1916, 1920." The message was repeated three times, then stopped abruptly. She wondered who would contact her, sat back on her heels, and looked out at the sinking bay, where a flock of angry seagulls squawked and yelled their way across the mud flats. The air outside was listless as if Mother Nature was deciding what to do next. She flinched at a rapid knock on her door, stood, and turned to see a shrunken old man holding a battered fisherman's cap in his hands, surrounded by a pair of tough-looking boys, whom she judged to be in their late teens. For a fleeting minute, she wondered how they had gained access to her flat but just as quickly dismissed that thought. Whoever she was linked to had vast resources, so getting into a building would be the least of their problems.

"Begging your pardon, miss, my boys and I are to be picking up something from you if you please." She stared at the old man, sure she had never seen him around the town before or in her travels. She mentally made a note to investigate how they had gotten access to the block, but she shouldered that thought away as she walked toward the trio.

"Well, I suppose you'll be telling me when," she asked, folding her arms across her chest. The old man bobbed his head, and the two young men just stood somewhat stoic, also holding caps in their hands.

"That would be 19 and 16, then again in 19 and 20." She nodded silently, turned, and pointed to the green box with its yellow stripe.

"This be yours, then, so take it with my blessings." The two boys moved to the crate, lifted it as if it weighed nothing, then walked out of the flat. The old man looked up, his gray eyes sparkling in the wan light, bobbed his head again, then spun his cap in his hands, pushed one into his pocket, pulled out a stained, crushed envelope, and handed it to Moriah.

"Thank you, missus. It's a great thing you do, and we'll not be forgetting it anytime soon. Good day to you." And as quickly as they had arrived, they disappeared. She closed her door, part thankful the strange event was over, and part curious as to what was in the box. She put it out of her mind and thought about what she would do next, rolling the envelope over in her hands. Now that she had some funds to work with, she ran down her mental list of everything they needed to do to secure their home and look after her people.

Given that she had come from a destroyed family, she smiled at the thought that she had managed to make the over nine hundred tenants in the building and the one hundred odd they had collectively picked up off the street, her very own.

The musings were broken when the transmitter yelled at her, and in clear English, she heard an invitation, one she would have to hurry to satisfy. She grabbed her cap and her small purse and ran downstairs and out into the gray of the day. She looked skyward, but the overcast was impenetrable and uncommunicative, so she hunched her shoulders and continued onto her meeting.

With whom?

No idea.

Why?

Likewise. But the excitement of having the box collected and euros in her purse blinded her to the potential risk of being outside in daylight by herself.

She need not have worried as a small sedan, painted bright blue, pulled up, the back door opened, and her professor from her university beckoned her in.

"Moriah, I'm glad to be seeing you again," the older woman said, reaching across to take Moriah's hands in her own. The driver, a younger woman, turned and smiled, nodded her head in welcome, then turned back and started the car.

"I'd be Catlin, and I'm pleased to meet you as well." The car started off silently. The only noise was coming from the tires as they hit the ruts in the road.

"Where are we going?"

"Not far. We want to show you something and have a quiet conversation." Moriah nodded, as comfortable as possible, given that she was headed for an unknown destination. She looked outside and saw the ravages of the gangs and disenfranchised youths mirrored in the piles of refuse and burnt-out vehicle bodies that lay strewn alongside the road. Seeing such wanton destruction in her small town hurt her heart, and she sighed heavily.

She wondered if it would ever be normal again.

They pulled up next to a long wooden shed, through the slats of which the ocean could be seen, rushing in and out with an undefined purpose other than obeying the laws of nature and the pull of the moon. The three women stood in the cropped grass, taking in the pure beauty of the seascape: small white caps cresting and falling with a soothing rhythm, gray and black gulls yelling, swooping, and flicking at the baitfish that were out for an afternoon surf.

The air was chilly, the slight overcast adding an overall gloom to the day, with little pockets of sunshine fighting their way through like torches of the gods. Moriah felt the musical wash of the ocean, the screaming of the gulls, and the flow of the sweet air through her exposed face and hands and shook her head at the wonder of it. Catlin moved forward, breaking the spell, and opened the rickety door, letting out a mangy brown cat, who immediately rubbed itself against Moriah's legs, meowing at the top of its voice.

Catlin snapped on a torch, revealing a stack of very old machinery piled high and partially covered by tarpaulins with great rents in them, creating the impression of a long-forgotten dump.

"It isn't much, but we believe you and your girls can bring it back to life and give all of Dundalk hope and a purpose that will create a beacon that will light up the whole world."

CHAPTER FOUR

Fay, now dressed in urban camos bearing no military insignia or rank, swept her auburn hair back off her face, mindful yet again that she needed to get it cut. Sometime in the distant future. Maybe she would tie it back to keep it off her face. Who knew? Because since she had transferred to Interpol from the FBI some weeks ago, she hadn't had a single minute to herself.

Not that she minded; the compressed International Law classes, combined with learning the latest combat hand-to-hand techniques and how to use a plethora of weapons she had never even heard of before, had kept her busy twenty hours a day. Then she had been unceremoniously plonked down at Da Vinci airport, only to be swept up by a gang of Indigo's ninjas.

And now she was back in Israel, sitting at a very old and rusted desk, waiting for her first interviewee—Reve Nazreen, a 20 year-old genius who had been a major player in designing the computer games that the terrorists used to kill the world. Her sister, Anaisha, waited in another cell, right alongside Rena Niele, a slightly older woman who had been the master psychologist behind the planning of the attacks that had so devastated the world.

Fay's agenda was simple: find out where the use of undetectable nuclear weapons fit into the women terrorists' plans. It made no sense to anyone involved in the investigation. On the contrary, it seemed to be the fastest way to lose any social capital the terrorists may have accumulated since the first attacks.

"On the door!" she called, and a pair of slightly built Israeli soldiers, creased camos giving them a lived-in look, marched in, the 20 year-old girl between them, chains linking her hands to her feet, leading back to a dirty brown belt that surrounded her slight waist. Her hair, usually a blondish brown, looked like a spider's web, tangled and untidy, and in the black coveralls, she looked like a child playing dress up.

And she looked unhappy—very, very unhappy.

"I'm Inspector Remer, Interpol. You have already been interrogated by others, so let's get down to the root of it. In all your game-play development and conversations with others, where does using nuclear weapons fit into your scenarios?" The young girl looked haggard, a little gray around the gills, her eyes dull and flat, and Fay wondered if the Israelis were drugging her to maintain control. She shook her head, sending her scraggly hair flying across her face. Tears suddenly flooded her eyes and ran down her sunken cheeks like little waterfalls.

"Never! We never, ever planned on using tactical nuclear weapons. Why would we? They're an abomination!"

She lunged forward, sinking her head into her manacled hands, and sobbed. Fay waited a moment, let the tears run, let the drama flow, then slapped her hand on the desktop.

The sound of a gunshot had the desired results: the girl snapped back into her seat, her eyes wide and focused. Fay smiled to herself. In was a pantomime, and she was being played. And she hadn't used the word 'tactical.' Well, she hadn't gotten to be a lead investigator for the FBI by accident, so she took a deep breath, held the girl's eyes, then slowly nodded.

"Let's skip the theatrics, shall we? Simple question, where did using nukes fit into your grand plan?" The girl held her eyes, didn't blink, just stayed focused on Fay.

"I told you before, we never, ever planned on using nukes. My job was to make use of very old-style weaponry relevant to a modern day attack—which I did, with the help of my sister and a lot of online gamers. We made a game, nothing more. You can buy a copy for 60 dollars last time I looked." Fay held her aggressive stare and, for a brief second, mentally saluted the young girl's resolve, then put a hard cap on it, remembering what the 60 dollar game had enabled the terrorists to achieve.

Cripple the Catholic church for decades by blowing up the Vatican and killing Cardinals and thousands of worshipers at the time of the Conclave; destroying the Wailing Wall and rupturing the Dome of the Rock; bombing West Point with a massive loss of life; numerous other attacks, but perhaps the most serious, killing the internet and most computers; then denying the world any oil, gas, or coal for eternity. Against all this, the attack on Avion, the Grand Mosque, the shooting down of the International Space Station, the destruction of Lloyds of London financial databases, and the bombing of random sports stadiums seemed trivial.

But they weren't, as the social upheaval that followed these atrocities created unprecedented riots in every street in the world, with religious factions attacking everything they could see and gangs taking advantage of the social unrest to maim, murder and bloody anyone unfortunate enough to be caught in their sights demonstrated all too clearly.

"If that is true, then how come we have captured over thirty nuclear-capable shells made with machinery produced in your mother's factory in Toyoko, and almost used by members of your female cadre. All of whom we have killed or captured, just so you know?" Her young face went from horror to disbelief and back to horror in a parody of a painted white-faced Japanese Butoh dancer.

"And just as a sidebar, two of the shells were used by one of your terrorist friends to blow up half of the Gaza strip." Fay paused to let that sink in, then formed an evil smile. "And again, just to keep you up to date, he and his friends are now just bloody mist floating on the wind."

Intuiting that she would not get any further information out of the young terrorist, she called for the guards and set about interrogating Nazreen, the elder sister. She got nowhere, not even a flicker of interest in nuclear weapons, and that left

Rena Niele, the master psychologist who had analyzed and predicted most of the behavior of the nation-states that had been attacked by using advanced computer modeling.

And she had proudly boasted when she had been captured that they had used a Cray supercomputer for years to help predict what the various governments would do and how to manage those behaviors. But it was obvious the women terrorists had badly underestimated the level and viciousness of the civil unrest, which had effectively pushed most governments into a defensive position since the first bombings.

Fay decided to take a different approach.

"As a world-renowned psychologist, you must be proud of the work you did before the attacks?" Rena Niele, a refugee who was just 29 years of age, but had progressed through the education system at an amazing rate, with both a medical doctorate and Ph.D. by age twenty-four, was super smart. And as a brilliant psychologist, she could easily interpret Fay's intentions. Use reinforcement and positive language to build trust. She smiled and nodded. Two could play this game.

"Inspector Remer, as a refugee yourself, and a smart one at that, you would understand the frustration we had with the majority of countries who chose to ignore the refugee problem or, worse, actively contribute to its disastrous growth. Putin's so-called war with Ukraine created over three million more refugees, nearly two-thirds of them children, and displaced over two million more, all while the world thumped its collective chest and let the USA fight a proxy war with Russia and China. Who benefited?" She stared at Fay, openly challenging her to refute her comments.

Fay felt the visceral pressure to maintain control of the conversation, but once again, she was a super smart FBI agent in her previous life, so she let the terrorist take control for the moment.

"The military-industrial complex and, I suppose, to some extent Russia."

"If you call being isolated by the rest of the world and treated as a pariah success, maybe, but the Russian economy collapsed, and millions of ordinary Russians were forced out of their homes and onto the streets. More refugees and none welcome anywhere in Europe." She waved her manacled hands as if to dismiss the topic, then suddenly tears appeared in her eyes, started to fall down her face, a face that had aged considerably in the last months, then turned her face up to the light.

"Putting all that aside, we still have 120 children under the age of ten dying in refugee camps every day, one every eight minutes or so, and you cannot tell me anyone but us is doing anything about that." Fay saw her chance to get control of the conversation again.

"Who is 'us'?" she asked in a soft voice, indicating sympathy with the terrorist's point of view. Rene Niele turned her head back down, and the tears slipped across her face, glistening in the harsh overhead light.

"'Us' would be the cooperative we formed some years ago under the guidance of 'Helen', one of the most talented women I have ever met. She and our benefactor, whom you know as Mohammad bin Azaria, put us together to right the wrongs in the refugee camps and gave us the support we needed to make it happen. My only regret is we didn't get as far with our plan as we hoped before you shut us down."

"So you don't regret the 30 million plus deaths that have occurred since your attacks or the fact that, in the main, they were just ordinary people going about their business?" Fay's face hardened. She simply couldn't help herself. "That's nearly half as many as were killed in both world wars." The terrorist smiled, but there was no warmth in it.

"I admit we got that bit wrong. All our computer modeling suggested that most countries would tamp down any insurrection quickly, that the main damage would be done to the major religions of the world that have created the disastrous state we currently experience, and that the attacks would cause major governments to think about what they could do to mitigate the refugee crisis."

"So, where did the use of undetectable nuclear weapons come into your plan?" Again, Fay's voice was soft, almost warm, but her eyes were as clear as glass and pinpoint hard. To her credit, the terrorist gave nothing away with her facial expressions, and her body did not react in any way. But a look flashed across her eyes at the speed of light, and Fay unconsciously registered it. She nodded, leaning back in her seat.

"You may as well tell me as you're never going anywhere again, not in this life, and we have captured or killed everyone who was involved in that part of your strategy, except for your terrorist friend, Amir Abbas, who managed to destroy himself and his followers in an uncontrolled nuclear explosion in the Gaza." Fay rippled her fingers on the tabletop, making a little drumming sound.

"Oh, sorry, forgot your roommate—what was her name? Ah, that's it, Maribelle Assiano. The US Navy blew her out of the water, literally, in a nuclear explosion that destroyed all the shells and nuclear material she had onboard her gunboat. Sorry about that." A dead silence fell in the small interrogation room as both the terrorist and Fay let her words sink in. The terrorist had gone sheet white, and Fay could sense the restrained fury in her adversary. Good. She pushed even harder.

"Who came up with the idea of nukes, and how did you intend to use them?" The terrorist flopped her head back down into her hands and sobbed. Fay waited patiently. Silence was a powerful weapon in any interrogation or conversation, for that matter, so much so that she almost closed her eyes.

"The development and use of the shells was a closely guarded secret. And if you really have captured all of them, then you know how they work. Or should I say don't work?" The terrorist looked up, her eyes full of tears, her sobs just occasional, fitting between her words like punctuation marks. Fay looked at the terrorist and nodded. She had just confirmed something Amira had told them all back in Venice.

"So it was an empty threat?" The terrorist wiped her eyes with one hand, bending to accommodate her shackles. The metallic noise they made was a direct contrast to her sobbing, which had now stopped. It was a wan smile Fay saw, and while she sympathized with the terrorist over the loss of her partner, compared to everything else, she deserved her fate.

"Not so empty when you find nuclear material has been stolen, and then a pair of incompetent terrorists roam across Europe and the Mediterranean with the shells. I bet you took that very, very seriously." Fay nodded. No reason not to acknowledge the truth of that statement.

"But what was your end game? How was that activity going to help your cause?" The terrorist sat up, straightened her back, and steadied.

"We believed—and our computer modeling agreed—that the demonstratable threat of a nuclear explosion on sovereign soil would be a sufficiently powerful lever to get the major governments behind our resettlement plan and remove the barriers you have erected—like all the Red Notices on our funding." Fay nodded. That had been her conclusion, as well as Jessica's. As soon as Amira had told them that the shells, once loaded and resealed with the nano bugs, couldn't be exploded by any means known, they had all thought 'blackmail' with a twist. Fay debated whether or not to tell the terrorist about the sinking of the ocean liner with over 5,000 refugee children on it but decided not to.

No reason and nothing to be gained but more pain. She called for the door, waited until the guards had taken her prisoner out, then looked up into the camera that had been faithfully recording every conversation.

"Tell Arie the results, please, and get me back to Venice."

CHAPTER FIVE

Lilian and her sisters had all come from the same group home in Scotland, where they had been given an excellent upbringing as well as first-class education. Each had gone a different route, choosing the particular educational stream that most appealed to them. In her case, it had been oceanography, and she had just started to work in the Caymans when her mother—the woman who had raised her once she had been recovered from the refugee camp in Dagahaley, Kenya—called her three months ago and asked her to come home urgently.

At just under six feet in height and with the trim, fit body of a professional diver, she looked tough, and her closely cropped jet black hair looked like a cap perched on her chiseled face. Her usual dress code was well-worn Rockport jeans and an endless supply of bright t-shirts, each with a different message. Today's said, 'Don't breathe my air, or I'll punch out your lights'. A photo of a goggled and masked diver holding a baby shark sat behind the challenge.

She did not know at the time that her sisters had also been summoned back to Scotland. They had all arrived within days of each other and were surprised to hear what their mother had to say. They were all refugees, all about the same age, but they had all been encouraged to follow different paths. One is a physical scientist, one is a geologist, and Lilian, an oceanographer. Their mother, unknown to them, had been working with 'Helen' for a decade and was, in fact, the sole remaining commander of the women terrorists.

Her mother had kept a watch as the mercenary terrorists had been either killed or captured and thanks to her link to the majority of the security data sites in Europe and the USA, links that had been perfected by 'Helen" and her team of professional computer hackers, she knew exactly what had been reported by Interpol. With most of the world's computer systems being crashed by terrorist attacks, it had made it easy to tap into the small number of working government systems and suck out their data.

And while all this was happening, the girls sat at home, watching all the chaos from a safe distance, getting more and more curious every day about being called back home.

And now their mother had just confessed to being one of the masterminds and planners behind the female terrorists, had shown her daughters the reports from Interpol, the FBI, NSA, CIA, and European Security Agencies in summary form, and had listed the objectives of what the terror attacks had been all about.

Lilian initially had trouble believing her mother, whom she had only known as a caring, warm, and supportive parent. Nothing of her amazing spy-like activities had ever leaked into the household, and to say she was dumbfounded was an understatement.

"Now, girls, I don't want you to be worried about what I've told you, but just yesterday, I received notification from a friend of mine that we are ready to proceed to the next phase of our operation, and I need your help."The three young women sat next to each other, balancing little cups of strong tea on their laps. An outsider would see a group of women sharing a moment, a family enjoying an afternoon together, not the beginnings of what would later be construed as yet another terror attack of massive proportions, albeit a benign one.

Even though in the two short months of the new attack, not a single person would be killed or injured by design, the world would gain a new renewable power source of immense value—for a price.

"My friend and her partner have designed and built something magnificent. It will change the world in a way that few can imagine. But to benefit from this amazing and creative work, we need to set the stage, as it were."

"Ma, what would you have us all do, then? Don't be talking around the point so much." The youngest, who had been saved from a child trafficking ring in Syria at the age of six, had been so badly beaten and repeatedly raped that it had taken her over a year to recover. Then she had worked every day to strengthen herself, studied longer and harder than her sisters, gone to university at sixteen, and graduated as a physical scientist of some note before her twenty-first birthday. The older woman, her hair now gray at the temples and the center part where her roots showed, her house smock patched in several places in defiance of its age and condition, studied her children, for that's how she regarded them, not as adopted refugees but as her God-given right and responsibility. She loved her daughters and feared for them, but she could not keep them out of the fray. They had been given to her for a purpose, and it was now their time, God willing, to fulfill that purpose.

And she was positive that with the detailed planning that had gone into every aspect of what they were to do and with their innate brilliance and trained abilities, she felt sure they would prevail and return to her unharmed. The fact that she prayed for this outcome three times a day at her little indoor shrine, topped by a weeping Mother Mary figurine, did not make her less worried.

"You each have unique skills and are the best in your fields, but now we need you to do something that will initially enrage people, then do something that will win their hearts. You will have help, also highly trained, and all the resources you need to achieve our objective. And when this is over, you will see the world acknowledge the tragedy in the camps and do something positive about it, and it will be due in no small part to your efforts." She looked at her three girls, smiled at their placid composures, mindful that none of them had ever ventured beyond what she had encouraged them to do, and pulled out a long paper roll, spread it out on the carpeted floor of the lounge-room, then got down on her knees to straighten out the edges.

"This is a map of Ireland, England, Scotland, France, and Spain. These red circles mark nuclear power plants. One in Scotland, eight in the UK, seventeen in France, and seven in Spain. Within the week, those that are still functioning power stations will be closed down peacefully. No need to talk about how, but the why is important." She looked at her girls, now all kneeling around the big map, fingers tracing the circles as if trying to divine a secret message.

"Each one of these beasts is connected to a major power grid, and that will become critical when you see what we want you to do." She looked at her daughters, fierce concentration on their faces, warmed by the depth of love in the room, each for the other.

"Your role will be to set up our new devices in seventeen of these locations, but before that, you will need to go to Ireland and set up a demonstrator model of what we have created. It will take all your skills to manage that because each one of you has a specific role to play in what you do, and the overall task is immense." She looked to the youngest and patted her on the shoulder. "For the truth is, once the authorities learn of what you will do in Ireland, it will be very much more difficult to complete your tasks in the other countries." She held the eyes of her girls, sensed total commitment, and smiled to herself.

"Else, you will need all your science skills to make this work. In a sense, you will be the mechanic. Lily, your geology skills will be paramount. You will have to read the earth and find its weaknesses. Lilian, as the eldest, you will be responsible for keeping you all safe and using your diving skills to great effect." She looked around at their shining faces, sparkling eyes focused on the map, curiosity pushing through in a way that made her heart sing.

"This is what you will need to do, mostly under the cover of darkness and with great stealth and determination." And she rolled out another sheet of paper and heard the gasps from her girls as they recognized what the picture and drawings meant. "Your transport has been arranged, and your support will be ready for you in two days." The girls all leaned further forward to study both the map and the drawings, nodding to themselves as they absorbed each point.

Their initial destination was a small town on the Irish coast, hundreds of miles away, and they wondered how they would get there in just two days. It had taken the youngest of them nearly a month just to get home from where she had been working in Spain.

And once they had completed their tasks in Ireland, depending on how long it took them to be successful, they had to find their way to Spain, France, Scotland, and England. Else could not help but feel the thrill of excitement build up as she thought about all the wonders she would see on this challenging trip!

It never entered her mind that she and her sisters were about to hit the top of the 'Wanted' lists in every country in the world, and specifically in the top ten of Interpol's 'Most Wanted', globally.

VAPOR WARE

The advantage of the C-17 Globemaster cargo lifter was that at a slow cruising speed of around 260 kilometers an hour, it could fly for over 18 hours and cover over 3,700 kilometers of territory. And that was with two drones folded on its cargo rails, computer workstations for eight people, and a significant pile of electronic equipment. At an altitude of 7,300 meters, the nano detector could scan a corridor 40 kilometers wide, which it had been doing for over a day as the aircraft had flown up and down the vertical length of Ireland.

They had literally scanned the entire Island from top to bottom twice and found nothing. The navigator, a nuggety little Israeli airman with long curly hair and a complexion that was anything other than Middle Eastern, sat with his legs folded under his backside, tapping his screen with one blunt finger, mumbling to himself. He looked around the cavernous hold of the aircraft, dimly lit by the glare from the computer screens and red safety lights, looking for a sign.

Nothing.

He lifted the minicomputer out of the pocket of his flying suit and dialed Fay.

"Inspector, we have nothing. Your instructions, please." At the other end of the call, Fay looked at the shadowed face of the navigator and saw the fatigue that was clearly evident in the bags under his eyes.

"Ito, can you do a run between the Irish coast and the UK? Have you seen any anomalies in terms of blurry spots?" The nuggety Israeli shook his head, his jet-black hair flying around his face like a small cloud.

"Negative. Everything is clear; the resolution is first-class. There simply has been nothing to detect." Fay gave it a minute's thought, then tilted her head to one side.

"Okay, fly the grid between the two countries, then scan the UK from Scotland to Wales, then grid search the western coast and the sea between the UK and Europe. Look hard at Glasgow and London. Let me know how you go."

"WILCO." And the mini went to a black screen, giving Fay a pause, and she hoped it was not a portent of things to come. She was less than 30 minutes from landing back in Venice, where she would hop on a transport to the new Interpol temporary headquarters somewhere in Italy.

The crew flew the grid search three times in the next two days, covering the area from Ireland to Italy, with zero results. The reported shell had simply disappeared.

So they did the unexpected. They parked the aircraft and waited.

CHAPTER SIX

The convoy of old wooden trucks, all converted to electric in the last year or two, made very little sound other than that of the worn tires slapping on the cracked tarmac. Overhead, a light blue sky allowed feathered high-level cirrus clouds to strut their stuff, warning of a cold, if not chilly, night to come. The sun, having given up on the day just minutes before, had left a faint trail of sparkling orange on the wet trees that surrounded the shed. A flaccid waterfowl squawked its irritation from the mud banks, where the tide had worn away the bottom in the shape of snakes fighting their way across a muddy shore.

From the opposite direction, an ancient tractor with a huge bucket and dangling rusted chains bashing on the sides challenged the leading vehicle, forcing it to stop in its tracks, the chains flicking insolently at the windscreen of the truck.

"So, boyo, where exactly would it be that ya would be wanting me to lift all this stuff to?" The words filtered around the stem of a pipe and came out in a heavy dialect reminiscent of an old Irish publican calling 'time.' The old tractor driver, leaning forward over his steering wheel in his dirty green jumper worn at the elbows and sporting large patches of various colors, looked harmless, but the truck driver knew him of old, as well as the double-barreled shotgun he carried under the bench seat in his cab.

"Henry, you old fart, get yerself out of our way. I'd be needing ya to unload all the trucks into the shed, which, if you could still see, has its opening at the other end of the road." Henry, true to form, slipped on a well-worn pair of glasses held together with sticky tape and, screwing up his eyes in concentration, focused on the shed door. He thumped the tractor into reverse, greasing the old and worn gears, and with a flourish, backed up to let the trucks move adjacent to the side of the shed.

"Patrick, yer just could have said that when yer left yer message instead of making it all sound like such a mystery." Henry just shook his head. His note had been quite specific. He had even drawn a diagram of where he wanted the tractor to work. While the trucks moved into position, Henry lowered the bucket, jumped out of his cab, and fitted a pair of well-worn and heavily rusted prongs into the face of the bucket. He looked over just as the first truck backed up to the open door, and judging the distance he had to work with, he figured he would unload from the side, swing around, then drive into the shed.

It took three hours to get all the crates and massive boxes unloaded, and as the last truck got ready to disappear into the murky night, Henry and Patrick shared a Harp beer, congratulating themselves on their success.

"Well done, Henry, and I'd thank ya in style if I had the time, but I'd be getting back to the missus, or I'll miss me supper."

Patrick just nodded, all too familiar with the idea; having lost his blessed Bess just two years ago, there was no one around now to make supper for him, but the thought warmed his heart for his friend.

"Aye, off yer go, happy to stay here and wait for the lassies, but if yer had another harp, it wouldn't go to waste." His old friend pulled another bottle out of his truck, patted Patrick on the shoulder, and climbed into the cab.

"When they get here, just be on your way, and we'll meet sometime later this week to settle up."

"No rush. It's not as if I've anywhere to spend it, but it will be nice to have a punt of two, even if all they do is rattle around in me pockets." With a whine, the truck turned around and left the tractor guarding the door in the gloom, taking on a prehistoric look. Henry sat on the steps of his cab, pulling an ancient, scuffed leather coat on to ward off the creeping chill that was advancing like a quiet fog across the trees. The sky had now turned black, and the brilliant star field flickered from horizon to horizon. The single lantern cast very little light, just enough to see the shadows of the crates and boxes stacked inside the shed.

The only sound was the whistling noise Henry made while sucking on his empty pipe. He watched the nightbirds ferret out their dinner on the mud flats, marveling at the jerky movements of their long necks every time they took a step. It was weird, he thought, the way they moved back and forth as if they were going somewhere, then changing their minds, and coming back.

He pulled his well-worn coat around his thin shoulders, listening for the women he had been told would arrive around ten or eleven. He wondered who they might be and where they might be from. Dundalk Bay was a small town by any standards, and he was sure he would know any of the locals on sight, having dug the drains and drained the ditches around the bay for over thirty years. He sucked his empty pipe contentedly, his ragged cap falling over the sparse white hair that surrounded his ears, staring out into the distance. With his cracked glasses back in his pocket, he didn't see the tiny spark of light weaving and bobbing along the track until it was almost on him. Then with a sigh, he pocketed his pipe, doffed his cap, and bent to open the door of the small vehicle that, even in the gloom, he could see was filled wall to wall with beautiful women.

"Ladies, good evening to ya all. I am Henry, to answer any questions ya all may have and to lock up after yer be finished. May I have your identification, if it pleases ya at all?" His smile lit up his entire face, his unshaven cheeks wobbling a little, creating the effect you might expect from a tame hobgoblin.

"Henry, hello, I'm Marlene, and this young woman is Catlin, who very kindly is driving us around, and I'm sure you know Moriah; she runs the big house up on Century Road."

"Aye, I do, and how are you then, misses? I haven't seen ya for some time now."

"Good, thanks, Henry. Can you tell us what we need to do?" She looked at him with curiosity in her eyes. For the life of her, she couldn't imagine what role he might play. But the way he was looking at them suggested that he might well know something they didn't.

"Patrick tells me that I'm to let you look at all those boxes and crates, then lock up after yer have done with it all. I'll be meeting with Patrick later in the week, and that's all there is to it, as far as I know."

"Thank you, Henry. We'll go inside now and see what's what." And patting him on his shoulder as she walked past, she led the two younger women into the gloom of the shed. The boxes and crates seemed to come in two sizes and were clearly color-coded with massive red and green stripes across their sides. The professor did a quick count, pulled out a notepad, mumbled under her breath, then marched from box to crate, tapping her finger on the pad as she did so. Catlin and Moriah followed her around, their curiosity building with every finger tap. She turned back to the old farmer, who had waited at the door next to the small lantern, his cap twirling around in his hands.

"Henry, thank you. You can go home now. I have the keys, and I will lock up after the girls and I check every box once again." He nodded, pulled his pipe out of his bib pocket, and with a tip of his cap, turned his back and walked back to his tractor. It rumbled into life belching smoke as its tired engine fought to catch, then with a jerk started off back the way it had come. The professor waited a minute to be sure Henry was on his way, picked up the lantern, and moved back into the shed.

"All right girls, this is what we need to do next. Catlin, we're going back to the university, to arrange for some equipment. Moriah, I'll leave the keys with you, you will need to have someone sleeping here every night and here during the day, casual, like no big deal, and only people you absolutely trust. You can expect to have some visitors in the next week. Catlin will bring them to you. My guess is from four to six, you will need to find them accommodation and look after them until they get established. Now, I want you both to make your own list of these boxes and crates, so you can compare them down the track. What we have here will start a revolution if we're not careful." She looked critically at the two young women, pleased that their eyes had not left hers since she started talking. She smiled to relieve the tension.

"Moriah, as well as your building, you'll now be in charge of this shed and everything that comes from it, and I'll give you more information once your visitors arrive." She walked slowly out the door, waited until the two women had followed her, then turned and snapped the three big locks in place. She handed Moriah a small electronic pad, turned it on, and showed a picture of the locked door. She pointed to the hidden camera.

"This will work back in your building. Charge it every day during your power-up cycle, and have someone check it at regular intervals." Moriah looked at the image of the locked door, then turned the pad off and flipped it into her purse.

"I don't suppose you'll tell us what's in those crates and boxes?" she asked. The professor just laughed, patting her on the back as she headed for the car.

"No, not yet, but I can assure you that the future of the whole of Ireland will be in your hands and that you will love the outcome!"

CHAPTER SEVEN

We had been moved during the night a day ago, and our workplace was now an abandoned, slightly ransacked hangar at the edge of a range of mountains I couldn't pronounce the name of—*Towente La Buliga*—a hangar we were told that had been the headquarters of a notorious Italian gang of smugglers some years ago. The outside looked as if it would fall down in a mild wind, but the local militia had refurbished the interior in a manner that allowed for three-star comfort if you didn't mind standing in an open shower with your bare parts hanging in the breeze. I promptly commandeered one corner and surrounded myself with boxes and crates, creating the illusion of privacy.

On a very large screen literally nailed to one wall, furious, colorful shapes waved in and out of focus as the images stabilized across the network.

In one box, Malcolm was buzzing, bouncing up and down on his seat, his face glowing with enthusiasm and his eyes alight with passion. In faraway Israel, his counterpart, Shami, mirrored his excitement. At the bottom of the screen, Indigo's brother, Stefarino, sat with Luigi and a string of geek heads in company, and while a little more reserved, he also had the 'I've got a secret' look, so I did the only thing possible: I sat back in my seat, waved my hands as if I wasn't particularly interested, and placed one hand on 'Just call me Sally's' vibrating shoulder to try and contain her. Her short blond hair was flying around her face as if it had a life of its own, and she was all but getting set to explode.

"Jessica, commander, ma'am, we have the most fantastic news!" The shout reverberated around the small space of my so-called office and bounced off the walls of the massive hangar, echoing along the way so that it reverberated almost to the point of canceling itself out. I took a deep breath, centered myself, nodded to the big screen, looked at the image of the monk, and smiled.

"Stefarino, what's all the excitement about?" He looked at me with his face flushed, his cheeks red with excitement, so I warmed myself up to reflect the power of the happiness bursting out of the screen and the bubbly vibrations from Sandra.

"Commander, we have just had the most marvelous luck. Using the services of all these wonderful people, we have intercepted and triangulated the signals from five communication devices used by the terrorists. I also believe from this we can track the movement of the missing shells." I held my hand up, to stop any comment.

"Where?" I looked as deeply as I could at his face, watching his eyes, which on the screen were now slightly shut, reinforcing the importance of what he was telling us. He was, after all, the head of a hidden order of monks, charged with recording the religious history of the world, not a professional spy.

"Ireland-specifically Dundalk Bay, where the destroyer pinged off a shell; Dublin, Glasgow, London, and Paris. It was almost simultaneous, the primary transmission came from Scotland, from as small town called Lochgilphead, on the top of Loch Gilp. Single transmission, on five discreet frequencies. And we were then able to track the movement of blobs from the five locations contacted, thanks to some really excellent work by Malcolm Luigi, and Shami. Commander, we have found your missing shells."

That put me back on my haunches, and looking around the piles of boxes and equipment in our new temporary base in the backwoods of Italy I wondered how to prosecute this information. Then I paused my thinking – I had been looking for a way to remove myself fractionally from the pointy end of the action, mimic the Boss to some extent, and here was the perfect opportunity.

I had five excellent leaders: Sandra, Fay, Tom, Bob, and Indigo, and if I had to reach further, there was the colonel who led the Israeli commando 104. We also had cross-trained Rapid Response Teams in the US Navy, at least two of them on ships close to the nominated locations of the shells. Maybe this was an opportunity to test my new leadership style, although part of me was hungering to be in the mix, leading my troops into the fray. I mentally choked down the instinct to lead everything from the front and thought through the possibilities of tackling six targets simultaneously in four different countries.

"Excellent work, team geek, really excellent work. I need the final location of each blob as soon as you have it. Can you nominate one contact for us to continuously monitor the situation in real-time?"

"We will do that, Commander. I would suggest Luigi and Shami share that between themselves." As Stefarino offered his suggestion, I opened up a discrete channel on my mini.

"Indigo, I need five RRTs stood up immediately, plus a squad of sweepers, Sandra, Fay, Tom, Bob, myself, and yourself in command, with teams of shooters as backup positioned in each location. I will coordinate on the move; make it so."

"*Subito comandante.*" Then I had a stray thought. Where was Fay? And how did I move five RRTs plus a sweeper team into position simultaneously? Then I remembered the admiral. I dialed him up.

"Admiral, quick question. Do you still have the RRT we trained in the Mediterranean?"

"Hello to you, too, Jessica. Nice to see you. Short answer, yes, but we trained up another three teams as backup. Why do you ask?"

"We think we have located the missing five shells, two of them potentially in Europe, and three others in Ireland and Scotland. I can cover Ireland and Scotland; it would be nice if you could cover England and France."

"It would have to be an Interpol exercise; we'll need documentation and in-country clearance." I had anticipated this, and while working with the US Navy was a real blast, their rules of engagement were so strict that it made it very hard for a flexible, fast-acting group like Section Five to be fully effective.

"We'll cover you with Red Notices and World Court documentation, and I can send one of my people to 'advise' each of your teams to fully protect you if you need that." His look said it all; his eyes tightened, and his face pulled into a hard frown. The mere thought of a civilian, even one trained by Interpol Section Five, managing a troop of sailors and marines was unthinkable.

"Before you say no, your RRTs may be required to shoot first and not bother with any questions; these are terrorists we're dealing with, and I can't see them giving us the shells with a polite smile." His face went thoughtful, his eyebrows lowering over his dark eyes like shutters on a window. We had both lost valuable men and women in retrieving the shells we had recovered so far, and I knew that weighed heavily on him.

"I'll give that some thought, and maybe accept that if they are on your military roster. No civilians."

"But Admiral, I thought you enjoyed our company last time we met!" He had the good grace to laugh, and his face relaxed into the happy version I was used to. Admiral Cranky was not a good look for him.

"If you need them, and I'll have to know in the next hour, I'll send you a Master Chief and a Major. Will that make you happy?" He just continued to smile, then I put the fork in his ribs, and he turned serious again.

"If you want them, you will have to pick them up from a location I'll give you when you make up your mind, and I'll need you to let them have a little leeway. As far as we know, these shells are inert, but we don't want to take any chances, and we do not know who the opposition is, their strength, or how well they are armed."

"So it's the usual Interpol crap shoot?" It was my turn to smile. I nearly switched him off, then thought of something.

"Admiral, would it make it any easier if we also provided a working member of Interpol from each head office?" He obviously gave that some thought because his head tipped up on the small screen, and he scratched his throat. His wedding ring flashed in the sunlight, yet another reminder that some of us had lives outside of our professions.

"No, not necessary. If we have your cover to enter and execute with UN permission, we should be fine. It would be handy to know there was no nuclear material involved."

"Understood. At this point, we have real-time satellite coverage, and we'll get you as much data as we can."

"Real-time satellite coverage?" His look was one of astonishment and mild disdain. "How, exactly, is Interpol doing that with all our satellites out of action?"

"Secret women's business. Sorry, that's all I can tell you." His face went blank again, so I just smiled and clicked off.

I had decisions to make, people to call, and places to go, and the clock was ticking. With the possibility of Bob and Tom heading for Europe, that left me, Sandra, Fay, and Indigo for Ireland and Scotland. Then I remembered I hadn't seen Fay for a day or two, so I dialed her up.

"Fay, good morning, where are you?" She looked relaxed, her auburn hair tidily held behind her head with some sort of tie. It was obvious she was rested, and I smiled at the thought. At least one of us was getting some quality sleep!

"Venice, I've been here just over half a day, looking at all the data we have collected in the last three months, trying to make some sense out of it."

"Conclusions so far?" She looked up into the camera lens, slightly perplexed at my question.

"Well, nothing really startling, but I have an opinion on the women and their structure if you want that." Being an ex-FBI, Fay's natural instinct was to pursue the data and look for the patterns and similarities in the behaviors of the people we hunted. Once upon a time, I had the same instincts, but they were now well and truly dulled by the repetitious need to gun up and go chase somebody down.

Now.

"Go. Surprise me." She smiled, enjoying the challenge. She brushed a stray ribbon of hair from her eyes, tucking it back over her ear, which I noticed was adorned with a minute diamond stud.

"Looking at their command structure, we know 'Helen' was at it for thirty-five years, at the very least, our deceased terrorist mastermind for at least that long, and a large number of bit players for a decade or less depending on when they were taken out of the camps and graduated into the ranks of the super smart and clever people they turned out to be. But we are missing something I can't quite put my finger on. Field commanders. You know what I mean—the people who make everything work and manage the teams, projects, and activities. I know we swept up some of them with the women we have taken, but the organizational structure is too one-dimensional. If you just look at roles and responsibilities, we have one or two women in charge of Point Roberts, the CEO, and the COO; two in charge of New Zealand; the women we swept up in Helena; both of them played a very small role; one from Roanoke, the psychologist, and her girlfriend, the skipper of the gunboat, but she was in Ireland; and we have the scientist, engineer, and pilot linking them all together. The pilot is my bet for inter-office communication, the engineer for initiating the plants, and the scientist for the nano work.

"Then we have 'Helen', and her crew of computer hackers, the CEO of Innomatchi, and her two refugee daughters. We know of at least five mercenary leaders, and the main man from the desert-Al Hemish al-bin Mohammad Karesish, or Mohammad bin Azaria as we knew him, and his accountant.

"We know there were over 350 girls taken, maybe more, but we have only accounted for around 26, including the masterminds from Point Roberts, Helena, New Zealand, and Japan.

"When I dig deep on Innomatchi, and I checked this with our local team, we find shipments of unknown hardware made to a number of locations a full year before the first attacks. Then we have the team we pulled from 'Helen's' headquarters, the ones who were generating the false IDs for the refugee girls and workers; look at the two youngsters who designed the games, and you find big holes in their order of battle.

"We know other male terrorists were involved, we swept them up, but overall I think we still have a thinker or two still out there driving the train, particularly when you look at what we are chasing now."

"Explain." I didn't mean to be gruff, but my tonality got away from me. If there were more heavy hitters out there, I needed to find them—and fast. She smiled again, letting me off the hook for my bitchy attitude.

"Well, we have the missing shells, for one thing. And even though the geeks have located them and we're now tracking them, who's running the show? Then you have 33 nuclear power plants in Europe going offline in the last week, zero information about who, just the silver clag turning up one morning, and zero power output. Who's running that operation? And now that the devil from South Africa is out of the picture, who's doing the fieldwork?"

If I looked startled, it was because I was; nothing about the reactors had reached me in our new headquarters. This was a serious omission, and I wondered how we had inflicted it on ourselves.

"And according to our own people, the attacks on the nuclear plants all took place within the same three-day period."

"Where were the power plants?"

"Scotland, the UK, France, and Spain. There is no working nuclear power plant anywhere in Europe, including Russia, and we don't really know about China." My blood ran cold. With no power for the last two or three months from coal, gas, or oil-fired generators, thanks to the terrorist attacks, and now none from the nuclear plants, Europe was going into a whole new world of pain, and the potential for further social unrest just went into the red. I thought about who I could have a conversation with about this and decided to park it for a minute.

"Have you estimated how many people it would take to attack that many power plants in just a week?"

"Yes, we figure no less than five, probably double that number in reality, but the only real clue we have is some scattered photos of people riding electric bikes carrying backpacks. But as you can imagine, with the constant movement of hundreds of thousands of migrants and refugees across every border, in every direction, even that data is almost useless."

"Any casualties?"

"None reported."

"So, to summarize, you project one or two masterminds still at work, and maybe ten Indians running around shutting down nuclear power plants?" She looked straight into my eyes, held mine, and didn't even blink, but I swear I could see her mind working at a million miles an hour behind those baby blues.

"Don't forget whoever is moving the shells. The masterminds could be as many as three or four-the Indians maybe ten or twenty, but who knows? I got one of the young geeks to model how he would take out three of the plants in France, just to get a feel for it, and his model did it in two days, easily. We still haven't unpicked what their real purpose was with the shells, other than blackmailing us into releasing their funds for the environmental plants." I let that sit for a moment, mentally appointing a mastermind to each of the activities we were tracking-one to the nuclear shells moving around, one to the zapping of the nuclear power plants, and maybe one to the overall oversight of the whole shooting match.

The trouble was, we were all just guessing, with no hard data to go from. I shook my head. It was time to move on.

"Fay, get yourself to Dublin, connect with Bob's RRT, stand by for a detailed briefing, and get there as fast as you can." Sandra, who had been sitting as quietly as a mouse for the first time in her life, stood, stretched, then turned to me with a question written all over her face. I just pointed, twirled my forefinger, then flicked it at the makeshift door.

"You and I are going to Scotland, Indigo," I called as I looked over to where he was still chatting with the geeks on a smaller screen, "need you to arrange transport for us all, please, and get yourself to Tom's team, then Dundalk Bay, stand by for a briefing." He nodded, turned back to the screen, and spoke in an animated fashion for thirty seconds, then his screen went black.

"Commander, the geeks have pinpointed every shell, down to five meters, some of the locations beggar belief." I raised my eyebrow and waved him over as Sandra disappeared. "The one in Dublin is in a pub-hotel; the one in Dundalk is in a school; London is also in a pub; Glasgow is in a boarding house; and the Paris one is, amazingly, in a little brasserie on the Seine. And commander, the cloaking mechanism has been turned off; the five shells are as clear as can be in the images."

"What?" Indigo looked at me with his hazel-green eyes sparkling, his face cut with a grin as he nodded.

"Yes, commander, clear as a bell." To say I was astonished was to understate my feelings by a mile. Why would the terrorists put their nuclear shells out on public display at least as far as our imaging was concerned? I pointed to the big screen, and he fiddled with his mini, then the shadowy outline of the five shells swam into focus, each showing a POI as described. They weren't on display or in the open, but they were visible to our scanners, and that couldn't be an accident.

"How long before our first team can make contact?" He fiddled with his mini again, muttered to himself under his breath, then, with more enthusiasm than I thought possible, flicked some calculations up to my screen.

"The Americans could be first on station if we cut them loose immediately two hours for Paris, four for London. We're three hours away from Ireland if we leave now, a little less to get a team into Glasgow." I thought as fast as I could that I would have to take a huge risk, but I had no choice in the matter. I dialed the admiral.

"I need two of your RRTs on station in Paris and London ASAP, without our people but with full UN and Interpol cover. Can you do that? And while you're working that out, can you get a third team into Glasgow as fast?" His eyes glazed over, and he looked down at me from under his bushy eyebrows, his mouth forming a thin line.

"Jessica, I don't like this. What has happened to change your strategy?" The look he gave me chilled me all the way to my backbone, which I automatically straightened.

"Admiral, all five shells have become visible to our scanners. They are for all intents and purposes out in the open. The terrorists, for some reason, want our attention. And they are all in very public places."

"They're not loaded?" This was the critical question, and we had no way of knowing without using the scanners we had on the Israeli C-17. I gave him my best, most positive look and even smiled a little, but he saw through me in a heartbeat.

"You don't know, but you don't think so."

"Correct. If I'm wrong, then we'll have a monumental problem, but what I am reading is a deliberate decision by the terrorists to attract us to the shells, for whatever reason I just don't know."

"It wouldn't be to let them off with you taking all the blame?" I smiled at that. The mere thought of being responsible for five nuclear explosions in major European cities was enough to make me go weak at the knees. But I went back to Fay's report from Israel and my own interviews with some of the women terrorists.

And the design of the shells, which Amira had proven, was such that the shells were designed never to explode once sealed by the nanobots, and they were only sealed if they had nuclear material inserted into them. So loaded or unloaded, no big bang! And as proof of that, when the US Navy sank the terrorist gunboat in the middle of the Atlantic Ocean, the unloaded nuclear material exploded with a vengeance that nearly sank an aircraft carrier and rolled a destroyer, killing all onboard. But the shells had come up on our scanners days later intact, thousands of feet underwater.

"Admiral, without actually seeing one in the flesh, as it were, I don't believe that they're loaded." I held his stare, mentally transmitting all my belief as hard as I could, he didn't blink, but slowly started to nod.

"Send me all the data; if you want us to take Paris, London, and Glasgow, I'll get on that immediately. But we won't be going in guns blazing, no matter what the situation is." I nodded. It was the best I could expect, but we didn't have to abide by the same rules, so I hustled Sandra and Indigo out of the building to our pocket jet, and headed for Ireland as fast as we could go.

ARRIVAL

The woman, tall and slender, with long jet-black hair falling evenly to her waist, literally sparkled in the warm light of the afternoon glow. The Irish weather Gods, usually a little capricious at this time of year, had left off the raging storms and chilling fogs for another day, allowing the sun to stream down from a cloudless, rich blue sky. Her tailored suit, in a misty off-purple, accentuated her curves, her long, long legs, and the rippled collar of her silk shirt showed off her generous mouth. Moriah thought her coffee colored skin had been painted on, so smooth and creamy it looked.

Towing a jet black carry case, she looked for all the world like a rich, successful executive, as she stepped from her dark blue jet copter, followed by two aircrew pushing large cylinders on trolleys. The park at Southend had been hastily prepared for her arrival, and a well-used slightly dented limousine waited to collect her.

Beside it, dressed in her very best Sunday dress, Moriah waited nervously, unsure of the protocol of welcoming such a regal looking person. Then she remembered what her mentor the professor has told her, and she fractionally relaxed her shoulders, and warmed her smile.

"Hello, that would be me Miss Katrina. I'm Moriah, your hostess. Pleased to meet you, I am, and welcome to Dundalk!" She moved forward, and held out her hands, which caused the arriving goddess to let her bag go so she could reciprocate. Her bag hit the ground with a thud, and the following aircrew nearly upended one of the trolleys, and swore under his breath in Russian.

"Oh, I'm so sorry! Let me get that for you." Moriah picked up the handle, then took one of her visitors hands, and started towards the vehicle.

"Moriah, relax. I'm happy to meet you as well. Please don't stress on my behalf. It's the first time I've been anywhere for a very long time," and her melodious laughter rang between the two women. Moriah put the carry-on in the boot and closed it, turned in time to see the aircrew load the cannisters in the small truck parked immediately behind, and watched like a hawk as they moved back to the helicopter.

Sassy, one of her sister's young tribe members and one of the few with a legal driving license, nodded her head, started the truck, then moved off. They had charged the truck from their precious battery supply for two full days to make sure it would run properly. Moriah started the limo and waited until the motor ran smoothly. The biofuel they were using was locally produced and of uneven quality at the best of times.

"Miss Katrina, you'll be staying in our building. I've cleared a top floor for you and your friends. I understand there will be three of them. Is that correct?"

Next to her, the woman whose newest invention would, literally, change the world, just smiled. "Moriah, thank you. The three girls will be here tomorrow, they are driving down from Belfast, they have their own vehicle, and they will have a charger that can be used to keep it running. As a matter of interest, how do you run your building?" Moriah slowed the vehicle, allowing the big car to traverse a very rough passage of road, destroyed by the flooding rains of the past months and unrepaired due to the local council no longer being able to function because of the civil unrest. They rocked from side to side, jerked front to back suddenly, then leveled out, and she was able to accelerate again.

"We have a supply of batteries we have scavenged from all over, and solar panels and wind generators on the roof. We limit the usage to two hours a day, mostly for cooking and cleaning. We use biofuel for lighting, and we run a generator occasionally for light and heating. Everything is rationed, and we barter some of the power for outside services." Katrina smiled to herself, wondering what Moriah's reaction would be when she got her project up and running. She just nodded her head and sat back to enjoy the ride. The rich green hills and valleys of Ireland were such a contrast to the sand and ocean she had just left, but the beauty was amazing, and a slow grin slipped across her lips as she pictured the future.

CHAPTER EIGHT

I f you stood perfectly still, shaded your eyes from the glare of the late afternoon sun, and looked straight up, out of the corner of your eye you would just make out a minute speck, leaving a white contrail behind it. If you had super powers and could zoom in your eyes, you would see the blue hexagon of the Star of David on the fuselage of the C-17 as it pushed through the frigid air some 37,000 feet above you.

You might wonder what it was doing up there, seemingly floating through the rich blue twilight without a care, but what would really get your attention if that super vision was working overtime would be the minute shape of the drone, crisscrossing the space immediately off to one side of the bulbous transport aircraft. The images that were being sent back to the C-17 were causing more than a little concern.

The navigator, who had been sitting on his folded legs for over three days, had his most stoic look on, trying to hold in his excitement. He was, after all, a professional airman, and a member of one of Israel's elite squadrons. He had a reputation, hard won in the defense of his country, and didn't want any dents in it.

Ito had been watching the drone images for days, looking for either proof of the shells or the blur that signified an electronic cloaking system that hid the shells from detection. The aircraft and its drones had scanned hundreds of thousands of square kilometers, from the west coast of Ireland all the way to the far reaches of the French/Italian border, then back again. They eventually uncovered all five shells and sent the locations to Jessica.

Just two hours ago, in what turned out to be an inspired move, the crew decided to shift the search area to the southern reaches of Ireland and scan all the way along the Atlantic coast.

And as they crossed a minor waterway that surrounded a small group of Islands held against the coast by who-knows-what, the detection alarm rang, sending shivers up and down his spine. He had recorded false positives before, so he took his time and requested the pilot fly a long, elongated racetrack pattern, not unlike the one they used when waiting to land at a busy major airport.

The north-south run was 50 kilometers long, the east-west base leg was 30 kilometers wide, and the drone was crossing the area being described by the C-17 at the diagonal, its scanners wound down to their highest resolution. In contrast, the high-resolution radar was in wide-aperture mapping mode, and the crew watched in fascination as the telltale shape of an oil or gas refinery unfolded, with a series of weird-looking concentric circles heavily grassed and reinforced, one on the eastern coast, one at each end of the Island.

Ito dialed his immediate supervisor and smiled when Fay's pretty face swam into focus.

"Inspector, we have a positive on some shells, eight in all, all at the same location. Sending you video now." And she watched, fascinated, as the scan image seemed to rotate around its own axis, indicating that the shells were stacked in proximity to each other. The mapping overlay was a confusing series of concentric circles, some of which resolved themselves as massive oil or gas tanks; others belied any rational description.

"Where is this, Ito?"

"On a very small Island on the west coast of Ireland, just north of Banty Bay. Our mapping software has no identification for it, but there are a few houses to the east and what looks like a small longhouse. I've sent you the latitude and longitude." Fay looked at the images, wondering what she was looking at. The problem with the scans was that they were in high-contrast black and white, and the mapping overlay was in washed-out colors, so the definition of anything on the ground left a lot to be desired.

Fay dialed me into the conversation, brought me up to date, and in complete silence, we all just watched the images of the slow circling of the shells. The obvious questions popped into my mind, but I kept them to myself. What were the geeks tracking, and where did these shells come from? I thought I had a solution for the last question, so I pushed the current image up to the top of my screen, isolated it, and dialed my substitute grandfather.

"Arie, I have a puzzle for you. You might have to involve the monks, but I've forwarded you some images; they are real-time and current, and when Amira confirms our suspicions, I need to know where they came from and when." His gray eyes looked tired, but his smile was warm and inviting, so I bit down on my instinctive need to ask him how he was. He just looked up at his screen; his eyes tightened appreciably as he made out the images, then he nodded, smiled at me again, and clicked off. But the lingering first question started to resonate in my mind— what, exactly, were the geeks tracking down on the West Coast of Ireland, and was this in any way related to what we had uncovered in Ireland, Scotland, England, and France?

Sitting, or more correctly, sprawled, across from me and watching me like a hawk out of slitted eyes, Sandra remained silent. I could almost hear her thoughts echoing mine. Was this another goose chase, running down the electronic blurs and the shells supposedly hidden under them, and what did the discovery in South-Western Ireland mean?

"Sandra, everything you can find out about that location, yesterday." She threw me a mock salute and buried her head in her mini. "Indigo," I called, turning around in my seat to face him, "We really need to know if those shells we have uncovered are still in place, and we need to know that now." He looked a little grim, having watched the screen over my shoulder and having heard both ends of every conversation. He flicked a quick look at his mini, then smiled up at me, which was reassuring in itself.

"Commander, the first RRT will make contact in ten minutes." The fact that he spoke in perfect English underlined his concern, but he held my eyes, didn't blink, and his happy face took the tension out of my shoulders, and I sat back, prepared to wait. There was something calming about working with a solid man wearing a pristine uniform who always knew what to do. Then Sandra popped up like the battery bunny she was, flicked data from her mini to the bulkhead screen, then sat sideways on the arm of her seat and looked expectantly at me.

I waved my hand at her. "Go."

"The latitude and longitude the C-17 is scanning is a small Island, with a wicked history. In Irish it's called *Oileán Faoide*, in English that translates to Whiddy Island. One pub, and around twenty permanent residents, and the long story of historical note is that back in the eighteen hundreds it was where the British built their first line of defense against Napoleon. They constructed forts and gun emplacements during the Napoleonic War. I'm guessing, but I suspect that is what the double built up circular structures in the middle of the Island are. More history, not so storied, it was an oil terminal, and back in 1979 an oil tanker, the French MV Betelgeuse exploded, killing 51 people; French, British, Dutch and Irish. Terminal subsequently closed, a little fishing and logging are the only recorded economic activities. It was the worst Irish marine tragedy in their history, unless we count the terrorist boat you took out in the Atlantic."

I nodded, accepting her analysis. Now the strange shapes in the drone images made some kind of sense. The oil tanks that had survived the fire were the huge vessels we could see stacked up at the end the jetty. The shells were hidden in the end one, which had a collapsed roof. My mini buzzed at me relentlessly, so I answered it.

"Arie, I was just thinking of you." He smiled, and he must have been thinking of me. It had been hardly five minutes since I had asked the impossible of him.

"Jessica, Amira believes the shells are the same as the ones you took down on the gunboat. Different to those made in

Afghanistan, no dolphin nose, and three times the size." I did the arithmetic; 18 plus kilos of nuclear material would equate to a very large explosion, probably comparable to the first atomic bombs dropped on Japan at the end of WW2. Now I got the cold sweats, and in the back of my mind, I revisited the scariest six minutes of my life so far—sitting out the tsunami caused by the destruction of the gun boat while aboard an American aircraft carrier, over 1,000 miles away from ground zero. A tsunami that lifted us up over 1,200 feet into the air, then dropped us like we didn't really exist. A tsunami that rolled a destroyer, killing all 200 souls on board. Later, much later, the technicians in the Navy calculated that the blast that had literally set the ocean on fire had been in the order of 300 to 350 kilos of plutonium, and 20 kilos of Uranium 235.

They had worked all this out using dark magic and samples of the residual radioactivity from both the ocean and the air, taken by the submarines that had so succinctly sunk the gun boat on my command. The admiral had his hand on the button as well, and I knew the US had taken a silent credit for the sinking, the explosion being blamed on a massive and just as mythical tectonic and volcanic upheaval.

Now I realized what we had avoided by sinking the terrorist boat when we did.

"Thanks, Arie. Looks like we dodged a bullet there. Have you been able to back-trace where these new bastards have come from?"

"In progress, Stefarino has the bit between his teeth. He'll let you know as soon as he can."

"Thanks, Arie. Appreciated." I shut him down, only to have the hairs on the back of my neck stand up. I turned slowly to find the source and nearly jumped out of my seat when Indigo leapt up into the air, filling the narrow aisle with his enthusiasm.

"Comandante, abbiamo messo al sicuro il primo dei proiettili, cosa vorresti che se ne facesse?" We had the first of the shells. It wasn't a wild goose chase. Now what? I thought furiously.

"Where did we find it?"

"The US Navy team, led by the master chief we met on the boat, reclaimed the shell in the French trattoria exactly where the geeks said it would be. No resistance, the shell was sealed, but when weighed, it proved to be not loaded. The admiral is asking instructions as to its final destination, and for the other shells, he expects to have them located within the next hour." I pointed back to the big screen at the front of the cabin and waved my hand around a little.

"Israel, get them to Amira, tell her to open them, check them out, and let us know what's what." He gave me a mock salute and sat back down, letting the light back into the rear of the cabin. I suddenly had another thought, turned to Sandra, and gave her my fiercest look.

"Divert us to the nearest airport to this Whiddy Island, contact Tom or Bob, whoever is the closest, and have them meet us there, ready to move." I dialed the Boss without looking at the keyboard. I had done it so many times now that my fingers knew where to go. She held her mini up to me and pointed to the word 'Cork'. I nodded.

"Boss, I need a fast helicopter at Cork ASAP. One team plus three, all loaded; we may or may not meet resistance, but we have found a new store of shells, the same size as the ones on the gunboat. I need UN/World Court cover for the Irish Government, Red Notices, all the usual. Sandra will give you the details." He looked at me with a thin smile, then tilted his head to one side.

"Hello Jessica, nice to see you. Glad you're having so much fun. The geeks tell me we have the shell from Paris?" I studied his face, looking for any tell. If he was this plugged into the everyday bitstream, something was brewing that I didn't know about. I started to form a question, then just let it dissolve unformed. I had my teams out in the field, I had my own priority, and it was best to leave any high-level mucky-muck stuff to him.

"Yes, I just learned that myself." He gave me a bland stare. I hoped I had surprised him by not asking why he was engaged in the day-to-day action. But then, he was a master at not letting you see what was in his mind, if he didn't want you to, so I rolled my shoulders and sat back in my seat.

"Comandante, la Marina ha recuperato il proiettile a Londra. Nessuna resistenza." Good, London recovered. No resistance. That just left Scotland and the two in Ireland, which my team had been planning on recovering. I noticed that the Boss had suddenly looked off to one side, then back at me, with a thin smile creasing his craggy face.

"We got London. Who have you in Glasgow?"

"One of the admiral's RRT's." He nodded and tilted his head again.

"You were taking Dundalk and Dublin?" I nodded.

"And then I was going after the transmitter that started all the movement in Scotland." He just looked at me with slightly crinkled eyebrows, neither agreeing nor disagreeing with my choices.

"Are you not worried about the timing with the other shells having been taken out of harm's way?" It was my turn to crinkle my eyebrows.

"No. Someone wants us to find them. This is a deliberate action, I don't know why, but I suspect we will find out once we have all the shells." He nodded.

"Are you getting the feeling we're being led by the nose?" My turn to nod. We were starting to mimic each other's body language, which might have been fun at some other time, but now it was just irritating me.

"There's some master plan in action here. The fact that the shells were hidden, then revealed as it were, and then we are being allowed to take them with no resistance suggests that they know we can track the shells and probably a whole lot more about us than we would like. It doesn't feel right." He nodded again and leaned slightly forward.

"Now that we have our own comms system, working satellites, and our fabulous geeks, we are better at coordinating what we do."

"There's no chatter anywhere, and I'm willing to bet that when you get to the location of the transmitter in Scotland, you find the same setup we found in Montana and the Middle East."

"An underground cable leading somewhere else?"

"Yes. Want to put five euros on it?" I shook my head. For him to be so sure made it a very bad bet. So I threw my metaphorical hat in the ring and held the metaphorical fire to his belly.

"What do you think is going on?" He looked up off-camera as if thinking about something. When he looked back at me, the steely glint in his eyes told me all I needed to know. He had our backs, and he had a good idea of what we were up against.

"Jessica, that would be spoiling it for you. I trained you better than that. Go get those extra shells out of the way, finish what you started in Ireland, then call me when you find the transmitter, and we'll swap notes." He grinned, a sure sign he knew something I didn't, but it couldn't be fatal because otherwise, he would have told me. His image faded from my screen. I closed the lid and wondered what he knew or had worked out that I hadn't.

Have to go without it, the cabin seatbelt fastening sign was flashing. Cork, here we come!

And before I could celebrate having survived another flight without getting shot out of the air, my mini buzzed against my thigh, demanding my attention. When I opened it, I was surprised to see the blond, unruly locks of my favorite American geek, Malcolm Tannery, beaming at me. A surfer by preference, he made it a habit to escape the dungeons of the mountain he worked under in middle America as often as he could, but my recent experience with his Boss's jet had temporarily grounded him.

As it had crashed and burned after being shot down by a missile-bearing drone midway across the Atlantic.

"Hi, Malcolm. What's up?" His grin was infectious, and the blond hair hanging over his shoulder was soon joined by the pretty face of his assistant, Rosalie, who was mostly hidden away in the bowels of the mountain somewhere. Her passion was horse riding, and she kept her saddle and riding clothes in her locker and used them at every opportunity.

"Hi, Rosalie. Good to see you. Why did they let you out today?" Her face lit up at the mention of her name. She really didn't get out all that much, and I could feel her passion through the screen of the mini.

"Commander, great to see you again. I'm out of my burrow because I'm the only one here that speaks Italian, and your geeks are working so fast our automated translation programs can't keep up. They have news for you, but they are too absorbed in the chase to let you know what's happening, so they asked us to call you." That got me worrying. What could possibly cause my geeks to get so busy they couldn't call me?

"Okay, what's the story, Rosalie? Don't keep me in suspense."

The front door of the aircraft had opened, and some of the troops from Commando 104 had started to pile out, and Sandra, seeing I was on my computer, locked into the conversation, motioned to one of the soldiers, and formed a physical barrier between me and the door. She was really taking this bodyguard thing seriously, and I would have to calm her down over it as soon as I had the time to scratch myself.

"Commander, the shells have been retrieved in Glasgow, London, and, as you already know, Paris. The team in Dublin has not reported yet. There are no nanites packed with the shells. All three are sealed, and all three are present as unloaded. They are now all on their way to Israel, as you instructed."

"So what's got everybody's head down?" This was very unusual behavior by the geeks, something I could not remember ever happening previously. Luigi and Shami were renowned for talking endlessly about everything geeky, so their silence was telling.

"The shell we were tracking from Dundalk Bay has disappeared. It was originally located in a school out on the edge of town, then it just started to move south. We still have the shell in Dublin. It's still in the pub, and your team should have it in minutes."

"What do you mean by 'disappeared'?"

"It was tracking down the main road towards Dublin, then when it was near Stamullen, the blur disappeared completely. We have the area under tight surveillance, and your people are running everything they have learned in the last three months to try to uncover it, which is why they asked us to talk to you." I gave that some thought. We had great respect for the technology the women had employed so far, but we had managed to unpick it bit by bit to the point where we thought we had defeated it. Just as I formed that thought, Bob's team sent through a "CQ" on my mini, indicating they had grabbed the shell in Dublin, and would be happy to talk to us if we wanted to.

"Thank you both. Please keep me in the loop. We're going to get the shells that have been identified in the refinery."

"WILCO" (Will comply). And the screen went blank. I put my mini back in my pocket and ignored the stare Sandra was giving me. I could feel the tension rolling off her in waves, motioned her forward with a casual wave of my hand, then picked up my pack and threw it over my shoulder.

"The geeks have lost the shell that was on its way somewhere from Dundalk Bay." She squinted her eyes, trying to work out what that might mean, started to ask me a question, then stopped herself. Good control, another aspect of her that I was starting to like.

"We have three 4WDs and two helicopters. How do you want to set the attack?" She looked around the grouped troops, all dressed in combat black, NVGs fitted, weapons slung, then turned back and looked me directly in the eyes.

"I have the latest images from Ito's team, and we have according to the airport staff approximately an hour before last light, around nine forty local." Without a word being said, the entire group silently surrounded Sandra and me, all facing out as if protecting us from attack. But every trooper had their head bent slightly back or tilted to the side, so they could hear anything we said—the mark of true professionals. I looked at the overhead shot of the old refinery and noted the sunken piles and ruins of the old wharf, the really old gun emplacement, and fort, and the alignment of the fourteen oil tanks. The shells were showing up as being stacked in the last (or first, depending on which way you came at it) oil tank, in what would be the third row of two tanks.

They were still being used to store oil, the commercial company responsible for them bought back into the site a decade ago. We did not know yet if the oil had been contaminated, as had all the oil in the rest of the world. So, we had civilians, potentially oil workers, and the two jetties towards the end of the Island looked clean and busy, so maybe fisherfolk as well. The tactical issue was simple if you said it fast—get the team into position, get the shells, and get out again without anyone noticing, and most importantly, no one shooting at us.

I needed more intelligence; I needed someone on the ground, and I needed real eyeballs on our target.

"Sandra, according to the data, there is a pub and boarding house to the northeast of the terminal. Take the best-looking trooper we have—and every hand went up—you're backpackers staying for a few days, doing the tourist bit, drive to the ferry terminal, look natural, soft clothes, small arms only. I need to know the state of the target and the probable interaction we might face."

"Commander…" She started to answer me back, saw the look on my face, then grabbed two troopers and pulled their faces in close to hers with one hand, then put one pointed finger in the middle of my chest with the other. "Keep her out of trouble. Don't let her out of your sight!"Then she pushed through the troops, looking left and right. "Who wants to be my boyfriend or girlfriend for a day?" Every hand still stayed up, laughter broke out, and she pointed to the tall Israeli who had fought side by side with us on three previous occasions.

"I'll take Shifrah; the rest of you can wait your turn." And she climbed back into the jet to change. The two troopers she had nominated flanked me, so I spoke to the master sergeant, whose responsibility had never been spelled out, but he had managed to be part of every briefing I had even given to the troops.

"Sergeant, find somewhere to bivouac, plan on at least one night, and keep our weapons out of sight. This is a public terminal; there is no need to scare the natives any more than we have already." The airport official, who had been patiently standing off to one side while we made up our minds, moved forward, causing my two bodyguards to try to get in front of me, which I stopped with a firm pushback with both hands. The official ignored the guards and looked directly at me.

"Commander, there is a large area behind the number two hangar you can use; the army has it fitted with ablutions and cooking facilities, and they use it occasionally for exercises." His bright yellow high-visibility jacket with its fluorescent stripes stood out in the dark, making a contrast with our dull black combat gear. I smiled and shook my head at the incongruity and walked back into our jet, where Sandra and her friend were just finishing changing. The dirty look she gave me said it all, but I needed my best set of eyes on the target, and if I couldn't go, she would have to.

'Sit down for a minute. Both of you." Sandra did, but her body was stiff, and I chose not to notice. "I need on-the-ground-eyeballs-this is a very large and complex site, and the chance of collateral damage is high. I need to know who is where, what they do, how often the tanks are guarded, if there are terrorists on the Island, etc. You know the drill. I'd like to be going in at midnight tomorrow. See if you can make that a possibility." I looked Sandra dead in the eyes, held her stare, saw her blink, nodded silently to her, then let her and her companion go.

Another large change in management style for me cutting loose the one person who the Boss had personally told to stick to me like glue, but we were a very small team, and I simply couldn't afford to have so much talent locked away guarding me. I dialed my mini.

"Indigo, where are you, and how goes it?" His smiling face gave me a boost after Sandra's cold shoulder and warmed me a little.

"Commander, we are abeam Skerries, around forty kilometers from Dublin, and our geeks have us very close to where we think the blur is. We're feeling our way, but there is nothing on the road or anything our drones have picked up at this time." I gave that a moment's thought, flicked the map of the eastern coast of Ireland up on my mini, looked at the alternatives, then made a decision that would either establish me as a genius or the dumbest person ever to have led an Interpol team.

"Indigo, go straight to the location in Dublin, coordinate with Bob, get the shell on its way to Israel, split your total team, half to go back and pick up the trail with the geeks, you and the remainder get here to Cork ASAP. Clear?" I could see the slight hesitation on his face, I had worked closely with him for over six years now, and I knew his strong desire to finish everything he started. It was almost a mantra with him, one I respected.

"Indigo, I need you here." He finally smiled, nodded his head, looked straight back into the camera, and gave me the full force of his incredible energy.

"*Sì, comandante, saremo con te il prima possibile. Rimani al sicuro.*" I would do my utmost to stay safe, and I mentally wished him luck. I dialed one more person, watched the craggy face of the boss swim into focus, took a deep breath, then started in.

"I need backup. The target is a very long site, with civilians, workers, and who knows what, it's an oil refinery, somewhat isolated, but there is no way a squad of fourteen can safely take it down. I'm informed that it is now used as the strategic reserve for oil storage for the whole of Ireland, so we can expect government traffic daily. I need a team from the Irish special forces, under my command, but acting in an official government capacity. I'm planning on attacking tomorrow evening, and I've sent Sandra plus one as backpackers to the Island to do a reconnoiter. What would be handy is the special forces landing tomorrow morning, sweeping the peninsular, getting all the civilians out of the way, so we can go in and get the shells." He looked at me, a slight smile creasing his face, his favorite look when thinking about being a bastard.

"What are you doing about transportation?"

"Undecided. These shells are three times the size of the ones that came from Afghanistan, plus there's an indication on the scan of several large barrels and their signature is quite faint, and our best guess is nanites. And it's an Island." He looked thoughtful and nodded.

"Would a big chopper carry the load?"

"If it was one of those brutes the Americans use—I think it's called a King Stallion—it might do it, they can carry up to 20 thousand pounds, but how do you get one to us in a day?"

"Call your friend the admiral. I'll work this end, and get back to you." He looked directly at the camera and went all serious for a minute. "You're doing great, Jessica, keep loose, keep thinking." I dialed the admiral. He came on the screen, his background was a cyclone of flashing colors; his hair was standing on end and I could feel his tension. Then the whole image steadied, and I realized he was standing in front of a massive vertical wheel of some sort. He moved to one side, and a huge black shadow covered his face, then resolved into a striped pattern that made him look like he had painted his face.

"Admiral, sorry to bother you, but do you have a spare CH-53 lying around anywhere close?"

"Close to where?" he shouted. The background noise sounded like several jet engines were revving for takeoff simultaneously. The shadows over his face softened, and he moved slightly back from the camera, revealing the starched collar of his khaki shirt, and the gold star of his rank.

"Ireland." He looked thoughtful, shaded his eyes with a hand, and nodded.

"You've got three of my RRT teams already. What do you need such a big helicopter for?"

"I have to lift eight shells and what looks like 20 big barrels out of my target zone in Whiddy Island." He squinted his eyes. Obviously, the ambient light, wherever he was, was killing him.

He nodded, looked off camera as the jet engine noise intensified, then back at the camera.

"Where do you want it, and when?"

"Cork, now, but no later than fifteen hundred hours tomorrow."

"It will be there." And the sudden lack of noise told me he had pulled the plug at his end, and I fed the mini back into my pocket. A battle plan was slowly forming in my mind, I might not be as quick as the boss or as detailed as Tom and Pete might be, but all the pieces were coming together, and all I had to do now was get everyone in the right place the right way, and at the right time.

I looked at the picture of the refinery, and like everything else in Ireland, the grass was greener, the ocean bluer, and the light seemed to have a heavenly hue, making the metal of the tanks with the red-lined rims glow slightly, a contrast between the white of the tops, and the metallic green of the sides. The small vehicles down the pier end fluoresced, and the roads looked swept and in excellent condition.

Difficult to imagine that such deadly weapons as nuclear shells could ever be part of this beautiful and timeless surreal landscape.

CHAPTER NINE

Sandra and Shifrah climbed off the car ferry with big, bright backpacks slung over their shoulders and almost matching floppy hats. At a little over six feet in height, even in sturdy and well-worn combat boots, Shifrah was not easy to miss, and as both wore stylish sunglasses, it was difficult to see where they were looking. The simple answer was everywhere; they considered themselves to be in enemy territory, in fact, behind enemy lines, and the puffy jackets they wore, as it was chilly so early in the morning, disguised that both of them had one hand well inside their jackets and on the grip of their weapon. As the sun was quite bright, almost washing out the early morning sky, the dark glasses wouldn't draw any particular notice.

They managed to remain in the middle of the group of tourists who had made the trip over on the ferry, a strange sight under the current circumstances, but the plethora of accents and languages suggested a well-mixed group of people from mainland Europe. The two women slowed their gait, making no effort to draw attention to themselves, and when they reached the main road from the jetty, both stopped, looked around, then dropped their packs and sat on them back to back.

"These civilians won't make it easy for us," Shifrah commented, burying her head in a spread-out guide map that they had purchased on the ferry. It showed a short walk to the one pub, which had short-term lodging available, subject to bookings. The oil tanks were all marked, the no-go areas indicated, the emergency phone numbers should something be amiss, even the number for the local Fire Unit, which was listed as a voluntary service the Island was very proud of.

"No, they could be a complication, but let's swap views and tell me what you see." They stood up, stretched, then sat down on each other's packs, now facing one hundred and eighty degrees away from their previous view. Sandra now looked at the small huts and vehicles parked on the verge of a fisherman's wharf, nets hanging out to dry in the moody sunlight, with men in dark green wellingtons and full-body rubber suits, colorful woolen hats bobbing up and down to some silent tune. Shifrah now had a clear view down the main road, all the way down to a long hut at the very far end before the road hooked to the right, behind the last oil tank.

What caught her attention was a miniature set of rails that ran all the way to the shed, almost hidden by overgrown grass and weeds. They were shiny, indicating they had been recently used, and the grass in the center of the rails held a telltale brown hue as if recently attacked by an oily flame thrower. She leaned back until it looked like she was watching the seabirds squawking overhead, no doubt telling the fisherfolk to hurry up and throw them breakfast.

She casually pulled her mini out of her pocket, and her hands, hidden by the map, snapped a series of short videos of the entire road.

"To the commander?"

"Yes."

"What now?" Sandra looked around. The tour group had mounted a small, open-sided bus and was heading up the road. The fisherfolk were finally throwing the waste from their catch out for the birds, it looked and felt like a perfectly normal day on a beautiful Island, and even the ferry, which had now pulled back and was turning for its trip back to the mainland, looked normal. But under it all she felt a fission of tension, and her well-toned back muscles, a true reflector of her instincts, had autonomously hunched her shoulders in an effort to make her less of a physical target.

"I've got an itch. Let's scratch it. Go for a walk. I'm putting in buds, so don't be quiet if you have something to say." She fitted two flesh-colored earbuds, shook her hair to cover her ears, rolled her shoulders, lifted her pack, checked the snap faster on the zippered compartment that held her H&K, waited for her companion to shake her pack into position, watched her check her own quick-release pouch, and then started off down the road, paralleling the tracks but well away from them.

They had originally planned to camp near the ancient gun emplacement, as it was close to their target, on a well-grassed area, which was clearly marked as a recreational park. Sandra now had a tactical decision to make. If the rails were what they both suspected them to be, they needed to take a hard look at the infrastructure at the end of the road. Their target oil tank was three rows over and close to the old gun emplacement, around 500 meters away.

To get there, they had decided to walk the entire peninsula, taking photos with their minis as they went. This meant they would walk up the long side of the storage area past ten of the tanks, back down between the first two rows, then finally back up to the remaining two tanks, one of which was their target. That had been their plan, which they would now modify. They hadn't gone far before they were hailed.

"Hello there, might you be going up to the pub then, and might you be needing a lift?" The melodious voice, obviously Irish, came from a red-headed woman of indeterminable age, driving a bright green open truck, which rocked back and forth on its springs when she braked. Sandra elbow-bumped her companion, smiled, pulled her hand out of her jacket, and waved.

"Hi! Thank you, but we're happy to walk. Need the exercise." The redhead smiled, waved, then drove off slowly, the unmistakable whine of her EV slicing through the crisp air. As the vehicle moved up the road, Shifrah squinted her eyes and rolled her shoulders.

"Pretty woman, I wonder if she will turn out to be one of our targets?"

"I had the same feeling, but we could both just be a little wired. She just might have been married for 20 years and have six bright and bouncy kids running around somewhere." Shifrah laughed and punched Sandra on the shoulder with her free hand.

"If that's true, then they would account for just under half of the published population!" Sandra laughed, then stopped, bent as if to check her boot laces, kneeled, fussed around some, then spoke in a low voice.

"Check out this. Get a photo of it if you can, but don't make it obvious." Shifrah pulled her pack off, pulled out a sketch pad, and cleverly palmed her mini under the pad. Then she walked back a step and started to draw Sandra on her knees with the long shed in the background. Sandra stood, looked over her shoulder, pointed to a corner as if critiquing the drawing, slapped her clever Israeli companion on the back, then waited until she had remounted her pack. They walked off, following the road around, noticing that it ran straight for around three hundred meters and had the same shunt-like attachments as the main road had.

"We have a choice. Keep going, follow the road to the pub, veer off to the fort, or walk somewhere else." Sandra looked into the distance, where she could see the target tank heading off at an angle to the twin rows with their red-lined tops. "Okay, I vote we walk around the backside of our target, get to that small block of buildings, one of which will be the pub, and maybe have a beer."

"Beer, no thank you. G and T, yes, Schnapps, yes, even sparkling wine, but not that dreadful black tar the locals call beer, thank you very much." Sandra laughed, happy to have such an interesting companion. One she knew was an expert markswoman, had provided overwatch on the last two combat missions, and had a deadly backhand in unarmed combat. But she looked the part of a young backpacker, and right now, that was her most important attribute.

"Hold that thought. There's the fort, and there's our target." Sandra pointed to the tank, noticing that the ancient gun emplacement was approximately the same diameter. She wondered if it was an accident or someone's silent tribute to their forefathers. She understood the Irish were very much like that, proud of their history and just as proud of their ancestry, having the world's record for being invaded by everyone with a boat over the centuries.

"There's something funky about these two tanks. Look at the base."

"Yes, I can see it. Access panels, some form of sliding doorway, are very large. You could get a semi in there without effort."

"But no tracks in the grass."

"No. Either they haven't been here for a while, or they've got concrete or Marston Mats under the grass."

"My money's on Marston Mats. Look at the pattern of the grass clumps." Sandra zoomed in her mini camera and saw the telltale circles cut into the PSP's (perforated steel planking). Developed for the US Army Airforce, which needed instant runways all across the Pacific Islands at the start of World War II, the PSPs were stamped out by the thousands and shipped all around the world and could still be found supporting grass airfields all over the globe.

"When you put what've found around the other side together with this, I think we need to have a chat with Jessica. Sit with your back to me. I'm going to give her a call." The women put their packs on top of each other, then sat down back to back, the Israeli opening her large map again to cover their actions. The deep green-tinted blue of the waterway sparkled in the light, and seabirds flew in swarms, looping the loop without a care in the world.

"Jessica, have you seen the photos we sent before?"

"Yes." I watched Sandra's face for her usual tells: a slight tightening of her eyes, the small lines at the corner of her mouth closing up. She looked relaxed, but there was tension in her voice. "You look happy, but I can see you're not. What's up?" My two Italian bodyguards, one on either side, turned to face out-wards, creating the illusion of privacy. The back of Shifrah's head was in focus, but the view was blocked by whatever it was she was reading.

"Jessica, this place is a military camp. We've spotted launching and retrieval rails for drones, and our target oil tank has access points for a semitrailer cut into its side. And there's a distinct possibility we've been made." That got a reaction from me, and I looked quickly around to make sure I couldn't be overheard.

"How?"

"We were offered a lift just after we got off the ferry by a good-looking redhead, youngish, around forty-ish, fit, driving a small truck. She was very polite and made no attempt to push her invitation to ride, just drove off with a wave." I tried to picture this in my mind; where was the threat in driving away? But rule one, trust your troops on the ground, so I took it seriously and started to work out how to back them up—they were only eighty-odd kilometers away, less than thirty-five minutes by helicopter—but I suspected that would only make matters worse if they had in fact been identified as Interpol or more likely as military or police.

"Do you have a suggestion?"

"Yes. Defer the attack, work out how to overload the Island with good guys, and wait for more intel." As I already had Irish Special Forces on the way, point two was possible, and if we had eyes on the ground, then maybe we could wait a day or two, but I was still very edgy about nuclear-capable weapons being within my reach and remaining free.

"Stand by, keep looking, and stay safe." I clicked off before she could continue the conversation, looked around the camp where my two teams were gearing up, waved to Indigo who had just arrived with half his people, Fay and all of Tom's, and he trotted over on the double.

"*Salve, comandante, siamo riusciti a recuperare i proiettili a Dublino, come posso essere al servizio ora?*"

"Thanks for that. Now I need one of your exceptional coffees, and five minutes of your time. Send someone else for the coffee." He laughed and waved to one of my guards, who took off at a trot. I waved Fay over. She had finished whatever she was doing with her troops and was looking a little worse for wear.

"*Cinnte*, commander, at your service." I smiled. This light banter relieves my stress better than a massage. We moved into the lee of the hangar. Indigo motioned the other guard away; he saluted and took off, and the coffee arrived on a beaten-up old tray that had seen the best of its days some decades ago.

"Indigo, here is the overhead of the Island. Sandra and Shifrah are here, between the road and the gun encampment. They have sent images of high-tech drone rails and catching mechanisms on these two roads." I pointed to where the women had seen the rails and flicked on the video. Indigo bent his head, then straightened. Fay duplicated his action and looked at me with her head tilted to one side.

"Might it be possible that this is where the drone that shot you down came from?" she asked, looking as pissed as I felt.

"Possible, not important at the moment. Look at this shot." I held up the closeup of the massive doors cut into the base of the oil tank, again she turned her head looking pissed.

"If these shells are as big as we suspect, then they would have needed a large transport to have gotten them there. Do you know if the ferry is large enough for a semitrailer?"

"From what Sandra says, yes. And that means that someone has seen this entire activity, probably passed off as something to do with the oil storage, there are quite a few workers around the site, lots of fisherfolk, and that's what I want to talk to you both about." Indigo's eyes twinkled, so I grabbed him with one arm, and Fay with the other and started to walk with them.

"This is a big area to attack. There are civilians all over the place, the potential for collateral damage is high; and we don't know the bad guys from the good guys, so we need a strategy to either clear the Island of people or isolate them somewhere while we go in and take the shells." He looked at me with his twinkling eyes again. I knew he wasn't laughing at me, but he was on the verge of mirth, and I didn't see the joke! Fay just watched this play quietly and stoically, probably as much at a loss as I was.

"Commander, it seems to me that this is your first really big battle, and you have nerves!" And he did laugh but patted me on the arm at the same time. "Perfectly normal reaction. I'm nervous as well. This is a really difficult assault for the likes of us. What are you planning?" And just like that, he turned deadly serious. I looked deep into his eyes, more for comfort than anything else, turned back towards our starting point, and noticed that we were being shadowed by my two guards. I just shook my head. I would sort that out later.

"My idea is to get the Irish Special Forces to mount an exercise on the Island, make a lot of fuss and bother and noise, wave around Government documents, act like they own the place, then slip in while everyone is distracted and get the shells out. I've requested a CH-53 from the Americans. It will be here sometime today, and we've now got Tom's team and your squad. What I want from you is your best idea on how to isolate the civilians and keep them out of the line of fire." He held out his mug to one of the guards, who raced off to refill it. He took my mini off me, zoomed in on the peninsula, scrolled back and forth, then looked up at me with a very serious look.

"Commander, you could force an evacuation using the Sciathán Fianóglach; they are first class, and we are known to them through the boss. They were briefed on everything we did a month ago, and I know they also got an after-action report. That way, anyone who stays on the Island could be considered a potential threat and dealt with accordingly."

"Could they do that?"

"Absolutely. Give the Island notice when they arrive here, and move everyone out by 18 hundred hours tonight. Two or three ferry trips should do it, and then let the commandos take up strategic positions to protect our team during the retrieval." I nodded. It was a great idea, I just wondered at the local reaction to being kicked off their Island by the military. In a sense, it was not my problem. Keeping my people and any bystanders safe was, so now I needed to work out how to get a message to the Island, given the current state of communications, manage the extraction of everyone on the Island, then plan the attack required to get the shells and whatever else was in those tanks.

And possibly destroy those drone rails and any infrastructure around them. I dialed Sandra and was comforted to see her still sitting with her back to Shifrah, taking in the rays.

"Do you have somewhere you can hide?"

"Not immediately. We've noticed a string of cameras on top of the oil tanks. Some point down, some point out." I nodded. This was expected, then I had a thought.

"Could you continue to wander around the Island, find somewhere to disappear for an hour or two while we get reinforcements on the ground?"

I could see Sandra thinking it over, then she leaned back and whispered something in Shifrah's ear. She pointed to the top of the map, and they both nodded. Then Sandra looked back at the camera.

"We can go walkabout to the far northeastern side of the Island, where there's another fort. It's near a large homestead and just north of where the Whiddy Ferry used to pull in before the terrorist attacks. Apparently, the jetty was destroyed by gangs who tried to take over the Island, just after the attacks on the Vatican and the Dome of the Rock. The locals, backed up by the Garda and a small force of Army reservists, beat them down. It's been written up on the map we purchased on the ferry over as a point of interest in some detail."

"Good to know. That will give our current operation a baseline to work from. Okay, I'm sending Fay over as backup. She'll arrive in the next three hours. Start your trek, and watch your back. There'll be a briefing in a couple of hours, and once all the troops are here." I turned to Fay, looked at her weary face, saw only determination in it, and nodded.

"Fay, take two of Tom's team, dress casual, day trippers, catch the ferry, then make your way to the top end of the Island, link up with Sandra and Shifrah. Try not to compromise them in the process. I want you all back in one piece!" This brought a wry smile to her beautiful face. She gave us a mock salute and took off. I turned around, started walking away with Indigo in tow, and dialed up my reliable Israeli navigator, currently at 35,000 feet above us, orbiting the Island.

"Ito, how goes it?"

"No change, commander. We have three hours before we need to refuel. Do you want us to continue?"

"Affirmative, but switch to ground mapping, FLIR, and GPR (ground penetration radar). Map the whole Island, please, as fast as you can."

"Do you want the drones to stay on station?" I thought for a minute. We had the location of the shells and an indication of barrels reading as if they contained nanites. Did I need to keep them in the air? I looked at Indigo, and he just shook his head.

"No, Ito, recover them. Thank you, get me that ground data as soon as you can please."

"WILCO". I turned as Indigo started asking a question.

"You suspect a setup like you found in Montana and Turkey?" I nodded.

"They have always had a headquarters somewhere, and the speed at which they evacuated both sites leads me to believe they were tactical, not strategic. Even 'Helen's' lair, while it looked solid, came apart very fast when we attacked, and taking her out of commission slowed them down but didn't stop them. There seems to be a rolling supply of leaders, well placed to continue their campaign. And Fay has a theory, and I trust her instincts."

"You think there are more women running things and that some of them might be here, in Ireland?"

"Yes."

"Why?" I looked at him, it was unlike him to challenge my thinking, but this is what I needed—someone to bounce stuff off, test my thinking, and force me to work at being correct. The Boss and I had developed a tempo and a rhythm that allowed us to bounce stuff off each other, which I had yet to do with anyone on my team. Maybe this was my chance.

"Indigo, just a few weeks ago, we bombed a subterranean work site out of existence just up the road and a tunnel that had been here for years. No pile, but we interrupted the loading of shells with terminal results. Add to that the woman and her patrol boat, nuclear material, and shells, all out of an Irish port, plus the terrorist Malik Badawi from Al Bar al Shirak, and his really big boat and shells, again, located initially here in Ireland, then add in Siobhan O'Cleary, the nuclear scientist, who holds Irish nationality, plus the two girls we took back in Helena, and you have a solid history of Ireland being at the center, or at least a major player, in everything that has happened over the last three and a half months." He nodded, looked very serious, then nodded again.

"If you take away the mercenary terrorists, the women have all come from either the United States or Ireland. We know there are boatloads of refugees headed for the US. Why not here?" My turn to nod, and a little grin started to form. This is why it helped to talk all this stuff out with someone you trusted and respected. I filled my face with a smile, clapped him on his broad back, and laughed.

"Exactly. We know there was at least one trust fund set up for Ireland, and we know a slab of that went on building Badawi's boat, but we haven't found the ship set that was sent here. Plus, think Dome of the Rock." He looked blank for a second or two, then turned his head and smiled.

"The drone."

"Yes, the drone. Israeli manufacturer. We suspected it was launched and managed from Turkey, but maybe it came from this little Island here. We haven't found any rails or catching equipment anywhere else."

"And you and the Boss worked out that it had the range to have been able to fly across the Mediterranean Sea." He dipped his head for a minute, thinking.

"What has Ireland got that makes it so attractive?" I smiled and slapped him on the back again.

"Great question. And I'm thinking of a million empty homes or houses, a strong innate rural farming background, strong community roots, and it's out of the way of the European bloc and all its troubles."

"But a home or house needs a family unit, someone to work the land and support the household." I looked up at the magnificent, crystal-clear sky, and tried to imagine how to manage a household with blended personalities, nationalities, religions, and temperaments. The terrorists had used existing family units in both the US and New Zealand, offering financial and social stability for families who adopted refugee children. The broad base for this work was the provision of incredibly efficient solar and power packs. Ireland had cloud cover half of every day on average, so the terrorists would need to supplement their solar strategy with something else if they wanted the resettlement plan to work at the same scale. And adults would be involved if they intended to fill the existing empty infrastructure. And the women did not like men or even little boys. So what would be their social model?

I knew who had the answer or could at least ask the questions from those that might, so I dialed the boss.

"Sorry to interrupt," I said, ogling his Italian cut suit, starched white shirt, and regimental tie. He caught my sarcasm and gave me the hurry-up signal, so I just laughed. "You look good. I hope you are enjoying all the mucky-mucks you have to deal with." His scowl told me what I had guessed. I was just very glad it wasn't me playing grownups in Lyon or the Hague.

"I need you to ask your contacts in Red Cross, Red Crescent, Médecins Sans Frontières, who they are moving towards Ireland, age, profession, quantity, and timing."

"Please."

"Please."

"Why?"

"I suspect there is a new refugee resettlement model in the works, and I want to get in front of it if I can." He looked puzzled for a second, tilted his head to one side. His close-cut black hair was showing a lot of gray, and his craggy face, scarred as it was, was never a pleasant sight by any means but looked well-polished and calm. The job must have suited him, or maybe he was growing into it. I crossed my fingers. I had an unrequited crush on him, something I was constantly aware of every time we spoke.

"How is the information going to help you with your plan to take the Island?" I paused and thought through my answer, mixing tactical plans and broader social issues never went well once the rubber hit the road.

"There's a deeper undercurrent here than we initially expected. In talking it over with Indigo, it occurred to us we should be aware of what their next step might be."

"What was Indigo's take on it?"

"He spoke perfect English the whole conversation." The boss looked surprised. Shot his immaculate cuffs out from his jacket sleeves, no mean feat balancing a mini-computer in his hand at the same time.

"That serious. It will take me at least two hours before I can make the calls. Will that fit your planning?"

"Yes, thanks. At this point, we're not going in until late tonight." He shut us down, the screen went black, and I put the mini back in my pants pocket. There were times I wondered about who his mother was and how he was raised, then stopped thinking about that as the sky filled with a massive black and gray cloud, punitive rotor wash, and sensationally loud jet engine noise. Our big-assed helicopter had arrived, so I held onto my cap and bent my head to avoid the flying debris the instant storm was kicking up. Indigo was following my lead, and we both looked up as the noise and the storm moved away. The C-53, the biggest helicopter in the American arsenal, was a massive 99 feet from nose to tail, just under 30 feet high, and its monstrous seven-bladed rotor reached 79 feet from tip to tip.

It sat down on the chipped tarmac at the front of the hangar so lightly it might have been a butterfly and immediately sagged down onto its wheels, and as the rotor spun down, the tips of the massive blades came closer and closer to ground level, finally stopping just a few feet up in the air. Up close, the sheer size was awesome, but the real surprise was the man who was first down the rear ramp, none other than the master chief who had worked with us onboard the carrier last month. On that occasion, he and I had a serious chat about the effect Sandra and I were having on his crew, and we openly discussed the differences in our approaches to combat.

As in, we shot first and never really bothered to ask a question, whereas his Navy was restricted to the Geneva Convention and all the rules and strictures that brought with it.

He also pointed out the rigid hierarchical structure the Navy had built around authority, planning, and execution, in direct contrast to us making it up as we went along and frequently changing our minds along the way.

Chalk and cheese. Asymmetric warfare had changed the rules, there was no doubt about that, and we had been deliberately stood up by Interpol, the UN, and all their members, to understand that and act accordingly. Which we did, and that had been the root of my conversation with him.

"Hello, master chief. What brings you to this neighborhood?" I held out my hand to welcome him. He pushed his visor up, a huge smile lighting his craggy face, his hand in its green Nomex glove reaching out for mine.

"Commander, good to see you. The admiral sends his regards."

"Nice to know. And the real reason you're here?"

"He wants his chopper back in the same condition it's in now, and I'm sworn to see to that." I laughed, clapped him on his broad back, noticed the six well-armed commandos that followed him out and steered him over to where we had set up our makeshift camp.

"Excellent. I don't suppose any of your people are trained in our RRT methodology?"

"Affirmative, ma'am. This is the team your own people trained up on the factory ship." I nodded. That was very good to hear. Now we had four RRTs to handle whatever we found, and with my mini buzzing at me again, I moved away, having passed him off to Indigo, who saluted the chief as a matter of respect and handed him a steaming mug of coffee. Indigo knew what the chief had gone through with Sandra and me in the chase of the ex-Iranian gunboat and its subsequent destruction in a nuclear fireball just a month previously. It felt like years. We were running up so many critical actions one after the other that it was really hard to keep track of such a simple thing as time.

"Yes, Ito, how can I help you?" The face of the nuggety Israeli navigator was partly shadowed. I guessed the aircraft was banking across the sun.

"Commander, I'm downloading the first scan to you now, but based on the material we reviewed after the attack in Turkey and your report from Montana, we have another tunnel system running from the tank farm to a large building marked here." And his map with a POI (point of interest) framed in one corner of the screen.

"Indigo, map of the Island." He rushed over, pulling his mini out, tapping it as he ran, then thrusting it under my nose with a bump. I dragged Ito's map over to Indigo's screen, and my shoulders sagged.

"Ito, what are these big circles?" I asked, looking at the two screens.

"Commander, the tanks are now painting as solid objects, using the ground scans we have activated. Sorry, I can't comment beyond that." I thanked him and switched off, dragging both maps onto my mini.

"Indigo, this POI is where Sandra and Shifrah were going to ground. We need to warn them, and I need to change our plan again. What time do we think Fay will be on the Island?" He looked at his watch, worn on his right wrist, face turned under an old soldier's trick, took his computer back and looked at me with intense scrutiny.

"She'll be off the ferry in half an hour." I held my mini against my forehead as if trying to divine a solution and then recognized what I was doing.

"Indigo, collect everybody, get them into the hangar, briefing in ten, take the chief with you. I'll join you in a few." He saluted, something I'm sure he did automatically, but maybe to bolster my ego. It was sagging, for sure, because we now had a huge problem digging out the shells. From the scan, it was obvious that this was a major operating base for the terrorists, on the same scale as the one in Montana, but this time we had an unknown number of civilians walking around and a perplexing set of photos that could be either very good news, or very bad.

Then a khaki-colored chinook darkened the sky, with a rubber duckie slung underneath, and three Irish Army helicopters and two gunships appeared out of nowhere. The helicopters landed, and the chinook continued on towards our target, its twin rotors making a wonderful sound as they thrashed the air unmercifully, the rubber ducky swinging freely in its swing, and I drew the conclusion it would put down in the water at Bantry, just opposite the Island. A gaggle of army rangers deplaned from the helicopters, the leader running over to the chief, whom he saluted, then looking a little startled when the chief pointed to me, and the next minute I had the youngest-looking soldier I had ever seen standing at attention before me.

I promise you, he looked about twelve, bright, shiny face, very short red hair, and a huge smile, and in his camos and battle dress, he looked like someone playing dress up.

"Commander, Major O'Leary reporting, Team Thee, Sciathán Fianóglach, at your service." His Irish accent was so musical I could listen to it all day.

"Your Chinook and boat are headed to Bantry?"

"Aye, that they are. We'll drop some of the girls and boys off there, then coordinate an approach using the helicopters and the boat to suit your purpose."

"Have you been briefed on what I want to do?"

"Maybe we have been a little, I would think, but to be sure more information would be welcome." I nodded, thought fast, and pointed to where Indigo was assembling the troops.

"Take your people, over there, get coffee or whatever you drink. We'll have a briefing in five." He snapped another salute and waved to his people, and I was pleased to see his aircrew joining the crews on the ground. In the type of asymmetric warfare we engaged in, everyone needed to know and understand every detail of our planning, even if we were going to change it minute by minute. Actually, that we the real reason for my paranoia about briefings.

I stood perfectly still, visualizing the Island, the oil farm, the drone rails, the building we thought might be the hangar, the oil tank where the shells were hidden, then the long tunnel that ran from the tank farm to the building that sat right next to the Napoleon era fort at the northern end of the Island. I had texted a 'hold' message to Sandra, so with luck, they would not yet be in the hornets' nest. I had told Fay to hold at the pub with her two troopers. I had assets on the ground, but in completely unknown circumstances. That worried me a lot.

I walked slowly over to where the mixed crews from the US Navy, the Irish Special Forces, Tom's team of mixed US, and Israeli commando 104 personnel, Indigo's RRTs, and the Italian Special Forces who had traveled with Sandra and I. Mixed in there were weapons specialists, technical experts on nuclear hardware, pilots and aircrew, sailors and ground pounders, long gun shooters, and close quarters combat experts. They needed a focus, and it had to be simple, and everything else had to be spelled out in a way that gave us the maximum flexibility with the maximum safety for our teams and the civilians on the Island.

I knew, utterly, that my people were trained for the job and very, very good at what we did. As far as everyone else was concerned, I would make sure they were put in positions where they could do their very best without compromising the mission.

No battle plan survived the first shot, but the people putting their lives on the line still needed direction and confidence in their commanders.

"Listen up." Every head turned to look at me, and apart from my shaggy hair, I looked like I always looked -rumpled, creased, but ready for anything. And I grinned at that thought as Indigo moved around the people distributing closed-net communication devices.

"I am Commander Riley, my second in command is Colonel Kashasini, and I have overall command of the entire mission. We have people on the Island, they will make themselves known to you if necessary, and you will take direction from two of them—Inspectors Thomas and Remer— and that direction will override anything you might be doing at that time." That got me some looks from the US and Irish contingents. The Israeli commander of the 104 just hid a very small smirk by bending her head down. At the end of the day, I would have to rely on their individual commanders to brief them further. The master chief had met and worked with Sandra and me previously, so he knew my habit of changing plans on the fly, and it was impossible at this point to anticipate why they would be issuing countermanding orders. But I wanted all the people involved in this to understand the potential for changes on the ground.

"Our target is this silo, where we believe multiple nuclear-capable devices are stored. We believe they are inert. The RRTs that will travel with me are equipped to neutralize these devices and will take care of any other materials that may also need to be neutralized." I looked over at the C-53 crew and saw the two women pilots and their flight engineer standing together, with four really tough-looking sailors in full combat gear milling around them. Probably chatting them up and looking for a date.

"Chief, you and your crew will fly from here to a small strip at Bantry. You'll find the Irish Chinook there. Wait for our signal, then I want your tail in, ramp down, at this point." I flicked him an overhead of the target silo, where we had marked the landing area as close to the side of the silo as we could. "Hold for a further briefing at the conclusion of this one." He nodded, turned to his people, pulled them into a group, and started a conversation. Whether or not the sailors got a date would never be known!

"Major O'Leary, I need you to empty the Island of civilians and eventually to create a people-free zone around the tanks we are targeting. You are authorized by the Irish government, the World Court, and Interpol to evacuate everyone off the Island, on the basis that there is a clear and present danger in the form of potential nuclear weapons. I want it clear by 1800 hours or as close to that as you can manage. Once you have the Island secure, I want you to stage your people in three groups, your discretion as to the makeup; one group here at the fisherman's wharf, one group here at the Napoleon gun emplacement on the north end of the Island, and one here at the head of the road where we believe a drone hangar is located. It is possible that you will be attacked by an unknown number of terrorists. You cannot take for granted that everyone will obey the evacuation order." I looked at the lithe red-headed major. I promise you, to shave he had only to stand out in a strong wind, but the Irish Rangers had a reputation not unlike the Special Boat Service in the UK, so I just held my peace until it was clear he had no questions.

"My teams—all RTTs and support personnel—will land by helicopter at three strategic locations: here, here, and here." I highlighted the landing zones in yellow for all to see. I was just getting into my stride when my mini yelled at me again, so I held up a hand and took the call.

"Jessica, we have a problem. Can you get secure?" Sandra's anxious face filled the screen, and I could see by the background that they were near the ocean. I walked away a few strides, and Indigo inserted himself between me and the teams sitting on the ground.

"Go."

"There's a well-disguised production plant on the western side of the Island, running full-bore as far as we can tell. I'll send you the location in a minute. It's disguised as a series of farm sheds. We only found it because an electric vehicle took off from a property we were near, and we got curious and followed on foot." The map with a blue scribble overlay popped onto my screen, and I could see that it was abeam the second old Napoleon gun fort, but on the opposite side of the Island, around half a mile away.

Interesting. This made the far end of the Island as important as the southern one with the oil tanks, and the tunnel we had uncovered with the earth mapping scan clearly linked both ends. And I was not sure if I had sufficient boots on the ground to attack both locations simultaneously.

"What caught your eye and can you tell what they're manufacturing?"

"The electric buggy was driven by the most beautiful woman I have ever seen, and her companion rated a one hundred fifty on the OMG meter. And yes. Power panels, but nothing like the ones we saw in Point Roberts or New Zealand. These are dull gray/black, and they look like roof shingles, but in wide planks. There are literally thousands stacked in the field we are in, covered with dirt and grass, and even a few sheep. You would never had spotted them from the air. We just saw a new batch unloaded, and a tractor covered them up in minutes. And before you ask, no, the drones would not have seen them. They were electronically focused on the shells." I thought about this very weird situation, but in consideration, we had already taken two operating plants out of service, or at least taken them away from the terrorists, having placed them under the control of the US Army and the New Zealand Government, both of whom were still operating them and supporting the re-establishment of thousands of young refugee girls.

In that respect, at least, the terrorists had been successful.

"How large is the plant?"

"Based on the buildings we have scouted, it's probably one-third that of Point Roberts. It's very compact, and the only sign it's working is the heat haze the buildings are sending up."Indigo, who had been listening in over my shoulder, had his mini out, and I could see him talking to our C-17 crew, and while I thought about my options, an aerial view of the area zoomed into focus: a massive huge bog covered with grass and trees, sheep, and what looked like a cow. Then, at the very edge, the telltale twin pipes led into the ocean, which in turn led to a blocky building that looked like a milking shed. The trees, shrubs, and natural foliage made it hard to differentiate the other buildings, but if you looked hard enough, you could just see the overgrown pathways cutting between them. Unlike Point Roberts and New Zealand, for that matter, this plant had been designed to be hidden from the get-go.

Brilliant camouflage. But then, these were brilliant women, possibly some of the smartest people on the planet if Amira and Fay were anything to go by. And once again, they had been in front of us for months, if not years. Now I needed to change our strategy or tactics on the ground, and I needed my brain's trust to ensure I missed nothing and minimized the risks. I group dialed Indigo, Fay, Sandra, the master chief, Sgan Aluf, and the major and texted them to come to me. I sent a message to everyone else via the miniature tight-band communicators Indigo had given everyone.

'There's been a slight development in our plans. Take ten. We will pick up where we left off. Relax, get a drink and sandwich, but be back here by 1150.' I moved a few feet away, shadowed by Indigo. The major, master chief and commander of the 104 marched up, and Sandra and Fay's faces were resolved in the mini-screen.

"People, we need to change our plan. Major, forget clearing out the whole Island, concentrate on the area south of the pub and its surrounding buildings, then establish a perimeter around those two tanks and a smaller one around what we suspect is the drone hangar. You will start your clearing operation in sync with our attack on the silos. Clear?" He nodded, referred to a physical map he pulled out of his pocket, made some notations, and looked at me with hard eyes.

"Are we likely to take fire from the north or the south once you move?" I held his stare. I had always believed in absolute truth. I nodded.

"Yes, major, I can almost guarantee it." He just nodded a few times, his face now closed off and looking a lot older than it had just seconds ago. I held my breath and let that information sink in.

"Chief, change of plan, I'll be travelling with you with my three RRTs, it will be a straight-in approach; we will take the shells and anything else we find, then you will fly back here. Questions?" He also gave me a hard look, but this one was tempered by what he knew of me and his past experience of working with us under the most deadly of conditions.

"No, ma'am. Will you be staying behind?" I nodded and pointed to Indigo.

"Colonel Kashasini will take his squad and link up with Inspector Thomas and take down the plant at the same time we attack the tanks. Once you depart, I will link up with Inspector Remer, hop across to the hangar, and dispose of the drone facilities. Then we will fly north to the plant and see what's what." There was silence all around as each person visualized their role in the operation. It was now a question of timing, and we had no option but to attack both ends of the Island at the same time because we could count on the terrorists having communications between their various facilities.

The one thing I was mentally counting on was that none of the women had ever fired a shot at us. It had always been their surrogates, the mercenary terrorists, and I hoped like hell there were none on the Island.

Now I had to consider timing.

It was a thirty-five-minute flight to the center of the Island, maybe five more minutes to get to the hidden sheds. Traditionally, an attack like this would happen after midnight to take advantage of the lack of light, and people's circadian body rhythms, which were at their lowest in the very early hours of the morning. But I wanted some visibility to give everyone the best chance to see anything coming at them. Luckily, the evenings were a long, drawn-out affair here in Ireland, with good light still being available up to nine, nine-thirty in the evening. That gave us precious time to fine-tune our planning and move everyone into position.

But the most urgent thing I faced right this minute was the need for coffee, and I needed it now!

FACT VS. FAKE

The President's executive team, comprising the directors of the CIA, NSA, FBI, Department of Justice, Homeland Security, ICE, and the Department of Health and Social Services, the military liaison, and two lesser mortals in the form of Malcolm Tannery, senior geek, NSA, and Anna Bernstein, Senior Supervisory Special Agent, FBI, and last but not by far the least, the President's newly appointed media liaison, Bertice Halestorm, met secretly in the electronically protected bowels of the White House for over three hours, while a strategy was thrashed out and tested severely by all the participants.

The loudest voices in the room were, as expected, the NSA geek, the FBI SSSA, and General Bridget Saunders. The three of them had been involved personally from day one of the attacks and had participated in every decision or action taken since that time. The tension in the room was palpable, the consequences of getting it wrong unimaginable, but backs stood straight, faces reflected the passion and belief in what they had done, and they were all, individually and collectively, prepared to stand by it.

Two hours later, the majority of the President's team met again, this time facing seven very upset and antagonistic politicians who only had one agenda: blame someone for the atrocious conditions that now blanketed America like a feral ice storm and save themselves from their constituents, who were literally crying for their blood.

The President of the United States sat stiffly behind her 240 year old desk. The light coming in through the large window behind her showed a restless weather pattern, with sleet, freezing rain, and gusty winds, all of which contributed to the gloomy outlook beyond the Oval Office. At other times, she would have celebrated the sheer power of Mother Nature as she enjoyed its capricious and multifaceted ability to impact the physical world. She still believed in magic, but was finding it harder and harder to remain centered and calm in the emotional storm that raged around her and her country.

The Leader of the House and six senior representatives, representing three from each side of politics, faced off with her new media Advisor, the heads of the CIA, NSA, FBI, Justice department, ICE, and Military Liaison, and sat in a semicircle facing her, and she could feel the heat pouring off some of them as they pointed their accusations directly at her. While her liaison and heads of departments sat stoically by, the politicians ranted and raved with such passion and force she wondered for a split second if she needed to clear the room and start the meeting all over again. After all, there were a lot of people in the Oval Office. She held one manicured hand up, the color of warm coffee, her wedding and engagement rings sparkling in the light from the overhead cove lighting.

"Stop. Just stop. If you want this meeting to continue, stop shouting at me, stop waving things in my face, and stop shouting over each other." It was as if she had poleaxed them as they paused mid-scream and suddenly looked like a group of nasty children who had been caught with their hands in the cookie jar.

"The situation is not of our making. We have been forced into it with no choice if we want to survive as a country."

"That's all very well and good, madam president, but how do we tell our constituents that a bunch of rag-tag refugee children, now recognized immigrants, take priority over them? What do we tell a starving family, one who has no work, no power, no way to earn an income, and in all probability, nowhere to spend whatever they managed to scrape up to support their families?" The room erupted again, with finger-pointing and shouting overwhelming the president's patience. It was hard to believe that just four men and two women could make so much noise!

"Quiet!" She slapped her hand on the desk, the resounding crack ricocheting around the storied walls of the office. She looked at the red, swollen faces of the supposed leaders that faced her and recognized not only panic but also fear. They had no story to tell other than the bare minimum that had been broadcast by civilians with old high-frequency radio transmitters—previously labeled as 'Ham Radios'—information that mostly had not been based on fact.

"You, senator, your party led the fake news war, the 'big lie,' story for over five years. You still are in denial about the outcome of the 2020 election. There have been two elections since, where your 'big lie' was exposed for what it is, and your party nearly decimated in both houses and in the court of public opinion. Haven't you learned anything along the way? How can you sit there and accuse me—or the government—of these impossible actions based on rumor and speculation when you know nothing? Are you hoping history will repeat itself?

"And you, Mr. Speaker, performed so badly in your own electorate that you had to get military help to get back here to the relative safety of Washington. Now settle down, all of you, and I will have my military liaison, General Sanders, and the FBI read you in on what's really happening. Just one proviso." And she looked into the eyes of everyone in the room, held their uncomfortable stares until they blinked or looked away, then nodded to herself.

"If one word of this conversation leaks outside this room, I will have the person or persons responsible picked up and thrown into the deepest dungeon I can find, under the Terrorist Act as modified in 2022. No trial, no hearing, no debate, just a rotten prison for the rest of your lives. Or maybe I'll just have you shot. Do you understand me?" A deadly hush swept the room, and no one moved. The president looked at her general and nodded, folded her hands on top of her desk, leaned back slightly in her chair, and created the image of calm she most wished for in the room. She was a firm believer in the axiom 'model the behavior you want to see in others'.

"Thank you, Madam President. As you all know, three and a half months ago we—and other countries—were attacked almost simultaneously, and in short order, we lost access to all oil, gas, and coal, our nuclear power plants were disabled, the internet crashed, satellites and computers made useless. Not to mention the wanton destruction of three religious entities, causing untold harm to their leadership and their followers. Then the riots started, and civil unrest became so bad the president and her cabinet declared that all the representatives in both houses should return to their constituencies and try to hold the peace." The general looked around the room and noticed that everyone was paying attention, so perhaps this meeting might achieve its objective. She didn't think so and had told the president of her feelings in private, but she then agreed to participate in a show of support.

In her mind, the politicians had gone too far down the rabbit hole with the 'big lie', five years of grief, disorder on a grand scale, outbreaks of violence all over the country, and the lowest level of trust in the government and corporate institutions ever recorded. And all caused by just one man and his sycophantic cultists, a successful grifter who had won the White House for one tumultuous term, then spread the 'big lie' unceasingly until the Department of Justice finally laid charges at his door, in the form of theft of top-secret documents concerning the nuclear secrets of an unnamed country and the Obstruction of Justice he had perpetuated in their recovery.

Almost as an afterthought, he was also prosecuted for his attempts to overturn the result of the 2020 election. At this time, the national guard had to be called into action in some states to maintain control over the roving mobs who shouted slogans as they shot at and attacked offices of both the FBI and the government, all egged on by the party that had spawned the grifter.

It wasn't quite a civil war, but so close to it that the very foundations of the republic were seriously shaken, and thousands died in the ensuing stupidity.

It had gotten seriously bad, then the grifter was taken out of circulation, held incommunicado under the domestic terrorist act, and the rhetoric died down.

When he was finally incarcerated in a federal prison with no outside contact, most of the 'big lie' noise died through lack of repetition as people looked for the next lunatic to follow and make their lives meaningful again. Cultism was successful for good reasons, and the power of personality fit right into those reasons at every visceral level of human existence. The need to belong to a recognizable tribe—to be talked about, to be held in awe, and most importantly, to allow people to act out their most vicious fantasies through the actions of a perceived super-star, one who thought themselves and behaved openly as if they were above the law.

And no sooner had the country started to recover from all this political turmoil based on the biggest lie ever perpetrated on the American people than the terrorists attacked and made things worse.

Much, much worse.

"I'll be frank—none of you did much good in the peace-keeper role, but then the job was probably beyond your scope." Seven filthy looks headed in her direction, and she smiled and waved her hand as if brushing the insulted looks aside. Julius Bronstein, the director of the CIA, dressed impeccably as usual in a dark suit with creases that could slice bread, highly polished Prada shoes, a silk shirt, and a club tie. He smirked. He couldn't help himself. He hid it to some extent with a polite cough, drawing the eyes of his fellow directors from the FBI and NSA.

"However, that was then, this is now. I would ask SSSA Anna Bernstein to take the briefing from here."

"Thank you general. There are three parallel activities I will draw your attention to: the first is the attacks on our infra-structure, the religions, and our communications network. That affected every country in the world, without exception. It wasn't just us. It was everyone—the Russians, Chinese, French,

English—you name them; they were deeply affected and continue to be so.

"The second is the fact that a very wealthy person from another country set up numerous trust accounts some years ago, with legitimate documentation and support from other wealthy people in many countries, ours included. These funds were set up specifically to enable the migration of refugee children. And this is perhaps where the most important aspect comes in." She looked at the faces of the politicians and failed to see any real understanding of what she was saying. She reached for her water glass, drank from it, then placed it back on the low table as if it were a live grenade. In a flash of insight, she thought about facing down the terrorists and fleetingly thought it might have been an easier proposition than trying to explain recent history to these angry politicians.

"People, you have to understand that what we're telling you is that the attacks and what followed were made by very clever people who had a single agenda behind which sat some thirty-five years of planning."

"Thirty-five years? Impossible! Who in their right mind plans something for three and a half decades?" The senator from the largest state in the union spluttered as he shouted, his face turning a bright purple color.

"This man did." And she posted the photo of Mohammad bin Azaria as he had been known prior to his death at the hands of Interpol, onto the huge screen that had been wheeled into the office just for such a presentation. How much more Anna showed them, the president thought to herself, would rely solely on their response.

"Who is he?" demanded the woman who currently sat on the Joint Intelligence Committee as its chair. Offended by the very inclusion of the other politicians in this briefing, which she viewed as her sole purview, it had stuck a claw in her throat from the get go when she had learned of the others to attend this briefing.

"Al Hemish al-bin Mohammad Karesish-or Mohammad bin Azaria as we knew him recently. He had been working on his masterplan for at least thirty five years, in partnership with an ex-Stasi spy by the name of Natasha Trotsky-or 'Helen' as she was called. She was a computer genius, a master planner, and had a broad network of sleepers, or hidden spies, in many countries, including here in the United States. Between them, they planned and plotted the attacks, and all that followed." Stunned silence filled the room, and for the first time the politicians looked at odds, as if having difficulty understanding what was being laid out for them. The honorable member for the great state of Texas who had been up to his eyeballs in the election denial, and had managed to get himself elected on the strength of the 'big lie', pulled himself erect.

"What proof can you give us that this isn't just some elaborate cover up for your political inadequacy?" he barked, having been sorely rattled by the president's earlier condemnation of him and his party. At his outburst, general Saunders stat straight up in her seat, her back a ridged line of tense muscle, her face a mask of fury.

"Senator, perhaps we should all ask what would you accept as proof given your predilection for living a lie?" she snapped, her forefinger pointing at him as if were weapon in her hand. The president leaned forward, her eyes never leaving the senator.

"Good question, general, and senator, may I remind you that under the terms of Marshall Law, and with respect to the Terrorist Laws as modified in 2022, instead of having a conversation with you, I can just order you taken to the cells in the basement and left there indefinitely?" His face puffed out, turned bright red, then the speaker of the house reached over and grabbed him by his arm.

"Bill, calm down, we all want to know what really happened. Madam President, could I ask you to request your general to concentrate on the briefing, and leave politics out of it?" The President smiled, knowing a conciliatory move when she saw one, and the fact that the opposition had come to his defense was not lost of the senator. The president motioned to general Saunders to continue, who merely nodded to Anna.

"Thank you, madam president. We have bullet proof evidence of everything we are telling you. From the moment of the first attack, a team led by Interpol acting under the United Nations charter has coordinated experts from Israel, Italy, the European Union, Canada, the United States, and many other countries. Our own FBI, NSA, and CIA were part of that team, and on behalf of the FBI I was part of every conversation and decision made." As Anna spoke, a brave single bright beam of sunlight started to move across the surface of the table, having sneaked its way through the outside trees, the bullet proof glass, and the awesome stone work that graced the front of the White House.

The president found herself fascinated by it, watching its snail like progress across the table, climbing up and over a glass, then a coffee jug without apparent effort. She smiled to herself, there was still magic in the world after all, all you had to do was look for it! Her attention was drawn back to her FBI agent's summary, as she clicked another slide onto the screen. It filled with the faces of refugee children in a camp somewhere, where the background was a burning pyre giving off an oily, dirty black smoke.

"The third parallel activity is the story of the refugee children, in that the master planner worked out a way to entice governments to empty the camps of children with a sound economic proposition. The first step in this part of their plan was to throw the whole world back to the mid twentieth century technology wise, and deprive us of all carbon based power generation. They wanted to create the same conditions, or very similar ones, to those experienced in the camps." She looked at her audience, saw seven suddenly very interested people, and seeing the relaxed posture of the directors and heads of departments sitting behind them, continued. She was 'on song' as it were, the agreed path the executive team had thrashed out just hours before.

"We had lost all carbon-based fuels, including nuclear, leaving only renewables-solar, wind, and to some extent wave generation. So the terrorists traded power for refugees, in a manner that was impossible to ignore." The room had taken on a deadly hush, the only sound the swish made by legs moving in pants or the rustle of a dress as legs were crossed.

"The terrorists offered a proposition-and the proposition was this." The screen filled with an aerial shot taken from a drone in Helena, highlighting all the colorful houses with their sparkling roofs and walls. Children could be seen playing in a grassed area, with adults looking on from the low fence.

"The terrorists recruited some of the cleverest scientists they could find, we think ten to fifteen years ago, funded them in university laboratories, then turned their work into a practical application by creating ecological plants that could be erected all over the world. These plants produce extremely efficient solar panels and massive power packs, but I'll get to that detail a little later." She held her breath, waiting for the explosion she anticipated from one of the politicians, but to her surprise, no one said anything. She looked at the general, got a nod, so continued. As did the shining blob of light as it continued to walk itself across the table, this time tip toeing across a yellow legal pad and glasses case.

"When we traced all the trust funds, we discovered that nineteen countries had been seeded, including America, so we found a plant running up near the Canadian border, New Zealand has one, and there are seventeen other countries that have the capability to build a similar system." The general held up her hand as the politicians started to talk over each other, and an uneasy silence once again ensued.

"Before you make fools of yourselves again, let agent Bernstein finish." Her voice was parade-ground stern, leaving no doubt in anyone's mind who was really in control. While the story was far from the absolute truth, it was close enough to pass the pub test, and the executive team had agreed to censor most of the detail in the background in the interests of not creating more problems than they already had. And they had agreed to keep the super smart refugee women completely out of the picture.

"What is this economic proposition you talk about?" the speaker asked, sitting back in his seat, which was immediately emulated by the other six politicians. The general looked at the Anna, shook her head minutely, and took over the briefing.

In the general's mind, this is where their story got a little sticky, so she crossed her fingers and flicked another image up onto the screen. This one had descriptors, photos, and numbers moving along a snake-like arrow, terminating in a photo of a nuclear family, obviously of mixed races.

"The terrorists provided the funding for the building of the ecological plants, then took advantage of the trust accounts set up years ago and made an offer to a small township as a demonstration site. In this case, Helena in Montana. They would provide the material to build ecologically responsible houses, each with their own power supply, fund the build, then pay local families to adopt one or two refugee children. The parents would get a stipend to support the child, free education and medical for the whole family, and the cost price of the house would reflect the labor cost, and a little for the materials. All this was done through the civilian trustees for the trust accounts, at arm's length from the terrorists, and set up years in advance.

"This turned out to be an excellent idea in Helena because over three thousand families had already migrated there due to the chaos and civil unrest in the larger cities. And there are more and more arriving every week. There was one other sweetener." The general paused, to see what impact her description of the Helena situation may have created. For the first time, she saw seven fully engaged people, all focused on the screen, no doubt scheming how to get this economic model up and running in their own electorates. She smiled to herself, never underestimate the natural greed of the average politician!

"As well as solar panels, many times more efficient than anything we had seen, they produced portable power packs, each one capable of running a small factory-say, 5,000 square feet. These are being distributed up and down the west coast as we speak by a series of tradespeople who were trained by the terrorists but have no other relationship to them." This was a sticky point, because every distributor was a refugee woman, albeit never involved in the attacks. And their family histories were intact, not wiped like the terrorists were.

"What do these power packs cost?" The speaker of the house asked, looking like a serious businessman for the first time since he had arrived.

"At this point, the cost of building and distribution is being met by the trustees. There is no apparent link to the refugee children." The speaker sat back in his seat, baffled by this, in all his experience, you never got anything for nothing, and in politics, everything had a cost with a tightly defined return.

"But that's impossible! Someone must be making a fortune somewhere?"

"No. As the general said, the production is handled out of their ecological plant, paid for by the trustees, the distributors are also paid by the trustees, as are the installers. To date, we have over three hundred factories up and running, and the excess power they generate is going into local grids. We now have probably over a million homes that have reliable power, twenty four hours a day." The seven politicians sat back, astonished at the outcome, rapidly trying to work out how to take advantage of it somehow. Free power? Magic solar panels? Anna just gave them all a neutral look, this reaction had been predicted earlier in the meeting, and the decision then was to let them work it through for themselves.

"Madam President, if this is true, then why haven't you allowed other towns and cities to participate and benefit from this technology?" The President paused, watching the little blob of light fall off the edge of the table, as if its walk across had worn it out. She smiled to herself, if only dealing with these politicians was as easy as watching a magic light show!

"We have a second settlement under construction, again funded by a trust fund the genesis of which is impeachable, it goes back more than half a decade, in Roanoke. This was agreed to some months ago before the terrorist attacks and before we knew of the technology. We were, in fact, in discussions with the Aid Agencies about it well before the attacks."

"These powerpacks, as they are not linked to any refugee issues, will they be available for us to use in our state?" The congresswoman for Illinois, a state the size of Italy, asked. A raven haired women in her early forties, she was dressed in a smart dark green suit with bright red high heeled shoes in contrast and a very expensive diamond necklace dangling between the top of her impressive breasts, which were suitable hidden by a warm pink silk bodice. It was true, the President thought to herself, that women dress for other women.

"Yes, our Army Engineers are erecting additional ecological plants on the east coast as we speak. They will be up and running within a month and producing power packs and panels a month after that. And before you ask, this technology is so far beyond our current understanding, we simply can't go any faster at this time." Anna looked at the President and received a nod.

"I can add to what the President has just said. I have worked with the technical teams who are solving this problem for us, and it is so advanced there is just one person right now who can create the process to make these plants work."

"Can you prove that?" demanded the honorable senator from Texas, his nose right out of joint at the volume of data he had previously been denied. It was all very well for the current regime to be getting things ordered in a world gone mad, but he owed his soul to very large vested commercial interests in oil and power generation, and he could see his cushy world disappearing before his own eyes. They had already contacted him with their demands, and if they found out about this from someone else he might just as well go back to his ranch and forget politics altogether. That's if he survived the trip back!

"As I stated earlier, I have been on the ground as part of the Interpol team from the first attacks and have met with and interrogated every person involved who we have discovered so far. I have also visited the plant and Helena, and Roanoke and can attest personally to the facts as stated here."

"Then when can we have enough of these supposedly miraculous panels and power packs for our state?" He almost shouted as he rose out of his seat to emphasize his question.

"Senator, sit down and contain yourself. I had had you brought here so we could work out a way forward to getting some balance back into our country, but I can see that I have made a grave mistake as far as your electorate is concerned." The President folded her arms, directly challenging his position. "It is never going to be about you or your lobbyists, or your donors or commercial interests ever again, we have a brand new game to play, called 'let's help the people' and the rules are simple." She leaned forward towards his shocked face, now almost white with rage. She held up one finger, her lacquered nail sparking a tiny flash of light at the end of her fingertip.

"One, the decision as to whom gets what and when will be made by a council under the command of the Army Corps of Engineers, advised by the Departments of Agriculture, Commerce, Energy, Health and Human Services, Urban Development, and Homeland Security and the Department of Justice." The senator relaxed back into his seat, finally realizing that the vested commercial interests who controlled his life would not be a part of the new order, at least not under this President, and he would give deep thought to that as he listened to the rest of her conditions.

Maybe, just maybe, if he could get to his money men fast enough, he could manufacturer a coup. He unconscientiously scratched his chin, a bad habit. After all, hanging onto the coattails of the ex-president, even after he went down, had worked for him personally. People would believe anything you told them over and over again, repetition somehow, making the simplest lie a powerful fact.

The country was already in turmoil, there were still raging gangs looting and killing all before them, and there were still thousands of people migrating to anywhere that looked safer than where they were now.

The opportunity was vast, as he thought about it, change the government, take control of these new technological marvels, whatever they were, and he would be set for life. His state could be the first to reorganize and could well end up controlling the whole country! He scratched the loose skin under his neck again in deep thought and nearly didn't hear the President's second point.

"The FBI, working with the National Guard and local Law enforcement, will control the program, whatever that turns out to be. In the meantime, you seven will be sequestered in safe lodgings while we work out the details of what to do and how to do it. You will be expected to contribute to the conversation, but we offer no guarantee of form or favor. Questions?"

"Shut in? Where? And for how long?" This time, his voice screeched, and he rose to his full five feet six inches, albeit two inches of which were provided by the heels of his cowboy boots, and waved his arms as if in a panic.

Which he was. How could he implement his master plan to overthrow the government if he was locked up in Washington? There were no mobile phones or computers; to call anyone he would have to rely on old-style analogue handphones, and as he just knew every line in and out of the White House would be tapped, he was effectively trapped. Inwardly he fumed, to have been outsmarted by a person of color and a woman to boot was intolerable. And he noticed that the President and the FBI agent were both smiling as he looked from one to the other. The hairs on the back of his neck and arms stood up in fear, and animal reaction to being trapped. They were up to something, and he had a sneaky suspicion he wasn't going to like the outcome.

"And to ensure you safety, you will be assigned a pair of Secret Service agents who will also help you with anything you need to get. Communications are severely limited, but you will each have a phone in your rooms, with no guarantee of a connection at some times of the day. Questions?" She looked around the faces of the politicians, saw interest in some, suspicion in others, and naked fear in the senator's.

"One last comment-the real world doesn't stop for your personal or political fantasies senator, and there's a lot more to life that pledging your soul to a grifter." She stood, signaling that the meeting was over. Seven secret service agents walked in, positioned themselves alongside each of the politicians, then taking them gently by the arms, led them out of the Oval Office. Once they had left, she sat down again.

"You were right about our Texan, Anna, I wonder just how much the others will contribute to what we do."

"Doesn't really matter." The general filled her coffee cup from the dispenser that the sparkling light had climbed so over effortlessly.

"Why?" the President asked.

"Because you are including them, involving them, seeking their input, that's all you have to demonstrate to Congress. And you can grow your base as large as we can cope with."

"Bridget's right," offered Frank Reynolds, filling his cup as well. "Party politics aside, we need to focus on getting the country running again, get the marauders off the streets once and for all, and try to get back to normal, whatever that will look like now."

"It's doesn't sound all that difficult when you say it that way." Anna sat back and folded her arms. "But we lost nine good agents just getting this group here in the first place. We can't take that ratio of losses every time and hold the country together."

"That was my mistake," Bridget offered, "I should have called out the Guard to support you. The truth is, we just didn't have good intelligence on the ground as to the real situation. And that jerk from Texas cost us three agents all by his intractable self."

"Did you see his face at the end?"

"Yes, not a pretty sight by any means. I wonder how fast he will realize he had no option but to play with us."

"Never happen. I could head him plotting your overthrow from where I was sitting." The director of the CIA stood, stretched, rolled his shoulders.

"Here's where I see we are-first tranche of politicians, for better or worse, inhouse, and working-or pretending to-with us. If we need more or different, we'll go and get them. But for now, I really want to concentrate on these new shells Jessica has found, and I want to understand the real level of threat we face and from which direction." The director looked at the faces of his contemporaries and saw their silent agreement. Anna nodded and stood up.

"What is keeping me going is what we are seeing in Helena. It truly is remarkable how well the little girls are fitting in with their new families."

"Yes, I read your agent Vernon's report. If only the rest of the country was getting their act together." The President stood, nodded to her directors and Anna, then turned to look out her windows. A light snow was falling, creating a wonder garden in front of the White House, and if you didn't look too closely at the tank barriers and armored personal carriers ranged against the fence, you could be forgiven for thinking it was a tranquil end to the day.

CHAPTER TEN

t wasn't particularly tranquil in Whiddy Island, a relatively small bump of land off Bantry on the south western Irish coast. Just three miles long and a mile and a half at its widest point, its only real claim to fame was that at the beginning of the Napoleonic Wars back in 1800, the British had built three massive circular forts and gun emplacements to ward off the French. A minor claim to fame lay in its oil tanks, which once had stored the Irish reserve before a massive explosion back in 1979 destroyed the main jetty and cause over 50 deaths.

The sudden storm that had blown in from the Atlantic of was such ferocity I worried about being able to get the helicopters airborne. Visibility was way down in the weeds, and the low hanging clouds spat a barrage of harsh freezing rain as cold as anything I had ever experienced. The Irish Sciathán Fianóglach would take off first, coordinate with their boat waiting for them in Bantry, then attack the Island in three places-the lower end where the fisherfolk worked; the oil tanks, which were in three rows, two long and one very short. And then provide a barrier between the two tanks, which were our objective, and the northern end of the Island where the pub and a few scattered houses stood. The Israeli commando 104 would reinforce them once our helicopter got in position.

It was an imperfect plan, we did not know who the opposition might be or their strength. But experience had taught us to play the hand we were delt, so I loaded up our three RRT's with the chief's team, then crammed the commandos from the 104 into the vast cargo hold of the massive CH-53 helicopter and gave the order to flap our way into the unattractive and untidy mass of air currents and lightning that filled the cockpit windscreen.

To say the ride was bumpy was to make the understatement of the century. The aircraft, big as it was, bounced up and down like a ping pong ball caught in the exhaust of a vacuum cleaner, rolled from side to side, and lurched violently every few minutes as if trying to empty itself of its self-loading cargo by ejecting us all out into the storm. To their credit, no one needed the barf bags the crew so kindly provided, but it was close if my stomach was anything to go by. We landed with a perceptible thud, followed by a huge sigh as the aircraft squatted down on its compression struts, then the back ramp dropped down, and like refugees from a sinking ship, we all raced out into the maelstrom, the Italians and the Israelis forming a wedge that the RRTs fell into.

The massive door that had been cut into the side of the oil tank was blown out without fuss, and we stormed into the equally massive interior of the tank. It was obvious that it had been a long time since oil had been stored here. The interior walls were painted a mute industrial gray color, the floor was epoxy over sealed concrete, and the machinery that had been left standing after its last use gleamed in our torch lights. Massive overhead neon's flickered into existence, giving us a view of a well-ordered and maintained workspace.

"Master Chief, where are the shells?" The commandos had formed an interior perimeter, leaving the four RRT's in the center. Mindful of the master chief crouching at my side, I turned slowly to scan the work area, my eyes tracking my weapon.

"Commander, we are getting a very strong reading from over there," and he pointed to a dark area not reached by the overhead work lights.

"*Colonnello, abbiamo una scala qui, scende!*" The shout was from one of the forward commandos, and the tightness in her voice told me that we had a serious problem.

"Down where?" I asked. Before she could answer, the master chief grabbed me by the shoulder.

"Commander, heat signatures coming from our left, now static. They've come out of some tunnel." I took the biggest gamble of my life.

"Hold fire! *Tieni il fuoco!*" And I held my breath. The work lights we had carried with us suddenly burst to life, showing a tableau that would be hard to imagine in any other job. Three really beautiful women, all very young, stood in an untidy group with their hands held high. Dressed in jeans, colorful shirts, and in some cases, lovely-looking jumpers, the juxtaposition between them and the hardened, comparatively ugly, fully braced Italian and Israeli commandos, weapons pushed forwards towards their targets, was startling. Now my focus was split. I still had to secure the shells and the strange barrels that had shown up on the scan, and now I had prisoners to deal with.

Indigo was off, surrounding the plant Sandra had uncovered; Fay was outside somewhere, either coming to us or staying away until we reached her. That left me with the amazing Josephine Aria, with her big thighs and massive shoulders, the colonel in charge of the 104, and the master chief. The chief had a highly trained RRT, which made my decision easy.

"Chief, secure the shells. Hold off on moving them just yet. Major," I felt in my bones his immediate discomfort. Getting a call in the middle of an armed attack would do that.

"Commander?"

"Any sign of resistance?" He paused, a good sign.

"Not at this time."

"Can you split off a section to penetrate the hangar at this time?" Another pause. I was getting to like this young man's style.

"Affirmative."

"Excellent. Look for a tunnel heading east, secure the location, send two troopers through, and expect no resistance."

"WILCO." Now to find Fay. I dialed her on my mini.

"Where are you?"

"Holding at the pub as instructed, enjoying a really good shepherd's pie, if you're interested."

"Tangos?"

"Nil. Not ever a ripple when you landed that monster against the tanks. Ten people here with us, very relaxed, almost as if they were expecting us."

"Funny about that. Don't move. Stay sharp." I dialed Sandra on silent mode, so as to not comprise her if she was in trouble. 'Sitrep?'

'Just joined with Indigo, working on a coffee as we speak.'

'Funny. Haha. Location?'

'Holding external to the plant, Indigo has 360 cover." I gave that some thought, knowing Indigo and Sandra would have the site well covered. I made one of my famous tactical decisions based on a gut feeling, which is not always a wise thing to do behind enemy lines. But the women had never fired a shot at us if you didn't count the number of times someone had tried to kill me, shoot me down, or blow me up. My gut was telling me the only real danger we were in was likely to be manufactured by ourselves!

'Hold until I reach you.'

'WILCO.' I focused back on my recent arrivals.

"Do you speak English?" asked the middle woman, who had to be at least twenty, her purple and green jumper climbing up her bare torso as her hands reached for the roof. She looked like someone from Europe on a summer holiday, dressed for something casual, but her eyes told the real story. Bright, alert, and very switched on. She held my stare across the floor of the oil tank, never wavering for a second. I instinctively knew exactly what I was facing. I had seen this look in the eyes of other refugee terrorists a number of times in the last three months.

"Aye, that we do, and may I ask if we can put our hands down now, and who might you be, and your purpose?" It was all I could do not to smile; here we were to remove several nuclear-capable shells and who knows what else, and I was being challenged by a smart-looking woman dressed for the piazza!

"No, you may not. Keep your hands high. We will shoot on the slightest provocation. Move over here." And I pointed to an empty area in front of a resting forklift, again, in immaculate condition. It had been used recently and serviced in sparkling condition. The three fully armed commandos emerged behind the women, and my suspicions were confirmed.

The women had come from the hangar, probably due to some type of alarm system. I motioned to the commandos to return, and they saluted and retreated back the way they had come.

"Commander, shells secure. There are eighteen of them, all on pallets and fifty containers, all with electronics plugged into mobile power supplies. If we can use the forklift we saw in the main area, we can have all these loaded in half an hour."

"Go. Once loaded, get them back to Cork, then return here." Within a minute or two, the choking sound of a gas-powered engine cut through the silence in the tank, and the forklift was driven off into the depths of the shadowed area. I turned back to the three women.

"Names." The leader, who was about three inches taller than her companions, both of whom looked very relaxed and calm considering the circumstances, smiled as if she hadn't a worry in the world.

"I'd be Shannon Berkley, and these would be my sisters, Faith and Roslyn, and if I may, who would you be then, I'm asking?" The Irish lilt in her educated voice was easy to listen to, almost mesmerizing, which had all my instincts screaming at me. Were we in a trap? Why were these three so calm and composed? They must know what was stored here, and they had to know who we were if only very heavily armed soldiers were pointing very big guns at them. There was something going on here, and I didn't have the faintest clue as to what it was.

"Colonel, please take these prisoners to the aircraft, secure them, isolate them, and follow protocols for the Terrorist Act as modified in 2022, weapons free at the slightest sign of resistance or non-compliance." The nuggety Israeli Sgan Aluf saluted, and in seconds the three women were cuffed, bags over their heads, and being led to the helicopter. I tucked away the interesting reaction the woman who called herself Shannon Berkley had exhibited on my instructions—a mixture of shock and disbelief. Now I had to disperse my forces to protect the hangar and the tank until we could determine what we could do with them, recover Fay and her companions, and get to Indigo and Sandra to face down whoever was running this s-h-one-t show from the plant.

I used the tight-beam communicators we had issued and set things in motion. "Colonel, give me four of your best, then secure this tank; Major, secure the hangar. Both of you consider yourselves well behind enemy lines. There is a tunnel exit/entry somewhere in here. You might care to look for it when you have time. I'm going to take some of my Italian friends and go walkabout." A salute and a grunt were my acknowledgment, so I moved out where the navy crew with the RRT's were loading the shells and containers into the maw of the massive helicopter, which made its own umbrella due to its sheer size. I broke into a trot, headed for the pub, flicked a quick wake-up call to Fay, and wondered how anyone could live in weather conditions like this.

I had been outside less than a minute or two, and every part of me was sodden, cold, and getting more and more sodden. Grit your teeth girl, this is what you trained for! What pissed me off was the overt ignorance of my team as they jogged beside me, seemingly impervious to the pouring, freezing deluge. We came in sight of the long structure I guessed was the pub, and sure enough Fay and her two companions were standing under the shelter of the wide verandah, waiting for us. I signaled for them to join us, and we continued on up the muddy road with boots sucking and breath steaming.

"Buggaring cold, thanks for the invite." Fay's face, encapsulated by her watch cap and her rollneck jumper which peaked out from under her hiking jacket looked relaxed, and her smile was streaked by the rain that battered her pretty face.

"Still glad you crossed to the dark side?" I asked between puffs. Fay had been a senior agent in the FBI before she joined Interpol just a month prior, and she was fitting into my team as if she had always been part of us. Her skills were remarkable, her intelligence incredible, and by chance she had been a refugee pulled out of the camps by Mohammad bin Azaria but not turned into a terrorist. And given what she had achieved with us it was his loss, and our gain.

"Hah! San Francisco was a tropical paradise compared to this. Don't know what you're complaining about!" Her smile was infectious, and it warmed me to see her as confident and as comfortable as she was.

"We've got quite the situation here. The terrorists we took back at the oil tank were really young, and as innocent-looking as you are. I'm not sure what we are running to, but stay on your toes."

"Sandra and Indigo are holding the fort?"

"Yes."

"Then it really doesn't matter. We'll cope." Her absolute faith in our team gave me pause, and then one of the two troopers who had come to the Island with her pulled up alongside, jogging as smoothly as if out for a Sunday run. He too was in civies, but now had a submachine gun slung across his chest, and looked the part of a hard-edged warrior even as he was covered in mud and slush up to his knees, and sodden wet, with water streaming down his face from the bill of his cap.

"Commander, Inspector Remer asked me to monitor the team tracking the shell down from Dundalk. It went off our detectors abeam Clogherhead, and the team are asking for a drone to over fly the area." I looked at the young man with his two-day-old growth, his tough Middle Eastern looks, and his chiseled face, and could imagine him on the cover of a Men's magazine. The one thing that this operation was proving to me, at least, was that it was the young taking over the world, so I inwardly sighed and nodded.

"I'll get a drone over there asap. Thank you." He sent me a loose salute, then jogged back to where his companion was. Equally young, equally good looking, I was starting to feel threatened by all these young, vibrant, alive people I had around me, then had a sudden thought. The fashionista was up ahead, and I wondered how I would look compared to Sandra? Weird thought to have on the way to a possible firefight! I looked at Fay out of the corner of my eye, her calm composure forcing itself on me.

"You picked well with your backpackers," and she just grinned.

Then the brush in front of us erupted, and Sandra dressed in stylish outer wet wear as befitting a young backpacker, stood up, accompanied by Indigo, thankfully wearing camos and all the necessary military accountments. I held my hand up to stop our jog, and without any further signal, the team formed a circle around us, facing out, but loose enough to hear anything we said. The sound of the heavy rain hitting the muddy track was a constant reminder that we were exposed to the elements and possibly surveillance. Time would tell.

"Commander, good to see you. We have troops surrounding the plant, all the way out to the first pile of roofing panels." He pointed to his left, where a huge mountain of grass and scrub sat on top of flat packed building materials. His team had dug a small section out of one corner, and the telltale shine of a solar panel was obvious. If the mound, which ran on for at least a mile in every direction, covered panels and they were stacked as high as the ones we could see, then there were literally thousands stored here.

That meant the plant had been running for a long time, and if I used Point Roberts as a benchmark, possibly years before the attacks just three and a half months ago. I looked around at the sparse countryside, the odd black faced sheep or cow doing whatever they did without any regard for us, and I mentally saluted our opposition for their excellent choice of location. We had found it by accident due to Sandra's curiosity about beautiful women out for a drive in atrocious conditions, and I intended to keep that luck running in our favor.

"Okay, Indigo, Sandra, Fay on me, everyone else cover positions, my intention is to breech the plant, but without a firefight if possible, so stay loose and focused." And with that, I started down the boggy track again, this time with just the four of us, but shadowed by our team. It took six minutes, but we arrived at the door to the plant, a very industrial-looking building with bland, flat stone walls that seemed to grow out of the ground. I reached forward to use the massive antique brass knocker, reminiscent of something you might find on an old-style manor house.

Before I could actually knock, the wide wooden door swung open, and one of Sandra's beautiful women stood before us. We had been under surveillance.

"Good evening, my name is Patricia, we've been expecting you. Please come in." And stood back so we could enter a long reception area that once again could have been cut out of a vintage English manor house, possibly eighteenth century. The carpets were well worn and very vintage, and the art work on both walls was as old as the house. The juxtaposition between walls of really old paintings and the modern outfits both Sandra and 'Patricia', if that was her real name, wore, was jangling. Then we entered another very large space, which took my breath away.

The room was painted a warm orange color and trimmed with a brilliant gleaming red, and the dark mahogany furniture added a elegance that was only enhanced by the series of rolling seascapes that followed the long bend of the feature wall. On the short side, a long, ancient armoire added its trim grace to the overall ambience. The colorful stained glass doors added a touch of spice, as rusty old weapons of war could just be made out if the lights were turned up high.

What brought the entire ensemble into the twenty first century were the long, high flat screens mounted side by side and the computer screens built into the long, time-aged teak conference table. We learned later that it was made up of over three thousand pieces of teak taken from the wrecks of boats that had crashed upon the shores of Ireland over the centuries, when you looked under the table you could see the individual shapes of the various pieces and not a single nail or screw. The desk was a work or art, the room an eclectic demonstration of the evolving style of its occupant, a magnificent women in her mid-fifties with long, rich red hair cascading beyond her shoulders, her skin a creamy white, and her lipstick a direct contrast to her highlighted eyes. The blue/green dress with its flounces and puffy cuffs she wore shouted wealth, privilege, and position, and I wondered not for the first time exactly what we had gotten ourselves into.

She could have graced any runway, the cover of any high-fashion magazine, indeed, if the fashion industry hadn't crashed due to the terrorist attacks, she could have been crowned 'Irish Queen Beauty', and she gave our very own Sandra a run for her money in the good looking stakes.

"May I introduce you to our governor, Lady O'Brian Flattery, and I apologize as I don't know your names." Patricia moved around the table to stand at the shoulder of the red haired woman. I didn't sense any animosity, in fact, quite the opposite, and I suddenly became aware that we were dripping water all over the antique Donegal carpet. How did I know the type of carpet we were presently destroying? In my early days in the NCIS, I had been stationed in England, where I was schooled in all things antique by my roommate, a died in the wool Anglophile. And she had dragged me to every museum to show me the way life had been hundreds of years ago, carpets, rugs, and furniture.

"I am Commander Riley, these are Inspectors Thomas and Remer and Colonel Kashasini; we are with Interpol, and madam, how would you have us address you?" I asked in all honesty, my experience of Lords and Ladies being on the short side of nonexistent. The magnificent red head smiled at my discomfort, probably having suffered ignorant fools like me all her life, waved us to our seats, which we ignored. Wet. Saturated. Dripping like a leaking faucet.

"Call me Fionnuala, for this is my given name, everything else was granted me because of my husband's position in the Irish Government. If you won't be seated, will you allow my assistant to take your wet coats?" I smiled to be polite, the strangeness of our situation starting to sink in. Heavily armed and very wet Interpol police facing down Irish royalty in an ugly brick block house outfitted as if it were a castle or royal palace on the inside.

"Fionnuala, forgive me my ignorance. I'm American after all, and my purpose here is to take you into custody charged with crimes under the Terrorist Laws as modified in 2022. Please stand away from the table and do not reach for any weapons." I put a sharp edge to my voice, mainly to remind my team who we were and what we were here for. The sheer luxury and wealth that surrounded us were breathtaking. Our usual milieu was a battered, smoking battlefield in the middle of nowhere.

Her reaction surprised me. She smiled, linked her delicate hands together, raised them so her elbows rested on the table as it in prayer, and smiled.

"Commander, I've no doubt as to your sincerity in what you say, but I'll not be going with you or any like you, if you please. My people and I are sanctioned under the 'Rebuild Ireland' statute of 2024, we are independently financed, and audited and monitored by the Government. Our objective is to refurbish one million empty houses ready for immigrants. If you wish to check our credentials, Patricia here will provide you the necessary contacts."

I'd never heard of her statute, but in any case the Terrorist Laws were written to transcend any national interest or vested control in favor of the World Court and Interpol. But she gave me pause, and as I didn't sense any immediate danger, I decided to play her game.

But by my rules. I gestured to the team to remain where they were, and sat down on a chair that was at least two hundred years older than I was, pulled my mini out, and set it up so we could both see the screen. I dialed the boss and quickly cut him off before he could ruin my strategy.

"General, apologies, please, for interrupting your busy schedule. I have a question for you." He looked polished, sharp, rested, and very much in control, and his background was a plush club of some type because everyone walking past his back was dressed either in an immaculate suit or full-dress military uniform. He looked as serious as he ever did, and I hoped against hope he had seen the woman and her assistant and sussed out what I was doing.

It was a version of the old 'third party referral' trick, where you empowered someone outside your immediate circle to endorse or advise you on your position, removing you from an immediate responsibility. It was a good trick when used well, and I had my fingers crossed.

"Commander, I'm in the Hague, a United Nations meeting of some import. How may I help you?" His gruff tonality told me he had trigged to my strategy, so I played it for all it was worth.

"General, again, my apologies for interrupting you, but we have a situation here in Ireland I seek your advice on." His eyebrows shot up, no doubt down the track I would get a pithy reminder that I never asked him for advice, but he played along.

"Get to it Commander, I'm due in a meeting with the Security Council" and right there I had the first part of my endorsement.

"Sir, I have Lady O'Brian Flattery, who I am arresting under the Terrorist Laws as modified in 2022 for acts of, and support of, specific acts of terrorism. She has just informed me she has state-level protection from the Irish Government, which would prohibit me from acting in accordance with the Terrorist Laws." He took on a serious look, I had no doubt what his reaction would have been if there were here in the room with us, and I smiled inwardly at the thought of the casual indifference he would have shown.

"Commander, correct me if I'm wrong, but Ireland is a signature party to the United Nations?" I looked at the red-haired woman, now sitting just a little bit higher in her chair, her face glued to the small screen.

"I believe so, yes, sir."

"Then, under Article 29A, Ireland will have signed their acceptance of the modified Terrorist Laws. My advice is to proceed as you see fit." And the screen went black as he cut the call. The significant thing in all he said was the statement 'proceed as you see fit." Did not lessen my authority in any manner. In fact, boosted it up as high as it goes-United Nations Article level. Now I stood, faced the two women, and repeated my earlier statement.

"Stand away from the table, both of you, and do not reach for any weapons. Under the Terrorist Laws, we can shoot you without further cause." As I spoke, Indigo and Sandra walked around the table, approaching the pair of women from either side, with Fay staring them both down, and without further conversation, we cuffed them and started back out. I checked Indigo's position, and nodded to Fay, who took over from him behind Fionnuala.

"Take a team and comb the factory; for now simply round them up, but keep them out of harm's way. I'll arrange transport." He tapped me on the shoulder, smiled that big full-face twinkling-eyed smile of his, and raced back out into the sheeting rain. I held our group back under the roof, jutting out from the massive wooden doors. Why get any wetter than I had to? I called the chief.

"Where are you?"

"Inbound to the Island, ETA (Estimated time of arrival) three minutes."

"Divert to my location, land on the track in front of the plant, and arse in. We have passengers to load."

"WILCO." I looked at Fionnuala and raised one eyebrow.

"Nothing to say?" She gave me a look that I am sure would have any hired help quaking in their boots and raised her head until she was almost looking down her nose at me, something I had never seen before.

"My barristers will be in contact with you, if not the Prime Minister or the President, when I will demand your immediate firing from Interpol and have a government sanction placed on Interpol forbidding any involvement in Irish politics." I laughed, joined by Sandra and Fay; it was a real laugh, deep from the belly, and Fionnuala's face, if possible, got even frostier.

"You know, the thing about the Terrorist Laws, there's no phone call, no legal representation, just the judgment of the World Court, followed by permanent incarceration or death. Think on that, ladies, on your short flight out of here." And I waved them away towards the open ramp of the CH-53. Sandra and Fay handed the prisoners over to the chief's men, who immediately bagged their heads.

"What now?" Sandra asked. Indigo had left us a squad of commandos. I called them in out of the deluge, working through my priorities as I did so. I called the chief.

"I'll want to interrogate everyone we have when I get back. Can you set that up, please? Something similar to the aircraft carrier would be excellent."

"Certainly, commander, my pleasure. How will you get home?"

"I've got things to do with the colonel and the major; I'll probably leave them behind for a while, so all I'll need is one of the smaller choppers."

"I'll have one sent to you. Navy out." I dialed Indigo.

"When you're finished inside, there's a tunnel somewhere leading out of this area to the fort, and from there back to the oil tank or hangar. Find it, leave us four of your best, and don't be surprised if you meet the Israelis or the Irish coming the other way."

Sandra bounced up and down like the battery bunny she was, and her smile could light up the fast-approaching night. Even Fay looked relaxed, shucking her backpack off with a flourish.

"Don't get too comfortable, girls; Fay, I want you to interrogate the staff we are rounding up, same as for Point Roberts;

find anyone who can stay and run this place; weed out the terrorists; you know, the drill. Sandra, you and I have exploring to do. Keep your partner, bring her with you, and get four of the 104 as a backup. I'll be with you in five."

Sandra started to protest, then saw the look on my face, grimaced, and then walked off with her fellow backpacker. Fay threw me a sideways look, mimed pointing up at the sky, and promptly reminded me to sort out a drone overfly for the east coast of Ireland.

I called Ito and got that started just as Indigo emerged from the guts of the plant. His bearing was one of cheer and happiness, in contrast to the weather, which was still pouring buckets of freezing rain.

The lightning was cracking at us only occasionally now, so it might be letting off to some extent.

"Commander, there are only fifteen people here, all secured. Where do you want them?" I pointed inside the blockhouse. He nodded and spoke rapidly into his communicator. We re-entered the foyer, and for the second time, I was engaged by the contrast between the ordinary, almost too ordinary exterior and the interior, so plush and rich and alive with history and artifacts. I had read about people so rich they could indulge themselves in dressing like these, but I had never seen such a combination of luxury and plushness outside a museum.

I wondered how rich our Lady in Shackles might be and wondered about her personal trajectory. She was rich, stylish, positioned, connected, and maybe even powerful in her own sphere, so why had she gotten herself mixed up with terrorists? And it would be a very big ask for her to deny any involvement—the hangar where the drones flew from, the nuclear-capable shells stored in the oil tank, and the damming evidence of thousands of high-tech solar panels, all made in the exact same way as the ones produced in Point Roberts and New Zealand by the terrorists.

And if that were not enough, the hidden tunnel that linked the hangar, oil tank, and her plant. No coincidence, just meticulous planning and a lot of money.

Now I had to track it down and have a lot of questions to ask, and I was feeling a little weary and wet to the bone.

I sat at the table, not caring about the vintage chairs. Indigo shepherded his prisoners in and sat them down with their hands shackled behind them. He indicated the four commandos he would leave with us, then briefly stood at my shoulder.

"I'd kill for a coffee, but that'll have to wait. What's the setup like?"

"Same as Point Roberts, except they make four or five nanoproducts—the panels and a slime of some type that ends up in barrels with an electronic power pack on top. The factory layout is a direct copy—same dimensions, same type of machinery, and all underground, but the plant shows a lot more wear and tear, so it may predate Point Roberts by a year or more." Perfect English, so Indigo was as pissed as I was. These arrogant, genius-level terrorists were so 'in your face', it made ordinary people like me feel very inferior and challenged our self-worth. We had all worked like dogs for months, only to find ourselves still years behind. I shook my momentary depression off and smiled up at Indigo.

"Good to know, thanks. Go find the tunnel. This might take a while." I looked around the table, met stoic looks with harder looks, and was satisfied that many of them blinked away my stare.

"Listen up, people, you are all to be charged under the Terrorist Laws as modified in 2022. We have already taken your leader off in chains. There's only one way to save yourselves, and that's to answer our questions accurately and fast. Would anyone like to offer an explanation as to what you are all doing here?" I looked around the young faces, all showing varying degrees of fear and confusion. I had a sense that we would run right into the 'we didn't know of any terror attacks' roadblock, so I mentally relaxed and settled in for the long haul.

I was good at interrogation. Fay was better, so I left it to her and sat back and closed my eyes. I could feel Sandra breathing heavily over my shoulder, like a hound that has sensed blood.

I reached back and squeezed her arm. I needed her calm and focused.

"Cool down, relax." I could feel her vibrating under my hand.

"Did it occur to you that someone here could have sent that drone after us?" she whispered, but the edge in her voice was clear. I just nodded, kept my eyes closed, listened to the line of Fay's questioning, and got a sense of her direction.

At Point Roberts, the first terrorist environmental plant we discovered, ninety percent of the workforce were local and not in any way involved with the terrorists, with the exception of being paid by them for what they thought was legitimate work. We had incarcerated the leadership and left the remainder to work with the US Army Corps of Engineers to keep the plant running. The power cells and panels were critical to the future of the US, and from what I was hearing, all but one of these girls or women were from the mainland, recruited through the social grapevine on the promise of work, which, in this remote part of Ireland, I guessed would be at a premium.

That left the one woman who definitely didn't fit the innocent mold. I sat up, looked at Sandra, stood, and walked out of the room with her. I paused in the magnificent hallway with its vintage artifacts and called the boss.

"Jessica, nice background." I smiled, still feeling weary but a little buoyed by his lighthearted greeting.

"I need someone to take over this environmental plant here in Ireland, same as we did in Point Roberts and New Zealand. I'll turn it over temporarily to the Irish commandos we have here, but I thought I'd give you a heads up." He nodded and looked off-camera, then back at me.

"I've got to go. I'll take care of it. What's your next move?"

"I'm going for a little walk in the rain to get a feel for what we really have here, then back to Cork to have a chat with a couple of terrorists." He just nodded, and the screen went to black.

"Sandra, call the major, get him to take over here, gather your partner and our four hangers-on. We need to take a walk."

She nodded, made the call, waved her hands around, and as if by magic, five very wet and sodden figures dressed for war emerged out of the gloom.

"Indigo ci ha detto di aspettarci qualcosa che funzioni con te, comandante, ma ho l'acqua negli stivali!" The whole squad broke down laughing, myself included, as the soldier pulled his boot off and emptied it out in the mud. Sandra propped him up as he tried to put it back on and nearly fell into the mud herself, which only earned her rude jibes in three languages.

"Okay, fun time over. We're heading to the house you saw the women leave from. Take point." Sandra walked forward and headed off, her temporary partner walking along side, as I was surrounded by three laughing Italians still enjoying the discomfort of their fellow trooper and my second in command. As they were all shorter than me by half a foot, I looked over their heads to keep Sandra in view. The light was not quite full dark, but not really light enough to see easily by, but the muddy track only led to one destination, which soon came into view.

Without a word, the seven of us spread out into a vee shape. I moved onto Sandra's shoulder, and when we reached the shelter of the porch, which ran right across the front, I held up my fist, then signaled for the commandos to move around the house, two on each side. Sandra's partner turned to face the way we had come, guarding our backs, and we opened the door.

"Interpol, with a warrant, is entering!" Sandra went left, I went right, and we cleared the living room and lounge area before we took a full breath. The rooms were lived in unmistakably by women, with pretty cushions on bright couches, and the carpets, which now had two sets of muddy boot pins, were high-grade but practical for the location. We both turned cold barrels, pointing towards the noise of the back door being forced, then faced off with our squad, who added more muddy boot prints to the polished floors of the kitchen and dining room.

"The house is empty, at least on this level. Check the bedrooms." Two commandos broke off, disappeared for a minute, then returned shaking their heads. This was an older-style residence, probably built back in the fifties, and as I looked around, I felt a sense of calm but couldn't put my finger on why. Maybe because women lived here? Who knew.

"There's no upstairs. Might there be something under our feet?" I looked at Sandra. She looked at the wet and dripping commandos. They all grinned at each other, then started to thump around the floor boards, looking for echo's. It only took two minutes, and in the corner of what we would call a mud room but was probably known as a laundry over here, between the huge washing machine and the dryer, we found a trapdoor, opened it, and three commandos immediately jumped down, disappearing into the gloom, just the odd flash from a hand-held giving them away. I signaled for the remaining commando and Sandra's partner to keep watch in the house and followed Sandra down into the tunnel.

It had that dry, musty smell of the earth. The floor was good-quality timber planking, sitting on cross beams to raise it above the mud, and the uniform shape suggested it had been dug by some type of boring machine. We followed the flittering flashes of the trio in front of us, and my mental compass told me we were now heading almost due south, so towards the oil tank and the hangar.

"Halt! Guns down." The shout had Sandra and I hitting the deck, literally, straining to see what the fuss was about, and then a melodic but seriously aggravated string of Italian and Irish told us that our vanguard had found the major. We got up and jogged to where the two groups were still eyeing each other off.

"Stand down everyone, good to see you major, if you go back the way we have come you will emerge into a house, the soldiers there will point you towards the plant, I want you to take it over please, and guard it until I send further orders." He saluted, waved his hand, called his men and women to order, and marched past us. I could still hear him grumbling something about 'bloody rude foreigners' or thoughts to that effect as he disappeared into the dark.

I had no doubt that what had saved both sides from a blood bath was our fluorescent arm bands, something so common I never gave them a thought.

"Lead on." And we followed the still-shaken commandos down the tunnel. In around ten minutes, my internal compass told me we had turned to the west, and then we started up a mild incline, which emerged into a chamber and a set of stairs. A helmeted head peered down at us, then disappeared. We all climbed up and found ourselves in the hanger, looking at two fully armed drones, proudly wearing the tail feathers of the one hundred and fifty-first bomber group and the unmistakable roundel of the USA Air Force. I laughed. I couldn't help myself. We had been shot down by our own drone! I pulled my mini out.

"Admiral, sorry to bother you, but I have something I want you to see." I panned the mini around the drones, focused on the air-to-air and air-to-ground missiles on their rails, red 'safe' streamers fluttering in the light air of the hangar, then did a close up of the registration and serial numbers stenciled under the wing root. I switched the video back to my side of the screen and looked at her confused face. He held his hand up before I could say anything, and the screen went blue. All that was missing was the elevator music! The screen came alive again.

"Well, I won't say it's impossible. I'm looking at them with my own eyes, but what you have there is the most recent and most secret version of our battle drone. Can you tell me where the missiles come from?" I got down on my knees, with Sandra holding a touch for me, and scanned each missile. The air-to-air carried Israeli identifications; the air-to-ground carried the USA's.

"We'll start a back trace immediately, but whoever got these got them in the last six months. That system only went online earlier this year. Can you get the chief to ship them back with the CH-53?"

"I can do that. The more troubling issue is how they got here in the first place and who can fly them." He gave me one of his 'I'm thinking' looks and tilted his head to one side.

"You took out a control room back in Montana, didn't you?"

"We think so, but don't forget they blew the tunnels, so we only recovered wreckage, which could have been anything, as we didn't have it forensically examined. Same situation in Turkey, and there we were visitors, so we had to tread lightly. If it's not a secret, how do you fly these bastards?" He smiled, and his whole face lit up.

"You need someone to launch and recover them, and either a preprogrammed AI or live ground or air-to-vehicle control. In the data you sent earlier, you specified launch rails and trapping gear, so they are either preprogrammed before flight where you are now, or you have another control point you don't know about."

"Maximum range between control point and drone?"

"With or without satellite links?" And there he had me: did the terrorists have satellites other than the French ones they had hacked for their telecommunications? We now had good global coverage, thanks to an American entrepreneur who had seven hundred satellites in orbit but isolated from the ground and effectively shut off at the time of the web and technology hack that had killed every electronic device with a MAC chip as well as the world wide web. And hadn't the young all around the world been aroused about that?

What did the terrorist have? We knew they were still using short-wave radios; we had tracked them through that since the time we detected their signals back in Montana. Not knowing your enemy could be fatal.

"Without."

"Preprogrammed AI is limited only by fuel, and the drones you are looking at have eighteen hours of duration at 140 knots."

"The one that shot us down was loitering in a holding pattern. Do you know how long?"

"If the question you're not asking is could that drone have been launched from your location, the answer is almost certainly yes. We haven't been able to track it that far because we got to the party a little late. But yes, the drone could have come from there."

"Good to know. Thank you, admiral." And I disconnected, thinking about my options in the coming interrogations. Sandra had gone back to fuming, unhappy that the drone that had shot us down had most probably come from here. I wasn't as worried; as I saw it, we had a much bigger issue. We had been chasing the terrorists for the last three and a half months from behind all the way, and somehow we had to get into a position where we could anticipate their next moves. We had to map the terrorist command structure to see where the holes were. My mini buzzed.

"Yes, chief, how may I help you?" His big smile broke my contemplative mood. It was always hard to resist someone smiling at you.

"Commander, all the materials we recovered are now being loaded into your C-17 for flight back to Israel. The admiral has briefed me on the drones. I'll have a team back to you in thirty minutes. Do you still need a chopper to recover you and your team?" I looked at Sandra, now just grumbling to herself as she stalked between the drones and the hangar door. I caught her attention with a hand wave.

"Inspector, one minute please." She turned, looked at me with a quizzical look in her eyes, then joined me.

"First time you have ever called me that."

"Had to calm you down somehow. Thought that would do the trick. Chief's sending a team to recover the drones and the munitions. Do you need more time here?" She chuckled, gave me a huge smile, saw the chief on the screen, and waved to him.

"Hi, master chief, good to see you." And she waved again, baffling me even more with her mood swings.

"What's wrong with you?" She just continued to chuckle ominously.

"Jessica, I just want to get at these bastards. I don't know what else we can do here, but I do know we can get answers back in Cork." I nodded, finally understanding her angst. She was taking the drone shoot-down personally and wanted to confront the person responsible. I had heard our special forces troops talk about this syndrome from time to time and even had a long conversation with Pete about it. They hated remote death—happy to die fighting mano-a-mano, with a knife in the guts or a bullet in the head—but getting killed by a remote-controlled machine of any type, where the operator could be thousands of miles away, sipping coffee in an air-conditioned van where the biggest risk was a paper cut, got their blood boiling.

I reached out and stroked her arm. I needed her on her game. And I had never seen her this upset.

"The chief is sending a helicopter now and is setting up the interrogations." I turned to face the mini camera. "Chief, thank you. Recover us. We need to be back in Cork." He gave the camera a mock salute, and I put the mini back in my pocket.

"You can take your anger out on the terrorists. Start thinking about the order you want to interrogate them."

"Well, we have the young ones from here, then the Lady and her cohort, plus any Fay might have identified. If we go with the established behavior, there will only be two or three at the most actually involved with the terrorists. Everyone else will be hired help. But these drones require servicing, maintenance, and an armorer to load missiles. I didn't get that vibe off anyone we've taken so far."

"You think we've missed someone—possibly at the pub or laying low. What did your instincts tell you at the pub?"

"We didn't stop or go in. We went around the far side of it to stay out of sight. Fay and Lizzie went in. They ordered some pie of some sort, local color, backpackers after all, we need to ask her." I nodded, Sandra pulled her mini out, and I watched her face go from warm and friendly to a hard-edged frown. She turned to look at me, her eyes shadowed by her thoughts.

"She thinks there were two of them at the pub, a man and a woman, who paid too much attention to them, and when she walked over to get a better look, they both left casually. Fay said she watched then walk slowly away and back down towards the wharf. They could be fisherfolk. Before she could follow, you swept her up on your way to the plant." I thought about that, and yes, I dimly remembered a couple walking in the evening twilight on the far road, heading south.

I had thought nothing more about it.

"And some fishermen are mechanically oriented, being able to keep boats going, which is perfect cover for someone working on drones occasionally."

"Is it possible everyone on the Island is involved in some way?"

"There's only one way to find out." Out came the mini. At this rate, I should have it stapled to my arm.

"Major, slight change in plan. Take the commandos of the 104 as and when you need them. Secure the plant. I need you to support Inspector Remer. You will need to sweep the whole Island and support her while she interrogates everyone. Clear?"

"Aye, commander, will you let the Israeli colonel know?"

"Yes, I will. Thank you." I dialed the Sgan Aluf, told her what we needed, and looked back at Sandra.

"We're in for a busy night." She smiled, a feral one that reminded me of the look on a wolf just before it ate you, and for a split second I felt sorry for those we were about to interrogate.

EMERGENCE

The three girls from Scotland, Lilian, Else, and Lily, arrived at the muddy football arena in a bright green corporate helicopter, claiming it to be 'ecologically responsible transportation', which was almost an oxymoron, as it had a biofuel jet engine that was badly tuned, so it spewed smoke and microscopic debris in its noisy wake like a dirty diesel truck. The girls didn't mind. It was their final leg for this trip, and they were a trifle lagged from all the convoluted travel. They pulled large wheelie suitcases behind them, were dressed almost identically in Rockport jeans and jackets, and apart from their difference in height and hair coloring, could have easily been taken for sisters, which they considered themselves even though they had distinctly different bloodlines.

Lilian was just under six feet tall, incredibly fit, and had a short cropped cap of jet black hair. She had a habit of wearing bright t-shirts with empathetic slogans on them, and today's was a simple 'Keep your hands to yourself, and I'll keep my boot off of your arse'. She was a highly experienced deep-sea diver and was itching to get started on this new job her mother had sent them on. As the oldest by one whole year, she had responsibility for them all and took it seriously. Her sisters often argued with her about her age, as, like them, she didn't have a birth certificate and didn't actually know how old she was when she was pulled out of the refugee camp.

In their minds, their cause was both understandable and just. As parentless child refugees taken from the worst of the camps some twelve years previously, they understood their mother's passion to get more children into loving homes as quickly as possible, particularly as the world had turned on its head as a result of the terrorist attacks.

The fact that they had ended up at the same home was a fluke of fortune, one that their mother reinforced every day of their lives. But in fact, it wasn't a fluke but a deliberately designed move. She had taken them in, nurtured them, loved them unreservedly, and treated them as her own blood. The fact that she was 'Helen's' highest-placed mole in the Scottish Government was never revealed, and the fact that she sat on the joint-services Intelligence committee for the United Kingdom gave her unfettered access to secrets both big and small. In her day, she was rated one of the best sources of information in the network 'Helen' had created in Europe.

And while they didn't know of their mother's past role, they did know she was a passionate supporter of solving the refugee crisis, and they had been imbued with that passion from their first day of arrival. Each had been allowed to go their own way, each had graduated very early compared to other children, and each had excelled at their chosen trajectory—science, earth sciences, and marine biology. And now they were on a mission to help turn the tide in favor of the refugee children by doing something that would shake the world.

As their mother had told them before putting them on the truck, what they did would turn the world in favor of the refugees and their plight faster than anything they could imagine.

"Welcome to Ireland, such as it is. I'd be Moriah, your host, and this would be my littlest sister, who'll take your bags. Get in the car now. This weather is filthy, and you've no need to stand about in it."

"I'd be Sharon, and it's a pleasure to meet you all, and I'll be your guide while you are here, so anything you need, just let me know."

"Hello Sharon, Moriah, my name is Else. This is my sister Lily; and this is Lilian. She's our very own giant. We count on her heading off the rain because she's so tall!" And the three younger women all laughed, the broad-brimmed hat Lilian wore shedding water like a waterfall. The bags and the large containers and boxes they had brought with them were loaded onto the truck, and the women climbed into the old car that rocked on its springs.

"You'll have to forgive me the car. It's very old, but it occasionally runs well, so today I hope to show you that." They all laughed, and while the three girls had distinctive Scottish brogues, they were charmed by Moriah's musical Irish inflections. Outside, the rain continued to pour down, and the track they were driving on had no more than two muddy ruts in the overgrown grass. The car nosily bumped and ground its way towards the road, bouncing up and down on its worn springs, and inwardly Moriah cringed at the experience she was giving her charges. Behind them, with a massive thumping sound, the helicopter took off, its rotor wash flooding down over the car, making it impossible for Moriah to see the road for a few seconds, so she let the car drift.

"The boys put the landing pad here just yesterday, so it's still a bit rough," Sharon said, turning to look at the women in the back seat. They looked comfortable, even a little amused.

"Maybe the understatement of the year!" Else laughed as she spoke, breaking any tension Moriah was feeling. She smiled, remembering that while the car was legally a wreck on wheels, she owned it. It was hers, and she took great pride in that.

"As a teacher, you see, I don't get much to spare on fixing the car up, so it has to do as it is."

"Moriah, chill, aye, it's a bit rough, but far better, I'm thinking, than walking out in this shite weather." Sharon punched her sister on the arm, so she started the car again and headed into the sheeting rain, which now was flooding the tracks. It was strange to her mind that this type of weather had only come around in the last year or two, and she wondered what natural imbalance was causing such a disturbance.

"You'll be meeting with a lovely lass by the name of Katrina when we get home, which is not far now, and she'll look after you all as well as Sharon here." The girls nodded, having been well briefed by their mother. "Initially, I've put you all on the same floor, but you might have to share a room later in the week, as I'm expecting some more locals to need a bed or two. You won't mind that, will you?" Lily, the youngest of the three, looked to her sisters and saw acceptance in their eyes. The difficulties their Irish hostess faced almost daily had also been explained by their mother.

In a way, this was why they would work their magic here in Dundalk first, as both a proof-of-performance test and a way to make it easier for Moriah and her team to do what they did best—looking after anyone in need in their general vicinity, which seemed from the reports they had gotten stretched from Dublin to Belfast!

"Moriah, please, we'll be fine. We'll not get in your way or take up much of your time. It's very kind of you to be carting us all around in this filthy weather. Would you happen to know where your power station might be and its condition?" Moriah looked in her rear vision mirror, the better to see Lily's eyes.

"Aye, I do, but it's not going to be much benefit to you, as it no longer works, as the gas supply that fed the boilers was destroyed by the terrorists some months ago." Again, Lily looked at her sisters. Both nodded, so she continued.

"Once we have our bags put away, do you think we might go and look at it? It might be that this Katrina you mention would like to come with us." Moriah smiled; she had no idea what these beautiful young women were up to and, in a sense, didn't want to know.

"Aye, I can do that. I'll send Sharon here along as your driver, as you not being used to our roads such as they are, it might be more than you would want to handle." The three women nodded, watching the rain fly by as if driven by some massive fan, and all three silently prayed that the Gods would be kind to them and their quest. Up ahead, the dark shadow of a building cut through the gloom, and a ray of sunlight cut through the clouds, briefly creating a spotlight.

"And there it is, our home, and would you look at that, lit up as bright as a button for your arrival."

Maybe the Gods were listening, Lily thought to herself, knowing that time would tell one way or another.

CHAPTER ELEVEN

We still couldn't find the missing nuclear shell. The chief had retrieved the two drones and the munitions and had arranged for one of the Irish helicopters to collect us. Before we flew out, Fay had rejoined us, and I had immediately sent her off with the Irish Sciathán Fianóglach to interrogate everyone on the Island. We needed to find out who was in on the drones and the plant. For some reason, I felt edgy about the whole operation. I couldn't put my finger on any one specific thing that had happened, but the unease I felt was reflected in Sandra's face. Maybe she was feeding off me, or maybe I was imagining things.

The simple fact was that we had arrived here to remove nuclear-capable shells and had discovered a covert drone facility and a hidden environmental plant, linked by underground tunnels.

There was one way to quell the stomach clutches.

The chief had set up the interrogations for us, so having stopped for a shower and a change of clothes, I marched over to the container where two of our Italian troops stood guard, read the notes that had been prepared for us, nodded to Sandra, who had also showered and changed, this time into a sexy gray pants suit, the cut of which showed her weapon and badge with little effort, and walked in. I made a solid heel-on-the-ground sound. She had put her rubber-soled combat boots back on, a distinctively odd look against her tailored suit. I would never understand her choice in clothes, nor would I ever look as glamorous and sexy as her in anything I put on, no matter how hard I tried!

Flat gray walls, a flat metal roof, a single fluorescent light, and a battered metal table with our first terrorist chained to it, hands and feet. No longer dressed in chic casual, she now wore a bland boilersuit, Crocks on her feet, and a bag over her head. I sat down, and Sandra positioned herself immediately behind the terrorist and leaned back against the wall. She looked at me, and I nodded, so she pulled the bag off her head, causing a mass of silver-blond hair to cascade out in waves. To make it worse, the terrorist shook her head, as if clearing something out of her ears.

"You called yourself Shannon Berkley. Is that your real name?" I watched her face for any signs of prevarication, any micro movements around her eyes, any tightening of her neck muscles. I put her in her mid-twenties, in the middle of the first group of refugees to be repatriated. She was a stunning-looking woman. Her skin had been well cared for, and her green eyes sparkled with controlled anger. She looked back at me with an arrogance I had seen before in other interrogations. Other young, intelligent, beautiful young women, all as innocent-looking as this one, were involved in various stages of the most ruthless and destructive terror attack we had even witnessed.

I decided to put our cards on the table and see how she handled herself. "Shannon, or whatever your name may be, you are charged with aiding and abetting known terrorists, planning and participating in acts of terror, and a whole bunch of sundry charges under the Terrorist Laws as modified in 2022, all of which will conclude with you being executed or incarcerated for the rest of your life. Whether it's option "A" or "B", is very much up to you." And I shut up, linked my hands on the desk top, and watched her eyes as they went from shocked, questioning, to brittle anger. She held my stare and got her emotions under control, which I respected. It showed an inner strength, and the only noise in the room was a creak from the metal structure flexing under the torrential downpour we were enjoying.

The weather on the Island had been brutal, but it paled in comparison to what came back with us to Cork. Our helicopter had indicated a ground speed of over 250 knots, more than half of it due to the ferocious tail wind from the storm. Needless to say, it made for an interesting landing!

"Commander, wouldn't it just be quicker to take her out and shoot her?" The edge in Sandra's voice reminded me she was still pissed at having been shot out of the sky by a drone, which we now suspected had come from the Island. I gave her a good, hard look, as if I were considering her suggestion. She was turning out to be an excellent partner in the interrogation stakes.

"Yes, Inspector, it would. Still," and I started to tap my fingers on the table top, as if I were thinking about her proposal, "we might just learn something new if Shannon, or whoever she really is, talks to us. Do you have a specific activity in mind?" Behind the terrorist's head, still leaning on the wall, Sandra sent me a beatific smile, and I could feel her excitement levels pumping up.

"Well, knowing who was in control of those drones might be a good start, but I suppose Lady Do-da will tell us that when we talk to her." The terrorist's eyes gave her away, just the barest flicker of surprise. She hadn't anticipated our line of questioning. And she hadn't known we had arrested the team at the hidden environmental plant. Which made us wonder what else she had been up to that we didn't know about. Ireland was a very long way from the strike points the terrorists had attacked, but recent activity pointed to Ireland being an important landmark in their plans, both long and short term.

Malik Badawi had his boat refitted so it could launch nuclear weapons, and that work had been done in Dublin. His partner, Siobhan O'Cleary, was a nuclear scientist trained in Ireland and had an Irish background. Maribelle Assiano had her renovated gunboat moored in Northern Ireland before she headed out into the Atlantic, sinking a fishing boat, shooting down a helicopter, and sinking an ocean liner full of child refugees, only to be retired by a coordinated attack by the US Navy. The nuclear fallout from that encounter was still circling the globe.

Then there had been the terrorist underground plant in Pollatomish, which had required a pair of US cruise missiles to take it out, and then the year-old web notice board, which had started the search in the first place for the nuclear shells and promised an Irish uprising the Thursday before Easter. Whichever way you cut it, Ireland was a prime location for the women terrorists.

And now we had a tiny Island with sophisticated drone technology and an environmental plant making nano goo and solar roofs, not to mention the cache of nuclear-capable shells stacked in a disguised oil farm, with the attendant underground tunnels linking various parts of the Island.

When you stood back and looked at what these women had achieved in what we thought was three or four years, it was staggering in its scope. Sandra cut into my thoughts, bringing me back to the 'now'.

"Commander, maybe if we brought in one of the other two women, what were their names? Ah yes, Faith and Roslyn, and offered them a bullet in the brain or a conversation, we might get an answer?" Behind the terrorist, Sandra was glowing like a candle, her battery bunny façade in full swing. I wasn't sure she didn't mean what she said! I held my hand up as if to slow her down, but in truth, it was all I could do to hide my smile.

"I don't think that will be necessary, will it, Shannon?" And I held her stare. She finally looked down at her manacled hands, then back up at me.

"My team was only responsible for keeping the drones airworthy and making sure the conditions were optimal for the storage of the chemicals." I shook my head.

"Sorry, Shannon, that won't fly. We confiscated drums of nanomaterial and nuclear-capable shells, not chemicals. And while we didn't find any AI programming hardware in either location, it would not be all that hard to hide. Want to try again?" Her response was to glare at me, tighten her eyes, then shake her head.

"Let's put this all into perspective then. The terrorist group you are part of is responsible directly and indirectly for the deaths of over fifty million people, the displacement of millions of others, and the economic destruction of most countries in the world. Bullet or conversation, Shannon, we'll give you five minutes to decide." And with that, Sandra and I left the container, making sure to slam the door to make our point. Our exit was spoiled by a waterfall sheeting over the edge of the container roof, which soaked us both to the skin before a trooper managed to get an umbrella over our heads.

"*Scusi comandante, non ci aspettavamo che finissi così in fretta.*"

"*Non c'è bisogno di scusarsi, andremo a cambiarci, poi potrai tenerci all'asciutto quando torneremo.*" Sandra and I walked off to our temporary quarters to dry off and change, get a coffee, and consider our options. The guards weren't responsible for us getting drowned; the filthy weather was.

"What do we really need to find out from her?" Sandra asked, stripping off her sodden shirt and revealing a lacy black bra that would do a catwalk model proud. I shook my head, ignored her wardrobe choices, and concentrated on her question.

"In retrospect, where the drone was launched from is moot. We've taken out their ability to use them from here. That's all that really counts. You have to let the shoot-down go. It wasn't personal. They were after me, not you." She practically exploded across the room, grabbing my forearms.

"Bullshit! It was an attack on us, Interpol, not just you, and while you're still the prime target, anyone with you is more than just collateral damage!" I looked into her face, her eyes ablaze, her whole posture one of aggressive anger. "And I'm not going to apologize for that." And she let me go and slumped on the bunk.

"Jessica, these bastards have destroyed the world and killed millions, yet profess to be only interested in the poor little refugees in the camps. What about the millions of new refuges they have created by their atrocious actions? Where do you draw the line?" I looked at her, a study in anger and fury, a side I had not seen of her previously, and I wondered what was under it. We had fought and bled together as we retired terrorists, but I had never seen her so visibly upset, even when she had been shot.

"What's really going on with you?" I posed the question as warmly as I could and sat down beside her. If someone had walked in on us, they would have seen two mostly naked women sitting side by side on a khaki-colored army bunk with dripping wet hair, sodden clothes, and slumped shoulders. But they wouldn't necessarily see the weapons we each had slipped under our thighs, a habit developed from living in stressful situations twenty-four hours a day.

She looked at me, her face smoothing down, the reddish color fading from her cheeks. Then she smiled, and I could see the battery bunny emerging from the shell of one very pissed-off woman.

"It's the contrast between the bastardry these women have perpetuated and the smiling, beautiful innocence we keep walking into. Not one of them has even looked guilty, ashamed, or even marginally scared, if you discount the disgust we get from time to time. I'm more used to the bad guy being really bad and acting out like a bad guy, not looking like they want to have a coffee and a croissant with us. I'll get over it, but Shannon pissed me off with her attitude that we just didn't matter in her view of her world."

"You want them to respect you—or at least the badge."

She gave me a brutally hard look, her eyes wide open and sparkling with energy, then broke into a grin again.

"No, not really. The bad guys never respect us. That's not it. Even back in Chicago working with the FBI, the bad guys behaved like bad guys. Look back at all the women we have incarcerated and compare them to the mercenary terrorists we took out. There's such a contrast it makes my brain spin."

"The mercenaries never hesitated to shoot at us, blow us up, or kill us. They shot first and, like us, never stopped to ask questions. You could rely on them to act like what they were."

"And the women don't act like terrorists, and if you discount 'Helen's' little firefight, none of the women have ever shot at us—and in 'Helen's' case, it was her mercenary terrorists who did the shooting, not the women."

"Exactly. And the reason I'm pissed off about the drone is because it's too impersonal."

"I get that. Pete and I had a long discussion about that some time ago. Our commandos hate remote killing. They see it unworthy of their skills." She sat quietly for a moment, lifted her shoulders, signaling she was getting back in control, stood, walked to her bunk, and started to dress.

"Back to my question. What do you want from Shannon?" I hand brushed my wet hair, considered it done, and climbed into my combat fatigues, my suit laying like a limp, wet doll on the bed. I slipped my weapon back into its holster and clipped it to my belt. I bent down and slipped my ankle holster on, taped the Velcro flap firmly shut, and pulled my pants leg down. Across the room, Sandra mirrored my movements, except she also fitted her H&K into her minicomputer case, which she slung across her shoulder. There was a knock on the door, which we both reacted to, each in a different manner. I called "Come in," Sandra slipped her hand into her minicomputer case, no doubt grabbing her H&K.

"Commander, inspector, do you have time for an update?" Indigo held out a small tray with two steaming mugs of coffee floating in a small sea of rainwater. His smile was infectious, and he had dressed in his uniform blues with red stripes running so far up his legs that he looked taller than he was. The clear raincoat he had on over his uniform was splattered with rain, and drops quickly formed a puddle at his feet.

"Indigo, you're a life saver, and Jessica and I would love to hear what's happening out there in the real world." Sandra finished her comment with such a huge smile, I sensed she was now back to full-power battery bunny. But I would keep my eye on her. She was showing signs of stress, and in this business, stress could lead to mistakes, which could get you killed very quickly. We were still, in my mind at least, behind enemy lines, even in the calm but seriously wet Cork! Indigo stood at parade rest, his hands behind his back.

"No sign of the missing shell. We've got continuous drone coverage of the coast from Dundalk to Dublin. The major holds the northern end of the Island."

He paused, watching my face for a reaction. I didn't give him one, so he continued. "The Israeli 104 hold the southern end of the Island, and they calculate there are now only fifteen people left, six in the pub, the rest at the fisherman's dock. Inspector Remer asks what you want to do with the Island from this point on." Again, that thoughtful pause, same result.

"Inspector Remer reports they have found three more terrorists. They are being shipped to us as we speak. She asks what you would like her to do now." Another pause. This time, a little smile crossed his eyes.

"Inspector, remind me when we get home never to play poker with the commander here, under any circumstances." Sandra smiled, looked over at me, and nodded.

"She is a cool one, but she has a tell."

"Really? What is it?" Indigo nearly forgot where he was up to with his report. He had been demolished by Jessica at the poker table since the first time he met her with the Boss six years ago. Sandra just shook her head and laughed.

"You'll have to work that one out for yourself." Indigo's shoulders slumped, a nice physical full stop to the temporary lightheartedness that had invigorated both Sandra and myself. Working with Indigo was an absolute joy, good times or bad, and I loved the opportunity to pull his chain.

"*Oh bene, torniamo al lavoro.* The major asks what you would have him do with the plant. He has secured it, and the remaining workforce are sequestered in the big room, awaiting your instructions. My feeling from talking to him is that he does not want responsibility for taking operational control of the plant." Now I had to make several decisions, and still that little uncomfortable bug wrestled in my gut, making me uneasy.

Every other site where we had chased the terrorists down, we had faced some form of resistance, even if it had been passive. Here in Ireland, apart from the evil look the CEO of the plant had thrown my way before we had bagged her, the fiercest opposition had been a group of smiling women emerging from a tunnel!

"Indigo, give me a minute, please. I need to talk to the boss." He nodded, put his hat back on, saluted and bowed at the same time, and prepared to leave.

"Certamente comandante, fammi sapere cosa vuoi che sia fatto." I looked at Sandra and raised one eyebrow. I waved to Indigo to stay for a moment.

"Well?" Sandra studied my face, tried to discern what my preferences might be, shook her head, and turned to Indigo. She was a quick learner.

"Colonel, ask Inspector Remer to return soonest. Ask the major and the Sgan Aluf to hold in place, be watchful, but not offensive to the locals." She turned slightly to look at me out of the corner of her eyes, seeking a reaction, but she got none. "Also, tell the major we will have a plan for him and the plant within the hour." He nodded, bowed slightly again, and with a very large grin, split his face. He collected our mugs and left.

"Now you can call the Boss." Sandra waved at me with one pretty hand.

I did. His craggy face slipped into focus, and the background behind his head was a blur, suggesting he was in a vehicle.

"Boss, I've got a logistical problem I need you to solve. I could make the call, but you know the players better than I do, and frankly, I need to get back to the interrogation of the terrorists."

"What do you need?"

"We've captured another environmental plant, producing nanomaterials and solar panels. We've taken the top two or three people in. I'm in the middle of chatting to them now. I suspect that down the line we will find valid reasons for keeping the plant running, but unlike New Zealand, the army doesn't want anything to do with it operationally. I need a team to take it over, run it, train the locals, you know the drill."

"What are you thinking?"

"You know the President of Ireland. You know the President of the US. It seems to me that a team from the Army Corps of Engineers trained in Point Roberts would be an excellent temporary solution." His face gave nothing away, but I could see his mind working at a million miles an hour behind his gray eyes, which had closed to slits.

"You're thinking like a politician." I smiled at that. Like most of my kind, I detested the normal political cadre with a passion and with few exceptions.

"No, I'm thinking like someone at the tip of the spear, needing a softer solution than one I could think up."

"Give me an hour. I'll see what I can arrange." Before I could thank him, he cancelled the call, so I turned to face Sandra.

"Let's go and continue our chat."

Just as we emerged from our tent, two massive umbrellas snicked open, and we were escorted back to the container and our prisoner. The chief was standing out in the rain, some sort of plastic raincoat over his fatigues, with streams of water running down his face like miniature waterfalls. He gave us an evil smile as he opened the door for us, looked hard at me, nodded to himself, then slammed the door behind us. We both sat on one side of the battered table, with Shannon, or whatever her name really was, on the other.

"Normally, I would ask you if you needed anything—water, food, a comfort stop—but the weather is so shitty I can't find it in myself to be polite. I believe you were to answer a question before we left?"

"Sorry, in all the fuss and bother of the last half hour, I've forgotten what it was." Her sarcasm cut across the table like a knife. I leaned back in my chair.

"Well, there's no rush. You'll either get a bullet or a very deep, dark hole, no skin off my back, which ever. It would be a lot easier for you, and those that follow you if you simply answered our questions. Inspector?" Sandra stood, put her back against the wall, and looked relaxed, but I could see she was wound up like a clock again.

"I only have one question. Did you launch the drone that shot down the US Gulfstream three weeks ago?" Shannon looked amused and rolled her manacled hands open as if to say, 'what?', but her body language gave her away.

"Let me be clear. My team looked after the drones, made sure they were flight ready, the munitions stored properly, then fused when needed. We launched and retrieved them as required, but had nothing to do with the targeting. Let me repeat-nothing to do with the targeting."

"Who programmed the AI, then?"

"I don't know. It was delivered to us an hour before flight time. We simply fitted it to its cradle, and closed up the airframe." I dropped my head slowly, looking at the desktop, framing my next question.

"What is the nanomaterial you were storing?" She looked up at the roof and scrunched up her eyes, her face showing some strain. If she was going to lie, now would be the time. She did.

"Don't know what you are talking about. Every few days we were delivered a truck load of sealed containers, which we transferred into the oil tank and made sure the electronics were connected and working. Never opened one up, never thought to ask what was in a container."

"Where do you get your power from?" Sandra spoke so quietly that I had to tilt my head to hear her. She pushed off the wall, rested her fists on the tabletop, and leaned forward in a very in-your-face stance. "Come on, we know the main power supply from the mainland has been cut for weeks. Where do you get yours from?" The acidic edge to her voice had me paying attention, and I wondered what effect it would have on our prisoner. She seemed a little startled at Sandra's increased aggression level, so I mentally applauded my partner because this was the first crack we had seen in her.

"I don't know. We have a permanent supply in both the hangar and the oil tank. I just assumed someone had a generator or something." For a smart woman, she was really bad at lying, and I couldn't figure out why she was prevaricating. I decided to crack her shell a little further open.

"Inspector, how many other terrorists have we taken from the Island?" I asked, not taking my eye off the woman for a second.

"Commander, three from the plant, three from the hangar, and another three from the general population. What were you planning to do with the nuclear-capable shells?" Brilliant! Now we would see what we would see.

Oldest trick in the interrogation book is to ask an unaligned question at the end of a statement, forcing the person being interrogated to switch mental gears rapidly. In this case, I suspected we were dealing with another genius, super smart being the baseline for these women terrorists, and watching the thinking raging behind her eyes confirmed my suspicions.

"Nuclear shells? What shells are you talking about?" Her whole face lit up with the question, and if I hadn't been a born skeptic, I would have believed her. Sandra delivered the killer blow, and I could not have been more proud of her. She leant right into the terrorist's personal space and, in a cool and deliberate voice, leveled her anger at the women.

"Listen, you foul-smelling rat, we pulled dozens of bimetallic shells out of your precious oil tank, where they were well hidden. You stored nanomaterial in the oil tank, had your very own private tunnel from the hangar, and obviously used it often. Don't lie to us, you scum sucking bitch, or I'll retire you where you sit." And to make her point, she pulled out her weapon, worked the slide, then snapped the slide release, and with a resounding 'click, snap' as the action slid home, pointed the gun right between the terrorist's eyes. Holding a smile behind tight lips, I placed my hand on Sandra's arm and felt her quiver with tension.

"Inspector, think of the mess we would have to clean up. If you have to shoot her, take it outside." You could hear the rain on the roof and feel the silence in the container as I held my pose, Sandra held hers, and the terrorist tried to unpack what was happening. There was both confusion and fear on her face now. Sandra had sold her 'bad girl' act with great style and passion, and from the moment she had pointed her weapon, her hand had not moved a single millimeter. She had such fine control. In all probability, facing down an unmoving, cocked automatic just inches from her face finally convinced the terrorist we were serious.

Sandra slowly pulled back, de-cocked her weapon, and then, with a fierce grin, looked at me.

"Can I take her outside now?" I gave her a studied look, tilted my head to one side as if considering, then pulled my hand off her arm.

"If she doesn't tell us everything we want to know, yes." We both looked at the terrorist, whose eyes had gone wide open, and waited. She slowly nodded, put her head in her manacled hands, and sighed. Sandra sat back down, her weapon now flat on the table under her hand, pointing at the terrorist. Another old police tactic was 'good guy, bad guy', so with Sandra visibly salivating at the idea of just shooting our terrorist in the head, I played the softie.

"Shannon, we don't want to play hard ball, but please understand the pressure we are under. We've already had two nuclear events, one that killed over ten thousand people and made a very big hole in Gaza, the other responsible for a radioactive cloud several thousand miles wide. Where does your electric power come from, and what were you doing with those shells?" She looked up at me, her eyes showing the strain she was under, obviously conflicted by her loyalty to the other terrorists and the need to save her own skin. But I could see a lot of calculation behind her eyes, so I knew we would not get the whole truth. Super-smart people always thought they had the edge.

"The power comes from the pub. That's why I told you I thought we had a generator somewhere. As for the shells, I know nothing about them other than a woman came here two months ago and asked us to store them for her."

"Who was the woman?"

"No idea. I wasn't introduced. I was just told where to put the shells and how to store them."

"How did they get here?" At this question, she looked up and stared at me, and the confusion she showed indicated that they were not at all prepared for us, at any level.

"She arrived on some sort of small ship, offloaded the shells, then took off."

"Who do you take your orders from here on the Island?" Sandra was leaning forward again, her weapon now only a foot from the terrorist's face. She was showing pure bitch. The anger and power rippled off her in waves.

"And you never answered my question about the drone." I looked at Sandra out of the corner of my eye to see if I had to intervene again, but she looked steady and focused.

"Shannon, who do you take your orders from?" She looked down at her manacled hands, then back up at us.

"There's a woman from the government on the Island who lives up in the north end somewhere. She's in change, and she sends all her instructions down through an assistant."

"Name?"

"Only know her as Patricia. She never stays long, just in and out as it were, and leaves us pretty much alone most of the time."

"Shannon, how can you get us to believe you knew so little when you walked out of the tunnel that is connected to the property where your mythical government employee lives?" She held Sandra's stare, but you could see how uncomfortable she was by the tension in her body. I sharpened my voice but still projected warmth and support.

"If you look at it logically, this is a very small Island, and the chances of you not knowing everyone important to you are very slim—in fact, I'd go so far as to say impossible. Who is she, what can you tell us about her?" The insolence on the terrorist's face suggested we had got all we were going to get. I stood up and rolled my shoulders.

"We'll give you a few minutes to make your peace, then we'll take you outside." I turned just as Sandra picked up her weapon, pointed it at the terrorist, and said "bang!" in a soft voice. We exited back out into the downpour; no umbrellas this time. It seemed the weather had gotten the better of our guards and escorts.

"It's like drawing teeth out of a frog."

"Frogs don't have teeth."

"Exactly. None of them have talked since day one. They just seem to be satisfied with their tactics. And it's not fanaticism, it's a deeply seated belief."

"Yes, their moral compass is somewhat screwed, but their belief in what they are doing and why they are doing it is cemented. I wonder if Lady Muck-muck really is related to the government in any way?"

"Are you suggesting the Irish government is complicit in this?" Sandra's voice had risen sharply, and the look she gave me was pointed. I held her look, thought for a second, and tilted my head to one side.

"Maybe. Possibly, probably not. We haven't found any government link to the terrorists so far, ever. The negotiations with the US State Department before the first attacks were innocuous and in good faith. But this does raise a question or two. Remember how Trotsky had all those women hacking government sites to create false IDs, permits, entry visas, and green cards?"

"Yes. Only too well, both you and Pete got yourselves shot." I unconsciously rubbed the bullet wound on my shoulder, which I had almost forgotten about.

"Well, consider this. If, as we suspect, someone on this lovely piece of real estate has a plan for a million refugee migrants, they would need at the very least IDs and visas acceptable to the European Union. Where are they coming from?"

"Trotsky had six women working on the US entry permits, and that was for just a few hundred thousand. We haven't found anything here mirroring that technology, so it's happening somewhere else."

"Yes, and isn't that an interesting thought? We might just have to go see the President of Ireland after all. But we know someone who knows someone else who might be able to give us an answer to part of this puzzle."

"The boss and his Red Crescent/Red Cross contact."

"Exactly. But not yet. We need to finish the interrogations." As we had now been thoroughly drenched again, sloshing through ankle-deep water and mud, when we reached our tent, I shook like a dog, throwing most of my excess water all over Sandra. She just laughed and reciprocated. Indigo sloshed up with coffee mugs, closely followed by the chief.

"You have news?" I asked, as they both shook water off their raincoats. We all collapsed into the wire chairs someone had found for us, forming a tight little conversation circle. Indigo looked thoughtful, the chief bemused, and I wondered what was entertaining him.

"Jessica, Fay is on her way back with the three additional prisoners, due in ten minutes subject to the weather; the major and the colonel are holding position as requested. Our C-17 will land back in three hours, and Ito reports no sign of the missing shell at this time." Indigo's use of our first names suggested a casual approach, very unusual for him in company, so something else was up. He was sitting calmly, but I watched his eyes, which scanned the room continuously. The chief had also picked up on Indio's casualness and was looking a little miffed at the lack of normal military manners.

I just looked at Indigo, held his eyes, relaxed, and gave him a little smile. Next to me, Sandra went on high alert. I could feel her vibrating through her wet clothes. But she held her seat, her hands loosely folded on her lap, her minicomputer bag with the deadly H&K in easy reach.

"I cannot be sure, but from the tone the major used during my conversation, it didn't feel right. And the ground staff we have here are acting very strangely."

"How so?" I noticed the chief was now more engaged, sitting up in his seat.

"I can't put my finger on it, but just minutes ago a pair of maintenance men walked past on their way to the civilian terminal, and the looks they gave me raised the hair on my arms."

"Chief, are all your RRT here?"

"No. One squad went back with the shells in the C-17."

"How many left?"

"Eight."

"Indigo?"

"We have half of Tom's team and eight of ours from Venice."

"Chief, how secure are the prisoners?"

"Chained in the back of the hangar, bagged and separated, and my team is watching over them." I gave it a minute's thought, working through the possibilities as fast as I could. We were on a civilian airfield, at the back of a hangar in a temporary Irish army barracks used for training, with the approval of the airport manager. Our helicopters had landed openly in front of the hangar, using the airport's control system. The C-17 had used the normal strip, and we had kept our weapons out of sight as much as possible. But we were dressed in combat fatigues, and the Israeli 104 had been dressed in ninja black, so we may have aroused interest somewhere.

But this was a civilian airport in the second-largest city in Ireland, and while no one locally knew what our agenda was, the fact that someone on the Island could have communicated with someone at the airport was not that far-fetched.

There had been no civilian air traffic movements while I had been on the ground. There were civilian passenger aircraft parked on the tarmac, and with the exception of the ground staff you would expect to see at any reasonably sized airport, civilians were few and far between. I looked around at my team and stood up.

"Let's go walk around a bit, see what's what. Chief, get your guards back on the container, make sure the prisoners are secure, and we'll meet you at the tower." I patted Indigo on the arm. I trusted his instincts, but more than that, I trusted him. He was the bedrock of my command now that the Boss had deserted us for a suit and tie. He had more field experience than I had, having been the head of Interpol Italy for a decade, and apart from his fantastic barista skills, he brought a sense of calm and absolute professionalism to every situation we found ourselves in, no matter how dire.

"Indigo, call a squad, loose protection formation, weapons slung, have them form on us." He nodded, used his communicator, fired instructions into it in Italian so fast I could hardly translate, then looked at Sandra with a wry smile.

"Inspector, are you and the commander dressed appropriately?" She looked at me and grimaced.

"No, we left our body armor here in the tent." He just looked at me with one eyebrow raised. I shrugged like a schoolgirl caught skipping out on school, turned, and went back into the tent. At least Sandra had to strip as well, fit the vest, and then redress. Donning lightweight plastic raincoats, we went out and joined Indigo and his team, who were now formed up in the classic wedge shape for personal protection.

"Gente, questa è una missione di scouting; non eliminiamo problemi, ma teniamoci all'erta."

"Sì, comandante!" They would stay on their toes, and they would keep aware. They were some of the finest commandos I had ever served with, and their loyalty and courage set a high benchmark for everyone else we worked with.

"Let's go, gang."

THE CHALLENGE

Moriah looked around at the women, now dressed in winter gear: mittens, caps with ear muffs pulled down, and thick down jackets. The three sisters, Lilian, Else, and Lily, wore identical red parkers, with a little gold angel motif sewn on the top pocket. Katrina not only the eldest, but also the tallest, dominated by her very presence as well as her intellect. She and her partner had perfected a technological miracle, and while her laboratory was now thousands of kilometers away, the results of her work were in the large barrel she had brought with her.

She took the lead, and looking around at the bright, intelligent faces, eager with anticipation for what they were to do, she focused in on the youngest.

"Lily, you're the geologist. Is that correct?"

"Aye, that's my profession, but I'd call myself a naturalist if I had my way about it." Katrina just smiled. She knew Lily's background to the second and understood her passion for studying how nature created the geological masterpieces that littered the hills of Scotland and other countries.

"I have a map here. I need you to tell us where we should concentrate our efforts." She handed over a detailed geographic chart that had geothermal gradients plotted on it, as well as stratification data.

"Will I be able to test any areas of interest?"

"Yes, you brought your gear with you?"

"Aye, we did that. Can you tell us how far down you want to look?"

"Our plan is to use what we build here as a working proof of concept, so I'd be happy if we didn't go below three hundred meters."

"On land or on the sea bed?"

"Doesn't matter. We've got an expert deep diver with your sister here. On land would be preferable but not essential, but whatever strata you select, it needs to represent what we might find in other countries."

"So you want a homogenous sample—do you have similar maps of the other countries where you want to do this?"

"I do. Would you prefer to work on this map first, then relate to the others, or look at all the maps at the same time?" Lily looked to her sister, the scientist, and noticed she was thinking deeply.

"Would you have a computer I can use by any means?" Else asked. It was Moriah's turn to look around the shed, as if seeking an answer in the timber walls.

"I'd be getting you one from the university. I'd be thinking, or I could take you there when you need it. Maybe taking you there would be the easier option, now that I'm thinking on it."

"You have a working computer at the university?" Katrina asked, a question mark in her voice. Moriah just smiled at the implied challenge and nodded.

"Aye, that we do. It's a well-kept secret, but we had some off-line and not working at the time of the attack, and we managed to get them up and running soon enough after, but we've kept mum on it, so as not to attract any unwanted attention." Katrina smiled. This was a bonus she had not counted on having.

"By any chance, might this computer of yours still be linked to the university library?" Moriah gave her a hard look. Her instincts had her hackles rising at this question because it suggested that Katrina was knowledgeable about such things, and to be truthful, Moriah was not at all sure her professor would be happy giving this information away so freely.

"I can't be telling you that. Just be happy for now I can get you to a machine that still works." Katrina looked at her host, confused about her response. She had been told by the sister's mother, who was the reigning senior planner still operating and went by the code name 'Mary', that the Irish team had been fully briefed and had accepted what needed to be done.

She decided to retreat and let things lie until they needed computer access. But a computer would be a fantastic aid, enabling them to look at multiple countries simultaneously, shortening the time they would need by perhaps months.

"All right then, we have all the gear we need for safety stored here, Moriah. You have security organized. Let's go back to the building and get a start, shall we?" The sisters nodded, happy to get back inside where it was warm. They had already started looking at the maps, seeking a solution they had never considered previously.

A strata formation that was unified and replicated in at least, from the number of maps, nineteen other countries. It was an intellectual challenge of such magnitude that it absorbed them during the drive back to the apartment block.

So absorbed, no one saw the hunched figure in the shadows, who watched them leave, then walk to the shed, where it rattled the locked doors, then retreated back the way it had come and disappeared into the night.

CHAPTER TWELVE

We walked out into sheeting rain so dense you could hardly see a foot in front of your face. The temperature had dropped several degrees in the last hour, and it was hard to tell if it was day or night.

We walked the line between the parked aircraft, past two of our Irish-supplied helicopters and the massive twin-rotor Chinook that had carried the boat to Bantry, and then past the massive US Navy CH-53 Super Stallion with its seventy-foot blades dripping down almost to the tarmac. It was so large that sheets of water cascaded off its fuselage as if it were being attacked by fire hoses.

Under the aerobridges, we passed parked tugs and refueling equipment, and as we did, the hair on the back of my neck stood up, and I felt the unease I had experienced earlier on the Island. We were being surveilled, of that there was no doubt, but by whom and why remained a mystery. Sandra felt it as well, as her hand had slipped into her minicomputer case, no doubt now circling her trusty H&K. Indigo had also picked up on our body language and had deliberately moved to a position that covered our flank. We reached the foot of the control tower, a blocky-looking structure sitting on top of a long, flat building. The chief and some of his RRT ran up, dripping like they had been swimming, so I signaled to Indigo, who set a perimeter defense at the base of the building, sent a long-gun shooter and a spotter right up on top of the roof, and waving to the chief, I moved up the stairs, Sandra leading, Indigo following, with the chief in the rear

"Guys, I don't want to make too much of this, but I had a very bad feeling out there on the tarmac." No one commented, a comment in itself. Old Intelligence Corps motto *'When there is doubt, there is no doubt.'* We reached the control tower, where a single woman sat in a high-backed chair, facing the slanted windows. She turned when we arrived, stepped down, and held out her hand. I took it. Warm, smooth, well-manicured, tiny, and neat came to mind. She was probably five foot six in her boots and had a waterfall of shiny jet black hair cascading over her shoulders, which contrasted with her eerie green and gold eyes. Maybe she was one of the fabled Irish fairies?

"You must be all the visitors we've been having these last few days. You are welcome to County Cork airport. I'd be Wendy O'Connor, and what can I do for you on this very wet day?" Her smile lit up the room, and I sensed no hostility from her at all, just mild curiosity.

"Commander Riley, Colonel Kashasini, Inspector Thomas, from Interpol, Master Chief Samson, United States Navy." She just widened her smile, then turned to look out the massive tinted window as her overhead speakers came to life.

"Cork Tower, Rebel fife-niner inbound two-two-six radial Cork VOR (Very high frequency Omni Range), three nautical miles DME (Distance Measuring Equipment), visual, request landing instructions." The Irish lilt in the voice was music to my ears. It meant that Fay was just a few minutes away. I gestured to the controller, pointed to the microphone, she nodded, I picked it up, and with Sandra at my back and operating purely on gut instinct, I made the call.

"Rebel fife-niner, hold, hold, hold, remaining fuel?" There was a distinct pause in the pilot's response, probably as she worked through my instructions and related them to where she was situationally.

"Cork Tower, holding as instructed, ninety minutes before bingo, we can land-on if required, plenty of open fields here, advise." And then the world took on a new look as missile smoke erupted from our west, cutting through the rain like a scythe, and suddenly the Chinook and the US Navy C-53 were blazing infernos on the tarmac. The shattering noise of the aircraft exploding reached us before the sound of the missiles. The controller snatched the microphone out of my hand, pressed a large red button on her console, and shouted.

"Everybody down!" She picked up a red handset. "Emergency response tarmac area fourteen, aircraft on fire, expedite!" And the howl of an emergency siren and then fire engines and emergency vehicles worked their way into the control tower, and cautiously looking over the control desk, I scoped out where the missiles had come from. The emissions smoke still hung in the saturated air, forming a dirty gray pillow.

"Indigo, the target is fifteen hundred feet behind a hedgerow; reference small green buildings; can't see the exact locus for the bloody rain." The distinctive crack of a high-powered rifle flew through the room, and instinctively everyone ducked again. "That's our overwatch. He has movement, a small vehicle, moving away from the buildings. Wait for one." Indigo had his communicator in his hand and was also peering over the control console. We all held our breath at the cacophony of explosions from the airframes, the sirens from the emergency vehicles, and the supersonic snap! of the rifle fire over our heads was very disjointing. I could see a dispersed group of commandos running across the tarmac, then across the runway, before I lost them in the rain. I snatched back the microphone from the controller.

"Rebel fife-niner, resume tracking. Look for tangos driving small vehicles your way, weapons-free. Reference small buildings east of the fire you will see. We have been attacked by missiles. Connect Inspector Remer." No acknowledgment, a distinct pause again, then Fay's cheerful voice crackled through the speakers.

"Commander, you called?"

"Fay, tango's heading your way, small vehicle. They just took out two of our helicopters. We think they are running. Challenge any vehicle you see, disable it if possible, and I would like someone to talk to."

"You have all the fun! WILCO." The commandos were leap-frogging each other, one group going to the ground to cover those still running, then the runners would drop to cover their team as they advanced. The first of them would be where it looked like the missiles had been fired in a couple of minutes, but the fact that they were not firing suggested the enemy had retreated. The rain was easing, and in the distance, I could see the navigation lights of Fay's inbound helicopter, which was zooming up and down and spinning on its axis. A short burst of fire came from the open door on the side, the fire looking like red and orange spurts of light, which were, in fact, the tracer rounds loaded every fifth link in the ammunition feeds. The helicopter rotated violently around its axis, nose down, then dropped like a stone and then flared, half out of sight.

"Report!" I snapped into the microphone.

"The vehicle stopped, and they shot at us, confirming their identity as tangos. We have one alive and two dead. We need to secure this location, then we'll come on in."

"Well done." I handed the microphone back to the controller, who was looking at me with wide, open eyes. Her mouth hung slightly open—a little shocky, if I were any judge. She continually pulled at a thread at the corner of her shirt collar, and her hands were fluttering like the wings of a little bird. I made another decision from my gut; we were at a huge tactical disadvantage, and I wanted to nullify that as fast as I could.

"Indigo, get Bob and his team here ASAP. Call in your reserves. If you need transportation support, let me know. Sandra, get a small squad to the target site. Get everyone else back here." I pulled out my mini, looking around the control tower. The woman had gone back to her raised seat, the microphone now clutched in her hand. Indigo was deep in conversation. The chief was standing behind me, looking amused, and Sandra was attached to my side like a leech, talking quickly into her communicator.

"Chief, you'd better tell the admiral he can collect his helicopter anytime he likes, but to bring a big brush and shovel and ask him if he could spare a platoon of marines." He looked at me, his eyes twinkling, his face showing his level of amusement. I'd get the blame for the destruction, of that there was no doubt, but he might get whacked as the messenger!

"Commander, are you serious about the Marines? You know you scare them half to death!" I reconsidered, then shook my head.

"Accepted. We'll get more of our own troops onsite." He nodded, turned to face the wall, and pulled his mini out.

"Commander, we've left two with the vehicle, heading in now, requesting landing instructions." Fay's voice was strong and edgy. Obviously, the short but deadly interaction had her adrenalin pumping. I looked at the controller.

"Where do you want them?" In contrast, her voice was shaky. I guessed she was still a little shocked by all the action around her.

I pointed out her window. "Right in front of the tower." She just nodded.

"Rebel fife-niner, land-on my location, tower, straight in approach approved, no traffic in the area, warning aircraft fire at the northern end of the tarmac, some visibility issues due smoke. The wind is six knots, zero-six-five, QNH (mean sea level pressure) one-zero-one-four."

"Rebel fife-niner. Roger all, straight in approach, landing at the tower."

"What would you be having me doing now?" the controller asked, her voice still unsteady but her face calm. She had stopped fluttering around now she was back doing what she was trained for. I looked out towards the thin black smoke of the terrorist's burning vehicle, then back towards the billowing dense smoke from our burning helicopters. The rain was still sheeting down, but now it was much lighter, suggesting it might well stop. I looked down at my mini, trying to remember why I had pulled it out.

The fog or war was relentless.

The puddles that had formed on the tarmac were reflecting the burning helicopters like a mirror, and suddenly the images were shattered and broken up into flying tiny pieces by the rotor wash of Fay's helicopter. It plonked down unceremoniously on the tarmac, bouncing on its skids, and was immediately surrounded by our troops. A hooded figure dressed in dirty combat fatigues hobbled out, accompanied by Fay, who, even in the constant rain, looked like she was just out from a day at a spa, and I smiled. Turned to the controller and gave her my best smile.

"Thank you for your help. Here is a communicator you can reach us on. I'd appreciate a heads up on any aircraft movements for the next day or two." I headed back down the stairs, straight out into the sheeting rain, which had again increased in ferocity, made eye contact with Fay, pointed down the tarmac to where our choppers were still burning, the thick acrid smoke billowing up until it reached the point where the heavy air could no longer let it rise, then curled down on itself, and ran vertically across the tarmac creating a false swirling and very smelly roof over our heads.

Talk about spooky!

I still had the mini in my hand, and I looked at it with disdain, but I remembered who I was going to call. It could wait. I put it back in my pants pocket, happy to just be in the open air and out walking with a few friends, albeit heavily armed and very dangerous ones. And very pissed off, I could sense the tenseness in everyone around me.

"What's your impression of your captive?" Fay turned to look at me, water sheeting off her sodden watch cap and across her face, one hand on the back of the neck of the hooded terrorist, the other holding a short-barreled machine pistol I didn't know she had. As he was manacled with his hands behind his back, she had the mechanical advantage in terms of moving him where she wanted him, with the occasional jab in the back from the barrel of her weapon.

"You won't believe me, but he's Slavic. I'd bet my life on it, and I wouldn't be surprised if he didn't turn out to be one of Shetani's boys."

"You're kidding?"

"Not in the slightest. Think about it-who had the technology and the ability to seed the gas lines and oil tanks with nanites?"

"How did they know who to shoot at and when?"

"Why would they have to know specifically? We've been here over three days, flying in and out. It would not be hard to work out who we were—and in all probability, the women on Whiddy Island were in contact with them." I thought about that, and a sudden cold chill ran down my back. I pulled my mini out and group-dialed the major and the colonel.

"Sitrep!" The faces of the Israeli Sgan Aluf and the head of the Irish *Sciathán Fianóglach* swam into focus side-by-side, both looking a little startled. I pointed at the major.

"Ma'am, commander, we have the workers secured in a big room, we have guards out on the perimeter of the plant, and we are as secure as we can be without more bodies." I waited for a beat. The stumpy Israeli with her massive shoulders nodded to the camera. Her over-the-head straps that held her helmet in place under her chin made her look rugged, and for some reason, just seeing her gave me confidence.

"Commander, we have some fisherfolk being held in a shed, some civilians in another shed, we have guards posted in the hangar and oil tank, but have sensed no opposition at this time." I nodded to them both.

"Thank you. The reason for the call is we were just attacked by a group of mercenary terrorists who we believe may be left over from Shetani's crew. Major, I'm sorry to say, your beautiful flying truck has been totaled. They also took out one of your smaller helicopters with the resultant fire."

"Well now, commander, who should I be sending the bill to for replacement? My boss is very understanding, but a bit of a penny pincher he is, at the best of times." We all laughed, relieving the tension, even Fay and Sandra, who were looking over my shoulder. Fay had passed the prisoner off to the chief, who was walking slowly ahead of us, his head cocked so he could hear us.

"Both of you be aware of the potential of an attack, they are highly trained and ruthless, and their weaponry is state of the art. They used missiles on us, type unknown at this point, then left in a small vehicle. Suggest you think about one to two-kilometer trip wires. Have you emptied the pub?"

"Affirmative, they are the civilians locked in a shed. They claimed to be locals and were passed by your Inspector." The Israeli colonel looked anything but happy, but she was one of the very best soldiers we had. So I did the only thing possible under the circumstances and mentally crossed my fingers.

"Thank you, stay sharp." And I cut the connection, not wanting to distract them any longer than necessary. We caught up to the chief and the prisoner, and skirted around the smoking hulks, now black-edged burnt and buckled metal covered in foam, with helmeted and yellow-jacketed firefighters rolling up hoses and little wisps of smoke fighting their way up through the overcast. The huge rotor of the CH-53 lay partially on the ground, the long sleek blades broken and bent, the effect not unlike that of an umbrella that had lost its cover in a very strong wind, revealing a bent and warped frame underneath.

"What was the admiral's reaction?" the chief turned and looked at me, an evil grin warming his face, which was being washed from top to bottom by the rain. Here was another reason to be confident. Calm in the middle of a storm.

"He wants your guts for garters and is sending you the bill." I just laughed.

"The Irish want to do the same. Looks like no more holidays or mink coats for me."

"As if," muttered Sandra under her breath as we rounded the burnt-out wrecks and came to the first of the chief's guards. We were waved through, and the chief took the prisoner off to the back of the hangar. I tapped Fay on the shoulder and formed a loose circle with Sandra and Indigo. At that moment, I would have cheerfully killed for a hot coffee.

"We have a logistics issue."

"Not enough hard bodies on the ground."

"Yes. We're now covering three potential attack sites on the Island, holding twenty or more people in two different locations, prisoners here, and we're still looking for the missing shell. Indigo, what's your take on our tactical situation?" He looked like a sopping wet garden gnome, his combat fatigues covered by his rain-slick, a weapon slung across his chest, and water dripping everywhere, particularly from the rim of his current favorite ballcap, this one representing some esoteric Italian football team.

"Commander, I believe we have distributed our forces equally to the risk of threat. The attack we just witnessed is a wake-up call, and as we are not really equipped to maintain a force in place, I suggest we get reinforcements from the Irish Government as soon as practicable." I nodded.

"I totally agree." The strength of his statement was that he said 'we,' not 'you.' We were all in this together, a genuine team dynamic, which gave me more confidence.

Section Five was a hammer, not a nursemaid. Our job was to get in, take the terrorists out, then get the hell out of dodge, leaving the clean-up and repercussions to the locals, whomever they may be. I wondered how the Boss was going to get the US Army Corps of Engineers to take over the plant?

I started to wonder about a number of other things, then my concentration was broken by one of Indigo's RRT arriving with a sopping wet tray full of coffee mugs. The chief nipped one off as he moved past, Fay and Sandra dropped their lady-like pretenses to snatch a mug each, and Indigo did the right thing by bowing slightly from the waste, gifting me the final mug.

"*Grazie. Apprezzato.*" He just looked at me with his kind eyes and smiled, motioned to the trooper, who sprinted off to get him a mug. "I owe you big time, Indigo. I can feel myself warming all the way up from my boots.

"Back to our tactical situation." I paused to sip more coffee, my head clearing for the first time since the attack on the airport. "I'm going to question our most recent prisoner and the CEO of the plant. Indigo, find out where the C-17 is, and warn them they may be shot at when they land. Get your teams out beyond the airport boundary, and create a tripwire so any further shooters have to get through you first to get in MANPAD range. Sandra, we need to work out who or what goes on the C-17, so we can turn it around ASAP.   "Comments?"   The four of us stood in the pouring rain, sodden but now at least internally warmed by the excellent coffee. The chief had taken his mug and his prisoner into the back of the hangar. Fancy a blue water sailor being afraid of a little rain!

"What are we going to do about the broadcast site in Scotland?" Sandra's face was almost in her mug as she inhaled the aroma. I looked at Indigo.

"Jessica, we may or may not have more terrorists in this area; we still need to find the missing shell. Tom and his RRT are on that; there is the broadcast site in Scotland we need to run down, as Sandra points out. We need to secure the Island. To my mind, this is one of our priorities."

"What about the recovered shells?" Fay asked, shaking her head and shedding water like a dog. I stepped slightly away from her to avoid the spray.

"The US Navy has the shells from London, Paris, and Glasgow. Bob has the shell from Dublin. I don't see any urgency in moving them anywhere, do you?" I looked around, catching the eyes of all three, noticing more than just a little fatigue. We all needed to catch our breath and get out of the rain.

"Everyone take ten, shower, change, and meet in the hangar" I looked at my watch and noticed it was nearly eleven PM local. Where did the day go? – twenty-three-twenty." Everyone nodded and broke off, except for Sandra, who stayed glued to my side. I just shrugged and moved towards our tent.

"You know, you will have to find a real job soon. I can't keep carrying you this way." She gave me a dirty look and poked at me with her weapon.

"Says you, the bullet magnet." I just laughed and held the tent flap open for her.

"I like the way Indigo ran down his list for us. Made me feel good to be a part of the team." I looked at her closely. With her watch cap off and her rain poncho at her feet, her innate beauty shone through. I really did envy her genes!

"Yes, he was inclusive, shows the value of working together so closely for a long time. Plus, it's sometimes hard to not feel isolated from external events because we tend to focus so tightly on our objective, so in his way, he was giving us all a hug."

"You manage us in a very different way to how the Boss used to."

"Better or worse?" I had most of my sodden clothing off now and was starting to lust after the hot feel of the shower.

"Neither. Different. I like your approach, and I notice you're delegating more and more to Indigo, Fay, and I. Don't mind that, but the Boss's instructions come first."

"I appreciate your candor, but I need you as a force multiplier, not a babysitter, and we need to solve that issue as soon as we can."

She just raised her shoulders, dumped his sodden clothes in a basket, and walked bare-assed naked into the small shower. Within seconds steam flowed out of the small temporary cubicle, so I decided to let it go for now and join her. Of course, being temporary, the water supply on my side relied on her side being turned off, so I tapped my foot impatiently, waiting for her to finish.

When I eventually got out, now warm all over, she had her luxurious hair wrapped in a towel, another around her breasts, and was sitting on the edge of her bunk with a forlorn look on her face.

"I'm down to my last change. You need to find us some good weather."

"Or we need to get some washing done."

"How?"

"We ask the master of logistics if Indigo can't solve it, no one can." She just nodded, looking thoughtful. She shook her hair out of the towel and started to dry it with long, pulling strokes. I just ran my hands through my short damp hair and called it a day.

"You know, you'd look good with long hair."

"Too much bother. Get dressed, *Sally*. We need to speed things up." I slipped into my last set of combat fatigues, these ones in a faint green pattern. I shook my head. When it came to military equipment, the forces had no style! My mini buzzed at me.

"Commander, who do you want to interrogate next?" I turned my head to think, I had fixated on the CEO of the plant before the terrorists had fired their missiles at us, and we now had one of them, a prisoner. What did we really need to know first?

"Chief, the terrorist, please hold the CEO in waiting. And I need you on the door, in a filthy mood." His evil smile and the glint in his eyes was the only answer I got as he disconnected. Sandra finished putting herself together, and again envy slithered around my spine. Even in crappy camouflage, she looked radiant, and I shook my head in defeat. We reached the container, where the chief was waiting with two guards and the prisoner.

"Thank you, chief. In case our decision is to execute the prisoner, have a firing squad on standby." He saluted us, made a big deal of opening the door, pushed the prisoner in, forced him down onto the metal chair, then linked his manacled hands to another chain on the top of the bent and rusted metal desk. But I had seen the terrorist's body language, and I didn't need to see his eyes to know he had understood me. Good. A little genuine fear went a long way in interrogations. And besides, the chief knew we didn't need a firing squad, just a summary judgment from the World Court, and Sandra and I would take care of it as duly authorized executors of the Court's will.

That was one of the less fine things about Section Five, and the chief had close personal experience of our methodology when we had been on the aircraft carrier a month or so ago. It seemed like months, but it was only a few weeks. Was it any wonder we were all getting a little fatigued?

True to form, he slammed the door, shaking the whole container. I smiled and gestured to Sandra, who was standing directly behind the prisoner. She pulled the bag off his head, and his first move was to shake his hair and yawn, clearing his ears. He was dark-skinned, dirty, looked disheveled, and his black eyes fired at me with some temper behind them.

"Kto ty, chert voz'mi, i pochemu ya zdes'?" Answering those questions would be easy.

"YA komandir Rayli, a ty nash plennik." Not the answer he was after, then when sitting across the interrogation table from us, you rarely got what you wanted. His eyes flicked, the tiny muscles alongside his eyes tensed, so he understood Russian as well as he spoke it. I decided to try another tack.

"Let's make this easy. Under the Terrorist Laws as modified in 2022, you will either be shot or incarcerated for the rest of your miserable life. Which one you chose is of little consequence to us, so let's make this fast.

"Name." He pretended not to understand English, so I let him have a little rope.

"Imya." Just a stoic look, as if he hadn't a care in the world.

"Sandra, message to the World Court please, trial in absentia, describe our prisoner, identify him as 'sole survivor of three,' specify the attack date and details, and request immediate summary judgment." She just nodded, making a big play of entering the data. She waited a minute, then, grinning behind the head of the terrorist, looked up at me.

"Summary judgment as follows: at the discretion of the arresting officer, immediate termination unless mitigating circumstances prevail." I tapped my finger off the desktop, beating in time to a rhythm that was running through my head. God knows where it came from, but in a strange way, it was energizing me. Being in Ireland was starting to get into my head. I looked at the prisoner and saw his thoughtful look. He understood English, of that there was now no doubt, so I let the silence hang a little longer.

"Your choice, we shoot you now, or you tell us what we want to know." My voice was soft, almost bored, definitely disinterested. It did the trick.

"What do you want to know?" his accent was very heavy. Fay had been right to peg him as Slavic. His 'w' sounded like a 'v.'

"How many are there of you in Ireland?" He looked at me with concern in his eyes, no doubt wondering how much he could bullshit us. After all, we were women, and where he came from, women probably did most of the house chores, carried the water, fed the animals, and kept the home fires burning for their men. Unfortunately for him, we were a little different-we hunted his kind with a passion and killed eye-to-eye without losing sleep. At least, I hoped so in Sandra's case. I had never thought to ask her. She had now assisted me in three retirements and who knew how many more before this was all over.

"And do yourself a favor. Don't think we don't know what's going on. We have captured or killed too many of your compatriots, including your South African wonder-boy, the almighty Shetani, who's now just dust, so please, keep it simple, and keep it real." His face seemed frozen in a rictus of hate, and his eyes now blazed with a passion I had seen in other terrorist eyes. But behind the anger was fear, so I nodded to Sandra, who drew her weapon, cocked the action with a loud 'click, snap,' and pressed the barrel to his ear.

He leaned away from the pressure, wincing, his hands reaching up as much as his chains allowed. I waved a hand at Sandra, who pulled the weapon back slightly.

"Vosem' nedel' nazad nas bylo chetyre otryada. Dvoye otpravilis' na materik posle togo, kak my zakonchili zdes', a my ostalis' s

drugim otryadom. My okazalis' zdes' sluchayno, potomu chto uvideli, kak na Uiddi prizemlilis' vertolety, i reshili posledovat' za vami."

"He claims that two months ago, there were fourteen squads. Twelve went to the mainland after they finished here, and his squad stayed. He says they saw the helicopters land on Whiddy Island and followed them here."

"That means there's still at least one squad on the Island?"

The prisoner nodded.

"Where is the other squad?" He hesitated. Sandra flicked his ear with the barrel of her weapon. He winched and tried to rub his ear, but his manacles pulled his hands up short with a loud clatter.

"Nort-End, zhenshchina v smene khotela uderzhat' kogo-to iz nas poblizhe."

"North end of the Island. She wanted them close to the plant."

"So uber bitch is in deeper than we figured." I nodded, thinking it through. If the CEO of the plant knew the terrorists were on the Island, that made her and everyone around her complicit in the earlier terror attacks and not just involved with the drones and the environmental plant. I stood, called for the door, the chief stomped in, Sandra threw the bag over the prisoner's head, and we all stood, the sound of chains rattling on the metal desk top filling the container.

I pushed the prisoner at the chief and ducked back inside before I got too wet, closely followed by Sandra. I grabbed my communicator.

"Indigo, when you can, coffee for two, and the CEO of the plant, please."

" Subito, comandante. Vuoi anche tu un aggiornamento?" An update would be nice, and I wondered how Fay was doing with the outbound planning for the C-17.

"Go."

"Commander, we have warned the major that there may be terrorists in his area. The C-17 is three hours out, and Inspector Ramer has the manifest ready; our overwatch at the tower reports no movement but warns that visibility is still restricted by the rain. The vehicle has been stripped, the bodies bagged, and they had some nano packages we have secured."

"Thanks, Indigo. Let's have the coffee and the CEO." A double click was his answer, and I suddenly wondered where Bob and his team were.

"Where was Bob last time you heard?"

"You had him and half his team with the Israelis."

"Good." I pulled out my mini. "Bob, are you secure?" His dripping face nodded, water cascading off the lip of his bush hat, which he preferred over a helmet. A habit he had no doubt picked up off Pete or the Boss.

"Detach from the 104, get to the tunnel, follow it to the house, then pretend you are looking for a terrorist squad wanting to kill us all." He smiled, shook his head like a dog after a bath.

"Anything to get out of this bloody rain. Should I be worried?"

"Very. They will be in that area somewhere and have no idea what their orders are. Knowing what we know now, I'm surprised they didn't turn up when we went in the first time." He just nodded, looked off camera, patted the top of his hat with one gloved hand, the military signal for 'form on me,' then looked back at the camera. He might have come from the Presidential detail, but he was one hell of a soldier.

"Should I ask the colonel for a few bodies?"

"Good idea. And get the colonel to ship all the civilians back to the mainland, voluntarily or in chains, then get her to sweep the Island from the bottom up until she reaches wherever you end up. Leave cover at the hangar and oil tank, but make sure there are no warm bodies left below the pub. Consider an overwatch on the oil tanks."

"WILCO." Sandra gave me a hard look, then relaxed.

"I see what you're doing. You've decided the whole Island is potentially enemy territory, so we occupy it, and they won't."

"Simple, but true. When you put everything that was going on there, you have a situation more complex than Point Roberts, and to be truthful, I'm worried about all the infrastructure work they have done; the tunnels, the drone hangar, the plant; it seems a lot of expense and work for very little gain." The knock on the door stopped me in my tracks, and Indigo poked his head in with a tray of coffee.

"Jessica, Sandra, coffee for my lovely ladies. Will you be wanting anything for your guest?"

"Absolutely not!" We all laughed. The CEO had introduced herself back at the plant as 'Lady O'Brian Flattery, and as an American, I had very little understanding of the customs or protocols of receiving Lords and Ladies, and frankly, I just didn't care. And then I suddenly had an epiphany.

"Indigo, tell the C-17 captain to execute a tactical under-fire landing, entering from the southeast. Tell the controller what we are doing. Explain this is a military requirement." He nodded, working through what I had just told him. The aircraft would execute a tight spiral down from ten thousand feet within the airport's perimeter, ready to jettison flares if fired on, but essentially would be down and landed before anyone could get a bead on them with a MANPAD.

This was a technique perfected in the dangerous and sometimes deadly mountainous corridors of Afghanistan during the American occupation.

"Look after yourselves, ladies. Your guest will be here in two minutes." He didn't slam the door like the chief did, but the look he gave me as he exited suggested both Sandra and I would be getting a talking too as soon as we finished with the CEO. He was a worry-wart, and I liked that about him. It was good to go into battle with someone who genuinely cared for you.

The CEO arrived, the chief did the usual dance with the shackles, and true to form, he slammed the door as he left. Sandra was about to pull the hood off when I held out my hand to stop her.

"Ms. Flattery, thank you for joining us. Before we get started, I want to inform you officially that we have a warrant from the World Court, which has tried you in absentia and sentenced you to death for your acts as covered by the Terrorist Laws as modified in 2022. Do you have any comment?"

The curses that came at us from under the hood would not have passed the 'Lady' test, but we got the gist.

"Before we unbag you, I want to inform you we have captured or killed your mercenary terrorist friends, and the one who survived confirmed that you have been in contact with them, in fact, passed instructions to them as to their disbursement. That makes you complicit in the original terror attacks, the aftershocks of which continue to reverberate around the world. Over fifty million dead, millions displaced, and the greatest economic crisis since the great depression. And that's just covering the highlights."

The bagged head suddenly stopped moving, slightly tilted on one side. I signaled to Sandra, who pulled the bag off with a flourish. The look the prisoner gave me might have curdled the stomachs of young children, but I was tired, it had been a very long day, and I desperately wanted some downtime to do some quality thinking.

"You will refer to me as Lady O'Brian Flattery, or as previously explained, Fionnuala, and at the first opportunity, I'm calling the President of Ireland to have you dismissed!" The icy voice had an educated edge to it, but the tonality left us in no doubt of who thought they were in charge.

"Madam Flattery, you will get no call. We are holding you under the Terrorist Laws as previously explained. You have no rights, you will have no representation, and if you don't provide us with information, I will shoot you myself." Her face turned deep red, and spittle dribbled out of the corners of her mouth.

"You will get me a phone now, or I'll have your guts for gaiters!" This time the spittle flew across the desktop, making a random pattern of little reflecting drops. Her hands bashed up and down on the desktop, the chains making such a racket that I held my hands up to stop her. Sandra just reached across and smacked her in the side of her head with her weapon. It had the desired effect, and then big, fat tears started to run down her face as the hurt from either the slap or the situation she was in finally sunk in. I picked up on the slap and grinned at Sandra.

"You're still pissed off about that drone!"

"Yes, I am. Can we stop this charade and just shoot her?"

Sandra's voice was modulated, just on the side of edgy but with an underlying tonality that suggested boredom. I gave her a hard look to see if she was playing or being serious. But the look of fear on our prisoner's face told me that something we were doing was working, so I plowed on.

"Were you in contact with the mercenary terrorists?" She looked up at me, her face set, tears falling, looking quite pathetic. Actually, it was a wonder she had been able to command her people, as she obviously had been able to until we yanked her out of her environmental plant. But her relationship with the mercenaries suggested she had input over everything that happened on the Island, and that meant the drone attacks, the nano seeding of the oil tanks, the construction of the hidden storage area, and the nuclear-capable shells in the oil tank, the construction of the drone hangar, and the tunnels.

In other words, she was in it up to her eyeballs. But what was I missing? Why was this little speck of an Island so important to the terrorists? I thought about what we knew, then I remembered the comment from someone about a million empty houses, and bits and pieces fell into place.

"On the door!" The chief entered with his ceremonious bang, and leaving the prisoner unhooded, I walked out into the rain, Sandra hard on my heels as I headed for the hangar we had commandeered.

"What's put a bug up your backside?" she asked, holding her hand over her eyes to keep the rain out. We shook ourselves off inside the wide door, catching our troops by surprise as they lay on their packs, obviously recharging.

"Stand easy. I need Colonel Kashasini."

"Ma'am, hea isa witha a teama clearing outa the wreckeda helicopters." The sergeant who offered this information had jumped up and stood to attention and snapped a salute before

the words were out of my mouth. His heavily accented English reminded me we were an International force, so I answered him in his native language.

"Stai calmo, scusa se ti ho sorpreso, torna a quello che stavi facendo." He saluted again, then sat back down on his pack, keeping a wary eye on us both. I walked over to the huge silver coffee dispenser someone had purloined from the airport lounge, found three reasonably clean mugs, started to fill them, and spoke to Sandra over my shoulder.

"Call Indigo. We'll find a quiet space. We need to talk. I'll call Fay." It took nearly three minutes, during which time I managed to inhale the fumes from the coffee, drink the first mug, and start on the second.

Yes, I was an addict. I'd go into a seven-step program as soon as I could!

Indigo and Fay joined us. We found a corner just behind the massive roller doors of the hangar, and with the blinding rain forming a silver curtain outside, albeit as a white-noise counterpoint, we squatted down as comfortably as we could.

"We have a problem." I looked at their calm faces, all eyes on me.

"I've just worked out why Whiddy Island is so important. And I think we are going to have a jurisdictional issue with the Irish Government."

"How so?" Indigo jumped up and took the four folding chairs off the young sergeant who had responded to our sudden entry.

"Grazie sergente, ben fatto." We all pulled them open and sat back down again, this time to the accompaniment of squeaks and chalk-like squeals as the bottoms ran over the rough concrete floor.

"Okay, where was I?"

"Problem. Not defined, but hinting at political bull crap." Sandra was quick. It wasn't exactly what I said, but it was perhaps closer to the truth.

"Does anyone remember a comment about a million empty homes in Ireland?" Confused looks on every face, so that was a big fat 'no,' then Sandra's face broke into a huge smile.

"Fionnuala, Lady Bitch—she mentioned it when we first interrogated her back at the environmental plant."

"Yes. Now think through what her statement really means."

"Passports, Visas, and IDs for a million refugees?"

"More likely two to three million, maybe as many as four or five, and that means a hacker set up like the one 'Helen' had in her desert lair." Where Pete and I had been shot, thanks for the reminder, and I unconsciously rubbed the wound.

"Hacking at that level, given the current status of most computer systems, would be a really time-consuming task and one that would not be easily hidden." Fay looked serious. As an ex-FBI agent, she was perhaps the most familiar with black-hat setups and processes. But Indigo managed a team of world-class hackers back in Venice, and if anyone could unravel this, he could.

"I'll call my brother." I nodded. That was the outcome I had hoped for. His brother, Stefarino, was the head monk of an Order that, before the terror attacks, had dedicated their lives to recording everything they could find about the rise of religion around the world and, as such, had developed skills that were usually only ever found in Government enclaves or darkened basements. Since the attacks, they had helped us at every twist and turn in hunting the terrorists down, often at the expense of their own work and personal security.

I looked into my mug, now empty, the bottom covered with minute coffee particles. I wished I could read tea leaves and make some sense of the disturbing but no doubt random pattern that just stared back up at me. But they were coffee grounds, not tea leaves, so I really was out of luck!

"He will call you back, commander. Have you considered the Irish Government's position in all of this?" I looked at him, seeking clarification.

"If you remember when the USA discovered that their State Department, ICE, and Social Services had been hacked, and IDs, Visas, and Passports generated for over twenty thousand refugees, they allowed the forgeries to stand." That they had, seeing no downside to allowing the young female refugees to resettle in the purpose-built housing the terrorists had created out of the technological marvels developed at their environmental plants.

Marvels that had stemmed from the original work done by one of our own long before the terrorists had become a focus. Amira Abramowitz, who was now a sworn member of Interpol and Israeli Intelligence, had been one of the first refugee children taken out of the camps by Mohammad bin Azaria, and she had turned out to be a very young genius and was placed in an Israeli home. She had literally invented the nanoscience that had been bastardized by the terrorists to cripple the world by permanently polluting all oil, gas, and coal planet-wide. Not to mention nuclear reactors.

I looked at him, aware that we had seen various governments wiggle and squirm when they had been identified as potential destinations for environmental plants and, by inference, young female refugees. Some had been happy, such as New Zealand, and some had been quite negative, like Sri Lanka. And in the middle had been most of the others, with, as I seemed to remember, Ireland, Canada, Greenland, and Chile open to further guarded conversations. It was worth mentioning that there were very strong economic reasons for countries to acquiesce to the terrorist's plans.

The master planner had set up trust funds worth billions in nineteen countries to support the refugees, money that filtered back into the local economy at a time when the world's economy was at the bottom of a pit.

We had obtained a Red Notice on the trust fund set up by the terrorists in Dublin, out of which the three-hundred-foot luxury boat that had been retrofitted with an electromagnetic rail launch system for nuclear-capable shells had been paid for.

We did not know what else it had funded before it had been closed down. Obviously, there was at least one other trust fund we had yet to locate. If what I thought was going on, maybe more than one trust account.

That was a good place to start. But before I did that, I had to consider the political ramifications of what we were currently doing. We could only operate when invited to by a sovereign government, which was one of the one hundred and ninety-four members of Interpol. Ireland had invited us in when we had found evidence of nuclear shells hidden on their soil. In fact, the first time they had invited us in was to take out a terrorist cell dug deep into the wasted peat bogs around the small village of Pollatomish.

That had ended with a twin cruise missile attack launched by the Americans, at our request, and the arrest of one of the prime terrorists we had been chasing all our Europe. It occurred to me in retrospect that we had never investigated its background, perhaps yet another blindness in my methodology. If you stop to think about it, the structure we found deep underground beneath the ruins of a centuries-old church must have taken years to build.

We knew a major portion of the construction was done at the same time as a gas line was installed, the legitimate construction acting as a cover for the illegitimate underground production facility. But it was now nothing but fused debris, and we had recovered a large number of shells and nuclear material and removed a few terrorists from the game board permanently. The Irish government had thanked us profusely, never really addressing the issue of the fake Garda, who we had also had to deal with.

Now it appeared we had, to some extent yet to be proven, a major operational base and environmental plant running freely on Whiddy Island under the control of a very senior member of the Irish parliament.

I decided to split my forces again and looked around the team.

"Okay, this is what we'll do. Sandra and I, with two of Indigo's best, will go visit the Irish Government. Fay, get all the prisoners and material on the C-17, get it back to Israel, and keep the drones looking for the missing shell; Indigo, secure the Island as planned, and find the other terrorists if you can. Questions?"

"How are we getting to Dublin?"

"We'll take one of the Irish helicopters. Contact the major, clear it with him." Sandra stood and moved away to use her mini. Fay stood and faced me.

"What do I do once the C-17 is airborne?" I gave that some thought. She was an excellent interrogator, her style was the exact opposite of Sandra's and mine, but once again, I was reminded we needed intelligence.

"Go with the prisoners. When you get to Tel Aviv, interrogate everyone from the Island, then start on all the other prisoners. I'll get Anna to join you. It's time we found out exactly what's what." She nodded and moved out into the sheeting rain, heading for the flight line. I called the major.

"I need to borrow one of your helicopters for a trip to Dublin." His face was dripping, his background a mishmash of mud and foliage. I had no idea where he was exactly, but wherever it was would be uncomfortable.

And wet.

"Ma'am, at your disposal. No sign of the terrorists here so far. The Israelis have joined us, and we are sweeping the top end of the Island. Major Reynold and his team have secured the house."

"Excellent. Stay sharp; they are somewhere, and they are deadly." I turned to Sandra.

"Let's go. The long twilight we get here will work in our favor time-wise."

"We need clothes."

"We'll get them in Dublin." And we both sloshed out to the flight line, seeking the shelter of the sole remaining flight-worthy helicopter, which stood proud against the carnage and destruction from the rocket attacks.

"Where will we get our crew from?" I pointed to the terminal, out of which three black-suited aviators were running, their flight bags slapping against their flight suits. Without ceremony, they clambered in, the two pilots fitting helmets and comms gear, the third rudely pushing us into our seats and fiddling with the door guns.

"Ma'am, apologies, but we've just been informed that a terrorist group may be adjacent to the airfield. I need access to the door gun." I shuffled over one seat, pushing Sandra. The pilot turned on the intercom.

"Where to?"

"Dublin. Casement Airport."

"Aye, commander, strap in. We've got to make a tactical departure, I'm thinking." We did, he did, and as we raced away from Cork at dot feet, weaving and bucking in what looked like zero visibility, I was reminded that skill came in all sizes and languages. The loadmaster relaxed and let his door gun drop on its hydraulic mount.

"There now, you can both sit back and relax for a while. It's pleased I am to tell you no one shot at us." I smiled, fitting my headset.

"No more than we are. Can you connect me to a landline in Dublin?" He nodded and spoke into his microphone, the copilot fiddled with an overhead panel, and the loadmaster mouthed, 'number?'. I checked my pockets, found the Boss's little black book, found the number I was looking for, and held it up to the loadmaster.

"Interpol Ireland, how may I direct your call?" The part voice lacked an Irish accent but resonated with an English one, so I put my most formal voice on and asked for what we needed.

"This is Commander Riley, Interpol Section Five, inbound Casement airport, ETA (Estimated time of arrival)"-and I paused, looking at the loadmaster-he held up five fingers, and made a circle with his other hand-"Fifty minutes. I need a car on the ground, and we will need to obtain civilian clothes suitable for a visit to the President." The line echoed my request, then another part voice spoke up.

"Commander, I'm Agent Robertson, Head of Station. I heard your request and will comply. For security purposes, may I have today's code?" I looked blankly at the loadmaster and turned to Sandra, whose eyebrows had shot up like small caterpillars running from something that wanted to eat them.

"I don't know what day it is, let alone any code. Meet us at the airport." And I made the cut-across-the-throat sign to the loadmaster, who mumbled into his microphone. I sat and thought for a moment, code? Why? The two Italian commandos sat facing us, their faces wary, reading my tense body language but not being in on the conversation. I couldn't know the reason for it. I held up one hand to calm them down, and they both sat back in their seats with an inaudible sigh. It was hard work being a bodyguard to someone like me. Sandra was just giving me the gimlet eye, letting me resolve my own issues in my own head.

We sat in stoic silence until we landed, and I was pleased to see an official vehicle surrounded by army personnel. We strolled over to the vehicle, and a leggy woman dressed in a well-cut charcoal suit with blue low-heeled boots got out, smiled at us, and held up her ID.

"Welcome, commander. I'm Agent Robertson. I apologize for the code query, I did not know you were in Ireland, and I did not know you were operational." The mild rebuke hung in the air until Sandra stepped forward, combat boots still wet enough to leave a small puddle on the tarmac. Our two Italian commandos stood relaxed at our sides, weapons casually pointed at the car and the welcoming committee, which was not lost on the army guards.

'I'm Inspector Thomas, and we would have advised you of our operation except for the fact we were being bounced all over Ireland, chasing terrorists and nuclear-capable shells." She looked a little taken aback. Sandra could do that to you, on the tall side, stunningly beautiful, and exuding an innate strength and sharp focus I was starting to depend on. She looked warm and female but had a very sharp edge.

"My apologies, inspector, commander. How can I assist you?" I decided to just take a practical path, not wanting to piss our local Interpol agent off any further. I'm sure I would have reacted the same way if armed members of my organization suddenly dropped in on me unprepared. Sandra would probably have just shot them and been done with it! I pointed to the helicopter and the crew, who were now standing beside the aircraft.

"Refuel the helicopter, provide food for the crew, and perhaps you could get them a dry set of flight suits and somewhere to rest up. I'd like to be airborne again within the next three hours." She signaled to one of the army guards, whom she briefed in a sotto voice. He saluted and raced off.

"Then we need professional clothes suitable for meeting the president, and we need that organized ASAP." She gave me a hard look from top to toe, took in my saturated, dirty, and creased fatigues, looked Sandra over the same way, nodded to herself, then turned and opened the car door.

"Get in. We'll organize the President on the way. I know a little boutique that can help you. They have full facilities." Good, we could shower and put our professional faces on before meeting with the President. I gestured to two of our guards to go with the crew, and with slightly worried faces, they moved off. Sandra just put her hand in her mini-case, no doubt foundling her pet H&K.   "Will the president know what the meeting is about?"

"Just tell his people it's Commander Riley, Interpol Section Five, and it's urgent." She looked at me with confusion on her face, and I took pity on her. "The President was aware of our operation, we entered the country with his explicit approval, and we're working with his very own *Sciathán Fianóglach*, so you shouldn't have any difficulties getting us an appointment. Just point out we're out of here and back on station in Cork in three hours or less if we can manage it. That should get his attention." She just nodded and picked up the car phone.

The streets of Dublin showed little of the carnage from the terror attacks and the ensuing civil uprising. The roadways were clear, with little to no traffic but no burnt-out vehicles or debris. In contrast, Chicago, which we had driven through just weeks ago, looked like a very bad moonscape, with trashed vehicles and smoking piles of garbage in every direction and buildings with their windows blown out. It seemed that Ireland, as a whole, has suffered much less than most other parts of the so-called civilized world from the civil unrest.

"The President will see you in an hour. He will be at his residence Áras an Uachtaráin, in Phoenix Park. His secretary asks if you have specific agenda items."

"Yes." She gave me a hard look. Sandra just smirked. Even the two commandos seemed to get the joke. I held my silence, our agent retreated to her car phone, and we stayed that way until we reached the garment district. Eerily empty, except for a dog walker, who shied away as soon as he saw us. We exited the vehicle, our commandos forming up on either side, one facing backward, and our agent's face displayed both annoyance and curiosity at the same time.

"Why do you expect to attack? Who here in Dublin would want you dead?" Sandra, her hand deep in her minicomputer case, leaned across me, forcing me to stop. She looked the agent squarely in the eyes and shook her head.

"I can't believe you don't know that there is a thirty million euro fatwa on the commander's head. Even in this charming backwater, you must get our faxed daily reports?" The agent looked shocked and pulled her head back on her shoulders, her eyes flicking to my face and then Sandra's.

"I didn't know. We have had no such communication from Lyon. But surely you don't expect to be attacked here in Dublin?"

"We did expect it in Chicago a few weeks ago and weren't disappointed." She looked horrified. We reached the door and entered, with one of our commandos remaining facing the glass window. She scurried over to a little gnome of a man dressed in a spotless striped suit with creases so sharp you could shave on them. He bowed from the waist, looking up at me from under bushy eyebrows.

"Miss Robertson wants me to outfit your booth for a meeting with the president?" His English was faultless, suggesting it was not his first language or he had attended an English boarding school. It didn't really matter.

"Yes, please, suits will be fine, a little room in the coats, plain shirts, we'll keep our boots. And we'll need bags to hold our wet clothes. Please." He stood up, and I realized just how short he was, the top of his head barely hitting me mid-chest. He had to tilt his head up to see Sandra.

"At once. Please use the facilities, and I'll have a selection for you to choose from." He pointed to a sign in Irish that I assumed said 'ladies' because of the stick figure painted over the words *'Leithreas na mban.'*

"I'll take the first watch. You clean up." Sandra squatted on the corner of a low couch, its red fluffed upholstery looking a little out of place in the wide bathroom. There were stations for applying makeup and long-hanging wardrobes, and the tiled floors were a reflection of good taste. The whole room was not overtly feminine, and I wondered about that.

A hand poked through the curtain and dropped two clothes bags inside.

"Commander, inspector, I can pass through the selections if you wish?"

"Thank you."

We were in and out in less than fifteen minutes, clothes bags secured, standing at the door while our agent settled the bill. The commando who had been on watch shook his head.

"*Finora nessun interesse, comandante.*" Excellent. No one interested in us. Time to go.

We did, the commandos took our clothes bags, and both Sandra and I flexed our shoulders in our new suit coats. They were not Armani, but they were well-cut and comfortable. The only disjointed thing about our outfits were our combat boots and our weapons on our hips.

"How do you want to play it with the president?" I looked at Sandra, then at the two commandos sitting opposite. Our agent was looking at us both, wide-eyed and uncertain of her role.

"Chi parla il miglior inglese?" They both looked at each other, and Edwardo, the one of our left, held his hand out, fist closed, and in seconds we had a game of 'rock, paper, scissors' going, and I guessed best out of three the way they went at it.

"I do, commander, my illiterate friend here would only embarrass you."

We all laughed, breaking the tension. Roberto had a sour look on his face, spoilt only by the grin behind his eyes.

"Fine. Eduardo, you will come with us as my adjutant. Roberto, stay with the vehicle. You'll be our forward trip wire. Keep your communicator on. Sandra, you do the same. First sign of trouble, yell.

"Comandante, quali sono le nostre condizioni di ingaggio?" Roberto asked, giving our local agent a strange look. Terms of engagement? Good question, great question under the circumstances. We were, as far as I was concerned, deep behind enemy lines until proven otherwise. It was hard to reconcile with the pleasant, peaceful environment we were driving through. Well-tended houses, clean streets, and everyone we saw was neat and tidy, going about their business in what could only be described as a normal manner.

"Are you armed?" I asked our agent. She shook her head.

"No, commander, Interpol agents do not carry weapons, as you would be aware."

"Is your driver armed?"

"Yes, ma'am, he is in the army."

"Good. Please tell him that any orders he receives from Roberto here are to be followed with utmost dispatch. I want you to wait in the car with him." She looked at me with curiosity shaping her face as if she did not believe what she was hearing. She turned to face her driver.

"Sam, tógfaidh tú d'orduithe ón saighdiúir seo anseo inár n-éagmais."

"Sea, ma'am." She turned back and looked at me.

"Do you honestly expect to be attacked while we are with the president of Ireland?" Her voice was incredulous, the denial shaping her body language. I felt for her because, right now, she was way out of her depth.

"We were shot out of the sky over the Atlantic, attacked leaving the ground in Tel Aviv, accosted by hoodlums in Chicago, and just yesterday, we survived a missile attack in broad daylight in Cork. So yes, the possibilitiy of the tangos knowing we are here, is quite high." Sandra delivered her rundown in a mild voice, her tonality almost amused, but the casualness belied her body language, which was anything but relaxed. She was wired like a high-tensile spring.

We arrived at the gate to the Áras an Uachtaráin, which was little more than a quaint hut with two Garda in full ceremonial uniforms, who saluted as we drove through. The long, narrow road curved around the magnificent gardens, and we arrived at the front entrance, four tall pillars supporting a roofed portico and a massive wooden front door that would make any four-hundred-year-old building in Washington proud. If there were any. The stark white of the brickwork was offset on both sides by climbing vines with red-tipped flowers.

A contingent of Garda carrying Heckler and Kotch MP7s slung across their chests were lined up as a welcoming committee, with a high-ranking officer resplendent in gold-colored lanyards over both shoulders of his blue jacket standing in the middle. He was only armed with a holstered weapon, and his service cap had the telltale gold braid on the peak of a senior officer.

We stopped, and our driver leaped out and opened the door for us. The Garda came to attention. The officer saluted, then moved forward, extending his hand to me.

"General, welcome to Áras an Uachtaráin. The President is waiting to see you." I looked him straight in the eye and saw what I wanted to see, zero hostility, a genuine welcome, so I braced myself like the officer I was supposed to be and looked at Sandra, then at Eduardo.

"Inspector Thomas, my second in command, and Staff Sergeant Ricci, my adjutant."

"Come this way." He turned on his heel and led us through the massive wooden doors into the most magnificent entrance hallway I had ever been in. The roof was lined with square frescos, dark blue iconic objects in white frames, and on the walls massive paintings, and for the first time, I regretted my lack of knowledge of local history. I knew the building went back to the 1750s, but the artifacts and historical icons that laced the corridors running off to the left and the right created an atmosphere not unlike that of an ancient museum. A huge golden harp featured high up on the front wall, with busts of no doubt very important historical figures positioned on either side of the walkway.

"The president will meet you in the State Drawing Room." Which turned out to be an understatement because the rich brocade, gold-painted vintage chairs, and antique wooden furniture reeked of the old world and era totally lost on me, having been brought up by a single mother who worked in a truck stop on the fringes of Chicago. If I had any culture, and I was never sure I actually did, it came from my study of languages. That I got. So I put myself into learning mode and waited patiently for the President to arrive. The Garda officer, who had stopped at the doorway, moved to the 'attention' position, and the President, accompanied by two well-dressed women, entered.

"General, please sit down. These are my invaluable advisors. How can we help you?" No introduction, no names, no apparent formality, but my hackles were up, Sandra was tense, and even Eduardo had stiffened up. The two women sitting opposite us on what might have been three-or-four-hundred-year-old chairs had big smiles, no notebooks or electronic devices I could see, and looked happy and relaxed like a fox licking its chops watching young lambs frolic in the grass. At our back, I was only too aware of the Garda officer filling the doorway.

I would put money on them being grown refugee children from the first or second tranches. Their apparent ages fit that. In fact, they reminded me of Amira and Fay. Amira had been one of the very first refugee children to be relocated, and Fay had been a few months behind her. They were now in their mid-to-late twenties. How to play this? I decided on an old Poker strategy.

Let the other guy make the first move, so I gave him a clear shot.

"Mr. President, thank you for seeing us on such short notice. You are aware of our operation on Whiddy Island?"

"I am. And I understand you have reclaimed several nuclear shells and taken some prisoners into custody?" I held the most neutral look on my face I could manage and never took my eyes off the two women.

"We have, thankfully, without any casualties."

"Excellent. You will turn the prisoners over to the local Garda, of course?" *Here it comes*, I thought to myself, rubber or the road.

"As is our policy, all terrorists we capture are taken to a neutral site and interrogated before the world court decides their fate. And in this case, we are working with your own *Sciathán Fianóglach,* so if there is to be any release, it would be to them." He studied me with an intensity I had only seen in the eyes of someone like the Boss, and I understood I had underestimated him. Badly. I shifted gears.

"Sir, we have also discovered some other activities that suggest that the terrorists have been working in that area for years, and I'm wondering how that could be without your government becoming aware of it, even if it were only the local authorities." He gave me a shrewd look, shooting the cuffs of his crystal white dress shirt. Little blue and gold cufflinks winked in the light like fireflies. The rich French-style brocade surrounding us was starting to close me in, and I clenched my buttocks to relieve some tightness I was starting to feel from the antique straight-backed chair I was sitting on. Pretty, yes. Comfortable, no.

"Our only interest in Whiddy Island, apart from it being an excellent place to fish, was that it held our strategic reserves of oil, which after the terror attacks, became moot. It wasn't until your office contacted mine for permission to retain the nuclear shells that we became interested in it again."

"I see. Are you aware of any infrastructure development on the Island, say, in the last three to five years?" He looked to one of his so-called advisors, who shook her head.

"It appears not. Why do you ask?" I looked at him, really looked at him. I knew he was smart, and I suspected he was currently sitting between two genius-level 'advisors' who were either working in concert with the Irish government or masterfully influencing it towards their own ends, in plain sight. And I didn't sense he was lying. I decided to use another Poker tactic. I threw my metaphorical cards into the middle, signifying I was finished with this round.

"Mr. President, thank you for your time. We'll get back to our base." We all stood, everyone shook hands, and I took the opportunity to look deeply into the eyes of the two 'advisors', still not introduced, felt the intensity from both of them, then turned on my heel and walked out. The Garda officer led us out, our driver held the door open, the Garda came to attention, and that was that. Before anyone could speak, I placed my hand on Sandra's leg, looked at Eduardo, and addressed our agent, who was looking a cross between curious and miffed.

"Can we retain these suits?" Surprise exploded over her face. It was obviously not the first question that came to her mind.

"Yes, I paid for them out of office funds."

"Thank you, excellent work all around." Now she looked a little anxious, then broached the question I had been waiting for.

"How did you go with the President?" I squeezed Sandra's thigh to keep her quiet.

"It went well. Thank you for organizing the meeting. Can you have our helicopter ready to lift as soon as we arrive at the airport?"

"Yes, commander." And she busied herself with the car phone, speaking very fast in Irish. Odd. The number of people who could still speak the old language could be counted on one hand. With the influx of Europeans migrating away from the chaos of conflict, fuel shortages, and constant economic pain, you tended to hear English, Italian, Greek, and even French more often than not.

And she was English, so she would have had to study it for quite a while to become so fluent.

I decided to let it go. There was something afoot here in Ireland, it was definitely terrorist-inspired, possibly at the highest levels of government, but for now, we'd let them think we knew next to nothing, which was the absolute truth until we were more able to manage the tactical situation.

Whatever it was or turned out to be.

I felt like a cork floating on a very rough sea, bobbing up and down, occasionally getting swamped and sucked under by a rogue wave, being taken somewhere I did not know but ever so gently.

I remembered the story my mother had told me about the frog and the pot of water, and I mentally made a note to get off whatever bus we were on before we unknowingly slowly boiled to death.

TURNAROUND

The Israeli C-17 spiraled down from ten thousand feet at a descent rate of six thousand feet a minute, so the final flare was both brutal and majestic, seeing as how big the C-17 was. In full reverse, it backed up to the turnoff from the main runway and stopped on a dime behind the burnt-out wrecks of the Chinook and the CH-53. As the massive rear cargo door dropped down on long, lean hydraulic rams, the loadmaster ran out, nearly colliding with Fay.

The noise from the idling Pratt and Whitney turbofans made normal conversation impossible. Leaning into the loadmaster's ear, Fay shouted her instructions, and immediately a small electric tractor towed the cargo to the edge of the door while a chain gang of terrorists, all manacled hand and foot and with their heads bagged, shuffled out of the hangar and into the passenger door in the side of the massive aircraft.

They were assisted by members of the Italian RRT, who were none too gentle. They had suffered major casualties at the hands of the terrorists, not the least of which was the attack on the Vatican when the majority of the Church's leaders had been killed. The terrorists we chained to their webbing seats, leaving two meters between them, the net effect being a scattered line of hooded and orange overalls-covered bodies distributed across both sides of the cargo hold, with massive pallets of equipment bolted to the floor running between them.

The cargo door came up, the engines accelerated, and the C-17 taxied out to the runway. Fay accepted a seat behind the pilots, fitted the padded headphones that were handed to her, fastened the five-point harness, and when she looked up, she saw the very end of the runway filling the windscreen.

"Hold tight!" And the massive Pratt and Whitney's roared into life at full military power, screaming like banshees, and with what felt like a kick in the backside, accelerated down the narrow strip, and Fay realized they were taking off from the overrun alongside the runway. Within a minute, the aircraft's nose shot skyward, the clouds obliterating all outside view, and she felt her body lean to the left as the plane banked. The pilots retracted the gear, flaps, trimmed out the excess force in the controls, then just seemed to slump into a relaxed pose she imagined was innate in most aircrew.

"Sorry for the gee-force, just keeping us away from any tangos."

"No problem. I'll just catch a few zzzz's if that's okay." The pilot, who looked like a skinny teenager, turned and gave her a huge smile.

"Be our guest, next stop Ramstein." Fay scrunched up her face, working through what the pilot had just said. Fuel. She smiled, nodded, and closed her eyes. It would be nice to wake up in Germany!

CHAPTER THIRTEEN

I had the Irish helicopter land in a grassed paddock in sight of the modern-looking house the women terrorists had been using on Whiddy Island. Nothing remarkable about it, but then the tunnel that led all the way back to the oil tanks was well underground. The night sky was just starting to poke through the thin clouds replacing the Atlantic storm that had drenched us for the past two days, and with the lack of artificial lights, the stars flickered and flashed with a strong visual vibe. I couldn't help but look up and nearly skinned my shins on a low stone fence.

"I wonder what the fence is designed to keep in?" I asked, stepping over it.

"Obviously not you." Sandra's sarcasm was pointed. I had stopped her from commenting on our meeting with the President and his 'advisors' all the way from Dublin. I knew what she was going to say, and I wanted the whole team to hear it for themselves. On the wide verandah, fringed by tall blue potted trees of some sort, the major, colonel, Indigo, and Bob stood, relaxed, a most unexpected situation.

"We know where the terrorists are, and we've got them bottled up." I looked at Bob, his floppy hat sagging still, and remembered he had done a masterful job in Germany, so if he said all was good, then all was good.

"Where are they?"

"We've got them trapped inside the Napoleon Fort, they have heavy weapons, but we've been sitting on them waiting for you to arrive."

"I'm only going to ask one question." I studied their faces in the gloom and saw Indigo break out into a grin just as one of his RRTs exited the wide doorway with a tray full of mugs.

The Irish major pulled a ten Euro note out of his pocket and handed it to the Israeli colonel.

"Thank you, commander, you've made me a rich woman!" The laughter broke the tension. We were getting into the habit of doing that, a good sign of an integrated unit. I just inhaled the smell, buried my face in the mug, then looked up into Indigo's eyes.

"This is almost as good as we get back home." He smiled and gave me a mock salute. "Okay, let's all sit down for a minute. I want to brief you on the meeting with the President." I took a long slow sip and let my mind settle. This might be the most important briefing of the entire operation. Time will tell. "Sandra, your impressions, please." She turned to look at me, and the bottled-up frustration that had been dogging her face cleared in a heartbeat.

"The commander, Edwardo, and I met with the President in his palace. He was accompanied by two female 'advisors'. They were not introduced to us. He denied any knowledge of infrastructure work here on Whiddy Island and appeared to have very little interest in it altogether. He asked we release our prisoners to the Garda. We left and flew back here." The only sound we could hear was that of some sheep or goats, which had bells around their necks. If I could have captured the eyes of everyone at the same time, I would have a series of identical looks of disbelief. I smiled inwardly, my team knew me, and they knew Sandra, so they waited patiently for the punch line. I looked at Sandra.

"You or me?" She grinned, stood, and rolled her shoulders.

"Well, the commander here did tell the Present that we, as a matter of policy, ship all prisoners off to a neutral site for interrogation, and if we ever did decide to give them to someone, it would be to you, major, and not the Garda." He laughed, scratched his ear, and shook his head.

"Aye, I'd be thinking that Hell might have frozen over before that happened, and besides, after all the trouble they've put us to, I'd be thinking I'd be inclined to just shoot the bastards and be done with it." We all laughed again, and I could see Bob's mind working furiously behind his eyes, which sparkled in the porch light now that his floppy hat was secured in his epaulets.

"Jessica, if the President claims he knew nothing about the development here, the locals have kept it a secret for years."

"Yes, we did wonder about that, but he asked the question of one of his 'advisors', and they confirmed the President's stance."

"Huh."

"Yes, huh! And pigs fly, and all the world believes in fairytales."

"What the commander is saying so eloquently is that the President is either stupid or being led by the nose-or his balls-by his 'advisors', who had a look and feel about them of fully operational refugee terrorists."

"We know what they look and smell like now, and of course, it's all in the eyes."

"What you are hinting at is a state-level support for the terrorists here in Ireland," Indigo emphasized his statement with perfect English, something that was not lost on any of us.

"But we've seen this before. Remember our experience in Germany when we were trying to trace the gold. The terrorists had penetrated the Finance Ministry, yet their influence seemed a little thin after the fact." Bob tilted his head, letting what he had just said sink in.

"How so?" This was from our Israeli colonel, who, in the dim light, looked like a thick tree trunk, her massive shoulders continuing all the way down to her hips. She was a stunning-looking woman but with a very athletic and solid build.

"We got the information we needed. Their influence seemed to diminish the further away we got from the ministry." I nodded. That was my take as well. It seemed our women terrorists limited their exposure to very selected people in government circles and were usually very targeted in terms of function. But then we now knew that they had penetrated our electronic systems for decades, and their hackers had had free access to every database worldwide and were able to change or simply delete data at will.

We had captured a whole team of hackers responsible for creating forged identities, visas, and passports for thousands of refugee children when we had taken down Natasha Trotsky, or 'Helen' as she had been known. A veteran of the East German Stasi, she had worked for Mohammad bin Azaria for over thirty-five years and had built up a network of embedded sleepers all over the world.

I briefly wondered how her work had impacted Ireland.

"We need to deal with what we have on our plate right now. I think I have a way of finding out what might be happening at the government level. Major, how many terrorists are at the old gun site?"

"We believe six. We saw three go in and recovered two vehicles. They are well armed, but according to our guards, there's no other way in or out of the building, and we believe unless they have cameras in the grass, they have no way of knowing what we are doing outside, left or right, or behind their backs."

"What's the top cover?"

"Hard-crusted peat, small rocks, some grass, it doesn't look like anyone has done anything but mow the grass occasionally. The outer ring is very old brickwork, flooded, with a few stumpy trees. The inner ring is angled upwards, maybe half a meter high, and again is made of very old bricks of some sort. Three buildings are in the middle, two are completely overgrown, and one is in use by the terrorists. It's been refurbished in the last few years, but it has grass and scrubs growing on the roof. We suspect it's made of corrugated iron."

"Tunnels?"

"Nothing showed up on the GPR (Ground Penetrating Radar)."

"Any outlet or inlet seaside?"

"The building is approximately one hundred meters from Killala Bay. We could see no pipes in or out." I shook my head. I didn't want to blow up a historical artifact, certainly not one over two hundred and twenty-five years old.

"How do we get them out?"

"Tear gas and flash bangs, we can only make a frontal assault unless you want to destroy the building.

"Not if we can help it. Have you got overwatch?"

"Nothing high enough, but we have a team on top of the roof of the middle building. They can see most of the target, but only from the rear.

"Our long guns are three hundred meters away, covering the front of the building. We will close them in, fire the grenades, then broach from the sides." I gave the attack plan a moment's thought and looked at Indigo, who was concentrating on the major.

"Colonel, comments?" The Sgan Aluf looked at me. I nodded at Indigo, and she relaxed.

"Good plan. Maybe we hit them with enough gas and flash bangs. They come out under their own steam?" He looked at me with a twinkle in his eyes, obviously enjoying the thought of flushing the terrorists out of the building. So did I. Less chance of us taking casualties.

"Colonel?" I asked the Israeli. She just nodded, looked at the major, then at Indigo, then back at me.

"Our Barrett's are fitted with fifty mil canister launchers. We can use them out to one hundred meters with an accuracy of half a meter. We can put ten rounds inside in less than thirty seconds." Everyone nodded. Now the plan was coming together.

"How do you get that close without getting shot?" Bob had stayed very much in the background, letting the younger troops have their say. Every head turned to look at him. His thoughtfulness and calm were attributes I valued.

"We lay down covering fire, our shooters come in from the sides until they have a good angle on the building, we can also lay down smoke."

"Let's assume they have infrared and thermal imaging gear, night vision, all the bells and whistles. If this shed has been refurbished, as you say, then taking it out simply means we rebuild it after we're done. The overall site stays intact. All good?"

"In that case, you want to collapse the building?"

"Not unless we absolutely have to."

"When do you want to move on it?" I looked at my watch and looked up at the cloudless sky, a rare sight since we had first landed on the Island.

"How about now?" Every head nodded, eager to get at it. We had come to eradicate terrorists, retain nuclear-capable shells, and anything else that took our interest. The idea of a firefight warmed everyone's heart. Then Sandra broke her silence, nudging me in the ribs as she did so.

"Have we collected all the data from the plant?" The major looked at her with a quizzical grin.

"Aye, that we have, Inspector. It all went to your people in Cork on the last flight." She nodded, looked at me.

"Then I suggest we maintain the blockage around the building and postpone any attack until we have sifted through the data." I tilted my head to one side. She was correct, and again, I had missed a critical step with my mission blindness. I was going to have to lift my game and quickly.

"Agreed. My fault. I was too keen to dig the terrorists out of their bunker. Fay and I will fly back to Cork, keep the lid on the building, and stay in contact." We left the real soldiers to their own devices and stepped over the low fence, scattering a few sheep in the process, their bells ringing in anger. I wound my arm over my head, signaling the pilots to start up. We climbed in, strapped in, and were surprised by our two guards who jumped in, pushed past us, then took their seats. I had forgotten all about them. Luckily Indigo hadn't. I shook my head. I really needed to get my head in the game.

"Who have we got that can help analyze the data?" The engines reached their point of maximum thrust, and the noise made talking other than by intercom impossible, so we fitted our headsets just in time to hear the pilot finish his briefing.

"………estimate Cork in fifty minutes." I looked at Sandra.

"If I know Fay, she will have loaded all that material on the C-17 and taken it to Israel." I looked at her, gave her the hardest stare I could manage, then just let it go.

Of course, she would have. A highly trained ex-FBI agent would take the data to the nerds as a matter of course. It was too noisy to use my mini. I'd just have to wait until we were on the ground.

PEOPLE POWER

Dundalk was, by most measures, a small town in Ireland, noted for really only two things, both of which had been made mute by the terrorist attacks. The Spirit Store was recognized as one of Ireland's top music venues, and the horse and greyhound track was the only all-weather facility in Ireland. For three hundred years, it had been the destination for Europeans and travelers from across the world, as the midpoint between Belfast and Dublin, but now it was mostly still. The civil unrest that had swept across Ireland had been a short-lived affair, with the locals banding together and basically running the thugs and marauders off. Likewise, the community had banded together to clear the roads and remove the burnt-out hulks of cars, vehicles, and refuse.

Batteries were a high priority on the scavenging list, and it was not unusual to find a vehicle in good condition, only lacking a battery to be able to run. And, of course, fuel, of which there was little to none.

Situated on the Castletown River and with a population of only thirty-odd thousand, which had been slowly diminishing for the past decades, its energy had always come from its young people. And Moriah had a team of such young people at her beck, both providing for the building she was managing and keeping a balance between those currently housed and the outside world.

Her recently added burden of the newcomers, the three sisters from Scotland, Else, Lily, and Lilian, and the lanky Katrina, who looked like a supermodel, had not posed too many issues so far. They were all out most of the day or secreted in the big room Moriah had provided for them at night and provided physical help when needed. Thanks to the money she had earned minding the green box, she was able to buy good quality food for them and was encouraged when Lilian, a very tall woman who looked as tough as nails with her close-cropped black hair and antagonistic tee shirts, had added to the pot with a large stack or Euros.

She had also offered hope in the form of a question.

"Moriah, we notice that the building next to yours is mostly empty. Could you manage it if it were repaired and fitted out?" Moriah was initially taken aback by this question. The next-door building was as tall as hers but broader in the base and had more apartments, most of which had been gutted, ransacked, or at the least trashed during the civil uprising.

"Aye, that would be the least of it, I'm thinking, but it will take a pretty penny to put it to rights, and that's for sure." Lilian nodded. This was the answer she had expected. She smiled as she handed Moriah a large carry-on travel case.

"In here, you will find enough Euros to fix it up, fit it out, and I'd be surprised if you didn't have a little left over for other things. Let's assume you can get it back up. What else will you need?" Moriah pointed to the single bulb lighting up her small apartment. It was the two-hour period of the day when electricity ran through the building freely.

"Power. We have a good balance here now with all the batteries we have accumulated and our roof panels. But next door will need a whole new setup, and I'd be thinking it almost impossible to find more batteries now, and we haven't any panels." Lilian nodded again. She had also anticipated this and was prepared.

"Can your truck-the one that brought our bags back from the oval-get to Waterford? It's around two hundred and twenty kilometers."

"We'd need to be able to charge her at Waterford. Would that be possible? Lilian smiled. Things were falling into place nicely.

"Yes, we can do that, and we'll give you a device that will extend your battery life in your vehicle by eighty percent as well. When could you leave?" Moriah looked startled, never expecting to be asked to do such a thing. She smiled to lessen the sudden tension, a little flustered.

"I'd be thinking I'd be sending some of the little's. I can't leave my building here for such a time." She was flustered again and very unsure of how to manage this magnificent-looking woman who the professor had made clear was a priority.

"That's okay. You have little's with driver's licenses?" She smiled as she spoke, the term 'little's' not one she had heard before in any language.

"Aye, at least three the last time I checked, but our eldest is my sister Sharon, you met when we picked you up. How many of the little's do you want to go with you?" Lilian gave Moriah a concentrated look, mentally working out the logistics. She needed at least four people. She'd take Katrina, as her view was critical; Lilian was the biggest of the sisters, so she needed one more.

"Sharon, you say, that's great. Can you lend us one more about the same size?" Moriah looked puzzled, but as the hostess in her took over, her innate manners came to the fore, so she just smiled and nodded.

"Jason is the biggest of our boys, a bit rough around the edges. His Mah and Dah were killed during the riots, so he's still carrying a bit of a chip. But he'll do you well, and a crack shot he is as well, should you need it."

"Can we pack some food and water so we only have to stop once?" Moriah nodded, wiping her hands nervously on her apron.

"Aye, you can do that. We'll pack a basket for you. Are you serious about starting off now, then?" Lilian nodded. The sooner, the better, she thought, this was just one stop on a long and lengthy journey, and she needed to be in France with her team within the month if she could manage it.

It took another half an hour, but finally, the quartet was on its way via a slight detour Katrina asked for just as they started off.

"Sharon, if it's not too much trouble, could you take us via the power station, please?"

Sharon looked up into her rear vision mirror, straight into Katrin's magic, deep blue eyes, sitting in the back seat of the cab. Truth be told, Sharon was both a little awed by Katrina's long blond hair, as well as envious of her well-rounded feminine form. She caught Jason looking at her out of the corner of his eye, a smirk firmly fixed on his unshaven face, nonchalantly pretending he was looking out the window. He had an unrequited 'thing' for Sharon, and while he could only admire and look at the new woman in awe, as he had never seen beauty such as hers ever in his life before, she was a *Gaill,* while Sharon was as Irish as the rich, clear air that flooded the cabin through the window.

"Aye, that we can do. It's not far off our track. Is it anything, in particular, you'd be wanting to see then? It's been shuttered these past months since the gas was killed by the terrorists." Katrina considered her options. The edge in Sharon's voice, when she described the power plant, was sharp enough to cut metal. She chose the truth, having learned the hard way that the bitterness in people's minds created by the terror attacks and their aftermath would perhaps never go away, but they could see and feel more positive about good, practical solutions that gave everyone hope.

"We might be able to get it up and started again. It will depend on our Scottish friend here," she said, poking Lilian in the side. Lilian, unsure of what to say, kept her mouth shut. Katrina took the hint and continued.

"We hope we have sustainable solutions you can start to use almost immediately. That's what this trip is all about."

"You have some sort of power generator on the scale of the power plant?" Sharon asked incredulously. Katrina laughed, making a rich, deep sound from her belly.

"Not quite as grand, but we think it might help." They traveled the next ten kilometers in silence, finally arriving at the tall barbwire fence surrounding the substation. Huge transformers could be seen, row after row, with massive towers of high-tension wires leading in from the dark of the night and smaller, lower current-carrying cables running out on the more traditional power lines most people were used to seeing. There appeared to be no visible damage to the plant or equipment. The towers in and out stood proud and true, the wires dipping towards the ground in massive 'u' shapes. There was an almost eerie feeling surrounding it, and a shiver ran up and down Sharon's back.

"Thank you, we can go now. Next stop, Waterford."

CHAPTER FOURTEEN

It was amazing what four hours of sleep followed by a hot shower, masses of coffee, and a hot meal could do for your system. As I sat in a metal chair in one corner of the hangar, with Sandra hovering over me like a wet blanket, I checked to see if we were within hearing distance of anyone, then dialed Fay, who by now would be halfway to Israel.

"Hope I didn't wake you." The red background lighting suggested the aircraft was in night flying mode, and we could see Fay was sitting at the navigator's console with two laptops open, the backs of which were blurred.

"No, hi Sandra, you caught me at a good time, commander. I would have called you sometime in the next half an hour anyway."

"Let me guess-you're looking into the data we took from the plant."

"Yes, and the data we collected at the oil tank and drone hangar. All linked, they had excellent communications, obviously the same sort of digital phone system we found at Point Roberts." That took me back. One of the great surprises we had at that point was finding a whole civilian community at the tip of Canada with working cell phones at a time when the entire telecommunications network worldwide had been hacked and crashed.

The system had been provided by the terrorists at the environmental plant as a goodwill gesture, as had been the provision of unlimited free electrical power. At the time, our investigation was very young, and Fay had been leading her FBI team based on Interpol finding out about secret trust accounts, with billions of dollars secreted away.

How we got that information was another story in itself.

"We believe that there are multiple mercenary terrorist cells around here somewhere. Do you have any information on that?"

"Yes and no. I've got the location of the trust account that is paying them. It's a firm not far from the airport. It seems that there are other trust accounts in play, but we haven't yet found their location, just references to them."

"We?" She looked a little sheepish and wiped her hair away from her face.

"I asked Ito to help me sift through all the data seeing I took his seat." Her smile at the mention of the little Israeli navigator's name suggested the possibility of more than just a professional relationship, but in this bloody asymmetric conflict, normal human comforts were few and far between.

"Good choice. Any idea where the terrorist might be holed up?" She reached forward and flicked one screen, and data started to flow across it like demented worms made of letters. She had set her mini down on something, the view we were now getting was the side of her face and the screens.

"It seems that they trained at the drone hangar and oil tank, became proficient in the use of the nano bugs, and probably practiced on the other oil tanks there. Then a large group bugged out on masse about two weeks before the first attacks in Rome and Israel. The last group left only a week ago, according to a briefing note, headed for England and France." That gave me pause for thought. We had been relying on finding the mercenary terrorists through the movement of their money, which had enabled us, with the help of various other government military forces around the world, to account for a whole lot of them in the first weeks after the initial attack.

In point of fact, until we had been shot at by the team we had killed or taken prisoner outside the Cork airport, with the demise of both Malik Badawi and Amir Abbas, who had taken out a chunk of the Gaza strip as well as a few thousand of his followers and himself in a nuclear explosion, we thought we had accounted for all the mercenaries.

Not by half, it seemed.

"What else have you found?"

"Your Lady Muck Muck is in it up to her beautiful eyeballs, and it goes much further than just her. She is seriously well-connected to the government. There are hints that the women have sleepers or even active agents well embedded in the government and have had for a long time. At first glance, it looks like a Northern Island thing." That was confusing, as our meeting had been with the President of Ireland in Dublin. And he had at least two refugee women on his staff as 'advisors'.

Or so we thought.

"Fay, any info on the drones?" Sandra leaned across me and pushed her face toward the small camera. I not so gently moved her back and turned the screen until we could both see it.

"Specifically, what do you want to know?"

"Did the bastard that shot us down in the Atlantic come from here?"

"Wait, one, I'll open that file." Again her screens looked like rabid lines of code trying to devour each other. One screen froze, revealing a map with targeting lines on it. She zoomed in on one part, using her fingers on the screen. Nodded her head, swiped the image away, and brought up another.

"It seems that they had a holding pattern worked out, covering either a northern or southern great circle route between the East coast and Europe, a non-specific destination but crossing S244 off the coast of Africa, or N343 off the coast of Ireland. Those waypoints are the published routes for all jet traffic-at least they were before the terrorist attacks."

"Are the holding patterns near where we flew?"

"The southern one is exactly on your route, but there's no flight plan or data to prove they targeted you."

"But they had the positioning and the route plotted in?"

"Yes."

"Did they fly a drone the day we were hit?" Fay scrolled through more pages and finally found one marked "Flight Log-D22". She used her fingers to move up and down the page, then swiped it off in favor of another. She expanded the data box so it filled almost a third of the screen.

"Launched drones D22 and D23 nine hours before you took off, they both flew to holding positions, orbited for nearly eleven hours, then the message 'contact' was received from D22, eight minutes later 'fox-2', then fifty-five minutes after that the signal was lost. D23 returned to base some hours later and was one of the two we took into custody." Sandra suddenly sat back in her squeaky chair, the legs making that horrible chalkboard sound, sending shivers up my spine.

"The bastards."

"Who are now on their way to Israel, where they will never see the light of day again." That stopped her in her tracks, and her furious look turned soft. She crossed her arms over her chest, sat back, and released a very pent-up breath.

"Okay, you win, but I'd really like to have punched them out for it." I reached over and pattered her shoulder.

"Same wavelength, different outcome. Let it go. We have bigger fish to fry." She nodded and signaled to one of the guards that lingered in our eye line but out of hearing distance. He broke into a huge smile, sent her a mock salute, and ran off toward the massive coffee dispenser. It was a move I could wholeheartedly agree with. But I started to think about their command and control setup. Who had given the order to shoot us down? Was it a local request or from some other player we hadn't uncovered yet?

"There's something that's bugging me in all this. Who put the fatwa on my head, and who is giving the orders now?" Sandra turned to look at me, her hard stare a reminder she was still pissed at being shot down by a drone. "And I'm really interested in where Ireland fits into it all. I think you need to work on that."

"Work on what?" I tilted my head, looked directly at her, and gave her my warmest smile.

"Ireland. I need you to do a deep dive on the politics, relationships, power bases, who's who in the zoo, where does Lady O'Brian Flattery fit in, and our erstwhile President and his two advisors." I turned back to the small screen.

"Thanks, Fay, good job. Let us know if you find anything we can use here." And I dumped the call, left the screen open, and looked at Sandra. Smiled again.

She took the hint, opened her own mini, and turned her back to me, the screech of her chair on the concrete making its own angry statement. I dialed the Boss. His face came into focus with his background streaming behind him, so he was in a vehicle of some sort. No gentlemanly pretense today, just a camouflage flight suit and a beaten-up leather jacket. His aviator sunglasses hid his eyes, and his hair was hidden under a dark blue baseball cap with a faded logo of the 150th. fighter wing. He nodded to the camera, said nothing, and that put me on my guard.

"Call me back soonest." And I shut the lid, dropped my head, then opened the mini when it buzzed at me. A message was sliding across the bottom of the screen. It was cryptic but explained why the Boss had blown me off.

"Sandra, when you've finished daydreaming, we need to have a chat." She looked at me over her shoulders, her eyes half closed, a frown dominating her face. She flicked her long hair back with a snap of her head.

"Make your mind up. I'm either the bloody researcher or your slave, which is it?" I just laughed, reached forward, and pattered her on the shoulder again.

"Let it go, girl, let it go. Before we finish this, no doubt someone else will shoot something at us. Who knows, we might even get killed!"

CHAPTER FIFTEEN

The car pulled up abruptly. The Boss climbed out, tugged his cap down further on his head because of the wind, tucked his head down almost onto his chest because of the sheeting rain and sleet, and shuffled as fast as he could into the guarded entrance. The soldiers in full combat gear moved aside for him, some saluting, others just watching with amazement on their young faces, the general's legend having preceded him from the airport.

He stopped in the small foyer, shook his head to get rid of as much water as he could, considered taking off his soaked leather jacket, then thought better of it. No need to advertise he was armed. He was led into a small anteroom, furnished sparsely, as was the style for the retired head of Israeli's Sin Bet (*Shabak*). He rose as the general entered, smiled, and moved in to hug him. The genuine warmth of the gesture was not lost on Colonel Shami Borowitz, who also stood, or on the audience watching on the massive video screen.

"*Shalom*, Aire, good to see you still in one piece!" The Israeli spymaster laughed, slapping the Boss on his arms.

"*Shalom* General, or can I still call you PJ?" The twinkle in his eye betrayed the tone of his voice, so the Boss just waved him away.

"Hi, Shami, and I see you've got the geek team here as well."

"Yes, we thought it would save you some time and perhaps make the commander's life a little easier." He looked up at the screen, where each participant sat framed by a blue box, their name listed under, and their location. The Boss immediately picked up that the FBI was also represented, so he waved at the screen, then gave the lower left square a mock salute.

"Hi Anna, great to see you again. And I see you've got your tame geek with you." She laughed and turned her head to look at Malcolm Tannery from the NSA, who, by a trick of electronics, appeared to be sitting beside the FBI SSSA but was, in fact, deep inside Frontier mountain fifteen hundred miles away, surfboard at the ready.

"Stefarino, Luigi, *ciao*, good to see you both." The Boss sat down next to Arie, and was immediately given a massive mug of coffee, and immediately inhaled. Arie looked around the room, then up at the big screen.

"PJ, I called this meeting firstly to provide a secure venue for the conversation and secondly to enable you to see first-hand what we have collected, analyzed, and get your opinion on where we go from here. If you can wait just one moment, please?" He nodded to Shami, who fiddled with his desk, then another image swam into focus, initially looking like a two-headed monster, but finally resolved to show Fay and Ito sitting side by side under the red lighting of the navigation station of the C-17.

"*Shalom*. Fay, thank you for joining us. We got your data, thank you."

"*Shalom*, sir, how can we help you further?" Fay noticed that the head monk had been included in the call, which in her mind, elevated the importance of the conversation to the highest level of geekdom.

"When we add the data you have collected from Whiddy Island to that we collected from Point Roberts, Helena, the terrorists we have incarcerated, and the information Mohammad bin Azaria and his accountant provided, the picture that emerges is a little more complex than we had originally thought." Arie paused, waiting for any comments, this was a group of some of the smartest technical and analytical people on the planet, and their minds all worked much faster than his at this point in his life. He saw nothing but anticipation on the faces before him, so he continued. Out of the corner of his eye, he saw Amira Abramowitz, the genius whose early work on nanotechnology had been bastardized by the terrorists to kill the planet, enter the room. She found a seat at the back, doing her best to remain invisible.

"In summary, then, we appear to have three distinct layers of organization. The first level was Mohammad bin Azaria and 'Helen'-Natasha Trotsky-ably supported by the mercenary terrorists commanded by 'Shetani'. Without a doubt, these were the plotters, planners, strategists, and implementors of the grand plan. The trio of refugee women we know as the pilot, scientist, and mechanic feature here, as do the CEOs and COOs of the plant in Point Roberts and New Zealand, and eventually the management of Innomatchi, the Japanese company that built all the nano manufacturing equipment." Still, no interruptions, except to see the huge screen suddenly lit up with smiles.

"Hi Amira, how are you?" coursed from the screen, and the Boss acknowledged her by moving to her and engulfing her in a bear hug. The seats were rapidly rearranged, and everyone quieted down when the Boss sat her down next to Arie.

"Sorry, Arie, it's just good to see our girl here happy and well."

"Yes, it is, and since I have forbidden her to work longer 26 hours a day, she has really perked up!" Everyone laughed, then a calm descended on the room and on the screen as Arie picked up where he left off.

"The second level was undoubtedly Siobhan O'Cleary, the Irish nuclear scientist, and her mercenary terrorist buddies Malik Badawi and the now radioactive Amir Abbas. The nuclear-capable shells were a great distraction to us all, and as I understand from the last communication from the commander, there is only one shell still missing." Fay nodded.

"Sir, while that is true, and we have the shells we have taken from the oil tank on Whiddy Island, we have no way of knowing if there are more hidden somewhere else." Very tentatively, Amira looked at Aire, seeking his permission to speak. He grinned at her, waving her on with one wrinkled hand.

"Sir, general, you have my report that it is our studied opinion that the first tranche of shells could never have exploded?" The Boss nodded. Aire looked at the screen.

"Is that the considered opinion of everyone?" Heads in their blue boxes nodded in unison. Amira sat up, gaining confidence from the unilateral support of her fellow scientists. Initially, she had not run physical tests on the nano shells, and it was only after prodding by Interpol that she did so and discovered the shells could never be exploded. In her mind, at least, she had failed her team by not getting to the answer quicker.

"However, I cannot say that about the second tranche, specifically the ones recovered from the plant in the old Milk Factory and the plant buried in Ireland." Looks of concern raced across the screen, and the Boss turned to look at Amira directly.

"As I understand it, the torpedo-shaped shells were designed so that once loaded, then sealed with the nanites, they became almost indestructible?"

"Yes, General, that was our conclusion. The shells that were blown up in the nuclear explosion in Gaza, according to sensor data, are still intact, albeit at the bottom of a very radioactive hole."

"So, as we surmised, they were a distraction to get us looking the wrong way while they prepared an attack that was headed for America." Amira nodded. While a genius-level scientist and one of the very few in the world that could shape nanomachines to work in miraculous ways, since she had been attached to Israeli Intelligence and Interpol, she had learned a lot about geopolitics and terrorism. And she was learning that asymmetric warfare was far from predictable.

"It may be that sinking that gunboat in the Atlantic, captained by Maribelle Assiano, prevented a nuclear attack on the USA."

"There's no doubt that it did. And remarkably," the Boss added, "the shells that sank with the remains of the gunboat have been detected intact on the bottom of the ocean floor."

"Intact?"

"Yes."

"Do we place any credibility on what her partner, Rena Niele, the psychologist, stated were the objectives of the original terrorist attacks?"

"To create a worldwide environment that emulates the refugee camps?"

"Yes."

"Well, ask yourself, did the strategy work?" The entire cadre of geeks and specialists went quiet, thinking through the question by the diminutive ex-spy.

On faraway Frontier Mountain, Malcolm put his hand up as if seeking permission to speak. His surfboard glistened in the harsh overhead lights, a reminder that the blond-headed geek had other passions besides work.

"Go ahead, Malcolm. We value your opinion."

"Thank you, sir. From all the data we have accumulated over the past months, I would say categorically the terrorists succeeded in creating refugee-camp-like conditions; look at the fact that over fifty million people are dead, another thirty-plus million displaced, we have no oil, gas, or coal, and the internet has been crashed; nearly every country is now without power, clean water, and food, not to mention communications. But their plan to force the migration of the refugee children would now, at least, seem to be at the whim of governments, in that some will allow the migration, some will not."

"As in the United States, allowing the falsification of IDs, visas, and passports to stand and accept the children in Helena and Roanoke."

"Yes, sir, there were an additional seventeen countries who had trust accounts set up and environmental plants sitting on their docks ready to be built, but so far, no country has agreed to proceed."

"What about New Zealand?"

"Sorry, sir, yes, you are correct. New Zealand has welcomed the children with open arms and is actively establishing more locations for the children to be housed." The room and the screen went very quiet again, reflecting on what the NSA specialist had said. Arie looked at the big screen and judged it was time to get the focus back on the 'now'. But before he could speak, the Boss stood, offered Arie a small bow, and then turned to face the camera.

"Apologies, Arie, but there's something else we need to consider. Why did the women use the threat of nuclear-capable shells in the first place? What was the end goal?" Again, the entire group went silent, considering the recently appointed Inspector General of Interpol's question. For the first time since the conversation had commenced, the head monk, Stefarino, offered his opinion. His order was charged with the responsibility of recording everything known about the rise of religion and had dedicated themselves to this task for centuries. And now that the Vatican and its vaults jammed full of icons and religious treasures, too many to mention, had been obliterated in the first terrorist attack, what the monks held in their electronic vaults was, literally, priceless.

"General, if I could offer a comment?" The Boss sat, nodding to the monk.

"At the risk of degrading their social capital gained by the placement of the child refugees, given the timing of the discovery of the shells, and Interpol's reaction to the terrorist attacks, I believe the nuclear message was no more than a threat aimed at the countries that had been nominated to take refugees, but had their trust accounts Red flagged. I suspect this was not just to make us look east while they prepared an attack in the west, but had it been allowed to play out, I believe we would have seen some first-class bargaining-we'll stop the nukes, you take the refugees." A number of the heads in their little blue boxes nodded.

"What do you mean by Interpol's reaction?" the Boss asked, agreeing with the monks' assessment but interested in his rationale. The smile the monk sent the Boss was beautiful to see and, by itself, removed any inference of criticism.

"General, you and your captain moved so fast. No one had a chance to develop any game plan before they were either taken off the board or incarcerated. You had Red Notices on the trust accounts in the third week after the attacks. In fact, before the target countries even knew they were in the frame for a forced migration program." The Boss raked his hand over his head and settled back into his seat, rolling his shoulders.

"We had a lot of help, not the least of which came from Arie and Malcolm and their various agencies. But you are correct—we did move fast, but not fast enough to prevent the civil unrest from tipping the world on its collective head."

"Once the Vatican, the Dome of the Rock, the Grand Mosque, and West Point were attacked, then the internet was taken down, computers and communication crashed, followed by the denial of oil, gas, and coal, there was little you could do to stop the madness. Little anyone could do." The Boss nodded again, he agreed with the monks' rationale, but it didn't hurt to hear it spoken by someone as revered and objective as he was.

"Thank you, Stefarino. I agree with your assessment. We didn't get to see their nuclear strategy play out, but in hindsight, it's not too difficult to see what they intended. The women used the mercenary terrorists as pawns and were happy to sacrifice them in the short term. Arie, you were running down the major questions before I interrupted?"

"Thank you, PJ. I think it's important that we all heard that." He looked around the screen, then at his companions sitting alongside him. "And that brings us to the next question, now that the major players are out of the way, who is running terrorist central?" Everyone nodded, and the room went eerily quiet again. Fay, encapsulated in the C-17 steaking across Europe at 35,000 feet, was the first to break the silence. The whine of the engines was a constant reminder that she was airborne.

"Sir, I've just confirmed to the commander that the drone that shot them down over the Atlantic flew out of Whiddy Island. Inspector Thomas was not pleased, and she feels the need to have a conversation with some of the women we have taken into custody." She smiled as she delivered this information, knowing full well what Sandra really wanted to do with the women.

One in the heart, one in the head.

"I bet she does. Can you summarize what Whiddy Island has added to the picture?" Arie sat back in his seat, suddenly weary from the constant need to examine every little piece of data, looking for snippets of intelligence that might enable them to get in front of the terrorists for once. He had here the key people who had cleaned up a lot of the mess the terrorists had created from day one, but it still seemed that they were constantly playing catchup.

"General, I'd prefer that the commander provide that summary." She sat back in her seat, shrinking her image. Arie nodded and looked at the Boss.

"I warned Jessica we were having this meeting. She can answer a call."

Arie looked at the technician managing the master control panel, nodded once, and within seconds I was looking at a screen full of people and a long box running across the bottom of my screen with the Boss, Arie, Amira, and Shami sitting side by side. The mini was way too small to enable me to see individual faces clearly, so I held my hand up as if to stop a speeding vehicle.

"Wait, one." I stood, walked over to where our techs had placed a massive screen sitting on a pile of ammunition boxes, empty, I hoped, pointed to it, and immediately was able to scroll the image from the mini onto the screen. "That's better. How are you all?" Lots of smiles, and the occasional wave, then everyone looked at me with expectation written all over their faces. The Boss had warned me what the topic would be, and since his electronic note had registered, I had been thinking through what we knew, what we suspected, and what we had yet to do.

Here was the brains trust we had been working with from day one and a smarter group of people I had yet to meet.

"I see you have Fay and Ito on screen. Have they brought you up to date?"

"Partially, as related to the drone shoot-down." I felt Sandra arch up alongside me, and I stroked her arm to calm her down. She really had to let it go. I signaled for more coffee and felt our Italian commandos at our backs. I immediately wished Indigo was on this call, but given his current tactical situation, I left him out of it.

"Arie, Fay is traveling with a number of prisoners, all of whom we have decided are directly related to the women terrorists. It's my hope that she will get the opportunity to interrogate them before they are incarcerated." He nodded, looking more frail than he had the last time I had seen him.

"I'll see that it is set up for her arrival."

"Thanks, Arie. As always, your generous help is appreciated. The next issue is we have a number of mercenary terrorists holed up in an old Napoleon-era fort on Whiddy Island. One of their ilk is traveling with the prisoners and the material we recovered from the oil tank and drone hangar. According to him, there are numerous other teams roaming around Europe, some of whom we have undoubtedly run into previously, and possibly some we have yet to meet."

"That might tie in with a report we just got from France, where three of their remaining nuclear electrical generating plants have suddenly gone offline. Guess what the French have found at each site?" Malcolm's comment cut through the screen with such import, and every head reacted in some way.

"Silver sludge!" Luigi almost said the words gleefully. From his perspective, the nanomachines were a true marvel, proof of what humans could do with the right motivation and resources. Or, in this case, the wrong motivation and vast resources!

"Yes, nanites."

"That's going to make a living in France, and some parts of Europe, even more uncomfortable." The Boss spoke so softly he almost wasn't heard on the multiple ends of the electronic conference, but I heard him clearly, and I knew what he was alluding to. Since the first days of the terrorist attacks, middle Europe-Spain, France, Italy, Switzerland, Poland, and the eastern bloc countries all the way to the Russian border had suffered tremendously from the aftermath of the attacks. Roaming armed gangs, civil insurrection, military troops turning on their own command structures, ordinary people panicking and rushing borders in every direction, and the constant pile-up of abandoned vehicles that turned into burning pyres, stinking up the air and polluting the sky for weeks.

It was the worst civilian tragedy in human history and showed no sign of abating anytime soon. Martial Law had been declared in most countries, and borders had snapped shut like sharks feeding in a frenzy. Surprisingly, many of the northern European countries like Sweden, Norway, Finland, Estonia, Latvia, and Denmark had very little civil unrest and only marginal infrastructure damage. That was something I'd have to put some thought into at some point, but not now. Malcolm suddenly became agitated again, his face a canvas of concentration, then he looked up into his camera.

"More bad news. Reactors in Scotland, England, and just now, Spain have all gone offline. No report on the cause yet, but I'm willing to bet nanites again." The silence across the conversation was absolute. Even the whine of the jet engines seemed to fade into the background. The Boss looked at Arie, whose shoulders had slumped to their lowest, and his once chiseled face had suddenly gone flaccid. He physically shook himself, regaining some of his earlier composure, his gray skin color slowly returning to a washed-out pink.

"Arie, are you alright?" the Boss's concern showed in his voice, and every head focused on the Israeli spymaster, who waved away everyone's concern with one gnarled hand.

"*Oi vey*, I'm fine, I'm fine. Commander, please continue." I could see the silent plea in Arie's eyes, he was embarrassed, but he was also not well, and that was plain for all to see. I respected him so much that I forced myself to continue, as if nothing untoward had happened, and made a mental note to get him seen as soon as possible. I scribbled a note to Shammy, who, as Arie's right-hand man, I knew would see to Arie's health as a matter of urgency.

"If it is the mercenary terrorists doing this damage, we can only hope that the local enforcement agencies can cope. Not to diminish this new situation in any way, I'd like us to concentrate on what we are finding here." Every head nodded in agreement, albeit some a little slower than others.

"Thank you. Arie, general, our major concern is that one of the women we are sending you is highly placed within the Irish government, and after a short conversation with the President, we believe that the women have penetrated the top echelons here and may be exerting a measure of control. Look at these images." I fired up shots of the power panels hidden under the grass and shrubs, the oil tanks, the containers we suspected held nanites, and shots from inside the environmental plant. They scrolled across the screen, each image pausing for five seconds, then retreating to a little dialogue box at the top of the screen, where anyone could pull them down for a longer look.

"We estimate they have stored over a million sets of roof panels to date. The plant is temporarily closed down. We had no option once we took some of the staff into custody. They have also produced canisters of nanites, purpose unknown. We have sent them on the C-17 and would appreciate Amira and her team giving us their conclusions as fast as possible." Arie nodded and turned to look at Amira. She put a hand on his arm to comfort him, then looked up at the camera.

"I will make it a priority for you, commander. As a matter of interest, how do these roof panels differ from the ones being produced at Point Roberts?" I looked at her sitting beside Arie, concern on her face. I knew exactly how she felt. I had always regarded Arie as the grandfather I never had. It was a very strong emotional attachment. She probably saw him the same way, having been a refugee child relocated by Mohammad bin Azaria in the first tranche some fifteen years previously.

"They are the one color, greenish black, and multiple panels are stitched in an inverted 'V' shape. Having seen some of the row houses here in Cork, I suspect they are designed to slip over the top of existing roofs with a minimum of fuss. To my eye, at least, it would seem to be a really simple installation."

"Will you restart the plant?"

"Maybe. I'll pass the request on to the Army Corps of Engineers the moment I get time. We have a much bigger issue than the plant-if we are correct, and the women have penetrated the government, we may find ourselves in a political bind." And this was my biggest fear. If the conversation turned political, we would find ourselves on the outer and the terrorists in control by default.

"Ireland is a member country of Interpol." The Boss's gruff response left no doubt of the underlying issue.

"Yes, but we can't operate on their behalf unless they ask us to, and the remit we have to date was based on locating the nuclear-capable shells and shutting down any terrorists. If the women are inside the government, we may find ourselves without a mandate." The Boss looked up at the camera as if he was looking straight into my eyes. His were a deep graying blue, with little gold flecks around the edges, and had mesmerized me from the first day I had shot him.

"Do you think that is a possibility?" He didn't bark, but his tone reminded me of a bulldog snapping at my heels.

"Yes. Sandra and I met with the President, and he had two 'advisors' who fit the women's terrorists' profile to a tee. That plus the protests from Lady O'Brian Flattery, the CEO of the plant, who is on her way to you, Arie, and you have definite signs they are inside the government. I have a question for you." The Boss looked thoughtful, still holding my eyes from thousands of miles away. He was a pure bastard to play poker with, and I could see no 'tells' in his face.

"And?"

"How much did you find out from your friends at the Red Cross, or Red Crescent, for that matter?"

"Find out about what?" I had him momentarily on the back foot. It was over a month since we had last discussed the agencies the terrorists were using to recruit and transport the refugees. I smiled inwardly at my shallow victory.

"" Numbers. How many children are being migrated, and which countries are they headed for." He looked thoughtful, scratched his chin absentmindedly, but held my eyes. I still couldn't read him.

"We got numbers for every country that was on the list, and as you know, five thousand odd that were headed for Roanoke were lost when they were sunk by the gunboat. I haven't looked beyond that-should we?"

"Yes. We know the women—Helen's crew specifically—created over one hundred thousand false identifications, visas, and passports for the American and New Zealand migrations. It would have been more, but we stopped them. We know the US has agreed to let the false identifications stand and will take around ninety thousand at this time. What happens in the future is very much up to the terrorists." I paused to let everyone catch up with the numbers.

"How about Ireland?" He looked blank for a second, then started to put together what we had arrived at, albeit over a period of days, not seconds, as he was doing. Did I mention my operational blindness? And how smart he was?

"Give me your impression." Now I could read his eyes. He was suddenly totally focused on the issue, his mind working at the speed of light.

"We think over a million children, maybe as many as three or four, but this is based purely on the roof panels they have already constructed."

"How in the name of God do you move that many children, given the utter chaos that is most of Europe?" Anna Bernstein, the FBI SSSA, had sat silently through all the discussions, and her quiet and cultured Bostonian voice cut across the chatter and mutters that had broken out at the mention of the huge numbers of child refugees like a hot knife through butter. Her crisp dark blue suit made a distinct contrast with her short bob of blond hair, her pale blue collared shirt, and her innate elegance belied her aggressive nature on the job. She held one manicured finger up to the camera, tipped with a clear polish as if she was admonishing me for mentioning the number we were guessing at.

I smiled back reassured her that she was on the ball. I had the exact same reaction when we first learned of the possibility. Or maybe an impossibility?

"That's a very good question, Anna, but it makes sense if you look at the infrastructure. We have been told that there are over a million empty homes here in Ireland, and if you look at all the potential occupancy models they could use, relocating two or three million children looks easy."

"Models?" She shot her cuffs, revealing the blue shirt was anchored by a pair of dull silver cufflinks. I had seen them before—a gift from her father she treasured. It made me long for my mother, whom I had secretly met a month before. I wore the little pink watch she had given me as a gift religiously.

"How many adults and how many children. We figure one adult per four children, with a majority of the adults doubling as teachers, nurses, and anything else you can think of that requires skill and commitment. It's not just finding the children's homes. It's the support infrastructure they will need to survive."

"In both the US and New Zealand, they used existing families to adopt the children. You're suggesting a different model?"

"I agree with Anna. I can't get my head around it. The numbers are too big. Are there that many skilled and educated women in the camps to provide, what, a million volunteers to look after the children?" Fay's voice was accompanied by the sudden acceleration of the whine of the jet engines, and every head turned to look at her image.

"Trouble?" I asked, crossing my fingers. I knew firsthand what it felt like to be shot down out of the sky. Fay's face revealed nothing. She was sliding from side to side, then bouncing up and down, then the weird motion stopped as suddenly as it started, and the engine sounds went back down to their normal intrusive drone.

"Just a little turbulence. We've got a bit of rough weather on the route."

"Haven't we all! Anna, we're not experts in accommodation modeling, and at this point, it's just raw numbers we are extrapolating from. The issue is, if it is in any way true, do we have an active state-level member of Interpol playing with the women terrorists? And do we have a million adults and three or four million young children on the move?"

"Yes, that is the real issue." The Boss's glum assessment cut across our emotional arguments very succinctly. Always to the point and to the heart of the matter. In a sense, the numbers didn't matter so much as the possibility of who and how they would make this scenario come true. No one on the call looked happy, the idea of state-level support for the women terrorists was daunting, and I wondered fleetingly how we might manage it. If we were still allowed to play. Moving five million people was a massive task for anyone.

"At the last count, and that was before the terrorist's attack on the Vatican, there were over forty-three million refugees, half of which were children under eighteen. If you do the math, the terrorists mean to relocate around ten million children, and God only knows how many adults."

"At the moment, it's speculation. Let me get more data from the aid agencies. Do you have anything else for us at this point?" The Boss was looking directly at me. I could feel the intensity of his eyes from sixteen hundred kilometers away. My heart gave a little 'thud-thud'. This man pushed my buttons, and there was no getting away from that, no matter how hard I tried.

"Only the small thing of the Irish Chinook and the American CH-53 being totaled by a rocket attack yesterday, collateral damage to a UH-3, no casualties, and as I mentioned earlier, the lone survivor of the attack is on his way to you, Arie, with the women prisoners."

"We can help with the forensic examination of the data you have retrieved. We know what to look for from our earlier work." The head monk had almost been invisible throughout the call, having sat silent and as still as a statue, something I envied him for. His calm and balanced disposition helped smooth out my nerves every time we interacted with him, and I hoped on this occasion, some of his calm might rub off on Sandra, who was still vibrating like a badly played cello.

"Thank you, Stefarino, that would be of immeasurable help. Fay, if you could send a copy to the monks, please?"

"At once, commander. We're only two hours out. See you on the ground, Arie." The old spymaster smiled and waved one liver-spotted hand as Fay's box cut to black. The sudden lack of turbine whine left an empty space in my head, and I wondered what the reaction would be to what I said next.

"Arie, Boss, I'd like to call the Irish government and request sufficient troops to take over Whiddy Island to ensure the terrorists are removed before we allow any civilians back. I'd also like to call in the Corps of Engineers, and Amira or one of her people, to assess the plant and perhaps get it back up and running if we see any benefit in that."

"When do you anticipate you can clear the mercenaries out of the fort?"

"Indigo has that under control. I'd defer that decision to him."

"Keep us posted." And the long rectangular video box with the four in Israel went to black, leaving me with the geeks in Venice and Anna.

"Anna, if you could stay on the line, please, everyone else, thank you for your contribution. Stay safe." One by one, the boxes emptied, and progressively Anna's face enlarged until it filled the screen. She smiled into the camera, and I sensed her power and innate calm. Maybe this would work on *'Just call me Sally'*, whose whole being was so tense I could feel the waves of anger washing off her. I remembered when she had first used her nickname on me and smiled. Good times. We were early into the investigation into the terrorists. The hunt was raw and edgy, and our focus and commitment were singular.

And that was the main problem I faced now. We were stretched too thin and doing things we were not good at, like babysitting an Island and worrying about how the government might interfere with our mission. We were Interpol's hammer. We trained to get in, fight, get dirty if necessary, then get back out. Here we were tied down by the complexity of the target and a list of unknowns as long as your arm.

"Thanks, Anna. First up, can you get the Corps of Engineers to send a contingent to Ireland? Can you get us an update on Helena, Roanoke, and anything else the President is thinking of, specifically setting up more ecological plants? And that brings me to another question, and I apologize for not asking it first. How is the President?" Anna's face looked a little grim as she considered her answer.

"Not as well as we would hope. The congressmen and women and representatives have all been returned to the capital under guard, those that survived, that is, and the President has had to make a few very hard decisions that don't sit well with the executive."

"Are you still under Marshall Law?"

"Yes, no change there, but there are signs that the National Guard and LEOs are getting control back in the major population centers, but the lack of fuel and power is creating the biggest headache."

"Commerce, cross border trading, all the normal things people do stopped in their tracks."

"Yes. The panels and power supplies that are coming from Point Roberts are making a huge difference on the West Coast, a new plant on the East Coast will be up and running in a week, but the truth is there is very little fresh food on the shelves, and with unemployment now running at over ninety-five percent you have an economic crisis never seen before."

"Tough times. And no way to accelerate a comeback."

"And what would that look like in any case?"

"Power to the people!" And I smiled. There had been a folk song way back in the sixties that had used those lyrics during what had been known as the 'flower power movement'. I had missed that period by a few decades, but my mum had played all the tunes from that time endlessly while I was growing up, and I remembered that the jukebox in the truck stop had carried most of them as well.

"Yes, power to the people. And right now, there is very little to go around. Those towns that had good renewable energy grids are doing okay, but as you can imagine, the migration into those areas is massive, and most are not coping well at all."

"Is Helena an exception?"

"Yes. They are building houses with the panels from Point Roberts at a good rate. In a way, they have created a self-sustaining economic model, with the money flowing back into the local economy and fringe businesses growing up around the city. With no plastics or oil-based fibers, they have had to revert to wood and natural materials, and as you know, Montana has a lot of trees."

"Yes. What rate are they settling in the children?"

"The first ship had one thousand one hundred and seven children and three hundred adults. All were absorbed in less than two weeks. The adults were all educated, skilled and slipped into the workforce seamlessly. Most of them were teachers and nurses, a few doctors, engineers, and a few religious types. There are now over three hundred families waiting to adopt, with one hundred and forty houses being completed every week."

"How many families took more than one child?"

"About half, and I'd like to think for the right reasons, but the financial offer for two or more refugees was very enticing."

"Do you know if there is another ship on the way?"

"No. Perhaps PJ can find that out for us. We can only guess the destination for the five thousand children that were lost in the sinking of the cruise ship in the Atlantic, but with the work in

Roanoke ramping up, there will be room for the next ship whenever it arrives." I shook my head. We still didn't understand why the terrorists had sunk their own ship, but then, we knew very little about their plans. And nothing about their future intentions.

"Are the power packs that are being distributed along the West Coast making any difference?"

"Huge. Better than forty percent of the factories and businesses up and down the coast are back up and running, but there is a desperate shortage of raw materials. No one—and I mean no one—and ever done any genuine studies on what the outcome of having no oil or gas would have on the manufacturing economy. No plastics, for example. No University had ever studied the effect of that. And the women have embarrassed us again with their technology because, as you know, they are mining sea water and sand for the elements they make their panels and power packs out of, and so far, every plant you have uncovered is using the same technology."

"Yes, even here in Ireland. There is a new nanite product. I don't know what it does, but we confiscated barrels of it earlier this week. It's on its way to Amira." Anna looked thoughtful, her beautiful green eyes sparkling in the low light, her face framed by her bob of pretty hair.

"You know, the terrorists have won. No matter what happens next, we simply can't recover from the disastrous situation they have created. It's a time thing. We can't repair the damage to infrastructure and the human psyche fast enough." My turn to look thoughtful, as the pointy end of the hammer, I had very little time to look at the bigger picture, and if the truth be known, no real skill at looking at it. But I understood what she was getting at. The terrorists had wanted to collapse the world into the same conditions found in most refugee camps-overcrowding, lack of hygiene, food, water, and little or no economic support.

We now had over fifty-five million dead and a further thirty-six million disposed people trying to migrate wherever they could get to, and on the whole of the European continent, most governments had shut their borders, some with deadly consequences. While there were reserves of biofuel and more being produced every day, with no commerce employing people to work, no one could afford to buy it. That, in itself, was creating a deadly paradigm. I had seen figures that suggested that better than eighty percent of the world's industrial base was currently stalled, either due to a lack of power or raw materials.

We were heading back to the stone age, from a highly industrialized society with no real capacity to produce anything useful.

Just thinking about it made my head hurt.

"Yes, they have won round one, but we're not letting them do a victory lap just yet. Stay strong, and give the President my regards. I'll get back to you the moment I have something new." I watched the image dissolve and felt my hopes mirror it. If Anna, one of the smartest women I had met so far, was despondent, who was I to be happy? I felt a hard dig in the ribs, tucked my elbow into my side to protect it, turned, and saw Sandra smiling for the first time in days.

"She got to you, didn't she?" I looked at Sandra, no longer vibrating, now looking almost relaxed.

"What's got you on such a high?"

"Anna. I know she sounded down, but when you look at the problems they've got in the States, it's no wonder. But she's not giving in."

"No, she's not. But her problems make ours look trivial."

"Like being shot down, blown up, attacked by rockets. Did I miss anything?" I laughed, slapped her on the shoulder, stood, and walked back out the big open doors where the rest of the day sat between low-lying clouds and sleeting rain.

"She's right about the time factor. There's going to have to be a massive readjustment of people's expectations and ambitions. It will take us years to recover from this mess, and the women have, to a certain extent, posted the technological signposts for us to follow. We just need the smarts to understand the science and duplicate it."

"Well, it all stemmed from Amira's work, so we should have the inside track." I gave that some thought, remembered how Amira had looked during the group call and nodded.

"Yes, you're probably correct. But who is the 'we' in this case?" She looked at me with a quizzical gleam in her eyes as she processed my question. She slowly started to nod.

"I see what you mean. It can't be Interpol. Not our role. Maybe the Israelis, but they have their hands full with the cross-border attacks. The Americans are the best placed, but from what Anna told us, they're not in the 'help humanity recover' space. We have environmental plants in seventeen other countries, but as you said, time and resources. What are you thinking?" I turned to face her. I wanted her to see the absolute truth of what I was about to say in my eyes.

"I think we're standing in the middle of it. Don't ask me how, or even why, just a feeling I have, but don't be surprised if Ireland turns out to be a core ingredient in solving the problems we all face." She turned her head to one side, obviously thinking through what I had just said. Then she smiled again.

"Well, I guess we'll find out soon enough. Are we going to rescue Indigo and his playmates anytime soon?" I sighed. She had a point, so I let my unproved speculation based on no more than a gut feeling slide back into its place in my consciousness.

Time to go to war again.

CLICK AND COLLECT

The truck was a kilometer from the abandoned factory when Katrina put a hand on Sharon's shoulder and asked her to stop. Outside the window, the heavy overcast created a gloomy atmosphere, but for now, at least, the rain was holding its breath. What had caught her eye was a young boy, no more than ten or eleven, sitting on a pile of burnt-out vehicles. Dressed in tattered corduroy pants, heavy, unpolished, and well-scuffed boots, and half hidden by a mottled blue and green jacket of some kind, he looked lost and forlorn. His red hair was tamed by a dark cricket cap of indistinguishable age, with untidy spikes leaking out the sides.

"Would you know who that might be?" she asked, drawing a puzzled look from Jason, sitting in the shotgun seat. Sharon took a long look, searched her prodigious memory, then shook her head.

"No, sorry, it is that I am. As handsome as he might be, I can't place him. What about you, Jas?" He bent to look out the window, which Sharon had wound down. He shook his head slowly, then looked back at Katrina.

"I don't think so. He vaguely reminds me of one of the littles that hang around our building. He probably lives locally. Why would you be interested in him, I'd be asking?" Katrina looked at Lilian and raised her eyebrows in a silent question. It was Lilian's turn to duck her head and look out the window.

"We could, if you judge it to be wise?"

"We have to start somewhere, and maybe this little man can do us all some good." She opened her door, walked to the back of the truck, and pulled a small container out of her pack. Sharon decided to stay in the vehicle, previous experience with the locals had imbued caution in her, but Jason climbed out to follow.

"Do you have a good memory?" Lilian's question followed him out of the truck. He stopped, turned, and looked back at her, still sitting in her seat.

"Aye, I do at that, at least as good as Sharon's, I'd be thinking." Lilian laughed and waved him on.

"Then watch closely because you will need all your wits about you to report what you see."

Katrina approached the young boy, who, far from being scared, looked slightly down his nose at her.

"And who'd ya be, missus, all dressed up like you're planning on partying?" He sat some five meters up on top of a sedan stacked on top of a truck, stacked on top of a bus. All had been gutted and burnt, and from the dark ash stains on his hands, it was not hard to guess where he had been. The paddock held hundreds and hundreds of wrecks, very few of which were not burned out, and for a fleeting moment, Katrina feared he was living in them.

Then Jason arrived, looked up at the boy, and held a hand out. "I know ya, little Seamus. What are ya doing all the way down here? And where's the gang you usually travel with?"

The boy slipped down the wrecks, leaving a mottled trouser mark in the ash, sliding in a way that suggested he had done it many times before. His cheeky grin filled his freckled face, and his bright green eyes looked up at Katrina in awe. He slowly reached out and touched the hem of her dress, today a peacock blue. She stood perfectly still, unaware that her dress would attract so much attention. She made a mental note to find clothes more appropriate for the area and the conditions as soon as they returned.

"Aye, pretty and soft. Wouldn't last a day on the wrecks."

"So that's what you're doing, scoping out what you can pilfer. Is you Dah around?" Jason eyed the boy suspiciously, looking for the lie.

"Nah, he stayed back, got some sort of cough or something. I walked down yesterday to see if there's anything worth saving." Katrina mentally winched, a little boy walking so far, by himself, under the prevailing social conditions, where anyone and everyone was a target for gangs and thieves, making her blood run cold. She made an instant decision.

"Seamus, is it? Well, I'd like to show you something, then if you approve, I'd like you to come with us to collect some hardware, then we'll drive you home with us." He looked up in awe. No one this well-dressed had ever paid him the time of day in his young life, and her voice was rich with a very educated drawl he had never heard before. He doffed his cap and bent his head.

"Missus, aye, I'd be Seamus. How can I be helping you this fine day?" and he looked up at her with his best smile filling his face. His hair had fallen down and now cascaded in unruly waves around his shoulders, dancing in the light breeze.

"Seamus, I'm going to show you how to turn these wrecks into different things, things you can use for making other things. When we get back home, I'll talk to your father and Moriah and show them how to manage the process. Would you like to see what we can do?" He looked up at her expectantly, not really understanding what she was talking about but encouraged by the presence of Jason. Jason was one of the people that Moriah used for both protection and getting work done in and around the apartment building, so he nodded and put his cap back on.

Katrina poured a tiny amount of nanites onto the wheel arch, took him by the hand, and moved back. In seconds the vehicle started to dissolve, and a small pile of metal started to accumulate on the burnt grass. Not able to help himself, Seamus bent down and ran his fingers through the thin stream of metal.

"Oh! Aye, I've never seen the likes of this missus. What is that you be doing here, exactly?"

Katrina capped the container and looked at Jason, who stood open-mouthed.

"We'd better go on now. We can talk about this in the truck. Come along, Seamus, we'll take you home." She held out her hand, and Seamus unhesitatingly took it, transferring murky black soot as he did so. They got back to the truck, where Seamus was squeezed into the back seat between Lilian and Katrina. He doffed his hat again, mindful of his manners, never having seen such beautifully dressed women before. Everyone he knew had patches on their clothes.

"I'm Lilian. Who might you be?" Her Scottish brogue was so distinct that the young boy almost couldn't make out her words.

"I'm Seamus, missus. This lady here invited me to ride with you."

"Aye, that she did, and I know you as well, young Seamus. What the devil are you doing so far from home by yourself?" The edge in Sharon's voice was unmistakable, and the young boy's face turned pale.

"My Dah wanted to see if there was anything else we could salvage from the wrecks, but he got sick, so I came on my own." Sharon shook her head and looked the boy straight in the eye in the rear vision mirror.

"We'll say nothing of it but mark my words. If Moriah finds out, she'll tan your hide good and proper!"

"Yes, um." He dropped his head and presented the top of his cap by way of apology.

They arrived at the abandoned factory, where a small vehicle was parked and where two tall, coffee-colored women in overalls leaned against the fence. They straightened up as the truck stopped. The woman with jet-black hair, cut short like a pretty dome that flowed just above her shoulders, opened the door for Katrina.

"Welcome to Waterford, sisters. Come this way." They led the quartet inside the massive shed, where stacks of solar panels ran as far as the eye could see. An equal volume of canisters ran around one side, and overhead, a rusted chain looping down from an equally rusted crane swung slowly from side to side as if restless. "Now that we've seen your truck, we can load what you need. It will only take a few minutes." As she spoke, a soldier of indeterminate rank walked in, a machine pistol slung across his chest, his uniform creased and showing signs of accumulated dirt and neglect. He gestured rudely with his weapon, pointed back outside to the gates, and spoke with a guttural growl.

"Finisha nowa, we closea gates in tena minutes!" She just looked at him and fluttered her hand at him. He slouched off behind the shed.

"Apologies for that. The hired help leaves a lot to be desired, but as you can imagine, we need good security with all this material here." Sharon looked at Jason and, comforted by the fact that their two visitors hadn't reacted to the guard, the women bent their backs to load the truck as fast as they could.

They made it through the ten minutes with seconds to spare and noticed the guard had been joined by six others, all looking as shoddy and unkempt as each other. He sensed the unease in the troops as if they really didn't know what to do, they all looked tired and worn, and he wondered about their living conditions. The two women climbed into their small car and waved out the window as they drove away. Sharon, who had plugged the truck into a charger while they loaded, pulled the cable out, wondering if they had enough power to make it back home. Katrina handed her a long, heavy container with a set of cables attached.

"Plug this into your battery; the guards will wait. It will extend your range considerably."

They made it back to the apartment building without further fuss. The only problem was that Jason didn't know what to say about what he had seen. So he pointedly asked the question. Katrin answered him succinctly.

"You tell Moriah everything. Let her decide what to pass on. You need to get to Seamus's family and get them to the apartment so we can brief them." He nodded, thinking the day had been one big surprise after another and that Lilian hadn't said very much other than her name.

Strange dynamics, strange women, even stranger people at the factory, and the confidence everyone exhibited made him wonder if they were living in the same world he had experienced firsthand these past months. But he knew what a solar panel looked like, even one as strange as the one he had helped load onto the truck. They looked very different from the panels he had seen before. They were larger, a light red color, bendy and flexible, and as light as a feather, and it was obvious they were designed to snap together like Lego bricks. It had taken the four of them to load each panel simply because of their size and the fact that they bent so easily. But they had stacked one on top of the other without issue, and now they sat waiting for their next adventure. He had a sense that they were alive somehow, and it made his skin crawl.

He would find Moriah, and then he would find out just what in the devil's name was really going on!

CHAPTER SIXTEEN

The scene might have been out of a video game, with the colors so contrasting and bright under the moody sky. The grass was greener than green, waving slowly in the mild breeze. The old fort, with its three-ring structure and long, stubby buildings, was well overgrown and looked like three massive wheels trying to hide unsuccessfully in the grass. The water trapped between the first two rings shimmered and sparkled every time the sun was brave enough to peek out, then turned moody when it hid again. Some sort of white long-legged bird strutted unconcerned along the circular lake, snapping its head down into the depths every now and again as it jerked along on its leisurely stroll.

What ruined the image was the three soldiers with their long guns peeking out from their ghillie suits, and the reflection of the muzzles of the other soldiers spread around the sides of the fort. Indigo, the Irish major, and the Israeli Sgan Aluf met us as we walked down the muddy road that linked the fort to the rest of the world. In all my days in Ireland, I had only ever walked on muddy roads!

"Colonels, major, sitrep, please." We formed up around the major's minicomputer and looked as he scrolled through various photos of the front of the fort, equally as overgrown as the rest but showing some signs of having been disturbed recently, as you could see the distinct shape of the door. There were no windows, but a small chimney poked its snout up from behind the middle of the center ring, well below the level of the middle infrastructure.

"Are you ready to attack?" I looked around at the expectant faces and saw how tired they were, but I didn't miss the sparkle of excitement in their eyes. These were some of the finest warriors I had ever served with, so I kept my concern about their physical state to myself. Sandra was vibrating again, so I put my hand on her shoulder, hoping the physical contact would calm her down.

"Aye, commander, that we are at your beck."

"Then let's do it." The major spoke quietly into his short-range communicator, and out of the lush green rolling grass spat red and orange fire and smoky trails as canisters of gas and explosives sailed into the door, creating a maelstrom of dense smoke and flame. It bucked, twisted, and hovered around for a second or two, then, as if sucked in by a massive vacuum cleaner, whooshed back into the fort, leaving a jagged hole that smoked in spite of the Surgeon General's warning. A trickle of ugly smoke leaked out of the chimney, to be swept away by the wind, which had suddenly picked up as if the Gods were angry with us for disturbing their peace.

Ireland was a tricky place to wage war. You could feel that in your bones.

The white bird, surprisingly, just snapped its head around with a jerk, looked towards the sound of the explosion, then went about its business as if driving terrorists out of a Napoleon-era old fort was an everyday occurrence.

"Team one entering," came over the net, and a group of camouflaged troops erupted from the grass and ran towards the smoking door. The snipers off to the sides held their fire, and I held my breath. If it was going to go wrong, it would be now. As the first team disappeared into the smoke, the second team erupted from the grass and ran, and as they hit the door, the sound of muffled explosions could be heard, probably from flash-bang grenades. I started to walk towards the fort, our guards from Indigo's *Gruppo di Intervento Speciale* forming a wedge around us. I loved the little Italians. To a man and a woman, their sense of humor was outstanding. They could be under fire and still find the funny in it. Most importantly, they understood my total dependence on the magic brown bean.

We stood clear of the door, maintaining combat spacing, our backs to the wall of the old fort. Nothing happened. An eerie silence settled around our shoulders as the heavens opened and a drenching cold rain fell, something we were getting used to. Thunder cracked across the grass, the flash illuminating the area in front of the fort, creating stark images of the stumpy trees and the goats, who continued to root out the grass as if nothing untoward was happening. And a small stone dance suddenly appeared in the after light, something I had not seen previously.

I guess if you lived here long enough, you would get used to the capricious weather, the mystical architecture, and the iconic ruins. Ireland had the reputation of having been the most invaded country throughout history. Apparently, anyone who had a boat crashed onto its pebbly shores at one time or another. I wondered if we would be regarded as invaders or saviors.

"You should see this commander," the major said, holding his mini up. The water sheeted off it as if washed by a fire hose. What I saw was a stockpile of military hardware, gloomy areas not reached by the torchlight, and nothing else but piles of rusted cannon balls.

"Where are the terrorists?"

"No reported sightings and our troops are now covering the entire interior of the fort. Their feeling is that they have left via some underground tunnel, as there are no infrared signatures anywhere."

"That means no one for at least thirty minutes," Sandra mumbled, shaking her head to clear her eyes. "And our aerial scans didn't show any tunnels over here. They stopped back at the house." I nodded. She was correct. But I wondered if a centuries-old tunnel made from dirt and rubble would necessarily show up on our scans, the tunnel we had discovered was made in the last five years, had been bored professionally, and lined. I looked around. The three long buildings were so overgrown they had almost merged into the landscape. I pointed to them.

"Any chance they have gone to ground in one of those?" The major followed my finger and tilted his head to one side.

"No way of knowing. The IR didn't penetrate the fort. It is possible. Only one way to find out." I nodded, and we moved as a group around the inner ring until we were standing between two of the low-set buildings. There were no apparent doors or windows, and three of the commandos raced back from having surveyed all sides of them.

"Nothing, sir." The major looked at me as if seeking permission. Not my call.

"Major, you are the senior representative of the Irish government here. This is undoubtedly an antique historical relic. I can't order you to breach it." He looked at me with wide-open eyes, smiled, and nodded.

"Commander, thank you for your consideration. I'll make that decision once we have really surveyed these buildings. Meanwhile, I suggest we maintain the perimeter we originally set, just in case." My turn to nod, and just as I did, his communicator squawked at him. He held it to his ear and looked at me.

"We found the entrance to a waste tunnel, and by the materials left there, it would seem our terrorists have left the building." I looked up at the angry sky. No relief there and no heavenly signs leading to our escapees.

"Search the entire premises, recover what you can, then work out how to reseal the fort. Make it as permanent as you can."

"And block off the tunnel," Sandra added, her shoulders slumping in frustration. I knew exactly how she felt. She still wanted a conversation with the people who had sent the drone after us.

"How far to the ocean?" One of our guards looked at his map and looked back at me.

"Maybe a hundred and ten meters."

"Thank you. Major, sweep the area to the coast, then start at the top of the Island and work your way south. Indigo, get your team together. You can come back with us. Colonel," I said, addressing the Israeli Sgan Aluf, "if you would, work with the major, and once you have cleared the Island, I'll get you all back to Israel."

"Certainly, commander, it is our pleasure to work with you as always." She saluted, then moved off. I wondered how I would get her and her team back home. Fay and the C-17 would be in Israel now, so I'd have to call the aircraft back. Then I thought some more about it and looked at Indigo.

"Can you organize transport for the Israeli commandos?"

"Sì, comandante, non è un problema."

"Grazie." I looked up at the unrelenting sky, then back at my leadership team, and made a decision.

"Colonel, major, rest your teams in squads, four hours off, four on. They can billet where they are. Keep sharp." Sandra, Indigo, and I moved away back towards where we had landed. I was mulling over my next moves when Sandra poked me in the ribs.

"You don't think the terrorists are still on the Island?"

"It doesn't make sense for them to still be around here somewhere. We know they had secure communications; they must know we swept up their team back at Cork, and they must know we have taken in several women from their command structure. Why would you stay?" She looked straight into my eyes, hers blazing with intensity. She physically stopped me in my tracks as Indigo looked on in amusement, and our Italian guards pulled themselves into a loose circle, all facing outwards. They were old hands as far as Sandra and I were concerned. They knew our moods and our habits.

"Because there's something here they're being paid to protect." I had the same feeling but couldn't explain it in rational terms. My gut told me we weren't finished here on little Whiddy Island, not by half. I asked an obvious question.

"What did we find in the oil tanks?"

"Silver crud from the nanites."

"Nothing else?" She lowered her eyes, thinking through the process we had used when we had first landed and attacked the oil tank that had been converted into a massive store and workshop. It had held the nuclear shells as advertised and canisters of nanites, purpose unknown. It had also been the hub for the tunnel system between the drone hangar, the oil tank, the women's house, and, therefore, the plant.

"As far as I know, the tanks were physically inspected, but it was top down, as that was the only way in we could find at that time."

"Exactly. And our scans didn't find the waste tunnel, so maybe they are hiding something below the crud." She looked back at me. This time her eyes were sparking with energy. She really was a battery bunny!

"I like that. I like that a lot. Can we go find out?" Her expectant look was beguiling. I'm sure it worked on members of the opposite sex. I just found it a light relief on a bitterly wet and long cold day.

"Sure we can, just as soon as you eat your lunch." She laughed, pulled an energy bar out of her pack, broke it in half, and offered it to me. As I tried not to break my teeth on her generous gift, we started walking again, this time heading straight down the muddy road that led past the pub to the oil tanks. Like everything else on the Island, it wasn't far, and as they loomed up out of the sheeting rain, the Italian commando immediately to our front suddenly dropped. The muffled crack of the long gun followed a second or two later, by which time we were all flat on our stomachs, hugging the muddy road, trying to be invisible. The dirt about a meter in front of my face suddenly erupted, flinging mud and putrid water up in a little geyser. Without ceremony, Sandra suddenly rammed my side, forcing me to roll into a truck tread gouged into the road. Somehow she managed to put herself in front of me, legs spread, her H&K locked into her shoulder. She fired three short bursts. They were for effect, the range was too great for her little pea shooter, and whoever was sniping at us probably was laughing in his beard.

My ears were assaulted by the sounds of heavy automatic fire as some of the guards joined in, laying down suppression fire. They did have the range to hit the shooter with some luck, but I noticed out of the corner of my mud-covered eye that one of our long-gunners was taking careful aim, his ghillie suit now stained by the detritus from the muddy road, making him look like a madman created by a child. He fired two measured shots and turned his head towards me.

"Tango down, commander. At least the one who fired on us."

"Thank you. Search for more. That bastard cost me my chocolate bar!" Laughter broke out all around me as we started a crawl toward a small rock fence. On one side were goats, unconcerned by either the weather or the firing. On the other hand, my band of mud-splattered commandos. Indigo had dragged the fallen soldier by her webbing harness and was applying CPR while the medic was ripping her jacket open to get at the wound. I crossed my fingers. If it had been an armor-piercing round, she had no chance. If it was a standard ball round, her vest might have kept her alive. The Italian came in rapid spurts as the medic wrestled with her clothing.

"*Giù le mani dalle mie tette!*" The shout was the war cry of women all over the world and music to my ears - 'Get off me!' She was alive and presently swatting at the medic's hands. He held them up in the air in surrender, the sweeping rain washing over his blue surgical gloves, creating a pink cascade of bloody water.

"*Piano, Milio, sto solo cercando di salvarti.*"

"*Allora fallo senza toccarmi le tette!*" Again, laughter broke out, the idea of the medic being told to take his hands off Milo's tits lightening up the mood. Indigo had watched all this with his usual calm, reached over and checked her chest, nodded to the medic and turned to look at me. It was an eerie sight—him lying spreadeagled across her legs, the medic sprawled at her head, surrounded by at least five of the commandos, providing a human shield.

"She will be fine, commander, her vest did its job, but she will have a very nasty bruise."

"Sandra, what can you tell me about the sniper?" I snapped out the question with a hard edge in my voice, for which I didn't apologize. She was still in front of me. All I could see was the spread of her legs and the bulge of her pack. She shimmied sideways and rested her back against the stone fence. The look she gave me was anything but pleasant. Here was a warrior who took being shot at personally. We would really have to have a conversation about that at some point.

"Good shot, poorly trained, and didn't know his target." I looked at her and held my tongue. The silence was its own weapon, just as useful in a conversation as in an interrogation. She knew it, and a weak smile flittered across her face and stayed in her eyes.

"Buggar you, I should just let you get killed or something." She flicked her wet hair out of her eyes, then leaned back into the fence.

"Properly trained would have known to make it a headshot. No one goes into the field anymore without some form of body armor." I raised one eyebrow in a silent question.

"And you're still alive, so they didn't know you were in this group."

"Or they're not interested in me, and they want to delay us." She screwed up her eyebrows in concentration, thinking through my comment. She slowly nodded.

"Could be, don't know why. And we have troops down there. Where are they?" As if by happenstance, my communicator burst into life, and an Israeli-accented voice demanded my response.

"Commander, cease-fire, tango down, intentions?" I looked at Sandra. Her face was a mess of questions.

"Inbound your position, would appreciate a heads up next time." The silence was constantly interrupted by the rain bashing itself to death on everything around us, including the stone fence.

"WILCO." I took that as a literal statement and motioned our team back up to our feet, the long gunner and his spotter remaining where they lay in the slush, the long scope and binoculars sweeping from side to side.

"No contact, commander." I motioned for us to move out, little Milo having pulled herself back together, looking none the worse for wear. She punched the medic in the arm as she passed him and muttered something I couldn't hear, but he smiled under his battle helmet, so she was probably thanking him. Did I mention these were the best soldiers I had ever fought with?

We trudged through the growing muck that was the road, and I noticed we now had two-thirds of our team walking in front of Sandra and me, and it was more linear than before. I had to have a conversation with the Boss. We were wasting valuable resources. We still didn't know who had issued the fatwa on me, but we did know it was now up to forty million Euros.

I shook my head to flick the thought and the rain away. It did me no good to dwell on it. The tanks loomed up like specters in the gloomy rain, and I gave a thought to the two snipers who had battled it out in appalling visibility over a thousand meters or more. One had inflicted pain and died for his skill. My team formed a solid ring around Sandra and me as Indigo broke out to confront an Israeli sergeant, standing in the rain, his weapon hooked into his bent arm, looking miserable. Behind him, some ten meters away, the rest of his squad stood in loose formation, watching our approach intently. Sandra reached into her bag, her whole posture one of anticipation. Her little H&K was no doubt being stroked like a kitten.

"Commander," Indigo said in perfect English, which only highlighted the importance he put on the conversation, "the sergeant here and his team were down at the fishing sheds and only became aware of the sniper when the shooting broke out. By the time they got here, he was dead and on the roadway."

"Ask where he was shooting from." Indigo turned back to the hapless sergeant, nodded once, then followed the pointed arm.

"He says the second tank." We looked up at it, the rain was creating little waterfalls all the way down its painted face, and the runoff was threatening to engulf the road. I turned to Sandra.

"I remember asking for an overwatch on the tanks. What happened?" She shook her head.

"There was a long gun and spotter on the tank when we left for Cork. They may have been pulled out when we instructed the teams to go north."

"Maybe, but I smell a cluster fuck here. That overwatch should still have been in place." I walked over to the team from the 104 and noticed they looked as fatigued as our other troops had but nevertheless very alert.

"How long have you been on duty?"

"Since the others moved to the top of the Island."

"Stand down now, bivouac in sight of the tanks, keep a sharp lookout. I'll send you relief if we're here much longer." The commando saluted, shouted orders in Hebrew, and the team moved away. The sergeant looked at me. I waved him after his troops. Indigo turned and looked me up and down.

"*Vedo qualcun altro che ha bisogno di dormire. cosa vuoi fare dopo?*" Yes, I was tired, mostly of grinding around the countryside and getting nowhere.

"*Fai perquisire i carri armati da cima a fondo, porta gli israeliani a casa, fai sgomberare questa maledetta isola.*" He nodded and looked up at the looming tanks, their tops nearly hidden in the low-flying scud.

"Getting off the Island might be a problem. I've organized transport for the Israelis. It will be here in five hours. I'll get the tanks looked at now. Why don't you and the Inspector grab a few hours down?" He looked pointedly at where the 104 team was setting up personal tents on the side of the road where the saturated grass rose majestically, swaying drunkenly in the wind. I walked over to look at the dead sniper.

He was dressed the same as the group that had attacked us at the airfield, his uniform a little tattered and very dirty. His weapon was another story. A pristine Russian Dragunov SUV. It had suffered in the fall from the top of the oil tank, but under the mud, you could see how well it had been cared for. The long telescope had been knocked off its mount, and one end of it looked up at me like a weepy eye, water and mud sliding down its face in a slow-moving parade.

"Indigo, we'll take the body with us."

"Certainly, commander. The tanks have been checked. They are solid with silver crud. The sniper must have been hiding somewhere else." I thought about that. We had a lot of resources on the Island. My gut told me the Island was important, but it didn't tell me why. I shook my head in frustration.

"Indigo, get the 104 back home, get us home, leave the major and his Team Thee of the *Sciathán Fianóglach* in control of the Island, get onto his command and get him reinforcements. I don't want any civilians back here until we know for sure the terrorists have left."

"*Sicuramente comandante, subito.*"

PROOF OF CONCEPT

The teapot was cracked slightly on one side, patched with some sort of white glue, which made the pretty rose picture look like it had been attacked by bugs. Moriah poured into the cups, a mismatched group she had collected over the years. One by one, the women took the cups, and sipped graciously, then the clink of cups hitting the saucer rebounded around the small room.

"Moriah, I'd be thanking you and your wonderful people for their hospitality. Sharon and Jason were a great help, and you can send them back to Waterford for more panels anytime you like. You can think in terms of fitting out as many buildings and houses as you need to. We'll leave you another bag of cash as well. And thanks to you, we have been able to help the young boy, Seamus, and his family, and we've given them more material they can use to convert those wrecked vehicles. They will need security, of course, but they have the beginnings of a great little cottage industry." Moriah acknowledged Katrina with a little bob.

"Aye, I'd be thinking it's us who should be thanking you, to be sure. You're making it very easy for us."

"Our pleasure. We're here to give you all hope and economic freedom, and it's great to see you so well organized." She looked around the table, the oddly matched cups, the repaired teapot, and the patches so evident on Moriah's jacket. Yes, they were doing it hard, but it hadn't crushed their spirit.

"The sisters and I need to get on with our primary task, so we'll be leaving you shortly. We'll camp at the old shed where you put our containers and packages. We can well look after ourselves, so you don't have to worry about that, and when we've finished what we came to do we'll get you to take us back to the football field so we can fly out to the next job."

"Aye, we can do that. Will you need anything else at this time?" Katrina looked at Lilian and got a subtle shake of her head, so she smiled and stood.

"Thanks, but no, we'll be on our way. If Sharon or someone else could drive us to the shed, that would be appreciated." The women stood, Moriah moved to hug them all in turn, and when they left, she felt an emptiness in her that she hadn't experienced before. Outsiders from faraway places, all beautifully dressed and polite, reminded her of the best times she had experienced at the university before the attacks.

She shrugged her shoulders and went to the window to see them depart.

Sharon drove with Jason riding shotgun and squeezed next to Else, the smallest of the sisters, and felt his pulse rate rise at the warm touch of Else's thigh. Mildly embarrassed, he focused his attention out his window. Else never having experienced the touch of a man before, did her best to ignore him and looked stoically out the window. She wondered at the strange feelings she was having but put them out of her mind as quickly as she could

They were both relieved when they arrived at the shed and were welcomed by Henry and his old and decrepit tractor. The women surrounded him as Sharon and Jason unloaded their bags and containers from the back of the truck.

"Well, now ladies, what is it you would have me be doing for you this fine day?" he asked, his old briar piper struggling to stay in the corner of his mouth. The rain had filled the bowl several times in the last half hour, but it didn't worry him in the slightest as he hadn't put tobacco in it for years. Katrina moved forward and held out her hand.

"I'm Katrina, and this is Else, Lily, and Lilian. We're from the far north, and all we need from you is to open the shed and help unpack the boxes if you please." He nodded. This was what he was expecting, so without further ado, he doffed his soaking cap to the women, opened the shed, then moved inside.

The boxes were opened, and the women made a neat stack of the wooden packaging material off to one side. Outside, the rain started to come down with a vengeance, and Katrina briefly wondered if the shed would flood. Henry saw her question in her eyes and smiled.

"Aye, ya should give a care for the rain, but it'll not be worrying ya in here, I guarantee." She looked at him, his weather-beaten face aged with the remnants of a hard physical life, his complexion ruddy, and his coat patched in several places with what looked like sheepskin. She smiled back. Her instinct was to trust this old man, the professor, and her network was obviously first-class, judging by what Moriah and her team had done so far.

"Thank you, I appreciate your help. Can we do anything for you?" He shook his head, doffed his cap.

"Ladies, thank you for your smiles. It's good to see happy people again." He walked back out to his tractor, and with a mighty snarl, it started up and rumbled away. Katrina walked back out to where Sharon and Jason sat in their truck.

"Sharon, thanks for all your help. Please give this to Moriah. Tell her when we need a lift to the field. This will light up." She passed the small wooden box with a red led on top. Sharon looked at it for a moment, then put it on the seat beside her.

"Aye, I'll be doing that. Are you sure you'll be alright here on your own? I'd be wondering?"

"We'll be fine. We have tents, plenty of food, and we should be done in a day or two."

"Okay then, we'll be leaving you to yourselves. Stay dry!"

Sharon engaged the motors and, with little more than a mild hum, drove away. Katrina walked back inside the shed, saw Lilian and Else unpacking one of the containers they had brought with them, then saw Lily working with a ground-penetrating radar gun.

"How long with it take you to decide on a location?" she asked. Else looked up from what she was doing.

"I think we will be able to sink the test lines within a hundred meters. The strata look good around here, so we can hide the system in here if you want."

"Is there any chance you could locate the unit at the power station?" Lily bent her head to her gun in thought, then looked up at Katrina with her blue eyes sparkling with excitement.

"That would be perfect. Among all those transformers and generators, it would never be discovered unless someone went looking for it. I'll set off now and test the strata."

"Not so fast, and never by yourself. Lilian, can you go with your sister, please? You know where the power station is from here?"

"Yes to both. But we need Lily to be sure." Katrina screwed he eyes up in concentration.

"Okay, we'll all go. Pack what you need. Maybe we camp at the power station tonight. In fact, let's plan on that." Within twenty minutes, the four women were back outside in the rain, backpacks covered with ponchos, heads covered with watch caps. Katrina locked the shed door, set the alarm and the little camera she had positioned, and then followed Lilian into the rain.

It took them half an hour, by which time they were sodden but cheered up by the sight of a maintenance shed in the middle of the transformers. In another five minutes, they were through the fence and in the shed, flicking and waving water off with some vengeance. Luckily, the workers had left their utensils behind, and an old cast iron kettle sat on the rusted hob of a massive wood stove. The women shed their ponchos and packs, quickly loaded up the grate under the hob, and started a fire. Within minutes, the smell of peat smoke permeated the shed, and after a brief reorganization of the old wooden table and chairs, the women had enough room for their sleeping bags and room to work.

Which they did in almost total silence. Katrina watched the sisters in awe as their nimble fingers moved from equipment to equipment, setting up what they needed. She found a very rusted tap, turned it on, and after some loud protesting from the pipes, a muddy fluid that soon turned into a clear liquid flooded the floor. She tasted it and screwed up her face in disgust.

"We'll use our bottled water, this might run clean, but it's not worth the risk."

"I'm ready to start the survey." Lily stood, holding the GPR, then placed it back on the floor to refit her poncho. The three women watched her go, glad they were able to stay and enjoy the heat from the stove.

"You don't want the locals to know what we're doing?" Lilian looked at Katrina, trying to judge her mood. Since she and her sisters had first met her at the apartment, she had been unable to read the willowy, tall woman with her long, jet-black hair falling straight to her waist. She dressed like a princess and walked with a grace that suggested some innate regal blood. To her mind, and she had traveled to many exotic parts of the world as a professional deep sea diver, she was the most stunning woman she had ever seen.

"It's better for everyone if they can enjoy the benefits without the detail, at least until the situation outside normalizes. Moriah is a very clever woman. She's managing a community of thousands, keeping them housed and fed, and she seems to be able to get whatever she needs from everyone around her. Not to mention the fact that she has her own security troops in the form of the young gangs-all of whom seem to adore her. This will give her more to barter with and more power-if you'll forgive the pun!" Lilian laughed, enjoying the joke. Else looked up from the equipment she was checking, smiling at the pair.

"If this works as we think it will, she'll have more than just power to barter with. She'll control the destiny of the entire area." Both women nodded, accepting the truth of the statement.

Outside, as if the Gods were enjoying the joke as well, the rain suddenly stopped, the clouds cleared marginally, and a weak sun fought its way through the scud casting a wan light over the power station.

Katrina looked up at the sky and took it as a portend that what they were doing was right and blessed by higher powers.

CHAPTER SIXTEEN

I hadn't been on the ground in Cork for ten minutes before my mini went crazy in my pocket, and my cursing was cut off at the pass because Sandra and Indigo were experiencing the same thing.

"You called?" The Boss looked serious, his face undeniably screwed up with concern. You could always tell because his eyes seemed to be retreating from his scarred face.

"Get secure. Get Indigo and Sandra as fast as you can, please!" I looked over at them, motioned to the hangar and its big screen, and called to the Italian guard on the door.

"*Avrò bisogno di privacy, per favore, e del grande schermo.*"

"*Subito comandante.*" We moved to the hangar, the guards took up their positions at our backs, and I flicked the Boss up onto the big screen.

"What's got you in such a twist?" We had the sound turned down, but the vision was very clear and very, very big. I hoped no one coming into the hangar would be scorched by the Boss's scowl.

"We've just got news from Colombia and Bolivia. Someone has bombed their forests with nanites, and almost both entire countries are covered in sliver slime. As you would expect, they are outraged and very scared, and as both are members of Interpol, we were the first on their speed dial." Why, in the name of God, would anyone blitz either country? Sandra got it before I did.

"Opium. Coca. The women are going after the drug trade." The Boss nodded, his eyes as weary as ours, so he had been putting in the hours at whatever it was that he did now.

"And you've got a little local problem that may cause you some grief." Now he looked sober as if recovering from a three-day drunk. His eyes hooded, his head sunk on his broad shoulders, weariness all over his torso, and he leaned into the camera as if to keep the conversation confidential.

"The Irish government has made a formal request for all prisoners taken on Whiddy Island to be turned over to the nearest Garda unit, or failing that, Major O'Leary and his Team Three." I giggled. I couldn't help myself. This was a little unexpected and, indeed, would cause us some grief. The prisoners were by now warming cells in Israel, something we would not admit to anyone.

"Is that an order from you?"

"No. You know better than that. An official government-level request was made to the secretariat of Interpol. Right now, the secretariat has no information on who they are, where they are, or what they will be charged with. I'd like to keep it that way for as long as we can." I nodded. I should have known the Boss wouldn't sell us short, so I put my thinking cap on.

"What was the premise on which we got our original permission to operate in Ireland?" His eyes pulled in, his gaze starting to really send out some power, a sure sign his mind was in high gear.

"The identification of potential nuclear-capable shells and radioactive material."

"That applied to the underground site we identified at Pollatomish. What about this time?"

"Same premise."

"Then we should be fine. The situation is identical to that we found in Point Roberts-long term employees engaged before the terrorist attacks, therefore assuming knowledge of the same, with the added bonus of a secret facility from which the drone that attacked the Navy G4 with Sandra and me on board was launched. Additional evidence of nanomachines and mercenary terrorists, the last of which we killed just an hour or so ago." He nodded, not yet having received our after-action report, as I hadn't written it yet. Maybe I could delegate that to Sandra. Sometimes you got the donut, sometimes the hole!

"Have you found the trust accounts that are supporting their efforts in Ireland?"

"Only the one so far, which we closed down a month or so ago. The geeks are on it as we speak." He nodded. He knew how good our geeks were, having worked with them personally during the first two phases of this rolling clusterfuck. I could feel myself getting irritated just because a Government wanted our prisoners, and it wasn't as if I didn't want to share, they were ours, and we had shed blood getting them. But this confirmed my instincts about Ireland. Something was afoot, but lacking any hard evidence, I would have to clean up here in Cork, get everyone home, and leave it in the capable hands of the major and whomever the government sent to reinforce him.

And I needed to keep a quiet, watchful eye on Ireland, and I had an idea how to manage that.

"What does your gut tell you?

"Never to wear red on Sundays, and always wash my hands. You can't go by my gut. It's too screwed up at this point. I'll clean up here, get back to Venice, and maybe visit Arie and Amira. Thanks for the heads-up." His face faded from the screen, and Indigo turned to me with a very solemn look on his face.

"You can't give the prisoners back."

"No. Not under any circumstances. The Terrorist Laws trump any political bent they want to use. The UN saw to that when they amended them in 2022. In fact, I wouldn't be surprised if the potential of political interference wasn't the reason they were modified as much as they were." He nodded.

"I agree, commander, so how do you want us to handle it?"

There was that magic 'us' again, reminding me I had an excellent team around me, all willing to share the lumps as well as the bouquets. Not that we ever got any!

"Pack us up, get us on the way home. I'll give you the final destination airborne. I need to connect with Amira, then Tom, then with our friend, the head monk. Sandra and I will set up camp near the door. Just one question."

"*Sì?*"

"Do we still have an overwatch at the tower?" He nodded once, his eyes glistening with intensity. He answered in English, a sure sign he was either pissed or very serious.

"Of course, which is why you are curious about it having been moved back to Whiddy Island." My turn to nod.

"Yes. I really want to know who called that off." Now looking serious, he cranked his head to one side and scratched the back of his neck.

"I'll find out."

"Thank you." Sandra and I walked to the end of the massive hangar, settled down just inside the stacked doors on our squeaky metal chairs, and opened the thermos of coffee we had been given on our way down. My blood ran cold from the shriek of the chair on the floor, so I sat without further ado and pulled out my mini. Sandra had managed to sandwich me between herself and the stacked doors, a classic close-protection move. I let it go. I was too tired to worry about it now.

"Amira, hello, how are you?" She looked pretty in her lab coat, she had swept her hair up into some sort of knot on the top of her head, and she had her sleeves rolled up like a manual laborer. Her pretty face was covered with a blue medical mask, goggles, and a clear face shield. She held up one hand, moved away, towing her mini, then plunked it down on a desk. The camera showed us a lovely view of her lab and someone's backside.

"Apologies, we are working around the clock at the moment, trying to keep up with you and all the things you sent us." Her smile told me she was happy about that, but I worried about her work habits. It seemed everyone in my orbit was running themselves into the ground on this case, and I needed to get on top of it before someone fell over.

"No need to apologize. Have you got anything for us yet?" She positively glowed, her excitement palpable.

"Yes. Watch this." She picked up a heavy glove, selected a small container, moved to an area where one of the original nuclear-capable shells lay, and poured the contents over the bimetallic torpedo. The front section dissolved before our eyes, and a puddle of what looked like water formed under the remnants of the shell.

"So we have nanites that will seal the shells, and now we have ones that will dissolve them?"

"Yes. Isn't that fantastic?" She literally started to bounce up and down.

"I guess so. What else have you established?" She looked straight into the camera, surprise all over her face as if to say, 'isn't that enough?' She pulled herself back from her emotive state, looked serious, and suddenly we were looking at a young genius unsure of herself. Flutters of uncertainty ran behind her eyes, and she waved her hair away in response.

"There were three color codes on the containers, the nanites that dissolve the bimetallic material is colored black. We have fifteen of them tucked away. The green-tagged containers, of which we only have twelve, are a 'starter' for manufacturing biofuel. If you remember, when you first interrogated me, I mentioned we had developed this in the lab, but not at scale and not like this. Someone on their team has the chops to make this realizable. They would be a world-class biochemist as a starter. I calculate one container will produce five hundred and fifty-five thousand US gallons of biofuel. And we will be able to replicate this specific nanite here in Israel." Before the attacks, I knew that only about two percent of aircraft and five percent of vehicles had been converted to run on biofuel. If we were talking about the same thing.

Electric vehicles were the order of the day, and in the three years following the 2022 COP meeting in Sharm el-Sheika, Egypt, the number of EVs being built and sold worldwide had doubled every year. The issue now was how to power the charging stations. Those with panels were marginally okay, depending on how many sunny days they experienced. But with no local power being generated, any charging station connected to the grid was as good as useless.

Biofuel was a complimentary product for EVs, not a replacement, and from what little I knew about the production process, you had to grow a lot of specific flowers or vegetables to make it worthwhile, and I wondered at this point in time where this might be happening, if at all. And how much time it would take to produce at scale.

"And the green container?" She looked at me quizzically, my question bringing her back into focus. She was with me, but I could see that a part of her mind was somewhere else. Then she did something I had never seen her do before. She pulled at her hair with both hands, then slowly stopped pulling and started to stroke it. She looked glassy-eyed, as if drugged, and I really started to worry about her. Before I could even find the words to comment, she snapped back with a vengeance, sat straight up in her seat, and looked directly into the camera lens.

"I only know partially what it does. It boils water or any liquid you mix it with. It's like a fluid fire starter without the fire. I have absolutely no idea what it's for." The look on her face was one I would remember forever—stoic resentment at not knowing something about her precious nanites! So this is how a genius handles not knowing everything. I swallowed my laughter, forced a mild look of concern onto my face, and was about to ask a question when Sandra cut across me.

"Had you done any similar work back at Harvey Mudd?" Amira looked flustered, then shook her head.

"No, nothing like it. It's a marvelous process to watch. The nanites don't dissolve, they don't seem to feed off the water, they just heat it up so it boils away."

"How does that work given the Laws of Thermodynamics?" I looked at Sandra with new respect.

"Well, there is an exchange of energy, the water boils off, but the remaining nanites are exactly the same as the ones that started the boil, so perhaps it's a one-dimensional process, with the energy balance in the water. Or the nanites are eating some-thing in the water and refreshing themselves."

"Okay, thanks." Sandra pulled her head out of my lap, let-ting me face Amira again on the screen. I decided to change the subject, picking on something I thought I understood.

"Are the shells from the Island different from the ones we took off the boat and the terrorists?" Amira suddenly smiled, all the worry she had just shown thrown away with a wave of her hand.

"The shells-yes, same construction materials wise, but very different functionality. If they were loaded, then sealed, they could be exploded using some sort of charge. And they are designed to hold fifty kilos of nuclear material, so you're going to get a lot more bang for your buck!" She actually looked happy, but my gut shrank to the size of a pea and bounced up and down on my stomach, where my ulcer would soon grow. This was not good news. For starters, we didn't know how many shells had been fabricated. Were there still some hidden away, just waiting for an opportunity to be used? Somehow, I had to get that information from one of our prisoners, and fast.

"Thanks, Amira. Keep in contact, please. Let us know the moment you find anything else out." I canceled the call and dialed up Tom.

"Yo from the bowels of Ireland!"

"Yo back at you, how are things, Tom? Any sign of that miss-ing shell?"

"Well, we've found what might be the shell, according to our scanner, but it doesn't look like any shell we've seen before."

"Explain."

"Well, look here," and the camera went fuzzy, then focused on a pile of material I couldn't identify. A hand scanner moved into the frame, and the indicator clearly showed the presence of copper, brass, and nanites, but the material looked nothing like a shell. Then I got it. It had been dissolved by the material from one of Amira's black canisters. Now we have even more questions. Who, how, and when? Just two days ago, our drones had identified a whole shell moving down the coast, then lost it completely for a day. Maybe this was why. But that meant there were active terrorists in Tom's area, and he only had a small squad with him. Leave him in-situ; send reinforcements? Bring him home? Ask more questions? I went with the latter.

"Did you get any details from the teams that picked up the other four shells?"

"Yes, almost identical details. Squad of four old Irish men, all carrying shotguns, and very surprised to see us. The shells had gone to ground, as it were, and the old men were keeping guard. No shots were fired, they surrendered after a flash bang or two, all are in custody, and all claim they were waiting for further instructions. No idea from where. They all had small burst receivers. We've confiscated them and have them being monitored."

"Who has the receivers?"

"Interpol France, and the UK. The shells, by agreement, were sent to Israel. Even the French wanted them gone with little or no fuss. The Spanish were a little harder to deal with, but eventually, they saw the light."

"Bob's team did a good job."

"First class. He and his team are holding in Paris, waiting on your orders." I thought about that. Where would he and his team be of most use? The obvious answer was wherever the shells were, and I didn't have the first clue about that. And from the looks of it, Tom's team was also now available.

"Tom, wait where you are. I'll have you picked up. Good work appreciated." I immediately dialed Indigo.

"Yes, commander?" His background was flickering, with falling rain and strobing background, so he was on the move.

"Indigo, did we find anything that looked like the production facilities for the shells we found previously, specifically Afghanistan?"

"No. The plant here, as far as we can judge, is making the nanites in the containers, power packs, and panels." I nodded to myself. Sandra elbowed me in the ribs, so I turned the mini so she could see Indigo.

"Hi! Question: we've cleaned up three production sites, including one here in Ireland. Did they all look the same in terms of hardware?" He turned his head up as if looking for inspiration in the dark clouds that seemed to be getting lower and lower.

"Sandra, the only difference in the three production sites was how they managed their seawater intake and effluent. If you remember, Afghanistan brought it in by trucks, used big tanks in-situ, then let it run out into the desert. The other two sites used a dual pipe system direct to the ocean."

"Yes, I remember that. Thanks, Indigo." And she sat back in her little metal seat, looking like the cat that just ate the mouse.

I ignored her for the moment and concentrated on my mental list of things I had yet to do. My gut told me Ireland was key going forward, whatever that looked like. I needed some-place well set up and quiet to work it all out.

"Indigo, please add collecting Bob and Tom's team to your long list of things to arrange. He'll have samples for Israel, and if I asked you where we should set up for a while to work things out, where would you point me?" He laughed right from the belly. It cheered me up just looking at him.

"Why, back home, of course. We're only a few hours away from here, and I will have my espresso machines!" I smiled. He was right, and not just about the coffee.

"Fallo così, Indigo, riportaci tutti a casa."

POWER TO THE PEOPLE

The little red LED started flickering, and even though the box was sitting on Moriah's kitchen table, she didn't see it for around five minutes. Then she did and panicked. Were the women in trouble? Then she remembered that the signal was simply to get her to collect them from wherever they were.

Next problem, where were the four women? Tossing her keys back and forth in her hands, now somewhat stained from the varnishing she had been doing, she went down the twenty flights of stairs without effort, not giving the elevators a single thought—they had been out of action now for over three months. If you had to choose between the comfort of an automatic lift between floors versus a hot meal, the hot meal would win out every time.

She hit the basement floor running, waving to Jason as she unplugged the truck.

"Hurry up, we have to find the women and get them to the field." Jason dropped what he had been doing-he had been repairing a broken table for the apartment next door, grabbed his satchel, and jumped into the vehicle.

"The boys tell me they moved to the electricity plant." She turned to look at him as she drove out the old wooden doors, her brow furrowed.

"Sharon dropped them off at the old shed?" Jason smiled to himself. His network of young boys and girls on the 'outside', as it were, gave him real-time intelligence on anything he wanted to know. And he made sure they were fed and could sleep in the basement any time they wanted.

"They moved to the plant soon after Sharon and I left them. They've been there these past three days." Moriah nodded to herself, remembering that one of the women had asked if she could go there, but with everything else happening, she had put it out of her mind.

Her truck was running better than it ever had, and Sharon and her team had made three trips down and back to collect more panels and power packs without having to recharge the batteries. She now had teams of men and women, supported by their children and friends, fitting the panels to all the row houses they could access. The building next door now had a full complement of panels on its roof and was within days of being able to house another seven hundred people.

Her little empire now numberd over three thousand and counting!

Everyone in her apartment who was fit and able was furiously helping to refurbish the apartments next door, rebuild furniture, and scavenge fixtures and fittings. The look on the faces of the families who had volunteered to move in once it was finished was one of hope, with a little suspicion thrown in due to past events. The damage to the housing and apartment blocks happened just a few days after the terrorist attacks. It was vicious, it had resulted in the deaths of hundreds, and it had soured the area for the past months. The gangs had now moved on or been crushed by the Garda and the military. But the wide-scale damage lived on and was a constant reminder that times had changed, and not necessarily for the better.

The truck skidded to a halt outside the massive metal gates of the power station, where a gaggle of young children sat on their haunches, dressed in dirty tracksuits and patched puffy jackets of various colors. One young girl, whom Moriah judged to be around nine or ten, stood and approached the truck.

"Hi ya, the lady who calls herself Katrina asked us to look out for ya, and happy to do that we were, given they looked after us."

"Did they know, and how might that be then?" The young girl smiled and pointed to a row of small green military-style tents rigged against the fence.

"They gave us those to live in and food. We might stay here forever!" Moriah laughed, knowing how precious food and shelter were during these darkest days.

"Well, that might be so, but if you want, I think you can come and live with the other children in our apartment. And we're just fitting out a new building, where you could probably have a whole floor to yourselves." The young girl smiled and hung her head. Moriah climbed out of the cab, walked to her, and embraced her in a huge hug. "You're not on your own now, little darling, and happy I am to be able to look after you and your friends." Just as she looked up from the hug, Katrina and the sisters walked out from the plant, carrying containers and backpacks.

Without a word, they threw all their luggage onto the truck, then stood looking at Moriah and the young girl. Moriah looked at them, smiled, let the little girl go, and then stood with her hands on her hips.

"Katrina, we'll be taking you and yours to the field, and then we'll come back and collect all these children you seem to have attracted, if that is alright with you." She looked over at the children who now stood, their backs to the wire fence. "You can all come with us in just a bit. We have a home for you. There are lots of other children for you to play with. Can you wait for us to come back, then?" As one, the children bunched together, seeking strength in their numbers. The one who had approached the truck suddenly moved a pace back, tucking her hands into her coat with a firmness that surprised Moriah. Before she could react, Katrina approached and whispered in her ear.

"Moriah, we'll wait for you. I think you need to take these children to your apartment first." Moriah nodded. The naked fear on the faces of the children told its own tale. Trust came hard when you were abandoned, lost your family, and left to your own devices amongst the wreckage of civilization, and you hadn't yet celebrated your tenth birthday!

"Aye, that we'll do, and I'm thanking ya for it. We've had plenty like them in these past months, and caring for them is a priority." She stood, then bent down so she could look the little girl directly in the eyes.

"Come with us now, then, all of you. Collect your tents, put them in the truck, and climb aboard. We'll take you all to your new home first, then come back for these lovely ladies." Ever so slowly, the children moved to the tents, packed them away, collected their meager belongings, and moved to the truck.

"You promise you'll look after us, all, then, at the one time? We'd not be wanting to split up, you see, and that's important." Before Moriah could reply, Katrina stepped to the girl and hugged her.

"As I told you all before, Moriah here is looking after the neighborhood, she'll look after you, and you can keep everything we gave you to share with others." Katrina's voice was warm, positive, and direct, and the children responded in kind. The three sisters, arms linked casually, looked on with smiles radiating their support.

"Okay then, we'll go with you, but you have to promise to keep us all together." Moriah, tears running down her face, nodded, then climbed into the cab. Some of the children crawled onto the flatbed, and Jason climbed out to make room for the others in the cab.

"I'll stay with our visitors." Moriah just nodded and drove slowly away, torn by the opportunity to get more precious children off the streets and with the growing concern about how she would look after them. They now had nearly three hundred parentless children in the apartment, some being looked after by existing families, some by caring adults. It was a constant problem that she had just added to, without a solution in mind. And as strange as it may seem, the elder children in the building had created a formidable resource in looking after the 'littles' as they were called, so perhaps this was a solution she could embrace.

Sharon met them at the apartment, Moriah explained what they needed to do, and within minutes the new arrivals were surrounded by a bunch of happy children, all welcoming them to their new home at the top of their voices. Moriah smiled as she drove back to the power plant. Somethings had never changed, and for that small miracle, she was grateful. She skidded to a stop again, and this time Jason and the women climbed into the cab.

"It's a fine and wonderful thing you've done, I'm thinking, and I thank ya for it." Moriah's voice was laced with tears, something Katrina noticed and appreciated. Sitting in the back seat, Lilian reached over and patted Moriah on the shoulder.

"They all just turned up on the first day, around noon, as polite as you like, asking if they could do a little work for us in return for some food. They had precious few belongings, so we gave them our tents and blankets and put them to work cleaning up the yard. We had plenty of food, and as you will soon find out, power to burn, so looking after them was easy. You'll do the hard yards now, I suspect, and we all love you for your commitment."

Moriah looked at the beautiful woman in the rearview mirror as she trundled along the gutted track. Piles of abandoned vehicles still dotted the roadside, and burnt-out houses littered the landscape.

"What do you mean, power to burn?" It was Else's turn to stroke Moriah's shoulder.

"What Lilian is saying is we're leaving you a control box that will allow you to provide power to your two buildings and progressively to all the row houses you fix up and repair and put panels on the roof of. You'll have to guard the box, and we suggest you feed the power out gradually so it's seen as a progressive thing, not all at once, and related to the panels." Moriah turned down the small road that led to the paddock that had been cleared for the helicopter, which waited like a patient black spider, rotors drooping as if tired from their previous flight.

"I'm a little confused. The panels and power packs, I understand, but what is this box you're talking about?" Katrina turned to face Moriah.

"We've got a plan in mind for you. We've left all the details with your professor. She'll be in contact. In the meantime, you have the beginnings for some industries now, things that will give people work and pride, and at the end of the day, hope. What with the metal recycling process, the rebuilding and refurnishing of the row houses, you'll soon find yourself the center of a bustling economy that will become the model for the rest of the world." Moriah sat back, engaged the handbrake, took her foot off the accelerator, and rested her head on the steering wheel. Her shoulders shook with a deep sigh, and she turned her head and looked straight at Katrina as if daring her to contradict her.

"A few weeks ago, I had a box to look after, and that gave me precious funds to use in our building. Then you come along with materials and money so everything can get bigger. I'm just a simple teacher at the university. What can I possibly do to model anything for the rest of the world?"

"You might be a teacher, but simple you're not. Look what you have achieved against the odds with your apartment—you're looking after thousands of people, directly and indirectly, and giving them hope every single day. All we're giving you is more tools so you can help more people. We treasure your skills, your compassion, and your heart. Here's the box; plug it into any outlet in your building, guard it with your life, and keep it a secret if you possibly can."

"Give it to Jason here. He'll know what to do with it. And I thank you for your kind words and I hope it's not a huge mistake you'll be making in putting such faith in the likes of me." The four women walked to the helicopter, mindful of Moriah and Jason standing by the truck. They turned and waved before boarding, then stepped into the massive cabin.

"You know, if we had more people like Moriah, we could manage this whole process so much faster and better." Katrina shook her head. "No, Else, she is one in a million, probably one in a billion, and as it has been throughout all of human history, it takes a crisis to flush out the really talented people who can and willingly do make a difference."

CHAPTER EIGHTEEN

If I had learned one thing working for the NCIS, it was that, in the main, in bureaucratic organizations, if you were on a task, you never got to hear about most of the important things surrounding what it was you were supposed to do. Something I immediately noticed was the exact opposite of working for Interpol. The context was everything, especially when you were chasing technologically superior and genius-level terrorists.

So when the news came through two hours into our flight back to Venice that Taiwan, Chile, Brazil, Ecuador, and seven states in Northern Africa had also been bombed with nanites, it came as no real surprise. Just the sheer scope and timing were a worry in itself. And every one of those countries, with the exception of the North African states and Taiwan, had speed-dialed Interpol for help.

So true to brief, the Boss had dispatched scientists from our European members, escorted by soldiers from each country, to prepare a report. We were essentially left out of it other than as a 'cc' for any information, as quite correctly, at this point, it was difficult to see any ongoing terrorist action once the opium and coca crops had been destroyed. With no oil or gas, the production of synthetic drugs would be a very hard task, and no doubt someone somewhere would reach into their deepest treasuries and find a way to make the raw materials, but that, as far as we were concerned at Section Five, was a problem for another day.

"It's the antithesis of the nanite that we developed for making biofuel. Nanite combines any organic material and converts it into energy-efficient combustible fuel with no carbon dioxide or other noxious residue. This nanite combines with the organic material and then destroys it, not unlike the bug that has eaten all our oil and gas." Amira's face turned serious for a second, and she swiped her hair away from her face. "Of course, I'm extrapolating here, as I haven't gotten a sample of the originating nanite yet."

"But you've worked all this out from your previous experimentation at Harvey Mudd?"

"Yes. And we got an early piece of a destroyed crop from Colombo, as well as a container we suspect, was used in propagating the destruction. Both had evidence of corrupted nanites."

"It wasn't airborne?"

"No. Like all the other versions of the nanites, it eats itself to dust when exposed to air—or, more correctly, oxygen."

"Explain how they poisoned the crops." My question came out more as a directive, and I shook my head in disgust. Here was the preeminent expert on nanites, and I was treating her like a common prisoner. "Amira, I apologize for my tone just now. Put it down to rudeness." At the other end of the call, she leaned back in her seat and smiled, looking all the while like a young teenager discussing her latest trip to the mall.

"You're forgiven, Jessica. I know the stress you're under. This was a low-level attack. I estimate no more than three terrorists per site, literally planting a canister of nanites somewhere, setting a timer, which we also have a sample of here, then departing for the next crop. We estimate one canister could propagate under the right weather conditions and destroy around one hundred thousand acres." Wow, big results for little effort. I wondered what order the terrorists had adopted because we had heard absolutely nothing about these attacks until yesterday, when the damage had been well and truly done.

"The timer we have was set for seventy-two hours, and the canister has a little mechanism that pops up out of the ground and starts the attack. It's an excellent piece of engineering, and I would suspect that it came from our Japanese friends. And the real worry is how innocuous this canister is."

How so?"

"It just looks like a local beer can." I shook my head in wonder.

"But this must have been carried out in the last two weeks?"

"I don't think so. If you allow for a lag between the attack, and the recognition of the attack, then the political response to the attack, you could add two weeks to the timeline and still be a week wrong. Safer to say within the last four to six weeks." I bent my head, tried to visualize what had been consuming our interest six weeks ago, and ran right up against the nuclear threat the terrorists had unleashed with Malik Badawi and Amir Abbas. Maybe that had been the entire point. We had always suspected that the shells were blind to get us looking the wrong way, and now maybe we could think about the wrong things as well.

But the bottom line was there were still terrorists out there, and we had to find them.

"Thanks, Amira. I want you to pack for a trip to Japan, I'll arrange it with Arie, and I'll have Nokomoto and Aikido meet you. Good work, stay safe." I thought for a minute, then dialed Nokomoto.

"Kon'nichiwa shirei-kan, watashitachi wa dono yō ni tasukete moraemasu ka?"

"Hello, Nokomoto. Lovely to see you again. I have a favor to ask." He bowed to the camera, his luxurious long black hair falling in a wave over his face, which he quickly wiped away with one manicured hand. His gray suit, impeccable as always, had a slight sheen to it from the light he had on in the background.

"We serve at your pleasure, commander. How can we help?"

"I'm sending you Amira Abramowitz, our resident nano expert." I paused.

"She'll have a companion, a colonel in the Israeli Army, and the best white hat I've met so far on this adventure of ours. I need you to let them loose inside Innomatchi, keep them safe, then send them home to me when they are ready."

His face had lit up, and the mention of Amira's name, and he positively glowed at the thought of meeting her in the flesh.

"It will be our pleasure, commander. When will she be here?" I thought about that, looked at my pink girlie watch my mother had given me, ran through the time zones and distance in my head, then took a stab in the dark. Before I could open my mouth to speak, Sandra leaned into the camera with a bouncy jiggle.

"Hi, Nokomoto, how's Aikido?" I sat back, outmaneuvered.

"She's fine, Sandra, running down some drug dealers as we speak. There's been a sudden uptick in shipments, so she and the locals are doing a little collecting of their own."

"We might know what's behind that, but I'll pass you back to Jessica." And she bounced back to her seat, leaving me staring at an expectant smiling face.

"Sorry for the interruption, but good help is really hard to find these days." He had the good grace to smile. Sandra just went into a full-on sulk. I left her to it.

"Let's say thirty hours, and we'll get them to text you when they're wheels up."

"Not a problem. Will this be a public visit?" I shook my head. The last thing I wanted was any public noise about what we were doing.

"Absolutely not. They'll be traveling as couriers, very low level, hopefully of no interest to anyone."

"I see. We will do our best on this end. Do they need any technical support?" I shook my head.

"Thanks, Nokomoto, they'll be fine on their own, and in fact, if you could, and I mean this literally, clear the entire plant a few hours before they arrive, that would be preferable." He looked serious for a moment, then dropped his head as he thought that through. Then he nodded slowly.

"We can make that happen. Is there anyone they will want to talk to?" My turn to think, my eyebrows scrunched up, telling me I was tired, the throbbing pain behind them a second-string warning.

"Good question. Let's leave it this way: if they do, they will tell you on the day, and you can work out how to manage that with a minimum of exposure."

"We can do that. Anything else I should know?" I looked at him in faraway Toyoko, clean-cut and immaculately dressed, his young face a mask of happiness, until you looked deeply into his eyes, which betrayed his experience and inner toughness. He was unquestionably suited for his role in Section Five.

"No, that's all for now. Give Aikido our regards, good hunting." I looked over at Sandra, now buried in her computer. I had an evil thought.

"Can you pack in a hurry?" She looked over at me, confusion in her eyes.

"Of course, I can. Why?"

"I want you in Japan with Amira and Shami." She seemed to think for a minute, then slowly nodded.

"I'll have to ask the Boss, then arrange a PPD for you with Indigo." I slumped my shoulders. Here we go again with this personal protection thing.

"I'll talk to the Boss, and I'll talk to Indigo. You start planning all the things we need to find out in that factory." She grimaced, looked back down at her computer, then at me out of the side of her eyes.

"Promise?" I nearly reached over and cuffed her ears, then realized I was just being anal, so smiled and nodded.

"You can listen in." And I dialed the Boss, told him what I wanted to do, got him to release Sandra, temporarily as he put it, then we had a short chat about the destruction of the coco and opium fields. Then we hung up, and I sat back in my seat with my eyes closed. The whole Irish thing was worrying me, particularly the part where they wanted our prisoners back. There was no polite way to manage that situation, and I wondered just how long before our Irish major and his Team Three of the *Sciathán Fianóglach* would remain on task.

"You know, all the Irish Government has to do is tell Interpol they're satisfied we have met our obligations, secure the nuclear threat, and we'd be done."

"There's more to it than that. That plant was producing power panels and nanites, those shells had to have come from somewhere, and we know Pollatomish was set up to manufacture them. Possession alone makes them subject to the Terrorist Laws. And remember what Amira told us was in those containers. That makes Ireland a primary site for us, and no one could argue that." Her stubborn look made me proud, but the fact was we worked at the pleasure of our member countries. When they wanted us, they yelled; when they didn't, the quiet could snap-freeze a lake.

We had prima facie evidence that the terrorists had bedded down in Ireland. What we didn't have was evidence of government involvement-if you discounted our intuition that the government had at least two of the women terrorists very close to the president.

"Have you had a chance to research the history of Ireland, specifically its political leanings?"

"Yes, I've got a report for you. I'll send it to your mini."

"Give me the high points." She bent her head and turned to look at me sideways. I could see her building her case behind her eyes, which were sparkling in the light, flitting across the aircraft window.

"Well, for the last three thousand years or so, anyone who had a boat or a canoe basically invaded Ireland for one reason or another. It's the most invaded country in the whole of Europe. Bottom line, the biggest export is its young people, the biggest political event, the 'Troubles', as they were euphemistically called, and right now, the country is caught between the technology crunch and the need for agriculture and food.

"You've got two Heads of State – Northern Island still recognizes the English monarch; Ireland has its own President, who we have met. However, one thing we may be able to use, both North and South are governed by their local Prime Ministers – known as the Taoiseach, who are elected by the populace.

"We received our mandate from the PMs on behalf of the whole country. It was the Northern Ireland Taoiseach who gave us the major and his team on behalf of the whole of Ireland."

"So the President might be an outlier in political terms. This could get interesting. I think I'll just flick all this to the Boss, and let him and Lyon sort it all out."

"Good idea. I got a headache just researching it. But the really fascinating thing is all the references to magic, fairies, and the like. The history books are full of it. Do you remember those stones we saw at Pollatomish? And the reverence our own brother Francis showed? Well, there's a huge volume of information on the stone dances and their role in Irish legends. It's very powerful stuff."

I couldn't help but smile, I remembered the warmth in the stones on a cold rainy night only too well, but I had put it down to some sort of local weather-related event-not magic. But they had been warm to the touch, and they had vibrated before the cruise missiles had impacted, so who knew?

"Any other fact you want to impart?" She looked bemused but took my pragmatism with good grace.

"Only to remind you that Major O'Leary's team came from Belfast. You might tuck that away for future reference." I nodded, and that might indeed become a critical conversation point with the government. I thought for a moment, bent my head in concentration.

"What would you do next if I wasn't sending you to Japan?" Her eyes blossomed, her whole face lit up, and she started bouncing on her seat.

"Oh boy! What would I do? Simple, really, go back and cuff those two arrogant women we met with the president, throw them into the deepest hole we have. Then I'd try to find out where all those panels were headed, I'll raze the drone hangar to the ground, then I'd get Indigo, Tom, and Bob to comb the entire Island for terrorists, and then…."

"I get the picture. You're still pissed about the drone attack." She looked over at me, a fierce expression on her face, her eyes thinned to slits.

"Yes, I am." I shook my head. Her plan was not a bad one. It just had a few edgy bits to it, like blowing things up and locking people away.

"You've convinced me. Pack your bag, get your bouncing backside to Japan, remember you are covert in transit, keep Amira and Shami safe, and find out everything about Innomatchi, especially the bits we are missing. Go back four years, track every delivery, get our geeks in Venice to back you up, and make us a map and a flight plan of everything they have done and where they have done it. Get photos, drawings, everything you can find to help us unravel this technological mess."

"Yes sir, ma'am, boss, Jessica, as you command!" and she threw me a sloppy salute and went back to her mini. I ignored her for the rest of the trip, preferring to put my thoughts together for what we would do next and how we would do it.

We landed at Tel Nof, dropped Sandra and the members of the 104 commando off, a lot of miscellaneous gear for the laboratory, refueled, then headed to Venice. My favorite master mariner whisked us back to our headquarters, and I only grimaced once as he bounced us across a wake from a small speed boat. I didn't kiss the stone steps when we drifted to a stop outside our headquarters, but only because I had an audience!

CHAPTER NINETEEN

The single dome of the nuclear power plant at Vandellòs, near the Coll de Balaguer pass in Catalonia, had lived peacefully with the locals for over half a century before it was attacked one night, its entire internal structure taken over by silver nanites. The nanites followed the path of the carbon dioxide cooling pipes all the way to the fissionable rods, now fused in place and rendered useless. While the plant had been closed and partially dismantled back in 1990, the working guts had been preserved due to their radioactivity. The whole site was planned to be razed in 2035.

A frantic effort had been made by the engineers to clear the scud, to no effect. In fact, if anything, they made it worse. After four tedious weeks, they and their management gave up and shuttered the plant again, leaving only a handful of security guards to roam the picturesque location. The outlier buildings, with their white-washed walls and tile roofs, looked like massive hotels but were now just empty offices with a spectacular view of the Balearic Sea as it ebbed and flowed against the sea wall and the rocky foreshore.

The sisters, holding hands, stood with their bare feet in the warm water, looking at an edifice of modern technology that had failed so spectacularly and now was so outdated as to be irrelevant. Katrina sat on the rocks, pouring coffee into three silver mugs.

"Will it work?" she asked, pausing to scan the beach. A few isolated fisher folks were casting long rods into the small surf, some just standing idly by waiting for a bite. She wondered what type of fish they might catch and if this might be the camouflage they needed to be successful. Lilian turned to look at her.

"That wall provides a cover for the cooling pond, which in this case is seawater. Originally this plant was cooled by gas, not water. The pond was their backup in case of failure, so we could go in direct from there to connect to the generators. We need to know their condition."

"This was a plant designed back in the fifties, so the generators will be very big, I and I suggest very robust. They may or may not have been maintained, but we only need one for our purpose. Else, we'll get you inside so you can scope out the possibilities, and Lily, you'll have to tell us where to situate the intake." She nodded, swinging her dainty feet through the small rippling surf. She had not felt so free and relaxed for months.

"Inside the breakwater wall would be the best, but Lilian will have to show us where." Katrina looked at the sisters, trying to imagine them living together as they had been for the past four months. Each radiated confidence and had a luster based on their superior skills, yet they didn't bounce off each other as you might expect with such highly talented people placed in close proximity to each other.

They genuinely seemed to be able to cooperate and not feel the need to compete, and she put that down to the way they had been brought up by their parents. It all started in the home. No matter what the influencers, talking heads, so-called experts, and social scientists tried to project into the nature/nurture argument. As far as she was concerned, nurture won out every time.

Yes, nature set the ball rolling, but as history has shown time and time again, if you didn't develop innate skills, they faded away like the early morning mist. And education and experience were the cornerstones of personal development. She shook her head, she had a task to complete, and while they were on the clock to some extent, she had allowed this pause in their routine because, after Ireland and the thrill of success, the sisters needed to decompress.

They were, each in their own way, brilliant yet slightly naive in their worldly experiences, and she felt a strong maternal instinct to look after them.

She lay back in the pebbly sand, watched a small bird fly across the horizon, smiled as a small wriggling fish shimmied and shook, trying to get itself off the hook in its mouth, and smiled.

Things were a long, long way from being better, but they had a start. And it had been a satisfying and powerful one to be a part of.

ALBA AN ÀIGH

Freya Gordon looked at the inbound TXT message on her satellite phone and grinned. Her daughters had completed their task in Ireland and had moved on to Spain. Their job would be far harder in Vandellòs because the power plant had been closed in the early nineties due to a fire that started in one of the turbines. It also used very old technology imported from France, in that its cooling process used carbon dioxide and not water. Perfect from her standpoint, it would make her daughter's task all that much easier.

And the terrorists had infected the radioactive parts of the machinery with nanites months ago, creating an impenetrable silver scum that effectively covered eighty percent of the guts of the nuclear power plant.

And in thinking about her daughters, she again thanked the Virgin Mary for her gift of three sparkling young girls twelve years ago from the refugee camps. They had arrived within a week of each other, each with their own horror story etched on their small faces, and dug deep into their souls. It had taken the best part of a year to enable them to not fear the dark, hide away food, and be prepared to run.

And trust their new parents.

Her husband of some twenty years took to the young girls as if they were his own, and until the time he died just a year ago, he had schooled his girls in everything they needed to know to survive in the modern world. Living in the Scottish highlands provided the perfect canvas, as did the indifferent weather, from freezing cold rain to baking hot and dry days when the sky was so blue as to defy description. He had also taught them to be self-sufficient, keen learners and readers, how to manage the digital world, and become critical thinkers, himself having been an engineer of repute who had adopted the digital age as willingly as he had adopted his daughters.

Unlike his daughters, he had known of his wife's association with 'Helen', the ex-Stasi German spymaster, and had contributed as much as he could to the development of the European arm of the organization. He had, on many occasions, asked himself why he would willingly help someone set up a network of homegrown spies throughout Europe and invade every Government and industrial database they could identify. And when 'Helen' had told him and Freya, over a whisky one cold winter's day, the fire smoldering in one corner, their shaggy arthritic wolfhound asleep on the hearth, of the grand plan to find loving homes for millions of young refugee parentless children at a time when the world would be ready to accept their responsibilities, he had cried.

Freya had been unable to conceive, their greatest disappointment in their union, and the promise of their own family, made just months before it occurred, was motive enough for him to have thrown his skills and talents into the pot that became the center of their world from that time on. And once the three parentless refugee girls had arrived, he had embraced them as his own and worked through the difficulties of belief and culture with a vengeance. And because they lived on a large property, assimilating the new family members into the community had been an easy affair, taken over years; and because of Freya's position on the local council and his as a digital professional, he was always ready to help any in need, where the girls had come from became moot.

Freya put the picture of her family, taken the day her baby, Lily, had graduated from Edinburgh University with honors, back on the mantle where it says proudly beside the older family photos taken when the other two girls had finished their formal schooling. A surge of pride filled her chest, and silent tears leaked across her flushed cheeks. She had been blessed with a family of smart girls, a loving husband, and a task so enervating she could not imagine doing anything else.

She thought about the timing of the next big step, a message in the clear to the American, European, and seventeen other countries that chose to house the environmental factories and coerced into receiving the refugee children being prepared even now for their bright futures.

Ireland was under control, two of her very best operatives we well placed to guarantee their planned outcome, and her mobile team had successfully run down the last remaining nuclear shell and disposed of it. Spain would soon know the possibilities and benefits of accepting the refugee children; America was already playing ball, with refugee centers well established in Helena and Roanoke and growing by the day; she was missing a ship in the Atlantic with over five thousand children on it, but she put that down to communication issues until she had learned that it had been sunk, by persons unknown. It had almost broken her heart, but as she had seven other ships already in transit to New Zealand and the United States, albeit some weeks away yet, her hope had been somewhat restored.

She knew 'Helen' had been captured, she was still inside some of the military databases in Europe, and she had an intelligence report prepared for her by her 'basement' of talented hackers-all local girls, all at the top of their skills, and all enjoying their daily venture into places previously secured against them. And they got paid for it extremely well, and there was no limit on where they could go in the hacking world, now that the internet had been crashed and working satellites so few and far between.

Why no limits? Because the crazy gray-haired lady upstairs had access to satellites and communication channels, a hacker could only dream of! So they roamed, hacked, and gathered the intelligence that was asked of them, with a few excursions off to the side, as it were, for personal pleasure and gain!

Freya turned towards the sound of a buzz, not unlike that of a honey bee seeking the next pollen store. She reached for an old-style satellite phone and turned it on, and smiled as the young face of one of her favorite persons swam into focus on the small screen..

"Crissy, how are you, my love?"

"I'm fine, Freya, all good at this end. Have you heard from Katrina?"

"Yes, they've left Ireland for Spain."

"Thanks. I've got some other news for you." Freya looked around her large secured workroom and made sure she was out of earshot of her girls, beavering away at their computers. "Yes, go ahead."

"I have a visitor. She just arrived and asked to speak to you." Freya racked her brains trying to think of who it could be, given her girls were either onsite in Spain, destroying nuclear power plants across Europe, or across the room from her in her basement.

"Put her on." And Crissy's face was replaced with one of a young woman, her hair scraggy and matted, her face bruised with dried blood streaking where tears had fallen, but her eyes, deep rich green with gold flecks at the edges, were sharp and intense, and a direct challenge to anyone looking at her.

"Siobhan! How are you, and what would ya be doing in Socotra?" The face on the small screen grimaced, then one long, delicate but incredibly dirty hand wiped a string of once blond hair from her battered face, feeding it behind one dirty ear.

"It's the only place I could get to safely from where I left Badawi."

"Are you hurt now, I'd be asking?"

"Only bruises and scrapes. I managed to steal a small boat, it's taken me weeks to get here, but I didn't know where else to go." Freya wondered at the grit and determination the girl must have had to make such a voyage by herself, then she remembered that while Siobhan had always presented as a socialite when building her cover in Ireland, she was one tough little girl when she had been pulled out of the camps some years ago. That toughness shone through the tiny screen now, and Freya thanked her God for small favors.

"And what would ya like to be doing now?" The image lengthened, until both Crissy, looking like she was at the beach, which she was, and Siobhan, in contrast, looking like she had just escaped from a flea market, were in focus.

"Get to Ireland, and start building my homes as I always intended." Freya nodded to herself. This had been Siobhan's passion from day one and the reason she had agreed to go with the terrorist two years ago as his consort to set up the blind they had perfected in the Mediterranean. Two terrorist organizations had been involved, but Siobhan's part had been to play the scientist, which of course she was, and develop the nuclear-capable shells in Afghanistan, and to do so publicly. Her role had ended badly after a plane crash in Libya when she had been able to escape the clutches of Malik Badawi.

"Well, that might have to wait a day or two, I'm thinking. Interpol has closed our plant on Whiddy Island and taken our girls into custody. The Irish government has asked for them back, but I don't see that happening anytime soon. We have the resources you need stacked in sheds, with several locations available to you, and your power plant is in boxes waiting for you at Killara Bay. Interpol also closed the plant at Pollatomish, we had finished there some time ago, as you know, but the terrorists had continued to use it and paid the price.

"On the good news side, my daughters and your Katrina have successfully set the test site up in Dundalk and are now in Spain." Siobhan nodded at this news. It was good to hear that their plans were still moving forward in spite of the multiple setbacks they had suffered at the hands of Interpol. She brushed at her hair again, this time a little nervously.

"Can you get me to Killara Bay, please?" Freya considered her options, it was a very long way by boat or helicopter, and her mobility assets were presently in Spain. Then she remembered where one of her electric planes still sat, worked through the timing in her mind, then nodded.

"Sure to be. I can do that. Give me three days, and I'll send a TXT with the details. In the meantime, I'd be thinking a good bath and a hot meal would be the very best things for ya." Siobhan smiled and nodded.

"Yes, it would. Bless you, Freya, and thank you." The picture went to black, and Freya snapped the phone closed, looking around at her other charges.

And thinking about the piece of luck that had delivered Siobhan safely to her doorstep, she started thinking about the message and its timing again. Now she had another piece of the puzzle in place.

A woman's work was never done!

CHAPTER TWENTY

The fact that Indigo had managed to sandwich two massive espresso machines into our main office was proof positive that we were all addicts, desperately in need of professional help. And I counted myself as possibly the most addicted of all.

I sat at my small desk, feet up on a box, looking at Fay as she worked through a report. It seemed that in our absence, every Interpol office around the world had sent us data on something or other, and now our people were sorting through it for information germane to our primary investigation.

I put my feet down, sighed, and dialed Ireland.

"Major, how goes it?" At the other end, his screen showed the drone hangar in the background, with soldiers walking through the frame, all looking very purposeful.

"Commander, it goes well. No sign of any more terrorists, and we have been joined by the fifth and sixth teams from the *Sciathán Fianóglach*. I remain in command."

"Good to hear. Any contact by the government?" He looked at me with a question in his eyes. He was too professional to give anything away.

"Directly, no commander, but my command center has received a high-level request to turn over all prisoners. I pointed out that would be impossible at the moment for tactical reasons, and they seemed happy with that response." I nodded. Not only was he smart, but apolitical as well, the very best position for us.

"Thank you, appreciated. If you get any more pressure, refer them directly to Lyon."

"Yes, ma'am. On another matter, a group of women has arrived at the lower dock, claiming to be managers of the environmental plant. I've had them held at the dock, awaiting your instructions."

"Do you have photo IDs?"

"Yes, ma'am, I'll send them to you immediately."

"Thank you, stay on the line." And a series of ID photos scrolled across my screen. I flicked them up to the big one on the wall by my feet. I smiled. It was always nice to have your instincts reaffirmed. The two women we had met with the Irish President were in the group.

"Turn them around, no civilians on the Island until further notice, the threat of terrorism, etc., etc., you know the story."

Yes, commander." And he left the screen, then realized what he had done, and stuck his head back into camera range.

"Apologies, still getting used to these little minis."

"No problem, major, stay safe." I thought for a minute this was an overt move by the president of Ireland, or at the very least, an overt move by the women terrorists. We would have to sort out which was which before we went too further. One real issue was that if the Irish did get their political knickers in a twist, and pulled the major and his teams, our only fallback as far as military support would be a UN Peace Keeping Force, and to be honest, I didn't know how that might play out in the halls of power.

Another one for the Boss and Lyon. But I forwarded the IDs to Fay with a request for a fast track and trace.

Before I could mull that one to death, Tom signaled he wanted a chat, so I stood, walked to the massive copper and brass espresso machine closest to me, ducked the hissing steam that suddenly spurted out of a long snout, refilled my mug, and motioned to Tom to walk with me. We got as far as the zig-zagging entrance before we were surrounded by four of Indigo's team, so we walked out into a bright early evening in Venice, pretending that all was right with our little world.

"What's up, Tom?"

"I've got a question for you. I didn't want to bring it up in the field." I looked at him, currently dressed in dull brown jeans and a longish leather coat, his scuffed parachute boots completing his simple ensemble. His hair was still wet from his shower, and the finger raking he had given it had left little furrows along his scalp. As he walked, his coat flapped open and shut in time with his cadence, and with each stride, the long gun he had strapped on poked its deadly nose out as if seeking a little fresh air. A small rusted badge sat comfortably on one lapel.

"Shoot!" I said with a smile, turning to sit on a bollard that still showed the effects of the blast we had suffered during an attack some time ago.

"My twenty is up in a week, and I was wondering if there might be a position I could apply for with Interpol." I looked at him, a warrior to the core, one who had my back multiple times in just the last three months, let alone the last six years. I detected a slight hesitation in his voice, so I paid him the respect he deserved and stood to face him.

"When you say 'Interpol,' you mean 'Section Five?'" He grimaced, shook his head from side to side.

"Busted!" I smiled and patted him on the shoulder. "I've seen how you recruited Sandra and Fay, so I wasn't sure if you wanted an old hand like myself." His tone was soft as if he were apologizing for even asking.

"Tom, I'll have you in a heartbeat. Who do you have to clear it with?" He looked slightly astonished at my enthusiasm, his eyes wide open in surprise.

"When I hand my papers in, because of my role in special forces, I have to submit details to the Military Oversight Committee if I want to work in an associated field." I rolled my shoulders, stretched my neck.

"Tom, I'll get the Boss to clear the way for you with the military. In fact, I'll call him now and tell him I want you full-time as my Milspec (Military specifications) advisor."

"You're serious?"

"Tom, with the Boss being promoted to his ultimate level of inefficiency, we lost our best field commander. I'm a good investigator, probably a little better than just good, and I dig the military side, but never to the extent that the Boss did. You would make my life so much easier if you were formally one of us. In fact, I'll even give you the Boss's little brown book!" He laughed, a deep rumbling sound that had our guards looking on, unsure of what was happening. I dialed the Boss.

"You again."

"Nice to see you, too." He grunted, leaning back in whatever chair he was sitting on. His background was blurred, which should have given me pause to think. But I was saved from embarrassing myself by a tiny prickle at the back of my neck.

"Can you talk?"

"No."

"Thanks." And I hung up, fed the mini back into my pants pocket.

"He's tied up. He'll call me back when he can. In the meantime, keep this to yourself, please, until the Boss and I have talked."

"Of course. And thanks, appreciate the opportunity." He turned and walked back into the office. I waited a little longer, enjoying the fresh air and sunshine, went back to my bollard, and sat. I was always fascinated by the myriad of personalities our little band of hard arses collected, from the trim but robust Indigo to the battery bunny *Just Call Me Sally*, and all the freaky talented geeks in the middle. And I supposed you had to include all the temporary duty people we encompassed, like Bob and his team, the head monk, Stefarino, the 104, the major and his teams, and if you put your mind to it, the list went on and on.

Food for thought. My mini buzzed in my pocket.

"Hope you're in a better mood."

"I am. Security Committee meeting, you should try one.

"No thanks. Tom wants to join us full-time in a week when his twenties is up." No hesitation, no prevarication, no Monday morning quarterbacking.

"Good. When he's free, send him to me, and I'll explain the ROI (Rules Of Engagement) to him. You might want to give him my little book." I laughed. It was a rare moment when the Boss couldn't read my mind.

"My thoughts exactly. Any more on the Irish situation?" He paused. I actually saw him think about how much to tell me. In the end, his stoic nature won out.

"Bad situation. The president has demanded the women back, and the two Taoiseach are neutral on the issue, so obviously, in the south, the President is not seen in a dictatorial role. However, he does have a lot of political and government pull, so we can expect more of the same. You're fine for now. This is still a government-level conversation."

"Are you aware that the two women we saw with the president and tagged as part of the terrorist group turned up on Whiddy Island?"

"No. What happened?"

"I had the major ship them back to the mainland. The terrorist threat, no civilians, you know, the drill. Sandra and I spotted them for what they were, and they recognized both of us. We could see it in their eyes and in their body language. Given we were with the president, we let it slide as it was his meeting."

"Did you get their names?"

"No. We weren't introduced."

"That's odd in itself."

"We thought so. Moving on, the major has three of his special teams working the Island now, any suggestions for what we do if they get pulled?" He looked at me as if I had just landed from Mars, then I realized he was teasing me with his 'shock, horror' face.

"They will not be pulled. Full stop." I thought about his statement and what it meant to me personally and to my team, who had shed blood clearing the Island and its surrounds.

"Thanks. I think." He smiled, thinking the same as I was—if they got pulled, we had a much bigger headache than losing control of the combat zone. I put that thought away for later, sensing he wanted to finish the conversation. "Okay, I'll send you Tom. You send me back a spec-ops master planner." And we simultaneously disconnected, a rare feat of cojoined thinking! I looked over at Tom.

"Better say your goodbyes, and see Indigo about getting to Lyon. The Boss will brief you, then your shabby arse belongs to me!" I smiled as I said it, but secretly this was a solution to one of my problems since taking over: in that, unlike the Boss, Pete, Tom even Indigo, I wasn't special forces trained, having worked my way up through the NCIS quagmire, then being purloined by the Boss. Was I good at directing the action? I liked to think so. But Tom would be better, faster, and more pointed if it came to that. Just as he turned on his heel, a huge grin splitting his face, my mini screamed at me again.

"Hello from geek land!" Malcolm's grin was infectious, and all the other geeks on the call shared his merriment. Left with no choice, I grinned back.

"And what makes you so happy today?"

He brushed his long blond surfer's hair from his face, kicked back in his seat, and pointed to the screen. "You remember we identified a location in Scotland as a locus for the burst transmissions?" That got me thinking, and I realized I had parked this data with a whole lot of other things when we had started our most recent hunt for the nuclear shells.

"Vaguely, yes."

"Well, Tom's team put two on the ground north and south of the transmission site, and guess what they've found?" I shook my head, I really had developed tunnel vision on this mission, and I had to do something before it blindsided us and hurt the people I was working with.

"Go."

"We've been able to plot the possible epicenter of the transmissions, and we have a whole lot of encrypted satellite phone calls which, when you hear them, will blow your mind."

"Give me the highlights."

"Contact with a team in Spain, a person identified as Katrina, contact with a 'Crissy' on a really small Island in the Arabian Sea called Socotra—off the coast of Somalia; and the cream on the cake-we've found the elusive Irish scientist, Siobhan O'Cleary."

"Where is she?"

"On the Island, Socotra. Just arrived, according to her, after a long boat trip. But that's only part of the news." I held my breath. Finding the Irish scientist was a huge weight off my mind, so I gestured to the screen for him to continue. She had completely disappeared during our hunt for Malik Badawi.

"There's some sort of test site in Dundalk just set up, no data as to what it is, and this Freya person seems to be controlling the traffic at this point, and she is arranging transport for our Irish terrorist back to Ireland, to a place called Killara Bay, on the North West coast. She-the woman called 'Freya'-said that the plant the Irish scientist wanted was waiting for her in boxes."

"So Ireland is in play, big time, I would suggest, even if we haven't a clue what they are doing."

"I think you're wrong there. Before you shut them down on Whiddy Island, we know they had made literally a million panels, and that means they have been at it for a while, and from the pictures you sent us, the panels are slightly different from those made in Point Roberts and New Zealand."

"How so?"

"These panels are shaped as if they are ready to be put onto an existing structure. And they are all the one color, suggesting a more pedestrian use than the others."

"You don't think they would have made houses and schools?"

"Not necessarily. I think—make that we geeks think—these are designed to go onto existing buildings, like houses, and a lot of them." I thought about that, and a comment from somewhere about a million houses being vacant in Ireland made a kind of sense, but what would the family unit look like?

In Helena and Roanoke, the terrorists had relied on existing displaced families taking children in as adoptees, using the houses they had built out of the panels as the bribe plus a cash stipend to support the children. It was a clever economic and powerful motivation because they promised education and benefits to other family members, as well as a very low-priced modern home. Just the work required to build the new homes and schools had created enough work for the majority of the people who had arrived in Helena to escape the brutal civil insurrection in the larger cities and towns.

Then there was the need for teachers, doctors, nurses, shopkeepers, furniture makers, and all the other support people who made up any viable community, and in a short period of time you had a new self-sufficient town established, with a strong survival instinct and a hard core of welcome child refugees at its center. In this respect, the terrorists had shown their true genius in understanding the motivations of the ordinary person. And the strength of the family unit.

"Thanks for that. Send your summary through. If you think of anything else, call me immediately." I dialed my favorite monk and was pleased to see him sitting in the sun under a colorful umbrella instead of his gloomy cavern under the ancient church.

"Stefarino, thank you for taking my call. It's good to see you outside." My smile must have transmitted across the video because he looked straight into my eyes and beamed at me. It was the only way I could describe it.

"Jessica, *ciao*, you look more refreshed than at our last call." I nodded.

"Yes, had a chance to rest, take a nap, plus the work your geeks keep coming up with makes my job a whole lot easier. I have another favor to ask." He nodded, sat back in his lounger, still beaming at me. It made me feel twelve years old again, being watched by my father as I played on a swing and the unreserved love that had flowed from him as he watched me. I shook my head to clear the memory.

"Stefarino, I need your brother Francis in the field again. It's a bit more complicated this time and might expose him to more risk." I turned my head.

"I have no alternative at this point that I can think of, and that's on me." He nodded and smiled, so I continued. By the time I had finished, his look had turned to one of concentration, and he sat forward with his arms resting on his legs, his hands in the folds of his gray Kāṣāya.

"Jessica, I see no problem here, and might I suggest we ask him to take one of his brothers along on the trip? It might make the whole task a little easier." It was my turn to look concerned.

"Are you sure? Risking two of your brethren is a lot to ask."

"On the contrary, splitting the task between two means we can cover more ground in less time. And I take it time is of the essence?" I nodded.

"Yes, unfortunately, we have precious little to go on, the women are years ahead of us, and the political situation in Ireland concerns me."

"Jessica, I'll call Brother Francis to get things moving for you. You have the latest summary from Malcom and his young friends?"

"Yes, thank you, I do. You have been a wonderful support from day one, and I can't thank you enough." He just smiled and sat back.

"No need to. Blessed be." I put my mini back in my pants pocket, thinking through all the moving parts. Section Five was a very sharp stick designed to poke the enemy in the eye, and I was starting to wonder if we were running out of enemies!

CHAPTER TWENTY ONE

Colonel Shami Borowitz, dressed in jeans and a tee shirt screaming "Rock'n'Roll Rocks' sat with his booted feet up on the seat in front of him, headphones secured to his ears and a murder mystery novel in his lap. Outside his window, half shuttered because of the late afternoon sun, the earth streamed by innocuously, some thousands of feet below. If he had been paying attention to the moving map display on the cabin wall, he would have seen that they were just crossing the coast of South Korea, sliding down the glide path to Osaka and its Itami International Airport.

Itami was renowned for having been a military base under both the Japanese and United States governments during and after World War II and got its name from a city in Hyogo Prefecture. However, modern Japan preferred to call it Osaka International Airport, while the aviation world recognized it by its official designation, 'ITM', reflecting its convoluted history.

On this occasion, little notice was paid to the sleek corporate jet as it landed perfectly, then taxied to a prearranged hangar on the commercial side of the airport, which swallowed the mid-sized jet like a whale snacking on baitfish. As the engines ran down, a protective guard made up of the *Tokushu Kyūshū Butai (SAT)*, the Japanese police equivalent of the military special forces formed up around the aircraft.

Standing tall and straight, in an immaculate dark black suit, crisp white collared shirt, and regimental tie (borrowed from the Boss some time ago), his shoes polished within an inch of their life, Section Five Head of Section Nokomoto Senji waited for the airstair to drop. His partner, a goth-dressed solid woman in long black boots, black webbed stockings, and her (today) long purple hair flowing across her shoulders like a waterfall, presented such a direct contrast many had, to their ultimate chagrin, underestimated both her intellect and her physical abilities. Aikido Namoki could easily have qualified smarts-wise as a refugee recruit for the women terrorists, if she had been a refugee, and if none of the three generations of her family whom she lived with hadn't killed the inquiring gaijin out of hand.

"Yōkoso, sandora san, taisa, misu amira, yatto o ai dekite totemo ureshīdesu." And he bowed fully from the waist, his arms held rigidly at his sides.

"Thank you, Nokomoto, Aikido, I'll stick to English if you don't mind, my Japanese leaves a lot to be desired." Sandra reached forward and took his hand, and Amira reached out with a huge smile and grasped Aikido.

"Aki do, yatto aete ureshī. Watashi wa anata no kami ga totemo sukidesu!" This earned her a sour look from Sandra.

"Show off!" They all laughed, and then Sandra noticed Shami standing back against the steps, so she turned and introduced him.

"Nokomoto, Aikido, this is Colonel Shami Borowitz, our Israeli geek genius." Both Japanese agents bowed again.

"Kon'nichiwa taisa, soshite yōkoso."

"Okay, all you linguists hold your tongues, Nokomoto, have you been briefed on what we need to do?" His sparkling eyes narrowed a fraction, as he turned to face Sandra.

"Yes, the commander has been explicit. We have emptied all the buildings and factories on the site. The area is being patrolled by the *Tokushu Kyūshū Butai* who you see here, and I have ID badges for you all that will allow you to both carry and use your weapons here in Japan. As you might know, owning or possessing a handgun is a capital crime here, punishable by up to fifteen years jail, or life if discharged in public."

"This says we are authorized to carry and use our firearms under the protection of the SAT?" Sandra turned the plastic ID over and saw her photo on the back. The impressive crest of the SAT dominated the reverse side.

"Yes."

"Do you need to know what we are carrying?"

"No. We trust you implicitly, and Interpol has a reputation that enables us to move and work freely as and when we need to. But I need to warn you—there is a strong chance you will get to use your weapons. The triads the terrorists got into bed with are a very powerful group, and so far we have been attacked three times in just the last month." Sandra looked at the tall Japanese agent with a somber look, remembering the background during one of their recent video calls.

The blood had been bright red, and plentiful, and the twisted and shattered bodies of the triad soldiers had made their mark on her memory.

"We'll be on our guard. On that note, to fully brief you, we have four Israeli special forces on the aircraft, they will stay with the pilot. Let's go." They climbed into a long shiny black car which she recognized as a modified Mercedes Benz, usually used for rock stars and Heads of State.

"Nice wheels, how long to the factory?"

"About ten minutes, traffic is very light, and the curfew the local government has in place doesn't expire for another three weeks. You will see many signs of civil unrest, but compared to other countries, our losses have been small. Our people proved to be our best defense, so things quietened down here faster than back in Toyoko." The urban landscape that streamed past the vehicle showed some wrecked vehicles, piled on the sidewalk, and some damaged buildings, but compared to what she had seen in Chicago, the damage here was minor.

"How have you managed the power situation?" He turned to face her, noticing that Amira was looking a little unhappy. He tucked that away for later.

"We get just under forty percent of our power from offshore wind farms and solar, another ten percent from hydrogen generation. We were already reducing our reliance on oil, coal, and gas, and our recycling is very efficient."

"So with industry shut down, you have enough to support the country?"

"Better than that. As of last week, thirty-five percent of our industry was back up and running. It's still a transportation and supply chain issue, but we have used electric rail for decades, so we are simply changing the way we do things. And yes, we have put our hand up for another environmental plant, even as we are on the original terrorist's list."

"Why do you think that was?" Amira asked, her voice soft, with a tinge of guilt that was impossible to miss. Nokomoto looked directly at her, smiled, and put his hand out to take one of hers.

"It's not your fault, Amira, your work was pure, what the terrorists did with it is shameful. We read your paper on biomass research conducted in North America, and our Toyoko University tried to adopt your science but was rebuffed by Harvey Mudd. You have nothing to answer for except being a brilliant scientist and having developed the best solution to petrochemical spills ever invented." His hand was warm in hers, and she smiled at the words, a heavy weight lifting from her shoulders. She still felt responsible, but there was a major player on the terrorist world stage telling her she wasn't to blame, and it cheered her.

"And to answer your question, Sandra, I suspect it's because of our existing population density. Getting little children refugees would help solve our diminishing population problem, but where to put them is still an issue. Having said that, our national Government has indicated to both the UN and the US that we will put our hand up for refugees. That conversation is going nowhere at present, as you would know any issue around the terrorists is red hot, and as usual, the social implications are lost in the rhetoric."

"It's a pity, if you look at the geopolitical world before the attacks, we still had wars, people being dispossessed, state fighting state. Now the world has nearly been brought to its collective knees, nothing has really changed, except the number of people being dispossessed has tripled, with more and more starving every day, and no one government putting their hand up to help."

"Exactly correct. I haven't seen how other countries are managing, but we have not had the massive migration you have had in the United States, and all across Europe. I wonder why it is?" Sandra gave him a hard look, her hands fisting at her sides. Then she broke into a huge smile, lightening the mood in the car.

"Easy to understand. Japan has a rigorous culture built around the family, and clans, generation after generation, and I would suggest more structured and solid than most other countries. Aikido, you still live with your parents?" She smiled and nodded, happy to be included in the conversation. All too often those around her took one look, saw the goth and the black, and formed the wrong opinion, and ignored her.

"*Hai!* Yes, my parents, their parents, and their parents, and some of the grandchildren as well; we have lived in our home for over one hundred and fifty years. It is hoped by my mother, at least, that when I find my life partner, we will move in with them, and take over the running and maintenance."

"She wants you to move in and do all the chores?" Everyone laughed, even the driver who had remained silent the whole trip.

"*Īe!* I mean no, not like that, but my parents will pass the ownership of our home to us, as theirs did to them so many years ago. From that point, the responsibility for looking after it and everyone's needs will be ours, and that is a great honor in Japan."

"And there you have your answer. The family is strong, the country is strong. We've seen the same dynamic in many of the Middle Eastern countries, where the family is the bedrock of the community. Not all, but some. The Western, and dare I say, the modern world has become too transitory, too mobile, too involved with things, status, the latest fad, and technology for technology's sake. Human values have been diminished, reduced to mathematical formulas and apps. Change everything as often as you can afford to, and you depreciate the perception of value. The migration we saw throughout Europe in the last thirty years has mainly been caused by war, politics, and greed."

"And the migration we saw after the terrorist attacks was based on fear, lack of identification with location, and the urge to find a better, calmer space that was perceived as safer. If people had stayed where they were and fought back, the problem would not have been so grave." Sandra nodded, accepting the last statement from Shami, whose country had also been built on the stability and roots of the family, under desperate conditions, given the constant attacks and shelling from across their borders.

"We're here. How do you want to manage this, Sandra?" She slung her bag over her shoulder, the fast access slot right next to her hand, putting her H&K just a few inches away.

"Amira and Shami are the principles, everyone else keeps them safe, no matter what, and we follow their lead. Questions?"

They exited the vehicle, ringed by the STA, and moved into the factory.

"Aikido will lead us. She debriefed all the senior staff when we took the factory over, and her team from Tekio Polytech compiled the dossier on where everything is, and what it does. Here, look at this floor diagram." He handed Sandra his mini, who immediately passed it to Amira.

"Apologies. I will send this to you all now." Amira handed back his mini, opened her own, and bent her head to study the detail. Her hair fell over her face in a cascade of highlights and ripples, something the tall Japanese agent appreciated, having had a secret crush on her since the first time he had seen her on the video screen.

"Okay, we need somewhere to sit and talk this out. Amira has the details for here. I'll dial up the Point Roberts plant data, Shami dial up the Afghanistan data, Nokomoto dial up the data from Whiddy Island, let's see how they differ." They walked into a large boardroom, hauntingly quiet and reeking of having been empty for some time, but in the Japanese tradition was spotlessly clean, even to the empty decanter and glasses on the long oak sideboard. The STA blocked the doorway, facing outward, leaving the group to their own devices.

It only took a few minutes for Amira to grasp the essentials from the excellent and detailed summary Aikido had prepared, and nodding her head, she played with her screen, then spun her mini around so everyone could see the small screen. Her excitement colored her voice, which was rich with energy and enthusiasm. Sandra relaxed, having feared Amira might melt-down during this visit. She still carried the scars from the terrorists bastardizing her work.

"Here's the big difference. This plant has produced the—I'll call them seedlings—for the nanomachines; think of it as a starter kit you would use for making a garden. In every instance, it has been left up to the individual off-site plant to develop their own versions. Point Roberts perfected the nanites for the solar panels and power packs and sent the data on how to do it to New Zealand. Afghanistan perfected the nanites for the melding of copper and brass; which was passed to three other locations, all of which we know, and have dealt with. Whiddy Island perfected at least three other types of nanites, and from the containers we received in Israel, they are for making biofuel, dissolving the bimetallic structures, and boiling fluids. They also shared all their data, so any site could have made any version- or in fact, can still make any version- should we let them. But the hardware would have to be supplied from here."

"So, to be clear, you're telling us that the plants we have still running, and the ones in boxes waiting to be built, can't manu-facture bimetallic shells?"

"Yes." Sandra looked down at her hands, which she had unconsciously linked to the tabletop. She turned her head to look at Amira out of the corner of her eye.

"What's the raw material they need to make the panels and power packs?" Sandra was not convinced and held her line with a tenacity that surprised both the Japanese agents. Shami just grinned, he had seen Sandra work up close before.

"Sea water, and sand. They're mining both as part of their extraction process." Sandra suddenly sat up, a gleam in her eye.

"We didn't find any nanites in the other plants that make biofuel or burn water, did we?" Amira shook her head. Aikido leaned across the table.

"Sandra, in my analysis I have linked the equipment manufactured here in Japan with what has been manufactured in every other plant. Point Roberts and New Zealand can only manufacture panels and power packs. While the nanite data has been shared with them, the equipment that would be needed to make the other nanites has not."

"So you're saying the nuclear-capable shells can't be manufactured in those countries?"

"No."

"Have we broken down a shipping list of the plant and equipment that was shipped to other countries?" Shami leaned forward, inserting himself physically into the conversation. A trick he had learned from years of competing with hard-nosed military types who looked down their noses at geeks, even if their military rank was colonel and they carried very big guns!

"Yes, we have, and the ship sets are identical, so you can expect Point Roberts and New Zealand to be replicated in terms of capacity and capability. Remembering, of course, you still have to build them, and then we need our science team to seed the sinter baths for the production of the nanites. And training in all the materials handling, etc., something our women friends have done exquisitely well."

"We're using the Army Corps of Engineers for the building, and Israel is responsible for the seeding." She hung her head again, in deep thought.

"There's something missing here, and I can't put my finger on it." Sandra looked down at her mini, schematics and data jerking and flowing across the small screen like a river turning at a series of rapids. Then the back of her mind released a thought half formed, which blossomed as she allowed it some freedom.

"Damn it! We've missed something. Give me five." And she stood and walked out into the corridor, and was immediately surrounded by the Japanese SAT, whom she acknowledged with a small smile and a wave. She dialed Jessica.

"*Kon'nichiwa.* Jessica, commander, sir, ma'am, I have a question for you."

"You can call me your highness, and your question had better be good." The smile on my face belied my tone of voice, but I could see that Sandra got the message. She had roused me out of a deep sleep, the deepest I had managed in a full week.

"Jessica, Your Highness, looking at all the data for the various plants, I think we have underestimated how many people they needed to set this all up."

"What do you mean?"

"We're looking at the schematics for all the known facilities, and if you take Point Roberts and New Zealand as the baseline, we know there was an engineer, a scientist, and a pilot supporting those plants. My question is how did the terrorists intend to build the other seventeen plants they had planned, who was going to set them up, and who would do all the training required?" She stopped me in my tracks. A very, very good question. We had always obsessed over how many refugee women terrorists there were, and we had identified a number because of their missing backgrounds. But if you just allocated two or three more people to each potential site, there were another thirty to fifty out there, and if you added in working roles as well the number could be in the hundreds. She saw the concern on my face and leaned into the camera.

"Not to add to your problems, we've always skirted around the command, control, and communications setup they may have or still may have, someone is making decisions for them, and controlling the troops on the ground."

"Explain." Even to my ear, I sounded like a rifle shot at a close distance. I smiled to take the heat out of my demand. Sandra, thinking herself immune to my mood swings, probably because of the distance between us, just relaxed back into her stance, pushed the mini slightly away from herself, and suddenly I could see the fully armed troops forming her background. She was, for all intents and purposes, in hostile territory, so I wound my anxiety down a few notches.

"Apologies. Didn't mean to snap at you." She just shrugged her shoulders as if it happened every day, which in truth, it probably did, flicked her hair back with one gloved hand, and tilted her head slightly to one side.

"Jessica, don't sweat it. But the C-three side worries me, because, in the last weeks, someone has successfully polluted the raw materials for drugs in several countries, set up some sort of test site in Ireland, and is now working in Spain, doing who knows what. Who's driving the train? Is it this 'Freya' person in Scotland? Is she even there? And who is this 'Katrina' that's suddenly popped up. And what's this Island, Socotra all about? And before you ask, Shami is the call."

"All good questions, and I have our people on all of them as we speak. Do me a favor. Get everything from that plant as fast as you can, and then get back here to Venice." The look she gave me was a mix of curiosity and concern, then she just nodded.

"WILCO." And she closed down the mini and walked back into the room.

"What did I miss?" She looked at Nokomoto, Shami, and Aikido in turn.

"We've got to the point where we think we know the questions, can we start looking through the plant for the answers?"

"Yes. Good idea, Jessica wants us back soonest. Aikido, lead on."

They started in the shipping area, and in minutes Shami had a list of every piece of equipment dispatched in the last three years. He dumped it onto a portable hard drive and waved the team on. The next stop was a manufacturing area, robots galore, massive machinery that Nokomoto identified as a Giga Press, a 3D additive printing machine, and a huge sinter bath where mono and bimetallic devices could be manufactured.

As they had all been shut down over a month ago, and left in the last position they had been when working, the feeling was that someone had thrown huge toys up in the air and let them fall randomly on the pristine factory floor. At some basic level, Sandra felt distressed by the sheer size of the layout.

"I wonder how many people they had working down here"

"Less than ten. The entire staff of this factory is only one hundred and thirty people." She shook her head in wonder, wondering what the staff were doing now that the factory had been shuttered.

It took another five hours to eyeball the rest of the factory, and as they piled back into the armored car Sandra wondered if their time had been well spent. She was reassured when Amira spoke for the first time in three hours.

"This has been good. Now I know what the machinery looks like that they have been making, and we know where they have sent everything to. The question remains whether or not we let the factory start up again." Nokomoto turned in his seat to look Amira in the eyes.

"Amira-san, it will be a question of how fast we can build new plants, where they are built, and where you wish to build even more. But there's more to this, as I suspect the good inspector Sandra here has realized." Sandra nodded her head. She had watched Nokomoto intently during the walk.

"Yes. Staffing a new environmental plant, training the staff, and providing technical support. I asked the commander for her input......." Her statement was cut off by a massive explosion, the car lifted up off the road and started to roll around its longitudinal axis, thumping on the roof at every rotation. Everyone in the vehicle, even those restrained by their seatbelts and expanding safety airbags flew around like rag dolls, until with a shuddering smash, the car came to rest on its side. Machine gun fire could be heard, but Sandra, deafened by the explosion, could only hear a muffled thump-thump-thump which she felt more than heard.

Blood ran down Nokomoto's face, his head, being closer to the roof because of his natural height, had hit it several times on the way around. His eyes were glassy, and Aikido threw her belt off and flung herself towards him. Because of the angle of the car, she fell into the corner, almost hitting Shami with her booted heels.

"Apologies Shami-san, excuse my rude manners." Shami, caught between Sandra and the sidewall, just grimaced. His airbag looked like a very badly dented balloon, with bright red streaks across its sagging front. Sandra released her seatbelt, and using her hands and feet to move between the seats, pulled her combat knife out and punctured the three airbags that obscured her movement. She worked her way towards Amira, who was sandwiched between three airbags and the sidewall.

"Are you okay?" Amira shook her head, trying to clear her ears, her hair flying all over her face, and her eyes narrowed. She was upset.

"Yes. Bruised where the seat belt caught me, my face hurts from the airbag, but otherwise, nothing broken." She wiggled her legs and arms as she spoke, then reached into her own boot, pulled out a wicked-looking knife, then attacked the airbags with a vengeance.

"Okay, take it easy, who's hurt?"

"Nokomoto is bleeding, his head is a mess, his eyes glazed. Might be shocked, might be a concussion." The perfect English which Aikido answered with alerted Sandra, who immediately drew a parallel with Indigo. She mentally pulled her head in as sharp raps cascaded across the underbelly of the vehicle, tracing a circular pattern. Then another resounding explosion shook the car back and forth drowned out everything else, and the woodpecker sound stopped.

"I think we stay where we are for the moment." Aikido was talking into a small handset, her tone demanding, her speech as rapid as the gunfire outside. She slammed the small transmitter shut with a snap that reverberated around the crowded but now silent interior of the car. " The SAT has taken casualties, but they think they will have it under control in a few minutes. We should all get ourselves on top of seats, ready for us to be turned upright." No sooner had she spoken that with a massive lurch and a piercing screech, the car rolled back onto its wheels, bouncing up and down as its massive weight settled. The back door opened with an explosive hiss, and a helmeted head filled the gap between the vehicle frame and the door.

Three handguns and an H&K 47 poked towards it until Aikido held both hands out over the helmet. "Don't fire. Friendly!" And she started a furious conversation in Japanese, with the helmet nodding and a muffled *'Hai'* filtering through the noise outside. The head disappeared, and Aikido motioned for them to exit. A ring of SAT troops had formed around the open door, and in the foreground, the smoking remains of a military vehicle hung lopsided on the side of the road. Spot fires burned unchecked, sending black curls of smoke up into the darkening sky.

A lone bird, species unknown, sat on the smoking and burned remains of a tree, its head twitching back and forward as if making an assessment of the battleground. Black-suited bodies lay skewed in all sorts of awkward poses, in some cases with huge holes in them, blood leaking from shattered limbs, with the odd military-dressed corpse breaking the monotony. The bird drew the only conclusion possible from its scan of the battlefield: it had been brutal, it had been fast, and it had been deadly. With a resounding screech, it took off from the polluted sky towards a rare patch of blue, happy to be away from the stench of burning flesh and rubber.

Sandra watched its departure with a grimace, her thoughts echoing the birds. It looked like thirty or forty bodies, weighed heavily in favor of the triad. She pushed her H&K back into her bag, looking around for Nokomoto. She saw him being stretchered back up the slight rise towards an armored personal carrier surrounded by SAT soldiers. She followed.

"Sandra-san, please go with the first vehicle, it will take you all to the airport. I'll stay with Nokomoto." Sandra bobbed her head in acknowledgment, gestured to Amira and Shami, who was covered in blood splatters, and started for the vehicle.

"Keep in contact, let us know Nokomoto's condition the moment you know it." She smiled and put her hand on the Japanese agent's shoulder. "You did well, thank you for that, *kore wa anata no seide wa arimasendeshita. Sayōnara.*"

All the way back to the airport, all Sandra could think of was who was responsible, and why they had attacked. They really needed to uncover who was running the terrorist end of things, and she felt in her bruised and battered bones they needed to do it quickly.

DISCOVERY

This time, when brother Francis set sail in his well-worn and often patched Kāṣāya brown robe, he had a partner. A young Jesuit priest who had volunteered to teach in the wilds of Ireland as part of his mission from God. In contrast to the monk, he was young, which caused him to draw looks from bystanders who wondered about the child-like priest.

His newish patent leather black shoes lasted a whole kilometer before he begged the monk's forgiveness, requested a quick stop, and replaced them with a pair of bright red and white high-tops. The incessant drizzle managed to wet him from top to bottom, get under his hat and down his neck, and now, thanks to his shoes, his socks were saturated. Standing alongside, Father Francis smiled at the young man and waved his hand to encompass the bright green landscape, the rolling mist-covered hills, the tilted and narrow muddy road, and the imposing gray and black clouds that swirled so low overhead you almost felt you had to duck.

"Not to worry, my boy, this be the slightest of it, for sure, best you put on that raincoat I saw you pack, this weather is just teasing us, I'm certain!" He laughed, from deep in his belly, reaching out to help the saturated priest up.

"Brother, how far did you say we have to go on foot?" His imploring look reminded the monk that the younger generation had expectations very different from his own—not necessarily better or worse for that matter, but different. And at best, he judged this thin young man to be in his very early twenties.

"Think of all that wonderful music you used to make, look at our glorious Ireland, and make the music in your heart bring the landscape to life!" The young priest smiled, shook some water off his hat, wiped his eyes with one muddy hand, rolled his shoulders, and shook his pack into a more comfortable position..

"Playing in the Opera house is a far cry from walking the muddy lanes of Ireland, but I take your meaning, and I'll do my best." He started walking again, his high-tops sloshing through the mud, making a little sucking sound every time his foot lifted. When he looked down, he could see little fairy lights flickering from pool to pool, as the clouds allowed faint beams of sunlight to work their way through the crud. He was still young enough to find the flickering amusing, and it lifted his sodden spirits.

They were picked up an hour later by a farmer on his way to barter his rolled hay for vegetables, by which time the priest was so sodden that he felt embarrassed to climb into the warm cab.

"Aye, lad, don't you be worrying about wetting the seat. It's been sat on by much worse than you be, of that I can tell ya!" An empty pipe stuck in one corner of his mouth, the ruddy-tanned face of the farmer had crinkles in the corner of his eyes, which never seemed to stop smiling. With one hand on the wheel and the other on a battered wooden knob on top of the gear shift, his faded overalls managed to hold in a prodigious girth, some of which seemed intent on escaping out the sides at any moment. The monk, pressed against the side of the door, watched the interaction closely. If the lad was to make his mark in Ireland, empathy with the locals was imperative. The obvious religious symbology of his collar would get him so far, but his understanding of the emotions, hopes, dreams, and everyday frustrations of the locals would enable him to cement his place wherever he decided to settle.

"Ron, it's a true friend you are to be picking us up on a day like this, and I thank ya for it." Then the farmer just nodded, the gleam in his eyes intensifying.

"Brother Francis, ya sister would have my arse in her wringer if I were to have left ya on the roadside, and well, ya know it."

Francis nodded, his sister being the fierce member of his family, not known for her easy temperament, and it had been three decades or more that Ron and she had dallied around each other in an on-again, off-again relationship that strained the good nature of everyone around them.

"And when will ya finally be marrying her, I'd be asking, for we need ya to take her off our hands." Bob laughed again, poked at the priest with his pipe.

"Ya see what ya getting yerself into; a man can't even stop for a cup of tea before someone tries to marry him off!" Francis chuckled, trying to get comfortable with the window winder and door latch digging him in the ribs, every time the truck hit a rut in the track, which was often.

"If ya been mooning around me sister, for nigh on thirty years coming in for a cup of tea, then ya need ya head read, ya git!" They both laughed, enjoying the joke. The truth was that Bob spent all his waking hours in the small shed out the back of Francis's family home, tending to his sister, who had been confined to her bed since the age of just fifteen, having broken her back in a fall from her horse. While she had a wheel chair, the farm was such that getting anywhere was a real effort, and Bob had found his place in the world when he volunteered to look after the pretty young girl.

He earned his keep by working the local farms as a general hand, driving the truck whenever needed, and spending all this other time 'romancing', as he called it, with Francis's sister. He had never moved in, in spite of being invited more times than Francis could remember, and he had never missed a day, something Francis was deeply appreciative of.

The young Jesuit knew nothing of this, of course, and was left wondering why relationships in Ireland seemed so strange. Before he could expand on this thought, the truck lurched to a stop. Francis opened the door and pulled him back onto the dirt track.

"Thank ya Bob. Give my regards to the family. See ya in a couple of weeks." Bob waved, shunted the truck into gear with a lovely meshing, grinding sound, and drove off.

"He's been doing that for years. It's a wonder the truck still has the wherewithal to run!" The Jesuit looked around at the small village, low row houses, and three tall apartment buildings jammed against the sea wall. The ocean, a filthy gray, was venting its anger on the bricks and concrete in massive explosions of spray, each flooding the road without shame, the water draining back into the ocean through slits in the wall. The entire circle of the explosion, spray, and then the rushing water seeking its home created a percussion-like rhythm, and the Jesuit found himself humming a tune in his head. Here was what he was searching for—the power and music of nature—and for the first time since arriving earlier in the day by boat, he started to feel comfortable.

"Why are we here, brother Francis?" he asked, keeping his rucksack well away from the flooding water. Francis gave him a sharp look and turned his head to look around where they had stepped off, making sure no one was in earshot.

"As I told you before we set out, my mission is to look and see, listen and feel, and get an impression of what has changed and how our people are adjusting to the new way of things. Your mission is to meet the people and find your place." The Jesuit nodded. He knew he had searched. Education was his task. It was in fact the whole point of his Order, and he felt that he would know where he was most wanted when the time was right.

The worn sign by the side of the road said *'Fáilte go Dún Dealgan'*, the once white letters now faded, and the sign was somewhat bent around the edges. The monk started to walk towards the tall buildings, grateful the scud had run away for once, leaving a soft but chilly feel to the air, with the moon trying its best to push itself up from the horizon.

The little church stood proud, its pointed spite reaching up into the gloomy heavens as if in search of the light. A single light bulb illuminated the portico over the massive wooden doors, on which was fixed an ancient, corroded brass cross, split down the middle to accommodate getting in and out of the church. Before they could knock on the door, one side opened with a creak, and a bent figure in a long, dark hassock hobbled out, his hand raised in welcome.

"Brother Francis, blessed be, I could hardly believe my eyes when I saw you get out of that truck. Would you be well now and share a cup of tea with me?"

"Father O'Halloran, a pleasure it is to see you again, and of course we'll spill over a cup of tea with you, as it's your very self I've come to see." He reached forward and hugged the priest, and was pleased to feel some strength.

"And who is your young companion?" The old man's face lit up, his eyes shone, and his smile was all but swallowing his face. He reached out with two arthritic, bent hands to welcome the young Jesuit. He pumped his arms up and down, getting a huge smile in acknowledgement.

"Father, I'm Paul Ryan, and I'm on a mission to find my place in the new world, where I can do the most good."

"And what would you be doing, if you don't mind me asking?" The young Jesuit smiled again, claiming back his hands.

"My order is dedicated to providing teachers to those areas of the world where education is hard to find, hard to get, or just missing from the importance of people's minds. I'm tasked with finding a parish here in Ireland where I can set up a school and provide the stimulus for young minds so they can build our future." The old man nodded, thinking of his church's attitude to teaching, and found himself hoping this bright young man could find his calling.

"And that would be an excellent thing, I'm thinking, in these twisted times. Maybe you should go on a ways and find where all the young people congregate these days. But first, I have a lot of questions for both of you. Help me set up for a good, nice, strong cup of tea."

And strong it turned out to be, as the old priest poured three fingers into each cup from a bottle that looked older than he was.

"You won't want sugar or milk. My special brew takes care of all that." And he rose his cup up in salute and drank heavily as if starved. "Now, Francis, me boy, what's happening out there in the big wide world? We get precious little information down here. It's as if someone cut off the telephone lines." Francis smiled. In truth, that was exactly what the terrorists had done, if only in a far more radical manner.

"Paul, if you remember from my last visit, the internet has been turned off. Most computers don't work, so we have to rely on old-style copper wire and handsets. But the problem there, you see, is there's no switchboard nearby, and the local government can't connect you or anyone for that matter outside the town limits." The old priest nodded. This is what he had been told by the young people who came to him every day with food and helped with the cleaning of the ancient church. Not that he ever saw any of them on a Sunday, he thought, but better to be thankful for small mercies and hope for better.

"The social unrest has worn itself mostly out. There are still gangs traveling around doing damage just for the sake of it, but little by little Ireland is coming back. It may never be the same in our lifetime, but there is hope in most people's eyes now rather than fear. What's happening around here, if I might ask?" Francis placed his tea softly on the bent wooden table, happy to have an excuse not to drink it. He had seen the Jesuit's face when he took his first sip, his eyes opening like saucers and his face going beet red, so he knew the brew was potent. The old priest seemed to be thinking, then slowly nodded to himself.

"I'll not be telling tales, young Francis, but I think you need to wander down to the apartments and speak to Moriah. She can tell you much more accurately than I can what's what."

Francis sat back in his seat, surprised that his old friend was shunting him off to someone else. He knew of Moriah. He had even met her once at the University where she taught. It was the same one where he studied and occasionally lectured on his passion, the magic of Ireland. He thought he may have seen her in one of his lectures, but it was some time ago, and he couldn't be sure.

"That's the same Moriah that was teaching up at the University?"

"Aye, that's her. Since the attacks three months ago, she's been managing the apartments, providing beds and safe space for people and children, keeping them off the streets, and now has about one thousand people under her care. They found some more solar panels somewhere, and they have put them on both the other buildings, and I hear she is opening them up as well. She is a treasure, and you mind your manners when you meet her." Francis nodded. Here was the epitome of hope, something he had seen very little of during his travels in the last few months. He stood, bowed to the old priest, and decided to save the Jesuit's stomach lining for another day.

"Father, as you said to us, blessed be, thank you for the tea. Perhaps we will call in again on our way back." He shook the priest's hand, smiled, then walked out, hoping the Jesuit was following him. They found themselves under a star-lit sky, the sun dying on the horizon, leaving a silver sheen on the puddles and pools of water that walked their way across the road and paddocks. Black-faced sheep and a few goats chose to ignore them as they walked by, content to let the intruders find their own way.

"That was the strongest tea I have ever had in my life!" the Jesuit said, wiping his mouth with the back of his hand. One side of his young face was now lit by the moon, giving his high cheekbones a subtle edge. Some might say he was handsome, but none could confuse the tight, dedicated look behind his eyes.

Man on a mission.

"Tell me about this, Moriah." His question hung in the chilled air for a second or two as Francis considered his options. Sometimes seeing and learning things firsthand was the best way. And he didn't want his own mind filtered by any prejudice. He needed to be able to report factually and with as little emotion as possible. He was very much aware of the intelligence ditty that went, 'it's the little things that you miss that get you killed', and as well as his mission for the Order, he was also responsible for getting the Jesuit to his destination, wherever that may be, safely.

"Let's wait and see. Moriah is a bright, make that very bright, young woman. She teaches at Belfast University, has no direct family I'm aware of, and lives over there in that apartment block, the one with the lights on."

"They have power?" the Jesuit asked, astonished. Before he had landed in Belfast, he had traveled through parts of Europe and England where no light shone after dark, and certainly not every light in one building, as he was seeing now. The building was lit up like a Christmas tree of old, with every floor pumping out a golden hue through its windows. Then he saw a row of lights come on in the dark building next door, and then, to his utter astonishment, each floor above the lower level lit up progressively until its radiance matched that of its neighbor. Before he could comment, Francis put his hands to his lips and started walking again.

They walked in silence, soon joined by a gang of young people, all dressed in warm attire and seemingly happy to just walk in silent companionship with the priest and the monk. As they reached the tallest of the three buildings, one of the young boys walked up to the monk.

"Ya would be wanting Moriah. I'd be thinking, she's probably way up in the tower. I can go fetch her if you'd like?" Francis was impressed by the politeness of the young boy, particularly as he had doffed his cap when speaking.

"Thank you, I'd be saying, but I'm not sure it's Moriah I'd be wanting. My friend and I just need a place to stay the night before we are on our way again tomorrow."

"Aye, it's Moriah ya wanting. She's running these buildings, kind of like the mayor, if ya understand what I mean." Francis nodded his head, noticing that the lights had suddenly come on in the third building and that he could hear laughter and shouting, something he had not heard in months. Even some of the row houses that ran off down the street suddenly came alive, with lights flickering on and off as they learned how to work after all this time in the dark. He hid his surprise, nodded, and placed a warning hand on the Jesuit.

The boy ran into the building, so Francis turned to look at the other children who had now formed up around them.

"Would you all be living here? I'd be asking." He received a mixture of amused smiles and outright curiosity, but no one spoke. He nodded, thinking that here was a group of children that someone was looking after and had installed a sense of purpose and discipline in them, not to mention they were all clean as a whistle, including their odd mix of clothes. The Jesuit knelt down, careful to keep his trousers out of the wet grass. He carefully lifted his rucksack off and balanced it on one thigh.

"My name is Father Ryan, or Paul if you would prefer that. Do any of you go to school?" Again, no one spoke, and as he tried to think of what to say next, Moriah burst out of the apartment block, the young boy in tow. She was quickly surrounded by the children and placed a supporting hand on the shoulders of two very young children who looked to be about four or five years old.

'Brother Francis, I know of you from the university; you're the one that's always looking for the fairies and the stones. Welcome. And what can I do for you today?" Francis paused and pointed to the Jesuit.

"Father Ryan is on a quest, seeking where he might be needed. He is a teacher, and is wanting to find a parish where he can give himself to the community. Myself, I'm on another matter, which I'd be happy to discuss with you if you have the time." Moriah's eyes widened at this information. In all her time as the unofficial manager of the apartment, she had never considered the issue of education, other than by providing adult supervision and informal lessons on the basketball court for as many children as they could round up. She herself was a teacher at the University up in Belfast, but that was before. The local schools had been the first places razed by the rioters, and the burned-out remains were a constant reminder that things had changed now.

For the first time in three months, she didn't know what to do, but her innate need to provide comfort gave her a solution.

"Come inside. We'll find you both a bed for the night and a good hot meal, and perhaps we can talk some more." The pack of children opened, and the two men walked in, following Moriah, who was thinking at a mile a minute about what she needed to keep from the two visitors and what she could share. Luckily, she had not yet used the box Katrina had left her, as the roofing of the row houses with the panels from Waterford was still in the process of being completed. While some were now with power, she could attribute that to the solar panels, which were easy to see even in the moonlight.

It would be a delicate balance, as Katrina had specifically asked her to keep some details of what they had done and were yet to do to herself.

"As for schooling, most of the teachers were killed or moved away when the attacks occurred, so we provide what we can down in our basement area. We have a few adults that volunteer to help. To be honest, our first thought every day is how to provide food and shelter for everyone who has been displaced; then we think about everything else. We have over a thousand families who now rely on us for housing, and as you have seen, there are a large number of children running around without parents who we also take care of." She said it in such a depreciating manner, Francis bent his head, looked at her, and smiled. He solemnly made the sign of the cross and kissed his fingers.

"Moriah, we support all that you do, and we will help as much as possible while we are here. How many children do you think are in the neighborhood without parents?" She looked back at the monk, her face scrunched up as she thought.

"Around three hundred, we think. Some only come in for a meal now and then, preferring to keep to themselves. They live in the row houses, in the empty factories, in little gangs. We provide food and clothes, and our own children roam with them when they can, so there is a strong sense of community. They trust me and a few of the other adults, and no one is scared any more, but with such an uncertain future, you can't blame them for wanting to maintain their independence." Francis bobbed his head in agreement. He had seen the same behavior in other small towns and villages up and down the coast.

But none with this level of organization, and certainly none with the sheer amount of power that these lucky people seemed to have at their disposal.

"What you are doing here is grand, and you seem to have it well in hand. Might I ask where all the solar panels came from? We haven't seen the likes of them anywhere else on our travels." Moriah mentally flinched. This would be a test of her ability to tell most of the truth but hide the details.

"We always had the panels on this building, and after the attacks died down, we sent out our people to scavenge car batteries, which we have linked up in the basement. We found out about a store of panels down South, so we trucked enough up for the building next door, then found we had some left over, so we did the roof of the other building as well." Francis nodded, taking it all in, thinking that there might be more to this story, but he would hold his counsel. But it couldn't hurt to ask another question.

"And the row houses we see out there with the lights turned on?" Moriah laughed to break the strain she was feeling, one worn hand over her mouth, the fingernails chewed to the quick, to hide her embarrassment.

"That'd be the doing of the littles, I suspect. They're the best scavengers, and we know some of the elder ones followed us down to where we found the panels. And there are lots of adults who would willingly help them out, especially as they are helping homeless and parentless children. We expect to see families and other people migrate back here as the news gets out that we have some power feely available." Francis took all that in, mindful of the fact that the Irish had always been strongly connected for thousands of years at the family level, and that the social circles formed in the pubs and clubs before the terrorist attacks had been strong and vibrant. The fact that so many young people had left the country for other countries only spoke of the lack of opportunity at the commercial level, not the societal one. You could be a farmer, and a great one, but still feel left behind in the materialistic world.

"Well, it's a grand sight to be sure, but don't you fear that if more people arrive, there could be trouble between your residents and the migrants?" She shook her head.

"We've done away with that. The attacks and what followed hardened us to outside influence, and we have well-trained adults who will stop any trouble in its tracks—not to mention the bright intelligence we get from the littles. They are out and about everywhere, so we hear of trouble before it can get to us." Francis nodded again. This is what he suspected from the behavior of the young gang that had met them and escorted them from the old church. It was very casual, almost accidental, but by its very nature, it was a self-managed community, looking out for its own best interests with the light of youth at its heart.

The pair retired to bunk beds after a welcome hot meal, met very early the next morning over a warm breakfast, said their goodbyes, and Francis left a few punts by way of covering their cost to the community. As they hit the road under a still pastel blue sky, the sun not quite having made its move to bring the warming light to the verdant countryside, their breaths puffed out in the chill, and the Jesuit had the strongest sense of comradeship he had ever experienced.

The monk was a huge bundle of confidence. His ability to interact with anyone they met on the road was unchallenged, and his warmth and genuine concern were a rock in the uncertainty of the times. He wondered where he would find his place in this most fascinating country, but knew he would and hoped it would be soon.

"Paul, if you wouldn't mind, I'd be taking a photo of you with this little gizmo. Could you stand just over there, if you please?" The Jesuit did as he was asked, doffed his hat with a huge smile, then bowed.

"Now that'll be ten euros for my modeling fee," he laughed, then started back on the road. Francis, with what he was beginning to believe was a good sleight of hand, dialed Jessica and sent the photos. He pushed the mini back into his robes.

"I'll be owing it to you all your life, rather than do you out of it," he replied, slapping the young Jesuit on the shoulder. He had to get further south. He had a feeling that's where the heart of the story lay, and he smiled to himself. This spy business was almost as much fun as hunting down the stone dancers and the fairy bowers!

CHAPTER TWENTY TWO

I sat looking at Fay as if we were having a staring contest or playing eyeball Ping-Pong. The coffee machines were puffing happily away, and the clicking and clacking of key boards reverberated off the walls. She knew the backgrounds of the two women from Ireland. Or rather, she had what we knew now to be a totally false background and identification on both, which confirmed they were who and what we thought they were and begged the question of what they were doing in the office of the President of Ireland.

Indigo, an expert at being silent, sat stoically off to one side, working on the big screen, where he had photos of the women up next to their fabricated backgrounds. There was a little pool of water at his feet, and the light from the roof bounced off it like it was on a trampoline. Our new Venice office was in the basement of a seven hundred-year-old church, and like every building in Venice, it leaked.

One of the women was identified as Liddy Cochran, supposedly a representative of an overseas Aid Agency. The other was Mary MacDonald, a Scottish academic with no provable history. We knew that they had attempted to get on the ground at Whiddy Island and had been sent packing by the major and his *Sciathán Fianóglach*. The question in our minds was how long he could keep them at bay, and would the President of Ireland stick his well-manicured fingers into our pie?

And now we had a report of the attack on our team in Japan. No serious casualties, but Nokomoto was hospitalized for at least the next few hours, and our team was now back in the air and headed home. The data Shami and Amira had collected was sitting on our minis and being examined by the rest of the geek team here in Venice, Israel, and the US. Indigo had, in fact, been going through it before we interrupted his train of thought.

The latest report from Whiddy Island was no change—no terrorist activity, no movement—but I had received a photo from Brother Francis of a solar panel setup outside the town of Dundalk that had sent my nerves jangling. It was a direct copy of what we had observed under the camouflage on Whiddy Island. The immediate questions that came to mind were: where did it come from, when did it come, and how were the terrorists moving it around so freely? Dundalk was on the exact opposite side of the country from Whiddy Island, though not so far if you looked closely at it. At just over three hundred and thirty kilometers, it took a little over four hours on a well-maintained truck.

If that was all there was to it.

And overlaying all of that was the information from our teams on the ground in Scotland about the transmissions they were tapping into. A test is running in Ireland; no details. Something is happening in Spain; there are also no details. And a whole bunch of names we hadn't come across previously. Freya, the sender of messages from Scotland; Katrina, the receiver, firstly in Ireland, then in Spain; and Crissy, on the Island of Socotra in the Arabian Sea. And our old friend, the scientist from Ireland and one of the terrorists that had started us on the trail of the nuclear-capable shells in the first place, Siobhan O'Cleary, soon headed to Killara Bay, where something awaited her packed in boxes.

But it was clear to me that Ireland, the most invaded territory in all of history, was the epicenter of the current terrorist activity, even though many of the players were now distributed across Europe and Africa. And the nagging thought at the back of my mind was the million-plus empty homes that went begging in Ireland due to the migration of over twenty percent of the population over the past ten years.

Which took me to a question I had asked the Boss. I broke the eyeball dual with Fay conceding a draw and dialed him, flicking his image up to the big screen, forcing the photos of the two women into little boxes on the bottom of the screen where they belonged. Indigo responded by stepping up to one of the espresso machines and gesturing to us. We both nodded, and the smell of freshly roasted coffee beans flooded the office. "Have you got Tom yet?" The Boss's look was relaxed, his background an outdoor sunlit veranda, and he had been reading because his glasses were still in one meaty hand. He shook his head. The collar of his bright blue shirt moved, revealing one of the many scars that littered his body.

"Not yet."

"Okay, I need an answer to the question I asked you about the Aid Agencies and how many children they are preparing to move and to where. And I need it now."

"You're lucky." And he held up a sheaf of papers and waved them at me. "Just been reading what they sent us, plus what we were able to compile from other sources. Makes interesting reading."

"I'm sure it does. Spill!" My rude and sharp tone only made him smile, and he shook his head.

"Somethings never change," he said with a laugh, "okay short summary, and I'll take questions. There are eight million people headed to Ireland. One and a half million female adults, six and a half million children. The US has seven hundred thousand children, unknown number of adults, New Zealand half a million, same story, and the same number for all seventeen countries that have been sent ecological plants. The timing is spread over five years, and there are seven boats already on the water holding a possible forty thousand souls but we're not yet sure of their destinations. Or for that matter, where they are, exactly." At the back of my mind I recalled the head monk, Stefarino, had the technology chops for that, so I mentally put him on my call list.

"How many ships do they have at their disposal?"

"We don't have an accurate figure yet, but the best guess is thought to be twenty or thirty. All purchased for cash during the pandemic, all rebuilt to similar specifications, again, paid for with cash, so if we take the extreme distance they have to travel in Europe, say Helsinki to Dublin, you are only talking five days. The US and many of the other locations are, of course, a much longer sail."

I thought that over, then held my hand up for him to wait and dialed in FBI Senior Special Agent John Vernon in Helena.

"Hello John, I've got General Anthony on this call, and Fay and Indigo are also listening in. I hope I have you at a convenient time?" He smiled gently, his background an office by the looks, and nodded. The office felt small, but maybe it was his football-tackle-width shoulders throwing off my sense of proportion.

"Yes, ma'am, how can I help?"

"John, how are you and your two children getting along?" He looked at me with curiosity in his eyes, but his face remained relaxed.

"Well, it's taken my wife and I a week or two to get used to having children, plus the new house, but I'd have to say we've never been happier."

It was my turn to smile.

"Excellent. And the girls are adjusting?" He nodded, his smile fading a little, but a twinkle came into his eyes as if he were enjoying a private joke or memory.

"Yes, they adjusted better and faster than we did. They've settled into their school and are already showing signs of relishing the new environment. They both now have a pet, Aya a dog and Kona a cat. They are inseparable. They've stopped hoarding food, and Aya is a whiz with a Rubik's cube! She's unbeatable, and I'm talking adults and math wizards from the university."

"Again, excellent. How many refugees do you now have in Helena?"

"The second boat landed a week ago, so that would be around 3,000."

"No issues with that number?"

"No, the houses are going up at a fast clip, we are all helping there when we can, and the whole town has got behind this in a way we initially found surprising. I think a lot of it is the fact that we now have stable employment and different support industries popping up all over, and people are able to look after themselves with confidence and gain a little self-sufficiency. The money we have been given for the children is going into the local economy, so Helena is looking a little flush right now, which brings its own problems, of course."

"Local crime?"

"Yes, but very little in truth, the locals tend to stomp hard on anyone who tries to do something stupid. It's as if the whole community has a collective conscience and they want this to work. And trust me when I say, this feeling starts with the mayor's office and filters all the way down to the lowest worker. It seems as if the entire community is behind the migration, and there's a sense of pride in everyone involved." I thought about that, and realized the terrorist's psychologist, Rena Niele, had been spot on with in her understanding of the cause and effect relationship between chaos, loss, fear, and uncertainty, and then the hope and pride that came from rebuilding and supporting disadvantaged refugee children.

"Are you running out of families to take in the refugees?" He laughed, stood up, walked his mini out of the building, and pointed the little camera at the street where a long line of vehicles were streaming slowly from one end to the other.

"This is just today's new comers, but it's like this all over town. People are migrating from everywhere. The area that the Westhall trust had set up originally was predicated on one hundred thousand new houses, plus schools, hospitals, commercial, and retail buildings, so there's plenty of land, and anyone who can handle a hammer or a spanner is working on getting the houses up. And I might add, getting paid a wage for their effort."

"Okay, do us a favor, please, and send a detailed report to us via your Seattle office; copy SSSA Anna Bernstein." He grinned, like a schoolboy being thanked for his excellent behavior.

"Commander, it will be my pleasure. Thanks for your interest." I cut the call and brought the Boss back into focus.

"You got all that-back to the boat question, and I have another one when we finish, don't let me forget. Now, if memory serves, the other countries that have environmental plants ready to be built are Canada, Greenland, Chile, Portugal, Denmark, Norway, Finland, Estonia, Sri Lanka, Solomon Islands, and Japan. They have a trust fund set up we know about.

"We know what's happening in the US and New Zealand. There's one big question that keeps rattling around in my mind, and that's, do we have any idea how long this has all been planned?" He grimaced, not a good look, as the scars on his face contorted into an evil-looking mask. But I loved him for who he was, scars and all, so I just ignored the obvious and dug for the hidden. "It seems to me it's all been going on a lot longer than we suspect. There's so much in play at present."

"I agree. Perhaps we now have the real reason for the attack on Lloyds. They destroyed all the shipping files, so no one could answer the questions we are now asking." I thought back to the interview with the man who had started it all, Al Hemish al-bin Mohammad Karesish, or Mohammad bin Azaria, as he had also been known. He stated that they had destroyed Lloyds to settle a centuries-old debt, in that the traders who had set up the insurance mammoth in the gutters of London had ignored the Arab traders, who were the most prolific sailors through the Middle East, and labeled them as 'unsafe' to carry insured commercial cargo. The fact that British, French, and Spanish galleons took over from their dowls and long boats also did not go unnoticed.

But the Boss's speculation was on the money—what better way to hide what you are doing than to irrevocably destroy the baseline data?

So the only people who knew how many ships the terrorists had, what they had been called, what flags they sailed under, and where they were located were the terrorists.

Maybe.

"You asked me to remind you of another question?" the Boss asked, breaking into my circuitous thoughts. Indigo had returned to his seat in front of the big screen, Fay was seemingly relaxed, monitoring the conversations, and the Boss had sat back further into his chair, which I could now see was a whicker bamboo-woven number with bright red and blue striped cushions. I almost asked him where he was.

"It's a question of jurisdiction. How far do we go? Our original mandate was to find the terrorists, then we morphed into stopping the nuclear shells from being used, and in the middle of all that, we discovered the environmental plants."

"I see where you are going. We gave Point Roberts back to the Americans, and New Zealand now has control of theirs, so you're wondering how we manage Ireland?" I just shook my head. His ability to anticipate where I was going was as frustrating as it was wonderful.

"Yes, in a nutshell. On the way through, we destroyed three other production sites where we judged the nuclear risk was the highest, and Whiddy Island had a stockpile of nuclear-capable shells. However, I acknowledge they were not manufactured there, most likely further north at Pollatomish."

You found no nuclear material at Whiddy Island?"

"None. Just the shells, which are now with Amira."

"So your issue here is, do you give the ecological plant back to the Irish government, knowing that at least two of the potential workers are terrorists?"

"That's it in a nutshell. And if they are really going to receive over six million refugees, how can we stand in the way of what they need in terms of infrastructure?" He seemed to be thinking, his brow furrowed, a glazed look in his eyes, his body perfectly still. Then he waved his forefinger in a little circle and nodded.

"The problem is simple. Think Corps of Engineers and Amira."

My turn to nod. I could see where he was leading me. "You're saying we still control the traffic because of our relationship with the US and Israel."

"Yes. The only real wildcard is that in both Point Roberts and New Zealand we were able to remove the prime terrorists by their association with the planning of the attacks. When we gave the plants back, both sites had to rely on us to make them work. You're afraid that if you let the Irish have Whiddy Island, the two women you have identified as terrorists, but have no associative evidence against except for their purged backgrounds, could introduce a new technological element we're not prepared for." I nodded. Indigo looked over at me, his head tilted to one side.

"Excusea me, commander, buta ifa I remembera, didn't they shoota youa downa?" I almost burst out laughing at Indigo's pidgin English, which he added to with a wild hand-waving flourish. Fay did laugh, so I noticed the boss did too.

"Okay, enough hilarity, but you makea gooda pointa," and I pointed to Indigo, who sheepishly sat back down.

"Then there's your reason to keep it shuttered for the time being: the shells you found and the drone that shot you down."

"I have another tiny issue, and it's to do with what Amira discovered about the nanites they are making onsite. Have you caught up with that yet?"

"No."

"They were producing and storing three new types: one identified as the starter for organic-based biofuel, different from anything we have seen before; one that dissolves metals on contact, leaving a sludge that can be reclaimed; and a version that causes water or liquids to boil. I can get you more detail from Amira if you need it." He looked interested, sat forward in his chair again.

"Any idea what they could be used for, except biofuel, of course?"

"None. I haven't pursued it as I was occupied with other matters. But the data we have from Amira and Shami via Nokomoto and Aikido shows that Innomatchi shared all their data with all three sites and included a data package with every environmental plant shipment, and in Amira's opinion, the nanites can be manufactured on demand by anyone with a running plant and a technician who knows what they are doing."

"From the reports from people you interviewed in Point Roberts and New Zealand, I got the impression that none of the locals had the scientific chops to make the nanites, startup a factory, or do anything really fancy. It seems to me the terrorists limited their key knowledge to the three you swept up in Helena and New Zealand—the pilot, the engineer, and the scientist. Would you stand by that?" I thought about the women who had been living together in Helena for over three years and had not volunteered a single word in their defense. In fact, all three had refused to answer any questions at all and were now wasting away in a small concrete cell somewhere deep and dark. Amazing genius-level talent and skill aside, they had also refurbished an old decommissioned missile base in Montana and used it to run the attacks on the Vatican, the Dome of the Rock and Wailing Wall, the Grand Mosque, the bombing of West Point, and what we thought of as their finale, the shooting down of the International Space Station.

They may or may not have been involved in giving the 'go' signal to Shetani and his mercenary friends, who took out all the oil, gas, and coal reserves worldwide.

"I stand by what we have in our interview reports. At that time, there was no one on staff at either plant that could technically run the factory or manufacture the nanites, in spite of the level of automation. They were being trained, but the secret sauce, if you will, was a carefully guarded secret." His head bobbed up and down, and his grin spilt his face in two, neither half particularly pretty.

"I spoke to Arie a while ago, and his comment on Amira's key frustration is that she has been unable to train anyone up to her level so far. And we are talking serious genius level people here, with the best laboratories in the world. A month ago, she asked Malcolm if he could tell her of anyone he knew, and he provided two names. We chased them down; one was a no-starter, the other has been with her for three weeks, and is struggling like the rest. So my take on this is that if you haven't already got the skills, it's going to take some time to develop them."

"But once a plant is up and running, keeping it going is not so hard?"

"Correct. As we proved in both New Zealand and Point Roberts. But the engineers are adamant that having watched Amira re-start Point Roberts, and they filmed it, and her number two was with her every step of the way, they cannot get the nanite process to work by themselves. It's as if Amira has magic hands or something, but at least we know how to do it."

"So, the two women who tried to get back to Whiddy Island may or may not have skills others lack?"

"Entirely possible. Only one way to find out." It took me no time at all to consider his suggestion and reject it.

"No. Just no. We spilled blood to be able to hold this Island. I'm not giving it back until I absolutely have to." His smile was wicked, like something I imagine an alligator might offer after a bloody meal in the swamp.

"Good. I was hoping you hadn't gone soft on us. As far as Interpol, and therefor the World Court, is concerned, the Terrorist Act as modified in 2022 still holds. You have proved prima facie attachment to the terrorists, their timing, and their attacks, so hang tight. Our mandate holds, and will continue to hold, until we say we're ready to step back."

I nodded, inwardly relieved that his view supported mine. I hated politics with a passion that, in my position, was somewhat juvenile, but I had a sneaky suspicion that of all the places we were dealing with, Ireland would become the hardest to manage. Then I had a flash of inspiration.

"Could we identify the nanites as the prime terrorist substance, based on Amira's original work, and as such get Red

Notices issues wherever we find nanites, and take them into our control?"

"Brilliant. I knew I kept you around for more than your good looks. I'll get Lyon onto it immediately with a 'to be released only under supervision by Interpol' and maybe or maybe not I might add 'Section Five'."

"Thank you. We can work with that. Amira is attached to Section Five, so keeping her in control will be easy once we identify other potential scientists. In the meantime, it gives us what we need to keep Whiddy Island under our thumbs." My screen went black, Indigo stared at me, and Fay looked like I felt a little weary and tired, so I got up to refill my mug. Fay followed me with a concerned look on her face.

"I'm not complaining or anything, but we still lack hard data on the terrorists intentions with the nuclear shells. They moved them all around the place, if you count Amir Abbas and his friend Malik Badawi, the three sites we obliterated, and now Ireland we have a really large area of Europe to cover. Have we confirmed that the metallic puddle reported by Tom as the missing shell?"

"Yes. The result matches the experiment Amira did."

"Okay, that's good, but apart from the accidental nuclear explosion in Gaza and the deliberate one in the Atlantic Ocean, there's been nothing to show for all the fuss and bother. Nothing." I looked at Fay. She had been the youngest Supervisory Special Agent in the FBI when I poached her for Interpol. She was no slouch in the smarts department, was fast on her feet, and was an excellent, quick, and thorough learner.

"What, specifically, are you worried about?" She gave me a hard look, wiped the hair out of her eyes, and flicked it behind her ears. Dressed in our version of daywear, light fawn slacks, combat boots, and a military-style jumper over an open-necked purple shirt, her weapon hitched on her hip, she looked younger than her twenty-eight years. Even dressed 'down' as she was, she looked like a runway model, and not a hardened investigator.

"In my experience, and in all the war games we played back in Seattle, when you had a toy as threatening and fearsome as a nuclear bomb you wanted something in return for not letting it go off. We've received no threat, no demand, in fact not a single word has been sent our way regarding the shells. Why? These are genius level terrorists, the smartest we've ever been up against, their planning has been both exquisite and brilliant, every strike deliberate and purposeful, all aimed at getting the child refugees into the nineteen countries they identified. They ever have a smart economic platform that is working without them being around – look at Helena, and New Zealand. What in the name of Hell where those shells really all about?" I considered her question, and I had to admit, it was one that concerned me as well.

"How do you think we could get that answer? None of the senior women have said a word; we only got the overview because Mohammad bin Azaria wanted us to know why his people had done what they had."

"We go back and interview the weak link." I thought back over the now-long list of women we had incarcerated, trying to see who Fay's weak link might be. She played that eyeball Ping Pong game with me again, never blinking, just staring right through me to my backbone.

"You win. Again. Who's the weak link?"

"Your Irish woman, the CEO of Whiddy Island, Lady Fionnuala O'Brian Flattery." Now Fay had me curious. That pumped-up highbrow woman had gotten on my goat, well and truly, trying to tell me her instructions from the Irish parliament transcended my Interpol authority. The Terrorist Laws as modified in 2022 trumped all and any statutes or laws as far as terrorism goes, so she well and truly lost that little battle of wills and now hopefully was well rested in a deep, dark hole somewhere.

"Why?"

"She, of all of them, has something to lose other than their grand plan for the refugees. I'd start with Patricia, her aide, then work upwards."

"You place a great deal of importance on those shells?"

"Yes. Way too much effort, expense, and exposure for them to be just a blind, and even if they were, what were they to blind us to?" I thought that over, then had my second flash of inspiration in less than an hour. Probably a world record! I called Sandra.

"Where are you?"

"Forty thousand feet up, somewhere over Bangladesh, according to the inflight map."

"Good. Tell your pilot to divert here. You have a package to pick up." I hung up before she could reply, confident that within the next five to six hours this problem would be on its way to being solved.

"Go pack, get yourself to the airport, and when Sandra lands, tell her to come here. When you get to Israel, I'll have Arie ready with your two women friends." She just nodded, looked over at Indigo, who just shrugged his shoulders as if to say, 'that's what she does all the time', then stood.

"Thank you, commander. I appreciate the trust and support." I smiled. My instincts in stealing her from the FBI had been spot on.

And maybe we could address the issue of why terrorists created the nuclear-capable shells in the first place. My mini screeched at me, so I opened it with some reluctance. It had three levels for getting attention: a soft buzz, an instant buzz more like a shake, and a scream. The caller got to decide what level to use, and the mini had no 'change ringing sound' setting to choose from.

Annoying.

Then my annoyance went away in a puff of guilt as Aikido's round face, framed by her beautiful dreadlocks, filled the screen.

"Commander, good news! Nokomoto has just been released by the medics, battered and bruised but with no permanent damage."

"Excellent news. Do you know who your attackers were?"

"Yes, commander, the same Yakuza tribe that attacked us in Toyoko. They took a huge risk, operating on another gang's ground, and will no doubt be punished for it. Have you got all the material we sent to you, and are Sandra and Shami okay?" I nodded at the small screen. Her goth look had been turned down a little, probably due to the seriousness of the situation. But I envied her free expression and her ability to make such a bold and strong statement while working for such a normally hide-bound organization. Section Five would do that to you!

"We are analyzing all the data, and Sandra's plane is on schedule to land in a few hours. What do you plan on doing now?"

"I'll take Nokomoto back to our headquarters in Toyoko. Keep my eye on him. We were setting up for a monster drug bust when you called us in, so we will see if we can pick up where we left off."

"Have you heard the latest from Lyon on the status of the drug-growing areas?"

"Yes, commander, and I suspect the Yakuza have as well, making this shipment all the more important." I nodded; there was not much I could add, given that both agents worked day jobs for Interpol in tandem with the SFGP (Special Forces Group) and the Toyoko Public Security Bureau. That was the way we liked it; it kept our agents in far-flung places on their toes and well connected to the local law enforcement agencies. It also meant a smoother acceptance when we had to move into their territories on a mission at the request of the Government.

"Okay, good, keep your head down, thank Nokomoto for a job well done, and keep me posted, please."

"*Arigatōgozaimasu, shiki-kan,-sō shimasu. Sayōnara.*" I shut down my mini, feeling the tension in my shoulders start to get aggressive, so I rolled them and thought of all the things I had yet to do.

Coffee first, then maybe a quick nap. Maybe even a long one!

LITTLES

It was nearly a full day of walking on slippery, muddy roads and walkways when the brother and the Jesuit came upon a swarm of children working in a controlled manner beside a huge pile of vehicles. They ran row after row, piled four high, as far back as the eye could see, in a field that had obviously been used as a dump for a long time. The number of rusted hulks spoke of gangs lighting them up for fun, and the plethora of different colors reflected the imagination of the manufacturers. The youths were dressed for the cold, and some had long black gloves and safety glasses on, making the littlest of them look bug-eyed. None looked hungry, and none were fearful of the approach of the two male adults.

There was a process and a system to their work, as some stripped off wheels and then removed the tires. Others pulled out seats and dashboards, creating little piles of materials up and down the rows of wrecks. Yet another group was bent over old oil drums, feeding in bits and pieces of the vehicles as they were cut off by older boys and girls wielding power cutters.

For a moment, Francis wondered where they were getting their power from, then he looked beyond the drums and saw a fancy-looking trailer with solar panels all over it. He looked up at the sky, judging the sun's position, and nodded to himself. A mass of old, partially corroded car batteries was piled behind the trailer. One of the boys, whom he judged to be around sixteen years old, approached them before they could get to the working area.

"Father, please stop. It's not safe to go into the field without the proper safety equipment, of which we have very little. And I know you, brother Francis, for I have seen you with Moriah back up at the apartments." Francis wracked his mind trying to recollect seeing the boy previously, being relatively tall, with flowing and boisterous flaming red hair, the greenest of green eyes, and skin like a porcelain doll. He was wearing a puffer jacket two sizes too big for him, creating the illusion that he was being swallowed whole by it. He walked the two away from the work area to where an old, battered caravan stood on blocks.

"I can offer you a cup of tea and some biscuits, if it pleases you?"

"Aye, son, that would be very nice, I'm thinking. And forgive an old man, but I can't seem to place your name?" The smile he offered split his face, and two tiny dimples appeared on either side of his cheeks.

"I'd be Shamus, brother, and who's this good-looking priest you have in your company?" The Jesuit took his sodden and battered hat off, his matted hair dripping over his shirt collar, which was now showing signs of some hard wear and tear, and reached out one hand.

"I'm Father Paul Ryan, and I'm very glad to meet you. Where did you and your friends get all this equipment?" He asked, pointing around the yard. Apart from the cutting torches, there was a small triangular hoist, yellowed with age, and two sturdy full-length metal tool boxes with multiple draws hanging open as if waiting for attention. A small group of children were rocking a car back and forth, trying to tip it on its side. When it finally fell and bounced in the springy grass, a cheer went up, and some of the children, again wearing gloves and glasses, started to bash at it with hammers. In a sense, it was the most viscous thing either of the men had seen in quite a while, but the sheer happiness and laughter of the children suggested a purpose beyond the obvious.

"Well, father, the idea of reclaiming all these bits and pieces came to us from a vision she was, so beautiful and full of light it was hard to concentrate. It was a woman who stayed with Moriah up at the apartments, off on her way to somewhere or other. But she showed us the way, and gave us some of the materials to work with, then the next day we got all the rest from a driver who had seen us from the roadside, and has a small garage down south. He helped us get started, pointed out which bits to keep, and which could be disposed of, environmentally, of course. And he and a few of his friends have arranged to buy what we reclaim off us, at a very good rate." Francis nodded, wanting a good look at the main working area, but took the tea and biscuits and held his counsel.

He would take photos of the power trailer and the drums and send them to Jessica for her to worry about.

"We'd be thanking you for the tea, but we have to be on our way. Do you know what's the next main town we might find?" The lad looked serious for a minute, remembered what Moriah had told him just this morning, and nodded.

"Aye, that'd be Drogheda. Not much going on there now. Most people took off after the attacks." The monk stood, shook the boy's hand, and started off. The Jesuit hesitated just a moment, then changed his mind, put his hat back on, and followed the monk back to the road.

"Brother Francis, I'm new to this country, that's for sure, but I suspect you're looking for things I don't know about. Would that be true? Francis smiled and patted the Jesuit on the shoulder.

"Aye, that may be, but we'd be finding you a spot for your school, and that's the most important thing I'm thinking." The Jesuit looked at the monk, a twinkle in his gray eyes, and smiled himself.

"Well, if you take all these children we saw back to Dundalk and those we just came across, there'd be a good start, I suspect."

"Well, I think you'll find most, if not all, of the ones we just crossed will live in the apartments or close by, but you have the right to it. Let's see who else we can find." They walked on in companionable silence, each lost in his own thoughts.

CHAPTER TWENTY THREE

Fay sat by herself, dressed in a black suit, a white collared shirt open at the neck, showcasing a small blue diamond on a silver chain, her hair shiny and combed, but not extensively, and her unmanicured hands locked together and resting on the table top. In this instance, the table was a solid wood antique, straight out of Arie's office, densely black with age but unmistakable to any collector. No cameras were evident, and there was no glass wall for someone behind to be watching from. The room was a converted office with warm colors on the walls and a row of modern overhead lights running on a rail. Her coffee mug had the Interpol seal on it.

The first woman was escorted in by two Israeli female guards, also dressed in black suits but not carrying weapons. The woman wore a lovely dress, flat-heeled shoes, and a light-weight cardigan thrown over her shoulders. These were the clothes she had been arrested in back on Whiddy Island. As she passed through the door, the guards remained outside, and Fay stood and held out her hands in welcome.

"Patricia, thank you for joining me. I see you are rested and well?" The younger woman withheld her hands from Fay and looked around the room like a startled bird, her face a mixture of fear and curiosity.

"Who are you, and why have you locked me up all these days now?" Her voice was somewhat high-pitched, which Fay put down to stress. She gestured to the visitor's seat at the end of the table, forming an 'L' shape.

"My name is Fay Remer, and I'm with Interpol. Please sit. We can have this interview over quickly, and then you can be on your way."

"You're letting me go?" she asked incredulously. Her hands flittered about until she got control of her nerves, sat down, linked her fingers to stop them shaking, and looked hard at Fay.

"The faster we can get the formalities out of the way, the faster you can be on your way." Fay held her eyes, unblinking, the model of sincerity and warmth. The woman held Fay's stare for a moment, then bobbed her head in acquiescence.

"Firstly, can we confirm that you are the assistant to the CEO of the Whiddy Island plant, Lady O'Brian Flattery, also known as Fionnuala?" The woman nodded, her eyes still distrusting and wary, the tension in her body plain to see. "And would you like a coffee or tea? Forgive my manners. I meant to ask when you arrived." The woman looked astonished and slowly nodded her head.

"Thank you. Tea would be wonderful. I've not had a cup since you took me into custody, for reasons that have not yet been explained to me." The accusation in her eyes left Fay in no doubt who was in the wrong, and she made a mental note to explain it well and truly before the conversation finished.

"While we wait for your tea, could we continue, please?" A nod and a faint relaxation of her body showed Fay her tactics were working.

"As Lady—or I'll call her Fionnuala, as that was what she asked us to do—assistant, you were in charge of running the plant?"

"Not technically, no, I was trained in engineering, but more on the project management side, and the plant was managed by the three Berkley sisters, who I have heard nothing of since my arrest. Two of them are marvelous scientists. They invented the nanites we use to make the biofuel, and Shannon, the eldest, ran the plant." Fay tucked that away for future reference. The three sisters had been taken in the oil tank after crawling out of a tunnel that led to the drone hangar. The door opened, and a tea set was placed in front of the woman.

"As Fionnuala's assistant, you were aware of all the production details—how many panels, where they would go, that sort of thing?" Fay watched the woman closely, especially her face, looking for little, miniscule signs that would indicate a lie. As a former FBI agent, she was regarded by her peers and superiors as one of the best interrogators the FBI had—another reason why Jessica had recruited her.

"I was in control of the various projects, yes, but only in terms of managing the project plans, and seeing everything happen when it should. The decisions were always made by Lady Flattery and the three Berkley sisters."

"And Fionnuala told us you were preparing panels for over a million homes. Is that correct?"

"Yes, we have a contract with the Irish government for a million homes to start, then as many as we could make thereafter." Fay nodded her head, maintaining the rhythm of the conversation.

"Did the government pay you for the panels?" She looked curious, as if Fay had asked a dumb question.

"Of course. They paid thirty percent on order, then would pay progressively as we delivered lots, until there will be only the last ten percent due, which we will get as they are carted away."

"Have you delivered any yet?" She seemed to think on this question, started to answer, then pulled herself back, dropped her head, and then looked Fay straight in the eyes again from under her eye lashers, almost coyly.

"I'd have to have Lady Flattery's permission to answer that question." Fay smiled and let it ride. The photo she had received from Jessica when she had landed clearly showed the Whiddy Island panels on the rooftops of the row houses outside Dundalk. No idea where they came from, but it was obvious that the plant had shipped a large number across the country to somewhere.

"What do you know about the drone operations?" She looked relieved at not being pressed on whether or not panels had been delivered, so she answered the question without hesitation.

"Nothing. The Berkley sisters ran that end of the business, as they did manage the goings on in the oil tank. In fact, when they weren't working in the lab, they spent all their time down there." Fay nodded, as if she accepted the woman at her word.

"Who brought you the bimetallic shells?" As she asked this, she looked straight at the woman, as if daring her to lie. She returned the look, even putting a little force into it, as if clearing her conscience of something.

"Those shells were an abomination. They came to us by way of an American woman, who pulled up to the jetty one day and demanded they be offloaded. Lady Flattery was furious and ordered them to be tucked away in a dark corner, and the woman left. I didn't get her name, but I saw her boat. It was some sort of big cruiser such as you see on TV, all long and sleek, like a greyhound. The Berkley sisters immediately started work on a nanite that would dissolve them, and I know they were successful, as I saw a test with my own eyes, but then your lot arrived and shut us down." Fay took all of this in, and immediately revised her planned strategy for her conversation with the good Fionnuala.

She knew the nanite existed, and she knew it had been used outside Whiddy Island, but not by whom. She had unarguable photographic evidence.

"I take it you and Fionnuala didn't want the shells on the Island?"

"None of us did. We had an angry meeting on that very subject when the American arrived. Even the sisters hated the idea of the shells."

"What do the other nanites do?" Fay caught the woman off guard, and she nearly answered. Then, with a little grimace, she shook her head.

"Again, you must ask Lady Flattery about that. It's not worth my job." Fay smiled inside and thought, 'what job?' knowing the future for the woman was a dark concrete cage. She thought for a while, holding the silence, then, after considering her options, turned her head to one side with a thin smile.

"Patricia, as you were no doubt told previously, you have been charged under the Terrorist Laws as modified in 2022 for aiding and abetting acts of terror and a whole slew of other charges relating to the terrorist attacks. Thank you for your cooperation, and I wish you well." And before she could react, the door opened, the two Israeli guards entered, took her by the arms, and marched her out. As they exited, Arie walked in with a fresh mug of coffee.

"You've got all that?" Fay asked. Arie nodded, pointed to the buttonhole camera on Fay's jacket, and then sat where the woman had vacated.

"You did well. Anything you need?" Fay shook her head, smelled the reviving odor of the coffee, smiled, then sipped gently.

"I think I'm becoming as addicted as Jessica." Arie laughed, collected the empty Interpol mug and the tea set, and walked out, leaving the door open. Fay stood and stretched, rolled her shoulders, looked at the far wall, which was painted a pretty warm color, and nodded. Within a few minutes, the same guards escorted a beautifully dressed Lady Flattery into the room. She stood and looked at Fay, looked around the room, saw no cameras or recording equipment, then sat with a flounce. She was wearing a stylish wool blend suit in pale pink, with a cream silk shirt under it and blue short heels, and looked dressed for the Royal enclosure rather than an interrogation. Her hair had been recently washed and treated, so it flowed over her shoulders in warm cascades that caught the light.

"At last, you people have come to your senses. Make no mistake, the Irish Government will be made aware of your transgressions and your illegal restraint of myself and my people." Fay held her tongue, letting the woman vent. The more assured she was that they were letting her go, the more she would tell her. That was why Fay had requested the women be allowed to dress in what they had been arrested in and not the dull gray prison overalls they usually wore. She wanted them both to think they would be freed as motivation to tell them what they needed to know.

"Lady Flattery, would you like tea or coffee?' Fay asked disarmingly. The haughty look the woman gave Fay was designed to shrink the confidence of a lesser person, but it just rolled off Fay like water off a duck's back.

"Tea, sugar, and cream." The request came out like an order, and Fay just nodded to one of the guards, folded her hands, and stared at the prisoner.

"Fionnuala, if I may call you that, your assistant has already told us all we needed to know, so before we conclude this conversation, may I ask you a few questions? Just for clarity's sake, you understand?" The woman sat as if she had a stick up her backside, body rigid, hands flat on the table top, which she stroked gently as she looked down and recognized it for what it was, a centuries-old antique in exquisite condition. She looked back up at Fay with curiosity in her eyes.

"You may." Sharp, direct, letting Fay know who was in change.

"Fionnuala, we understand you had an order from the Irish Government for one million sets of solar panels. Is that correct?" A frigid stare was followed by a short head bob. Her face was a rictus of scorn, and her eyes were flat.

"Yes."

"And the government paid you a third on order, and would make progress payments as you delivered into store?" Another short bob.

"We know you delivered some to the other side of Ireland, and you were paid for those as well?" Another frosty look, but this time a little anxiety behind the mask.

"Of course." The door opened, and a tea set appeared. Fay took it and placed it in front of the woman. For a half minute, they stared at each other until Fay broke into a full-face smile.

"Fionnuala, my apologies, but if you're waiting for me to pour your tea, it'll get cold." And she laughed at the distress that rippled across the woman's face. "Now, while you sort that out, we know that one of the nanites you manufactured can dissolve bimetallic objects. And we have seen for ourselves firsthand the results of that south of Dundalk." Fay watched the woman's face as it cycled through distress, surprise, anger, then finally puzzlement. Giving nothing away, she mixed her cream and sugar into her tea, then, stalling for time, blew ladylike on the top of the Wedgwood cup, then sipped at it. If she had known the trouble Arie had gone through to find the tea set, she may have been impressed.

"And another thing, what were you storing nuclear-capable shells on your Island for?" At this, she put her cup down with a snap, rattling the teaspoon on the beautiful saucer with its golden edges, and she leaned forward towards Fay.

"Those shells were an abomination! If I hadn't been instructed to take them, I would have sent that aggressive young American packing." Fay watched her face closely, then in a voice that was soft and gentle, as if she were sympathetic to the woman's point of view, she asked something that had just come into her mind.

"And what was Freya's rationale for hoarding the shells in the first place?"

"She said they had gone to a lot of trouble to manufacture the shells, that you-Interpol-had run most of them down, and if we were to succeed long term, we needed them safely stored. And we were the only facility left under our control." Then with her hands over her mouth, she forced out an 'Oh!' and her eyes widened as she realized what she had just said. Fay pressed her advantage.

"How did Freya intend to use the shells?" The woman froze, then slowly breathed out, letting her shoulders slump. She had a decision to make, and she weighed the truth of the matter against fabricating an answer, then realized it was of no consequence. Interpol had the shells, and every factory that had been able to manufacture them was now just a pile of rubble. She looked straight at Fay, and for the first time, a weight seemed to have been lifted from her shoulders.

"It was felt that after the original attacks, it would still be necessary to force some countries to accept the refugee children and that a nuclear threat would be sufficient to achieve our aim. Unfortunately, some of the people we were dealing with took matters into their own hands. We took advantage of the chaos they created while we organized the movement of the children.

"Here in Ireland, we were able to negotiate a peaceful solution with the Government, which wanted both the money and the population increase."

"You acknowledged the Irish Government paid you for the panels. How much?" She rolled her shoulders again, comfortable now with the arc of the conversation. Fay still had a few surprises up her sleeve, but she was happy to be patient.

"They paid us one thousand euros per house set." Fay thought that over. In reality, it was a small amount for millions of refugees, but she made a mental note to track where the funds had come from in the first place.

"Did you ever ask where the funds came from?"

"Yes. They were upfront about that. It was a legacy from an old Irish family who donated it to the Government years ago on the basis they used the money for the benefit of Ireland."

"How much are you offering each family that accepts refugees? We know the figures from Helena, Roanoke, and New Zealand. What's your business model?" Again, the woman seemed to pause and consider her answer. Again, she judged, that no damage could be done if Interpol knew the details.

"Unlike in America and New Zealand where we have to bribe families to take the children, here in Ireland our intention is to place families of five or six, all refugees, who will look after themselves, become part of whatever community they go to, and build their own story. Each adult will get twelve thousand euros every year, we will build schools, hospitals, commercial centers, and develop the farming and growing of both food and agricultural products to make Ireland self-sufficient. This plan has been accepted by the Irish Government at the highest level." Fay held her breath, the sheer audacity of the plan was mind blowing, not just the financial figures, but the sheer scope of the plan. There was a trust fund somewhere with billions in it, and she wouldn't mind betting that the Government had got its funds for the panels from the terrorists as well, likely disguised as the fanciful bequest.

The sheer enormity of the plan was mind-boggling. Moving five or six million refugees from where they were in camps throughout Europe and Asia to Ireland alone was a monumental task and could, literally, take years. It would also transform Ireland; of that, there was no doubt.

"Thank you. You have been a great help. Just one last question. Who gave the order to shoot down the American jet?" The woman screwed up her eyes and almost laughed. Here they were talking about her dream coming true, and this agent wanted to know why they had sent a drone into the Atlantic!

"To get rid of you, of course, or at least the more bothersome of you. We didn't set the target. Those instructions came from others. That's all I'll say."

"Then in kind, this is all I'll say. Enjoy the rest of your life in your concrete cage." The door opened, she was marched out, and Arie came back in. No coffee this time, just a big smile.

"She spoke at the last as if she were still in Ireland, still in charge. And their plan for Ireland is simply beyond belief." Fay stood, as weary as she had ever felt.

"Yes, it is, but it's under way, and somehow we have to figure out how to wrangle the terrorists and separate them from the good people who have brought into this dream of theirs. Our mandate covers the terrorists, the nuclear shells, but not the refugees."

"Well, Jessica and PJ had an idea on that. While you've been busy, they have had the Hague and Lyon jointly declare the nanites a weapon of mass destruction, so you now have a reason to stay in the fight. Well done, by the way, getting them washed and polished before your conversations was a brilliant idea. You will not be the most popular Interpol agent as far as they're concerned!" They both laughed, feeling positive about the outcome of the charade but not so positive about what still faced them all.

PARLEZ VOUS FRANÇAIS

The one thing Freya had total command of was a brilliant international transport system. Set up a full year before the attacks, she saw that biofuel and aircraft were converted and stored in numerous hangars, mostly on small airfields out of the way of the main stream. She had personally witnessed the training of ten young women, all refugees, all living in wonderful homes, all graduates of different flight schools, and all with professional careers, right up until a month before the first bomb was dropped on the Vatican.

Katrina and the sisters were collected from a small paddock at the edge of the breakwater, flown to another paddock across the border with France, and landed in a paddock that looked a lot like a crop circle.

Their work in Spain had been an unqualified success, and all that remained was getting the right communication to the right people at the right time. That did not concern Katrina in the slightest, knowing that Freya had the master plan in hand and that they were unstoppable.

The nuclear plant at Golfech, slightly northwest of Toulouse, had been commissioned way back in 1991 and had, by all accounts, a checkered career. Shut down more times than it was open, the only thing it lacked was a consistent political view of its future, which had been made mute by the terrorist attacks. Like every other nuclear plant in the world, the 'hot' parts of the reactors, piping, cooling towers, and power generating plant were now covered with an impenetrable silver slime of nanites.

In the case of Golfech, this wasn't really a disaster, as the government had turned it off a year before as part of the constant struggle France was having trying to maintain its internal delivery of electricity as a bulwark against the Russian and Chinese gas manipulation, which had started in earnest when Russia invaded Ukraine in 2022. The nuclear generating plant, which straddled the Garoone River, had been controversial from day one, being blamed for pollution, killing fish, stinking up the environment, and just generally upsetting the locals to the point of constant irritation. Stained and crumpled protest signs lay in heaps against the security fence as a reminder of the locals anger.

Now that it was shuttered, a single security guard made the rounds in a golf cart twice daily. When the tall, striking woman dressed like a top executive in an impeccable suit, accompanied by three equally striking women similarly dressed, approached and presented impeccable credentials from Électricité de France (EDF), who controlled all the nuclear power plants in France, he bobbed his head in welcome, unlocked the front door, and ushered them in. He was handed a red-bordered security statement, sworn to secrecy, and asked to leave them alone. It may have been a day or two, but the 'investigation' work they had to complete was required by the government at the highest levels, and it wasn't worth his pension to create waves.

"Lilian, you have your choice of which side of the river you want. Else, you may have an opinion on that when you see the plant. We have three days budgeted; unpack your gear and let's get to it". At just under six feet tall and with a trim and fit body, she shed the three massive bags she had on her shoulders with a sigh. Her sisters just smiled, used to her antics. Today her tee shirt challenged all males to 'get it up or put it away forever' with a cartoon of Elmer Fudd dropping an ice cream on his shoes.

"As this is a more traditional layout for a nuclear power plant, I don't think which side we plumb will make much difference."

"Mum warned us that this plant might be difficult, so let's take our time and have a good look around." Both sisters nodded, Katrina acknowledging that on this site her skills with the technology would be critical. But she kept a watchful eye on Lily, the youngest of the three and possibly the most brilliant. Her eyes sparked with enthusiasm, and she often tread where the Angles feared, through excessive passion. They couldn't afford any mistakes on this mission. It was critical to the overall plan for the refugees worldwide to come to fruition.

But Katrina had to admit that the three sisters worked together as if reading each other's minds, and the myriad of technical issues fell before their brilliance. She had a similar bond with Crissy, and she missed her.

The unique work they had done to create the technology had taken them the best part of three years to perfect, and they had failure after failure. Crissy's constant, happy bounce-back attitude had made the difference and promoted their eventual success. But now they had a full-scale test running in Ireland and a second site in Spain, so the thrill of changing the world filled her with hope.

Hope that the world reacted as their smartest psychologists had modeled. In her short experience, people were too individually different and resistant to change for a computer to be able to predict their behavior, so in this regard, she was unsure of the eventual outcome. But they would have done their very best and demonstrated that critical thinking, applying first principles with honor, integrity, intent, and passion, could save the world from itself.

They spent seven hours crawling all over the plant—the massive cooling towers, the administrative offices, the clagged-up control room, and the massive turbines. They had their evening meal on a small electric cooktop and drank cold ginger beer they had brewed themselves before leaving home. They carried the root stock in a thermos flask and only had to mix it with water and drop a special minute nanite cube in to get the coldest, fizziest ginger beer in history!

By the time day three was drawing to a close, they had finished their work and were ready to move on. Two down, sixteen to go.

CHAPTER TWENTY FOUR

"The way I see it, we have multiple fronts to fight this on, and my gut tells me timing will be critical." I looked at Sandra over my coffee mug, with Indigo sitting beside me for a change, drinking his own coffee. Bob sat off to one side, working on his mini. He was listening to us with one ear, and his odd comment now and then suggested he was absorbing everything we were saying. A useful trick in his position. Sandra shrugged, her long arms reaching out as she stretched, pushing one hand in front of the other.

"You know, I should go back to Chicago. Life was a lot quieter there!" We all laughed. Her description of the attack on her vehicle in Japan was underplayed, but we all saw it clearly in our minds. "It's not that I'm complaining, but since joining you I've been physically shot, shot down twice, and blown up in vehicles twice. All in a little under ten weeks. Not a good look if you're just a pretty girl out for a stroll." We all laughed again, relieving the stress. She was a pretty girl, no doubt about that, but as for being out for a walk, one look at the fierce, concentrated look in her eyes and her constant poised-to-strike posture would dispel any notion of 'just a pretty girl'. I punched her on the shoulder.

"Yeah, that's likely, and you can't blame me this time." She turned her fierce eyes on me. Her face went grim, then she smiled and punched me back.

"But maybe they thought you were on board." I waved her comment away. We hadn't heard anything more about the fatwa on my head. It seemed to have stalled at 30 million euros.

Still enough to motivate the crazies, but that was life as we had come to know it. Our definition of the 'new' normal.

"Back to my briefing. We need to resolve our strategy in Scotland—let this Freya woman keep doing whatever she is doing a little longer, in the hope she gives us more data on what the terrorists are doing or planning? Then there's this Crissy person on Socotra, as in what in the name of Hell is she all about? The three—or is it four?—in Spain, and what was this test in Ireland? And do we pick up our favorite Irish terrorist before she gets to Killara Bay, or after she arrives? And what about Cochran and MacDonald, and Whiddy Island? We need to cope with all of these issues. I guess what I'm asking you all is, based on our experience so far, how do we set our priorities?"

"Commander, this Irish scientist, Siobhan, is the only one we can place so far with nuclear material and the shells. She had all the equipment on Badawi's boat capable of loading them, and a delivery system we believe would have worked. I think, perhaps, she presents the most danger." As he delivered his opinion in perfect English, Indigo was indicating he was deadly serious. I nodded my agreement but held my tongue. The silence was broken by Sandra, who lit up her mini, pushed the image onto the big screen, then scrolled through a shipping manifest. Unintelligible schematics and data flowed across the screen.

"Here's a list we took from Innomatchi before we got blown up on what they shipped to Killara Bay. This was a full two years before the attacks. And the indication is that the crates were inspected by Irish Customs on arrival in Belfast, passed, and moved on by truck. It is interesting to note the manifest matches exactly everything shipped to Point Roberts and New Zealand one year earlier. Neither of them were making shells, only panels and powerpacks, and Point Roberts biofuel as well." The silence descended on the room again like a curtain of fog as we each considered this information. On the screen, images and drawings of machines and output schematics continued to roll down, each full-page image jumping to the next as if chasing its predecessor.

"Okay, Sandra, dial in Point Roberts and get one of their engineers to verify this manifest. If all she's going to do is build a plant, we can let her get started at least. However, how will she seed the nanites?"

"Maybe she doesn't know we have the engineer from Helena." I nodded at that. We had never published a list of those we had sent to concrete cages and probably never would.

"Maybe she's smart enough to do it herself?" Bob asked from the sidelines. He had turned in his chair so he could face us. "I seem to remember when we took the ship we collected packets of nanites as well, which we now know open and close the shells permanently. We found similar nanites with each shell we recovered from our most recent jaunt around Europe."

"Definite possibility. But what's the bet there are already refugees in Killara Bay who will staff the plant. Maybe one of them has the smarts."

"Doesn't matter. What sticks in my mind is that those shells were never meant to work, and once loaded and sealed, they were just very expensive door stoppers. I'll bet my next paycheck she knew that going in." Sandra stood as she talked, rolling her shoulders, and finally stood behind Bob. "Have we heard from Fay?" Bob held out his mini.

"I've been reading it as it came in. You'll get the summary, but Arie sent me the progressive feed. What's the question?"

"What were the terrorists going to do with the shells?" I asked, turning so I could see both Bob and Sandra, who was now fidgeting with her hair.

"Well, firstly I'll give Fay credit for a very clever tactic with her interviews, and the consensus from Israel is that the women terrorists never wanted the shells in the first place, their agenda was hijacked by the mercenaries, which we suspected; the larger shells we took from Whiddy Island were manufactured by a splinter group, which looks like it was controlled by Maribelle Assiano, who we know was taken out by Jessica and the US Navy. Reading between the lines, the analysists feel that Assiano and a small group of mercenaries, probably with help from Badawi and Abbas, cooked the nuclear threat up themselves, then ran off and played with it. It's possible the women seeded the group with O'Cleary to ensure nothing went 'boom' at the wrong time. We can get Fay to question more of the heavy hitters we have in cages, but the data is fairly clear." I sat back, turned around, if the Israelis had come to this conclusion, we could take it to the bank. They had all the data and the best and most experienced analysts this side of the Atlantic. But it never hurt to have a second opinion.

"What does the US think?"

"They concur. I checked with the general just moments ago. Malcolm has been working with the geeks in real time, and the NSA and CIA agree with the findings. Interestingly, Anna made a comment that made me think." I nodded. Now I had two first-class opinions to work with, and it rarely gets better than that in the terrorist game.

If the nukes were a side issue and were now off the table, then that simplified things from our point of view. And we were still in the game well and truly because there were still mercenaries and women terrorists out there, not to mention nanites, now classified as a WMD. And most of the countries that had their drug crops destroyed had contacted Interpol for our help. Then what Bob had said sank in.

"Anna? What did she say?"

"She said from the outset, given the way we found out about the shells and the players, it was blind to what the women were really doing. The FBI head-shrinks and analysts couldn't find any plausible explanation for how a nuke threat would help the women sell the idea of refugee resettlements."

"We felt the same way."

"Agreed, but they sure as hell kept us busy, took us a lot of time and resources, not to mention the getting shot bit." Sandra paced back to her chair, rested her hands on the back of it, and faced the big screen, a scowl on her pretty face. She wore her small carry bag with her H&K slung across her back, and I wondered who she thought might attack us here inside our HQ in Venice.

"The situation as I see it is the planners, who were literally years ahead of us and probably still are to a certain extent, because we're still reacting, have won, and if we comb through your list, we're still chasing our tails. The children moving to different countries is a done deal. The only question in my mind is how many, to where, when, and what might happen if it goes wrong. And it will, we all know that.

"We already have five thousand refugee children on the bottom of the Atlantic Ocean, thanks to Maribelle Assiano.

"We'll have to release the funds we Red Flagged in those seventeen other countries at some point, get the engineers to help build the plants, then Amira and her gang to seed the nanites. No matter how we feel about it, all that is going to happen. Agreed?" You could drop a pin; it was so quiet, even the espresso machines had stopped huffing and puffing. On the screen, the data had stopped flowing. Fixating on the Innomatchi logo, a reminder of the attack in Japan just a day ago,

Sandra looked at all of us in turn, dropped her head, then looked back up, her face a mixture of fury and concern. Her hair had taken on a life of its own, flying around her pretty face every time she moved.

"We know these women are super smart-look at our own Amira and Fay for example-and the old man of the desert and his wicked companion from the Stasi had years and years to set all this up. They have deeply embedded agents everywhere. We know they were-or may still be-in every digital system on the planet. We also know they had buckets and buckets of money behind them, more that we have ever seen before in a terror organization. We know what they plotted and planned, right up until a week or so ago, and then boom! While we're chasing out tails In Ireland they take out a bunch of nuclear power plants, and poison every drug crop on the planet. They have boots on the ground, and those boots are trained, motivated, and directed by someone, because the timing on all this is not coincidental.

"They're coming at us in planned waves!"

She took a breath. We could see her chest expanding and contracting. There was no doubt she was worked up, and I suspected the recent attack on her in Japan was behind her anger. I knew she still took the drone attack on our aircraft over the Atlantic personally, but I had not seen her this emotional since she joined us.

"Jessica, commander, ma'am, sir, sorry for the spew, but I'm tired of being a target. If you want my take on the priorities, we go and destroy this Freya person as soon as possible; then this Crissy character in Socotra, wherever the Hell that is, and on the way find and sweep up Siobhan O'Cleary. We know her hands are dirty, we know she played with the nukes, and we know she played with Malik Badawi-the worst of the worst-he definitely was going to try to blow shit up." In the background, the espresso machines had started a puffing duel, but apart from that nothing stirred to spoil Jessica's rant.

She had made good points. Very, very good points. And I felt ashamed that I may have been going a little soft around the edges when I should have been at the pointy end directing traffic. She was absolutely correct. We had to take down their command and control capacity and capability, and we couldn't leave a known terrorist with the skills to build bimetallic shells and nanites floating around the world at her leisure. And Socotra could be another plant or design factory. We needed to shut it down no matter what.

And where exactly had the latest, bigger shells been manufactured?

"Indigo, what intelligence do we have on this Freya woman?" I asked, to start the ball rolling. It was time to get everyone invested in the outcome again.

He stood, walked to the espresso machine, refilled his mug, filled a new one for me, brought it back, and handed it to me with a little bow.

"We first pickeda upa hera transmissions a montha ago, instructing unknowna persons on the movementa of the shellsa down the Irish coasta, and in France and England. At a that timea the geeks had her pinpointed to an area around here," he said, pointing to a red circle on the digital map he had up on the big screen. "Lochgilphead was the epicenter. Bob senta foura people to investigate, posing as backpackers. They walkeda in from a drop offa on Lock Long. They founda the site of the satellite uplink, scanned it, and found no dark fiber leading anywhere." He moved the map, zoomed in on a small town called Aberfoyle.

"Now, youa mighta aska whya this towna?" He looked at Sandra, who was smiling now, enjoying Indigo's heavy Italian accent, which he put on like most people put on their underwear. The tension in the room caused by Sandra's impassioned rant dissipated like morning fog in a thunderstorm. I waved my hands at him, mouthed 'English', crossed my fingers. "That would be a very good question. Anyone want to guess except Bob?" Everyone shook their heads.

"Bob, over to you, please." Bob put his mini aside, stood, and walked to the screen. He acknowledged Indigo with a head nod and pointed to the map.

"We found a tiny microwave transmitter on the base of the antenna, pointed due east, so we took a bearing, and Ottoline, our most experienced stalker, walked it out. She found a repeater on top of Ben Lomond, just here with a 360 degree view of the countryside. It took her three days, but eventually she reached Aberfoyle. Population less than a thousand, a few miles north of Glasgow, ancient Scottish history is part of its story, but we didn't spot any microwave dishes. There is one there somewhere, but well hidden, and our best guess is indoors and protected, and only exposed during specific transmission times. We can intercept it, but only while they are transmitting, and that will give us a narrow direction, and the contents."

"We can still intercept from the dish?"

"Yes." I thought about that for a moment. Every Scott I had even met was as canny as any genius, and if we were dealing with one of the woman terrorists, then super canny might apply.

"Could they bounce the microware off in another direction?"

"Yes, they could."

"So they could be anywhere?"

"No. Microwave is strictly line-of-sight. Ottoline found no repeaters on her trek other than the one on the mountain, so she placed a detector with a laser sight aimed at where we suspect the receiver is, and when they use the dish again, we should be able to pin point exactly where it is. It would help if we could put a drone over the top, long duration, using a REDMAP detector. That will track and trace any outbound microware transmission, in case they are redirecting the stream, and will give us a direction."

"Explain that to me, please." Bob paused, frowned, and collected his thoughts. Indigo took the opportunity to refill everyone's coffee, and Sandra sat down at last, no longer vibrating. She was a battery bunny at the best of times, and when she got worked up, you could physically see her body shimmer and shake!

"A conversation usually consists of two parts—sender and receiver. We know they use burst transmissions, one way at a time, with the outbound preceding the inbound by at least five to seven minutes. There has only ever been the two bursts, so the sender is, from our perspective, aiming at the repeater from Aberfoyle. The return transmission comes from the dish, to the repeater, then to the sender. What the team has done is in the line from the repeater, and where we think the sender is, they've set up a laser that will read the direction of the microwave transmission, but not the content. We'll still get that off the dish."

"Is there any way to spoof the dish?" Sandra was leaning forward in her chair, her head being held up by one hand resting on her knees. The intense look in her eyes made it clear she was very much into this conversation. Her hair had settled back into its normal place, framing her face and stopping just above her shoulders. The room lighting created a shiny, rippled effect, and I wondered how she managed that given the relative primitive conditions we had just enjoyed in Ireland. I smiled to myself. I couldn't compete in the good-looking girl stakes!

"By spoof, do you mean duplicate or smother?" She turned to look at me.

"You want to keep them talking?" I thought about that. The conversations had given us excellent intelligence on what they were doing now, and maybe we'd get more by waiting, but I agreed with her earlier assessment—cut the head off the snake as quickly as possible. "No, on second thought, we locate the sender, then go in and collect the terrorists. Bob, what has been the period between transmissions?"

"The longest is three days, the shortest is six hours." I considered that first we had to track and trace, then set up a covert approach, possibly in an area full of civilians. I dialed the Boss.

"When will you give me back Tom?" His look was neutral, his eyes flat, but I could see the wheels turning in there somewhere. He had something on his mind, and I sensed it might not be good news.

"Hello to you too, Jessica. Lovely to see you again. Yes, I'm well. Thanks for asking." His sarcasm rolled across the ether like mercury across a steel plate and straight off my back. I ignored it. I realized I had been rude, but my sense of urgency was starting to catch up with my battery bunny's.

"Tom. When? And what's got you in such a tangle?" His face turned serious. I could see him take a huge breath as he let his frustration with me go, but his eyes focused on me like lasers.

"Tom you can have back, he's on the way, you can divert him if you need to. And our Irish problem just got a little trickier as the President of Ireland has directly petitioned the World Court, the UN, and our HQ for the release of the Irish prisoners. We've shuffled them off chasing due process, and the World Court will not reverse its decision, but the political noise is very loud. We've challenged them to produce an alternative solution, but from my experience and the advice I am getting here is that the noise will get louder, and black marks will be issued, and you'll be front and center in the complaint file." He smiled, a wicked smile that transformed his face from scarred to handsome. No way would he let anyone change their mind. "I may have to discipline you." Ha ha.

"Let the cards fall where they may; black marks don't worry me, but it's interesting, isn't it? We have our first nation-level complaint about how we have handled the terrorists, and from a first-world country, at that."

"Put it out of your mind, just be ready to lose the major and his *Sciathán Fianóglach*. I've already spoken to his direct boss, who is totally on our side, but she will have to issue the recall if the politicians request it. You might like to get in front of that, and you need to think about what we need to do to hold the Island and where to pull them from, and yes, they can be identified as Interpol. In fact, I will insist on it. A peacekeeping police force I think suits best under the circumstances, but gunned up and ready to fight."

"Thanks, appreciated. What are we doing about the drug crops?"

"I've got investigators in some countries, nailing down the time-line, looking for evidence, if we sniff out any terrorists you'll get the call. High level at this point, we're not stalling, but we haven't fast tracked it either for obvious reasons. The American DEA is champing at the bit, so we need to be thorough."

He had our backs in every way. All I needed to do was come up with twenty or thirty crack troops with first-class leadership that I could control. I looked over at Indigo. He nodded and started to map our current resources on the big screen, and I bet myself four hours down in my rack that we would end up calling Arie, Admiral Paul Rogers, or General Bridget Saunders.

Or all three of them.

I did a quick mental count. Bob had fourteen left from our ringfence in Scotland; we would eventually need more for the takedown whenever that occurred. Tom had a full complement of sixteen; Indigo had our standard issue of twenty, half from the elite Col Moschin, the 9th Assault Parachute Regiment, and half from our HQ contingent. All Indigo's men and women were

Section Five qualified, multilingual, and gutsy, fierce fighters, as they had proved on past occasions. And they loved espresso!

I did the math—ten plus eight plus eight plus a boss—which would give me more than we needed to secure the Island, given that we had removed all civilians and, as far as we were aware, the mercenary terrorists. Now, who should put in the change? Bob, Tom, or Indigo? If we called in the Israelis, could the colonel, *Sgan Aluf,* who ran the 104 commandos, manage a cross-national force? And the answer was, of course, yes. She could do it on her ear. I waved at Indigo to get his attention.

"Eight from Bob's team, ten from yours, and we'll get Arie to lend us the 104 again. I'll talk to him in a minute." He nodded at my suggestion.

"Bob, lend us eight. Keep the rest for Scotland." He nodded. I dialed Arie. It took a minute to connect, during which I had an epiphany. The boat we had taken off the mercenaries. Where was it? How could I get it? I made a mental note to follow that up when Arie's craggy face swam into focus.

"Arie, how are you?" He smiled, and once again I lusted after the grandfather I never had and inwardly sighed. A hug from the Israeli spymaster would have kept me going for weeks.

"Jessica, good to see you. I hear you need our 104 again?"

"Yes, please, your colonel with them. They'll be warranted under Interpol, it's a police action, ostensibly, but the truth is I just don't know yet what it might turn into. I'm combining Bob's RRT's, and Indigo's Col Moschin, and they will all replace the Irish major and his three teams of *Sciathán Fianóglach.* The Boss suggested we get in front of any recall, and I agree. Josephine Aria will lead the teams, reporting directly to me, or Tom, if that's okay with you?" He nodded, a little smile forming, as he recognized what I was doing.

"Excellent idea. Do you expect trouble?" I paused. All my instincts had caused my hackles to rise when it came to thinking about Ireland, and I could get sweaty under the armpits if I thought about it too long. Why had our overwatch been removed from the oil tank, and who had allowed a mercenary sniper to put us in their crosshairs? Plan for the worst and hope for the best.

"Arie, I just don't know. But my gut tells me Whiddy Island is important to the terrorists, and we have the government at the highest level sticking their oar in trying to get the terrorists we took into custody released back to them. Also, we have a bimetallic shell being dissolved on the east coast, from the batch made in Afghanistan, and terrorists attacked us at a major airport in daylight. The signs are not comforting." His face had taken on a serious look as I spoke, and I could feel his piercing gray eyes staring through to my backbone.

"You also lost the American and Irish helicopters, didn't you?"

I nodded. I had forgotten about that. No one was injured; just melting, stinking plies of rubber and metal with the huge blades hanging down like gigantic alien spider legs. How quickly you could erase a firefight from your mind when there were no human casualties!

"Yes. Where is Fay?" He looked at me, his eyes sparkling, a warm smile now covering his rugged face, and he took on a softer appearance.

"She is quite the interrogator. It's been fun to watch her work. She was packing up, then decided to take a run at the two young game programmers, Reve and Nazreen Anaisha. She finished about an hour ago, so I expect her back momentarily. Do you need to talk to her?" I shook my head.

"No, she sent through verbatim reports. Bob gave us the summary. I'm hoping we can put the nukes to bed once and for all." He nodded in sympathy, then looked off camera as something caught his attention. He seemed to listen for a minute, then leaned forward and smiled.

"Got to go. Stay safe, Jessica. The 104 will be with you in twelve hours."

"Thanks, Arie, appreciated." And I shut us down, leaned back, and worked through the next step.

"Indigo, I want you to go with the teams back to Ireland, at least initially. Make a smooth transition with the major. Make sure he knows he isn't being sacked. It's political. We might need him again. Brief the Israelis, settle them all in, then give me a call. I'll want you in the Scotland takedown, I just don't know when that will be. And I might have an interesting diversion for you." I smiled, and so did he, the thought of a diversion bringing happiness to every part of his solid frame. He literally started to bounce on his highly polished dress shoes.

"Commander, at your service!" And saluted me, causing Sandra to jump up and emulate him. I waved them both down. Motioned Sandra over and pointed to the big screen. She was back, and I thanked my lucky stars that she could pull herself together so quickly. The rant and rave had been entertaining but wearisome.

"Call our friend the admiral." She looked at me, curiosity in her eyes. She nodded, attacked her mini, and then the weather-beaten, dark face of my favorite admiral swam into view. His aide, Jordan Summers, was in the shot, slightly behind him, and I could see the head of the huge, flat tracking compass, so they were standing out on the bridge arm of their ship. The wind whipped at his hair, forcing him to put his squadron cap back on.

"Jessica, Sandra, good to see you. What's up?" He pulled his aviator sunglasses off and scrunched up his eyes against the sun to peer at the tiny camera.

"Admiral, you're looking relaxed, and it's good to see you as well. Are you still in the Med?" He smiled.

"Maybe. Maybe not. How can we help?"

Behind him, his 2IC moved away, probably to give the admiral some privacy.

"Where's our ship, the one we took off the terrorists?" He looked at me with a quizzical frown and tilted his head slightly to one side.

"Tied up next to one of my destroyers in the Med. Why?" I thought about how much to tell him, then jumped in with both feet. He had given us unqualified support during the toughest part of our operations so far, and while he was restricted by Navy rules and regulations, he had pushed them to their very edges in support of me and my people. He had also lost sailors and marines in an attack on a terrorist boat and sunk a rogue ship in the Atlantic, creating an atomic mist that had filled the airspace over the ocean, caught the attention of the rest of the world, and taken the lives of the entire crew of one of his destroyers.

The fact that my hand had been on the button with his was a secret I would take to my grave.

"I want to borrow the boat so we can mount a force projection in Bantry Bay. Unknown enemy, unknown capacity or capability, but the portends are strongly in their favor at this time. Remember your magnificent helicopter? Same bastards, different location."

"Do you anticipate it going into action?" he asked incredulously, the thought of a civilian boat being used in a naval engagement not sitting comfortably with him. Even one that had been fitted out with a nuclear-capable delivery system in its recent past.

"Quite possibly. Remember, this boat was fitted with the means to launch nuclear missiles at civilian targets, so it's not exactly a virgin." He had the good grace to smile at my metaphor.

"Whose flag?" I had to think about that: Interpol police action, unfriendly nation-state, sovereign waters. Only one option.

"I'll get Lyon to cover us as part of the police action Interpol is mounting in the area. So the US will be insulated from any blowback." He nodded, his eyebrows drawn together as he thought things through.

"Crew?" He got me again. I hadn't gotten that far other than to think in terms of getting Indigo aboard.

"Well, I haven't gotten that far, but I was thinking that Colonel Kashasini might like to play captain."

"I met him during the fuss in the Med—your fierce, solid Italian commando."

"Yes, he heads our Italian office, reports directly to me, and makes the best coffee on either side of the Atlantic." He started to nod, a small smile creasing his face, as the shadows crossed behind him, an indication they were moving at sea somewhere. In the background, I could just see a destroyer, its radar mast rotating like a Mixmaster. So he was still in the Atlantic on his carrier. Good.

"Yes, I remember. Well, I could give you a crew. You would have to warrant them. Then there's the question of weapons. The nukes are off the table, so you'll need medium and short range protection, possibly ground to air. Does that sound about right?"

And I suddenly realized why I had asked the Boss to induct Tom as my master-at-arms. Yes, I could lead from the front, shoot and kill when necessary, and use any weapon in our arsenal, but I was an investigator, not a soldier, and I needed a specialist to tell me exactly what firepower I needed and how to best use it. The Boss had said I could divert Tom on his way back, so that was a given.

"Admiral, do you remember Master Chief Tom? He was with us in the Med as well. He's just transferred to Section Five permanently. I can have him to your destroyer within hours, and it would be my preference for him to nominate what weapons we put on board."

"Excellent. I'll look forward to how that all works out. Keep in touch. We'll get the boat ready, as far as its systems and engines are concerned." And he ended the call, leaving me to wonder how Tom would find the destroyer. No need.

I dialed Tom.

"Commander?" His face was partially hidden by a seat, so he was airborne, heading somewhere, hopefully home.

"Get to Venice. Indigo will meet you at the airport. You'll chopper in to the US fleet in the Med and sort out what we require by way of armaments for the boat we took from the terrorists. I'll have more for you later. Enjoy your trip."

"Indigo, you heard both conversations. Get dressed for sea duty. I'll send Sandra in your place to Ireland. Pack a go bag for Tom. Take it with you. In the meantime, work out what weapons and crew you want on the boat. Your brief is to stop any vessel from entering our declared no-go zone, which you will set and post, plus I'll have a specific brief for you shortly. Organize a chopper, which you will keep on the boat, and make sure it has big guns." I switched targets.

"Sandra, go do what Indigo was going to do, get everyone pointed in the same direction at Whiddy Island, then get back here asap." As I finished, the two smiling Italian commandos, dressed immaculately in their blue and red striped uniforms, who had shadowed me during Sandra's previous absence sauntered over, as casual as you like, pulled up chairs, ignored me, and took mugs of coffee off Indigo. I was effectively boxed in, and somehow I had to stop this waste of manpower. Indigo and Sandra left for their quarters, and fuming just a little, I reviewed what I had just set in motion and noticed Bob was sipping coffee and giving me a quizzical look.

"Something on your mind, Bob?" I asked, rolling my shoulders to get the tension out of them. I not only needed sleep, I also needed a hot bath.

He just smiled, looking like a relaxed schoolteacher on afternoon break. His smiling face belied his canny nature and his smart mind. Then, working directly for the President of the United States wasn't for just anybody.

"Jessica, I've seen you up close and personal under combat conditions, so I know you can change tactics in a heartbeat, but to be honest, the speed with which you act is blistering. I can see why the Boss gave you command." If only he knew! I was fast and speedy, but confident in all my decisions, I wasn't.

The game we played against the terrorists had few rules. They broke them as a matter of course, and we broke most of them at one time or another. Asymmetric warfare required hard-nosed choices, not always ones that sat well with traditional soldiering or public opinion. Bob had come to me from the Presidential Guard in Washington, and he and his team had distinguished themselves in Montana and again in the hunt for the nuclear shells across Europe. I had him stake out who we believed to be the current head of the women terrorists, and it suddenly occurred to me that he had fitted into our little team seamlessly.

"Thanks Bob, I appreciate the vote of confidence. Before Indigo takes off, get him to lend you the drone you want, fit it out how you like, and get it overhead Aberfoyle and Ben Lomond. Then start planning how we can take Freya down without civilian interference." He stood and saluted me with a big smile.

"Yes, commander," he said, and he walked out in the same direction as Indigo and Sandra. That left me with my two bodyguards, the geek team, beavering away at their consoles, and a choice. I stood.

"*Signori, potete ritirarvi, sarò nei miei alloggi per le prossime quattro ore.*"

"*Sì, comandante, goditi il pisolino.*"

I would, indeed, enjoy my nap!

ˈALˠAPƏ

Torness nuclear power station is located approximately 30 miles east of Edinburgh at Torness Point near Dunbar in East Lothian, Scotland. The reactor had become infamous back in 2022 when cracks were found in the graphite cores that leaked radiation out into the ocean. Scheduled for final closure some years later, the terrorist attack that littered the power station with silver-colored clag made any future closure moot. Interestingly, the nanites had chased the radioactive particles all the way out to the final lengths of water pipe, creating a visible scar on the rocky beach. Fisherfolk still plied the choppy waters, but swimmers were still a little reluctant to risk their health. No leak had ever occurred, but it was the gist of the public outcry against the power plant, and as everyone came to know, the media ruled credibility, fiction over fact.

From a distance, the power station looked like a massive white concrete block house, with smaller blocks of buildings at its feet. Up close, all it looked like was tired, abandoned, and somehow seeking a better future. Under the empty blue sky, the direct sunlight cast long shadows between the buildings, as if it were seeking to lure you into one of the bright green doors that were now barred and locked against all comers.

Run by EFF Energy, who had their hands full from the forced closure of all the other nuclear plants they controlled, the 500-person workforce had been reduced to just one lonely guard on a single four-hour shift. His lot in life consisted of punching a mechanical clock with a time/date stamp, then finding the shadiest spot to sit, read, and smoke his life away.

The helicopter, flown by a thin woman wearing a black flight suit, a black helmet, and dark black glasses, her dark hair cut short, had landed on a small isthmus just south of the unhappy site, giving Katrina, Lily, Lilian, and Else about a half-mile walk on the bitumen road. When Katrina asked the pilot the reason for landing so far away from their target, she simply replied, "not safe closer," in guttural English. She had also been a victim of the lies about the leak.

Katrina was wearing a radiation detector on her wrist, which was as passive as her watch on her other wrist, but rather than argue, she helped the girls unload all their cases, which on this occasion were considerable. She also pulled out three hand carts, which they loaded everything onto. They had barely reached the perimeter of the rotor blades before the pilot took off, tail high, nose to the ground, backing away from the plant as if it were contagious. The cyclonic rotor wash was fierce and almost blew the women off their feet. Katrina made a mental note to let Freya know the outcome of the drop and hoped for a more accommodating pilot for their next leg.

"Okay, head for that small covered area. I think I can see the guard."

Against the hand cart and its stacked boxes, Lily looked like a diminutive fairy, her blue pants suit and colorful blouse offset by her pretty bowl of reddish hair, capped by a wide-brimmed fedora-style Panama, which she now fought to hold onto her head. No one would pick her to be one of the world's top physical scientists. No one would pick her as a terrorist.

Which she definitively did not believe herself or her sisters to be. The way she saw it, remembering her own dreadful past before the age of eight, when she had been beaten and raped repeatedly in the refugee camp simply because she existed, and then the sheer amount of time it had taken her to recover after being rescued, she and her sisters, both with similar stories, were now the bringers of hope to a world currently trying to destroy itself because conditions had changed. Conditions that had sucked many people into a spiral of digital disgust, love of things, loss of respect for the real, and the constant habit of one country attacking another.

She acknowledged that the human race had warred for as long as it had existed, with fear, greed, power, envy, and politics all being drivers for unceasing carnage and destruction. And in a funny way, she saw the current climate as a potential circuit breaker because most of the power structures that had previously been erected on the backs of disenfranchised people, ecological disasters, fossil fuels, and outright greed were now crumbling in the wake of the so-called terrorist attacks. She clearly saw the tragedy in the attacks and their aftermath. The social unrest had been epic. She knew the death toll worldwide was now approaching sixty million, with possibly one or two hundred million more displaced by the fury of the gangs, the raping, pillaging, and sheer wanton and senseless destruction. But ordinary people were starting to fight back.

Families had been forced to migrate to rural areas, learn to farm and grow crops, barter, and use their skills for the communities they helped form. The world didn't need sixty thousand lawyer-lobbyists, it needed sixty thousand farmers, shopkeepers, builders, craftsmen, and women. And as for the massive conclaves of overbearing and overpaid members of the so-called United Nations and other worldly political groups, all they had managed to do for the last one hundred and twenty-five years was talk, endlessly talk, apply sanctions that hurt ordinary people, and look good on the six o'clock news. The day of the international institution was on the clock, and most had failed the smell test.

The world had been broken long before her sisters had launched their attacks, and as she saw it, as her mother had said on many occasions, the only real mistake they had made was in linking with the mercenaries. She had been privy to none of the conversations the organizers had held. She had been away learning on the job right up until a few months before, when her mother called her home. And, she had to admit, at first, when her mother told her what was to happen, what role she was to play, what the role was that her mother had played for years, and what she and her sisters would be asked to do, she initially felt very disconcerted and unsure of her path.

That had changed when Katrina and Crissy had made contact and ran through all that they had been developing for the last four years. It was simple, it was brilliant, it was irresistible, and it would change the world for the better and give ordinary people the hope they deserved to live a full and fulfilling life. Would greed, fear, power, lust, and politics diminish? She had a sense it might. Distributing the very core of what had crushed the modern world into its political and secular divisions offered the ordinary person the opportunity to make their own way, find their own balance, and build their own communities without so much artificial economic and political push and shove.

You didn't need a new technology-driven phone every year. You needed a phone that would last for years and do what it was supposed to do at a price the average person could afford without having to go into debt.

They reached the guard, who stood at their approach, hiding his burning cigarette behind his back. Katrina reached forward and held out a sheaf of papers.

"We're from EFF Energy. We'll be inside for some days. Please don't let our visit disturb you." She smiled as she spoke, to take any perceived rancor out of her statement. He looked at the letterhead, scanned the page, then awkwardly one-handedly pushed it back to her.

"Aye, you've got the right to that. Is there anything I can be doing for you while you are here?" His brogue was thick, laced with the music of his country. Katrina eyed him over the papers and smiled.

"Thank you, but we'll be fine. We're planning on doing our inspections as fast as we can, and we won't interrupt you at all." He bobbed his head, still trying to hide the cigarette behind his back, but a thin wisp of blue-gray smoke gave it away. "Perhaps if you could give us the key for the workshop door?" The smoke made a trail towards the ground as he fumbled for his key ring, but he found the one he wanted, slipped it off the chain, and handed it to Katrina.

"And we thank you for that. Have a lovely day." The women moved off, the sisters towing the trolleys, until they reached the blue and white striped door. A massive sign warned of the horrors within. A huge radioactive sign was centered on the door, and yellow and black police tape was crossed from top to bottom, left to right.

Katrina cut through the tape, rolled it up, and handed it to Lilian. She opened the door, and they pulled their trolleys into the dark space of an equipment hangar.

"You can feel the emptiness," Else said, pushing her trolly.

"Lonely, sad building. I feel sorry for it." Katrina looked at Else and smiled. She pulled the pale yellow silk scarf from around her neck and opened her houndstooth coat, revealing an aqua collared blouse with long, clean, knife-edged sleeves.

"This plant has had nothing but trouble from the first day they started to build it. The people who live around here didn't want it, and hundreds were jailed over the years because of the protests, and when the bricks started to leak, the writing was on the wall."

"It's a pity we have to use its infrastructure. If the locals could see what we have, I suspect they would fall in love with it." Katrina pulled a massive case off a trolly, letting it thump onto the concrete floor.

"You're not wrong, but the consensus is we need to hide our technology, at least until we have the agreements with the governments we seek. The beauty of this system is that it is self-sustaining; it can be located anywhere within reason. They can be scaled up and down with ease, and they will change the balance of power forever. Don't lose sight of that." Else tipped her head to one side and smiled indulgently, her hazel eyes sparkling in the work light.

"Do you think we'll have enough time left over to visit mom?" Katrina returned her smile and waved towards the dark.

"For sure, but we need to finish up here first. Let's go."

CHAPTER TWENTY FIVE

I woke up slowly, realized the light outside had changed, looked at my pink watch my mother had given me years ago, and realized I had been out for nearly seven hours. I stretched, rolled my shoulders, made little fists of my toes, and headed for the shower. The fact we had multi jets in our quarters was a well-kept secret from the boys, who for some reason only had a single shower head. I used every one, letting the hot water pummel my aches and pains away.

I picked out my fawn military-style trousers, pulled on a brown t-shirt, a lightweight jacket with pockets and flaps all over, strapped on my weapon, stuffed my combat knife into my boot, noticed they needed a good clean, made a mental note to take care of it sometime, and headed out for life-saving coffee.

The twin monstrous brass and steel espresso machines were huffing and puffing in concert, the smell of freshly ground beans filling our HQ. During my sleep, the room had been cleared and cleaned. Every workstation was now a neat testament to the style and panache of the Italians, one of the reasons I loved working here in Venice.

I checked the movements board and saw that Fay was due back in an hour, Sandra was more than halfway to Ireland, the 104 were twenty minutes behind her, Indigo was due to touch down on a destroyer in the Med in fifty minutes, Tom had his entire team on a rest break, there was no movement in Scotland, the drone had been provided by Indigo and would be over the target in three hours, and I noticed that they had organized refueling and a temporary control point at Royal Air Force

Kirknewton, a RAF base in West Lothian. Close to Edinburgh. Handy to both our targets at Aberfoyle and Ben Lomond. The base was essentially only a glider station, so its selection was both strategic and tactical.

I now had my troops scattered to the four winds, and it would test both my patience and control. I wondered where my Italian guards were, then noticed them sitting at a console updating the board. The lights were turned way down, so it looked like two black-suited figures working magic in the gloom, the red stripes on their uniform trousers forming an interesting inverted 'L' shape. Both had their caps off, both had that luxurious black hair that favored the Italians, and both had cheeky, warm smiles when they turned to face me.

"Buonasera, come vanno le cose con voi due?"

"Bene, grazie comandante, hai dormito bene?"

"Sì. Più a lungo di quanto io aspettassi, ma vedo tutto tranquillo?"

"Se puoi darci cinque minuti, possiamo finire di caricare i dati attuali."

I nodded. I could give them the time they asked for, took my seat just behind them, looked at my desk, and saw a handwritten note from Sandra. We had all become so used to digital stuff that something handwritten had a real impact!

'Jessica, commander, your majesty, sir, ma'am, I have your PPU updating the board. Indigo has sorted the drone; Bob is offline until 1900; we gave the geeks the afternoon off. They are all exhausted and will be back by 2000 or earlier if you need them. Copy of the full report from Fay on your mini. I think you will appreciate her tactics with the two women from Whiddy Island; very clever of her. The Boss called to warn us that the Irish Government will rescind permission for the use of the major and his Sciathán Fianóglach from 1700 tomorrow, but we will be in position well before then, so no drama. Amira wants a long chat with you when you have time, and if you could, I'd like to be in that conversation.' It was signed Senior Inspector Sandra Thomas (acting), and I wondered who had promoted her, then laughed. She was pulling my leg; we had no such rank. Good, she had her humor

back, she was dialed in, my battery bunny was back up to full speed, and heaven help the terrorists.

But I gave thought to the Irish situation. It was escalating, and I could feel it in my bones. I checked my watch again and mentally worked out what time it was in Ireland—just the one hour difference—so I called my favorite monk.

"Jessica, hello. Lovely to see you again. How is everybody?" His smile lit up the late afternoon, his background looked green and lush, and he was sitting against a tree. "Say hello to Father Paul Ryan, my friend who has joined me on this leg of our journey." A young, innocent face pushed into the side of the screen, all smiles and wind-blown brown hair and lily white skin, his head held up by a white collar in a black neckband of some type. He waved one hand, which was badly in need of a wash.

"Hello, I'm Paul, and I'm happy to make your acquaintance." He disappeared the way he had arrived, leaving Francis front and center. Francis turned his head to one side, and I could see the small scar running down his throat from his ear.

"Paul, why don't you walk to that little shop and see if you can get us some tea?" He handed him a punt off camera, then focused back on me.

"Jessica, I'm glad you called. There are things I need to tell you."

"Who is this father Paul, and why is he with you?" More aggressive than I planned.

"He's a Jesuit priest and educator, and his calling is to set up a school somewhere here in Ireland. He's good company, if a little young with it, but we all have to learn some time." I sat back, running this complication through, and couldn't see any obvious traps. I trusted Francis with my life, and had seen him sit in the middle of a massive fire fight as calm as could be, while people died all around him, and the earth literally erupted and rose up from exploding underground cruise missile strikes, moving an old church way up off the ground.

If he wasn't concerned, neither would I be.

"Okay, I trust your instincts. What gives?" His smile faded slightly, and he imported a series of images, which he swiped through slowly.

"These are the panels being fitted to the row houses outside Dundalk, and we've seen another two trucks full of them pass us in the last day. By my count, which admittedly is rough, they will have panels on over two or three hundred houses by week's end." The light blue 'A' shaped panels looked like miniature roofs, so it was easy to imagine them on top of a row house. A long gray cylinder was attached, with a series of orange and blue cables running to and from it.

"What's that cannister?" He expanded the view with his fingers, and using a ladder behind it for scale, I judged it to be around six feet high and two feet in diameter. Big dude, about the size of an old-fashioned water heater, and a stack of them were off to one side in the last photo.

"My best guess is a battery of some sort, or possibly a transformer." I nodded. That made the most sense, and we didn't really have to know every detail. It was capacity, capability, and intent that most interested us, so I moved onto the next question.

"Do you know where they are coming from?" He shook his head, his roughly cut hair flying all around his face. He lifted one hand to wipe it back, revealing yet another patch on the cuff of his Kāṣāya. I knew he wore the robes as a sign of penance and to show he had forsaken money, position, and power, eschewing most modern artifacts, but the skill he was demonstrating using the minicomputer we had given him suggested he was a quick learner and not necessarily adverse to modern technology.

"My best guess is down south. I can keep going if you want me to." I thought about that. Was there a benefit to knowing where they had stored the panels? They had obviously been made on Whiddy Island. The photographs from both locations proved that. The terrorists had a million house plan. What we were seeing was part of that, and again, the downstream detail wasn't all that important. Catching the terrorists was. As Sandra had pointed out during her rant, the terrorists had won as far as migrating the young child refugees were concerned.

And experience had taught us that at least one or two terrorists would be in any prime location that was being developed to take the refugee children.

The pilot, scientist, and engineer had been living in Helena for two to three years before the building of the houses started using the panels and power supplies developed at Point Roberts.

Our infamous Maribelle Assiano and her master psychologist lived in Roanoke years before it was developed. We have picked up women terrorists in New Zealand, Japan, Pakistan, and now Ireland. We knew we had at least one lurking somewhere in Scotland and at least two more in Ireland, and from the damage being done around the world to nuclear power stations and drug crops, it appeared there were a lot more to be accounted for.

Or it could be a different crop of mercenary terrorists.

We had been attacked in Ireland twice, once on Whiddy Island and then at Cork airport, and while we had killed or captured those involved, it didn't mean we had rooted all of them out. Some had escaped from the old fort.

"Francis, if you don't mind, wander back to Dundalk very casually and find a safe location where you can stay for a few days, perhaps the apartments.

"And just look around as if you are searching for a location for your friend's school." He nodded, looked down slightly, then back up at the camera.

"We can do that, and in truth, that would be an excellent location for his school in any case. There are over three hundred children without parents there. It would be a big help to the people managing the apartments and row houses."

"Do you know any of them?"

"Yes. Moriah particularly, she's the unofficial mayor of the entire town. She runs the apartments, manages the children, sees that they are fed and clothed, and provides beds for them when they want to come in. She's a teacher up in Belfast. Her university has been shuttered by the riots and civil unrest, so she's been looking after everyone in Dundalk, where she lives."

"She sounds like a wonderful person." His face lit up, remembering the warm and comforting hospitality he and Paul had received just days ago.

"Aye, that she is."

"Did you encounter any other strange activities on your way south?" His face broke into a beatific smile again, just as he was handed a go-cup, probably with the tea he had requested his companion get. The way he pushed his nose at it suggested it more than met with his approval, his eyes closing momentarily, his eyebrows lifting as he sniffed, a little 'aahhh' escaping.

"Aye, we did at that, a whole lot of youngsters working at a makeshift recycling site, pulling anything of value from abandoned vehicles. They also had some way to melt the metal panels. I don't know how they did it. They had no visible fire going that I could see, but they were filling old rusted forty-liter drums with cut up pieces of the vehicles, and the filled barrels we saw had a silver sheen to them. Many of the children were from Dundalk, as we recognized them. I gave that some thought. It might just be local ingenuity, or it might not. And we knew the women had invented a nanite that dissolved bimetallic shells. Maybe one that did the same to aluminum and steel was not a step too far away. Something to chase down later, perhaps.

"Thank you. Do you need anything from us?" I asked. He shook his head.

"No thank you, Jessica. We'll be fine. Be safe." And he made the sign of the cross and disconnected. I went back to my mulling, not quite a brood, definitely not a sulk, and I noticed both my guards had stopped what they were doing, and were looking directly at me. I waved them down, brought up Fay's report, and immediately agreed with Sandra's assessment of her cleverness.

Letting the two Irish women dress in their original clothes and spruce up their hair and cosmetics as if they were to be released was a very smart way to get them talking, which, of course, they had.

Her report on her conversation with the two young girls who had created the game program from which the terrorists had created their war plan was a different matter. Both were not yet twenty, both were undoubted geniuses, both were confused as to why they had been locked up, and, as they pointed out, a lot of the development had been done online with hundreds of other contributors. That gave me pause for thought.

Then I remembered that one of them had been taken at the New Zealand plant and the other at Innomatchi, so their protested innocence went straight out the window. Did I feel guilty about that? Their war plan had set the world on fire, so no, not one bit. Asymmetric warfare was bitch. Finding and capturing genius-level refugee women was proving to be even harder.

I put my mixed thoughts away and dialed Amira. She swam into focus surrounded by laboratory equipment, had a huge pair of safety glasses on, and what looked like yellow rubber kitchen gloves. The mini was obviously on some sort of stand, as I could see far more than usual behind and around her.

"Hi Amira, can you talk?" She sat further back, and I could see her white-stained lab coat flap open, revealing an equally stained pink shirt. Whatever she had been doing was all over her, so I sincerely hoped it wasn't toxic.

"Yes, thanks for calling me. I wanted to bring you up to date with what we are finding with the nanites. Let me get a drink." And she moved out of camera range, then slipped back in, taking off her gloves, then used her long, lovely fingers to pull the cap off an orange can. She tipped it up and slurped it, and I could hear it going down all the way from Venice! "Ahh, that's better. The problem with working in a biolab is that it gets hot, and you tend to dehydrate.

"Now, the nanites. You've caught up with the different versions that came out of Whiddy Island?"

"Yes, one for biofuel, one to dissolve the bimetallic shells, and one that boils water, is that right?" She nodded, slurped another mouthful, pushed her long hair back behind her ears, and glowed. I could see the happiness flowing out of her like a bright fog.

"You're really hyped about something?" Big smile, sparkling eyes, head bobbing up and down as if on springs.

"You could say that. Whether or not I could have gotten this far so quickly without the development the women have done with the nanites is a moot point, but I've been able to build on it, and we now have a far bigger understanding of what we can do with them than ever before." Her tone was so upbeat and so positive, I nearly forgot we had classed them as WMDs.

"Where are you heading with all of this?" I was curious. The nanites had effectively killed all oil, gas, and coal deposits, been used to make nuclear-capable shells, taken out most if not all nuclear power generating stations, most nuclear warheads and missiles, and last but not least, all the drug crops around the world. And we now had versions that would make biofuel, dissolve bimetallic substrates, and boil water, and for the love of me, I couldn't see the reason for that version.

"The early work we did, when we made the nanite that ate the oil spill, was designed to consume itself, sink into the ocean floor, and break up. The trick was attracting it to the carbon in the oil, getting it to eat it, then self-replicate and transform all the way into an inoffensive and neutral biomass. What the women have done is take our design principle and apply it to different compounds, while essentially keeping its self-replicating capability. The way they designed it, once it consumes its target particulate, instead of dissolving into harmless sludge, it feeds on the oxygen it generates, then hardens into the silver clag we have found everywhere.

"It's brilliant. Genius even." I watched her finish her drink, then crush the can top to bottom with one delicate hand. I had no idea she had such strength! "And did I mention the amazing way they designed it to attach itself to their target molecule?" she continued, bubbling over with excitement.

"Good, I'm glad we now understand it. Can we reverse it?"

"No. It's a transformative molecular change. Once done, it's finished. But now we know what they did, and the biofuel nanite is in a class all of its own."

"How so?" I was genuinely curious. All I knew about biofuel was what I read in papers, magazines, and on the web. Most articles started with the oil and grease from restaurants, which I found most unappetizing.

"Well, if you take a biomass rich in fruits, vegetables, or flowers, the nanites attack the carbohydrate, carbon skeletons, and mineral content, consume the biomass, and convert it into carbon-free fuel. It's several iterations and generations beyond where we were back in normal times. And it's a force multiplier—one kilogram of nanites will convert one hundred thousand kilos of biomass." I thought about that, then asked the obvious question a dumb person like myself would always ask.

"Is it easy to convert petrol or diesel engines to run on it?"

"Simplicity itself. And its knock point is so close to carbon-based fuels as to be not noticeable." I'd have to look up 'knock point' to fully understand what she had told me, but I got the gist of it. We had cheap power-based technology on our hands, so I asked the question that was most on my mind.

"How long before we get pushback on nanites being WMDs?" She stopped smiling and went almost rigid, as if I had punched her.

"WMDs? You serious?" She had lost her sparkle; her face shuttered.

"When did that happen? And why? These nanites are miracles with which we can make an ecologically responsible future!" She didn't shout, but the force with which she spoke caused me to pause, and I realized she had ownership of the nanite development we had tended to ignore, pushing it back five or six years ago in our minds, at least, to when she had perfected the first iteration. Of course, she was invested. She was the first genius to manipulate the nanites to do her bidding. I realized I had made a huge, fundamental mistake in leaving her out of our discussions. As far as leaders went, I still had a hell of a lot to learn.

"Amira, I apologize, and no 'buts', it was a decision the Boss and I took in order to be able to continue to prosecute the women terrorists. Once the last nuclear-capable shell had been removed, we needed something to keep our sponsors focused on so we could continue to work the terrorist problem." She looked at me, her facial features slowly returning to her normal warm countenance, and she held one hand out as it reached out to me.

"Jessica, I'm sorry to have snapped at you. You took me by surprise. I don't see them as WMDs, but I support your reason for having them designated as such. The problem you face—sorry again, we face—is that the nanites offer us a way forward previously thought unattainable. A carbon-free, biologically, and environmentally responsible way of doing things. I suspect as the wider world learns of them and what they can do, you will be pressured into removing the WMD tag." I thought about that, and in principle I agreed, but I knew from the inside how long a government—or for that matter, a quasi-government—entity could keep the lid on, if only through self-interest, so I wasn't overly concerned.

As it turned out, I should have been. I asked another dumb question.

"Can you lay out for me how the biofuel nanite might be used?" She looked inward, her eyes defocused, her brow furrowed, and her hands started to roll around each other. I noticed her fingernails had been trimmed and polished and wondered, not for the first time, how women managed to do that in times of war. She came back to me with a huge smile and literally jumped up in her seat.

"Jessica, you'd need a very big tank. You fill it with your biomass, then inject the nanite under pressure from a small system that we could build here in the lab; and you could then get someone to manufacture. Trivial really, it would take no effort at all." A plan was starting to hatch in the back of my mind, only whisps at this point, but I could feel the tug.

"Can these nanites be manufactured in the environmental plants the terrorists designed?" She went blurry again but bounced back in just a few seconds.

"Absolutely. The samples we got were from Whiddy Island, and by samples I mean the twenty-five-liter containers. I'd have to look at the plant where they produced them, but the starter kit should be able to be duplicated. Where you would build it remains a question, now that you have shut down Innomatchi." Japan again, we kept going around and around in the same geographical circles.

"How many people do you know who can manipulate the nanites? Control them, develop them, manufacture them?" She linked her fingers together, sat back, and looked serious.

"I'm training a group now, but to be frank, apart from the three you know about from Harvey Mud and my ex-friend Michele, not many seem to have the instincts or the patience to work at the sub-atomic molecular level. I may have one guy. He's brilliant, youngish, and driven, like most Israelis, but he still needs a lot of time. Remember, we suspect that the women only had one or two in their entire line-up who could manipulate the nanites, and they traveled from site to site to keep all that going."

For a fleeting moment, I wondered what 'youngish' was in Amira's lexicon. She had barely turned twenty-seven or eight herself and looked like a teenager.

"In all the material we got from Innomatchi, was there a set of plans for making these starter kits?"

"Yes, and a lot more besides. But I can tell you from the shipping data that only the plant at Whiddy Island has the technology to produce them. It might be a question of development time or a question of priorities." I gave that some thought, reached no conclusion, and tucked it away for another day.

"What's with the boiling water nanite?" I had wanted to ask that question for days. She sat back a fraction, looking a little guilty.

"Sorry, I haven't gotten to that yet." I nodded. We had a ton of data to unpick, and in the scheme of things, the boiling nanite could wait.

"Okay, thanks, Amira. Is that all you wanted me for?"

"No, I have information for you on something else." I looked at her, curiosity popping out of my eyes.

"Go."

"Well, we pulled several thousand documents and data sets out of Innomatchi, and I have a team going through them one by one. But on a quick flick through, I found this drawing stapled to a blueprint, with very little explanation attached, but important enough to have been in a sealed vault we had to break into." She held the drawing up to her camera, and I took individual screen shots of it. Then she turned to the blueprint, and I took shots of that.

"What is it?" I asked as I scrolled through the shots. Not a geek!

"It looks like a small turbine, the sort you would have in a midsized jet engine. The blueprint is for a CAD/CAM 3D additive printer, but the hand-drawn sheet suggests they haven't made one yet, or it turned into something else."

"What got you curious about this particular drawing?" I could see no reason behind it that fit with what we knew the terrorists had done so far.

"It doesn't fit into any logical category we have found. It's as if someone had a great idea, tried it once, then simply filed it away. I know the feeling. That's how I used to work. My cupboards were filled with bits and pieces of paper. In fact, I had to leave most of them behind when I took off. I use a notebook now."

"Uh." I wiped my face. It was time for more coffee, and I noticed the geeks slowly filing back to their work stations, some slurping down cartons of noodles. Seeing them made me realize I hadn't eaten since breakfast, a long time ago.

Now we had an unidentified object, whose purpose was unknown, that had caught the eye of our genius scientist. I would not let this slide. Instincts were as important in this business as facts, and Amira was years ahead of all of her contemporaries and had been for her entire life. She may have started at age seven or eight when she was pulled out of a refugee camp and given to loving Israeli parents, but from that point on, she was at least a decade ahead of all who came before or after her. University at fourteen, first doctorate by seventeen, second by nineteen, major scientific breakthrough in her very early twenties, and that was what we actually knew about.

I earmarked the drawing and blueprint, clicked them into a little blue folder on my screen, and paused. I was missing something. It tickled at the back of my mind. I stared through the camera and into Amira's eyes, saw her looking at me with a wishful look, and it clicked.

"You want to make one of these things?" She broke out in a huge smile and clapped her hands. Her excitement was palpable.

"Yes, but I don't want to ask Arie or distract from what we are doing here in the lab. And you are the only person apart from Arie I know who can give me permission to do it." I felt flattered. Here was a world-beating scientific genius asking me for permission to run an experiment. Not a geek!

"Do you have the equipment to make it there?" She nodded, obviously prepared for my question.

"At one sixth scale, we only have a small printer, but that will tell us enough to figure out what it is, and hopefully, what they have in mind for it." I nodded. I didn't know much about additive printing, but I did know the machinery for it was large, very large, but if she said one sixth scale would be okay, I wasn't going to challenge her.

"Go for it. Anything else?" She shook her head, her wonderful hair flying all over the place again, and I was reminded just how young she looked.

We disconnected, and I dragged the video of the conversation I had made into the folder and sent it to Jessica. She had asked to be included in the call, but I wanted her to focus on her immediate task, which was to do a handover or takeover in

Ireland while preserving our relationship with the major and his specialist teams. We might need them in the future, and I wasn't about to let politics rob me of potential resources—especially great shooters.

I made a mental note to fill Arie in the next time we connected and blinked when the overhead lights came on at full strength.

I opted for a meal, stood, and was immediately blocked in by my two Italian studs, so I waved them forward and headed for the small mess we maintained in our HQ. And the situation in Scotland pooped into my head, unbidden and unwelcome. I'd eat first, then look at it in detail. A half-hour wouldn't make all that much difference.

SASSENACHS

They were at 10,000 feet, flying in and out of clouds, with long patches of sunlit countryside fleeing underneath them. Green, built-up areas, but silent, green, more green, more quiet cities and towns. The English countryside passed with a flourish, but the lack of road traffic was very noticeable.

She had been able to count the vehicles on the roads but had yet to reach double figures. Katrina could not help but feel lucky that this pilot seemed to have no fear of radiation, as he had landed right next to the doorway of the maintenance lab at Torness nuclear power plant, and with the help of the more than willing guard, they had loaded and got away in less than twenty minutes.

The pity of it was that Torness, because of its hard shutdown and prior history with fractured bricks, was much harder to work on, and it had taken all of the five days she had allocated. So there was no visit to Freya, and her girls were not happy about that. In fact, she thought that if Lily pouted any harder and the wind changed, her face would set in a really ugly mask!

Their destination was the most recent and modern of the nuclear plants in the UK, some three and a half hours away, and she smiled when she remembered it was also managed by EFF Energy. Sizewell B had been a pressurized water reactor, a massive lattice-woven dome sitting on top of an unremarkable squat and square building. In fact, the dome wasn't sitting on the building. It was an optical illusion, as it sat on its own little block at the rear.

Seen as the technological lead in the design of future nuclear power plants, it was an unmitigated disaster when it was abruptly brought to a hard stop by the nanite contamination. The scientists and technicians had tried everything they knew to free it up, but to no avail, and like the rest of the reactors throughout Europe, it now only had a skeleton staff or lightweight security. The mandarins at EFF Energy and their counterparts in the UK Government had pulled their hair out at the sudden loss of electrical capacity, and with the world's record for overcast and rainy days, they were now surviving on the wind farms scattered along the North Sea.

It wasn't enough; less than 26 percent of the electrical power the country consumed came from wind farms, so the deficit was noticeable and poignant.

The rioting and civil unrest had erupted violently after the initial terrorist attacks and were just as violently put down by police and the military with a hard-edged nation-wide curfew. The major arterial roads had been clogged by stalled vehicles and cleared by military trucks fitted with front tractor blades. The countryside looked quiet and collected until you looked closer at the burned-out wreckage and piles and piles of building refuse. From the air, it looked like a giant hand had smashed and then swept the rubble along the countryside in dirty streaks, maybe in an attempt to level it.

People had fled the big cities, but unlike Ireland and, to a certain extent, Scotland, the rural areas were well developed and populated, and they tended to want to hold on to the little they had. So the civilian conflict had rolled around the country, from the north to the south, from the east to the west, until an uncomfortable and unofficial truce was declared as people settled into the new 'normal'. Bartering was both a survival mechanism and the only reliable currency, as in most of Europe, physical money was in short supply, and without the Internet and digital banking, no one could access their funds.

As they crossed the A1 between Sheffield and Leeds, she could see the flattening of the houses and buildings, and while the woman in her wept for the death and destruction, the optimist in her saw the future, one she and the three sisters were dedicated to bringing to fruition, no matter what. She pulled her head away from the window, having reached a decision.

"Lily, because I love you and your sisters, when we finish down in Sizewell, we'll take a detour on the way to France to see your mom. I promise, no matter how long it takes us to do what we have to do." The pout disappeared and was replaced with a smile in seconds, the remarkable change in her young face reflecting her inner passion.

"Thank you, Katrina. I understand we are on the clock, but the thought of not seeing mom for months is hard to accept, especially when we are so close. And I know once we hit France again, we will keep heading east until we're finished." Katrina nodded. It was true, they had twenty or more power plants to visit before they were finished. She was counting on Freya to let her know if the ones at the end of her list were a possibility. They had sixteen for sure, plus their test site in Ireland. But as the last four were deep in what she considered enemy territory, she was keeping her fingers crossed that they wouldn't get the 'go'.

Time and politics would tell, as they usually did. Even in the new 'normal'.

WEAPONS FREE

The first shot zipped through the fuselage of the monstrous twin-rotor helicopter, creating a light beam that then raced across the floor towards the booted feet of the loadmaster, who pulled his legs up instinctively while at the same time yelling "We're under fire, port side!". The next intrusion came in a five-round burst, slicing a neat line to the rear of the first shot and impacting on the unlucky loadmaster from chest to crutch. The pilot, a combat veteran from the wars in the Middle East, rolled the CH-47 Chinook on its side and dived, then jinked back to straight and level just feet off the ocean's thirsty slap.

There was a momentary pause, the sound of the screaming rotors filling the cockpit, then the sounds of more rounds impacting the aircraft, followed by a much heavier impact that had the pilot swearing as he muscled the nonresponsive controls in an attempt to save the crew.

The Chinook hit the water mostly horizontally, and while it was designed to float on the water under controlled circumstances, this was anything but, and it started to slip beneath the choppy sea, the blades protesting with hard slaps.

The copilot, a young woman with short, cropped hair, popped up, her life jacket a yellow blur against the sinking aircraft. Then a second yellow blur popped up, and the pilot, with blood running down his face, waved and splashed his way out from under the cockpit. Both ducked the flapping blades.

"Frankie, are you okay?" he yelled, the sound from the still-running turbines and the rise and fall of the waves making normal conversation impossible. She waved her arms, spitting salty water out, and started to dog paddle, moving away from the slowly sinking wreck. The pilot on the other side of the aircraft did the same, wondering if his loadmaster was alive or dead.

With a series of hisses, gurgles, bangs, and farts from the engines, the huge fuselage sank, leaving spinning pools of tortured ocean in its wake.

From the shore at the fishing dock, three soldiers watched in horror, then one of them jumped into a ribbie, started the engine, and powered out to rescue the crew. A thousand feet above, the second CH-47 thundered along, with a gunship tearing up the sky and chasing the drone. In an almost soundless explosion, the drone erupted, filling the sky with debris and flame. Pieces started to rain down on the unhappy crew, and a large piece missed the rescue boat by a foot.

The crew were picked up, the ribbie returned to the ramp, and as word got out about the attack, the major considered his options.

He would hold until his relief arrived, and he would sharpen up his air defenses immediately. He wanted to tell the Interpol commander, but first he had to tell his battalion chief. That might be a very interesting conversation.

The Irish army had six CH-47s, and he had effectively lost two of them!

CHAPTER TWENTY SIX

"Do you want the bad news, the very bad news, or the disastrous bad news?" The Boss asked, his background this time looking like a tree-lined park. He was wearing one of his show-off suits, all sharp edges, flowing lines, discrete pin stripes, and a white collared blue shirt with a tie showing the emblem of the Irish Guard, circa 1888. Weird, even for the Boss. The green three-leaf clover with its three crowns on the red diagonal cross on a large silver star and the motto 'Quis Separabit MDCCLXXXIII' sat puffed out slightly by the pressure of his tailored jacket. I briefly wondered where he had gotten it and who he was trying to irritate by wearing it.

"Start with the worst, work your way backwards." He smiled, his face warming slightly, his cragginess smoothing out just a fraction, and I sensed that while I wouldn't enjoy the news, it wouldn't put us in the ground.

"Okay, you asked for it. The Irish President has informed the UN and Lyon that they are withdrawing their request for Interpol assistance, as of now. Thank you very much, but pack up your shovel and spade and go home. Our operation is in Ireland proper, not the north, and he is claiming jurisdiction."

"I have a note from Sandra, who is due there very soon, that the major and his *Sciathán Fianóglach* will be withdrawn tomorrow at 1700 hours local. Or maybe that's today. I'll have to check." He took that in, paused, then continued.

"That was the bad news. I've spoken to the major's battalion commander, who is on our side, and the First Minister, who has no love for the President, and they will authorize TDY back to us if you need it."

"And the very bad news?" I was starting to worry about what Sandra might be walking into, and as we had already lost one Sgan Aluf and two helicopters and troops in Ireland, I wasn't ready to lose any more.

"Have you heard that one of the Irish Chinooks has been totaled on its way to Whiddy Island?" I stared at him, open-mouthed, it was critical tactical information, and I didn't have it.

"When?" He looked at his tactical watch, then back at me.

"Nine minutes ago." I relaxed. I had no doubt I'd be getting a direct message from the major anytime soon.

"What has Lyon told the UN and Ireland?"

"We are chasing the source of WMDs. Whiddy Island is in the middle of it, and we won't be going home anytime soon." I nodded, as I expected.

"Any crew lost in the Chinook?"

"Yes, sadly, the loadmaster. The flight crew got away and were picked up by their own troops."

"Who shot them down?"

"Unknown. Drone, according to the gunship that shot it down.

"No rockets, just machineguns. You didn't pick up any other drone sites when you scanned the Island?" I shook my head. We were totally focused on finding the nuclear-capable shells, and Whiddy Island has been our center of focus. We literally tripped over the drone facility once we landed on the Island and took control.

"I'll warn Sandra and the 104. How long can you hold out against the politicians?" His grin made him look evil, his eyes lit up, and he leaned into the camera.

"Forever!" He laughed. I joined him, and he moved back so I could see more of him again. "And another thing, there's a rumor going around that the UN and NATO are falling apart. Over one hundred countries are withdrawing their support, there's no money to fund it, and the local issues seem to outweigh any global issues at present. The US, France, Spain, UK, India, Pakistan, Japan, most of the Northern European countries, and New Zealand and Australia are holding the line, but the signs are there that membership will be reduced and a number of global alliances will shatter."

"Russia and China?"

"Non-committal for now, but both looking for a target to bomb back to the stone age in retaliation for the loss of their petrochemical pipelines and mines. Of all the problems we face, that is perhaps the most unstable." I thought about that and remembered a conversation with the general who looked after the president and a comment made to me by the commander of the missile silos in the mid-west.

"Well, a little bird told me—make that little bird colonel—that they had lost control of their nukes, on land and at sea. Any chance that might apply to the Russians and the Chinese?" He stared at me so forcibly I could feel his eyes on my backbone. "I'm sure that was in one of my many reports."

"Jessica, if you weren't so far away, I'd boot you in the arse. When did you find this out?" It was my turn to stare as I tried to pinpoint when I had been in Montana. I waved my arms around in a gesture of defeat, then gave him my most whimsical smile.

"That would have to be somewhere between 6 and 8 weeks ago."

"Explain!" Short, sharp, and direct, leaving me in no doubt that he had missed this bit of news. Which I found amazing because he was now mixing with all the hobnobs in power from all over the modern world, and surely something like this would have leaked?

"The missile commander in Montana confirmed they had lost control of their silos, and that was confirmed by General Bridges with respect to their nuclear subs. In fact, the hint was that any weapons system that was connected to a server was locked out, and at that time they hadn't found a way around it." He went into deep thinking mode, a frown creasing his face, his eyebrows arcing down to meet in the middle. He looked back up at me from under his eyelashes, still frowning.

"Operational blindness. We only considered the effect on the US and their allies. They were the only ones that called us in to sort out the terrorist attacks. If they were in our IT systems back in 1999, and 'Helen' was ex-Stasi, Russian trained, why wouldn't they be in their IT systems as well? Bloody hell, I feel like an idiot." I took pity on him. It was a big miss, but it had started with me.

"Apologies. At the time it was just more data. It didn't relate to finding the terrorists, so it probably went unnoticed. There is a way to check the current situation." He looked at me, this time his face clear and calm, his eyes open and inviting, and a small smile formed on his lips.

"Arie or the general?" I just smiled back and waited him out. He slowly started to nod.

"Okay, keep on top of Ireland. Watch your six. I'll get back to you." And he hung up. I folded the mini and slipped it into my pocket. In thinking about it, if it had been a unilateral attack on nuclear weapons, then India, Pakistan, France, the UK, Russia, China, Israel, and North Korea would have lost their biggest bargaining chips.

And I wondered if the social unrest in Russia and China had reached the same proportions as in the rest of Europe. The reporting was scarce, to say the least. Not to mention North Korea. I put it all in the 'think about it later' basket and went back to obsessing about Ireland. I pulled my mini back out.

"Where are you?" Sandra looked relaxed, no doubt having slept all the way across the Mediterranean. Her eyes sparkled in the slanted sunlight working its way around the cabin through the oval windows.

"Landing in Cork in ten, why?" I knew her plan was to take a small helicopter into Whiddy Island, while the 104 would truck in to Bantry, then catch a boat over. The airfield at Bantry was only 450 meters long, far too short for a mid-size jet. The hackles on the back of my neck came up, and a chill ran down my spine.

"Take a truck—better still, wait for the 104, and go with them." She looked at me with a quizzical furrow on her face, one eyebrow raised.

"Why?"

"The Irish just lost one of their Chinooks to a drone attack. I don't want you bitching and moaning about how you got shot down again, so wait." Her face cleared immediately, and her eyes tightened.

"Anyone lost?"

"Yes, the loadmaster." She nodded. The stream of light moved across her face, suggesting the pilot had turned the aircraft. She looked out the window.

"According to the briefing we got, there were two Chinooks and a gun ship." I nodded. I had picked that up on the board. She seemed to think for a minute, then relaxed back into her seat.

"When will we have our own boat, and what armaments will it have?"

"Ask Tom. He's our new weapons expert, and Indigo and he should be aboard by now. Middle of the Med to you will probably take three to four days, depending on exactly where they start from, so you have what the 104 and our boys and girls come with. Did you pack MANPADS, and how many boots have you got with you?"

"Yes. Six. Plus we've got those sexy laser anti-drone weapons I'm dying to try out. As for boots, I've got all eight of Toms and four from Bob. Can't you hear them snore?" I smiled, my battery bunny had obviously made a full recovery, her enthusiasm shining through the transmission like a searchlight. Twelve troops, plus the 104, would give them another dozen, unless we ran into an army that should be sufficient to hold the Island, especially once our private navy, with a complement of four from the Admiral, Indigo, and whoever the Admiral had sent to look after his sailors.

"Sandra, I need you back here soonest, so do your handover, make sure everyone is comfortable, then come back with Tom. Be safe." And I hung up, little trickles of doubt running up and down my spine. We had to hold the Island until we knew exactly what the terrorists were up to. The plant would have to get back up to speed at some point, just like Point Roberts and New Zealand. And we had to find the Irish scientist at or before she reached Killara Bay, as well as this Crissy person on Socotra.

We were thin on the ground. I'd have to prioritize, perhaps call in more resources from somewhere, and we still had Scotland to resolve.

It was going to be a busy week. And just as I started to work through it all, Fay burst in at the top of her voice.

"Coffee. Now. Who do I have to kill?" I could feel my face light up at her bouncy approach, and as she threw her go-bag onto a chair, which immediately fell over with a crash, she caught the attention of the whole room.

"Give the girl a coffee, please, before she destroys the office!" The laughter was contagious. It rippled around the office like a hurricane. "And when you have satisfied your neanderthal urges, walk with me." I started to move towards the zig-zag corridor that led to one of the most famous canals in the world, flanked by my two pristine guards, now grinning at Fay's antics, and she joined me at the doorway with one of Indigo's prized gondola mugs gripped in her hand as if it were the most important thing in her life.

"Good to see you've got your priorities right." She ignored me, burying her head in the top of the mug.

"Easy for you to say, sitting on your backside between two of Indigo's beautiful espresso machines, but man, I love the Israelis, love them to death, but they can't make coffee!" I smiled, remembering my own reaction. I found a clean spot to sit on—the concrete edge of the foundations of the museum that sat next door to our very old church. Our protection detail had grown to six. I waved them away, and they faded back into the walls, their automatic weapons sticking out like someone poking a bee hive with a wooden stick.

"That technique you used with the Whiddy Island women was masterful. I would love to have seen their faces when they were stripped and taken back to their holes." She looked at me over the top of her mug, her eyes alight, her face a canvas of beauty and calm.

"Did the job. It's clear to me there are at least two separate agendas, not necessarily coordinated, but one side definitely took advantage of the other."

"As in, one group was happy to let us chase all over the Med after the shells while they did their thing elsewhere?"

"Yes." She looked at her nails, noticed that they had become a little torn and rough around the edges, and shook her head. "One advantage of working for the FBI in Seattle is that I could get a manicure once a month. I almost forget what it's like to be a pampered woman." I smiled. Living on the move, as we tended to do, bouncing from hot zone to hot zone, sleeping wherever we could, didn't make for pampering. Quite the opposite.

"What was your take on the Anaisha girls?" She put her mug down in her lap and looked deeply into the canal as if to see an answer. The flickering of some spilled light on top of the small waves was almost hypnotic, but she shook her head slowly.

"The Terrorist Laws were written the way they are for a reason, and by any stretch of the imagination, I can't see them not knowing what the outcome of their work might be. That and the fact their mother worked so closely with them. But they're so young, it hurts my heart to know they will only ever see the inside of a concrete cage until the day they die." I nodded. I had similar feelings a number of times when we were sweeping up the women terrorists, particularly the two young Irish women we took from the Westhall property in Helena, but as Fay had said, we wrote the Laws the way they were for a reason.

"Have you heard about Ireland?" She looked at me with puzzlement on her face, her eyes partially closed as she concentrated.

"Not in the last day or so, why?"

"We lost another helicopter, one crew, to a drone." She sucked her breath in, making a face that screwed up her lovely features.

"Buggar. What will we do now?" A very good question, one I had pondered for the last hour or so since speaking to Sandra. Or rather, ordering her to go by land, not by air, from Cork to Whiddy Island. I stood, rolled my shoulders, and motioned to the guards, pretending to be part of the stone walls.

"I've got Sandra and the 104 going in by vehicle. The major will make his own mind up about his exfil. One Chinook won't hold all his men. But he has a gun ship with him, and I'm tempted to ask him to leave it there for us. The problem is I just can't see the strategic advantage Whiddy Island offers the terrorists. We emptied it of civilians, the mercenaries we blocked off at the fort escaped out into the ocean, we took the shells and nanites, and we shut the plant down. What's left?" She stood beside me, rubbing her thumb around the rim of her mug. She looked into the canal again. If anything, the sparkles off the water had intensified, and the wind had picked up and was working against the tide.

"My feeling is that this is another diversion. We have never taken fire when arresting the women. Not once. While our attention is fixated on Whiddy Island, what are they doing somewhere else?" That got me thinking on a whole different level, and I ran through the data we had received in the last few days. Specifically, the transmission from Scotland mentioned a test in Ireland. If we could hold Whiddy Island for the foreseeable future, maybe we could uncover this 'test, whatever it turned out to be. And just as this thought was forming, my mini went mad in my pocket, screeching at me—a new sound I didn't know it was capable of. I pulled it out, ready to curse whoever it was that was interrupting my chat with Fay.

It was Shami, with Malcolm, Luigi, Bob, and Stefarino in the frame. I tempered my response. The last thing I wanted was to get our geek squad offside.

"Gentlemen, how can I help you?" It seemed that all their images were frozen, and all but Stefarino disappeared.

"Jessica, apologies, I had the others on a different system we are experimenting with. Let me fill you in, then you can decide if you want them all back on the call." I nodded and moved so Fay could see the screen over my shoulder. I was viscerally aware that our guards had now formed up around us, all facing out, but we still had the stone wall of the museum behind us, so I didn't feel all that exposed.

"Hi Stefarino, I'm happy to talk to you anytime. What have you got?"

"We intercepted another transmission from Scotland. Bob and his team have got a possible location for the transmission source in Aberfoyle. He's holding, waiting for your instructions. His team think they have pinpointed the Aberfoyle location down to fifty meters. But it's the content of the calls I'd like to relay to you." The back of my neck came to life, and I could feel the hairs standing to attention even in the slight breeze coming off the canal.

"Go."

"The transmission from Katrina to someone called Freya. The conversation was about a minute and a half long, and here is the transcript." And the message scrolled onto my screen, rising up row by row.

Transmission commenced at 1645 UST.

'Katrina—we've finished here in England. It was a difficult site, but we're heading out in an hour. Thank you for changing our pilot. The new one is a treasure.'

'Freya-happy to help. How are the girls coping?'

'Katrina, they are doing a fabulous job. They work together like a well-oiled team, and as you suggested, Lilian has taken charge, but your young Else is simply brilliant. They want to come home to visit you before we head east.'

'Freya, good to know. I'm sorry, but they can't come back here until you have finished. We can't risk it. I will not confirm the locations at the end of your list at this time. Your pilot will have more equipment for you—enough for the next three locations—and you can pick it up as you go. God speed, and know that you are making a huge difference.'

Transmission end at 1647 UST.

"So these mysterious women have been in Ireland, Spain, France, and England and are heading east. And we now have three names—Katrina, Lilian, and Else. What the hell are they doing?"

"As you would expect, there is a black hole covering their movements. We have cracked the code, but all we have is the same blur we worked with two months ago. To make matters really confusing, we are picking up multiple blurs, so there's no way to know which one is our prime target."

"Can you map the movements by time?"

"Yes and no. Some are static, and the ones that move seem to be random. But we have got a definite location on two of their transmissions—the first was over a week ago in Spain; the last just now is in England."

"Send me the latitude and longitude, please. Well done, and thank you for your brilliant work."

"Not mine. Your geeks and Malcolm did all the real work. We just sorted it out a little." His smile was infectious. You would never think he was the head monk of a centuries-old order whose normal day job was cataloging religious artifacts from around the world. The screen went black, and I immediately dialed Bob.

"You're holding for instructions?"

"Affirmative. I've got the original four on the ground, and I have four from Indigo's team packed and ready to go on your say so."

"Get your people on the ground to scope out somewhere they can go to ground safely, keep them in position, and move yourself and your team to Scotland. Unless something develops, I want to be able to listen in to them and hope they give us a location for the team they have moving around the place. We don't know what they are doing, but as you probably heard, we have two locations which we will follow upon. Comments?" His face looked serious as he digested my instructions, and he slowly started to nod. He hadn't shaved, and the dark scruff made his face look hollow. Once again, I was reminded that I was working everyone overtime and, in some cases, pushing them way too hard by most people's standards. But we were not normal people, and asymmetric warfare rarely gave you a day off.

"I'll ask Arie for transport. I'll find an airport close to Aberfoyle, get a ground vehicle, and go in that way. We will not be seen, I guarantee that."

"Excellent. Keep in contact. Remember this Freya person is at least one of their senior leadership, and she will be well prepared for you. We took casualties bringing down 'Helen' we have no reason to think this will be any easier. If we decide to take her, you will have support. Get eyes on the area, try to work out their establishment."

"WILCO." And the screen went to its usual black, so I interrupted yet another member of my team, and in seconds Amira's lovely face swam into focus. I had a wild-hair idea and couldn't keep it to myself. Behind me, Fay sighed, reached out, and put her hand on my shoulder.

"Amira, good to see you. I hope I didn't disturb what you are doing." She had the good grace to smile and shake her head.

"No more than usual. Hello, Fay, how are you?" Fay leaned forward, dropping her head into camera range.

"Good. Happy to be home." I could feel her smiling, and Amira mirrored her.

"Okay, enough already. Charm school's out. I have a question for you. In all the material you brought back from Innomatchi, was there a list of any equipment shipped to Socotra?" She gave me a funny look, then turned in her chair and bent her head, obviously working on a keyboard. Her hair swung to cover her face, creating an eerie look. The speed at which she worked bewildered me. Somehow, these geeks of ours could pound a keyboard ten times faster than us mere mortals. Her face swung into view, her hair flying around her head, and she casually brushed it behind her ears with both hands. I could see yellow stains on her fingers and hoped she hadn't hurt herself. Looking straight into the camera, she posted images on the screen below her face in a line of boxes and talked over them.

What she muttered was unintelligible. She enlarged them one by one in a flash of data and illustrations that reminded me of a cartoon drawn on a paper pad and flipped through on the edge, creating the illusion of movement.

"Sorry, that was a bit fast. I can give you a summary or take you through them one by one." I rolled my shoulders, and the not-a-geek side of me won over my innate curiosity.

"Summary, please, as slow as you can." Fay laughed, patted my shoulder, pulled her own mini out, and linked into the conversation.

One drawing opened up full screen, seemed to fade in and out of focus, then steadied into a crisp image. "This is a manifold of some type. You can see where the ports rotate around the barrel, and this," a second drawing swam into focus, "is probably what connects to the manifold. Wait a minute!" The exclamation was almost a shout, and the frame filled as she rose and walked off camera. We were left looking at the back of her laboratory, static and empty of people. She slid back into frame, holding a gray propellor-like wheel, and as I frowned, trying to make a link, Fay reached over my shoulder and tapped my mini screen.

"That's the object you were printing when I left." Amira rolled the device in her hands. It barely filled them, and I remembered that she had said that it would be one sixth scale, so the real object would be around two feet in diameter.

"Yes. Now I need your permission to make all these other bits and pieces on these drawings. It will take me a day or two. I think we've found something that will be of great interest."

"Go for it. I'll tell Arie. In a way, you've answered my question. In another, we have a puzzle I know you will solve. Thank you." I closed the screen, held the mini in my hands for a minute, and turned to look at Fay, who was putting her mini pack in her pants pocket.

"You saw Amira before you left Israel?"

"Of course I did. I really respect her. She has dealt with a huge amount of conflict and tension, yet she shines in everything she does. Plus, she has the same refugee background as me, and I feel a strong connection because of that."

"I get that, yes, but you have to admit she is in her natural element working in Israel."

"She'd be just as happy working here with Indigo or Stefarino. I don't think location is important to her—just the challenge of working everything out. She carries a lot of guilt because of the nanites." I nodded. I was aware of that, and even now there was still the odd rumbling or two from the talking heads on both sides of the Atlantic about her role in the development of the weapons that took out all the oil, gas, and coal. She was mine now, and Arie's, and obviously Fay's, and I knew firsthand that Indigo, Stefarino, and the geek squad had her back, so she had the makings of a first-class cheer squad. And she looked impossibly young to have achieved the brilliant breakthrough she had delivered to the world.

"It will be interesting to see what she discovers. How tired are you?" She looked at me as if I'd spoken Martian, shrugged her shoulders, and smiled.

"Not a bit. Slept on the plane. Used the maniac and his toy boat to wake me up. I'm ready to go. What do you need?"

"We've got a lot of options on our board." I let that sink in and turned to her.

"We need to prioritize them and work out what we might need for each operation. We're stretched a bit thin at present and still way behind the terrorists. Come inside, and I'll bring you up to date." I followed Fay along the zig-zag entrance, half our detail walking in front, the other half trailing. She stopped at the espresso machine, raised one eyebrow at me, I nodded and smiled, and continued to my little open office. The massive mission board was still being updated, this time by a pair of members of the Italian *Gruppo di Intervento Speciale* team. One was obviously a woman, her long black hair pulled up into a bob, and her companion was equally identifiable by his hair, which had been mown down to the skull and shone in the overhead lights. Neither looked old enough to walk into a bar and buy a beer. Both had small automatic carbines slung over their backs, and the way they moved across the floor suggested excellent reflexes and a high level of fitness.

It wore me out just looking at them.

Fay scanned the board, pulled a copy onto her mini, and made notes in the margins with a little electronic pencil. She was FBI-trained and the youngest Senior Special Agent at the time we recruited her, about a month ago, and the way she had managed her team, both older than her, and the entire situation that had developed on the West Coast is what had drawn me to her.

"Okay, I see what you're planning in Scotland. When we go in, we'll need more troops on the ground and possibly military or police reinforcements. That's a big urban area, and the potential for collateral damage will be high." I nodded, my thinking exactly. Also, one of the reasons I had instructed Bob to sit and watch.

"What's with this Socotra and Crissy?" She turned to look at me, the question in her eyes, her hand poised over the mini.

"Not a clue yet. That came to us from an intercept. We know our favorite Irish scientist, Siobhan O'Cleary, managed to get there when she ran from Malik Badawi. You would have missed all that, being on the other side of the world."

"I might have missed the action, but I have read all the reports on your chase of the shells, so I know the players to some extent. You said she 'ran' from Badawi. How did she manage that?"

"She was in the same plane that crashed outside Bagdad, one the Israelis had shot at. Badawi took off with some of his mercenaries. It appears that she just took off by herself."

"So you want to bag her before she gets to Killara Bay?"

"If we can, yes. If not, definitely when she hits the West Coast." Fay nodded, made little scribbles, nodded again, then turned and looked at me again. "You have Sandra and Tom going to Whiddy Island again. And Indigo on the boat that you captured?" I smiled, enjoying her voyage of discovery.

"Indigo has a master mariner's ticket, among other things, and that boat—or ship, because it's bloody big—was originally fitted out to fire nuclear shells at who knows what. My plan is to use it as a circuit breaker around Whiddy Island until we can figure out what the hell is happening there—or is going to happen there. It's become a bone of contention with the Irish President."

"I see that in the footnotes you made recently. Is having Colonel-sorry, that's General Anthony in Lyons and the Hague helping or hindering the political agenda?"

"How well do you know the Boss?" She frowned; something I was noticing took up her whole face. She was very expressive, holding nothing back from what she was feeling. But I had seen her interrogate terrorists, so I knew this was only one side of her sparkling personality. And while I wouldn't play poker with her, I had also seen her play hard-arse with the best of us, so she definitely had the chops for Section Five.

"I worked with him in Seattle, Point Roberts. You were there, and I read him as decisive, intelligent, a great leader, a little bit laid back, but in a constructive way, and someone who trusts you implicitly." I nodded, so I asked her question back to her.

"So how do you think we do in the political stakes?" She frowned again, looked down at the floor, then back up straight into my eyes, and smiled, her whole face lighting up, her eyes glowing.

"I suspect he gives them hell, holds the line, or simply moves it out of the way if he has to. I liked him a lot, particularly the way he managed my Director, the head of the FBI, and the president's general. You were all in a sticky situation because initially you had limited critical information to your own team, but he managed to bring everyone into the game without friction." My time to smile and light up

"He's very good at that, something I'm not." She just tilted her head slightly, as if considering my statement.

"What do you think is really going on at Whiddy Island?"

"I don't know. We took the shells, the nanites, the drones, chased a bunch of mercenaries away, closed the plant. That should have been it. But they persist in shooting at us, or at least our aircraft, but for the life of me I can't see any advantage for them. Their attacks are limited, don't really affect us or our planning, what are they gaining?" She looked at me with an evil grin, and I thought to myself for the second time in as many minutes I would definitely not face her over the green sway of a poker table.

"They're doing it to us again. Look one way, do something somewhere else. What if the drone attacks are no more than an exercise in keeping us focused on Whiddy Island?"

That slid home with a thud. It was something I had never considered. Another beard—a feint to keep us focused on the wrong end of the world. I rolled that thought around for a minute or two, then started to nod. It made total sense. They had done so—or simply allowed their mercenaries to distract us for nearly three weeks, chasing the shells all over the European continent and the seas between. So where should we be looking? Ireland was still important, of that I was sure. The Irish President was still trying to get us out of the country and the two women terrorists back onto Whiddy Island. So I made one of the snap tactical decisions I was becoming famous for.

"Fay, you may have a point. So here's what we'll do. Pick four members of Indigo's Col Moschin—the 9th Assault Parachute Regiment—you're looking for people who can go deep cover as civilians, possibly backpackers, you'll sort that out, plain clothes, but vests and concealed weapons. Work out how to get to Killara Bay as inauspiciously as possible, and find a safe place to stay. We have the delivery destination for the shipsets, so find it, reconnoiter it, and set a trap for her. No collateral damage if you can avoid it, but I want her in Israel in chains." She nodded. It made total sense when I heard it spoken out loud, and Fay could handle this in her sleep. Transport might be an issue, but she'd sort it out.

"Excellent. A holiday in Ireland sounds like fun. And you ask me why I was so happy to leave the FBI for Interpol? A decision like that would have taken days, if not weeks! When do you want me to leave?" Her smile was infectious, so I slapped her on the shoulder, warmed by her not-so-subtle endorsement.

"Pick your team, pack your bags, and I'll speak to Arie about your transport." She moved away, and I mentally crossed one item off my 'to do' list. I dialed Arie.

"Hi Arie, I hope I'm not interrupting anything important." He gave me a wan smile. His background was muted, so he wasn't in his normal office. "I have a request, please. I need eyes and ears over Ireland; one of your AWACS would be perfect. We have a drone problem, and I need to irradicate it as soon as possible." He looked at me, the serious look causing him to marginally close his eyes, and he leaned back in his seat, and as the camera followed his movement and refocused, a magnificent statue came into view, sitting on a polished wooden plinth. I didn't know what it was, but it was made out of glass, and it literally took my breath away. The rainbow effect was shooting all over the wall and roof. He saw me move my eyes from him to the statue and grinned.

"A piece of Murano glass was given to me by the President of Italy some time ago. It's wonderful, full of life, and reminds me why we fight so hard for what we love."

"If you ever get bored with it, you know who to send it to." He just smiled and wiped his hand across his face, and I realized he was tired. "And can you lend me a small jet, please, to ship five people over to Ireland?"

He grimaced, tilted his head to one side, uncrossed his legs, rubbed his thighs, and looked at me from under his bushy eyebrows.

"How about we pick them up from Marco Polo and drop them off in Belfast?" I nodded. Excellent solution, and one less aircraft to worry about.

"Thanks, Arie. Will we be able to talk to the AWACS directly?"

"Yes. I'll see that the pilot gets a mini."

"Thank you. All your help is appreciated. And we have a secure fuel store in Belfast, as well as hangar space. I'll arrange access." Then I helped my hand up to forestall any further conversation as I remembered the chat I had earlier with the Boss. "Have you had any difficulty with your non-traditional munitions lately?" His eyes frosted over, giving me the answer. Then he just smiled and closed the connection.

So, nukes were out of play in Israel as well. Interesting.

That left Scotland, on hold temporarily while we waited for more transmissions, and Socotra, which I didn't have a single clue about other than the name 'Crissy', and that our Irish scientist had managed to flee there. I was thinking through the issue when my mini pinged, and two sets of longitude and latitude scrolled up my screen. I pushed it to my big screen, asked a bot to show me both locations, and two very different images swam into view. Both were nuclear power stations, one in France at Golfech, northwest of Toulouse, and the second in England at Sizewell B. What the hell were the terrorists doing at the power plants? They had already put them all out of commission with a nanite attack, which started some two months ago. And we knew from the transmission we had intercepted from Scotland earlier that the 'Irish experiment' was associated with whatever this current activity was. And Ireland didn't have a reactor.

Okay, Killara Bay was covered; Scotland was covered; Whiddy Island was covered; that left this mysterious activity at the nuclear power plants and Socotra to resolve. Who did I have left?

The easy answer was, until Sandra and Tom got back, me. I decided to learn as much about Socotra as I could. I used the big screen, now linked to an ultra-secure system provided by the monks, and ran a search. Apart from being a mishmash of small saw-toothed mountains, bare earth, and dry, dusty-looking roads, the population was sparse, the towns quite small, and the most outstanding physical features were a number of very old-looking mosques and the hexagonal control tower at their single airport. With a ten thousand-foot runway! Why so long?

It had a reputation for pristine white sandy beaches, strange-shaped trees, and outstanding coral reefs. It was controlled by the UAE but was officially part of Yemen. A footnote claimed that ancient texts had identified it as the original 'Garden of Eden'. The language was *Soqotri,* a south Semitic language spoken by the indigent population and the two other tiny Islands nearby, Abd al-Kuri and Samhah. I knew for a certainty that we had no one I knew that spoke that language, but it was a derivation of Arabic, so we might be able to muddle along. If we went there. The Island was Heritage Listed, and that was a problem all unto itself. Both countries were strong members of the United Nations Assembly and Interpol, going back to the middle 1970s. Neither had partitioned us so far to act on their behalf, so I sent a text to the boss and asked him to start the diplomatic dance: WMDs, terrorists, yada yada, all unspecified, as we had diddly squat right now except for the names of the two women.

The length of the runway stuck in my mind. Ten thousand feet would take the biggest transport aircraft known, so why on such a small Island did they build such a long runway? I thought back to 1999. What was happening then? The data included references to invasions by the Saudis, the Russians, the British, and, of course, the French, but all had packed up their sandbags and gone home long ago, leaving the Island officially managed by Yemen.

I put it all away and dialed Sandra. Her background bumped and shook with considerable force, causing the mini to shake. Her voice mimicked the movement in a staccato fashion.

"Can't t-t-alk now, ca-l-l back later." And that was that.

SHOPPING EXPEDITION

om and Indigo stepped out of their helicopter onto the deck of the destroyer they had been given as their destination, straight into the arms of the master chief who had worked with them before. This time he was dressed in day blues, a camouflage pattern that looked like something a three-year-old might do in finger painting. And get a gracious 'D' for it.

"Colonel, master chief, welcome aboard, Gordon McKenzie." He reached out one meaty hand and took theirs in turn, stooped at the waist to prevent the rotating blades from taking his head off at the shoulders. The three men moved out of the reach of the spinning rotors, then stopped just outside the hangar at the stern of the vessel. The rotos wound down, and two sailors raced out and fitted tie-down chains to the undercarriage.

"My brief is to give you anything you want within reason, have it installed on your ship, introduce you to your crew, and send you on your way."

"Did the admiral put you here specifically for this?" Indigo asked, remembering the solid, broad-shouldered sailor from the first time they had met under different circumstances with his admiral.

"Yes, sir, he did. He made it clear to the captain that I had the discretion to help you in any way, no questions asked, and had me select your crew. You are going into harm's way, aren't you?" The look he gave Indigo was firm and deep, and Indigo returned the compliment.

"Yes, Gordon, in the last hour we have lost another helicopter near Whiddy Island and a crew member, so your help will be truly appreciated." The sailor braced his shoulders, looked at Tom, and tilted his head to one side.

"The brief said the Colonel here would be master of the ship. What's your role?" There was no rancor in the question, but Tom was wary of not having worked with the sailor previously.

"Well, the good Commander felt my experience with weapons might be useful in gunning the ship up." A hard stare flitted across the sailors face, then softened into a smile.

"Well then, master chief, let's go shopping!" And he led the way into the hangar, then to an open-sided lift that took them into the bowels of the ship. The armory, as you would expect, was extensive, and it took the best part of an hour for Tom and Indigo to agree on what they wanted. Boys and their toys!

The master chief waited until they had finished, then, with a stoic look on his face, ushered them back to the flight deck, then stood at parade rest. "The admiral wanted me to ask you if you wanted a little help beyond the crew we're providing." Indigo looked at Tom, and they both turned to look at the master chief. "What did you have in mind?" He smiled, pointed to his chest. "Me."

Indigo smiled, nodded, and looked at Tom. "The master chief was a great help when we captured this boat, and he will make an excellent 2IC." Tom smiled, seeing no potential danger in the posting. He looked serious for a minute and scratched his chin. He now had a different responsibility than just being a shooter.

"Master Chief, your rules of engagement will be those of Section Five, the ship will carry the flag of the United Nations, and you and your crew will be TDY'ed to us for the duration. Will you need to get that cleared with your Admiral?" The sailor pulled himself erect, gave Tom a hard stare, held it for a while, then broke out into a grin, and slapped Tom on the shoulder.

"I understand the rules. I have worked up close and personal with your teams previously. It's pretty much a 'shoot first, don't worry about the questions' mantra, and if I'm wearing your colors, I'm yours. And yes, I will clear it with the Admiral as a matter of course." Tom nodded, noticing that Indigo had stood silently while the conversation had taken place. He looked at him to see if he had broached his territory, stood on his metaphoric toes, as it were, but only saw the sturdy Italian smile.

It was nice to know that as new on the job as he was, he had the open and wholehearted support of the head of Interpol Italy and Jessica's 2IC. Although he quickly remembered that the beautiful model-like Sandra often worked with Jessica, he wondered how the FBI agent she had recruited would slide into the team. Before he could wallow in his thoughts, trying to work out the hierarchy of Section Five, Indigo clapped him on the back and turned to the sailor.

"Let's go and fit out our ship. We haven't named her yet." Tom scratched his eyebrows and tilted his head. Then he shook it from side to side.

"Just call her *'Scáthán'*, because anything that tries to get you will get something back threefold!" Indigo and the master chief both looked at Tom with the same question in their eyes.

"What does that mean?" Indigo asked.

'Mirror in Gallic." The laughter followed the three across the deck as they walked back out into daylight to peer down at their ship, happily sitting alongside, held at bay by large black fenders. Indigo nodded and pointed to the ship.

"She looks too pretty to be a killer, but underneath she's got the bones for a good fight. *'Scáthán'* it is then. Do we paint her name on the bow?"

"No. Let's keep it a secret." All of them nodded, then went about the work of turning a once-nuclear-capable weapon into a modern-day Q-ship.

CHAPTER TWENTY SEVEN

Sandra was fighting for her life, the armored personnel carrier she was in rolling across the sideroad like a spinning bottle, only the five-point harnesses keeping her contingent of special forces troops in one place. But the equipment stacked on the floor and in overhead racks raced around the interior like unguided missiles, slapping and hammering at exposed faces, hands, legs, and feet. She protected her face with her mini. The passenger compartment had separated from the chassis as designed, with the anti-tank mechanism working to perfection. Two out of the three carriers had been rammed, and the gunship flying top cover had attempted to frustrate the attack, but each time the gunner lined up with the truck cabs to kill the drivers, they found they were empty.

The spinning and rolling stopped with a jarring 'thump', and the passenger compartment shimmied and shook for a few seconds before settling down on its weighted flat bottom. Sandra looked around at the wreckage of the interior, saw lots of blood and jumbled gear, but managed to count the twelve heads she had started with. The rear door burst open, and the two shooters closest forced themselves out, their weapons tracking from side to side, seeking something to shoot at. Sandra waited until the soldiers before her exited, then followed, finding herself standing in the middle of a battered and bruised team looking for vengeance but lacking any discernible target.

The other compartment lay alongside, scattered only as far as its kinetic energy had allowed, and slowly it emptied of troops, who immediately mirrored the actions of her team. The Israeli colonel walked up to her, a shooter on either side.

"Injuries?" she asked, reaching for her radio. She looked up into the sky, finding their aerial escort hovering over the remaining carrier. "Sitrep?" she barked into the handset. There was no gunfire or smoke from the wrecked prime-movers, which now lay in various stages of discomfort, one on its side and the other upside down.

"Drivers?" barked the colonel, looking towards the wreckage. Her handset barked back at her.

"One dead, one ambulatory. Advise." She looked at Sandra.

"We need a medivac, we need to secure this location, and we need to find out what the hell happened." The colonel barked into her handset again, listened carefully, then dropped her head in thought.

"The suggestion is that the remaining troop dismount, we load the dead and injured in, and they drive back to Cork with the gunship overhead."

"Do it. Move everyone back up to the road, bring everything we can salvage, and keep everyone below the skyline." Within minutes, the compartments were stripped, the gear carried just below the roadside under the hedgerow, and all thirty-two soldiers were in a defensive position protecting the surviving carrier. A number of small head wounds were being treated by the medically qualified soldiers, but discipline was strong. There was no whimpering or moaning, just a purposeful movement from soldier to soldier.

"The trucks that hit us were autonomous. No drivers." The colonel looked at Sandra, as if seeking an answer, and there was only one she could give.

"Mercenaries using control systems designed by the refugee terrorists." The colonel nodded her agreement.

"Same system as they used back in Israel when they bombed our supermarkets." Sandra thought about that. She remembered reading reports of robot trucks at football stadiums and the discovery of the little black boxes in the wreckages, all of a similar nature. Including the aircraft that had been used in the attacks.

"This is absolute proof we are facing both mercenary and female terrorists. Give me five." Sandra rolled onto her back, pulled her mini out, thankfully not destroyed in the roll-over, and dialed Jessica.

I answered immediately, her last aborted call setting me up for too many imagined scenarios, all ending in death and destruction.

"Speak." She had dried blood running down the side of her face, only a small amount, and before I could ask the obvious question, she answered.

"Location one click past Drimoleague, on the R586. Autonomous truck attack, 2 Prime movers hit, carriers separated, one DOA, one injured, shipping injured back to Cork in the surviving carrier, covered by the gunship."

"Fuel state for the gunship?" I could see Sandra talking into a little handset. She nodded once, then turned to face me via her camera. She looked furious. That was the only way I could describe it. I saw the Sgan Aluf creep into the corner of her screen, just half her head turned away from Sandra.

"Eighty minutes. We have fuel at Bantry Bay, approximately eighteen klicks away." I thought that through, on foot, carrying all the materials they had with them, it would take them at least four or maybe five hours, but these were all special forces trained troops, so it was well within their capabilities.

"Tab until the gunship gets back. Go to ground. I'll contact the major. Some of his team will meet you on the road with transport. Talk more later. Stay safe." And I swapped one uncomfortable military situation for another.

"Major, your relief force has been attacked, approximately eighteen klicks from Bantry Bay, highway R586, can you get trucks to them please ASAP?" He stared into the camera, his face expressionless. I knew his commander still supported us, in spite of the recall order initialed by the Irish President. "Commander, we will not rotate out, and yes, I'll have trucks to our people as fast as I can organize them." I smiled inwardly at his 'our people' comment.

No matter the circumstances, a brotherhood existed between the different nationalities of our teams that was as tough as nails and just as unbreakable.

"I'll pass the word up the chain. Consider us here until you don't need us anymore." He looked grim, as if the attack had been personal and on his own people.

"Thank you, major, very much appreciated. You're getting thirty odd special forces, including the Israeli 104 with whom you worked previously. Will you share your command with their Sgan Aluf? He nodded, a thin smile flitting across his stern countenance, remembering the tough woman with the massive thighs and fully body smile.

"That will be a pleasure. I assume you have a briefing for us?"

"Yes, Inspector Thomas will brief you before returning here. I've also arranged a ship to work with you. It'll be there in four or five days, commanded by Colonel Kashasini. You've worked with him as well. When he arrives, I'll let you sort out your establishment. But your orders have not changed—hold the Island at all costs, no one to access by sea or air, no matter who they say they are or who sent them. Clear?" He nodded and looked back up at me.

"We will hold. Whiddy Island out!" So I dialed up my favorite General, hoping he was in a better mood than the last time we spoke. He wasn't, and after I relayed what had happened, his face clouded over in preparation for a royal spew. He held his hand up, took a deep breath, leaned back, and then looked directly at me with a very hard stare.

"I hope the irony of this is not lost on you, Jessica. You had the 104 there a week ago, and now you're trying to kill them getting them back." I gave him stare after stare, and he finally smiled and softened his face. "Just making sure you'll be on the ball. What's your plan now?"

"Get the team onto the Island, wait for the ship to arrive, get Sandra and Tom back here, then think about Scotland and

Socotra." He nodded, looking quite relaxed, which was a huge difference from the last conversation.

"I'll inform Lyon, and I'll speak directly to the Irish President, and read him the riot act. He'll have to toe the line or quit both the UN and Interpol, and I can't see him doing that." I gave that some thought, weighed keeping my conclusions to myself, then remembered the Boss had trained me to share, take risks, and most importantly, use all the mental horse power I had all around me.

"I can. They have a massive plan for the refugees—I believe from what we have learned, some five or six million children could be involved. That's going to make waves all over the world, and if you look at it clinically, that's nearly half of the total children in the refugee camps." He nodded, as quick to make the connection as I had.

"So you're saying we have a genuine political gun loaded and pointed at our collective heads?" I gave that some thought. He always figured stuff out in military speak, but I understood what he was saying. It was a deep-seated fear I had carried around in my gut every day since I had seen the two women terrorists in the office of the Irish President.

There was no doubt the terrorists had won the first round; refugee children were being shipped to America and New Zealand, one thousand at a time, wave after wave, with both governments choosing to accept the falsified IDs and documentation that the terrorist hackers had cemented into their systems. Systems they had been deep inside for nearly twenty-six years. I looked at him with my most serious face, held his eyes, and opened my hands in a gesture of total belief or surrender, depending on your point of view.

"Yes. What he might do is threaten to leave the UN and Interpol; demand the women back for the plant, plus all the trained workers; restart the plant as a matter of urgency, even though they have thousands of roof panels and power packs already-we have proof they have already shipped a thousand or so; get rid of our troops at Whiddy Island and possibly get us out of Ireland all together; plea his humanitarian case before the world, and I have an idea how he might achieve that; certainly petition the US and other major countries for their tacit approval, if not some form of technical or financial support. His mantra would go something like, 'Look what we're doing, little old Ireland, we're taking half the refugee children in the world into our arms and we will look after them, shame on you for not doing your part.'"

"When you put it like that, I can visualize the outcome. By your count, how many refugees do you think will make it to the United States?"

"Excluding the five thousand souls lost when Maribelle Assiano sank their ship, I can see the US absorbing a million or more, maybe two. New Zealand will probably only do half of that, and the other seventeen countries that have plants waiting to be erected may take another five to six million between them."

"Did you count all that in your head?" I smiled, all too aware that the total number very nearly matched the probable number of children in refugee camps. Except for the new ones being made daily by the social unrest as a result of the original terrorist attacks and the subsequent loss of power across the world. That could be another million or so with little effort.

"Yes, I did. Unlike you, I can do two things at once." He just smiled, the smile he sent me when he was humoring me. "Well, when you put it that way. It will be interesting to see how this develops. Stay safe." And he cut the connection. Which left me with two targets to consider and my team in Ireland with an uncertain future.

Sandra didn't see their future with any uncertainty. She had pulled the Israeli colonel to one side and bluntly laid out her tactics. The Sgan Aluf kept her counsel, immediately saw the logic and brilliance in Sandra's plan, and moved on to implement it. Sandra called the half of Tom's team who were with her on the lefthand side of the culvert, pointed to the sky, and watched as they set up the portable laser drone disruptor. A MANPAD team set up next to the drone team. At the direction of the colonel, the same setup rapidly appeared on the other side. The remaining troops spread themselves out until there were some five meters between them, each one alternating the direction they faced. It was eerily quiet. Even the birds seemed to have gone to roost, and no road traffic ran the gauntlet. She dialed the major.

"We're dug in one klick from where we were hit. Watching for drones or any surface activity. Have your driver stop 5 klicks from our location, sit for ten, see what eventuates. We'll decamp and come to you." The major looked worried. He'd been on the Island for nearly two weeks, and apart from the sniper and the mercenaries who had fled out into the ocean, it had been uneventful. The Interpol section seemed to be bullet magnets. Wherever they went, trouble followed. He smiled at the thought. It was good to be in the action!

He couldn't know it, but Sandra was having similar thoughts as she cautiously scanned the sky with her bulky binoculars. The compass rose reflected into her view slowly, and just as it passed the North mark, she made out a tiny dot at around ten thousand feet.

"Possible target, bearing zero-zero-two. Does anyone else have it?"

"Affirmative. Second possible target lower and ten degrees to the left." Just as Sandra adjusted her sight line, a sharp callout chilled her from boots to backside.

"Missile fired, missile fired."

She shouted over the callout, "everyone over to this side, move!" and like an anthill having hot water poured over it, the troops on the far side rushed across the road, dived for the ground, and crawled into the earth as deep as they could manage. Sandra looked across the road, saw the drone gunner maintaining position, swore under her breath, then pulled her head in to her shoulders as two MANPADS fired, aiming for the blazing trail each missile was dragging behind it. Both anti-drone weapons fired with their distinctive 'fizzzzzzzz', and the two drones simply evaporated in massive explosions. The MANPAD projectiles fitted with proximity fuses took out the missiles, and apart from four beautiful sets of flaming suns, arcing up and down ever so slowly, with yellow centers, gray and black smoke trails that reached both up to the heavens and down to the lush green countryside, and the rolling thunder of the airbursts, the deep blue sky maintained its dignity, and the countryside quietened.

"Move one click west, go go go!" she shouted, watching as her ant hill emptied again to reform further down the road. The gunner and his partner, who had remained on the far side, slipped across the road, gave Sandra a wry smile, bobbed their heads, and tabbed down to where the rest of their team had gone to ground. Sandra merely shook her head, not for the first time acknowledging that the 'special' in 'special forces' was a truly potent and accurate descriptor.

She stopped her forward motion, dropped into the prone position, and scanned the horizon again. She held her position until she heard the call that told her the team had resettled, then rose and joined them. The question that ran through her mind over and over again was, why? What were the terrorists trying to achieve?

She sent a text message to Jessica, checked in with the remaining carrier driver to get the condition of the wounded driver, texted the major, then lay on her stomach, her binoculars scanning the silky blue sky. The light wind had blown the smoke away to the east, and she wondered at the natural beauty of the Irish countryside—the blooming wild flowers, the swaying stunted dark green trees—and why the general population who lived all around where they had gone to ground had not reacted to the aerial destruction, or at least poked their heads out of their houses at the sound of the explosions.

The simple answer was that there was no one home.

Literally.

POWER ON POWER OFF

Moriah had been warned by a note Katrina had passed to her that she had to be judicious in the way she introduced the additional power to the neighborhood; she didn't pretend to understand how the girls had managed what they had done at the transformer station, and deep down she didn't really care. Her community had grown to over two thousand people in just the last week, and the number of parentless children had swollen to over four hundred.

Thankfully, the children who lived in her apartment block, and now those that had been moved into the one next door, provided the best and most trustworthy reference when it came to getting other children off the street. As soon as they realized the adults were genuinely there to help them, give them shelter, food, and comfort, the roving gangs dissipated until even the hardest of them either moved into one of the rooms, where clean bedding was provided and the only thing asked in return was that they care for their rooms and furnishings and help out wherever they could, or moved far away from what they regarded as an overcontrolling environment.

It was heartwarming for her when she realized more people stayed than left.

Moriah's biggest problem had been getting enough fresh food for everyone under her care, but the unpaid workers who helped put the panels on the roofs of the apartments and row houses soon turned into barterers and providers and formed a human link between the residents and the farmers. Moriah had gone to the biggest of the farms, protected by her original gang of children, and asked for a meeting, and to her surprise, every farmer in a thirty-mile radius turned up. She offered power and muscle for food, and when she was able, she also provided panels and batteries for them. She was swamped with offers.

The farmers were then faced with a resource management issue. They had over six hundred men and women willing to work on their farms for no more than a daily midday meal. They had the promise of power; the panels they had seen on the apartments brought the light back into the world, and they had envied it from the first time the lights had been switched on.

It took three days for the men to dig a trench and run a cable from the nearest row house to the nearest substation that had served the farms. It took only two days for a willing workforce to top every farm building with the panels and connect them to the substation. At first, Moriah made it clear that the power supply would mimic what they currently had—two hours in the morning and two in the late afternoon. But she promised to double that in a week and then double it again in a month.

The magic of it all was that the community was helping each other without rancor, greed, or fear of favor.

It was now beyond mere survival and into economic necessity.

It was now consideration and care. For each other as much as themselves.

It felt different—less pressure, a more balanced and happy outcome for everyone in the bartering chain. Some people were even smiling as they worked.

One man was whistling an old Irish tune, not heard in a pub in the last three months.

The children running the recovery business were having the time of their young lives, stripping everything that could be salvaged. The tires were being recycled as footwear and other essential objects, and all the plastics were bundled into sacks to be sold at the market. Shamus, who was their unofficial leader, had mastered the art of bargaining for what was needed up at the apartments and row houses and had provided a steady flow of furniture and fixtures that had been stripped out during the riots.

Using the silver material in the container the women had given them, they turned the stripped vehicles into puddles of metal. They had worried at first when the one container they had been given ran out, but within a day, two well-dressed women who were immediately tagged foreigners' because of their deep Scottish accents drove up in a small electric vehicle and handed over six more, with a promise of another six in a month.

Downstream, the metal traders who were taking the results of the children's efforts were glad of the supply, the ease with which they could obtain it, and the many uses they could put the recovered metal to. They were selling what they manufactured using a forge and fire, as they had no power, and passing a fair proportion of the money back to the children. When two immaculately dressed women approached them and offered them panels for the roof of their foundry and small manufacturing plant, they simply told the men to thank the children and never take advantage of them.

So, with no apparent effort, in the middle of the most socially difficult time in Ireland since the height of the 'troubles', a small corridor of commerce developed, with a balance of supply and demand, without the usual commercial avarice that had blighted the world just three months before.

Moriah turned the little box over and over in her hands and, helped by Sharon, plugged it into an outlet in the kitchen of their apartment.

"Here goes," she said as she turned the rheostat. The building, which had a sophisticated inverter and battery monitor, courtesy of one of the young lads who studied electronics, showed forty-four percent load, and within seconds the needle was pegged at the one hundred percent stop. She smiled. It was truly remarkable how they did it. "Sharon, tell the boys and girls to spread the word; power now eight hours a day."

Sharon ran off, Moriah put the kettle on to make tea, and not for the first time, she thanked her professor for putting her on this path. While she had enjoyed her life at the university, looking after so many and seeing them recover little by little, day by day, and the littles being given homes and protection warmed her heart as teaching never had. She brushed her long red hair back from her face, her skin glowing in the lamplight, her smile infectious and radiant.

She looked out the window to see a long line of row houses come to life, their porch lights coming on one by one, row by row, and she could sense the joy of the occupants, some of whom had come outside to look at their lights, working for the first time in three months.

The panels had been fitted by a volunteer workforce in return for meals, and the batteries had been connected, but nothing had worked since the installation started two weeks ago. The provision of mainstream levels of power would charge up all the batteries, allowing individual use between the times that Moriah would provide the extra push from the hidden power source.

And more than half the row houses were now occupied by people who had fled the civil unrest in the bigger towns and cities, and many were providing a home environment for the orphans who had been wandering the streets in gangs. Willingly, warmly, and with open hearts.

By coincidence, almost at the exact time the first row lit up, Brother Francis and Father Paul crested the small hill that led to the apartment. As they rose up, more and more of the twinkling lights came on, creating a fairyland lit as if by magic, and some people started dancing in the streets, their joyous shouts and laughter filling the still night air.

"Well now, Paul me bucko, isn't that just a wonderful sight?" The Jesuit was dumbstruck, having resigned himself to never seeing a well-lit building ever again. They both stood, their hands on their hips, heads rolled back, excitement in their eyes, and a smile on their faces. Paul slapped Francis on his broad back and laughed.

"You're right. This will be the perfect place for my school!"

On a farm some twenty miles away, when the lights came on, the cows started to moo, thinking it was breakfast time. Fred McNeil, who had worked the land with his father and his grandfather before him and now with his sons, stuffed his unlit pipe in a corner of his mouth, pulled his cap off, and scratched his balding pate with fingers bent from arthritis. Multiple colored patches ran across his vest and across his stained overalls. He laughingly called them his 'coat of many colors' after the musical he had seen way down in Dublin as a boy.

"Well now, she delivered, just as she said she would, and this is extra young Murphy, as I know our batteries are flat as your sister's chest." Both laughed, not intending any harm in their joke at young Bridget's expense. Indeed, had she been present, she would have agreed, then sulked as only an eight-year-old can, in love and envious of the old picture of a young, well-endowed model her father had dug out of the hayshed some time ago.

Power, faith, and hope had been restored. An eclectic community formed, and only one person outside the immediate area knew about it.

Freya looked at the automated text message sent by the power unit her daughters had installed, confirming that the Irish experiment had been successful. She immediately forwarded it to Katrina and her girls, feeling like the weight of the world had lifted off her shoulders. None of the other units would be in use for weeks, possibly months.

She still had the problem of working out how to bargain for what they all wanted with Scotland, England, Spain, and France, and the irritating issue of what to do about Russia and China. None of them wanted anything to do with helping either sadistic regime recover quickly, but as in all things political, it was the ordinary person in the street who struggled and suffered, never the power makers or the power brokers, and her heart bled for the trauma and distress the starving populations of both countries were presently suffering.

She had a team in faraway Canada working on a solution, modeling possible ways to break the stranglehold the oligarchs and dictators currently enjoyed, but with the capture of their most brilliant psychologist, Rena Niele, in Roanoke a month ago, the work was going slowly.

In faraway Venice, deep below the level of the canals, in the basement of a six hundred-year-old church, a team of modern-day geeks tracked the automatic transmission and fired off another message to their counterparts in Interpol's HQ. Eleven minutes after the message arrived, I used the software bot to show me the locations, and an image of an Irish transformer station swam into focus, followed by a POI in Scotland and a POI deep in France. The Scottish POI resolved itself as a three-story building in the heart of a built-up area in Aberfoyle, which I immediately passed onto Bob. The French POI was another nuclear power plant that was supposedly shut down a month ago by terrorist activity. I just obsessed over that. What in hell are the women doing at shut down nuclear power plants?

I worried about it for a few minutes, realized I couldn't do anything about it at this point, and tucked it away with all the other stuff I was avoiding.

Scotland and Socotra were still very much at the top of my list, and with the new data on Aberfoyle, I wondered if it was nearly time to resolve that little problem.

CHAPTER TWENTY EIGHT

The armored truck, sitting high on its massive wheels, looked like a prehistoric predator poised to strike with its huge headlights, massive bull bar, and blacked-out windows. Jessica could see it out of the corner of her eye as she scanned the sky. A soldier stood proud of the roof hatch, a MANPAD locked and loaded, scanning the horizon. Her eyes met his as their searches intersected. He waved one gloved hand, and even from the distance, she could see his intense focus. The truck had stopped less than four hundred meters from the 104 who had gone to ground, and as she watched, a second vehicle slipped around the first and provided a shield to those in the gully.

"MANPADS and drone exterminators, to the rear. Everyone else head for the trucks. Keep your heads down!" she shouted into her little communicator. The adrenalin was still pumping after the drone attack, and her senses were on high alert because the two trucks made for a simply wonderful, easy target. She moved sideways, scanning the sky, in automatic lockstep with the Sgan Aluf, who was two hundred meters further on, almost behind the second truck.

"Get everyone onboard, keep the exterminators free, and make sure they have a good field of view." The Israeli clicked her communicator twice, acknowledging Jessica's order. The instruction about keeping the terminators free was redundant, but she understood Sandra's attention to the smallest detail, a habit she appreciated. The ant heap cleared in double time until Sandra and the Israeli colonel were the only two left. She took one last look, then jumped into the cab, opened the window, and continued her scan. The convoy reformed one hundred meters apart and turned on its heel for Bantry.

The trip took just under ten minutes, and the boat ride to Whiddy Island took another ten, and the sky remained clear. The major walked down the ramp and saluted the colonel.

"Good to see you both in one piece. We'll put a MANPAD and drone unit on top of the oil tank they used as a store. I suggest the second unit be placed further north, perhaps adjacent to the plant." Sandra shook her head.

"No, first position is excellent. The plant will never be a target. Go wider, near the fort where we took on the mercenaries." He gave her a hard look, his eye brows raising, then nodded his head.

"There's a lot going on I don't know about." His flat tone underlined his discomfort, so Sandra put one hand on his shoulder and looked directly into his eyes. This is what she was here for—to disseminate information and gain trust.

"Major, we are the targets, not the plant, the Island, or anything they have set up as infrastructure. Organize your establishment with the colonel, and I'll take the four who came with me on a little tour of the Island."

She walked off, leaving the two officers to work things out without her interference. The four Italians, members of Indigo's Col. Moschin's 9th Assault Parachute Regiment, who had come with her as her body guards at Jessica's insistence, maintained their silence, rotating their heads as if on swivels. Their instructions were specific: bring her back to Venice in the same condition she left it in, or don't come back. Having seen firsthand what the woman could do in a firefight, neither took their roles for granted. She led them to the first Napoleonic-era fort, bent down, and studied the grass growing around the culvert.

She pulled her combat knife out and scraped some of the tangly moss-like undergrowth away, revealing a metal surface that, to her eye, wasn't anywhere near two hundred and thirty years old. She reached into a pants pocket and pulled out a small frequency detector. She ran it around the edge of the exposed metal and got a null reading. She rolled on her back, pulled her mini out, and dialed the Israeli AWACS.

"Thomas."

"Inspector, Pauly, copilot. Go."

"Need you to sweep Whiddy Island with GPR (Ground Penetration Radar), Lidar, and anything else you have, specifically the three forts on the lee side of the Island. They'll each paint as three concentric circles. One to the south, two in the north. We know the one in the middle is hollow. Also, suspect drone launching facility five miles north of Drimoleague, off their route 586."

"Got it. We've just cleared Belfast airspace. Be with you in thirty."

"Roger that, out." She leaned back, working out her next moves, when the top of the fort suddenly levered up, and three people dressed in black carrying very large guns emerged. Before she could even think, her two bodyguards rolled around her and opened fire simultaneously. She drew her trusty H&K and shot the next two out of the hatch with economical three-round bursts. She bent to rise, looked at both her partners, got a nod from each, then exploded up and over the edge of the trough, ran up the slight incline, and in total harmony with her Italian guards, pulled a grenade out of her vest, pulled the pin, and dropped it down the manhole, then pulled her head in and ducked.

Three muffled explosions followed, with body parts flying up from the compression wave that raced out of the manhole like a banshee. She cautiously started towards the edge, only to be restrained by one of her guards, who shook his head and, in an almost invisible whisper, admonished her.

"*No signora, non così in fretta. Lascia andare Roberto per primo.*" She reluctantly nodded, and Roberto crawled to the edge of the manhole, dropped the barrel of his weapon over the lip, and fired a long burst down the hole.

"Now, my inspector, she should be okay to peek," he said with a huge grin, removing all the tension that had built up since the hatch had first opened.

She crawled to the edge, looked down, saw only a bloody mess, and decided to wait for the major and his boys and girls on the basis that the fort on the top of the Island was probably holding terrorists as well. She thought about letting the AWACS know, but saw no reason to do so. But the attack had pushed a more urgent question into her mind: why? What was the drone campaign all about? Why were the mercenaries protecting the Island?

A squad from the 104 ran up, the Sgan Aluf leading, and immediately surrounded the fort.

"Anyone hurt?" she asked, watching Sandra's face for any telltale signs. Sandra just shook her head, slid down the grass slope, and regained her feet to jump back over the shallow culvert.

"We need to clean it out, then move to the one at the top. It's probably got some tangos in it as well." The colonel waved to three troopers, who scurried up the fort, emptied their magazines down the hole, waited a few heartbeats, then disappeared from sight. The communicator the colonel held in her hand rumbled and squawked. She nodded to herself a few times and looked up at Sandra.

"Lots of blood and guts, around nine bodies, they think, plus a massive store of ammunition and supplies. Lots of those containers we took from the oil tank." Sandra nodded, working out how to get the containers back to Israel.

"Secure the containers, mine the ammunition, set a trip wire, leave the bodies, and seal the hatch." The colonel gave Sandra a wicked grin, imagining the surprise the next mercenary would get when and if they ever managed to get back into the old fort.

"Not worried about blowing up a national treasure?" she asked, tongue in cheek.

"No. If it goes up, it's because the bad guys are sloppy. Not our fault." She signaled to her Italians and started to walk towards the third fort. The Israelis formed up on either side of the muddy road, spread out in a classical combat formation, and matched her stride for stride. The colonel walked up to her shoulder and, in a soft voice, asked the question that was on everyone's lips.

"Why are we being attacked? What are they protecting? What don't I know?" Sandra did some deep thinking, decided that the Sgan Aluf should be read in, a decision she would defend to her death, and brought the colonel up to speed. As she spoke in an equally soft voice, the colonel's eyes opened to the size of saucers, and she shook her head from side to side.

"This is way bigger than what we thought. Is Arie aware of all of this?" Sandra turned her head to look the colonel directly in the eyes.

"Of course. What we know, he knows, and vice versa. Arie was the first to involve Interpol. His geeks and ours have a constant love affair. I just returned from Japan with Amira. We are very close to Israel in every way possible."

The colonel nodded at this. Troops in the field rarely learn the big picture, being focused on their objective tasks and operational requirements. At best, they got a broad overview, but never the meat in the sandwich. She herself had been involved in two operations since her predecessor had been killed in action, and while she had read and reread the after-action reports of those who went before her, the information was always just a little bit of the overall picture. What she suddenly realized is that her walking companion, the long, lean, very beautiful, and single-minded Interpol inspector, was playing a far bigger role than she ever let on. She tucked that thought away for another day.

"What do you want the major and I to do here?"

"Hold the Island, no matter what. No one gets to land here, by sea or air, or submarine for that matter. You'll have 24/7 AWACS cover, and if you need more we'll provide it. The US Navy is just a few hundred klicks that way, and I have their admiral on speed dial. Oh, by the way, I forgot to mention you'll have your very own ship in a day or two. It's traveling from the Med. Colonel Kashasini is at the helm. He runs our Italian office, as well as being in the hierarchy of Section Five. It will be gunned up appropriately. I think its main use will be aerial protection and an at-sea deterrent."

The colonel simply nodded, adding more pieces to the puzzle. She sensed her team had gone on alert and sank down on one knee, looking over the sights of her weapon. Beside her, Sandra stood with her binoculars fixed to her eyes, scanning left to right. The colonel reached up and pulled her pants leg twice, and Sandra took the hint and kneeled.

"What?" The colonel pointed to her troops, all of whom had gone to the ground.

"Someone smells a threat." Sandra nodded. Instinct and the hairs on the back of your neck were very reliable early warning devices, and while hers were currently neutral, she trusted the soldier in the field. In the distance, she could see the third fort, this one with much heavier undergrowth surrounding it. It was also closer to the sea, and she remembered how the terrorists in the middle fort had gotten away.

"Send a team to the ocean side. watch for terrorists emerging from tunnels or pipes." The colonel signaled to the right, waved her hands in the air, held up fingers, waved again, and four troops moved off. The only sound was the two clicks that came back from the communicator.

"Trip wire, two meters to the front!" The call came in, and everyone froze. Sandra looked over to where the soldier who had called out was and saw two bodies crawling forward, hugging the ground. They stopped, one meaty hand raised in a fist, the universal military sign for 'halt'. The communicator in the colonel's hand came to life again, and the colonel turned her gaze on Sandra.

"The report is that the entire approach from this side of the fort, at least, is mined. They are crawling around to see where it ends." Sandra just nodded, keeping her binoculars on the top of the fort.

"You know, there's something that's bugged me from the get-go. Why no electronic surveillance? In all the time we've been chasing the mercenary terrorists, we've never hit anything electronic."

"You did in the underground factories." Sandra turned her head and looked back at the colonel.

"Agreed, but that can be explained by what the terrorists were doing in those tunnels and underground facilities, but never in the field." She turned her head as if giving it more thought, then pulled her H&K out of her bag and sighted on the head of someone who was slowly emerging from the ground immediately in front of the culvert that ran around the fort.

"Contact, front, twenty meters, hold fire," she whispered, as the head turned into a torso and was soon joined by three other heads. In the fading light, given the overcast conditions, the figures resolved themselves as dark shadows, and when fully erect, they moved off to the right, turned, and started directly towards Sandra and the colonel.

"No NVG, there's the breach in their trips. Close up behind them, but keep your people out of the line of fire." Sandra flattened herself into the ground, keeping the shadows in the center of her illuminated sight. She felt more than she saw a team move along the line of trips, then fade back towards where the shadows had emerged. They turned towards the ocean, and the colonel clicked her communicator to warn her people of the approach. Suddenly Sandra stood, fired a three-round burst into the ground at the feet of the shadows, and yelled in Russian.

"*Stoy! ili moy sleduyushchiy vystrel ub'yet tebya!*" She fired a second burst to make her point. The squad on Sandra's right stood and quickly surrounded the shadows. One of them raised their weapon aggressively, and Sandra dropped him like a smelly bag of manure, causing the others to try to scatter. They were stopped in place by the Israeli commandos with less fuss than wrangling a stray cat. The shadows up close resolved into men, poorly dressed in dirty combat fatigues, unshaven, but with clean, gleaming weapons. Within a minute, they were all cuffed on their stomachs, gagged, and bagged.

"With me!" and Sandra ran to the gap in the trips and hovered over the four Israelis, covering the point where the shadows had emerged. She saw another hatch, not unlike the one back at the first fort. The colonel put her hand on Sandra's arm and whispered.

"Wait. We'll learn more if we wait. That group looked unhealthy, as if they hadn't eaten in days or had any water.

"I suspect they have been left to their own devices since we first got here three weeks ago." Sandra paused, not a natural state for her, but respect for the Sgan Aluf overwhelmed her instinct to get it done and dusted. She still harbored a lot of resentment over being both shot at and shot down by the terrorists, but she sucked in a breath, rolled her shoulders, and relaxed fractionally.

"How long do we wait?"

"A day or two, then we go in. From here we can cover the fort as well. I'll let the major know what we are up to." Sandra nodded her head.

"Okay, I'll take my boys and finish my tour. You've got this. You understand our ROE. It's all yours." She signaled to her Italian studs, who were standing by and grinning so big they lit up the area with happiness, turned, and walked back towards where the environmental plant was located. Neither had fired a shot this time; both were excited to see how fast and positively Sandra had reacted and how clean her shoot had been.

To say they were enjoying the experience was a gross understatement.

Sandra led them to the walkway, where they were challenged by two of the major's men. Sandra held up her Interpol credentials; the two Irish and Italian soldiers eyed each other off, reached no obvious conclusion, then relaxed, recognizing like for like. She walked into the building, humming to herself, thinking through all that she had learned about these plants since she had first stepped foot on Point Roberts.

She now knew that all the infrastructure had been designed and built by Innomatchi, then shipped over in boxes to be assembled locally. All the buildings had the same dimensions, the layout was the same, and the only differences were where the nanites were produced. In Port Roberts and New Zealand, where only two types of nanites were used, there were two giant cistern baths. In building six, if she remembered. Here she expected to find at least four baths, maybe more.

And she did. Six in total, one well hidden behind the moving travelator.

Now inert, bathed in shadows, deep, dark, and mysterious. She pulled her camera out and filmed the entire section. She knew Amira would at least be very interested in the video. The plant was as silent as a graveyard, and she was happy to leave it. On the way out, she turned to her guards.

"Excellent job. I think it's time we got ready to pack it in and go home." Both broke out into infectious grins, home being the magic word.

She texted Jessica a short summary as she walked back out into the gloom and took a light shower. The rain steamed off her as if she were an electric bar heater, and she smiled at the temporary mist.

Ireland was a magical place after all. Then she had a sudden thought and attacked her mini with a vengeance.

DISCOVERY

Amira was super smart, possibly one of the innately cleverest people on the planet, and one of the first in a long line of genius-level children orphaned in a refugee camp in unimaginable conditions to be rescued by the 'old man of the desert', Mohammad bin Azaria, and placed in a loving home in another country. In her case, Israel, and then encouraged to bloom into the magnificent woman she had become.

In her very early twenties, she had invented a nano bug that lived to consume oil spills, turning the greasy, stinking, rainbow-colored filmy pollution into a harmless, carbon-three, environmentally neutral element that sank to the bottom of the ocean, degenerating into the natural muck and slush of the sea bed from which it had originated millions of years before.

Naturally, the terrorist woman had stolen all her work.

Naturally, they had further developed her work to do things she had only envisaged as experiments at the time of her early work. As in, eat all the oil, gas, and coal on the planet. Consume radioactivity in a manner that renders all nuclear weapons inert. To balance the cruel with the good, they also created incredibly efficient solar panels and batteries. And as Amira has seen firsthand in her lab, they had also created nanites that did other things, like boil liquids, dissolve metals, returning them to their base elements, and join metals, making an electromagnetic neutral-state composite of whatever metals they were activated on. And perhaps the most significant was one that, when combined with any vegetable or plant matter, produced a totally environmentally neutral biofuel with an incredible low ratio of nanite to biomass.

And as the nanites, panels, and power packs were manufactured out of the naturally occurring minerals and metals in sand and sea water, the environmental impact was zero.

And all this came from her original work before she was twenty-two.

She shook her head in frustration, her long hair swirling around her face like an out-of-control waterfall. She had a collection of blueprints and drawings pulled from the files at Innomatchi, the factory that had produced the software that had taken down the internet, and neutered every chip and processor in every computer, router, switchback, phone, and electronic device connected at the time of the attack.

She had 3-D printed several parts, all at one sixth scale, but for the life of her, she could not divine what the ultimate device might be. She had bits and pieces of it. She held in her hand a small turbine wheel, similar to one you might find in a jet engine. On her desk lay a small duo of pipes, joined seamlessly in a perpetual figure of eight. Next to it lay a really weird manifold, in that it had a disproportionate number of entries compared to its exits but had no accelerator or force-multiplying device she could determine.

In short, a bunch of technologically superior junk!

She pushed her chair back, closed her pretty eyes, let her head loll back on her shoulders, relaxed her hands and arms, curled her toes in her battered Rebooks, and muttered a relaxing mantra under her breath. That was how Shami, a colonel in the Israeli army and a master geek, found her. He knew how hard she was trying to offset her assumed guilt for her role in the invention and development of the nanites and the destruction they had rained on the world, a guilt no one else in the know attributed to her. He decided to let her rest, slipping the handwritten note and the data chip on the corner of her working space. He idly picked up one of the pieces she had lying around and marveled at its intricate design and flawless perfection.

Just like Amira, he thought to himself.

Something about the piece tickled at the back of his mind, but it was so fleeting that it faded away as fast as it had tried to appear. He tiptoed back out of the laboratory, happy to see her resting for the first time in days.

As he worked his way out of the laboratory, he suddenly remembered what the piece had reminded him of. Back in his youth, growing up in his kibbutz, his grandfather had once shown him an incredible wooden device that barely filled his palm. Made from the Juniper tree root, it had a little piece of plastic tubing running through it, and when you ran water through the tube, if the wooden bit was in the ground, as it got wet, it shrank and closed up around the plastic tube, stopping the water.

It had been invented by a friend of his grandfather's, a farmer from one of the West Bank orchids, as the solution to the sheer lack of water in Israel. It was an automatic, super-low-tech drip irrigation system, and it had ensured a part of Israel's survival for seven decades.

He turned on his heel and ran back into the lab. The noise his feet made on the tiled floor woke Amira, who looked up in surprise when she saw Shami slide to a stop, his face alive with happiness.

"I know what that little piece there is for!" he exclaimed, almost bouncing up and down on his toes.

"What?"

"That little bit there," he said, his enthusiasm overflowing to the point where Amira found herself smiling in concert with him for no reason other than his infectious joy. She picked up the small piece and turned it over in her delicate fingers, the clear lacquer on her nails reflecting in the overhead light.

"This bit?"

"Yes. It's an automatic fluid controller." He pointed to her cupped hand.

"It works by shrinking a tube of some type, like an automatic controller." She screwed her eyes up, a furrow forming between her eyebrows.

"An automatic controller?" She set the piece down, put the strange manifold alongside, and started to nod.

"Okay, I see it now. I'm still missing several pieces, but I'll draw up what I think should be here and give you a look." He beamed at her, took her now empty hands, kissed her knuckles, then the side of her pretty face.

"You're the genius. If anyone can work it out, it's you!" Amira's face flushed. She couldn't stop it as embarrassment flew through her in direct opposition to the warm feeling building in her belly. She stood to break the tension, smiled, and put her hands in the pockets of her lab coat, out of harm's way.

"Thanks for that. I was stumped. Come around anytime." She laughed to further dispel the mood and saw just the flicker of disappointment in Shami's eyes. He picked up the note he had left with the data chip and, still smiling but at a much reduced wattage, handed it to her.

"Here's the latest report from Jessica and some photos from Sandra in Ireland." She took both, careful to minimize her hand-to-hand contact. Shami left, thinking to himself that she was very young, didn't have many real-life experiences, had been hijacked at an early age to use her genius for a supposedly environmentally important development, then betrayed by her coworker and lover, so in that department trust was probably something she would have to develop slowly.

He'd put in the effort. She deserved it. And him, he thought, smiling. And him.

CHAPTER TWENTY NINE

It was with very mixed feelings that I read John Vernon's formal report of his first month as an instant father to his supervisor in Seattle, who had passed it to me through Anna in Washington. The report was positive in the extreme, highlighting all the things the children had accomplished, including Aya's skill with a Rubik's cube and their progress with language. Being home tutored for the interim, as expected, progress was a little slow, but reading between the lines, I saw hints of comprehension and understanding beyond what was expected for the ages of his children. I put the report aside. He was giving us an accurate insight into what the parents in Helena were involved in: taking one or two refugee children who had been in some of the worst refugee camps on the planet and exposing them to American culture, but in a family environment.

I crossed my fingers that it wouldn't go sideways. Nothing I could do in any case. The whole refugee migration issue was out of our jurisdiction. We were a hammer, not a nursemaid, and while we actively chased child predators, this migration was meticulously planned and fully funded, and the terrorists had seen to it that once accepted by the countries taking the children, it couldn't easily be stopped. They had gone to the trouble to hack into the systems that provided identities, visas, and passports, and as they had been inside our IT systems for over a quarter of a century, what they had presented to a shell-shocked world was a fait accompli.

The United States and New Zealand had been their test cases, with both countries having no real choice but to accept the children. There were seventeen other countries slated for children as well, with more than half already informing the UN that they would build the ecological plants and take their refugees.

The time bomb in the entire scheme was Ireland, which we believed was shaping up to take between five and six million children as part of their 'one million empty homes' status. And this was my real focal point, because I had just received a summary of the latest attack on my people on Whiddy Island and, like Sandra, had no idea what the terrorists were protecting or trying to achieve with the attacks.

We had an AWACS scanning Whiddy Island and keeping an eye out for drone launches. We had the captured terrorist ship refitted by the US Navy on its way to Ireland. I had three teams from the Irish *Sciathán Fianóglach,* supported by a team from the Israeli 104 commandos, plus commandos from Tom's former team as well as Indigo's, and quite frankly, I'd put them up against anyone and expect them home for tea. Or, in our case, coffee! Which I desperately needed. And I was becoming so predictable that one of my guards stood in front of me with a new steaming mug. I just looked up and smiled.

"Grazie Antonio, apprezzato."

"Comandante, vedi se questo ti aiuta a pensare."

I took my first sip, let the flavor roll around my tongue, and thanked the ancient Greek goat herder reputedly responsible for the discovery. What a guy. Little did he know at the time that he would be creating billions of addicts!

The AWACS aircrew had reported that Fay and her playmates had been unloaded in Belfast to make their own way to Killara Bay. That might take them a day or two, depending on their transport arrangements. As they were posing as civilians, it not only had to be in character but also pass the local smell test. The idea was to set a trap, not scare the terrorist away. But my gut told me Fay would make it work, so I relaxed and waited to hear from her.

My thoughts were interrupted by a data transmission that caused both my mini and my huge screen to ping, then click, buzz, then ping again, a sign that the anti-hack software provided by the monks had cleared the transmission. I booted up the big screen, my eyes blurring in the reflected glare. I tilted my head to one side, trying to understand what I was looking at. Geek time. I dialed up Amira, saw the happy smile on her face, and saw her flick her hair away from her eyes in a manner that suggested someone else was in the room.

"Hi, Amira, I've got your data, but I'm at a loss as to what it means." Amira, still smiling, turned in her chair, hit a key, and suddenly she was in one corner of the big screen. I shut down the mini and concentrated on the drawings and diagrams that scrolled slowly down the screen.

"Apologies, commander, what you have now is our best guess as to what the device is that was on the blueprints from Innomatchi." I nodded, so far so good. The diagram was exploded into tens of parts, each joined to another by dotted lines. Some of the parts were in black, others in blue, some in red.

"The black parts are ones we have made using the 3D printer—one sixth scale, as I told you before. The blue are parts we have drawings for but are not complete. The red is missing and so they are our best guess."

"Who's we?" She sucked her smile in, tried to look embarrassed, but only came off as uncomfortable. Interesting.

"Colonel Borowitz helped me interpret the missing parts from things he had seen previously."

"Did he? Is he there?" Amira looked sheepishly to her left and nodded.

"Hello commander, no biggie. As you know, Israel has had a severe shortage of water for generations, so some of us got to be very clever when it came to working with what we have. A friend of my uncle invented a little wooden-based valve. All I did was tell Amira what I had seen, and she immediately worked out the rest, as you would expect." I nodded, seeing a dynamic here I had never considered. It wasn't as if our people didn't fall in and out of love or even lust, but it rarely happened during an operation.

"Okay, that's the background, but remember, I'm not a geek. What am I looking at?" Amira broke into her biggest smile again, her face filling the little box. An obvious hand reached into the frame to sit on her shoulder.

"Commander, if we have guessed correctly, this is a self-powered closed-circuit fluid system of some sort. I need more parts and more data, but that's what this is looking like." I smiled, not having the first idea of what use you would put such a device to in my little world, but it excited two of my best and most intelligent geeks, so no doubt its purpose would be revealed in time.

"Thanks, Amira. You too, Shami. Great work." I closed the connection, sent the data to the massive file we were accumulating on this operation, and sat back in my chair. I still had to resolve Scotland and Socotra, get Sandra and Tom back from Whiddy Island, and backstop Fay in her ambush.

And work out what the hell the terrorists had planned for Ireland?

CULTURE SHOCK

With a little under a thousand homes finished and another thirty being finished every day, the massive plot that had been Westhall Senior's dream started to take on a shape that he would have been proud of.

Five schools, one university, four shopping centers, and parks are all linked by winding grass walkways and lined by three varieties of local trees. Multiple parks and gardens, basketball courts, football fields, and extraordinary playgrounds designed to stimulate young minds. A medium-sized hospital and medical center were a week or two away from being finished, and from the early foundation work, it was clear to see the potential for another three thousand houses or more. More shops, more recreation areas, and even more unimaginable buildings might see businesses in the Helena CBD move their offices.

The same standard contractor rate was being paid to every person who turned up to work, male or female, and that currently numbered in the tens of hundreds. The money they collected with big smiles every Friday went straight into the Helena economy at so many levels that the locals spent many an evening cheering, and more than one ended up in the cells overnight for exceeding their personal capacity for alcohol consumption!

If there was a worry, it was centered on the university, which suddenly saw itself in competition for students. That angst was erased when the Town Council called a meeting of the Boards of the six schools and universities that currently operated in Helena.

The offer was open and very attractive. Each educational facility would be 'gifted' one of the new buildings as a second campus and named in part for the Westhall family. The only stipulations were that every school and university had to hire a minimum of ten qualified teachers from the migrant refugee adults, introduce new and varied language and cultural courses, and not discriminate in any manner between local and refugee children.

If they agreed, an annual stipend would be paid on the commencement day of each school year. When the Boards read the fine print, their collective eyes shot open as they registered the number—three million each for the junior, middle, and senior schools, and ten million dollars annually for the university—for thirty years.

They were all aware that the trustees were already paying all the fees for the refugee children and intended to do the same for the children of the families who adopted them. To be blunt, no one around the table could see how they or their educational facility could lose. In fact, this was the most encouraging and remarkable thing to happen to any of them in the past one hundred years! One by one, they nodded, signed the agreements, then stood and shook hands.

One of the parents who had adopted two refugee children probably wasn't thinking about how lucky he was. He just wished the school year had started as he faced down an incredible mess in his kitchen. Paint in every color known to man dripped over his walls, across the double-door refrigerator, across the handmade wooden table, across the floor, and, to his consternation, all over both the cat and the dog, who continued to run around spreading the colorful joy. His two adopted refugee children, happier than they had ever been, sat on the floor, amazed at what they had created, dripping finger paint, which adorned them as if applied by some modernist painter.

Luckily, the parent was the new FBI supervisory senior agent in Helena, and just as luckily, he remembered the finger paint was water-based and would probably clean off without too much fuss. Giving up on the two pets, who now ran around chasing each other as if demented, he sat down between his two new daughters and picked up the drawing that had inspired them to redecorate the kitchen. It looked like a lopsided person of some sort, with stringy rainbow hair and splotches all over what he assumed were a shirt and pants.

Kona, the youngest, looked up at him from under her brunette hair, also carrying the results of the painting expedition. She grabbed the cat on its way past and hugged it to her paint-stained smock. Aya, with streaks of paint hiding the scar that ran down her face, looked up at John Vernon and smiled.

"Is it the good we have made for you?" she asked in halting English, looking very shy and uncertain. Her dog stopped in its tracks when it heard her voice, its stumpy tail wagging in unbounded joy. With love in its eyes, it belly crawled over to her and put its yellow, red, and black-painted head in her lap. She unconsciously stroked the dog, spreading more paint across its furry back.

John, remembering the suggestions they had received from the psychologist assigned to their family, relaxed his shoulders, put on his best and most sincere smile, and nodded.

"Yes, Aya, it is the prettiest picture I have ever seen. And your pets look wonderful in their new coats." Both girls laughed, happy for what they had done but more happy that they hadn't been yelled at or beaten, something they would have automatically expected just weeks ago. John secretly wondered how he could clean the kitchen up before his wife returned, but after looking at the paint-splattered room, he decided to leave it. It was the first time the girls had played inside, as the driving storm with its thunder and lightning had scared them both, and as the finger painting had been his idea, he'd take any heat that came his way.

When he looked over at the kitchen table, he could clearly see two distinct sets of finger trails that formed a bulb around the salt and pepper shakers, fell off the table, then jumped back up to the bench, across the refrigerator, and around the walls.

Being an investigator, he quickly worked out that the girls had pained their hands, then, in concert, ran the colors across everything together. The cat and the dog had spread the joy across the floors and across the base of the bench and the cabinets, so it has been a real team effort!

He had never been happier in his life, and as he looked at his two girls, he wondered how anyone could ever refuse to help or acknowledge a refugee child. He knew the camps were still full of them, and he knew the cost to the world for what he now held in his heart, but as hard as he tried, all he could see were his two little girls, happy, content, and safe, and his newly redecorated kitchen.

CHAPTER THIRTY

It had been easier for Fay, Luca, and Gabriella to move from Belfast to Killara Bay than had been expected. Within the first hour of walking alongside the road, they had been offered a lift in a faded green timber truck, driven by a tiny, crusty, wizened woman, at least eighty by Sandra's count, dressed in a many-times patched smock over rough overalls and a woolen jumper, with massive scuffed leather patches on the elbows. Her short gray hair stood up as if she had been electrocuted, with just the faintest trace of a purple rinse. Her glasses perched almost on the very tip of her nose, as if wanting to be somewhere else. The truck was electric and not a factory conversation, as evidenced by the constant grinding sound the transmission made, but it beat walking in the sheeting rain, and the conversation was stilted, to say the least.

Thankfully so, the three agents thought to themselves, their smiles welded on their faces in a rictus mask.

"Yer all going to stay at Killara, then, are ya?" the driver, who identified herself as Patricia O'Malley *but call me Pat*, croaked in a broad Irish accent. She had the disturbing habit of looking sideways at her passengers in the front seat for long periods of time, during which the truck slid ever so slowly towards the deep gully running along the road. When she looked back, her first instinct was to jerk the truck back on course, throwing her passengers across the cab in no uncertain manner. The three agents had squashed into a space barely big enough for two, their rucksacks and bags either on their laps or on top of their feet, forming an unsteady and dangerous pile of potential missiles.

Comfortable, no. Dry and somewhat warm, certainly. Fay kept this at the forefront of her mind as she crushed Gabriella on one side and Pat on the other, depending on whether or not Pat was talking or driving. The windscreen wipers, having seen better days by far, did their best, squeaking and grinding across the windscreen, the corners of which were elbow-deep in dirt and muck. Every now and then a new mud slide would peel off the roof, slipping down and fogging the view until the half-moon shapes the wipers made managed to clear enough to see the road or the encroaching ditch.

And the rain pelted down, the harmony of it happily banging on the dented roof like a brass band warming up for a march. Every now and then, Pat would reach forward, rubbing one sleeve on the windscreen, clearing the fog. On those occasions, she stayed mostly on the road, just shaking a little at the start and finish as her shortish arms reached across the steering wheel.

Fay tossed up whether or not to start a conversation, local knowledge could save them hours, maybe days, so she risked it by nudging Gabriella in the ribs. She squeezed herself a little more to her left until she almost couldn't breathe.

"Pat, we're thankful for the lift. Do you know any small boarding houses where we can stay?" She held her breath as Pat made one of her steering corrections, then turned to look Fay directly in the eyes.

"Aye, that I do, but Killara Bay is all about the sea. Where would you really want to stay, supposing it's not the middle of the bleeding ocean?" Fay stared back at her, hoping against hope Pat would look back at the road before they drove into the culvert, which she judged to be at least 2 meters deep.

"We were just given that as where we should be. Are you saying it's not an actual town?" While Fay was covering her tracks somewhat, Pat broke out into a cackle. That was the only way Fay could describe it.

"Oh, dear girl, someone's been pulling ya leg, that's for sure. Ya want Palmerstown, Killala, or Inishcrone?" Fay looked out the window, felt the swerve, and mentally forced herself to relax while she thought through the alternatives. She had a survey map of the area and a satellite overlay about one year old, so she knew about the towns Pat had mentioned. But she was unsure which to settle on, as she had been from the get-go. She screwed up her brow in thought, remembering what Jessica had said to her. The destination of the terrorist, Siobhan O'Cleary, was Killara Bay. They not only had to find where the crates containing the ecological plant had been delivered but also lay a trap for the terrorist, who they guessed was at least one or two days behind them.

Maybe.

The terrorist women had shown a propensity for moving around the globe rapidly, freely, and mostly undetected. So Fay revised her mental timeline by a day. She pulled the satellite photo out, looked hard at the detail, and nodded to herself. The roads to all three went through Ballina, but if O'Cleary arrived by light plane or helicopter, they would be way behind the eight ball. She knew the plant required direct access to sea water, so to her eye, Killara or Inishcrone were the closest. And of the two, without the benefit of a ground survey, she suspected that the northern end of Inishcrone would be the target because of its proximity to the ocean and a lot of undeveloped land against the seashore.

So they'd start there. She waited until the truck was on the straight and narrow, nudged Gabriella in the ribs again to get more space, crossed her fingers, and asked the question she knew was on the minds of her companions.

"Pat, if you were setting up a new factory in Inishcrone, where would you most likely go?" Pat tilted her head from side to side, giving the matter considerable thought. These three backpackers didn't look like the industrial type. The tall one was way too pretty to get her hands dirty by far, and the other two were obviously foreign by their looks, not that either of them had said so much as 'boo!', didn't look the laboring type. She shrugged her shoulders, no skin off her back, and in these most troubled times, they might even do some good.

"I'll be dropping this load off at a big paddock next to the sewerage plant, just below Dún na Sí. There's not a factory I know of anywhere there, but the order is for five truck loads, and this is the fifth, so I can take you that far or drop you off somewhere else of ya liking. There be plenty of bed'n'breakfasts, and a motel or two on Cliff Road. Ya might find them more accommodating." Fay stayed absolutely still. The terrorist women use extensive timber framing and infrastructure to support their power panels when building their environmental plants. She remembered the design and layout of both Point Roberts and New Zealand. Could it be possible they were traveling with one of the suppliers for the proposed new plant?

"Pat, how long have you been hauling timber all the way out to the Killara Bay area?" She hoped she sounded curious, not necessarily invested in the answer, and to lessen the impact, she rolled her shoulders and looked out her window across the untidy laps of her two partners. Pat did her swerving trick again, throwing Fay against Gabriella, now watching the ancient driver like a hawk. Gabriella pushed Fay back to her place, a wan smile crossing her eyes. Pat sucked her breath in through her teeth, making a sound not unlike a locomotive starting up, and scrubbed fruitlessly at the fog on the windscreen again.

"Well now, I got the order three days ago, made two trips the first day, got too tired, so only one each day since. The timber yard made it clear they wanted all on site by close of business tomorrow, even wrote a penalty into the contract. I nearly told them to buggar off, but business being what it is, I let it go. Need the money, no shame in that." Fay nodded. She absolutely understood the brutal economic conditions most towns and cities were experiencing. The lack of power had crippled industry worldwide, and it would be a long time before any sense of equilibrium would be achieved.

But her mind was ticking over at a million miles an hour, and her gut was clenching and unclenching as she thought through the possibility that she now had a defined time frame and possible location for the appearance of one Siobhan O'Cleary, now the most wanted terrorist on the planet. She needed to get into Inishcrone, she needed to talk to Jessica, and she needed to talk to Amira because, at the back of her mind, an idea was forming that might just change the outcome of what they were planning.

"Pat, drop us off at a motel or hotel, please. Pick the best one you know. That will be great for us." Pat swerved and turned to look at her, a question in her eyes. She shrugged her shoulders, then let it go. These foreigners would do whatever they came to do, with or without her help. The resolve was strong in their eyes, and she had always believed in people having a purpose, which was why she was still driving a truck with her eighty-fourth birthday far behind in her rusted and fogged rearview mirror. She had three generations to look after, and her grandma was sick.

"Aye, I'll be doing that. We'll be there in ten minutes or so." Fay nodded, working out her next steps. Beside her, Gabriella was unobtrusively looking up data on her mini, shielded by the massive pack on her lap, which was hitting Fay in the ribs at every twist and turn of the truck. She tilted the screen so Luca could see the data. They nodded to each other, then she slipped the mini back into her pocket.

"Sei perfetto con Inishcrone, i geek hanno una trasmissione aerea che stanno monitorando." Fay looked startled, then realized she had turned her mini on silent when getting into the truck.

"Grazie Luca, tieni quel pensiero." Pat immediately gave them both the eye, then smiled, her aged, wrinkled face falling into a soft, warm shape. She pointed one bony finger at Luca.

"I knew you were a foreigner, but I'd never guessed eye-talians!" She chuckled to herself, banging her hands on the old chipped steering wheel. Fay just smiled and elbowed Gabriella in the ribs as punishment. She had seen the sly look at the mini and even felt the buzz of the alarm through her thigh-to-thigh contact in the cramped space. But she didn't want to give Pat anything to talk to others about.

"Do you speak Italian?" Fay asked, hoping against hope that she didn't.

"Nar, those foreign languages are beyond me since I left school early, but I've got a bit of Gaelic if you're wanting it." Her eyes lit up at the thought of talking to these foreigners without them knowing a single thing she was saying. It might be considered rude, but at her age, you got your jollies where and when you could. Fay nodded.

"That would be nice, Pat."

"*Uill a-nis, tha thu coltach ri luchd-turais, ach cuiridh mi geall nach eil thu!*" She turned her head again to see if her passengers had understood anything. Smiled a wicked smile when their faces remained expressionless.

"*Ach tha mi a 'geall ort bhon riaghaltas fuilteach an àiteigin, tha mi an dòchas gu bheil thu suas gu math.*" Fay nodded, smiled, then risked patting Pat on the shoulder.

"Yes, Pat, we are up to good. You can count on it." The shocked look on Pat's face was its own reward, and all four broke out into stress-relieving laughter.

HIGH SEAS JINKS

The good ship *'Scáthán'* was making better than twenty-eight knots through the light choppy swell of the western edge of the Mediterranean Sea, with the southern coast of Portugal passing to starboard. At this rate, they would be at Whiddy Island in two days, give or take, due to weather.

The crew had settled into a cycle of training, repairing, training, sleeping, and eating, and the deck was always littered with walking or running sailors, keeping their mobility at its peak. Inside the converted middle deck, where the rail gun sat off to one side, ignored other than for somewhere to put discarded equipment or the boxes it came in, a new control center had been strung together, a series of very large screens sitting on black crates along the starboard wall. While there were seats for six, only one in the center was consistently filled in four hourly shifts.

Everyone on board, now numbering ten with Indigo and the master chief, cycled through the control room in rotation, Indigo's philosophy having been sharpened at the sides of both the Boss and Jessica, both of whom believed in everyone being able to do everything. If either of the two senior officers felt the need for more exposure to the control room, then a second or even a third chair might be occupied for a few hours, but the authority remained with whomever sat in the middle chairs. The reason for the extra crew was as simple as the master chief, after seeing Tom's shopping list, realizing they would need more hands and calling for more volunteers. He had to beat off the unsuccessful sailors and marines with a broom stick!

The ship had been fitted with an antiaircraft radar with a one hundred and twenty nautical mile range, a surface detection radar with a seventy-two nautical mile range, and automated close quarters attack radars attached to fifty millimeter gatling guns and a brace of surface-to-surface missiles. And two drone killers, one mounted on each side of the bridge. All of these weapons were hidden by false deck structures, giving the beautiful sheer lines of the original hull their due. The terrorists had paid millions of dollars for the boat and its original fit out, and both Indigo and the master chief wanted to honor their foresight and return the favor with interest.

In short, well below the armament level of a small destroyer but significantly more than the usual gunboat favored by the Mediterranean nations that had sea lanes to protect.

"How will we identify drones as enemies?" the master chief asked Indigo, both talking an extra turn in the control room. He, as a commissioned sailor in the United States Navy, had a code of ethics and Rules of Engagement that limited his ability to launch an attack until the foe had been clearly identified. While the ship was now under the UN flag and controlled by Section Five of Interpol, he still worried about the hard line Interpol took in combat.

Shoot first; don't bother to ask any questions.

But Interpol usually had the advantage of a specific, defined terrorist target, not the potential disaster of an open-sea encounter with friendly national or civilian forces. He had signed on back at the destroyer, knowing the ROE, but it still worried him in the back of his mind. Indigo was used to this situation arising with traditional soldiers and sailors and had a ready answer.

"Well, Gordona, my frienda, my second choice is to let thema opena firea on us first; thata makes ita clear, yes?" Indigo smiled as he closely watched the long-range air defense radar scope, which was presently showing three targets all heading away from them and out across the Atlantic. Thanks to the geeks, they now had a digital library of drone signatures, which he could pull up in a second simply by highlighting the target with his cursor. He had deliberately accented his English, knowing the master chief was internally fighting his training and his code.

He dug back into his memory to remember what it had been like the first time he had gone into combat as a newly minted member of Section Five, alongside another master chief, this one a retired marine, only known as 'Pete'. He smiled at the memory. Black Pete had been all laid-back fire and brimstone, and the engagement was so fierce and absolute that he hadn't had time to consider his conscience. Just focused on staying alive. They were chasing child smugglers, part of a human organ trafficking gang, and he remembered being so incensed at the cruelty and horror of the thugs that he had no hesitation in shooting first and shooting to kill. Alongside him, the Boss, Black Pete, Jessica, and a few other chosen commandos tracked and ambushed the thirty traffickers, with outstanding results. All the children—forty in all—had been handed over to the Red Crescent, relatively unharmed. Traumatized, yes. But now safe.

He also remembered the fierce way Jessica had interviewed a couple of unlucky survivors, then shot them for their efforts without so much as turning a hair. The deep black holes that were her eyes and the sheer, controlled fury on her face told the story, and he was as proud of her then as he was now.

Some things no one should do—like kidnap helpless children, traffic them across multiple borders, then sell them to crude facilities that harvested their organs for the slimy and infamous—as long as they had the money.

This scenario was a little different, he silently acknowledged. They were chasing terrorists who had been directly and indirectly responsible for the deaths of over sixty million people and turning the world on its head. And the terrorists had developed the habit of whacking at them a few times now, all unprovoked and all, as far as he was able to see, totally unnecessary.

Sniping at them on the ground at Whiddy Island.

Blowing up helicopters on the tarmac of the civilian airport in Cork. Popping up out of an ancient fort and trying to kill everyone in sight. Then a drone attack on the convoy heading to the Island to relieve the Irish contingent. Whether or not the terrorists had planned it this way, they had drawn Section Five's attention to the Island, and they were getting it in spades.

While Indigo had been musing, Gordon had been deep in thought, watching his screen with an intensity any ten-year-old playing an online game would recognize.

"Indigo, your poor English doesn't fool me for a second. My point is, how will we know we will be under attack, especially from the air? I'm not worried about boats, big or small. They have to get into range, and we have the edge there except for a destroyer or bigger. But attack from the air worries me."

"We can recognize any drone within a second. The radar you had fitted goes out to one hundred and twenty nautical miles, and remembering it's a drone, no people on board, if we splash the wrong one it's no great loss. Sincere apologies, reparation, take our money and we're really very sorry, etc., etc." Gordon nodded at that. Killing a civilian drone wouldn't even rate a mention in the daily dispatches given the current condition of the world's media, so he rolled his shoulders to relieve the stress he was feeling.

"What if they come at us by gunship or armed jet?" Indigo turned to look at the broad shoulders moving like an egg beater, smiled, then patted one muscle-packed shoulder between rotations.

"Our geeks have programmed in all probable attack profiles based on weapons and platforms that we know of, and we will get a heads up in plenty of time. Same with a seaborne attack. We have preprogrammed ring fences at one hundred, fifty, and twenty-five, then every nautical mile all the way in, the one thing we probably couldn't do much about would be a ballistic missile, but then the CQC guns would come into their own, and we'd have to cross our fingers."

"Cross our bloody fingers? Very funny. You've got more bells and whistles than we had on the Ruben." Indigo nodded. It was true that the Interpol geeks, in conjunction with the monks, had taken a leaf out of the terrorists playbook and gamed every scenario they could think of. Then Gordon suddenly turned in his seat, his face a mask of concern.

"What about a sub attack?" Indigo just smiled, pointed up at the black roof over their heads, and grinned like a schoolboy caught smoking behind the bike shed.

"The AWACS we have over Whiddy Island can help there, and if they detect anything we can slow to eight knots and deploy a dipping sonar. The AWACS has anti-sub missiles, and with our plot plus their data it should be okay."

Gordon turned back to his screen, screwing up his face in the process. He tilted his head to one side, stretched his legs out, crossed them at the ankles, and released a really deep breath. "I get you, Indigo. We're as prepared as we can be, but don't forget the prime rule of combat."

"No battle plan survives the first shot?"

"No, the one about mice and men."

"Mice and men?"

"Yeah. Working-class stiffs like you and me have little real freedom and are often at the mercy of their circumstances." Indigo shook his head.

"Too deep for me, my friend, too deep for me." They both laughed, one a little morosely, the other slightly confused, but both bonding due to the unknown variables and inculcated stress of their mission.

CHAPTER THIRTY ONE

Fay seemed preternaturally calm on her end of the call, standing in a little garden with the ocean behind her. I could see Luca and Gabriella standing guard, facing outward, but so casually that anyone seeing them would think they were being polite and giving Fay room to talk. The mini was small but bigger than a big phone, and Fay was using her silky hair to hide most of it.

"We have a question for you. Can you contact the local council here and see if there are any building permits outstanding for the area around where we are standing? Also, look for big housing development proposals." I looked at the small data block on the bottom of my screen, which showed the latitude and longitude of the call. I waved Luigi over, he took one look, I whispered in his ear, and he took off back to his seat in geek land. His shirt was badly wrinkled at the back, and his jeans were creased so badly they looked like they were hitching themselves up his backside in a wedgy. I wasn't looking after him properly, and I'd have to pay attention to that.

"Wait one, Luigi is on it for you now." Fay scanned her surroundings, giving me a glimpse of a low multi-window structure, I'd guess at thirty years old at least, from the old brown brick, a paved drive way, and a swinging sign that proclaimed *'Leabaidh is bracaist as fheàrr ann an Èirinn'.* If it were the best in Ireland, they would at least be comfortable. Data from Luigi flashed up onto my big screen, and I scanned the results before swiping them to Fay.

"Yes, the sewage plant is to be upgraded to a biologically neutral facility, producing biofuel, quantity unknown, but slated for completion early 2026; there is a permit approved for twenty thousand houses, schools, shopping centers, plus sports fields and recreation parks across two areas, one near where you are, and one on the other side of the Bay at Killala. Approval given five months ago, security deposit of fifty million euros paid at the same time. There's the name of a Trust given as the sponsor, we'll track that down for you. The deposit will be used in part to build universities, recreational and council facilities on each side of the bay." Fay looked shocked and hid it well, but her eyes had turned into big saucers of question marks.

"There couldn't be more than two thousand people here in total, and Killala is minute by comparison. If we assume the women are behind this, they intend to migrate thousands of refugee children. How in God's name will that work?" I shook my head. She was right to ask the question but wrong to assume any responsibility. The data indicated that the local councils had enjoined their facilities some years ago in the interests of providing services to the very small population spread out around the bay. Each of the three small towns provided the mayor for a year, taking turns. And a historical footnote listed Killala as the location for the rebellion against the French in 1789, and the town still had the now-ancient forts to prove it! Major tourist attraction before the terrorist attacks.

Was there a theme going on here? Whiddy Island had forts built during the Napoleonic era; Killara Bay had forts built during the same period; and the web site that had brought our attention to the nuclear threat two months ago had postured as a rebellious Irish interest, going all the way back to the 'troubles'.

But the conflict in Ireland had ceased years ago, and early in 2023, the Irish, UK, and EU governments had come to an agreement on Brexit that smoothed the way for trade across the Irish borders without checks and penalties. In effect, this moved the border into the middle of the Irish Sea, creating a commercial unification within Ireland that still mystified many.

Also not our problem.

"Fay, get someone over to Killala, maintain a watch where you are, stay covert, and don't apprehend O'Cleary until we fully understand what's going on. I'll try to find out what the latest political position is and get back to you."

"Don't take too long. We seem to stand out. Our foreignness has been pointed out a couple of times, and the feeling I get is that the locals are sensitive to outside influences."

"You're posing as backpackers?"

"Yes, on a fact-finding mission on behalf of a university, interested in the architectural history of the area. The outstanding features are the baths, built like an old fort, and the lighthouse built into a row of double-story apartments. Half the town is painted white, but many of the apartments, or row houses as they call them here, are very new, built in the last decade to my eye. We're staying in a bed-and-breakfast tonight, then moving into a hotel. The sea wall has been built out of stone and bricks that go back to the rebellion, and when we asked a casual question, one of the locals arced up and got defensive."

"Transport?"

"Electric bikes—we've hired them for three months, to allay any suspicion." I put my thinking cap on, remembering the diatribe we had pulled off the web site about Finnian's men, and wondered how bringing back all the fear, hatred, and terror the troubles had created would help the women terrorists' agenda. I shook my head. It wasn't getting me anywhere; the biggest concern I had was whether or not to beef up Fay's contingent in Killara Bay.

"Do you want some backup?" She moved the mini until I was looking at a close-up of her face, which was looking a little chilled. I checked the OAT (Outside Air Temperature) at her location and was surprised to see it was only 4 degrees Celsius. She was dressed for it, in a puffy jacket that came up beyond her collar, and she had a knitted cap of some sort on her head. Quite fetching!

"Right now, no thanks, but I might change my mind when we find out more. My biggest issue is the physical distance between here and Killala. Five kilometers as the crow flies, but six times that by bike. That might leave one of us slightly out-numbered if the s-h-one-t hits the fan." I nodded, my thoughts exactly, and just as I was about to respond, my mini flashed an 'Urgent' message at me.

"Hold, wait one." I switched between Fay and the incoming. Saw Sandra's wind-blown and dripping face fill the screen. She was huddled in the lee of one of the armored trucks, against some heavy ground cover. She did not look happy.

"Where are you?"

"Environmental plant on Whiddy Island. I just did a walk through, all quiet as you would expect, but I found something we missed. Checked back on our earlier reports, all the data we have accumulated, so I'm sure of this."

"This what?"

"We missed a sinter bath. They were making more different types of nanites than we mapped. There's a bath for the panels, one for the power supplies, both clearly marked. Then one designated 'BF1', one 'BL1', one 'BMD', which we related to the three types of cannister we took from the oil tank. And one we missed because it is in a separate section hidden behind the packing line, I only found it by accident. 'CD1' is its designation, they have stacked canisters I count at around the one hundred mark, maybe more somewhere, and these cannisters have a blue stripe, same size as the others. A data card attached to one of the cannisters describes how to prepare the ground, with photos of every sort of substrate you can imagine. What for? No idea. There must be more on their computers somewhere, can you get the geeks to take a look?" My turn to look unhappy, how did we miss that? Simple answer: My continuing fixation with the immediate mission gave me a narrow focus and blindness to anything out of scope. I would really have to open my eyes and overcome that. It might get us killed if I didn't. Then there was the nanite version that killed poppy and coca plants. Jessica hadn't mentioned that. It must have come from somewhere else. But where?

"My bad, I pushed everyone to get that plant closed down post haste. Good catch. I read your after-action report on the shooting, not much detail." I held her look, eyeball to eyeball. She broke first and dropped her head, a wan smile creasing her pretty face.

"Didn't seem all that important. The major has it under control." I nodded, reading between the lines. I had not only not looked after Luigi, but Sandra was getting jaded—too much, too often, too fast. Somehow, I had to rest my team in the middle of all the chaos.

"Okay, when Tom arrives, get back here ASAP. Is he flying to you or coming aboard the ship?"

"No idea. Indigo texted me he had reached the tip of Spain a while ago, so they are two days out, weather permitting. To be honest, I'd feel a whole lot better if you came here. My sense is something's brewing, and it's making me edgy." I gave her my hardest look. This was very un-Sandra-like, and for her to be suggesting something like this was counterintuitive. She ruled her roost.

But to be frank, it mirrored my own feelings about Whiddy Island. I made one of my snap decisions, for which I was becoming infamous.

"Luigi and I will be there in eight hours. Find us a secured location to set up, make sure the major and the Sgan Aluf know what we are doing, you'll need room for Tom, Indigo, you, Luigi, myself, plus the major and the colonel, maybe one of two more from time to time, take a good look at that hotel in the middle of the Island. Good call, see you soon." And I switched back to Fay, who had been patiently holding throughout my little chat with Sandra.

"Fay, we're moving HQ to Whiddy Island, so we can back you up fairly quickly, no more than two hours. We'll have transport. I'll arrange that now. Stay with your plan, be safe." I clicked off and dialed my favorite admiral.

"Jessica, I won't say it's good to see you again. It is, but it's becoming a habit!" I smiled. He was standing relaxed on his wing deck. I could see the boiling ocean behind him, and the wind was whipping up a veritable wave-chopping storm.

"You too, admiral. I need your help again."

"You've already stolen a bunch of my people, one of them my master chief. What else could you possibly want now?"

"A couple of gunships and a fast passenger helo with guns. Park the helo at Cork airport, sometime in the next six hours. It's to take me and my team and a few odds and ends to Whiddy Island. The gunships should be overwatch, and need to stay with us on the Island. Did you leave a chopper on the ship?"

"Yes, with a marine pilot and an empty gunner's seat." I nodded. I was starting to feel more positive every minute. "We'll need a gunner." I thought for a second and rolled a few options around in my mind, looking for the best solution.

"Did Tom stay with your destroyer or go with the ship?" He looked at me with a sly grin, and I knew I was about to be embarrassed again.

"Losing a senior member of your team is sloppy, Jessica. Not kosher at all." His laughter rang true, his whole upper body shaking with mirth. He made a whirling sign with his hand, then fired it towards the west.

I just smiled and let the joke play out, in spite of the direct insult to my command abilities. I had stood on the deck of his aircraft carrier in mid-Atlantic, with his large, meaty hand over mine, as we pressed a command button to unleash a nuclear explosion that sank a terrorist gunboat, rolled one of his destroyers, killing all aboard, and created a tsunami so huge that it battered the beaches of every shoreline exposed to the ocean on both sides of the Atlantic. I knew this man—he knew me—so I let the insult ride.

"Temporary lapse. You still haven't billed me for the CH-53."

He laughed again, the image of the blown-out hull of the massive helicopter with its rotors sagging all the way down to the tarmac lurking behind the blackened, destroyed wreck of the Irish Chinook fresh in my mind.

"You'll get it. Why the continued interest in Whiddy Island?" He looked directly at the camera, his face now as serious as I had ever seen it.

"There's something we're missing there, and we've been attacked again in the last two hours. No rhyme or reason we can see. Frankly, I need your firepower and your manpower. With the political situation turning nasty, the locals have already been ordered home, only staying because they are professionals and don't want to see us blindsided." He nodded, turned to look out to sea, and tilted his head in thought. When he turned back to me, his blue eyes were sparkling, his frown turned into a full-face grin, and his short brown hair with its gray streaks was waving in the breeze. He was charismatic, that's for sure. I would never admit it, but he stirred my juices.

"You know, I've been looking for somewhere to exercise the marines. I haven't had them off carrier for weeks. Would you care to formally invite me to your party?" I couldn't help it. I smiled so big, my face ached! That would change things in my favor, satisfy the local politicians in that their own people would be taken out of harm's way, and give me the ability to prosecute the Island the way it should have been from the start. Balls to the wall, inch by inch, and not just reacting to someone else's agenda or ducking when we got shot at.

"Admiral, I'll have the request cut within ten minutes, thank you. I owe you yet again." His smile was infectious, and I felt myself warming again.

"Be sure I'll collect. The lieutenant colonel in charge will report to you and anyone you delegate. This is an Interpol police action. We're just providing the muscle."

"I'll call General Saunders and make sure she's in the loop. Thank you, and I mean that personally." He finger saluted me and cancelled the call. I thought for a minute, then dialed the general and got a blank screen. I looked at my pink watch, did the math, realized it was just shy of 0230 hours in Washington, and cancelled the call. I sent a text instead, outlining my plan and asking her to call me when available.

Then I remembered Fay had wanted to call Amira, so I dialed them both up onto the big screen.

"Fay, you wanted to talk to Amira?" She looked a little shell-shocked, surprised that I had remembered. She nodded.

"Yes, thanks. Amira, hi, sorry to bother you, but from your research, would the nanite you identified for the production of biofuel work on sewerage?" I immediately saw what Fay was getting at, clever girl. There was a good reason I had stolen her from the FBI. Amira looked curious, a frown on her young face.

"Give me ten."

And she disappeared from the broadcast, her camera suddenly showing an empty work area, with the massive electron microscope that rose up through the roof and disappeared down through the floor in the background. Someone in white coveralls and a mask walked through the view, unaware they were live on air. I thought about closing us down, then decided to use the time to explore Fay's thinking a little more. Keeping one eye on Amira's lab, I slid Fay into her own box and kept clicking until I had two boxes of equal size.

"Fay, while we wait, describe the area you are in for me, please."

She nodded, looked around, then panned her camera for me to show the double-story row houses or flats, all orange and brown, with windows all sparkling in the cold wind. I wondered who lived there and how they kept themselves alive. There was a massive white block house further down the road, and it towered over every other building. I'd look it up later and find out what it was.

The data showed seaweed harvesting and fishing as the main industries, with tourism making up a very large slice of their revenue. Since the terrorist attacks, very few tourists have visited. In a sense, if there was another five or six billion trust fund hidden away in that area, using it to build the houses and infrastructure for thousands of refugee children might well keep everyone employed and alive.

The terrorist's model was working brilliantly in Helena, Roanoke, and New Zealand, as far as I was aware, and I could see no reason why it couldn't in Killara Bay. And as a sidebar, fourteen of the seventeen countries that had trust funds and ecological plants ready for assembly had agreed to the terrorists terms, so they were getting unilateral support by stealth.

"Sorry to be so long," Amira said, flopping back onto her chair, her hair flinging around her face in a veritable storm. She looked up at her screen and rapidly hit several keys, the clacking coming through the transmission. Then looked back directly at us.

"Simple answer, Fay, is yes. The yield will be different, but the nanites will act like a bioremediation agent and produce usable biofuel." Fay nodded, as if the answer confirmed her thinking. I could see where this was going, but I want it to play out between Fay and Amira. Ownership of an issue was a powerful motivator.

"That might explain the permit for the sewerage plant. Have you had time to survey where the houses might be built?" Amira looked interested, but I clearly saw fatigue building under her eyes, so I thanked her and disconnected.

Fay blinked rapidly, taken by surprise.

"Did you want Amira for something else?" She shook her head.

"No, I still haven't gotten used to how fast you work." I smiled to relieve her tension, then decided to let her get on with it.

My little office in the corner of our Venice HQ suddenly felt empty. Just as I was standing to refresh my coffee, Tom walked in, threw his go bag onto a table, and then stood with his hands on his hips.

"Who do I have to kill to get a coffee around here?" One of my guards nearly tripped over his own feet getting to the puffing espresso machine; everyone in the room laughed. I let it roll, then stood and faced my new master-at-arms.

"Tom, welcome back. You look like you enjoyed yourself?" He took the mug from my guard, sniffed royally, his eyes closed. The silence built, then suddenly they snapped open.

"Who do I thank for this excellent brew?"

"Indigo, but as you left him a few thousand kilometers away, just thank your lucky stars." He nodded, acknowledged the geeks, and holding his precious gondola mug in both hands like an expectant father would a new-born child, he moved over to my corner. "I was just talking to the admiral about you. He was complaining about you stealing his master chief." Tom shook his head, pulled one of the little metal chairs over, and squatted on it. My other guards, having wrested my mug out of my hands, returned with it filled. I mimicked Tom's reaction, silently blessing Indigo and his huffing espresso machines.

"Gordon volunteered. I practically had to fend him off; he was so keen. But he's professionally conflicted over our ROE, but I left Indigo to sort that out." I nodded. Most professional soldiers had the same issue.

"You obviously enjoyed yourself?" His face lit up like a schoolboy getting his favorite Schwinn on Christmas day.

"Never had the opportunity to shop in a store like that. I could have spent weeks there. Every toy imaginable, Indigo had to hold me back!" We both laughed. Then he looked serious.

"We fitted the ship out with the best gear we could get. Indigo is training them all the way to Ireland, and being navy, they have the bones to do what will be necessary. I just hope they don't get into too much trouble." I nodded and sipped my espresso.

"Well, you'll get a chance to find out. We're moving some geeks and us to Whiddy Island. Sandra is finding us an HQ. We leave in thirty." He looked at me with open eyes, nodded as if confirming something to himself.

"Good. I'll shower, change, and be ready in twenty. Do you want to know any of the operational details?"

"No, not now. You can brief me on the plane." He nodded, stood, his chair making that irritable squeaking, scratching chalkboard sound, which sent a shiver up my back, and headed off. I signaled to Luigi.

"Pick a helper or two to bring with, pack for a mobile HQ, and make sure we can link to the monks, Malcolm, Arie, and here." He nodded, went into a huddle with his team, and I sat back to enjoy five minutes of calm.

Didn't get it. The Boss's ugly face swam into view on my big screen, and not for the first time I wished he was on my mini!

"The Irish have formally withdrawn support. Politely asked us to vacate the premises, I refused, quoting the Terrorist Act and threatening a Red Notice on the entire government if they pushed it. Then I suggested a meeting of the minds, to which they agreed, I'll meet you in Dublin, bring your Armani." I looked at him with a fixed stare as my mind worked through the sheer difficulty of issuing a Red Notice to a sovereign government, one that was both a member of the UN and Interpol, and various other military and political groups, did some quick math in my head.

"I can be there in eight hours, ten for sure. Can you collect me from the airport? I'll get Sandra there as well." He nodded, his face a mask of anger.

"Good. It's your meeting. Come prepared. I'm only along for the ride." I smiled. That was as likely as me winning the lottery, all of which had been cancelled by the terrorist attacks. But now I had to get my backside moving, because the stakes had just become much higher.

I texted Sandra with a movement order to get her backside moving. Thought about what else I had to do. Put a call into Bob.

"I was wondering when you would call us again."

"Don't be like that. We're busy saving the world."

"Ha ha. How can I help?"

"Sitrep."

"Target positively identified, set up a ringfence that will work so long as there's no more than a cat and a dog in there, we are really thin on the ground if you decide we need to go in. This place is massive-three stories, and spread over a whole town block. Shops and a pub on the ground floor, our suspect is in the middle and upper floors, the receiver has been pinpointed on the corner of the middle floor, behind a sliding façade. It's open for around fifteen seconds, then closes. We don't have floor plans, only long distance visual surveillance." I thought about that, thought about my diminishing resources, remembered I had sent a bunch of his team to Whiddy Island, then figured the marines could take over their roles, so I held up my hand to stop any further conversation.

"Wait one." I froze his screen, dialed Sandra, and caught her by surprise.

"Yes?"

"Ship Bob's team to him in Scotland, soonest. Get the Sgan Aluf ready to receive a bunch of marines. They'll have a light colonel. Work out a holding plan for everyone, then get to Dublin. Suit, clean shoes, no armor, but you can gun up, but concealed. We're calling on the President again." She looked unimpressed, so I hit her with the rest.

"And the major and his teams will be decamping completely in the next eight hours; the marines are their replacement. Tom will set us up on the Island in our absence. Send him the location you have selected." Now she just looked pissed, as if having all these moving parts shift on her again was too much bother. She brushed her hand through her hair, her scowl making her usually beautiful face look compressed.

"Tell me this is the last time I have to rearrange everything here?"

"Sure. It's the last time, I promise." I paused deliberately, trying to draw her out. "Until the next." She broke down and smiled, then laughed and pointed to me.

"You're a proper bastard, make no mistake, but you're my proper bastard." And she broke the connection. I went back to Bob.

"The rest of your team will be with you within ten hours or so, maybe faster, depending on transport. Work out where you want them to land and how to penetrate your zone. Send the instructions to Sandra. Do you want more bodies?" He gave that some thought and looked away from the camera as if sizing up his target. Behind him, a small flow of people moved back and forth, obviously doing their daily shopping or just going outside for some sunlight and fresh air.

"If we're just observing, no, but if we go for a takedown, then yes, the potential for collateral damage is too great for a small force." I nodded. The last thing we wanted was a public display of our aggression, with its attendant civilian casualties.

"You'll have them. I may well be there myself." He looked amused at that, so I let him go while he was happy. I turned to my guards. I was taking them with me mainly for protocol. On my last visit, I had Indigo, and I wanted to maintain the illusion of force projection.

"Dress 1A's, pack combat as well as civilian clothes. Don't know how long you might be away. We leave in twenty." They both saluted, raced off to their quarters, and were immediately replaced by two others, grinning from ear to ear.

No doubt about it, when it came to excellent coffee and being happy, you couldn't go past the Italians!

PAS DE POUVOIR POUR TOI

Before the terrorist attacks, France had produced over 75 percent of its electrical power from nuclear stations spread out all over the country. Some fifty-six reactors, some as old as forty years, inoculated France, to a certain extent, from the vagaries of the EU and its power interruptions due to squabbles over gas and oil supplies, and the deadly consequences of the incursions made by Russia and others that shut off major supplies for years.

One by one, the reactors went quiet, and as it happened almost within the same twenty-four-hour period, by the time the scientists and engineers recognized the problem, it was too late. Immovable silver sludge hardened to concrete wherever there was the faintest trace of radioactivity.

The Civaux nuclear power plant sits at the edge of the Vienne River, between Confolens and Chauvogny. Also run by the EFF, it had a checkered history going back to the late 90s. The proposed target of a foiled terrorist plot to fly an airliner into it and a leak had been detected in 2021 during a routine 10-year maintenance program; subsequently, the return to operations had been delayed by some ten months. But it went back into service, until the terrorist attacks using the silver nanites killed it once and for all.

Like most other EFF stations where the staff of some one thousand three hundred had been sent home, two security guards shared twelve-hour shifts, one using the time to read, the other to smoke. In the two months since the shutdown, neither had been bothered by so much as a curious visitor. So when four immaculately dressed women turned up with credentials and a letter from the president of EFF giving them access to the facility, they were politely shown in and left to their own devices.

The guard on duty showed his compatriot the letter at the change of shift; the new guard shrugged his shoulders and promptly filed it with a number of other innocuous documents in the filing cabinet clearly marked *'Pièces de rechange uniquement!'* What the letter had to do with Spare Parts was a mystery that would remain unsolved for another few months.

Once again, the quartet stood hands on hips, staring up at the massive infrastructure, now covered with a thin layer of dust. Their attention was focused on the huge turbine, one of four, which by itself could provide better than thirty percent of the output of the plant. Like many of its sister plants, Civaux used ambient air and water for cooling, in this case sourced from the Vienne River, which was perfect for the women.

The plan was simple: Lilian would dive into the river and find the inlet pipes; Else would strip the generator and find the connections they needed; and Lily would find where they could locate their interface. Katrina didn't feel left out in the slightest, happy with her role as minder, protector, and master organizer.

It only took three days, but when they packed up and left, all four were smiling the smile of the righteous and satisfied.

The helicopter picked them up two hundred meters from the front gate. The guard on duty saluted them, then went back to his book.

"Freya, we've finished. Need more equipment. Your girls have done well, very well, in fact. It's as if they have been trained for this for a very long time." Freya, only able to visualize her girls smiling and happy, dipped her head in a silent salute. She missed them dreadfully.

"That they have been, Katrina, that they have been. Slight change in plans. Your pilot will take you to England, where you'll get another helicopter to take you to Ireland. I need you to meet up with Siobhan O'Cleary. She'll have all the equipment you'll need. When you're done with her, you'll go back and finish the other plants in France as planned. You'll like Siobhan. She's one of the originals." Katrina rolled her eyes. 'one of the originals' sounded to her just a little pompous. Crissy and she had been pulled out of the camps the same week, sent to the same country, and adopted by two sets of loving parents who coincidentally lived next door to each other. They had been in Mohammad bin Azaria's second tranche of rescued refugee girls but didn't know it.

They had grown up as both soul mates and sisters of the heart, each recognizing the utter bastardry they had survived, forming a unique bond their parents respected but, fundamentally, never quite understood. When they both enrolled in the same STEM university, both not yet thirteen years of age, they turned heads but were unstoppable. They graduated first and second in their class, with Crissy moving onto an advanced degree in nanotechnology and Katrina one in plasma physics. They both had doctorates by age nineteen, and at twenty, after a wild month on the Rivera together, they went home, hugged their parents and siblings, and disappeared.

A member of the local government met with the parents and told them that their daughters had been recruited into a secret organization and that the stipend they had been paid every year they had the girls would continue indefinitely. While not particularly happy about the news, the parents settled back into their routine with their natural children, who were also being provided for health-wise and education-wise, and wished with all their hearts that their girls were safe and would one day come home again.

They would never know that the two girls, now women, would make a breakthrough that would change the face of the world. That their genius would shine a light on a fractured world that would help heal billions. And that they would never hear from or see their girls again.

CHAPTER THIRTY TWO

Agent Robertson's Interpol office in Dublin was a chaotic mess. In one corner, back to the masses, I was hurriedly changing into my Armani suit; next to me, equally turned around, Sandra was hiding her silky underwear under a beautiful woolen suit the color of grapes. Our Italian guards, resplendent in their dress uniforms, red stripes up their long legs, black polished Sam Browne belts and pistol holders, and patent leather shoes, sparkled in the doorway, having a last smoke, their cheeky caps under their armpits.

The Boss had wisely vacated the battlefield and was presently sitting in the back of our limousine, pretending he wasn't watching his watch. Our travel plans had gone to the dogs almost from the first minute. But we were all here now. Tom was on his way to Whiddy Island with Luigi and a contingent of our best geeks. The major and his teams from the Irish *Sciathán Fianóglach* were on their way back to Belfast, and my admiral was delivering his marines to the Island. He had also moved some of his fleet vessels a little closer to the west coast of Ireland, a move he said was just 'normal maneuvers', but I sensed he was providing both physical and moral support.

My chat with General Saunders had not gone well. Her point of being an undefined threat was a poor reason to strip one of her battle fleets of its marine contingent. I pointed out it was only the one contingent from the Admiral's aircraft carrier, and her eyes had lit up like sparklers. But in the end, she had endorsed the temporary 'loan' as she called it, and we had spent the last few minutes of the conversation with her updating me on the situation in America.

Which, by any standards, was grim but a little better than it had been a few days ago. The Guard, Army, and various Police forces had managed to wrest power from the thugs and gangs, and apart from the stinking smoke from burning vehicles and buildings, things were getting back to the new normal.

The streets were not filled with people, but there were some brave souls moving about, no doubt trying to find food, work, or a purpose beyond mere existence. Schools were still shuttered, but the power packs and panels from Point Roberts were starting to help create little pockets of commerce up and down the West Coast, and the general was quick to point out that I would have to release the plant on Whiddy Island very soon if we wanted Ireland to survive.

Sandra led us to the vehicle, her Hermes carry bag over one shoulder, and not for the first time I marveled at her supermodel looks and upmarket artifacts. A less likely look for an Interpol agent, let alone a Section Five agent, was hard to imagine. Luckily, our resident Dublin agent, Shelia Robertson, brought me back down to earth with her smart light gray suit and flaming red hair tied up in a bun, making her neck look naked and exposed. She was pretty in her own way, with long, sculptured legs and a little lean in the shoulders, but she trained every day to run marathons, so her lithe fitness suited her from top to bottom.

While she wasn't Section Five qualified, her innate smarts more than made up for this lack, as her briefing showed as the vehicle started off to Áras an Uachtaráin in Phoenix Park. The Boss crossed his long legs at the ankles and shut his eyes, as relaxed as I had ever seen him.

"The two women you tagged are staying in the Maritime Hotel in Bantry, on the N71. I have one of the girls from the office staying there to keep an eye on them. She's very young, works part-time for us, but super smart, and can blend in. The women have tried to get to the Island twice, the second time by a private boat, but it was turned back from the northern beaches by

Israeli soldiers." She paused to look at her slim notebook, flipped a couple of pages, and nodded to herself.

"The President has been busy-drove down to Waterford, toured an old factory, was met by a very tough looking group of people, no weapons visible, but my money's on mercenaries, and one women, stayed an hour, then drove back through Dublin and onto a small village called Dundalk. He walked around some row houses, met with some local people, one woman in particular, a university professor who now manages the apartments, one Moriah O'Sullivan. She has managed to tame and look after some five hundred homeless children, and is managing accommodation for over three thousand people in the area. She's viewed as the unofficial mayor, and is held in very high esteem by the locals. And she has power." I listened closely, I already had Brother Francis's report on the O'Sullivan woman, and the power panels and batteries she was fitting onto her buildings and the row houses. I also knew about the children recycling materials from destroyed motor vehicles, which Shelia hadn't mentioned. I wondered if the Irish President had missed that as well.

The panels were reportedly coming in on trucks from the south. But Brother Francis had made a comment the last time we talked, and I was still puzzled about it. While he was not an electrician or an engineer, both he and his Jesuit companion felt the whole power thing was a little 'off'. Neither of them could tell me why they felt that way. But I was a firm believer in the sensitivity of the experienced gut, so I had made a mental note to follow up on their instincts and find out what it was all about. But right now, I have no one to send.

"As you can see by the condition of the roads, the LEO's have got control again, and little by little things are getting back to a semblance of stability. Very little power, industry, and commerce are still non-existent, but the President seems to think he has a solution. You might like to ask him about it?" She turned to look at me from where she had been studying the outside road conditions, her eyes asking a question I didn't have the answer for. Yet.

She gave me a vague look that made me uncomfortable, then continued.

"The Irish *Sciathán Fianóglach* have shipped out back to Belfast, the marine contingent has arrived and established themselves on Whiddy Island, and the two colonels are dividing up the landscape awaiting your orders." She looked at me again, the question still in her eyes, and I just shook my head.

"I can't guess what's going down on Whiddy Island. I can't guess what the President is doing, or what's in his mind, but I have been warned by others whom I respect that we may have to release the plant sooner rather than later. Good summary, thank you." Sandra lifted her head from her mini, her eyes glazed over somewhat.

"I got all that, thanks Shelia, and I just got an update from Amira. She's done some more work on the nanites, and from the samples she got from South America, the atomic structure—if that's the correct description—is the same for the biofuel bug, the metal dissolver, and the unknown CD1. It's different for the water boiler, the power panels, and the power supplies. But they all owe their genesis to Amira's original oil eater. Same family, slightly different function, but she says they all work fundamentally the same way." She laughed, smiled, and ran her hands through her short blond hair, which was shining in the light filtering through the windows. At her worst, she was happy and bubbly, and she managed to infect everyone around her with her cheerful demeanor.

She made me feel old! Happy with the state of her hair, she continued.

"You know, that might be the simple way to describe these buggars: oil eaters, plant eaters, drug eaters, dirt eaters, metal eaters, water boilers, and power makers. Beats the hell out of all those capital letters and numbers." We all enjoyed her joke. The technology side of this operation has been mind-blowing from the get-go. It was nice to hear such simple language describe one of the greatest inventions of the last thousand years or so.

And the fact that all these marvels were made out of sand and seawater made them all the more impressive and mysterious.

"Add radioactive eaters." The Boss's deep but soft voice broke the mood, and I realized he had made an excellent point because the nanites had taken out the nuclear arsenals around the world, including nuclear power plants. Funny how you tend to forget things just a week or two after you deal with them.

I held my hands up in mock surrender, wanting to focus us all on our strategy and tactics for the upcoming meeting. I looked at Shelia.

"Anything else we should know?" She shook her head.

"That's it for now. I want to know how you're going to approach the President." I gave her a hard look. The challenge in her voice was unmistakable. Maybe she was talking about an Irish view of everything, but I didn't think so.

"My plan is simple—Inspector Shinny Hair here", and I pointed to Sandra, "is going to set the scene. Then I'm going to ask why Whiddy Island is so important to him. Then I imagine I'll end up reading him the riot act."

I paused to let that sink in, waiting for the Boss to add something. He remained mute, so I put the words in his mouth.

"Then General Anthony, if he can stay awake long enough, will outline the potential effect of a Red Notice, and then maybe we can negotiate. But I had a flash a minute ago, based on something General Saunders said to me."

"What?" The Boss opened his eyes, his long legs still crossed at the ankles, his whole posture one of a relaxed but coiled panther waiting for its prey to make a mistake. He oozed charm and danger in equal portions. It was one of the reasons I had an unrequited crush on him. From the first day I had shot him six times, center of mass.

"Bridget pointed out that in the interest of Ireland's survival, we will have to reopen the ecological plant and resume production. And that has just turned into a big question. Do we let Innomatchi open again?" The sudden quiet in the car was spooky; being electric, the only sound was the soft imprint of the tires on the bitumen road. Sandra wriggled and squirmed. She had been to the factory most recently and had been attacked for her troubles. Shelia looked a little blank, maybe not up to speed on the Japanese plant that had made the equipment that produced the ecological plants and nanomachinery.

The Boss just looked like the Boss, but his eyes held mine, and I tried to discern the message hidden in those lovely blue irises. Then I got it.

"Okay, apologies. One potential disaster at a time, delete any reference to Innomatchi. My bad, I got ahead of myself." Sandra smiled.

"'Gee, Jessica, that's not at all like you!" And we all broke into laughter, enjoying the joke at my expense. I relaxed. I had rarely worked with a more brilliant team. They had my back, and I had theirs. And as I looked around the interior, I noticed both our young Italian guards were watching me intently, neither smiling. I wondered what was going through their minds. Corporal Edwardo Ricci had accompanied us inside the President's office on our last visit, so I asked him point blank what he was thinking about. He shook his head, saying nothing. I let it go. He was one of Indigo's highly trained *Gruppo di Intervento Speciale*, or the Special Intervention Group, so he was no slouch.

I wrestled with swapping them around this time, then thought better of it. Edwardo knew the battlefield, a definite advantage even in peacetime.

We pulled up outside the white-painted guard house, got a fast scrutiny from the uniformed officers, and were then waved through. We stopped outside the stone steps to the flat-roofed building, and I marveled again at the green vines growing on the sides of the walls, creating an effect that made you feel like you were in the arms of a big, loopy bush. We were marched into the President's office, past the impressive corridor that held busts of his predecessors and other Irish icons, past the three hundred-year-old antique table and chairs where we had sat so uncomfortably last visit, and halted before a massive Queen Anne desk, so well-worn it had turned black. The President gestured to the chairs set before it, and as we moved to take our seats, he made an imperious wave with one hand, shooing our corporal back towards the door.

I turned, held my hand up discretely, and pointed to the side of the huge doorway. Edwardo nodded imperceptibly, and I took up a position at ease, but facing the President. The Boss turned to look at me as he slid into his seat, a thin smile cracking his scarred face. We ended up next to each other, bookended by Sandra on my side, and Shelia on the other. Interestingly, Sandra had her hand inside her bag, a sure sign she was fondling her favorite pet.

"Mr. President, thank you for seeing us on such short notice." His look was anything but welcoming, and I could see his emotions waring behind his green eyes. An old-style fountain pen lay on a green blotter, with a slim note book alongside. The cover was made up of deeply etched Irish magical symbols and icons, with the figure '6' sitting proudly in the center. I recognized that, from my research on the Irish Troubles, it was the universal sign of the six counties put down by the British. His stare would cut an ice block, and it was all I could do to not burst out laughing.

"Commander, general, I'll make this as clear as I can. As I said in our last conversation, I want you and all your people off Whiddy Island, the workers from the plant reinstated, the ecological plant returned to full service, and for Interpol to vacate our country completely, once and for all." He held his pose, hands clasped on his desk, shoulders back, his immaculate white shirt covered with an equally impeccable suit coat, with shiny black lapels, reminiscent of a formal dinner suit. His tie was very old-school, a series of knots popping out of the tongue in an intricate pattern of the three-leaf clover.

The Boss shifted in his seat, tilted his head to one side, and turned to look at me. I nodded and looked at Sandra. "Inspector Thomas?" She nodded.

"Mr. President, in order, attacks have been made on us from Whiddy Island by a drone, which shot down an American jet; a sniper, who shot one of our soldiers; a terrorist group who used missiles to kill two of our helicopters on the runway of Cork airport; and more recently, another drone attack on a personnel convoy sent to relieve your Irish soldiers; and at least two more attacks by terrorists on the Island itself, launched from the Napoleonic era forts you are so proud of." She sat back in her chair and flicked her hair back with a casual stroke of one hand. The hand that was not holding her H&K in her tote bag. She held her silence for a few heartbeats, then continued in the same measured tone.

"As a sidenote, I had the pleasure and privilege of killing two of those terrorists personally.

"Now, to be sure, this all started when we were chasing down nuclear-capable shells that were stored in the oil tanks on the Island, shells that were manufactured at an Irish plant to the north. Not to mention the nanites we confiscated, all related to the ones that destroyed our oil, gas, and coal infrastructure, all the way back to the first of the terrorist attacks three months ago." She paused again, relishing the change in the President's face, which had now gone hard red, either from anger or embarrassment. My money was on anger. She was playing him like a Stratovarius.

"Oh! One last thing, I almost forgot Pollatomish, in County Mayo, where we destroyed a complete factory that was making nuclear shells and other weapons of mass destruction. We also took into custody one of the worst mercenary terrorists imaginable, but that was last month. You've probably forgotten that by now." I reached out and put my hand on her unoccupied arm, taking control of the room again. She was vibrating from her own internal anger, but I knew she would hold onto it. Having been shot down in the Gulfstream had really pissed her off, and she still hadn't recovered from the insult.

"You see, Mr. President, your country has been involved, whether by accident or by design, in the terror attacks that have destroyed so much of the world, and as such, you are very much under the scrutiny of Interpol, on the basis of the Terrorist Laws as modified in 2022. I'm sure you know what they are?" I asked in my most respectful voice. He started to fidget, picked up the pen, slammed it back down, and visibly shook. He started to say something. His mouth opened and shut like a guppy fish, and his grimace was not unlike the one someone would make after eating a rotten egg. I took full advantage of his emotional condition and asked the one question that had us all confused.

"Mr. President, why is Whiddy Island so important to you?" You could have heard a pin drop in the ensuing silence. No one moved so much as a muscle. Then the President's face relaxed, his color returned to its more ruddy complexion, and he took a huge breath, so much so that his shoulders rocked back. He picked up his pen again and tapped it on the blotter to some internal tune.

"General, commander, I deny any knowledge of any terrorist activities in Ireland until after they had taken place. We were not aware of the underground facility at Pollatomish, nor were we aware of the attacks you have outlined.

"Some three years ago I was openly approached by representatives of an aid agency and a private trust, who told us that certain funds would be made available if we were to approve the free migration of a number of refugee children and their support staff in years to come. All costs would be met. All that was asked of us was that we approve the building of an environmental plant at a designated location and the eventual fitting of panels and powerpacks on the million or so houses we had empty at the time. Lady O'Brian Flattery represented the trust and later took up the role of CEO of the plant.

"As this was a secret but formal request, made at government level, we signed a non-disclosure agreement. They paid a hefty deposit, did their research, and picked Whiddy Island as the location for their plant. They also submitted proposals to build new houses, hospitals, shopping centers, schools, and infrastructure to support the massive migration they planned, again all paid for by the trust.

"One year ago, Whiddy Island came on line and started producing the panels. I don't know anything about drone attacks, mercenary terrorists, or helicopters being blown up, other than a report from Cork that two helicopters had been destroyed in an accident at the airport, with no reported casualties. So I'm having difficulty seeing where we are in the wrong or associated with terrorists in any way."

I took my time to answer him. It was possible he was telling the truth, but the intent of the Terrorist Laws was to sweep up any and all persons even remotely associated with an attack, and it beggared belief that he could openly participate in this grand plan for three plus years now without some knowledge of what the women had planned, or at the very least, were doing. And we had Irish-grown refugee terrorists up the wazoo, and two of them had been with him on our last visit.

"Mr. President, if you can produce documentation to support what you have just said and the people who have worked on this with or for you immediately, I might be encouraged to change my mind." He gave me a hard look, as if to say, 'who are you again?' and before I could put him to rights, the Boss straightened in his chair and flexed his shoulders, a gesture that was not lost on the man sitting now a little uncomfortably on the other side of the table. To make matters worse, at least from his perspective, Edwardo had moved up until he was standing at my back, still in the 'at ease' position but physically threatening none the less.

"Mr. President, Commander Riley has the full support of the UN, Interpol, and every member country of those organizations to prosecute this case as she sees fit. If you and your government don't pass her smell test, then I will contact Bonn and Lyon and have your entire government arrested under Section 54 of the Terrorist Laws. We have a Red Notice prepared, and we can implement it in minutes." There goes that pin-dropping silence again, and this time the color drained out of his face, leaving a white, pasty mask of shock. But his temper and arrogance got the better of him, and he stood with an aggressive movement with his fountain pen, which resulted in Sandra pulling her H&K out of her Hermes bag and pushing it towards his face. I didn't raise my voice. Much.

"Sit. Now." I said, pointing at him. "Corporal, cuff him."

"*Immediatamente, comandante.*" And before anyone else could react, Edwardo was behind the President and had him in cuffs with his hands pulled up behind his back.

"At ease, corporal, let him sit." My tone was still warm and friendly, but with a sharp enough edge to have the Boss grinning and Sandra glowering at me out of the corner of her eye as she reluctantly put her H&K back in its little upmarket home. If you have ever tried to sit with your hands tied behind your back, you'll know how hard it is to get a comfortable position, and the President wiggled and squirmed like a rabbit with its leg caught in a trap.

"Now, back to my request: documents and all staff involved since the initial approach by the Aid Agency and the Trust, or I'll let the general do his thing." Edwardo now stood behind the uncomfortable President, one hand on his shoulder, holding him down in his seat. I wish I had a camera!

"It is my intention to report your rude and unnecessarily aggressive behavior to your superiors and the UN and have you court-martialed!" He almost spat the words out, the wriggling and squirming reaching some sort of crescendo.

"It's my intention to see you rot in a deep, dark concrete hole for the rest of your miserable life, and in case you missed the memo, my superior is sitting right there in that chair. Complain away!" I pointed to the Boss, ankles crossed, as relaxed as someone watching a boring football game on the TV. He casually brushed some imaginary lint off his coat, a gesture that was so out of his normal milieu that I nearly choked. Wearing all these expensive suits had gone to his head!

"Mr. President, all documents, and access to all staff who have worked on this grand plan of yours since day one." The President squirmed in his seat, probably thinking about his options, which, in fact, were none at all, because the way the

Terrorist Laws had been written, the simple knowledge of a terrorist act even without participation got you the proverbial noose. His intransigence had led us down a rather limited path, and now I had to pull us back to an operational level that made sense.

I pulled my mini out of my pocket, and in seconds, the scowling face of General Saunders swam into focus. She just raised one eyebrow, her uniform jacket with all its fruit salad hanging over the back of her seat. She was holding a large coffee mug with the crest of the 85th. Airborne on it, and I wondered who she had killed to get it. Okay, I had coffee envy! It had been hours since my last fix, and a girl was entitled to a little comfort now and then, even while chasing terrorists.

"General, I need Senior Supervisory Special Agent Bernstein and an analyst team over here ASAP, please." She immediately clued in to my use of Anna's formal title. She knew my movements, and I saw the implications of her putting two and two together and getting five flash behind her eyes. She put her mug down, clasped her hands on her desk, and leaned into the camera.

"Commander, she and her team will be with you in twelve hours."

"Thank you, general. I appreciate it." I put my mini away, let the uncomfortable silence hang, then looked the President right in his eyes, which were now tightly focused and shooting darts that would probably be fatal to anyone who cared.

"Mr. President, I'm going to uncuff you, and Agent Robertson and Corporal Ricci will escort you to our vehicle. You will wait in our office until our investigating team arrives from the United States. They will forensically examine all your documentation and interview all your people. Seeing as we are starting from the point where you are guilty under the Terrorist Laws, it will be in your best personal interests to make sure we have access to everything and everyone involved. Do you have any questions?"

"You have no right to hold me here. You have no right to make such requests of me. I am the President of Ireland. Ireland helps pay your salary!" He shouted the last, and I just couldn't let him get away with that stupid remark.

"And we all thank you for that. Could I suggest that while you wait, you read up on the Terrorist Laws so you can see exactly what is in your future? I'll see that a copy is provided for you. Now, if you continue to act like a spoiled child, I'll put the cuffs back on you. Your choice." I looked at the Boss, he stood, we followed, he thanked the President for his time, and we left his office, followed by the President and his new friends.

Sandra waited and positioned herself directly behind the President, and I could feel his skin prickling from ten feet away.

As we reached the first of his guards outside the office, I stopped and waited until I had their attention. The President and his escort continued outside. The guards looked very uncomfortable but stood their ground.

"The President is under house arrest under the Terrorist Laws as modified in 2022. There will be more Interpol agents arriving shortly and a contingent of FBI Agents. We will inform your command, but as of now, this facility and all supporting administrative functions come under the aegis of Interpol and therefore the UN. Do you understand what I have just said?" His rank was that of a major if I read his badges correctly, probably the senior officer on location. He drew himself up to his full height and looked at me as if I had crawled out from under a rock.

"Madam, you cannot take our President away."

I looked at him, sympathetic to his position but in no mood to vacillate or prevaricate. "Major, I can and I am. I'll be leaving our local Agent here to see that nothing is removed from the President's office. He will not be incarcerated at this time, but will remain in our office until we have satisfied our curiosity." His frosty look, if anything, dropped a few more degrees.

"Then I will send my men with him." Mexican standoff. The Boss leaned forward and, in a very soft voice, entered the fray.

"Major, I'm General Anthony. That is a good solution. Please have a vehicle made ready to take the President, your team, and three of our people to our Interpol office." The major looked at the Boss, confusion in his eyes, but heavily outranked, fell back on his military training and discipline, and saluted.

"At once, sir!" He turned to one of his guards, issued his orders, then moved towards our vehicle, where the President and our people were congregated, expectant looks on their faces, except for Sandra, who predictably scowled. And the President, who looked angry enough to chew on anyone he could reach.

"Corporal's Ricci and Roberto, wait for the President's vehicle." It took a few minutes, but both vehicles loaded up, and as I sat back in the plush seat, Sandra leaned over and patted my leg.

"Very ballsy, taking the President of Ireland out of his lair in broad daylight. I like that. But can we actually hold him?" The doubt in her eyes was real, and again the differences between the normal functions of Interpol and Section Five reared their ugly heads. I just nodded, pushed back in my seat, and closed my eyes.

The Irish major was one of the guards accompanying the President, and I respected that, but I started to worry about the size of our office and its security. When the Boss, Sandra, and I had to change earlier, we were close enough to each other to be in sin most of the time. If the Irish guards arced up and forced us into a defensive position, blood would flow, and none of it would be ours. That in itself would create a major shitstorm in both Lyon and Geneva.

The Boss was reading my mind and my body language, sitting in the seat opposite me with long legs crossed at the ankles, his favorite position of late.

"Three-step process. First step, secure the President, keep him away from any form of communication. Second step, keep the Presidential guard away from him—I would suggest in sight but out of physical contact. Third step, your choice—do you want to wait until Anna arrives?"

"Before what?" He grinned his evil smile at me, the one that reminded you of an alligator just before it took a muskrat. I could feel it even with my eyes closed.

"Before we leave for wherever you need to be next."

I reached for my mini, having worked through my own three-step process called the Sgan Aluf.

"Josephine, how's it going?" Her stoic face filled the screen, but her background was moving.

"Commander, just fine, we have a really lot of good-looking boys and girls running all over the place, Semper Fi and all that. A girl could get sidetracked in a heartbeat!" Her exotic accent was lovely to listen to, and I thought about the massive thighs on our Commando 104 colonel and doubted that any marine could keep pace with her, let alone get her off message.

"I need eight of your best. Chopper them over to Dublin, coordinates to follow, full battle dress, body armor, weapons visible. Their mission will be to secure a political prisoner and work in lockstep with a team from the FBI. It might be a week or so deployment, but you'll get them back eventually." She just nodded, used to my strange requests, and seemed to think for a minute.

"I'll send Lieutenant Brookneal. She wants my job. This will be good practice for her. Who does she report to?"

"Our local Agent, Shelia Robertson, or myself in the interim, or SSSA Anna Bernstein, will be here in twelve hours or so and will be in charge of the investigation. Your team will provide pro-tection and backup. This is high-level political stuff. They might come under fire, either verbal and/or hot metal, so they need to be on their toes. And one other thing—this is a Section Five operation, and our ROE will apply." Her look changed slightly, more interested but definitely not negative in any sense. She had worked with us and our ROE before and survived.

"WILCO." She dropped off the line, and I looked over at the Boss.

"My three points—one, you go back to Lyon or wherever, make sure our backsides are well and truly protected from any political blowback. And there will be plenty, you can count on it. Two," and I held up my two middle fingers facing outwards in the time honored 'f you' signal, "we'll let Anna and the marines work it out between themselves, and three, the moment she arrives, I'm off to Whiddy Island for a holiday in the rain." He just grinned, obviously satisfied with my points. He settled back, folded his arms over his chest, closed his eyes, and looked incredibly relaxed for someone who was about to face angry ambassadors and maybe even a commissioner or two from the UN.

I was glad it would be him and not me.

CHAPTER THIRTY THREE

"Where are you exactly?" The tension in Fay's voice was palpable. She was standing on the shoreline at the far corner of the fenced-off area that held the small sewage plant. Beside her, feeding off her nervousness, Luca kept scanning the empty paddock as if expecting an attack by rabid dogs. It wasn't fear. It was the potential for embarrassment in screwing up the mission. Their instinct was that the shed inside the fence might be where the environmental plant was stored, as they hadn't found any other likely building on their side of the Bay. If it were, then they were potentially standing at terrorist ground zero. Plenty of space exists to land helicopters or even short-field transport aircraft.

And very few residents—make that none—for around five hundred meters to the nearest houses. Which, when they walked past, appeared to be empty.

"On the beach opposite the processing plant, off Quay Road. When the tide is out like it is now, the water is about two kilometers away. There's a river of sorts that comes in from Killala Bay and a massive sand bank that guards the entire beach front. No way they could build a plant here without massive and very visible infrastructure, even though there is plenty of room in this plant to store a lot of crates." Gabriella paused, took another look around.

"As for somewhere to build a few thousand houses and support buildings, there are literally acres and acres of space everywhere you look. Population estimated at less than two hundred." Fay shook her head. She felt that they had underestimated the resources she would need to secure the location, and she was worried that this would become a problem sooner rather than later. She dialed Jessica and was amused to see her asleep in a room somewhere and equally surprised to see Sandra's head pop into frame.

"Hi Fay, our illustrious leader is catching forty winks. How can I help?" Fay thought for a second. She had seen Sandra glued to Jessica's hip for days, so the chances she would know the current disposition of their resources were high.

"Sandra, let her sleep. She probably needs it. On the other hand, I need more troops. Minimum eight, preferably ten. They need to be in soft clothes, with a legitimate reason for being here." At the other end of the conversation, Sandra looked over at the sleeping form of Jessica and debated with herself whether or not to wake her. One look at the dark circles that pooled under her eyes made her decision for her.

"Italian, Israeli, or American?" Fay looked bemused, not sure what Sandra was getting at.

"If you're offering up the 104 or Indigo's Special Intervention Group, I'd have to choose the ones with the coffee maker." Sandra laughed, feeling more comfortable every second she was in conversation with Fay. The strain was showing on Jessica's face, even in sleep, and the whole process of taking the Irish President into 'soft' custody had left its mark on her. Sandra would never let Jessica know how great she felt about that. Some secrets a girl just had to keep to herself. But she knew she had a wicked smile on her face. She couldn't help it, and she was secretly glad Jessica couldn't see her reaction.

"I can send you some lovely young, fresh marines if you'd like that?" Sandra saw Fay go into thinking mode, her eyes shuttering, her face smoothing out as if being massaged.

"Maybe they have to be either students or backpackers, young, inoffensive, and able to survive on their own and maintain discipline. We have a hugely distributed target area, separated by ocean. Prime locations are a minimum of thirty minutes apart, and there is no clear indication where the enemy will establish themselves." Sandra gave some thought to Fay's tactical situation and shook her head. A tough one in anyone's language, but Jessica had sent Fay into Killara Bay for a reason, and not just because she looked pretty and unthreatening.

She had shown her chops while still in the FBI in getting Point Roberts sorted and secured, as well as smoothing out the chaos in Helena, showing an ability to think on her feet and take direct action, which had attracted Jessica to her. And if she had learned one thing in the last month that stuck to Jessica's side at the instruction of the boss, it was that Jessica was a genius at unpicking fast-moving tactical situations and changing the game to suit their purpose. And was really good at putting the right person in the right place at the right time.

Sandra rapidly ran through the faces of the people they now had in the field at Whiddy Island, then remembered Tom's team, which had been split into two and then reformed when they had taken the last of the nuclear shells out of circulation. Or, in this case, located the melted puddle of bimetal sludge that had once been a shell.

"I can send you Tom's team. You remember them. Their strength is back up to ten now, with a new team leader, a warrant officer from England. She's very sharp. You'll like her. Her name is Rosie Hammond. She's been in the background a bit, worked across teams from day one, ex-Special Boat Service, the English version of our Seals." Fay nodded. She didn't need any more convincing. She mentally worked out how to get them to Killara Bay under the radar.

"Land them at Ballina, get them on bikes, and let me know their ETA. One of us will meet them near the Abbey Street bridge." Sandra looked at her tactical watch, worked out the time and distance at both ends, and made a snap decision just like Jessica would have.

"Three hours should give you time to get someone back to Ballina." Fay nodded, wondering how to manage her surveillance of the sewerage plant for the six or seven hours she would be on her own. Watching Luca watch her gave her all the confidence she needed.

"Luca, mount up. You're going back down to Ballina. When you meet with Tom's team—now Rosie's—send five to Gabriella, bring the rest back here, but to the hotel, maybe spread out a little. See if Rosie will take Killala. That will give us command on both sides of the Bay. I'm going to ground here and will let you know what to do when you get back."

"Roger that, Inspector. From memory, Tom's team was roughly fifty-fifty male and female. If they pair up, it will look more natural." Fay held her hand up. "Wait one." Fay dived into her mini and found what she was looking for.

"Book them into the Acres B&B—they have the room, and bike parties are part of their milieu. They can be American students caught on this side of the Atlantic by the attacks, spending time riding around while they wait for a way home. Send six, including Rosie, and bring the rest back here."

"Will do. Stay safe." And he mounted his electric bike and wobbled off back down the main road. Fay took one last look at the sewerage plant, then decided to hide herself in plain sight by parking her bike in the driveway of one of the empty houses that littered the area with military precision. Every house looked the same: an 'L' shape with a basic gray roof on the same small plot of land, obviously built by developers with economy and a cookie cutter in hand.

She and Luca had biked around the whole area, finding every house from the small shopping area on up empty. Clean, neat, and tidy, but no occupancy of any type. She had counted three hundred and sixty before concluding the area was vacant. When she had idly inquired back at the hotel, their hostess had simply said half the town was now empty, as very, very few tourists came through any more, and wasn't that a shame?

There was a massive row of stunted, low-profile wind power generators out on the cliffs, and she guessed that with less than forty percent of any day having sunshine, solar was not really viable. The national grid had gone down after the terror attacks, being predominately gas-fed. Interestingly, a number of power stations on the west coast were peat-fueled and were working overtime trying to make up for the lack of gas. But there was obviously some power because they had unrationed lights and heating in their rooms at the hotel.

As she set up her hide, her mini buzzed against her leg. Sandra's face swam into focus, looking a little peeved.

"Okay Fay, you have your bodies. They will be with you in one hour and twenty, landing at Ballina Airport. We decided to go formal. We've got letters of introduction from Belfast University, thanks to our friendly monk. They will be officially government sponsored students researching the history of the area, preparing for 'better times'. Still stranded by the attacks, still wanting to get home, but happy to have something to do with themselves. That's not why I called." Fay looked at Sandra. The room was still dark, and the sleeping form of Jessica didn't look as if it had moved in the interim.

"Don't keep me in suspense." Sandra laughed, and the untidy look morphed into a full-face smile.

"The AWACS is tracking a flight of two large helicopters heading your way. We don't have an initiation point yet, but it looks like it was somewhere in France. They are using a civilian squawk for their transponders, supposedly a Scottish Government code used for civil defense work. All above board, all squeaky clean, what gave them away was the transmission we traced—a call from Aberfoyle to Katrina changing their destination. At their present speed, they'll be somewhere in your airspace in the next fifty minutes."

"Is this the same group that did some type of experiment in Ireland, then bugged out to, where was it? Spain?"

"If we trust the intercepts, and I trust our geeks, then yes, most likely."

"Do we know what they did there?" Sandra rolled her eyes up to the ceiling, screwed her face up in a grimace, then looked back down at her camera.

"Short answer, no. But we know they visited a number of nuclear power stations; what they were for, we have no idea yet. The stations were all closed due to nanite contamination." Fay suddenly looked her most serious, thinking as hard as she could to join the dots. She shook her head in frustration.

"We don't know enough. Okay, I'll surveil them as best as I can, but my prime mission is to track O'Cleary and keep tabs on her."

"Want my best guess?" Fay smiled. She had a feeling Sandra's best guess wouldn't be far from the hard truth. She waved her hand in the 'come on' gesture.

"O'Cleary will connect with the Scottish team for some reason." Fay nodded. That would make her team's job a lot easier.

"I'd like that. We'll have both sides of the Bay covered, thanks for the heads up." She settled into her hide, dialed the AWACS up on her mini, selected the remote track function, and watched the two-minute green dots move slowly across the screen. A data block showed the squawk code, the ID, which was undoubtedly false, and the height and speed over the ground. A compass rose gave their current direction, and an arrow predicted their next position in a moving display. The arrow quivered as if it had a life of its own. In contrast, the two dots were steady. The moving ground map had them passing over the top of Tullamore. Interesting: the great circle route up from France was a bottomed-out curve that missed Dublin to the southwest.

Some twenty kilometers further south, having used the little electric motor more than he would have liked, Luca hit the outskirts of Killala, so he slowed to a moderate pedal speed, wary of any traffic. The number of cars on the road could be counted on one hand, and there were very few signs of the normally bustling commerce the town was known for. Tourists.

Back in 2017, Mayo Power Limited proposed a new gas-fired plant be built to get employment back up, and industry back into the area. After a three-year fight with the locals, who did not want a carbon-polluting plant in their backyard, the proposal was voted down by the Chamber of Commerce. In 2022, the council approved the sale of the former Asahi site, where the plant was to have been built, for the development of two data centers. That ran straight into a policy block by Dublin, which took the stance of 'no power' to be used for data centers until the national grid had been sorted out and the existing data centers, paid for by the central government, were being fully utilized. Underlying this conversation were the county-wide blackouts suffered intermittently throughout the next three years.

Frustrating, but that's politics!

Luca passed the first bridge, slowed ever further, and pulled to a stop at the Upper Bridge, as it was known. There was an old man with a flower stand on the corner of the road, sitting on a ratty chair, cap askew, head drooping as he snoozed, but surrounded by the most beautiful flowers Luca had even seen.

Florescent reds and blues, bright yellows and pinks—the colors cascaded across the small wheelbarrow like an out-of-control waterfall sparkling in the late afternoon sun. For some strange reason, he felt impelled to buy some for Fay. He held off, his soldier instincts overriding his male ones. He laid his bike on the pavement and sat with his back to the Ardnaree Abby Graveyard, hoping against hope that the ghosts were all still asleep. A staunch Catholic, he had been personally shattered when the Vatican and the hierarchy of his church were destroyed, but the strength of his upbringing had carried him through, and now he both served and fought to regain some semblance of balance in the world.

And hunt down the terrorists who had wounded his religion, which was the foundation for his entire family going back centuries.

He was eternally thankful for people like Inspector Remer and the amazing Commander Riley. He was part of a solid, professional, and focused team and was respected for his skills. So now he would use them and make sure he made contact with Tom's team. Or was it now Rosie's? He just shrugged. He was certain he would recognize a bunch of Americans cycling down the road, probably on the wrong side!

And he was not wrong, as a gaggle of colorful puffer jackets, helmets on cap-covered heads, and massive backpacks tied to rear pavilions bobbed and weaved down the road to the blare of Bruce Springsteen. He heard them well before he saw them, and when he did, he stood, making sure there was no oncoming traffic. They rode up to him, stopped, propped their bikes up on the tarmac, and he saw they all wore dull brown combat boots, a sure giveaway if ever he saw one. He sighed. This might turn out to be harder than he expected. One of the riders pushed up to him, large red-framed glasses on a pretty round face, her blue bike helmet made of silver and black ridges running from the front to the back of her head, where curly brown hair floated in abundance. Her naked lips were in contrast to her rosy cheeks, which he deduced were due to the nearly freezing wind.

"Benvenuta, signora, sono Luca." He bobbed his head, saw a lack of comprehension on the faces of some of the group, gathered himself, and tried again in English. He was used to working with people who were genuinely multilingual, with Italian and Spanish being as natural as English to most. But these were Americans, after all.

"Madam, welcome. I am Luca."

"Ciao Luca, grazie per averci incontrato." She smiled, nodded, then switched to English herself. "Good to see you, Luca. I am Warrant Officer Hammond. Do you have directions for us?" He scratched under his chin with one hand, the other holding up his bike. Her accent was hard-edged Jordy, which he knew was referred to as Tyneside English. He had never heard such an edgy accent used by a woman before, but he hid his surprise and pointed across the bridge.

"Inspector Remer suggests you and five others ride on to Killala, about a fifteen-kilometer ride. There you will be met by my partner, Gabriella. You'll know her as she will know you. The rest of your team are to follow me to Inishcrone, where the good Inspector will brief us all. One warning: once in position, we will be only six kilometers apart as the drone flies, but thirty plus kilometers by road. A small boat would be ideal, but you need to be mindful of the tides and the sandbars, but I'll leave that up to you."

"Why does the good Inspector want us separated?" Luca gave her a hard look. He was not used to anyone second-guessing his commanders, but he did not want to hold them up and possibly draw attention to them, so he answered. However, his cool tone let her know his attitude toward her asking questions, and to make his point, he copied Indigo, who he most wanted to be when he grew up.

"Wella, nowa, maybe shea has gooda reasons for thisa, whya not aska her yourselfa, whena you get therea, or even nowa, if you cana take thea timea?" Her response was to smile, nod, then issuing orders in a fast, deliberate manner, mounted, and pedaled off with half her team across the bridge. The old flower seller had woken and half-heartedly waved at the backs of the riders. Seeing a possible sale receding from him, he promptly went back to sleep.

Luca looked at his half, saw no animosity, just open curiosity, mounted up, and headed back the way he had come. This time a lilting Irish voice filled his ears, celebrating the death of her loved one in one of the many invasions that had plagued Ireland for thousands of years. In his experience, every Irish song was sad and about losing loved ones!

At the other end of the road, Fay watched in fascination as the radar image on her mini morphed into reality as two massive Russian MI-26 helicopters started to settle down in the bright green grassed paddock opposite her hide. The noise was incredible, so much so that she didn't hear the electric golf cart drive past, literally a handspan from her face. She hunched in, made herself as small as possible, and peeked over the top of the shrubbery that lined the fence. The rotors on both helicopters wound down to what she guessed was ground idle, and four fit-looking women jumped out of the first wallowing beast, then unloaded a series of boxes. As soon as they were stacked, they ran to the second helicopter and pulled an equally impressive stack of boxes and cylinders out into an untidy pile.

Then they stood back, still in the rotor wash, and just watched as the two monsters flapped and crawled back up into the chilled air. Dropping their noses, they both achieved transitional lift, pointing down at the vast ocean, then slowly climbed away as if it were a major effort. As the noise receded, the golf cart moved to the pile, and the women were greeted by yet another woman, this one with long red hair flowing from under a watch cap. Hugs were swapped freely, and then the impromptu labor gang loaded the golf cart. It sped off, straight into the sewerage plant, where she couldn't see it being unloaded due to the angle.

It seemed to be only minutes before it sped back to the women and the diminishing piles, reloaded, and then did its disappearing trick again. Three loads later, the women climbed aboard, and once again Fay had to literally shrink herself to avoid detection as the cart rumbled past her hide. It ran off down the road. She took a deep breath, then thought about the incoming team and decided to let them arrive at the hotel as planned, even at the risk of them being seen by the women. They were, for all intents and purposes, a legitimate group of students participating in research commissioned by the university to help bring tourists back to the area.

She was counting on Luca to deliver that message. Her mini buzzed against her thigh. She debated whether or not to answer it, bent upright, checked for people, saw none, heard none, so she laid on her back on the lush grass and answered.

"Remer."

"Hammond. Laying down on the job, I see?" said Hammond with some humor, so Fay let the mild sarcasm go.

"Are you in Killala?" The background was too compressed to give a clear indication of where the English woman was calling from.

"Yes, I checked in, all quiet. I'd like to know your plans."

This time she spoke with some sharp edges, and Fay immediately thought that Tom would not have spoken to her in this tone of voice. New team leader, new rules—she'd adapt as best as she could.

"Warrant officer, I'm point on this operation. Originally we were to have collected a terrorist when she got here. Plans changed when we became aware of another group, possibly also terrorists, due to arrive. They have, just now, so from this point on I'd appreciate communication discipline." The English officer's face had gone a little redder, as the use of her rank struck her as both aggressive and rude. But she knew Tom, her predecessor, had worked with this woman in the past under very treacherous and difficult circumstances, so she swallowed her pride and apologized.

"Inspector, I'm sorry, we got off on the wrong foot. Splitting my team makes me nervous, and your little Italian wasn't very forthcoming."

"That little Italian has been working up close and personal with our Commander, so he probably asked you to call me for details, choosing discretion over confusion."

"I get that, and I apologize again. How can I help?"

"Get Gabriella and yourself to a secure location, and I'll fill you in."

"Yes, ma'am. Give me five, please." Fay cut the connection, hoping against hope that the new boss of Tom's team wasn't going to turn out to be a royal pain in the arse. If her accent was anything to go by, just understanding her would be the biggest issue.

Fay dialed Luca, saw from his background that he was in a room, noticed some shadows behind him, and assumed they were the second half of Rosie's team. She split the screen, brought up Gabriella's mini, saw Rosie sitting beside her, and then, just for fun, brought Sandra into the conversation. Jessica was sitting beside her, obviously in her office. Fay decided to set the tone from the get-go.

"Commander, Inspector, we are established in Killala and Inishcrone. I've split the incoming team into two. Two MI-26's were unloaded; four women, all in our target profile, have headed towards the town. I'll track them down later. A number of boxes and cylinders were unloaded and transported to the sewage plant."

"Thanks, Fay. Rosie, welcome. I understand you've taken over from Tom?" I asked, watching her face for any tells. I had not worked directly with her before, but she had been across the teams once or twice but never seemed to be settled anywhere. I knew she was an ex-SBS and had done two tours on exchange with the US Navy Seals. She had not been on Tom's original team.

"Commander, thank you. Yes, I have Tom's team, half here with me and the other half with the Inspector." I acknowledged her statement with a nod, for that is what it had been. Her accent did nothing to disguise her tonality. Now I understood Fay's formal approach to the call.

"Fay, the AWACS is now scanning Ireland, top to bottom, and watching for any aircraft entering the AIDZ (Air Identification Defense Zone). The lack of traffic is working in our favor, and the US Navy in the Mediterranean has a high-flyer at forty thousand feet that looks likely. Unable to track its origination due to distance. But its transponder code is civilian, and it will be with you in around fifty minutes. Your orders stand, do not reveal yourselves, let O'Cleary land, and watch her for the next few days to see what she is up to."

"Do we know what the test here in Ireland was all about?"

"No, but we have assets investigating it. We also have a technology team from the AEC (Atomic Energy Commission) back-tracking the reactors they visited, so we may have an answer for you soon." Fay looked a little worried, the crease between her eyes deepening. Finally, she shook her head.

"Okay, worry about it when we know. I've instructed the West team—the one with Rosie—to hire a boat if they can, to shorten the physical contact time between teams. Do you have anything else we need to be aware of?" I looked at Sandra. She had set all this up while I slept, so she had a direction in mind.

"Yes, get out and be seen, prove your credentials, make a noise, but keep clear of the women if you can. There's no evidence of the women ever resisting arrest or attacking us one-on-one, but be aware that that might change, or someone else might take a shot at you, because we still don't know all the players." I nodded my agreement and pointed to Sandra.

"What she said. Okay, everyone, stay sharp, see what you can see." And I pulled the metaphorical plug on the conversation, then dialed Fay back up onto the big screen.

"What aren't you telling me?" She looked down the barrel of the lens, as if sitting opposite me, and shrugged her shoulders, which were highlighted by brilliant green grass. I realized she was lying on her back for some reason and smiled. Lying down on the job was not what she was doing. She was way too fast and bright for that. She was one of the genius refugee children, after all.

"Not sure about Rosie. Luca wasn't either, and Tom's team, as you know, is one of the very best. Luca's only real comment was they were all wearing combat boots when they rode in on their bikes." I tucked my head down on my chest, letting that statement filter through. The instruction had been soft cloths, then Sandra leaned across me and into the shot.

"Fay, reissue the instruction on soft clothes. We'll see what happens." Fay nodded, glad to have been given overt control of the local situation. It was something she really appreciated about the way Jessica ran her team—no second guessing, no Monday morning quarterbacking, just one hundred percent support at every step. The FBI had been good. Interpol was better.

"WILCO. Let me get to it." The screen went black. I sat back just as I was handed a new mug of coffee, silently thanked the Gods of the magic brown bean, and just inhaled the scent.

"You know, there's a five-step program for people like you." Sandra laughed as she accepted her own mug, a beautiful green elongated glass gondola with a pair of small wings on the handle that you could rest your thumb on. I wondered how many of these amazing mugs Indigo had packed.

"You did good while I was sleeping. Now I want to return the favor, and I want you down for the next six hours, no argument, and give me your mini." I held out my hand, and with a tremendous sight, Sandra handed it over.

"Next, you'll want my H&K. Not fair." I smiled and tucked her mini into my pants pocket.

"No, keep your toy gun. Go get your six. I'll call you when Anna gets here." She sighed again, then wandered off to our assigned quarters. My two Italian studs move over unobtrusively, one on each side.

She really had done well. She was turning into a great tactical thinker, which is a huge advantage when fighting an asymmetric war. And I was particularly comfortable with her making major force-projection decisions in my absence, which surprised me. Maybe, just maybe, I was getting the hang of being top dog.

I went over my to-do list again. It was growing by the minute, but the key items were now interviewing the Irish President, gathering all the data and analyzing it, solving our Scottish problem, getting to Whiddy Island, and the list went on. It occurred to me that I had more people at my disposal than I had at any other time in any operation in which I had participated for at least six years, so either it was a sign of the times or I was getting sloppy or lazy.

With that pleasant thought running through my mind, I walked outside to see the last of the fading orange sun slowly sink behind a thin black band of clouds. The air was crisp, promising more rain, but dead still, as if waiting for something.

I knew exactly how the air felt.

CHAPTER THIRTY FOUR

The Sgan Aluf of the Israeli 104 commando, broad of shoulders from power lifting, thick in the thighs from endurance running, coming in at around 110 kilos and 160 centimeters, faced her adversary, a marine light colonel, built like a linebacker, weighing probably 240 pounds in his jocks, 6'3", tattooed arms rippling with toned muscle. His butcher's block of a hand was stretched to its limit, veins popping up like worms running from an attacking bird. In contrast, the colonel's hand was delicate, her matte-polished nails neatly trimmed, and her forearm barely straining. Across from them, amused and amazed at the hidden strength in the Israeli woman, Tom sipped an incredibly bad cup of MRE's (Meals Ready to Eat) coffee and looked on in awe.

The colonel didn't appear to be straining in the least. Her forearm was upright, and her supple fingers seemingly relaxed in the marine's meatgrinder of a fist, which almost completely enclosed her hand. Her head was tilted to one side, and a warm smile filled her pretty face. Dressed in day camos, it was hard to discern any specifics of her body shape. In contrast, the marine literally pushed the seams of his camos to their limit. The word 'bulging' sprang to mind. Behind the small kitchen table that was the focus of the action, marines and commandos alike yelled and taunted each other, as happy as you can be in a combat zone.

"Colonel, I have chores. Can you please give in so I can get to them?" Her lilting accented English was warm and bubbly, suiting her overall appearance, but from the strain on the marine's face, he was thinking she was anything but a soft touch.

"Ma'am, if I concede, I'll have to resign my commission." His face screwed up in concentration, he pushed as hard as he could without taking his offhand out of the curled finger grip of his opponent.

"Oh, well then." And without apparent effort, the Israeli crushed the marine's hand to the linoleum-covered tabletop, to the cheers and boisterous verbal salutes from her troops. She stood, put her hand out, took the marine's, shook it, smiled, and both sides of the crowd started stomping their feet and clapping their hands. Stomp-stomp-clap. Stomp-stomp-clap. And once again, the famous rock piece from better times ruled the air.

"Gentle people, thanks for your support. Please go back to your squads and stand by for the briefing." The stomp-stomp-clap slowly faded as the troops moved out of the kitchen, and Tom noticed that the two groups were intermingling on the way out, each trying to convince the other of the superiority of their commanders. The colonel sat back down, the marine with a wry smile stretching his hand, huge fingers opening and closing, a massive smile splitting his tough face from corner to corner.

"It's going to take me a while to live that down," he said, his smile softening but his deep brown eyes glowing. "Where did you learn to do that?"

"Krav Maga. Four brothers growing up and being the runt of the litter." The marine nodded his head, his look now a little skeptical. She was anything but the runt of the litter. In civies, she could be easily taken for a high-class woman of style and culture walking the streets of any major city and looking like she owned them. He shook his head, accepting his defeat.

"Okay, you win, but if we get the time, you have to teach me how to do that."

"It will be my pleasure."

"About that." Tom grounded his mug, happy to have an excuse to leave his coffee mug, so-called, half full. "Unlikely we'll have much time for playing games in the next two to three days. Our personal navy will be here within twenty-four, and the commander wants us to deep-clean the Island, top to bottom. The

AWACS is sending us a magnetic and LIDAR scan. We'll have the composite from our geeks in the next hour. Your briefing packs will have that on your minis when we release them. In the meantime, we need to sort out roles and responsibilities."

The marine looked at the Israeli colonel, then back at Tom. His face was now all business, the crease between his eyebrows deepening in concentration.

"Where do you fit in?" There was no challenge in the question, which made Tom happy. He needed a unified, single-minded approach to what they had to do, and he had seen the start of that forming as the troops had left the building. It had given him an idea he would pursue at the end of the briefing.

"Right now I speak for our Commander, Jessica Riley, and in turn General Anthony. When Colonel Kashasini gets here with the ship, he will take over as the Interpol Section Five representative, and you'll both report to him. The Commander has labeled this a Police Action, to discover and remove any weapons of mass destructions, and terrorists involved in same, and we are operating under the strictures of the Terrorist Laws as modified in 2022. You're both familiar with the Laws?" The Sgan Aluf nodded, she had operated with Section Five previously under fire executing the letter of the Laws, and the marine had been given both an electronic and physical copy personally by his Admiral before he had shipped out.

He remembered the last words the admiral had spoken: "These people shoot first to kill and don't often bother to ask questions. You and your people will have to do the same, so you need to prepare them." And he had handed over the thickly bound manual with its impressive red and gold cover. He had briefed his people and had his team leaders run repeat sessions, but he suspected he would be questioned at the daily summary session. He considered asking Tom to participate, then decided against it. He had a chain of command, he had well-trained troops, and with good discipline, he would make it his business to see that everyone under him could do what they may need to do without hesitation.

"What are your orders, sir?" he asked, unsure of Tom's rank or even if he had one. Tom returned his smile and flipped a paper map over the tabletop with a swishing sound. He reached over and pointed to the first fort, just below the oil tanks.

"We chased mercenary terrorists out of her just recently. The colonel was involved in that. We also came under fire up here," and he pointed to the fort in the middle of the Island, "and subsequently moved on the top fort. The terrorists escaped to sea in both cases, through tunnels that didn't paint on our equipment." Tom watched the face of the marine for any reaction and only saw a slow nod.

"In all three cases, the forts had underground cubbies full of weapons and explosives, all modern and all in excellent condition. The Colonel here and some of our own troops mined the forts on their way out." The marine looked up, straight into the eyes of the Israeli.

"Why did you do that?" She held his eyes, a small grin forming.

"Well, it seems Interpol here," and she pointed to Tom, "are a bunch of pussies. Rather than blow up three hundred-year-old forts listed as Heritage sites, they decided to mine them and let the terrorists do it for us, if they bothered to return." The marine relaxed. He understood the pain of Heritage sites. He had gotten mixed up in them once or twice himself and still had the bruises to prove it. He nodded. Tom continued.

"We need to find how they got to the coast and how they escaped. So first task, find the end of the bolt holes, backtrack, but don't hit any trips, and work out how they got away." Tom looked for any questions, saw none, and continued.

"Second task, same priority, when we get the scans, we want to track down any underground facilities and neutralize them. Your task is to make sure the Island is one hundred percent terrorist free, no surprises. Politics are in play, bigtime, and if you need a reference for just how big, the Commander personally arrested the Irish President under the Terrorist Laws a few hours ago and is flying in top FBI agents to rip apart the parliament and government offices. This is as serious as it gets, so any questions, get them out now." Both officers seemed to be thinking through the conversation, then the Israeli turned her head to look directly at Tom.

"Inspector Remer was with us the last time we were in action. She freely joined in the firefight as we did. What are our ROE this time around?" Tom returned her look, turned to look at the marine, and put his hands flat on the table.

"It would be nice to have someone to question should you come across any tangos, but the word is 'nice' not 'necessary'. The Commander wants the Island as clean as a baby's backside after a bath, and while I'm in charge, I want zero casualties on our side." Both officers nodded. From a purely military perspective, no casualties was a great outcome, and they both wondered how they might achieve that given the terrorists knew the Island inside out, had been here probably for years, and were proving very difficult to find.

"I have a suggestion. You both might like to consider mixing your teams, keeping them small, maybe squads of four. I'll leave it up to you." He stood, nodded to both officers, then walked back out into the drizzle. With no hat or coat, he was soaked in minutes. He continued walking until he came to a three-sided little shed, where he pulled out a very tattered plastic chair. He pulled his mini out.

"Hi Tom, sitrep please." He looked directly at me, his gray eyes flat, so I knew he was in thinking mode.

"Hi Jessica, all quiet, teams just briefed, just waiting on the AWACS data."

"Good. How can I help?" I gave him a concerned look. It was very un-Tom-like to call just for a chat. He was new to the position, and while he had worked with the Boss for some years and myself for the last three months, that had been in a very different capacity. As in he had been the team leader of a squad of SEALS, TDY'ed to Interpol Section Five. Now he was my master-at-arms, or quartermaster in the old language, responsible for weapons and squad tactics and implementing any hairbrained scheme I came up with. And now a critical member of my small command team.

"Commander, the Boss left my rank up to me. I can keep what I achieved in the SEALS, or adopt a Section Five one. Which would you prefer?"

"Master chief you were, and unless you want an internal rank, I'm happy for you to remain a master chief. Remember, Black Pete was also a master chief, and he never had issues with gaining authority over anyone." Tom broke out into a genuine smile, remembering the tough, lanky Australian card-sharp who was recovering from multiple gunshot wounds. Jessica was right—no one had ever questioned Black Pete's orders or suggestions.

"Good, that makes me happy. Although I was a bit shy at first telling two colonels how to play our game."

"I bet Josephine Aria didn't give you any trouble?" His grin grew until it filled his face.

"No, ma'am, quite the opposite. She arm wrestled the marine right into the table top. It caused quite a ruckus." My turn to smile. I would have liked to have seen that.

"What's really troubling you?" He looked down for a second, then back up at the camera. His background was a dark blur.

"I don't feel comfortable sitting on my backside while everyone is out chasing tangos." I smiled. I had the exact same feeling when the boss pulled me out of the NCIS, where I was an active field investigator responsible for an overseas US Naval base.

"I know how you feel. When the briefing is complete, gun up and wander around. Tour the Island, walk through the plant, get the feel for the topography. Your observations will be invaluable in planning how we hold it. Don't be afraid of being seen by the troops. They will respect you all the more if you're out in the field with them." His whole body language changed. He suddenly looked happy and focused.

"Thank you, ma'am, WILCO." And he cut the link and left me thinking about the change in roles and the effect it always had on everyone involved. It was a truism that human beings didn't like change and that homeostasis was the most comfortable state for most of us. But the world had changed, and we had to change with it. But the fact that he had addressed me in three different ways suggested I would need to quietly help him find his balance in his new role, which I was determined to do.

OPEN WATER

The good ship *'Scáthán'* ripped across the Atlantic current as if it didn't exist. Averaging 22 knots, it was eating up the distance to Whiddy Island at a gallop. The six- to seven-knot tidal effect was helping, giving the boat an over-the-sea-bed speed of 29 knots on occasions, something Indigo was eternally grateful for.

He knew that Jessica was worried about the Island and had been brought up to date on the political status, and after a quick chat with Tom, in whom he sensed an unease he respected, he wanted to get there as soon as possible. To his surprise, he and the master chief had synchronized their teams extremely well, and he had no fear that they would not do the job they had come to do.

But there were now non-identified blips on the long-range radar—two of them, both at 20,000 feet—and they were all headed his way. From the size of the blips, he guessed small passenger aircraft or drones. The on-duty radar woman, one of the chief's marines, was running the data through the recognition system the geeks had sent, and as they had left the coastlines of both Spain and France in their wake and were now headed out over deep water, the Bay of Biscay was also receding in the background.

"Chief, two bogies confirmed, drones, linking to the AWACS now!" Her voice was soft, with just a hint of urgency in it, and Indigo waited to see what would happen next. They had practiced for just this eventuality, trained hard for the last day and a half, shed their egos, and worked as a team, which was now being put to the test. Indigo was on the bridge, the chief was down below at the control center, and everyone on board was now in their positions, linked by a hardwired comms system rigged by the crew.

The chief's voice, also soft and lacking any signs of stress, sped around the men and women at the speed of light via the fiber optic cable they had installed. Jam-proof and immune to any electromagnetic effect, it was old-school but proven in a thousand modern-day battles.

"Sir, two bogies confirmed. The data suggests no over-the-horizon capable weapons. Your orders?" Indigo watched as the deck repeater showed them now within 100 nautical miles of the ship and made his decision. Better to ask forgiveness than ask for permission; besides, like Sandra, he was personally offended at the number of times they had been attacked by drones and had the true soldiers' hatred of automatic human-being-less killing machines.

"They cross the 80 nautical ring. Bring them down." The irony that his missiles were automated escaped him as he watched the scope. He heard the chief's call to 'shoot', and watched the fire and smoke trail head off and up into the gloomy sky, to be swallowed in the low scud.

He could hear everyone on the bridge holding their breath, and the radar operator started counting down the seconds to impact. At Mach 4, the missiles would take just minutes to reach their targets.

"Splash one, splash two." Her voice again lacked any perceptible emotion. "Sir, AWACS confirms a good shoot and wants to know if we want their assistance."

"Thank them, ask them to backtrack the launch location, please, and report the same to the Commander. Keep a good watch. They may try again."

"Aye, sir." The entire crew relaxed but stayed at their posts, the two who had fired the long-range antiair missiles hastily reloading their tubes. These were, in the main, sailors and marines who lived to fight at sea, and all had been on the aircraft carrier when it suffered the wrath of the tsunami in the Atlantic Ocean when they had called for the sinking of the terrorist boat carrying nuclear missiles. That had been the ride of their short lives and possibly the scariest moment they had yet lived through.

The chance to give the enemy some of their own made even the most hardened of them bubble with anticipation.

"Sir, new targets bearing three five-five, 3,000 meters, 120 nautical miles. Same identification as for the previous targets."

"Chief, what's it look like to you?" Indigo watched the screen and the dots, now with targeting data overlayed. His crew were doing an excellent job, and he watched the helmsman wrestle with the wheel as a large rogue wave crashed over their bow, sending spray all over the decks. The sea state was increasing. There was no doubt there was a storm in their immediate future, and not all of it was from the enemy.

"Sir, they are salvoing, either trying really hard to sink us or run us out of ammunition." Just as the chief finished his statement, two more little dots emerged on the edge of the scope. Within seconds, the recognition software had identified them as drones, so now they had four targets.

"Range of our drone killers?" Indigo asked. He knew the answer but was using the question to get the entire crew thinking about their tactics.

"Sir, out to 25 nautical miles. Our missiles can go to 80."

"Chief, what range might their missiles have?"

"Sir, no more than 20; more likely, from the size of the drones, ten to twelve".

"Hold the long-range missiles at the ready-ready short-range antimissiles, and open up our Phalanx CIWS (Close-In Weapons System). Gunners, hold to 25 nautical miles; fire drone killers at your discretion; if they fire on us, let their missiles get in range, then take them out with the AMM's; if we have to, use the CIWS. I want them guessing at what we have and at our real capability."

"Aye, aye, sir!" rang through the network, and Indigo could hear the chief smiling all the way two decks below, in spite of clanging and bashing noises.

The cover flew off the CIWS, revealing the multi-barreled Gatling gun with its little targeting dome. No one could mistake it for anything but what it was—a deadly answer to an enemy that got closer than two and a half nautical miles without an invitation, something they were not getting issued with at this time.

Asymmetric warfare often favored the terrorists, but Indigo had worked with the Boss and Jessica long enough to understand the benefits of being totally unpredictable and striking like an enraged panther at any exposed throat.

"'*Scáthán*' this is AWACS on relay. We have the location of their base, transmitting now." And the latitude and longitude popped up on the data box, which Indigo ignored for now. His blood was up, and he was having the time of his life. Then he had a thought.

"AWACS, can you drop something on them for us?"

"Negative at this time. Target is in an urban area." Indigo clicked his microphone twice to acknowledge the transmission, then went back to his radar repeater.

"No more targets at this time. The first wave is closing on 40 nautical miles." Her voice carried no strain. Her master chief was in the seat next to her, arms folded over his broad chest, seemingly relaxed, and the young gunner on her other side concentrated on the firing controls. A ripple of excitement ran through the crew. This, in many ways, was like playing a Nintendo game! And this time, they might get to see some crash and burn debris if the bastards got close enough.

"30 nauticals." Time seemed to stand still, and the crew was holding their breath in anticipation. The overhead shield would prevent any visual contact unless the drones fired their missiles. Then they might get lucky and see the AMMs at work, or even the CIWS. No thought was given to them being impacted by any of the enemy missiles. It was beyond their comprehension to think that they could really be attacked.

"25, and the second tranche now at 60." The wine of the drone killers reverberated through the ship, then with a snap! Two ultra-blue energy rings flashed and raced up into the scud, and on the far horizon, two simultaneous sunbursts illuminated the sky.

"Splash three-splash four; targets now at 50; alert-targets changing course." The chief made an instant decision.

"Fire long-range missiles."

"Two away, Sir, tracking." Above in the bridge, Indigo heard the order and response and nodded to himself. Good tactics to not let the enemy get their weapons back. The countdown to impact continued in the background, and he watched the horizon for any sign and then put his binoculars down on the coming.

As he mentally counted off the seconds to impact, he felt the ship shudder from the sea state and called for a slower speed.

"Five splashed, six splashed, no targets."

"Great work, good call chief, nice work gunners, put everything away for the next time." And the banging and clanging reverberated through the ship as missile ports were closed, CIWS were stowed, and the ship took on its normal unthreatening appearance. Indigo acknowledged the chief as he entered the bridge, reaching for his mini.

"Really good call, Gordon. You beat me by seconds." The master chief just smiled, then stood with his legs apart, bracing against the sharp thump and crash of the hull as it tackled the growing waves. Outside, the dark sky was descending slowly to sea level as the storm built in intensity.

"You ground pounders always have to think longer than us Seabees. It's in your blood." Indigo smiled, motioned for the chief to take his position behind the helm, then moved back to the settee that ran against the bulkhead. He dialed Jessica.

"Hello Jessica, will you accept a collect call from the good ship *'Scáthán'*?"

"I might if one of your espressos went with the call." Indigo looked as happy as I had ever seen him, so something was up or had happened, and I wondered what.

"Did you get the latitude and longitude from the AWACS?" I looked at the data block sitting on the big screen, silently flashing with an unnerving blink.

"Yes, what is it?"

"The location of a base where some drones emerged from"

"Emerged, as in hatched, or flew out of, and did they attack you?" At the other end, the screen suddenly rose and dropped so rapidly that Indigo's face blurred. "Woah. What's going on?"

"Just a little rough sea, is all, and the drones were on an attack course, so we splashed them." His face lit up like a kid at a candy store, so I decided on a little background.

"Where are you?"

"About 20 hours to run." They were making good time, but if the sharp movement of Indigo's mini was any indication, they were in a rough sea.

"How many drones?"

"Six in total, three waves of two. We splashed them. I thought you might like to know." Six more drones—just how many did the terrorists have? I knew Sandra's team had accounted for two on the way in to Whiddy Island. But the bigger question is: how did they know we were sending in a ship, and who was giving the order to attack us? What was their purpose? They had to know we had the weapons and the intent to destroy them. I could not work out what they had to gain by sniping at us all the time.

"Stay safe. I'll join you at Whiddy Island when I finish with the Irish Government. Keep a bunk for me; I might like to spend some time with you. Tom has set up an HQ for us, you and the master chief included, in the hotel in the middle of the town. It's about half way up the Island, if you remember."

"We'll keep you a bunk, *'Scáthán'* out."

On the good ship, the seas continued to build, the helmsman had to move several degrees off the rhumb line to meet the white-capped waves bow-on, and the boat had slowed considerably. Indigo mentally calculated what this would do to their time line, then settled back to watch the chief and his crew work the boat. He just loved playing sailors; more, he loved watching sailors work the sea, a constant battle between nature and the desire to get somewhere on a man-made artifact.

CHAPTER THIRTY FIVE

Sandra emerged from her downtime in a sultry mood. She was rested but unhappy that she had missed all the action. The fact that it had been a 1,000 miles or more away did nothing to ease her twitchiness. Wearing a well-cut black pantsuit that effectively hid her weapon, her carry bag with her H&K slung across her chest, and her black flat-heeled boots looked casual but were anything but. She checked the temporary status board and saw that Anna was due very soon. A contingent of Israeli commandos under the command of Lieutenant Brookneal had already arrived and had been billeted at the hotel next door to the Dublin Interpol office. She was handed a mug of coffee by Shelia Robertson, the Dublin AIC (Agent in Change), who was wearing a stylish blue suit that seemed to sparkle in the room lights.

As the AIC, she had seen the myriad of details that had erupted in Jessica's wake as the ramifications of the 'soft' arrest of the Irish President hit home. The old-style landlines had practically melted under the strain of incoming calls, and she had assigned two agents full-time to manage them. Not bothering about public relations or answering questions, the conversations so far have all been one-sided.

The office was not as packed as the last time Sandra had been in there changing to meet with the Irish President, so she asked the obvious question, eyeing the two agents with phones glued to their ears, working old-style desktop computers. She wondered where they had found them.

"Thanks, Shelia, where's everybody?" The AIC pointed to where Sandra had just come from.

"Commander Riley has commandeered the ballroom next door, set it up as a temporary base, and has moved all your team there. I'm surprised you didn't trip over them on your way here." Sandra's face fell, her eyes opened wide, then she broke into a full-face smile.

"I really did need that time down. Thanks, can I take this mug with me?"

"Of course, if it doesn't come back, we'll just add it to your bill." Still smiling, Sandra made her way back to the hotel, this time working her way towards the ballroom. There were a lot of suits in the foyer, and Sandra figured they were for local police or maybe soft-clothed military. Every head followed her, and two people stood and cut her off before she could reach the stairs. They both pulled little brown folders out, showing the badge of the Garda Intelligence Bureau. She couldn't make out their names, and she unconsciously slid her hand into her carry-on bag.

"Who you be, madam, and where you be headed then, I'd be asking." The Irish lilt under normal circumstances would have been charming, but Sandra was caught holding a coffee mug in one hand and the hidden H&K in the other. The pair of agents made no overtly threatening move, but it was clear they would not let her go until they were satisfied. She handed her mug to the short female agent.

"Here, take this, please. I'll get my ID out." The woman, taken by surprise, reached out to take the mug before it hit the floor, and with a deft move across her body, Sandra pulled her credentials out and flipped them open, all the while covering the duo with her hand inside her bag.

That's how I found her at the base of the stairs, thankful I had gotten to her before she shot the local cops.

"The Inspector's with me." I spoke just loud enough for them to hear me but not loud enough to carry to all the other suits, all of whom were now watching the tableau with fascinated eyes. Several started to stand. I waved them back and walked down the staircase. I saw Sandra visibly relax, pull her hand out of her bag, and reclaim her coffee.

"Thank you," was all she said, then walked around the two open-mouthed agents to my side.

"Did you invite them to the party, or are they gate crashers?" She looked at me, then turned her head and looked back down over her shoulder. The agents hadn't moved.

"They invited themselves. I've had the entire alphabet soup drop in, local security, and Shelia and her liaisons with the Feds and the Army have quietened things down, but we don't have much time before someone does something stupid. Two of his guards came with him. We convinced them we had cause, and they have helped to an extent, but I'm waiting for the local Taoiseach—that's their equivalent of a Prime Minister—and his team to arrive so we can get a measure of control over the local situation."

"Isn't he selected by the President?"

"Yes, but he has to maintain the confidence of the three major parties to keep office, so he carries a lot of weight. In this case, I got the Boss to reach out to him and brief him on what we are doing and why. He's not happy, but understands the consequences of not playing well with us."

"Does he know of the refugee migration plans?" I turned to look at Sandra as we crested the stairs and ran into the first of our commando 104 guards. They were dressed for war, fully armed with armored vests and combat helmets, and it wasn't just for visual impact. One thing I loved about Sandra was her sharp mind and her ability to join the dots.

"I intend to find out when he arrives." She gave me one of her skeptical looks from under her eyelashes. Her mouth curled up in distaste. She flicked her bag back behind her shoulders and waved her hair back behind her ears.

"You'd have to be a moron to believe that something this big, countrywide, was a secret from the man ostensibly responsible for running it." I nodded. I agreed with her, but the telling point would be how much he knew and when, because we had a fine line in the sand as far as being able to sweep terrorists up on this case, and it all depended on whether or not they knew of the terror attacks in advance.

Was it possible to know about the plans for migrating five or six million refugee children without knowing about the attacks? To my mind, no. But I had to prove it, and in this case, we were aiming for the very top of the political tree. And the Boss had let me know in that didactic way he had that we were being watched by a lot of very important, powerful, and angry people whose countries were laying in ruins and were looking for a target to vent their wrath on.

"Where have you got him stored?"

"In a private room annexed to the ballroom, under guard, we have commandeered this entire floor, with orders to hold at any cost.

"Do we have enough people to do that?"

"Just. But I'm counting on the locals letting it play out, at least until we have to move him, then it might be a different matter."

"But you've got the admiral on speed dial and marines on Whiddy Island."

"Bridget's already had a heart attack on giving us what we asked for, but I'm sure you can talk her around if we need more green on the ground." Sandra looked at me as if I was crazy and laughed in my face.

"You're kidding!" I laughed back at her and patted her on the shoulder as we reached another pair of commando 104. They opened the door into the ballroom, which now resembled a poorly laid-out garage sale. Equipment boxes were stacked haphazardly all over the floor. Huge computer screens sat on top of flimsy-looking banquet tables, and Luigi and his geeks looked like they were having the time of their lives.

Everyone was carrying weapons with a casualness that suggested comfortable familiarity, a good sign under the circumstances. And to Sandra's surprise, in one dark corner, a small coffee machine puffed away. I saw Sandra's reaction and smiled.

"A gift from the hotel catering division."

"God bless Irish sentimentality. What's your plan?" I looked at her. The rest had at least removed the dark bags from under her eyes. There was a little of the original sparkle in them, and her posture was relaxed yet watchful.

"When Anna gets here, we'll start a proper interrogation, develop the time line, search the documents, and do an analysis of who knew what and when. I've asked the Boss to ask Arie for more support from the 104, and they have two squads flying out as we speak."

"Why didn't you go directly to Arie?"

"I wanted the request at a government-to-government level, because if this turns out the way I think it will, we're going to need big brass balls and a lot of support to get the President to Israel to be interred." Sandra nodded. She had a similar thought, but being on Jessica's shoulder as she had been for over a month had taught her she was always ten steps ahead of everyone else. She modeled the possible outcome in her mind's eye, ran through the resources and timing, and nodded to herself.

"And by any chance would the 104 be arriving on an aircraft big enough to carry the President and his supporters, plus some of our people, all the way home?" I just smiled at my padawan. As usual, she had put the dots together.

"I want you to interrogate the president's cohort, singly, establish a time line, I'm leaving Anna the President, then she can help you clean up, and I'll take the Taoiseach and his crew. I've made it clear to the President's guards that we mean no physical harm, and we will need access to documents and offices, so we'll use the 104 to provide support as we go. And I want Shelia to lead the charge in the president's office; she's local, knows the ground, so to speak, and I suspect there will be less resistance to her locally." Sandra nodded, her eyes turning to the huge screen that was now carrying the status update.

"When in hell did that happen?" she asked, her voice a full octave louder than normal. I saw she was pointing to the drone attack on our ship.

"Three hours ago, six splashed. They came in waves. Tom's guns and Indigo's trigger finger did the rest." Sandra's eyes squinted, her distaste for robot weapons an overwhelming visceral dread.

"That makes the case against the president even stronger. Do we know where they launched from?" I nodded. That was the good news amid the threat of attacks.

"Yes. The AWACS has painted the location. They can't drop anything on it due to the potential for collateral damage. I'm thinking about how to resource an attack." Sandra nodded. She was only too aware of how stretched we were, but the excitement started to build up in her gut as she envisioned leading the charge to blow the drone base to hell and back. Vengeance would be hers!

"No." I looked at her. Reading her mind was easy. She had a feral grin on her face, and her body had gone on alert. She turned to me, a sly grin sliding across her pretty face, as if to seduce me into letting her go play with the drones.

"No." I shook my head to make the point. "We'll clean them up once we know where we stand here. Indigo has the weapons he needs, Tom has his thanks to your convoy getting to the Island, the drone killers are excellent, and the ship has long-range anti-air missiles that have already proven their worth."

She went into a full sulk and almost pouted. I just laughed at her.

"Hey, you got to play with them. Let someone else have some fun." The disappointed look on her face reminded me of a child denied candy at the fair, but I knew she would bounce back, and as I moved my mind to more important things, Anna and her team arrived, escorted by a pair of commando 104 and our AIC. Sandra immediately deserted me and moved to Anna, giving her a massive hug, embarrassing the commandos, and drawing a wan smile from Shelia.

"She's being mean to me," she said sotto voce. I ignored her and took Anna's hand.

"Get any sleep on the plane?" she nodded.

"Plenty. I understand you have ratcheted up the political trauma?" Her smile belied any attack, and knowing her, she wasn't even being sarcastic. She was the number-two FBI agent in the USA and held her position for a very good reason. She was beyond excellent at her job and had been of invaluable help to us since the first attacks.

"Just a little. Let's get you a coffee, and we'll talk about it." We sat down at what would usually be used for a buffet, a wide wooden table that had bent legs as if holding the table top up was too much of an effort. Some kind soul had put a starched white tablecloth over it, which the geeks then insulted with all manner of technological trash. I brushed some of the debris away, making room for us. I turned and invited the two Special Agents with Anna to sit as well. They might be note-takers, but I wanted everyone on the same page, and if Anna had selected them, then they were some of the sharpest tools in the FBI box.

"What we have here is political dynamite. The Irish President and perhaps the government as well would appear to be involved with the terrorists. They have a national plan to migrate some five or six million refugees and house them in vacant homes and new-build ones similar to Helena. Just to recap, the ship we confiscated that had the rail gun and nuclear shells in the Mediterranean was modified here in a Dublin shipyard.

"We had a little altercation with mercenary terrorists at a place called Pollatomish, up in county Mayo—they were in the process of loading nuclear shells with fissionable material in a huge underground facility. We shut down an environmental plant over at Whiddy Island. It was building panels and nanites in four or five flavors—I'll let Amira fill you in on the details of the nanites.

"The Island also had a store of nuclear shells and containers of nanites. We cleared the Island, were attacked two or three times in the process, with light casualties, and there have been at least two attempts by women we have identified as likely terrorists to get back to the Island. Incidentally, both women were in the company of the President when we first met with him. What have I forgotten, Sandra?" She leaned forward and took control of the table with her body language effortlessly, a skill I admired.

"We tracked a vessel, captained by one Maribelle Assiano."

"She was the partner of Rena Niele, the psychologist we took into custody in Roanoke." The look on Anna's face was pure intensity, her eyes closed to little slits.

"Yes, she was. She created some mischief getting out into the Atlantic from the Belfast area with nuclear materials, and your navy, with the help of my excellent commander here, took care of her, but not before she sank a ship with five thousand refugee children on it." Anna looked shocked, and I heard the two agents suck in their breath. Sandra looked pleased with herself after getting such a visceral reaction from the FBI. She was a terror, but she was my terror, so I let it go.

"I knew about the navy action. We lost a destroyer and her crew, but no one mentioned the refugees." I thought on that, and I wondered why the admiral had left that out of his report. It had been in mine, but maybe that hadn't gotten to the US yet. I would have to think about that as well. It might mean our communications had broken down somewhere.

"We also have proof that the panels produced at Whiddy Island are already being shipped and installed in a small town north of here, Dundalk. We have an agent onsite there now. He has reported an anomaly with the supply of electricity, which we haven't yet run to ground.

"And if that's not enough for you, we confiscated nuclear shells from three locations, and we traced several calls from Aberfoyle to a location here in Ireland, from someone we believe to be high up in the command chain. And there was talk about an experiment here in Ireland, facilitated by a group of women led by a 'Katrina', with a 'Lily, Lilian, and Else' in tow. They conducted whatever the test was here in Ireland, then moved onto Spain, France, Scotland, and England, where they played around with shuttered nuclear reactors.

"We have a team backtracking that now." The reaction of the agents was open-mouth shock. Their eyes glazed over as the information sank in. Anna just looked at me, smiled at Sandra, and clasped her hands together on the tabletop. I couldn't help but notice the bright red fingernails, most unlike her.

"You've been busy little beavers, haven't you both?" Sandra laughed and sat back in her chair.

"Hey, that's not all. We've tracked the so-called test team to a port on the west coast called Killala Bay, specifically a small village name of Inishcrone, or Irishcrone if you believe the locals. Fay's there now with a contingent of Tom's SEALS, waiting for the arrival of Siobhan O'Cleary, who, if you remember, set the whole nuclear thing off when we picked her face up from a satellite picture taken over Afghanistan." Anna held her hand up to stop Sandra for a moment.

"Wait. She got blown up in an aircraft crash with Malik Badawi in Iran."

My turn to bring her up to date. "No, she didn't. She managed to run and ended up on an Island called Socotra, in the Gulf of Aden. Paired up with a 'Crissy', partner of 'Katrina' before she emerged here in Ireland. And before you ask, no clue what they are doing on that Island. It's on my to-do list, but at the bottom at present.

"Where's Tom?"

"Setting up a base for us on Whiddy Island."

"Bob?"

"Sitting on our head terrorist 'Freya' in Scotland with his team."

"Indigo?"

"Piloting the ship we confiscated in the Mediterranean to Whiddy Island."

"And Fay is in Inishcrone."

"Yes."

"My God, you're covering a hell of a lot of territory, and it's all related to the original terrorist attacks?"

"Yes."

"Does Julius, Frank, and Roger know all of this?"

"You didn't know about the refugee ship being sunk, so I'd have to say no at this point."

"Bridget?"

"Same story. Whether our reports are being censored somewhere, I don't know, but I intend to find out."

"You need an army." I looked at her. Her face had lost its shine, and genuine concern had replaced her happy smile. Her eyes were like pinpoints, and the crease between her eyebrows stood out like a series of linear sand dunes in the desert. I needed to calm her down and get her focused on the immediate problem. Was the Irish President in bed with the terrorists or not?

"Anna, yes, we have a lot of moving parts, but I'm confident we have a handle on it. We're moving on things one at a time. We have excellent support from yourselves, the Italians, and the Israelis. We're fine for the moment. If that changes, you'll be the first to know. I need you focused on the President; is he, or isn't he in bed with the terrorists?"

"If everything you have listed is, or has been, happening here, it is hard to understand how he could be ignorant of the terrorist plans. And as you know, knowledge alone is sufficient to get him locked up in a concrete cage." I nodded. She had the right of it—just one piece of data that showed he knew there would be attacks, no matter that he didn't know the details or even the when, and he was mine. My train of thought was derailed by one of our commando 104, moving swiftly up to me and whispering in my ear.

"Comandante, il primo ministro e la sua gente sono qui. Dove li mettiamo?"

"Metteteli nella seconda cabina, date loro del caffè, sorvegliate la porta."

"Sì, comandante, subito." The look on the FBI agents' faces told me neither spoke Italian, so I translated for them.

"Our Prime Minister and his entourage have arrived. I've tucked them away out back. We need to plan our attack." Anna nodded, pulled her mini out, and looked at me. I signaled to

Sandra, who swiped a copy of our summary over to Anna. She looked at it and nodded.

"I want a few days with my team to digest all this. How do you intend to get a timeline?"

"Sandra will take the President's cohort. I'll take the Prime Minister. When you finish with the President, move to anyone who's left in Sandra's group, then move onto mine if need be. Between us we should get a solid timeline, and to help with that I'm sending our AIC with our geeks to the palace to take all the data we can get our hands on." She nodded, I stood, Sandra mirrored my movements, and I left Anna to her own devices. As we moved to the door, a pair of the 104 moved with us, and I realized our young Lieutenant had worked out the disposition of his forces. My usual Italian studs weren't intimidated in the slightest. Simply put themselves between us and the 104. I held my hand up, nodded to the guard on the right, and told him what should have been obvious.

"Thanks, we have our own security. Let your Lieutenant know." He bobbed his head and marched off. As they were from the 104's original team, I had jumped and fought with both of them, so they knew me and what to expect. I was about to start out again when Anna called.

"Jessica, one minute, I want to change the interrogation structure." Sandra and I walked back to the table but stood rather than sat. The two agents looked uncomfortable. Anna had demonstrated a familiarity with me that they hadn't anticipated, and I suspected that the sheer magnitude of what we had to do had hit them hard. But once again, if they had been picked by Anna, they were potentially the best, so I did something I would never normally have done.

Looking straight at them, one hand on Sandra's shoulder, and in the softest voice I could manage, I told them why.

"When you've shed blood with someone, using their first name is allowable, as rank has no sway when the bullets start flying." They both looked a little uncomfortable but nodded. I suspected that, like most FBI agents, they had never drawn their weapons in anger, something I envied them for. I gently pushed Sandra into her seat, took my own, and folded my hands on the table top, making it clear that Anna had the room. She looked at me, smiled, then grinned and bobbed her head in acknowledgement. We really did know each other!

"Thanks, Jessica and Sandra. I want one or both of you in with me and the President, and I also want to take the Prime Minister. Swap around between the two, check them off against each other. Same as we did with Mohammad bin Azaria and 'Helen'. I nodded. I had wanted her objectivity in the interrogations, and the conversations she had referred to had all worked extraordinarily well.

"Sheila has set up multiple rooms. Take your pick. How do you want to handle the underlings?" Her open-eyed gaze skimmed the two agents, then focused back on me.

"I'd like to start with Ron and Richard as a team. I'm after the time line. The geeks will no doubt bring back tons of data we'll have to mine; that will take some time. And there's a major issue we need to focus on."

"And that is?' Sandra asked, her voice as soft as mine. Her respect for Anna was absolute, and she knew why I had insisted on getting her over here to chat with the President.

"If you remember, when you cleaned up 'Helen's' lair, you also took a number of women in who had been hacking into our data bases loading false IDs, social security data, and the like. There's no way Ireland could manage such a significant migration without documentation of some sort. The EU, for one, would arc up and create a massive political storm. Where are their computers, and who's doing the work?" I sat very still. There goes that operational blindness again. This was so basic I felt sick not having thought of it before.

"Hopefully, Shelia and the geeks will ferret that out." She nodded, letting me off the hook. I decided to confront my mistakes head-on.

"What else have I missed?" She looked at me with a wry grin, her hands now clasped on the table top again, her posture relaxed.

"Not much, and I don't think you missed the ID issue so much as had it far back in your mind. But if we want a timeline, establishing when they started to prepare for the migration may tell us about a lot of other things." I nodded. She was absolutely right, but she was being polite, and I mentally thanked her for not making me feel more stupid than I already did. Not being a geek meant that I often got to the geeky bits a lot later than others. It was a bad habit I'd also have to work on. Sandra put her hand on my arm to stop me from talking again.

"Anna, have you given any thought to the family model they might use?" Another great question that might tell us even more about the time line.

"Well, Helena, Roanoke, and New Zealand have depended on an existing family unit to adopt one or two refugee children. I can't see that happening here in Ireland. They have over a million empty houses and not a lot of spare families. Also, in the States, the mass migration out of the big cities and towns due to the terrorist attacks and social unrest helped with that, and the bulk resettlement established a baseline for the refugee intakes."

"You're saying that because, say, 10,000 families migrated to the Helena area out of the big cities, the refugee intake was easier to promote and manage?"

"In a nutshell, yes. The economic drivers were the extraordinary low cost of a new home, the provision of free education and medical care, not just for the refugee children but any natural children already in the family, plus the financial stipend for each child adopted, and the process became irresistible. Remember, we have an FBI agent as one of the adopting families, so we have very accurate information, on Helena at least." I remembered that Agent Vernon had brought a house and adopted two refugee children, and his reports were nothing but glowing. I tilted my head to one side, thinking through the whole opportunity here in Ireland.

"According to the socioeconomic data I read, Ireland has been losing young people for the past 50 years, as fast as they turn 18. The population is as low as it has even been, so I can see the benefit of growing the community. Do we think that refugee adults might be involved this time around?" Anna shook her head.

"Don't know. I only started to think about this on the way over here. But that same data you reviewed indicated that agriculture only makes up two percent of their GDP and that the services sector is very big. Pharmaceuticals, technology, medical devices, and financial services with food and beverage make up the rest. And, can you guess what the common denominator is in all of those?'" I thought hard, then saw the light go on in Sandra's eyes.

"Power." Anna nodded.

"And according to that data again, Ireland has a national grid that runs out of Belfast. They were dependent on importing oil and gas until the attacks, and only forty percent of their power comes from wind and solar."

"So they've lost sixty percent of their power supply?" I asked. Sandra nodded. And again, I saw the light bulb go on, and she started to vibrate, as she did whenever she got particularly energized.

"You know, I'm having an epiphany. What's the biggest unanswered question way up there in Dundalk?" I looked at her, thought through what brother Francis had said in his last report, and the light bulb went on for me.

"They've got a new power source!" She nodded, looked at Anna, and waved her hands around a lot, her excitement palpable.

"Anna, we've got the world's most wonderful and gentle agent up in Dundalk, a member of Stefarino's monks. Do you remember him from your earlier visit?" Anna looked at the two agents, mindful of what no one was talking about on either side of the Atlantic, and almost prevaricated. She was saved from herself by the arrival of Shelia and Luigi, escorted by two of the 104.

"Commander, we have the Red Notices, and we're off to the Palace and the administration building in the city. We have solid support. Do you want us to report progressively?" I gave that some thought, worked through Anna's change in strategy, then nodded my head.

"Yes, please, but only for data relating to the timeline." I pointed to Luigi. "I missed the whole computer/records ID thing. Look for how they are doing it and how long they have been at it, please." He nodded, a big smile plastered on his face, black hair curling over his collar, and turned on his heel to follow our AIC, looking as happy and relaxed as I had ever seen him. All signs of his earlier tiredness were gone, so he must have gotten a good rest somewhere. Anna used the interruption to change the subject, ending any possible further conversation involving Stefarino and the monks.

We looked at each other, Sandra picked up the ball, and she brought us back on point.

"Power. That was what the experiment was about." I shook my head.

"We need proof before we leap in that direction. We'll get the report from the nuke power plants soon. That might be illuminating—and I apologize for the pun! It was unintentional." Everyone at the table laughed. Sensing the tension had lessened, Anna asked the one question that was at the forefront of my mind.

"Even if it is, how will that help their case here in Ireland? Moving five or six million people of any persuasion is a monumental exercise that will take years, and that's in normal times, and these are anything but." Her question hung in the air like a huge black balloon ready to burst and cover everyone with sticky stuff.

"Well, if you look at Ireland's GDP, it's the second highest in all of Europe. That may have changed after the attacks, but Ireland is also one of the most expensive countries in the EU-lack of competition. If you take the Helena model, every 100 families that adopt have five million USD to put back into the economy.

And that's at one child being adopted. I can't see that model coming here, the migration is too low, so they have another economic model. But either way, it's definitely a pay-to-play process, and if you do the sums around supporting an extra five or six million people here it's easy to see the attraction to the government." Anna made good points, but I was getting twitchy about our guests, and my need for information.

"Okay, let's leave that for another time, or until we have more information. Any reason why we can't start asking questions to the people we think have the answers?" I looked around the table. My tonality had caused the two FBI agents to smile. Even Sandra was leering at me. I stood. No one spoke, so I moved away towards the door.

"I'll be twenty minutes before I'm ready for round one. See you soon." I turned to Sandra and looked directly at her. I was about to spoil her day.

"Get dressed in field kit, khakis, no vest, visible weapons. I want to offset the FBI suits and make a point to the President. Get copies of the Red Notices. This might still be a police action, but we have military support, and I want to shove that in his face. And if you wear those ridiculous frilly knickers, make sure we can't see them." She just smirked, knowing I was poking at her because I could, not because I needed to.

Our Italian guards cleared a path through the crowd, which had doubled since I had gone upstairs, and I suspected that if trouble broke out, it would start down here in the foyer. As if to underline my intuition, Sandra had her hand back in her carry-on bag, no doubt fondling her favorite toy.

NO CUENTO CUENTOS

The Vandellòs power plant looked exactly the same as it had for the last 55 years. The inspection team, this time a legitimate one, poured over the outer buildings, and the inner guts of the reactors and turbines, or at least as much of them as they could get access to, seeing that the silver nanite crud covered more than eighty percent of every internal surface.

They were professionals from the Atomic Energy Commission, as well as three members of the senior management team of the site when it had last been functional, two months ago. Areas of the massive dome had been searched using the latest in detection equipment, and the entire volume of the interior had been electronically scanned and mapped.

The team had compared the data to the plans and drawings that had been generated during its long life to locate any differentials.

There was evidence that someone had been around the number three generator, as the footprints left in the dust had been very clear. A team of specialized mechanics had been called in, and they had taken two days two laboriously break down the generator and its massive turbine as far as they were able, given that, once again, the silver nanite crud covered nearly every moving part and most of the static ones.

And nothing that was covered in nanites, even using lasers cutters and diamond saws, revealed so much as a scratch, as the nanites refused to budge.

Of course, being engineers and inspectors, the logical approach was the only one they knew, so they ignored the deep water inlets, the channels that had been driven up into the phased machinery, the turbine shafts, and the outlets and pipes that originally carried the carbon dioxide cooling gas.

Theirs was very much a top-down inspection, by the book, which several of the team members were quick to point out they had contributed to the writing of.

Their approach was flawless, competent, and became the model that other teams used in France, Scotland, and England to rip apart their own reactors, looking for what the women terrorist team had supposedly done.

Frustratingly, none of the teams found a single clue, other than in some locations, according to security, they had spent three days, and in England five.

The guards were only too happy to hand over the access paperwork they had religiously filed, and the documents proved to be world class forgeries.

That was the only negative element in any of their reports, and it was soon just passed off as an aberration. No physical evidence, therefore no change to the plants. A summary reached Interpol HQ in Lyons, and was immediately passed on to Commander Riley, with a note asking why she had initiated the searches.

CHAPTER THIRTY SEVEN

I had our Italians in their dress blues, which were black, impressive red stripes all the way up to their arm pits, patent leather Sam Brown belts, holsters, and shoes gleaming in the overhead lights, and the SEALS in full battle dress, looking drab and dull by comparison, including vests and weapons slung across their chests. The 104 were in soft clothes, beautiful Italian suits of varying colors, mostly grays and blacks. No one could confuse them with civilians, you only had to look into their eyes to see the controlled focus and ice lurking just behind their eyelids.

And their battle-hardened body postures exuded an overt threat.

Perfect.

I had scattered them amongst the people congregating downstairs, as well as along the hallway leading from the rooms where we had temporarily stored the President and the Prime Minister to where we were having our 'chats'. The eclectic mix of armed and seemingly unarmed warriors was meant to put everyone off balance, create a little uncertainty in the minds of any potential threat. They had our backs, of that I was absolutely certain.

I had the scene set, called for the President, had him escorted into the first room, very politely, it was still a 'soft' arrest, but that could change in a heartbeat, and secretly, I was really hoping we could take him away in chains, and lock him away in a dark concrete box for the rest of his life.

The primary reason I had asked for Anna to conduct the interrogations was that I felt I had lost my objectivity somewhere during our on-again off-again campaign here in Ireland. The stakes were too high to make a mistake.

The Israeli lieutenant was on the door, looking like a super fit basketball player wearing an expensive suit. He stood well over six feet, and had that lithe grace of an athlete at his peak, and as he opened the door his coat swung back revealing the automatic weapon he had slung beneath it.

Also not an accident.

Anna and I stood when he entered, and we had had lounge chairs brought in and a small coffee table on which sat a teapot, a coffee warmer, and cups and saucers, all decorated with the finery of the catering service for the hotel. Little green four leaf clovers, linked by a gold band.

"Sir, may I pour you a tea, it's Oolong, which we understand is your preference." I dipped my head in false servility, keeping my eyes on his the whole time.

'Mr. President, I'm Supervisory Senior Special Agent Bernstein of the FBI, and I believe you've met Commander Riley of Interpol, the head of Section five." Anna reached for his hand while I poured his tea, then handed him his cup. Anna and the President sat, the President looking a little off balance, so I continued with my womanly duties, pouring coffee for us. I had a feeling it wouldn't be the only cup I'd need to get through this. Anna took her cup, placed it delicately on the table.

"Mr. President, as you were informed when you were brought here, we are investigation actions by senior people in your government that may show you were complicit in the recent terror attacks on the Vatican, the Wailing Wall, and other targets of opportunity. And as your barristers have no doubt told you, under the Terrorist Laws as amended in 2022, no legal representation is accorded to anyone charged under the act." Anna's voice was smooth, almost welcoming. Mine was the exact opposite.

"Ireland is a signatory to the UN Charter, is it not?" he gave me a stare that would cause most people to shrivel up and die, I just smiled at him.

"As a charter member of the UN, you would have taken part in the voting on the Terrorist Laws, isn't that so?" Another deadly stare, also allowed to go through to the catcher.

"Either way, we know what we know, and really, we only want to know one thing from you. Drink your tea, it will get cold." He put his tea cup back on the saucer with such force I was surprised it didn't break to bits.

"Commander, or whatever your name is, I'm the President of Ireland, and you will afford me the proper respect!" he shouted out, spittle flying across the room like little shining stars. Good, I was getting to him. Anna, playing good cop, tried to calm things down.

"Sir, I apologize for my companion, she's a little upset at the number of times her people have been attacked here in Ireland" Anna let that statement hang, and so did I, wanting to see his reaction.

"I'm not responsible for any attacks on you. You had our Army working with you, what more can we do?" he wore his anger like armor, I could see the beginnings of a halo forming over his head. Self-belief was a wonderful, powerful thing, but for it to work to maximum effect there had to be absolute truth behind it, or the back of your brain where the beast resides will betray you subconsciously by your body language. As it was doing here with the President. The micro movement around his eyes and his constant jittering gave him away. I took immediate advantage of it.

"When did you learn the attacks would take place?" he spluttered again, started to reach for his tea, stopped himself, glared at me, shook his head.

"Ridiculous! I never had any knowledge of any terrorist attacks until they happened, just like the rest of the country." Interesting, I hadn't mentioned the word 'terrorist'.

"When did you start working on your million home project?" he spluttered, pulled a silk handkerchief out of his pocket, wiped his forehead where beads of sweat had started to gather, ready to flood his face.

"Three or Four years ago, when we were approached by a Aid Agency, whose proposal was to migrate refugee children to Ireland, under the banner of a beneficial trust. It was an economic windfall for us, and good for the refugees."

"So three or four years ago, you started to plan to migrate five or six million refugee children for no better reason than you were asked to do so?" he looked a little shell shocked, not sure of the arc of the interrogation. He just nodded and put his handkerchief away.

"When did you give the terrorist permission to build their factory on Whiddy Island?"

I..." he started to answer, then played back in his head the whole question.

"Never. The trust offered the funds to build an environmental plant, our university did some research, and as Whiddy Island was already being used to store oil, as part of our strategic reserve, and had good access to the mainland, it was chosen to be the site."

"Did you ever go there and inspect the site?" he puffed up, obviously thinking he was on safe ground.

"Yes, of course, it was a big project for us, an important one in our million home resettlement plan."

"Why?"

"The people running it said they would make very efficient solar panels and power packs for all the empty homes we have, making them independent of the centralized electricity supply."

"When did you give the terrorists permission to build an underground munitions factory in Pollatomish?" he blinked so rapidly I could almost feel the wind wash my face. Again, he opened his mouth to speak, his brain caught up with it and he snapped it shut. He waved his manicured hand though his silky hair, the evil look he was sending my way was now getting sharper edges, and I almost smiled at him again.

"The only construction at Pollatomish I know about was the gas line that was being built in from the coast."

"Is that right. Tell me, what did you make of the drone hangar and launching facility on Whiddy Island?" He sat back, very unsure on how to answer me.

"Mr. President, we have absolute proof that a drone launched from your Whiddy Island shot down an American corporate jet over the Atlantic. You claim to know nothing about that?" Again, the calm of Anna's voice offset my acidic one, and he was getting more and more irritated by our questioning.

"Did you ever inspect the drone facility?" His eyes opened like saucers, very unsure of his ground.

"Yes."

"Did you ever ask what it was for?" His eyes glazed over, he saw the trap, and simply didn't know how to avoid it.

"It was explained to me that the drones would be used for communication, and tracking the progress of the installation of the panels."

"When you toured the plant, did you ever ask about the nanites? What they were going to be used for?" he visibly blanched, his gut was telling him one thing, his mind quite another. I piled it on.

"When did you meet Lady O'Brian Flattery? Or Liddy Cochran, or Mary MacDonald?" he suddenly sat up straight in his chair, pulled his coat down at the sides, folded his hands in his lap.

"Lady Flattery was introduced to me by the Aid Agency, four years ago, as the representative of the major Trust Fund that would pay for the migration of the refugees. She also took over as CEO of the Environmental Plant after her husband died."

"And Cochran and MacDonald?"

"Never heard of them, don't know who you are talking about." I looked at him straight into his eyes, he must remember the first meeting with Sandra and I, the two women were sitting at his side in his big royal office. They hadn't been introduced, and we had seen that as deliberate. We had since sussed out their names, and established they were most likely part of the women terrorist group. The lack of backgrounds and family histories pointed to that conclusion.

"The two women in your office when we first met. You don't know them?" I asked in all innocence. "They've been using your name, and the weight of your office, to get access to Whiddy Island since we shut it down. I might mention the second time they tried was a run-a-round, and they ended being kicked off the northern beach by our troops." His skin had gone a lovely shade of gray, he probably hadn't been caught out in so many lies since he had left boarding school. I decided to play my biggest card, and pulled out the copy of the Red Notice our AIC was serving on his people and the government employees working on the million home project. And the central data center.

"Mr. President, this is the Red notice we have issued, covering the retrieval of all data from all sources concerning your little migration project. If we find any discrepancies between your answers and the data, you'll end up in a concrete cage." His face, which had turned pasty, suddenly flushed red, and he stood clutching his fists, leaning across the table to get in my face.

"Why are you so consumed by the need for years of documentation when all you have to do it let us get Whiddy Island back up in production, and we can resettle five or six million refugee children and clean the camps out once and for all?" Spittle flew out of his mouth again, this time almost reaching me, and I held my hand up in defense.

"I could do that, but the cost has been too high for the rest of the world. Sixty-maybe seventy million dead by now, millions more displaced, economies ruined, the societal fabric shattered in a way it may never get back to normal." I shook my head, this was the problem I faced. The outcome of the attacks was a wonderful program to get refugee children into homes and out of the camps. Unfortunately, the terrorists, in creating camp-like conditions for the rest of the world, had manufactured such a shock the world was bruised, battered and disjointed as never before. Not something I or Interpol for that matter, could let go, or justify in the interests of the children, even as my heart bled for them.

"On the door." Anna and I left, leaving the President to his now cold Oolong tea, and the chance to reflect on his position. I stood outside the second door, leaned back against the wall, took a very deep breath.

"He knew." Anna stroked my arm, facing me, calming me a little. She nodded her head.

"Yes, he knew, but now we have to prove it." I nodded, due process was there for a reason, but it didn't make me feel any better.

"It's going to really piss me off if he slides because of a technicality." Anna rubbed my arm a little harder.

"Take a breath. Let's go talk to the Prime Minister, and see what he has to say." I did what she said, sucked in a huge lung full of air, dribbled it out slowly through my toes, rotated my shoulders, stretched my neck. Looked the Lieutenant in the eye, smiled, and nodded at the second door. Throughout the entire exercise, our two Italian guards had stood perfectly still, eyes focused on a spot on the wall, pretending nothing untoward was happening. It didn't worry me, they had seen me melt down before, it was nothing new.

We entered the second room, where the Prime Minster sat, he acknowledged our approach, and stood. A short, well-dressed man, close cropped tan hair, clean shaven, white starched shirt with some sort of regimental tie. His smile was warm and genuine.

"Commander, and I assume the SSSA FBI agent from the States?" his voice was well modulated, and his entire body shouted warmth and welcome, a sharp contrast to what we had just endured next door.

"Sir, I am Agent Bernstein, thank you for your kind welcome. Has it been explained to you why you are here?" he nodded, and gestured for us to sit. He had utilized the tea set, so I leaned forward and poured from the coffee warmer, and handed a cup to Anna.

"Well, as I understand it, you are interested in the details surrounding the Environmental Plant on Whiddy Island, and our million homes refugee migration plan, is that correct?" I decided to match his calm presence, and looked at him over the rim of my cup, which I was nearly inhaling the smell was so gorgeous. Who knew? Great coffee in Ireland!

"Sir, who briefed you on this meeting?" he looked a little confused, then turned his head to one side.

"My office received an official invitation from your Interpol office here in Dublin, and it mentioned the reason for the meeting. My people sought clarity, and were given a list of possible topics. Then my office learned that you had also invited our President to a meeting, and we learned from his people your intent." He straightened his head, looked directly at me, his face calm, his tone measured.

"There was also mention of the President being taken into custody, but when we spoke to your office they denied that, and said that the President had gone with you willingly. Is that so?" Now I faced the consequences of our earlier actions, and all my instincts were telling me that this man, the Taoiseach, or Prime Minister of Ireland, was asking for an honest answer. I sensed no hostility in his questions, so I laid it all out for him.

"Mr. Prime Minister, we brought the President here because there is concern that he or his office may have colluded with terrorists, in that he or his office knew in advance of the terror attacks, and did nothing about it. Under the Terrorist Laws as modified in 2022, such knowledge would earn him a concrete cage. My apologies for any rudeness, but I have to ask you some of the same questions we asked the President." He still looked calm, but now a little concerned. He sat a little straighter in his chair, and Anna picked up where I had left off.

"Sir, when did you become aware of the million home refugee project?" he smiled a little smile, more like a grin, and relaxed.

"I was elected into this office back in 2022, and my predecessor briefed me and my staff on taking office that the Irish government had been approached by an Aid Agency, funded by a Trust, to willingly accept five to six million refugee children and their support personnel. We had set up a new department to look at the issue, in fact that department has all the documentation involved in the plan. My 2IC chairs it, and he reports to me weekly now, it used to be monthly but we're getting closer to the arrival of the first tranche." Now it all made sense, at least some of the logistics required for such a huge movement of people.

"Were you aware of the Environmental Plant on Whiddy Island?" he looked confused for a moment, then his eyes cleared, and he really did smile.

"Yes, wonderful thing that, although I don't pretend to understand the science, the idea of all those empty houses getting their own electricity supply independent of the national grid is a god send." It was my turn to look confused, I sensed no guile in this man, so I asked another question we wanted an answer to.

"Did your environmental people sign off on Whiddy Island?"

"Yes, without hesitation. Everything is one hundred percent recyclable, there is zero waste in their manufacturing process, and they use natural sea water and sand for all their ingredients-if that's what you call them?" he looked a little bemused.

"I should say I'm a lawyer, not a scientist, so my technical knowledge is very thin I'm afraid, but some of my people in the department can give you chapter and verse if you need it."

"Thank you, Prime Minister, did you ever visit Whiddy Island?"

"Yes, about a year ago, they were just finishing off a set of panels, it was fascinating to watch." I nodded, it would have been to any outsider, and being honest, I had to admit what the women had done with Amira's nanotechnology was amazing, to say the least.

"What deadline were, or are, you working to for the first tranche of refugees?" His eyes brightened at the thought, here was a man that genuinely cared, it would be a real problem for me if it turned out he was complicit in the terrorist attacks.

"In three months we expect the first thousand to land up north, their homes are being prepared as we speak, from panels that were moved from the plant some time ago. I am not up to date on where they are up to, but again, one of the project managers will have all that detail." I nodded, as if accepting everything he said at face value.

"When you visited the Island, did you see any drone activity?" His eyes open in question, he shook his head.

"No, not to my knowledge." So I threw my curve ball at him, to see if he would swing or flinch.

"What was your reaction when your strategic oil reserved turned to silver sludge?" he looked shocked, not the reaction I expected.

"We only learned of that five or six weeks ago, we lost all the imported oil and gas supplies for our power generation eight weeks ago, and I can tell you, it was a real shock. In fact, the result of the terror attacks here in Ireland had been quite mild up until that time. Luckily we have renewables that are at least keeping the lights on, and a few peat fired generators to help. We also have a lot of electric cars. But the loss of our reserves was a massively disruptive event."

"How did you find out about the loss of your oil?"

"Lady Flattery informed us, we sent inspectors, and they confirmed a silver sludge had consumed all our oil. We passed the information onto my counterpart in Belfast, informed the President's office, and the UK."

"When did you become aware that the first silo had been emptied, and turned into a store for nuclear shells, nanites, and linked by tunnel to the drone facility?" he moved his head back, his eyes compressing, furrows popping out on his forehead.

"What? Not possible. Our technicians would have spotted that in their monthly surveys."

"Very possible, we recovered nuclear-capable shells, nanites, drones and weapons, and I was there myself." I sat back, I was not reading anything but genuine shock, he was telling the truth, and I suspect he had been as much a victim of the terrorists as everyone else had been.

"How do your inspectors check the contents-determine the amount of oil in each tank?" he looked a little uneasy as the implications of my statement sunk in. He rubbed his hand over his head, ruffling his hair in an unconscious gesture.

"We have automated gauges, and every so often the engineers use a laser device to ping the tanks."

"From the top?" he looked curious, as if I had asked a really simple question.

"Yes, of course, the only way into those tanks is either through the manhole cover on top, or in through the outlet pipes which are underground." I nodded, we had checked that, and found it to be true for every tank except the first one. The inflow pipes and valves were all seaside and visible to all.

"Did you think to ask Lady O'Brian or any of her staff what the silver sludge was?" he looked bewildered, as if I had missed a step somewhere.

"No, why would we? They were not affected because they generate one hundred percent of their own power. Not tapping into the national grid was a condition of their approval in the first place."

"How many people are in the department that is managing the relocation of the refugees?" he looked startled, the rapid change in topics was getting him unsettled. I picked him for a straight, logical thinker, someone who wanted their arguments one at a time, and in order, which is why I was changing my line of attack so much, and bouncing all over the map.

"It has a director, a deputy, both of whom report to my department, and I think at the last count around sixty or seventy staff."

"How closely do you work with the President or his people on this?" he looked thoughtful again, then looking me straight in the eyes, unknowingly sentencing his President to a concrete cage.

"If memory serves me, we have only had the same contacts with the President's staff for the three years or so-two women, one from the Aid Agency that is sponsoring the entire migration, and one a Scottish academic who works closely with our university people on the psychology and social support elements, education and training. As you can imagine, there are a million things we have to set up to handle such a large influx of people."

"Do you know their names?" He furrowed his brow again, dipped his head in his thinking mode, then looked back up at me.

'I met them once at a social event, over a year ago now, I think their names were Liddy Cochran, and a Mary? Margaret? I forget, but her last name was MacDonald. She had a fabulous Scottish accent, and I remember laughing with her about it, because she commented on my English one, and she was curious."

"You migrated here from the UK?"

"Yes, five years ago, at the request of the Interdepartmental Brexit Commission. They were positioning me for the role I now have."

"The one million homes project was running when you got elected?"

Yes."

"What role has the President played in the project?"

"His office is the primary sponsor, they signed the agreement with the Aid Agency on behalf of the country a year before I arrived, I watched the process from the sidelines as it were, while the parliament debated the opportunity. With the President's overt support, it all happened very quickly. It is now our main focus for economic recovery, especially after the terror attacks crippled so much of our industry."

"What is your relationship with the President?" He smiled, and there was no prevarication in his answer.

"We meet once a month, occasionally at a social event, I have his trust and respect, and it is reciprocated." I let that go, it didn't seem to be they were BFF's, it sounded more like a professional relationship, which in such a small country, didn't really stack up. But then he was English, and the President was Irish, so there may have been some residual cultural resentment. Ireland still remembered the 'troubles', the six counties still lamented their lack of freedom from British influence, and it was easy to see the positioning of an Englishman to become the Prime Minister in Ireland as a provocative move.

"Agent Bernstein, do you have any further questions for the Prime Minister?" I looked at Anna, watching for her reaction, and true to form her face gave nothing away, she just smiled that gentle smile she used to disarm people for all sorts of reasons.

"Thank you Commander, I'm satisfied at this point, perhaps we could meet again in a few days?" he stood, pulling his double breasted suit coat around his chest, and did up the buttons. I watched his fingers, no tremble, no shimmy or shake, just push, pull, and all done. If he was lying to us, he was a master at it, and it would take a more ruthless approach to shake his story.

"On the door!" He bent to shake Anna's hand, then mine.

"Thank you for your time, sir, we'll be in touch."

He walked out, and headed back down the stairs, where he was enfolded by his personal guards, and without looking back, exited out to the street. I stood with my back to the door again, this time with one foot flat on the wall behind me, pushing my knee out into the corridor. I tapped my fingers on my knee, letting everything settle.

"He didn't ask if we were releasing the President. In fact, he didn't ask any questions about him at all."

"We know that constitutionally, the Prime Minister and his council run the country, the President rubber stamps what the parliament wants to do. But we have clear evidence that this President, at least, is driving a major project where the Prime Minister's people are doing all the heavy lifting.

"And you know, we never released the information that the oil pollution was due to nanite infestation, so his not asking lady Muck-Muck makes sense."

"It's complicated, I'll give you that, I asked for a CIA briefing before I left Washington, and even they have trouble sorting through all the different angles at the political level. Ireland as a convoluted system, for sure for sure." I worked hard not to laugh at Anna's sudden use of the Irish brogue.

"The web site that started us chasing the shells purported to be a Finnian related venture. That would make its focus here, not in Belfast. But I just don't get it." I stood straight, rolled my shoulders, wondered what to do next. We still had no absolute proof of the President knowing about the attacks.

"Okay, you take the Prime Minister's people, I'll take the President's, find out how Sandra is getting along." I moved up the corridor just as Sandra was stepping out of one of the rooms.

"How's it going?" She smiled at me, bouncing up and down on her toes, reminding me of her nick name, the 'battery bunny; she preferred her alter ego, 'Just call me Sally.' Either way she could exhaust you just with her presence!

"Fabulous. Great people, all dedicated to their jobs, all absolute believers in the grand plan, and half of them absolute liars. But I'm getting a theme, and it might help us nail the top dogs. The two women we met with the President are the brains behind the plan, also the movers and shakers as far as anyone in government is concerned.

"They give orders, layout project plans, are involved at every level, every step, and have been for all of the four years they've been at it. And all ostensibly for and on behalf of the President. They use his personal imprimatur with gay abandon, so much so many of the staff are very wary of the women, and cross check with the Prime Minister's senior staff at every opportunity."

"That's going to piss them off in a hurry."

"Yes, and a number of the people I have spoken to believe they have overstepped their authority on a number of occasions."

"Example?"

"Well, " Sandra started, then paused, rubbed her ear which was looking a little red, "got an ear ache, sorry. One example would be the women wanted to push through a raft of rezoning permits, to allow for the building of houses and infrastructure. It and of itself, no biggie, but where they wanted the permits to apply to was."

"Why?"

"Because every area was the province of a county council, and by law they have a right to approve any rezoning application, the women wanted to void the normal process and just get the government to pass a revised by-law and remove the county's opinion from the equation."

"Where did the drive come from?"

"The Office of the President, all in capitals. The government refused point blank to implement it, and it caused a lot of friction at both levels of government. In fact, it's still an issue of contention."

"Interesting. Any other key issues?"

"Yes, and a very interesting one. The airspace over Whiddy Island is in the Dublin Control Area, and once the drone facility was recognized by one of the inspectors, the fact that no one had applied for permission to use the airspace for that purpose created a row between the President's office and the Irish Aviation Authority. It's still unresolved, and I'm told that every launch has been recorded for the past two years."

"Has it now? Need I ask the obvious question?"

"No, I already have, and I've given the time and date to the woman I interviewed, and she promised she would send the tape to me by courier. She seemed anxious to do it from my perspective. There are a lot of axes to grind at the government level, and you don't have to dig down very far to find them."

"Nothing like local politics to get the blood moving." We all laughed, trivializing something that could have had major consequences. Well, it did. We got shot down, remember?

"Anna here will sit in on your remaining interviews, then you can both catch up to me." They nodded and moved off. I wandered up and down the corridor for a moment, collecting my thoughts.

We needed hard evidence. And we had yet to find it.

BÀGH BHEANNTRAÍ

The mid-size jet landed at Ballina airport, once a long grass strip now covered in tarmac, taxied to a corner where small buildings huddled as if hiding, and was met by a very big truck with rollup sides. Rich mud covered its wheels and splashed up over the front of the cab from the drive in through the magnificent trees and bushes that lined Airport Way. The aircraft was unloaded efficiently, the temporary ground staff in their red helmets and yellow safety hi-vis vests reflecting the early morning light with their silver bands around legs and chests. The boxes and crates were bulky, and two men worked for nearly an hour moving between the jet and the truck. The foreman reached into the now empty hold, visually checked it was empty, casually threw one of the tie down straps back away from the door, then pulled his head out and waved to the truck driver.

"I'm thinking you got it all, boyo, nothing left here but the loading gear." The truck driver waved, climbed into his cab, and with a silent snort, rolled his rig out behind the sheds, and onto the well-worn road. Beside him the only passenger on the jet sat, partially hidden by a shapeless black burka, dark glasses and a headscarf which hid her hair and half her face. She sat stooped shouldered, reducing her height considerably. No one would recognized one of the most wanted terrorists on the planet.

"Where it be we would be heading, then missus? I only got the general location of Inishcrone, and while it's not the biggest town we have around here, there's plenty of places we could drop this here load." He gave the woman a curious look, then just shook his head and watched the road. Business had crashed when the oil and gas had been cut off from Ireland, and all the computers had stopped working, and his little company was hanging on by its teeth, so this job was very important as it would feed his family for a month. He reached over and took the small piece of paper his passenger poked at him, held it on top of the steering wheel with one hand to read it, peering through his small wire framed glasses, nodded to himself, visualizing exactly where the sewerage plant was, and how to get there on the limited roads available.

Inishcrone, like so many small towns in the area, restricted where trucks as big as his could drive, although for the life of him given that more than half the population of the town had left in the last year or so, he didn't see his truck as that much of a threat. He put the map in his mind, and headed off up towards the bridge he would cross to get onto Sligo Road before cutting across to Harbor View.

It took the best part of an hour, but he finally pulled up outside the wire fence of the sewerage plant, where four of the most beautiful women he had ever seen stood patiently waiting. He jumped out, tipped his cap to the one who looked to be in change, a tall women dressed in a gray pants suit, her raven hair held on top of her head in a bob, her sensible heeled boots carrying cut grass and a little mud. The contrast between her boots and her suit was startling.

"Good morning to ya missus, it's happy I would be to help ya unload all these here boxes, where will you be wanting them, then?" Katrina smiled at the wizened old man who she guessed must be at least eighty years old, and handed him an envelope. His thin wisps of white hair fluttered in the breeze.

"Just unload them all here thank you, we'll take it from here." Her smile was so radiant the driver simply shook his head, pushing his cap back in its place. He slid his hands through the bib of his overalls, pushing the envelope into his inside pocket, looked around and saw a small hand cart, then nodded to himself. He would do exactly as asked, his mother had beaten manners into him at an early age, withdrew his hands, and moved to roll up the truck sides. The women, while looking a bit on the young side, surprised him with their strength and speed, and in half the time it took to unload the jet, the pile of crates, cylinders and boxes sat on the wet grass. Scratching his head, he looked a little befuddled, not quite knowing what to do next.

Then his passenger dismounted, and was immediately taken into a massive hug by all four women, and he found himself smiling at the warmth of the welcome. Putting his stained cap back on his head, he muttered to himself and remounted the truck, and with a casual wave, drove away. As soon as he was out of sight, the burka came off, the scarf thrown away, and the glasses pulled off her face, revealing the beautiful woman the satellite camera had seen all those months ago, and had started the search for nuclear-capable shells.

"Siobhan, welcome, we have worried about you for months. Linking up with that creep Badawi was good for our cause, but not out hearts! How are you?" Katrina looked at her friend, someone she had grown up with here in Ireland, gone to college with, plotted and planned with, until 'Helen'–Natasha Trotsky-had given the signal for the women to take their places in the world-wide organization she had established. Once in the field, Trotsky had passed control of the women over to Freya, who was managing the European theatre for the terrorists' attacks and all that followed.

"Katrina, I never thought I'd see you again. Crissy sends her love, and apart from being lonely, is working on more derivations of the nanites. You'd be Lilian, Else, and Lilly, right? I've heard about you of course, your mother talks highly of you all. How did your experiments go?" The women stood toe to toe, clasping hands, the boxes, cylinders and crates temporarily forgotten.

"Well," Lilian said, her tee shirt with its challenging logo poking out from under her puffer jacket, "our first attempt is working well, according to mum.

"They're still rationing the power, taking it easy and slow, using the panels for the baseline, and we could only do a systems check at the power plants for obvious reasons, but we think it will work." Siobhan's face lit up in a huge smile, this was the best news she could get, because she couldn't hope to do what she planned here if the technology the three sisters represented didn't function. She looked at Katrina.

"Crissy told me your system was perfected before you left Socotra, how do you feel about it all?"

"I'd have liked more time at the power plants, but we had guards at every site, so we had to be a little circumspect. But every test we ran read in the green, so I have a high level of confidence it will all work."

"Any problems on site?" Katrina laughed, remembering the difficulty working around the nanites had created, and slapped Siobhan on the shoulder.

"Next time don't make them so hard!" They both smiled, relaxing for the first time in months, sensing no immediate threat. They moved to the hand trolley, which had been fitted with a slim battery, and loaded the first of the boxes. They went through a double gate in the fence, and then into the large shed on the corner.

"We have planning approval for the work on the sewerage plant, how long do you need for that?" Katrina turned the empty trolley around and drove it back out into the chilly air. She looked up into the overcast sky, sensing it might get very cold and possible snow, so she quickened her pace.

"If everything comes together as planned, this is a very small plant, two or three days should do it. Which one of the girls is our diver?"

"Lilian. She did a tremendous job in France, diving alone didn't seem to worry her."

"She'll have to block the out-fill lines before we start, then thread the infill, what's the water like?"

"Apart from bloody freezing, you mean?"

"Yes, apart from that." They temporarily abandoned the conversation while they loaded the next load on the trolly.

"Ask her yourself."

"Lilian, how is the water here for your dive?"

"The tide goes out a very long way, the pipes just get to the water, and its only about three meters deep where they outflow. Very shallow, apart from the long walk, or wade depending on the tide, half a day should do it."

"Can you do it at night?" Lilian stopped walking, looked up into the overcast sky, looked out so sea.

'If you all can carry what I need through the boggy sand and mud, yes, I will only need two or three tanks. Maybe we can make a sled out of something."

Katina put her hand up, leaned towards Lilian. "Don't worry about that, tell me what you need when we get back to the house, and I'll either have one built or build it myself." Lilian nodded, she was used to everyone she worked with being able to do things, so Katrina's offer was no surprise.

"Do you have a compressor to fill your tanks?" Lilian jut nodded, thinking about the sled.

"Will I have to dive again while we're here?" Katrina shook her head.

"No, everything else will be landside, both here and over at Killala."

"How many systems do you want us to set up?" Katrina turned the handcart into the shed, and started to unload.

"Good question. When we get home, I'll show you what I plan. We have no existing infrastructure, so we'll have to lay them out where it makes sense to run connections and feeders. I noticed in France, particularly, you used three different sizes of hardware. At the time you told me it was to do with the rating and condition of the generator, or the turbine. How will you set them up here?" Katrina looked at Lilian, who turned to her sister.

"Else, you answer that one." She turned to her sister, completing the triad.

"Lily, you're the geology expert, what say you?"

"Can't comment until I see the ground."

"And that's my answer as well. We need to plot out exactly what you want to achieve, then I can plan out the hardware. Will we have access to the ocean at Killala?"

"Depends on where we set up. The town has a massive sandbar running across its face, with what amounts to a sea water river running along the foreshore. But if we go north, then we can get direct access to the ocean."

"How far north?"

"Maybe a kilometer or two."

"Houses?"

"Supposedly abandoned farms, but we will check it out."

"How much can we do in sight of the public?" Katrina looked over at Else, she had anticipated this question, and had a really good idea to share.

"I'll give you my idea back at the house." The third and fourth load came and went, and as they started on the fifth, little snow flaks started to fall, creating a picturesque scene that had the women laughing and sweeping at the flakes as they fell. Siobhan decided to float her agenda, she was impatient.

"My plan is to get the biofuel production started, then use that in generators to provide enough power to build the environmental plant. Then we can produce panels and power packs to run everything else, and use the panels to cover everything else we will do."

"You're talking six to twelve months, we need to be back in France in six weeks. In that time was can plant four to six systems, depending on the surface and substrate conditions. Plus your biofuel plant." Katrina looked at Siobhan to see her reaction, and was comforted to see that her timeline hadn't been objected to. Siobhan sighed inwardly, six weeks was very short for what she needed.

"I've got ten to twenty women ready to work with me, they are all living within 100 kilometers of here, nothing to do with anything that happened before, and they are all very smart, and very keen to help me set up my program. We also have the permits and council approval for everything we intend to do."

"How do you talk to them?" Katrina asked, mindful that she and the sisters only had the tight band system that used the French satellite for its link to Freya.

"Before I took off with Badawi I set up a comms link using the local newspaper, classified ads. The paper I used was off line for the first ten weeks or so, but has had two issues printed in the last month." Katrina nodded her head, very clever, but then Siobhan was a genius, just like her and the sisters.

"Well, let's finish this, and I'll take you through how I think we can stay out of the public eye and still do what we have to do. Agreed?" The four women nodded, and moved to load the final trolley.

Siobhan realized she had been out of the loop while she had been fleeing to Socotra, and she also sensed that Katrina was the driver of the young team, and she had their trust. If she could rid herself of the stench of her association with the mercenary terrorist, she would work hard to earn respect and trust from the team.

But that would take time, and she hoped the six weeks she was being offered would be long enough.

In an abandoned house just a mere five hundred meters away from the corner of the sewerage plant, Fay and two of her troops from Tom's old team, now the quirky Warrant Officer's, watched and recorded everything they could see. And thanks to a hidden 'quiet' camera that they had placed in the shed, they pretty much got all of it, including the conversations within range of the micro transmitter.

Now she had a decision to make, put her head down on her hands, worked through her choices. The terrorist women climbed into their golf cart, and drove off down the service road along the rocky foreshore. She dialed Rosie Hammond.

"Hammond," the tonality tight and curt, almost demanding. Fay smiled to herself, she was being tested.

"Hi, Rosie, just a heads up, but you can expect a group of up to five women to come your way in the next day or two. I'm sending you headshots. They'll be travelling together, electric vehicle is my guess. They will work the area from the fish plant north for two or three kilometers, likely along the shore line, and inland possibly as much as ten klicks."

"You want me to take them?"

"Absolutely not. Not under any circumstances. You are to observe and get as much data as you can without revealing your presence. Of it you do, you need to make sure your credentials are first class. I don't want them spooked, I want them back here doing whatever it is they came here for." Rosie looked anything but comfortable with her orders, she was Special Boat Services (SBS) trained, had served as an exchange officer with the SEALS, where she had been recruited into Tom's team, and her view of 'watch and observe' was decidedly negative. True soldiers fought, not sat on their arses watching and waiting. Her impatience communicated itself, because as Fay watched her small screen, her hackles went up.

"Rosie, this is a police action, under the jurisdiction of Interpol. You're in civies for a reason, and I really hope you have all lost your combat boots." The W/O's face was stoic, and the edges hardened perceptually. Fay thought for a moment, then looked directly into the little camera.

"Stand by, I'll get back to you." And she disconnected, then dialed Tom.

"Fay, how are you up there?" His warm smiling face relieved some of her tension, so she did her best to smile back.

"Tom, I might have a problem with your replacement." His eyebrows shot up, his face one big question mark.

"How so?"

"She doesn't seem to like the idea of watch and report, soft clothes, don't get identified." Fay held her breath, telling tales on someone in a military squad, one as highly trained as Tom's, usually didn't go well. Tom released his face from its curious look and morphed into a concerned one. If Fay hadn't seen it with her own eyes, she would not have believed such huge expressions could be shown by any face, especially Tom's!

"Fay, she's new to the team, she hasn't had a permanent home for some time. Let me talk to her." Fay sighed from genuine relief, her resources were stretched to the limit, and she needed everyone on the same page, and totally committed to her task, or she ran the risk of letting Jessica down. Not to mention the possibility of the most wanted terrorist on the planet escaping.

She rolled onto her back, and closed her eyes, mindful that her two companions had heard every word of her conversation with their ex-leader. And she knew from their casual chats they both revered Tom as one of the best of the best. She smelt it before she saw it, but one of them had lit a miniature camp stove, and was brewing coffee. She smiled, thinking about how long she would wait before calling the W/O to reaffirm her orders. As she was forming this thought her mini buzzed.

"Remer."

"Inspector, I want to apologize for my earlier conversation." Fay let the comment settle, then decided to push ahead.

"It's what you didn't say that worried me the most. We have to keep out of sight for weeks, or worst case, only be seen to be doing what our cover allows for. This is a critical mission for us, the Commander is counting on both intelligence and taking the women terrorists into custody. But we don't do that until we have learned everything we can, clear?"

"Crystal clear, Inspector. I'll post pairs along the beach, and one team about two clicks in, and I'll take the Fish Shed. There's not much civilian traffic at the moment, it shouldn't be hard to spot them."

"We'll give you a heads up when they leave, and a description of their vehicle. They have to swing through Ballina, so you'll have at least an hour's warning."

"Thank you Inspector, appreciated." Fay debated whether or not to call Jessica, decided against it , better to wait for more information. She peeked over the parapet, saw no movement, stood, took a mug of steaming brew, then rolled her shoulders to relax.

"This is good, you'll make someone a good wife one day, Paul."The laughter did its job, they all mentally relaxed, but kept one part of their minds on the outside.

Never pays to get sloppy in a combat zone!

CHAPTER THIRTY EIGHT

The interviews had wrapped, we had confirmed a solid time line, and even had a copy of the project plan as approved by the President's office. It was ten years long, this was year five, and nowhere did it hint at attacks of any sort, and if you took it at face value, it was an excellent blueprint for migrating five million refugees from across Europe and Africa to Ireland.

Like any good project plan, there was an entire section for the PERT (Program Evaluation and Review Technique) plan, which contained all the dependencies and alliances required to make the project successful, in a neatly labeled section title 'GANT Plan – 1 million homes'. This was where we would have expected to find reference to the disruption created by the terrorist attacks-but all we found were three vague mentions of 'potential acceleration points', which offered solutions to a possible time compression enabled by such disruptions.

Our geeks pointed out that there were six months of these acceleration points, and we were right in the middle of them. They also pointed out the need for rezoning which had not been achieved on the desired timeline, and now had its own red flagged section labeled 'Blockers'. There were no mitigating strategies offered, the only comment was 'work in progress with designated authorities-see personnel list for persons responsible.'

Sandra and Anna had interviewed one of these persons, and they described an almost siege mentality on behalf of the government, who listed what the president's office-albeit through the mechanism of the project plan, were trying to force on the counties.

Interestingly, one country had agreed to a partial rezoning, on the basis of a monetary compensation on a per-lot basis, and surprise, surprise, it was county Mayo, and the areas described were 'Killala and an area of thirty square kilometers, and Inishcrone, and an area of forty square kilometers.' The size of each lot had been left up to the local councils, but the timing was interesting-the plan called for houses to be built within the next year.

I sent a summary to Fay, she brought me up to date on the movements of the women, I considered sending her more troops, then backed off, she would ask for them if she needed them. I wanted another go at the President, and maybe the Prime Minister, but on Anna's advice I had slept on it. Metaphorically speaking.

And then the golden nugget dropped in my lap with a call from Malcolm under Frontier mountain in Nebraska, with Luigi and Shami sharing his screen. Anna and Sandra leaned over my shoulder to better see our geeks.

"Are you sure?" I asked, my blood pumping with optimism.

Here might be the hook I could hang the President's neck from. I could feel Sandra vibrating. In contrast Anna was her usual calm, smooth self.

I looked at the images of Shami and Luigi in their little boxes, no bigger than an inch square, and their placid grins told me they were all very sure of their analysis. And their eyes sparkled with an intensity I was starting to enjoy.

"Yes, Commander, every computer in every government department except for a few 'test' laptops were turned off and disconnected for two days eleven weeks ago. The order came from their CIO-that's Chief Information Officer-who logged the event as maintenance on demand, due to a notional national threat, on the orders of the President's staff. There is even a detailed list of every computer, department, and time-down. A report on the laptops ran only one paragraph on one page, and simply describe the complete destruction of the chipsets."

"Who authorized this shut down?" I asked, knowing the answer.

"The executive Portfolio Manager, on behalf of the office of the President, one Doctor MacDonald. She and her assistant, another woman but unnamed, visited every government department with the CIO one week before the deadline, and personally briefed all the Information Technology and Communications people, from department heads on down. The story was that in light of the on-going world-wide attacks, the government was expecting a massive denial of service (DOS) attack from terrorists, not identified, and from all reports the Information Technology world in Dublin shat its collective pants and did what they were told." I nodded, exactly as I had suspected. Then something Malcolm had said registered at the back of my brain.

"You mentioned Communications people-does that mean they had their phones turned off as well?"

"All the cell towers in a one hundred kilometer radius, the central servers, and every handset they could reach with an SMS message."

"And no one bitched?"

"Apparently no, most were in shock at the attacks on Rome, Israel, and the Grand Mosque, no one mentioned West Point or the Space Station, possibly too distant to be of interest."

"When did the rioting start over here?"

"According to the CIA, serious social disturbances started to register in the second week, then snowballed downhill from there. The biggest uprising was from the Catholics, as you would imagine, that was after all one of the roots of the 'troubles'. But the Army and the Garda stomped pretty hard and fast, so the major damage was limited to around a month all told."

"Did anyone question the event post the two days?"

"Yes, several departments, but the destroyed laptops were offered up as evidence of the DOS attack, and everyone went back to their business as quickly as they could. No one was prepared to challenge anything that had been said or done, as the proof was on the laptops."

"Any complaints from civilians not in government service?"

"Well, there you have an entirely different story. No one told the public, and apart from some public servants who took their own precautions, and told a neighbor or two, the attack had the same effect as it did every else. The only difference is that the phones worked within the shutdown radius of the towers, but everyone outside that radius lost everything."

"Guys, give me a minute please, I need to ask Anna and Sandra for their comments. They have done the bulk of the interviewing." I switched the call to 'hold', looked at both women, Anna now standing with her hands on her hips, Sandra with her arms folded defensively across her chest.

"As unbelievable as it sounds, all that could have been done without the President knowing beforehand. I can see where a trusted advisor could alert him to a possible attack, and suggest a solution, without him ever being complicit."

"You're supposing the two women had that much control?" Anna looked uncomfortable, the whole scenario setting her teeth on edge.

"Yes, I am. One representing the trust fund and its billions of euros, the other the Aid agency sponsoring the migration. Or did they sponsor it, or merely provide services paid for?"

"My money's on paid for." Sandra looked pissed, as the possibility of the President sliding out of any responsibility dug into her gut. I nodded in agreement, something I could check on with the Boss.

"Okay, here's how we play it. Get the geeks report, then we'll go and ask the President a couple more questions. Maybe we add the two women to our list for concrete cages?"

"Not the Aid worker, surely?" Anna asked.

"Yes, both of them, can't have one without the other. Where are they now?" I turned the mini back to 'live', the three geeks had been talking amongst themselves, and stopped the moment I intruded.

"Thanks gentlemen, appreciate all your good work. Summarize and report please, let us know if anything else turns up." Sandra looked up from her mini.

"The women haven't been sighted since they were forcibly kicked off the beach at Whiddy Island. The small boat they had hasn't been seen since."

"Did we get any photos?" Sandra bent to her mini again, slid data across to mine.

"Yes. Photo and registration, not that it will mean anything." I looked at the blue hull, about thirty feet long, aluminum bottom with inflatable sides, small cabin on top, not unlike the ones the Coast Guard used. They were fast and had a good range, so the boat and its occupants could be anywhere. And there were four figures in the boat, so they had help. That gave me pause to think. I looked around the small space we had commandeered, seeking inspiration from the bright colorful walls lit by little French lanterns, a clash of style that could only exist in Ireland.

"President." I pointed to the room where he still sat, the lieutenant on the door, watching us approach.

He open the door with a flourish, and our Italian guards moved to the opposite wall and took up their positions.

"Mr. President, apologies for the delay, but we've had such a good time going through all your paperwork-must congratulate you on that-especially the part about turning off your computers for two days. What, exactly was that all about?" I had taken him by surprise, the look on his face said it all, he had been about to blast me when my question threw him for six.

"Any by the way, this is Inspector Thomas, she's had the privilege of interviewing a lot of your public servants." I let that sit, as Anna and Sandra found seats opposite the President.

"Now, about that pesky computer thing?" And I held his eyes, watching for the inevitable prevarication. To my utter surprise, he didn't even flinch. His voice calmer than it had been during his initial interrogation, he laid out for us what he thought he believed.

"Commander, firstly I'd like to apologize for my behavior the last time we met. I was extremely upset about the way you took me into custody, and I felt-and still do to some extent-that you were overreaching your authority. I've read the Red Notices you left for me, so I have a much clearer view of what you are prosecuting now. Before I answer your question regarding the computer shut down, let me just say that no one in my department, no one in my government, as far as I am aware, had anything to do with what is described in the Red Notices. No one had any foreknowledge of the attacks, or we would have been better prepared.

"Now, if I can get another cup of tea, I'm happy to tell you everything I know about the computers." I nodded at Sandra, she got up, taking the tea set with her. She deliberately left the door open, showing the lieutenant and our two guards watching the room. I smiled at her nice touch, intimidation was a useful tool in any interrogation. She was back inside a minute, placed the tea set on the table, bent to pour a cup, and handed it to the President with a smile. One like you'd see on an alligator just before it took a swamp rat for breakfast.

The president didn't smile, but the rictus on his face softened slightly. He was still pissed, and I liked that. People riding on their emotions made mistakes, and I was counting on him making one or two I could take advantage of. Anna got the ball rolling again. She sat back in her seat, as relaxed as someone in a movie theatre, face shining and hands at rest in her lap, emoting calm. She was the top interrogator for the FBI for a reason, and it wasn't just her good looks.

"Mr. President, in the second week of the terrorist attacks, your department ordered a shutdown of every government computer, except for a few laptops, and the telecommunications network for a one hundred kilometer radius of Dublin. Why?" he placed his cup down on its saucer, this time adorned with an intricate rose pattern looped with four leaf clovers, so I guessed this time he had the convention center's best China. And he didn't bash it down like he had earlier.

Interesting.

"Agent Bernstein, the attacks on the Vatican and Israel took us by surprise, as no doubt it did the rest of the world. We have a very large Catholic community, as you would be aware, and the shock and horror of those attacks unsettled the majority of the population. Initially there was the usual calm before the storm, then as the other attacks became known, panic set in. Rioting started around week two, and we had to declare martial law as did everyone else in Europe. Sometime during week two, the rumor started about radioactive fuel, and things went from bad to worse.

"Here in Dublin, we had managed to maintain most government services, then our consultants met with our CIO, and suggested we prepare for the possibility of a country wide attack on our IT infrastructure. I reviewed their suggestion, and frankly, given that we were down to less than ten percent of our staff making it in every day, I agreed to their proposal. We had learnt how to manage at-home-work during the pandemic, so it seemed to be prudent to protect the infrastructure that supported that.

"The proof of their claim was justified when the rest of the world was attacked, including all of Ireland that had not obeyed the mandate." He sat back in his seat, letting his last statement hang. Sandra jumped on it before I could comment.

"You're telling us you sent out a message during week two of the attacks to the whole of Ireland?"

"Yes, I issued a Presidential order countersigned by the Prime Minister and it was sent to every government agency and council. We have no way of knowing who took our advice and who didn't."

"Did it occur to you to warn the EU?" He looked surprised, as if he had never considered the question.

"No, we did not. After a rather fractious conversation with the PM in Belfast, we decided to manage our own backyard."

"How confident were you that you would be attacked?" My voice was pitched low, in an attempt to reset the tension in the room. He looked at me, his brow wrinkling in concentration.

"We had worked for nearly two and a half years with the consultants, they had proved very reliable, and their expertise had been demonstrated time after time. They helped identify the opportunity with our empty homes, they helped select Whiddy Island for the environmental plant, get it built and operational, and they helped survey the entire country for locations where we can build more homes and support them. Their advice coming just after the attacks made sense to us, and we wanted to protect what we had."

"What if I told you your consultants are part of the terrorist group that caused all the damage over the last three months?" I watched his face closely, because if he was going to lie, this is where it would happen.

"Impossible. Ms. Cochran has been coming here for six years, and has made Dublin her home here, she is dedicated to help us migrate the refugees and has worked tirelessly both here and in other countries setting everything up. As for Dr. MacDonald, she was introduced by Ms. Cochran nearly four years ago, and she has been the driver for getting Whiddy Island up and running."

"Who warned you of the net attack?" he looked befuddled for a second, then his face cleared.

'You mean the computer attack. I believe it was Dr. MacDonald." I nodded, the answer was expected, so I tried another tack.

"Why have the county's arced up over the rezoning proposals?" he looked befuddled again, then turned his head to one side.

"Commander, Ireland is a very small country in the scheme of things, and the six county's guard their sovereignty closely. We are a very old culture, built upon the bones of our forefathers and too many wars to count. We've been invaded more times than any other country in Europe, and still wriggle under the imposition of British rule, or a part of us does.

"We have wanted our own identity and freedom for centuries, and the county's see their role as the keepers of our culture and our heritage. But to achieve our ambition of migrating five million refugees here, we need them to allow us to rezone a lot of their territory, or we simply can't fit the number of homes and infrastructure in. It's that simple."

"So how do you intend to manage that little issue?" I wasn't baiting him as much as genuinely wanting to know what they planned.

"We were to have held a referendum later this year, but that has been postponed in view of the current situation."

"So your plans to migrate the refuges has stalled?" He shook his head.

"No. We are fitting out abandoned homes with panels and power packs as we speak, no one has any objection to that, and we plan on the first of the migrants to be here later this year." I studied his face, so far I hadn't got anything on him I could work with, so I threw out a 'hail Mary' to see what happened.

"Tell me about Killala Bay." For the first time he looked shocked, as if we had done a 'Star Trek' and gone where no one had before. He pulled at his jacket, his face morphing through multiple expressions, until he was left frowning, and looking very uncomfortable.

"Killala Bay? I'd have to check our project plan, I don't remember it being very high on the list." I let that sit, it was such a barefaced lie I saw no reason to let him elaborate.

"Thank you, Mr. President. We'll ask you to wait again for a short time until we can conclude our conversation. Lunch will be brought in for you. We appreciate your patience, and having read the Red Notices, you will appreciate the seriousness of our inquiries." I stood, Sandra and Anna mirrored my movement, and we headed out the door, which the lieutenant closed behind us.

"You got him with Killala Bay," Sandra said, brushing her hands through her hair, shaking her shoulders to release some stiffness, and almost dancing on her toes. Next to her, Anna just stood quietly, looking at me.

"I haven't caught up with Killala Bay. What's going on there?" I suddenly realized I hadn't brought any of our external team up to date, but quickly excused myself on the basis that I was genuinely occupied elsewhere.

"Long story short, Fay has half of Tom's team monitoring Siobhan O'Cleary and a group of women who have been moving around the place setting up something in shuttered nuke plants. They're tied to 'Freya' who you know about up in Scotland, who I also have under surveillance, this time with Bob and his team."

"You've been busy." I just smiled. Hadn't we all?

"You're letting them run?" I switched off my smile and grimaced.

"No way, José. I'm letting Killala Bay play out until we know what it is they are doing. The report from the nuke plants was a goose egg. They couldn't find any proof of what was done apart from some foot prints. And O'Cleary has come all the way from Socotra, which we will also have to clean up at some point. She brought a lot of stuff with her, and we want to know what it all does."

"Some new development in the nanites?" I just nodded. Anna had put the dots together from minimal information, a sure sign of a smart mind, and a well-tuned one at that.

"We'll just have to wait and see. The other women with O'Cleary ran some type of experiment here in Ireland, and we're running that down as well." Anna gave me her motherly look, her eyes twinkling. "Do you want me to go home when we're finished here?"

"Hell no. Now that I've got you here again, I'll put you to work somewhere. But we're not finished here by a long shot. We still need to make a bullet-proof case against the President, or let him go, and frankly, I'm not inclined to do that yet. What's your gut tell you?" Anna gave me a long look, one that had her eyes scanning the whole of me, inside and out. Did I mention she was a formidable interrogator?

"On the surface, it could be said he simply followed the advice of his 'consultants'-but the fact is he was aware of a number of things-not the least of which was the probable date of the world-wide attacks. That six-month timeline suggests that years ago, when Trotsky and Mohammad bin Azaria started to plan this all out, they set a specific six months apart for the attacks and the follow on. It's in their precious project plan. And the warning about the computers was self-serving at best, and too specific to be overlooked. The relationship between Cochran and MacDonald is key here, we need to go deep on that. And one other point." She paused, ran her fingers with their pink nail polish, another thing she had adopted since going back to the US, through her shortish auburn hair, almost as an afterthought. She had glammed up a little but still retained her hard edge, wrapped in a pretty package.

"And that is?" I asked, comforted by her summary because it paralleled mine so far, giving me confidence I was on the right track.

"He flat out lied about Killala Bay. It's much more important to him than anything else we spoke about." I nodded, another uptick on the confidence meter. I had a deep-seated feeling that if we could unwrap Killala Bay, we could puzzle out their plans for the future, and that might just give us the edge for the first time in this frustrating and seemingly never-ending tail chase.

"Sandra, what's your take?"

"He's an evil, slimy, horrible bastard of a man, and I would love to give him the Badawi treatment." I tried to smile, but it never reached my face.

"Don't hold back. Tell us what you really think." She and I had shot the terrorist on the lift of an aircraft carrier, and then let the sharks enjoy a free meal. She had the good grace to smile, albeit a slightly lopsided one, as she remembered where she was and who she was with.

"Apologizes Commander, I let my emotions run away with me. But he is evil, and he is slimy, and he is undoubtedly guilty by association, and we've locked up a whole pile of young women on far less." She had the right of that, but this was the highest-ranked person we had in our sights, so we had to be very sure, as the political ramifications could be as severe as the terrorist attacks. And there was that nagging fact that the country was preparing to take in some five million refugees—an amazing opportunity to end a lot of suffering. Then Anna caught me off guard.

'By the way, we don't see much movement by Interpol on the issue of the nanites taking out all the drug crops." She gave me a bland look, so it was hard for me to tell if she was having fun or just interested in my perspective.

"And your point is?" I asked with the same bland face. She held her look for another half a minute, then laughed. Sandra was about to crack up, so we all let it out. Tears ran down my face. Sandra was swiping at her eyes, and even the usually relaxed Anna was sniffing.

"I get it. Don't blame you. We see it as an opportunity as well. But there is one question I think we need to address."

"And that's how they hit so many countries and areas so fast?" Anna looked surprised, but we had people on the ground from Interpol digging into it, just not Section Five yet.

"Yes, we wondered about that. Our own DEA are looking south as we speak. They haven't turned up any evidence of mercenaries or women, for that matter, but we have a rough timeline in South America if you're interested." I raised one eyebrow and opened my hand to indicate I wanted the information.

"Well, from start to finish, frankly, we don't know the start, but the crops all took on a yellow/blue look a day before they turned into sludge, and a day later they were as hard or brittle depending on who's telling the story.

"What do you mean by brittle?" Sandra had been playing with her mini the whole time we had been talking, just looking up every now and then to indicate she was still tuned in.

"Unlike the nanites in the coal, oil, or gas plants, these can be broken down physically when they turn into a silver shower of dust. Our people tell us they do not corrupt the soil, but we're waiting on laboratory tests to confirm that." I let my mind wander for a moment and tried to visualize the logistics involved in getting thousands of acres of drug crops across half the world all in the same fortnight. Hundreds, if not thousands, of people would be needed. I shook my head. At that scale, someone would have seen something. How the hell did they do it?

Then it hit me. You had to water the crops.

"Water!"

"What? Do you need a glass?" Sandra popped up like a spring.

"No, but thanks for your concern."

"You're saying they poisoned the water." Anna had also sprung up, mirroring Sandra. I was warmed by their automatic response to help me. Nice to know.

"How would you do that?" Sandra asked, hitting her mini again.

"Well, first things first, you would have to design the nanoparticles so they would pass through a human or animal gestation system without any ill effect. Then you'd need to target a specific biological feature of your target plant, or you'd end up killing everything."

"And that might get noticed,"

"And that might just wind the good guys up, yes. Is all that selectivity even possible?" I pondered the question; remember, not a geek. But I knew someone who was and would know the answer. I dialed her.

"Amira, hello from the far west. How are you today?" She looked bemused, her hair mussed up, flying around her face as she moved her head, goggles on, as well as a protective face mask. She held up one finger, then disappeared, leaving us looking at the back of her lab. The huge electron microscope that ran through the roof and the floor loomed in the corner like a hibernating prehistoric beast. The camera moved so violently that the background blurred, and when it settled, Amira's smiling face reappeared against an office background.

"Sorry, you caught me in the middle of an experiment. How goes it in sunny Ireland?" I laughed.

"Sunny it is not. They call it the Emerald Island for a reason. Lots and lots of rain, very little sunshine. We have a question for you. Remember, I'm not a geek, so forgive me any wrong words."

"Jessica, the entire geek squad has given you a lifetime exemption for your wrong descriptors. What's your question?"

"Hypothetically, could you design a nanite that a human or animal could drink or ingest without any effect, but that same nanite could attack a specific type of plant?" She looked amused at the question, screwed her face up, scratched at the back of her pretty neck, and drummed her fingers on the table top. We could hear the drumming but not see her fingers. They were below the sight line of the camera.

"Humans consist of carbon-12, one of the five elements in our DNA, and it's one of the most stable isotopes of the element. Cocaine has C-17, poppy plants have C-2, and cocoa has C-7. Artificial drugs like methamphetamine and ice share similar bonds, C-10, but I'll have to run a few experiments here to prove your hypotheses. But frankly, considering how fast and how broad the attack was on the drug plants, it is a good guess. Well done."

"It was a team effort. Blame Sandra and Anna when it blows up in your face." We all shared a laugh, breaking the tension that had unintentionally built up. "And don't send me the bill." She smiled, waved at us, and cut the connection.

"Did either of you understand any of that?"

Sandra patted me on the back platonically to soften her words.

"Well, maybe a little. The one thing that these nanites have shown us is that you can design them to do almost anything. Now, I'm not saying you're right, but it looks to me as if you're at least on the right track. Let's play a little geography game." She bent to her mini and called up a graphic that showed water sources in South America, and the river system that linked itself to and from the Amazon dominated the screen. And more importantly, the major systems in the south all had tributaries shooting out all over the place.

"Look at Africa." She swiped her finger across the screen and stopped at the west coast of north Africa. And lo and behold, a tributary system ran from the coast to the inland and smack through the middle of the prime drug-growing areas.

"Now you're talking about a small group of people dropping canisters of nanites into selected areas and patiently waiting for the nanites to dribble downstream and into the watering systems of the druggies. If you were super smart, I bet you could calculate how long it would take to do that." Sandra laughed, pointed at me, and shrugged her shoulders.

'Maybe not you, but I bet someone in Anna's team could, and the geeks could eat the problem for breakfast."

"Let's put your theory to the test." I called Luigi.

"Question for you. Imagine you had a little plastic boat. You dropped it in the headwaters of, just for arguments sake, the Amazon River. Could you calculate how long it would take the boat to get to various parts of the river system?"

"Of course, Commander, do you want us to do that for you?" I shook my head and smiled.

"Thanks, Luigi. That's all we need for now." I looked at Sandra, bouncing on her toes again, and Anna, looking calm and relaxed.

"This whole thing is so simple, it's brilliant." Both nodded, thinking about the genius women we still chased and marveling at their incredible use of the technology our own Amira had invented—or discovered, whichever was the correct terminology. And the miraculous things they had created. If only they had been able to let their genius flourish without destroying the world!

Time to move on.

QUIET TIME

From the top deck of the good ship *'Scáthán'*, the rising sun looked like a glorious yellow and orange globe that inched up bit by bit, the water shimmering in the far distance, brilliant white seagulls flying through the haze with imperious confidence. Gradually, the big globe, having forced its way up and out of the darkness of the ocean, began to split, forming a figure of eight, and slowly, ever so slowly, the two halves pulled apart, the top one turning into the sun, the bottom one sinking silently back into the black waves.

Indigo, finishing up the 'dog' watch, felt at peace with himself, and after witnessing such a miraculous start to the day, at peace with the rest of his world. Back in Venice, sunrise always happened over the tops of buildings, and always later in the morning. He turned at the approach of the chief, carrying two steaming mugs of coffee.

"Thanks, Gordon. Appreciated. Did you by any chance see the sunrise?"

"Aye, just the last of it. I can never get over the way it peels away from itself." Indigo sipped his coffee, watching a school of dolphins race the bow wave as they drove towards Whiddy Island. The blue/gray glistering skins seemed permanently bent in the middle as the big mammals slipped in and out of the water. The ship was doing 24 knots, and the dolphins were matching that with ease.

"How's the training going?"

"Good. We have cross-trained everyone now, and while some will be naturally better than others at different tasks, the least competent of us will still make anyone's eyes water if they attack us again." Indigo looked at the dark shape of the headland they were approaching. Their plan was initially to circumnavigate the Island and scope out where they could safely anchor. It was a big ship by any standards, and its draft of three meters required a lot of water under the keel.

"Nothing on the scopes?"

"Nada. We got a flash from the Inspector about a 30 foot ribbie, carrying four, potentially both mercenary and female terrorists. They want it detained or sunk, but the crew taken alive." Indigo nodded. He had seen the text message from Sandra and had posted the photos on the electronic navigation board. Easier said than done if the terrorists opened fire on them, he thought to himself. Returning fire was never a delicate matter. Then he had a thought.

"Do we have a long gun shooter on board?" The sailor nodded, a wan smile creasing his tanned face. Dressed in jeans, a hoodie, and a black watch cap, he did not look like the master chief of an American aircraft carrier but like a fisherman out to catch a meal or two. The dressing-down was deliberate.

Indigo wore what could only be described as designer jeans, a sleek fitted shirt, over which he had pulled a deep blue woolen jumper, with a roll top around the neck. Even his boat shoes looked handmade, which, of course, being Italian, they were. He looked like he owned the ship on which fisherfolk were working, and certainly not like the head of Interpol Italy or a senior member of Section Five.

"Yes, young Eric is a trained sniper and has his rifle with him. Why?" Indigo gave the chief a hard look, as if considering.

"Chief, I'd like to get him set up on our top deck, one eighty-degree field of fire, and if he needs his spotter, set him or her up as well." The chief looked interested and scanned the sky.

"That will take two from our tactical defense team, but I can adjust the shifts accordingly. What's your plan?"

"If we need to, a little excising with precision and skill, rather than having to use the CWIS. You recall she asked for the crew to be taken alive?" Gordon laughed, raising his mug to hide his smiling face.

"At sea, if someone shoots at me, I always regard requests like that as optional!" Indigo joined in, sensing he and the chief would really work well together, something he really wanted to achieve. But there was always the lurking difficulty of the ROE.

"Chief, no problems with opening fire before they do?" Indigo watched the chief's face, saw his eyes close partially, and saw the lines around his mouth harden. He turned his body to fully face Indigo.

"Colonel, this ship is under your jurisdiction, that is Interpol Section Five. My Admiral gave me chapter and verse on your ROE, and I've seen you all in action one or twice before. I trust your judgment and will obey any order you issue so long as it does not, in my judgment, risk this ship and its crew." Indigo nodded, reached out, and took the chief's hand.

"Good, because we just picked up an image at our one o'clock, we're in trail at this point, but we should get ready to find out what it is." The chief looked at the repeater Indigo was pointing to, nodded, reached for his communicator, and called all hands. Indigo pointed to the top deck. The chief nodded, and he used his communicator again. Two sailors, dressed as fisherfolk, ran up to the deck, then started to climb onto the roof. Indigo grabbed the blond-headed sailor with the long rifle bag across his shoulder on the way past.

"You'd be Eric?"

"Yes, sir."

"Okay, set up your nest. If the target is what we expect, I want it disabled at maximum distance with minimum casualties. I want the crew alive, copy?" The young sailor looked up at the sky, felt the wind whipping across his face, hoped most if it was from boat speed, and looked over the side where a half-meter swell was being pushed easily along the hull.

"Sir, I can probably take out the engines, and if it's the ribbie you have on the navigation screen, I can take out the inflatable sides. I won't aim for any of the crew, but I can't guarantee they don't move into my shot."

"Accepted. Go."

"Chief, take the helm, please. Man all stations. Keep weapons locked for now. Monitor the air radar closely."

"Aye, aye, sir." The chief moved behind the wheel, pulled the electronic control for the throttles back a fraction, scanned the instruments, and then fitted a pair of headphones that would connect him to the crew. Indigo watched the approaching boat through a pair of stabilized binoculars, scanned both sides of the inlet, and saw clearly the massive white oil tanks on the end of Whiddy Island. The little boat was turning slowly to take up a course that would cross theirs, and the range was now down to around one and a half nautical miles, a very long shot at a moving target from an unstable platform.

"Chief, can we lessen our movement?"

"Yes, slightly. See here." He turned the little wheel and moved the bow ten degrees to starboard, and immediately the ship steadied, now heading directly into the light chop. He also reduced their speed. The net effect was that the target was now moving slightly away from them, but they were still gaining ground because of their higher speed.

"Can we confirm the target vessel?" the chief called. Indigo scanned the foreshores again, checked the area behind the boat, and nodded. They were now around ten nautical miles from Whiddy Island, running between Shot Head and its opposite peninsular and up the guts of Bantry Bay.

"It is a ribbie as described: blue hull, gray topsides, small cabin. I can't make out the registration. The angle is too extreme."

"Are they showing any signs that they have seen us?" Indigo leaned his elbows on the coming, squinting as he tried to see every detail of the small boat.

"No, not yet. They look like they are slowing, waiting for something." He thought about what Sandra had told him about the Israeli 104 booting them off the northern beaches. They were now well and truly to the south of the Island. Perhaps they were waiting for a signal from someone on shore.

"Eric, can you get a clean shot at the engines?" Through his binoculars, the two massive black outboards stood out against the green background of the Island.

"Sir, I can."

"At your discretion, shoot!" The inevitable pause followed, then the crack of a fifty-caliber rifle echoed across the deck, followed by a second shot, then a third. The echoes had barely stopped when a round slapped into the window beside the chief, creating a spiderweb of fractures in the glass. The crack of the fifty rang through the boats again, and Indigo could see the boat listing to its port side. The chief wiped the blood off his face, cut by the flying glass, and shrank himself below the level of the helm. Indigo registered the shot with an autonomic flinch but chose to ignore it otherwise.

"Eric, one into the bows, one into the stern."

Two shots followed in rapid succession. The chief accelerated the ship to its maximum speed, and Indigo called for the CWIS gun ports to be opened. Indigo grabbed the loudhailer microphone and was about to speak when three shots in rapid succession slammed into the deck, followed by the boom of the fifty-caliber. Ahead of them, Indigo saw one of the shapes literally blow apart. Then the other three shapes held their hands up high, their small boat now rocking from side to side.

The chief motored at full speed around the boat, creating a wash that punched and slapped at the sides and eventually flashed over the edges of the deflating inflatable tubes, flooding the little boat. He retarded the throttles, and the ship slid to a stop under reverse, rolling in the artificial swell. Indigo called for a boarding crew, and in minutes, four Seabees armed to the teeth pulled alongside the wallowing ribbie. Two women and a young man were taken off, clothes soaked in sea water and blood, and Indigo turned to ask the chief a question and saw him holding his arm against the side of the cockpit, leaking blood over the deck.

"Chief! How bad?" His skin looking pasty, his face a lesson in anger, he peeled his lips back and spat out a mouth full of blood.

"Bastards couldn't shoot for shit! Got me in the shoulder, and they had to bounce the bloody round off the side to do it." Indigo pulled the emergency first aid kit out of its holder, grabbed a compression bandage, and rapidly applied it to the wound. The chief grimaced, obviously in pain, and the moment Indigo secured the bandage, he pushed him away.

'I'm fine, go see to our guests." Indigo motioned for one of the Seabees who had come up from the control room over to the chief, called for the CWIS to be retracted, and went to the side where the dingy was unloading their guests. Hair matted, cloths soaked, the two women didn't look even close to their photos, and for a split second Indigo thought they may have shot at the wrong boat. Then one of the women looked up at him, fire in her eyes, furiously wiping her soaked hair behind her ears, shedding pits and pieces of the terrorist who had been shot as she did so.

"Sure, I don't know who the fuck you are, but I'll have you shot by the President of Ireland's personal guard." Indigo just smiled. Right boat, right terrorists. Now all he had to do was clean up the chief and figure out how to get them all back to Jessica.

"Dr. MacDonald, I presume, Ms. Cochran, and friend. Welcome, and you are under arrest in accordance with the requirements of the Terrorist Laws as modified in 2022. Take them below, one room each, cuff them please." The seven people disappeared under the coming, the dingy bobbing in the swell, the sounds of the engines idling the only noise coming off the water. The ribbie had taken on a more severe list, and Indigo made a snap decision.

"Hold the bridge, Chief, will you be okay for ten minutes?" The crusty master chief read Indigo's mind, and now slumped down against the bulkhead being treated more thoroughly by a Seabee, he knew he could do anything required of him if his head would just stop ringing and thumping at the same time and his eyes cleared, even for just a few seconds!

Indigo jumped into the dingy and quickly motored over to the sinking ribbie, climbed aboard, retrieved three rucksacks out of the cabin, made a quick search of the rest of the boat, then headed back to *'Scáthán'*. He arrived back on the top deck with a flourish.

"Chiefa, is alla thata blooda yoursa? Becausea ifa it isa, we'rea going to have toa givea youa a transfusiona, and I'm a little rustya witha thea needle!

The master chief laughed, letting the Seabee root around in the hole he now had in his back, only grimacing when he absolutely had to. The stumpy Italian was okay for a landlubber, but he knew how to wage war, and that rated highly in the chief's estimation. He worried about his wound and how long it might keep him sidelined.

He didn't give a single thought to the Rules of Engagement that had them opening fire before any signal of hostilities had been given!

CHAPTER THIRTY EIGHT

I got word of the chief's injury and the collection of the three terrorists; the 104 had got their medic to run over the chief before letting him leave the Island, and they were now all flying back thanks to the helicopter the Admiral had left on the *'Scáthán'*. Indigo had dragooned two of Josephine Aria's 104 commandos to replace the chief and was now circumnavigating the Island, mostly to be visible to any terrorists in the area. He decided to have his CWIS on display, just to give anyone thinking of taking a pot shot pause to reconsider.

We now held Whiddy Island, and I was comfortable with the situation for the first time since we had first heard of it. We now had the President's two advisors and an unknown male. More fodder for the President: I needed to talk to the Boss to be certain I was on solid ground when it came to Liddy Cochran, the Air Agency representative.

"Jessica, you're looking a little better than the last time I saw you." I looked at his craggy face, shaded by some sort of hat, the background behind him looking regal and very expensive."

"Where are you?"

"In the delegate lounge at our HQ, you can talk freely." I looked around my work space, no more than a chair pulled into a corner, with my two trusty guards standing between me and the corridor, facing outwards. It was as much privacy as I could hope to get without going all the way up to my room. Anna and Sandra had gone downstairs to take the temperature of the milling crowds, which had grown in the last hour. I suspected they both wanted me to take a break, which I simply couldn't do under the circumstances.

"I need to know how the whole Aid Agency thing works for the refugees: how they are paid, where and when the money comes in, what exactly they are paid for, and how they are delivering the refugees."

"You don't want much, do you? Do you have a specific incident in mind?"

"Yes, a Liddy Cochran, here in Dublin, supposedly came here six years ago, and moved permanently a year ago. She is responsible for the five million refugees the Irish have decided to take." He gave me a hard look, then put his thinking cap on.

"I've spoken to the senior leadership of most of the Agencies, and only a very few are involved with the refugee children we are seeing moved around the world. They are mostly focused on the local programs they support in the camps, and on raising money to support their agencies. As for the three who are of interest to us, I had them audited by our finance office, they came up clean, in that all their funds were from, at the time, legitimate sources. The fact that so many trusts were set up is because there are commercial and private support groups around the world what are sympathetic to the cause, again, all above board-example the Westhall Trust in Helena. And all established five of even six years previously, and by the family, not the terrorists."

"Enough time for the money-washing process to be clean and neat."

"Yes. But it gives us a pattern, and once we showed them we were not interested in standing in their way but rather getting rid of the terrorists, they gave us more information. They did challenge us on freezing the funds held in trust in the nineteen countries that have environmental ship sets, but we told them we would release the funds for each country as they agreed to the migration plans. And we've done that in seven countries so far."

"Did you mention we controlled the scientific and technical assets they needed to start a plant from scratch?"

"No, for now, that's our dirty little secret. And we never mentioned nanites."

"Have we still got the cover of nanites being WMDs?"

"Absolutely. There is some major push back from some countries who have learned of the technicalities of both the attacks and the aftermath, and what is happening in Point Roberts and Helena is getting a lot of amateur airplay. The panels are seen as a god send, and the portable powerpacks, now in over one hundred locations down the west coast, as the means to ending the power drought. Towns and cities all over the US are screaming for them."

"And I just bet many are choosing to forget how they came about and the incredible cost to the world?"

"Naturally, local politics and survival trump all, even common sense in some cases. The screaming is working its way up Constitution Avenue, even as the President makes the point that America is on the way back again, but it will take time."

"So, enough of the history already. How are the Agencies getting paid, and when did it all start?" he glared at me, I promise you, with a full-on steely glare. I gave him one back, scrunching my eyes up to make my point, leaving my mini on the tabletop to fend for itself. "Well?" His craggy face broke into a smile, and he sat back and folded his arms.

"You always were picky. The agency that is feeding in children through the Red Crescent and Red Cross negotiated with both fifteen years ago for the help with identification, management, housing, transportation, and now bulk moving of targeted refugee children. It is a very sophisticated and professional operation, as you would expect from two of the world's best Aid Agencies. But the key here is that they are subcontractors, not instigators, and yes, they have been paid in advance for the past five years. Both opened their books to us, going back fifteen years in some cases.

"We've dug very deep and can't find a single thing wrong with what they have done or how they have done it. Some of the funds they have redirected into the normal programs with the permission of the trusts. Now, one very interesting development in the last week." He paused. The bastard was building tension, and I really didn't need any more than I had locally at the moment. I opened my hands in supplication and put a 'what?' I had a look on my face and was about to spew when he answered.

"When news of the ship being sunk in the Atlantic by persons unknown spread, the prime Agency halted all further shipments. That's nine vessels, possibly as many as twenty to thirty thousand children, all of whom are being looked after on board. The ships are spread around the Mediterranean, and they have given us the location and identification of every vessel. Guess what they want?" I looked on in mild shock, anticipating his answer. They wanted us to offer protection!

God in heaven, how could a simple 'find the terrorists and kill them' operation get so screwed up?

"I know you're not kidding. Did they suggest how we might achieve that?"

"They quoted the charter of the UNHCR at us." I looked at him with astonishment running across my face like the mumps, more confused than ever before in my relatively short life.

"They said, and I quote, 'the terrorist attacks seem to have stopped, and we are now executing a peaceful migration of refugee children to a number of willing countries, and we are asking for a guarantee of safety at sea to enable us to deliver on our commitment.'"

To say I was gob smacked was the understatement of the year—make that the century. The UNHCR charter, known as the Refugee Convention, was written way back in 1951, mainly to meet the needs of the millions of refugees created by World War II. It dealt specifically with refugee protection. What they—the Aid Agencies responsible for moving the millions of refugees around the world—were asking us to do was separate the terrorist attacks from the migration of refugee children and see them as two separate events.

"I'm only going to ask one question. How many of our terrorist women have penetrated these organizations?" He looked bemused, as if I had taken him off topic.

"If you think for one minute I've gone soft putting on a suit, forget it. I've started a deep dive into the background of everyone involved, and yes, we have some women geniuses involved, but they all have solid backgrounds, families, documentation, and all are way qualified for the roles they are playing. Were they part of Trotsky's and Mohammad bin Azaria's rescued children? Without question, and every one of them is prepared to tell their story.

"And of course, that includes how they were pulled from the misery of the camps and given to willing families, educated, and supported in their life choices until they found their calling in the Aid Agencies. And the bit that really rubs, is we can't do a single thing about it." I sunk into my chair. First, the terrorists had manufactured worldwide catastrophe by destroying the head and the heart of the Catholic Church, enraged Muslims with an attack on the Grand Mosque, attacked the Dome of the Rock, then launched a few other attacks, followed by cutting off all oil, gas, and coal, and the Internet, crashing most computers worldwide. Creating the conditions you would experience in a refugee camp.

Some sixty million plus people had been killed subsequently by civil insurrection. The world was in a mess it would take years, perhaps decades, to recover from, and now the terrorists were asking us to protect their ships with the refugee children onboard. It wasn't bad enough that we had been silently forced to let their environmental plants continue to work, providing the panels and power packs the world needed to stay alive. It wasn't enough that we had to provide the manpower and expertise to build more plants. Now we had to protect the refugee children from attacks by terrorists!

And let's face it, it had been the terrorist's very own Maribelle Assiano who had deliberately sunk a ship in the Atlantic Ocean with over five thousand refugee children on board for no apparent reason. Yes, we had, in turn, sunk her in a radioactive cloud that had circled the earth, but that had been deliberate to prevent her from getting her nuclear weapons in position to wreak havoc.

I could imagine the look on the Admiral's face when I gave him this news.

"They've beaten us at every turn, haven't they?" The Boss looked at me, putting a warm smile on his face, but I could see it was a little forced and thin in the making.

"It might look like that, but you and I know what we have achieved so far, and with what you have by the tail in Ireland, you might just put them all in concrete cages once and for all."

"I've having another shot at the President, with the new information we have mined, but I'm still not certain at this point we can nail him." He shook his head, pushing his lips out.

"Do your best, then clean up Whiddy Island. Then you've still got Scotland, Socotra, and our friends at Killala Bay. Plenty to keep you out of mischief." The smile I gave him back was worse than his, so I just closed the connection and slumped in my seat. Sandra and Anna found me all but sucking my thumb, and their evil grins snapped me out of it.

"Hey you, why so glum?" Sandra was laughing at me. I could feel it.

"When will the women get here, and how's the chief?" I sat up in my seat, signaled for coffee, and invited them both to pull up chairs.

"The chief is ambulatory. We'll give him a desk job until he can return to his fleet. The women are being processed now by our AIC, and she'll have them up here ready for a chat in ten minutes. We also have a male prisoner, a probable mercenary. You haven't heard the latest?" I asked, knowing they hadn't. But I decided to distract them first. The news about the boats still sat in my gut like a rusted and badly bent nail.

"How are we downstairs?" Anna looked uncomfortable, and Sandra bounced up to her feet, swinging her carry bag behind her back.

"Better call the riot squad. They could go feral at any moment." Anna smiled at Sandra's summary, and for once I couldn't tell if she was joking or not.

"Sandra's letting some of the chit chat get to her. I think we're okay as long as we maintain our professionalism and keep the information tight. The biggest threat we face is from the Presidential Guard. They are unsure what their role is, so we brought them up to speed. The President is helping clarify some details. We're waiting on more of his people to arrive so we can sort out a lot of the confusion and conflicting information. He's not under arrest; he's the only one that can help us, yada yada. They accept the authority of Interpol, but they don't like it."

"Will they hold?" I asked. Anna looked serious, so I looked up at Sandra, prowling like a corny cat.

"Yes, the local Garda and the Army contingent are on our side. They understand the stakes, and the Prime Minister's team has briefed everyone, which has helped a lot." I nodded in acceptance. The last thing I wanted was a civilian bloodbath over jurisdiction.

But the fact of the matter was that we were holding the President of Ireland incommunicado and under 'soft' house arrest without charge or representation, while hundreds of his people milled around downstairs, waiting for his release. And Sandra was still prowling like a caged animal at the zoo. What was wrong with her?

"Sandra, what's bugging you?" She stopped her pacing, turned on her heel, and lanced me with a look that would slice through an ice block. A very, very big block of ice, come to that. She pointed at me. Physically puffed up, she had a stunning look at any time. After all, she had the stature, look, and innate beauty of a runway model. And wore silk knickers under her combat clothes as a reminder.

"I've read every interrogation you have ever done, been in a few lately, and really came to like your style and aggressiveness. But with the President, it's as if you're walking on eggshells. Why?" Her face was now a mask of accusation, and she stood perfectly still. Anna held her face neutral, but her eyes never left Sandra. Inside, the rusted, bent nail turned over, creating a phantom pain that I recognized as the truth smacking me in the face. She was correct—I was dancing around the President, so I waved her to her chair, put my head on my hands and my elbows on my legs, and forced my head up so I could see her eyes, and more importantly, she could see mine.

"I've had a fear since we first met with him that if we got it wrong, the unintended consequences of my mistakes could unravel much of what we have achieved. We hold all the women we have captured so far because they had the intent, and the physical relationship with either the terrorist's plan or its execution. The women at the plants we hold by direct association, in that they could not have done what they were doing without prior knowledge of the timing of the terrorist attacks. We now have proof that the President's office, at the very least, expected some disruption over a six month period, unspecified, and had prior warning of the Internet attack. But it seems that the source was their advisors, and it's within his rights to take, or not take, their advice."

"And the mercenary terrorists, in the main, are all dead."

"Yes." I looked at Anna. "Very good point. Although I'm still not convinced we have cleaned them all out of Ireland." Anna nodded. Once again, her implicit support raised my confidence level above zero.

"I'll give you the consequences, but how can he claim to be the President if he doesn't know all the details?" Sandra's hostility was lessening, something I was grateful for. I needed her support, not her anger.

"Politics. It's easy for a head of State to point the finger at the executive or administration branches and totally isolate him or herself from the actions of the same. That's how the game is played."

"Jessica's correct. I've seen that behavior in every level of government I have served in." Sandra finally sat, letting her shoulders go soft. She ran her hands through her hair as she did. There was still tension, but it was more controlled.

"I don't have to like that answer. And I don't. What's next?"

"We go and have a polite chat with the two women." We all stood and moved to the first room outside, where our lanky lieutenant stood, a tray with five coffee mugs on it.

"Will you marry me and give me babies?" Sandra asked, taking one of the mugs off the tray. Anna grabbed the second, and unashamedly, I grabbed the third. He just laughed, and in that beautiful Israeli-accented English, he thanked Sandra for the kind offer, then told us he was married with two young children! I shook my head all the way into the interview room, where the good-looking Dr. MacDonald sat, her hands manacled to the desk. The fury in her eyes was palpable, and her body language spoke of severe damage to me and mine if she got loose. In contrast, she wore bright blue leggings with a pale yellow jumper over them, and her silver hair was cut short like a cap of sunshine. She looked like she could eat me in one bite.

Not going to happen. I had her on too many counts for her to slip away.

"Good afternoon, I'm Commander Riley, Interpol. This is SSSA Bernstein, FBI, and Inspector Thomas, also from Interpol.

"Aye, I know who you are. You're the shagging trio who's been killing and locking up my sisters!" The velocity of her voice reverberated around the small room. Her whole body rose out of her seat, and only the manacles stopped her from gaining her feet. I looked at her with the calmest face I could manage, looked deep into her tight, black eyes, and willed her to open and listen.

"Dr. MacDonald, the two women we killed were proven terrorists, one an ex-Stasi Agent, responsible for crimes against humanity too many to list here, and the captain of a gun boat carrying nuclear missiles on its way to attack the United States." I had a sudden flash of memory, the Admiral's hand over mine as I sent the command to the submarines to torpedo the gun boat in the Atlantic, causing the ensuing radioactive cloud and tsunami and the loss of the entire crew of a destroyer. And a ride on an aircraft carrier, I would never forget when the giant waves from the tsunami hit us.

We had no idea of the composition of the crew of the gunboat, except for Assiano, the captain. But I was sure of 'Helen', or Natasha Trotsky, as she was formally known. I had shot her myself in the head in an underground jail back in Venice. Sandra had been my wingman on that occasion—or woman—and I had also shot her, but in the heart. It was an old mantra for a reason.

"What about the five thousand innocent children you killed in the Atlantic?" She spat at me. Only the distance between us created by the table stopped me from getting a face full, and her anger shone on her like a radiant light. I waited a second for my nerves to settle, looked at Anna, then Sandra, whose hand had slipped unconsciously into her carry-on bag.

"We did not sink your refugee ship. That was the action of your very own Maribelle Assiano and her crew. I admit to sinking the gunboat after it attacked your refugee ship." The silence in the room was absolute as she digested this piece of information. It must have been quite a shock to learn that her own 'sister' had sunk the cruise ship.

"Not possible."

"Very possible. We have it on video. Would you like to see it?" She shuddered, her face now a mask of confusion. She shook her head as if freeing herself from the images in her mind, and she turned to me with an almost pleading look on her face. "We also have the Coast Guard helicopter and the fishing boat she needlessly attacked on video as well."

"Why would Maribelle do such a thing?" Her voice had dropped several levels, and it was clear she was in shock. I let it play out for a minute, then started in on what I wanted to know.

'We know you are one of the terrorist women. Your background is fake, your family doesn't exist, and you've been at this for over six years, so in all probability you were in the first or second tranche of refugee children taken by Mohammad bin

Azaria. The timing fits, and we know some of your classmates. We've had a lot of fun locking them up. So the only real question we have for you is: when did you tell the President about the net attack?" She looked more curious than scared. I had to give her credit for recovering quickly. She shook her head.

"Never did. We fed it to the IT geeks, and they did the rest. Once we got the President's seal on the overall plan, we didn't need him for anything other than the authority of his office. The day you met with him was the first time I had been in his office for months."

"Where did you spend your time?" She smiled at me, as you would consider a kindergarten child asking a stupid question.

"That's for me to know and you to find out." I stared at her, her sudden bravado surprising me.

"Do you have the feeling that you will walk out of here and go back to what you were doing before we arrested you?" She smiled and nodded her head.

"Yes, you can't hold me or Liddy either, or the plan for Ireland will collapse like a pricked balloon."

"So let it." Sandra's voice was harsh and whipped across the room like a bullet. The horror on MacDonald's face was like those made famous in scary movies.

"You can't do that. The lives of five million or more refugee children rely on the Irish project's completion." Now she faced us with her hands held out as far as the chains would allow, almost in a pleading gesture. Sandra leaned into her space, her eyes slitting with barely controlled anger.

"Our role is not to help you move refugees around the world. It's to stop bastards like you blowing the world up. Don't you think that all the chaos and destruction your attacks have caused is too high a price to pay for your precious project?"

"Don't you value the lives of refugee children?" She shouted, spittle running down from the corners of her mouth. Sandra sat back, folded her arms across her chest, and glared at Macdonald.

"Yes, I do, very much. Everyone in this room does, but we're not going to kill the rest of the world in the process." MacDonald looked down at the top of the table, folded her fingers into each other, and shook her head.

"It's the only way we could get your attention." Sandra laughed, a genuine belly laugh that boomed around the room like a drum solo.

"You have our attention—you could say undivided at this point—but tell us, before we lock you in a concrete cage for the rest of your miserable life, where does the Aid Agency person, Liddy Cochran, play into all this?" Sandra had dropped her voice again, and I was really starting to like her tactics. She was keeping the suspect off balance by using fire and heat and then being cool and calm. I was seeing yet another side of *'Just call me Sally.'*

"Liddy only knows what we tell her. She knew nothing about the attacks. In fact, when she found out about them, she threatened to withhold her support for our project. In fact, she did for a whole month, until we convinced her that the attacks were by others."

"Your hired mercenary's?"

"They serve their purpose." Both Anna and I picked up on the use of the current tense. Sandra did too, but you would never know it from her reaction—or lack of it.

"Why were you so intent on getting back to Whiddy Island?" She looked at Anna in a curious way, as if she had forgotten she was in the room with us.

"My business, not yours." I decided to finish what I had started, so I stood.

"Agent Bernstein, in your opinion, does this prisoner meet the criteria for permanent incarceration under the Terrorist Laws as modified in 2022?" Anna stood while Sandra continued to lounge in her seat, now offering a 'I don't care what they do with you' posture, as clear as if she had shouted it from the rooftops.

"Yes, Commander, she does."

"On the door!" It opened, and I motioned our two guards in, pointed to the prisoner, and looked at the lieutenant.

"Fetch the other female prisoner, please."

"At once, ma'am." The door remained open, and I saw two more of the 104 slide into view, so I moved to Sandra and punched her in the arm.

"Ouch!" She looked up at me, a scowl on her face. "Why did you do that?"

"Where are your manners? You're supposed to stand when a lady walks in or out of a room." She burst into laughter and pulled herself erect in her seat.

"Didn't see no lady, just a scumbag too full of herself to understand the trouble she's in." I let the use of derogatory language go. I felt exactly the same, and my anger had been building, interview by interview. We had been inside the belly of the beast for over three months. It was ugly, and it was personally uncomfortable, and it was getting harder and harder every day to keep a balanced perspective as far as the genius women terrorists' went. As Sandra had so rightly put it, the cost had been too high. And the terrorists were winning by default, having created situations where we had no choice but to continue their plan as far as relocating the refugee children were concerned.

It galled.

The Aid Agency woman arrived not in chains but held firmly on each arm by our guards.

"Commander, your prisoner." I gestured to the recently vacated seat.

"Thank you for coming, Ms. Cochran. Make yourself comfortable. My head office has spoken to yours, so we have a fairly detailed view of where you have come from, what you have done, and why you are doing it. Let's start at the beginning. Where did the million home project start?" She looked calm, too calm when you considered just hours before she had been involved in a high-velocity bullet exchange with a heavily armed ship, then bundled up and taken prisoner, shipped by helicopter across the country, allowed to shower and change into someone else's clothes, then bundled unceremoniously into an interrogation room, where the environment was anything but warm and fuzzy.

"May I know who is questioning me?" Her well-modulated voice suggested education, manners, and breeding, and I wondered if she was one of the genius children rescued by Trotsky or Mohammad bin Azaria.

"Were you a child refugee?" Sandra asked, on the same wavelength.

"Yes. Who are you?" Same calm voice, no edge that I could detect. This might be a very interesting interrogation.

'I'm Inspector Thomas. This is Commander Riley, both from Interpol, and SSSA Bernstein, FBI. Which camp?" Her eyes opened at the question. Sandra had the ball, and I was happy for her to run with it.

"As best I remember, as I was only six or seven, St. Ann's refugee camp in Kenya was closed by the government a year after I left. I was told that by my adoptive parents."

"Not a nice place to grow up?" For the first time, she smiled, almost wishfully.

"It was okay if you didn't know what was going on in the camp proper. We lived in a tent village on the fringe, and the people I lived with did their very best for me and the other children."

"How were you recruited?" She gave Sandra a hard look, as if insulted by the implication.

"I was taken out of the camp with two others by a Red Crescent woman, and after a week or two, given to my adoptive parents."

"Where?"

"In Canada. In Toronto, in fact, they're still living there with my sister and brother."

"Still alive after all the attacks?" She immediately looked uncomfortable.

She gave Sandra a strange stare, as if looking for some sort of hook. Placing her hands on the tabletop, she linked her fingers and worked very hard to conceal the involuntary shaking her body was doing. Fear or guilt? Time would tell.

"So, back to my question: when were you recruited to work for the Aid Agency? And what was happening in the refugee camp that was so bad?" Now she looked confused. A typical thinker's personality profile was where you had to go in order to enable them to feel comfortable answering pointed questions. One, two, thee, etc., and give time for a considered answer.

"On the day of my graduation, Lady Flattery approached me with an offer I couldn't refuse. She represented a trust set up to help refugee children like myself, and she introduced me to the Aid Agency people who trained me, then sent me back to her in Ireland." She paused, sucked in her breath, and her face suddenly took on a pasty look.

"As for what was going on in the camp, there were several warlords who had made their camps within our boundaries, and every so often they would shoot, kill, maim, rape, and pillage until a complete section of the camp was cleared for them. They fought all the time, took several children in as slaves and for other purposes, as we were just the inconvenient fodder for their wrath, the fresh meat in the sandwich as it were. Hundreds of children were killed, and hundreds more just disappeared. Getting out was the best thing that ever happened to me."

"What did Lady Flattery tell you she was going to do?" Now she looked calm again, as if we had crossed some unknown Rubicon. What have I missed? I replayed her answers while she answered Sandra.

"She said that they had a plan for Ireland. It would take a few years, but she had someone in mind to lead the project, she had the funds, and she wanted my Air Agency to do all the ground work in the the refugee camps. I couldn't have been happier." Just as she finished, I got it—the point where she had relaxed. The attacks. I moved my hand on the tabletop to get Sandra's attention. She got the message and sat back.

"Where were you during the terrorist attacks?" She went pasty again, and I could see her hands shaking even as they gripped each other, her knuckles turning white.

"I was here, in Dublin. I had just returned from Ethiopia, where I was visiting a camp. In fact, the attacks started the day after I got back."

"Lucky for you." I let that sit and remembered what MacDonald had told us. "Dr. MacDonald said you threatened to refuse further services because of the attacks." She looked extremely uncomfortable.

"Yes. Until she showed me the attacks had been made by mercenaries, I thought she and her sisters might have been involved. She proved to me she was at the plant on Whiddy Island during the attacks, and it soon became known that mercenaries were creating the chaos. In fact, she was instrumental in warning us about the internet hacks that shut down the world wide web and stopped all those computers. She warned the government, and they took action to protect what we had here."

"Did you ever think to ask where she got her information from?" She raised her eyebrows.

"Of course. She said that we had a network of people around the globe who were monitoring the terrorists and predicted the net attack. She was a refugee as I was, pulled out of a really bad camp a few years before me, and she said that many of the rescued children had formed a casual intelligence community around the world who were actively helping us to do our work. I believed her. I even checked with the professor up in Belfast, who was also running a refugee project here in Ireland." New information, but I had a suspicion where that project might be located.

"She introduced you to the President?"

"Yes, and to other members of the government, the Prime Minister, and his staff. My responsibility is to get the refugee families and children ready to migrate, based on what the project needs at any given time."

"The project was running before you came here?"

"Yes, for over two years. I visited as I needed to, then moved here permanently last year."

"Have you been to Whiddy Island?'

"Yes, several times, I've been amazed at what they can produce there."

"Do you know anything about Killala Bay?"

"Where? No, I don't think so." She looked deep in thought, then shook her head. "No, I haven't." I looked at Anna and gauged her reaction. She raised an eyebrow at me, and I raised one back. I looked at Sandra.

"What if we told you that the attacks had been planned and executed by a cadre of refugee children just like yourself, pulled out of the camps, placed with loving families, educated and grown up, then trained to wreak havoc on the world?" Sandra held her eyes, and the shaking started again, Cochran unable to hide it as successfully this time.

"No, no, you can't be serious? That's impossible." Sandra drummed her fingers on the tabletop, watching Cochran like a hawk.

"Not only possible, but absolutely true. You must have sensed it in your partner, didn't you?" She visibly shook, her whole body given to short sobs, and in spite of myself, I felt for her. I could imagine the sense of betrayal she felt, because in her I saw a dedicated worker who believed in her cause and her mission. Her passion came through as clearly as her fear.

"Liddy, didn't it feel strange when the two men with you started shooting at the ship? And why were you and MacDonald trying so hard to get back to Whiddy Island?" She wiped her eyes with the back of her hand, sniffed, and pulled herself upright.

"The two men with us were guards. In case of terrorists, there had been reports of activity out at the airport and along the road to Bantry Bay. When your ship bore down on us, they assumed you were going to attack us. And Mary wanted to get back because she said that some of the production processes would spoil unless they were tended to. I went with her because for the past three months we have stuck close together because of the civil unrest."

"Back to the attacks. We can show you irrefutable proof that the major attacks were made by refugee women, just like yourself. Mercenaries were used all around the world to shut down the oil, gas, and coal centers, and a lot of other stuff in between. What of your project now?" Sandra looked just a little feral, leaning forward again, her lips pulled back, showing her teeth. I nearly told her to relax, then thought better of it. So far, we have learned a lot more than we had expected to, so why screw with the arc?

"I don't know. I have millions of refugees being prepared in camps and holding centers all over Europe. I have some five thousand due here in three months. I have an order for thousands more over the next year, all dependent on the houses being fitted with power panels and supplies and infrastructure being built—schools, shopping centers, hospitals, all the things you need for a growing community. Are you suggesting the Irish government will pull out of the project?" I looked at Sandra, who was sitting back in her seat, happy for some reason with her response. I looked at Anna. She raised her eyebrow at me again, and this time I just shook my head.

"We'll take a look at that question and let you know. For the immediate future, you'll be given a room here for the duration, and we'll send someone to your apartment for your things. You will be monitored, but we will let you know your status as soon as we can. Thank you." I stood, pointed to the door, Anna rose and opened it, and the two guards came in and escorted her out.

I dialed Indigo.

"Did you shoot at the ribbie with the women on board first?" He smiled at me, was about to burst into Italian, then saw the serious look on my face.

'No, commander, we approached them openly. We did have our CWIS out and visible, but the men in the boat shot at us first. How is the chief?" I smiled. There was that immediate concern for our people again, no matter where from.

"He's fine, probably on his way home by now. Thanks for the intel." I closed the mini, looked at Anna, and Sandra was sitting back with her eyes closed.

"There are a million more questions we need to ask her." She spoke so softly that I doubted if the lieutenant standing at the door could hear her.

"Yes, we'll pass her onto a local team. Anna, same question as for MacDonald?" She gave me a considered look and slowly shook her head.

"No. Remember Amira and Fay, same background, different outcome. In this case the women terrorists recruited her for her skills in managing the refugees, not to attack or fight. Did she know about anything in advance? I think not. Even with her knowing of the possibility of the net hack and her suspicions about her 'sisters' as she calls them, she acted properly and consulted another senior woman she knew was involved with the refugee project. If you wanted to, you could get her on the net hack, but I don't see her as complicit. Sandra?"

"As much as it pisses me off, I didn't sense anything but honesty. She sensed the women were involved, did something about it, took the evidence presented to her, then made a judgment in favor of the project, which is where her heart lays in any case. A bit like you, operational blindness." I wacked her across the back of her head, just a gentle tap, but her point was well made.

"Guilty as charged, Miss Perfect. Now for the male?" She smiled at me, straightened her hair where I had mussed it, and rolled her shoulders.

"Guilty, let's just shoot him and get it out of the way." Anna smiled, not knowing about the two occasions where Sandra and I had done exactly that.

"Blood thirsty, at your best. We need information, and it won't hurt to be able to parade him around for the locals to see." I called for the door, explained what I wanted, and before I could get back to my seat, a tray with three steaming cups of coffee appeared, followed by a thin man in dirty combat clothes, hands shackled, and attached by a chain to his ankles. His shuffle was both awkward and noisy. His hair was a mess, and his caramel-colored skin was partially hidden by camouflage makeup.

In short, he was a mess. But according to Indigo, he had surrendered his weapon when his partner had been blown to bits and put his hands up high in the air, so perhaps he had a brain.

"Name?" He looked at me with a blank expression on his face, his eyes two black pinpricks.

"The two women you were captured with told us you spoke excellent English, so don't pull the dumb fucker on us. Name. Now." Sandra was at it again, full of piss and vinegar, and as lies go, this was well told. He looked pointedly at the coffee. Sandra just picked up her mug and slurped a mouthful, then literally smacked her lips. Torture of the highest order!

"Name, or I'll just shoot you here and now and save us any further aggravation." And she reached into her carry bag and pulled the deadly little H&K out, racked back the slide, tipped it on its side to examine it, then placed it on the table top with a 'thunk'. She drummed the fingers of her gun hand on the table, creating tension with a flourish.

"My name is Padroni Musfir, and I claim protection under the Geneva Convention."

"My name is fuck you three times over, and you are arrested under the Terrorist Laws as modified in 2022, so let's just get on with it, shall we?" He visibly quivered, the impact of the Terrorist Laws hitting home. No representation, a trial in absentia if necessary, and a dark, rank concrete cage were the best he could ever hope for. Or, as Sandra has already indicated, a bullet in the head if the World Court passed the death sentence.

"Why did you open fire on our ship?"

"We thought you were terrorists! And the woman told me too."

"Did she now? How interesting. You weren't fired upon. What made you think we were terrorists?"

"Your ship had big guns everywhere and bore down on us quickly. The tall woman told us to open fire."

"And you always take your orders from a woman?" He visibly shrank as the implication of that sunk in. In his country of origin, that was a big cultural no-no.

"Where did you come from here in Ireland?"

"We were guarding roof panels down in Waterford when we were called up to Dublin."

"How did you get to Bantry Bay?"

"When you closed the Island, we were driven to Bantry."

"So you've only been here a short while?" He looked confused at the question. I could see it in his eyes.

"Where did you stay?" More confusion. He didn't know how to answer the question.

"How many are in your group?" He visibly winced, imagining the potential payback he would receive if he gave anything about his fellow terrorists away.

"Now, you see, that just doesn't sit well with me. Commander, I'm for the bullet." She picked up the H&K and pointed it at his head. "Agent, you should move a little to the side," she said, motioning Anna offhand. His face went sheet white, sensing Sandra was absolutely going to shoot him. Another lie well told: she was really getting good at playing the bad arse. He held his hands up as far as the chains would allow, a pleading look on his painted face.

"No, please, I'll tell you. We were eight in Waterford. Four of us went to Cork Airport two weeks ago. My brother and I traveled first to Dublin the next day. We stayed in a house where the women were, then we moved around. We drove to Bantry Bay five days ago, with the two women. That's all."

Sandra lowered her H&K, reluctance all over her pretty face, and with a sigh that was audible, pushed it back into the carry bag.

"What a pity. I was really looking forward to splattering your brains all over this room." I reached over and patted her on the shoulder.

"He's still not out of it. The World Court will decide his future. You may yet get to shoot him." Anna had watched the byplay with a stoic look on her face, and she hadn't moved out of range when Sandra had indicated she was about to shoot.

She let her hands fall onto the tabletop with a 'thud' and looked the terrorist straight in the eyes.

"Mr. Musfir, my advice is to speak while you can and quickly, because I haven't had a proper meal in some time and I'm getting bored." Her voice was as soft as Sandra's had been and all the more effective for it. Beads of sweat broke out on his painted forehead, and his eyes showed his fear. Where he came from, women weren't allowed to be educated, had to be covered from head to toe, and were subservient to men in every way imaginable. Here he faced three well-dressed, stunning women, dominant by their very body language, their attitude very much 'in your face', the very antithesis of what he had grown up with. And at least one of them wanted to shoot him here and now, in a bright and pretty room in a hotel, with hundreds of people milling around outside!

"Where are your other friends?" Sandra mimicked Anna's soft voice, and she resumed her finger tapping. I would have to ask her later what tune she was playing in her head. He looked scared, then dropped his head.

"The ones who went to Cork didn't come back. The other two were still in Waterford when we left." I nodded. We had killed his fellow terrorists after their rocket attack on our helicopters at Cork airport and taken one prisoner, and his story had been similar. Suddenly I had an epiphany: I knew how to test the President.

"On the door!" And he was marched out by our guards, and both Sandra and Anna looked at me as if I had gone mad.

"Lieutenant, get the President back, please." He disappeared from sight. "I want you two to play along with me. I've figured out how to prove once and for all the President's involvement." He arrived walking tall, obviously not sensing any danger, and looked well fed and rested. In fact, very presidential. I remembered Anna's comment about food and felt sympathetic hunger pains roll around my gut where the rusted, bent nail sat.

"Sir, I have a question for you," I asked before he even had time to sit down. "What would you do if we could prove to you that there are terrorists in a facility in Waterford?" He half bent as if to sit, then straightened, smoothing his club tie in the process. He looked me directly in the eye, made no attempt at prevarication, and stood, if possible, a little taller.

"I would immediately order the Irish Special Forces to mount an operation and take them into captivity."

"Would you allow your Irish *Sciathán Fianóglach* to shoot to kill?" He looked insulted for a second, then tightened his face.

"Commander, you don't send the special forces on a grocery expedition."

"Would you allow two of our troops to participate, possibly even in command?" Now his face showed concern as he worked that through. I pushed a little harder. "You might recall we've had several teams from the *Sciathán Fianóglach* working with us to secure Whiddy Island, even if those did come from Belfast." He nodded. No doubt he remembered. He had been screaming at us to release them for a week.

"Why your troops?"

"Because we will be able to identify the terrorists."

"Whom did you have in mind?" I pointed to Sandra.

"Inspector Thomas is experienced with dealing with terrorists. And I'd also like to send one of our guards to keep her safe." She gave me a dirty look at the implied necessity of a guard, but she had been bugging me for weeks at the Boss's instance, and this was my chance to see how she liked it!

"I would ask one favor of you, sir, and will take your word on it. Do not call anyone at Killara, for any reason. We will know if you do, and we will take that to the World Court to have you prosecuted under the Terrorist Laws as modified in 2022." The look he gave me would have shrunk the balls of the toughest commando, but I was a woman, so he completely missed the mark, unless he was after the pair Sandra swore I carried under my armpits. He looked puzzled, then nodded.

"I agree. But you do realize Killara is the one place we have county permission to amend the bylaws for housing and infrastructure development?" he paused, as if thinking how much more he should add.

"And we expect to have at least three thousand refugees ready to move in later this year. You won't prevent that from happening?" My turn for the steely look as I thought through my options.

"To the best of our ability, we will do nothing to prevent that outcome, providing no terrorist activities are detected in that region. That is nonnegotiable." He looked unsure, which told me he knew far more about Killara than he had let on. Not the time to push, and we had Killara covered.

"I can accept that. Will you keep my office informed, please?" I nodded and signaled to the lieutenant.

"The president is to be escorted to his vehicle. Please let everyone downstairs know he is going back to his office and that we will be mounting a joint Army/Interpol operation, details not available at this time." He saluted me and walked out with the President.

"Sandra, where's our chopper, the one that carried the prisoners and the chief here?"

"Still on the ground at the airport."

"Good, get there, take Edwardo Ricci, he's been in the field with us before, vests and hard hats, NVG's, have him wear his Gruppo di Intervento Speciale regimental patches, fly to Waterford, scout out the location, then wait for the Army. Do not attack the terrorists unless they try to run. I want to see what the Army does. Remember, this is a test of the President's noninvolvement." I pointed at the door. "Go!" I dialed my favorite geek in the whole world.

"Luigi, *ciao*, good to see you. I need you to do something posthaste."

"What?"

"I want to know every conversation the Irish President has for the next seventy-two hours. They have working computers and phones, were tipped off about the net hacks. Can't be traced back to us. I have a Red Notice if you need cover, let me know."

"Commander, can I get help from Stefarino and his people?"

"Yes. But keep it to yourself and them for now."

"WILCO, Commander, will get on it immediately." One down, three to go.

"Boss, I need cover for telecommunications intercepts of all calls made, digital or analog, computer or phone, or even carrier pigeon from the President of Ireland, to all and any destinations. Send it to Luigi."

"You're letting the President go?"

"For now." He nodded, his background this time whizzing past him at a furious speed, so I guessed an electric train. I hung up and dialed again.

"Fay, how goes it?" Her background was a muted green out of focus, something or other, with rain flooding down all over her. Big drips leaked off her bush hat, some even making it to her collar, which she had pulled up to the top of her throat.

"A little wet, as you can see. What's new?"

"I was going to ask you that." She smiled and shook her head, flinging water everywhere like a shaggy dog.

"The women have taken over an empty house near the sewerage plant, from the lights and noises they are doing something inside we can't see. However, one of them in full diving gear and accompanied by a second pulling equipment on a cart walked all the way out the shale at low tide, that's around one and a half kilometers, did a dive, lasted 45 minutes, then towed everything back to the house. Dead of night, even with enhanced night vision we didn't get much detail, except the tanks were ordinary compressed air, no exotics, and the tools looked like your standard underwater rip, tear, and hack types. I can tell you that from our mapping of the area, it looked like they worked at the end of the outflow pipes." A puzzle to be sure, but we knew from the council approvals that the sewage plant was being converted into a biofuel generator, so maybe that's what the work was all about.

"Fay, there might be some trouble headed your way. Be alert for any change in the posture of the women. We are monitoring their comms, so you will have warning."

"Okay, our biggest enemy here is the weather. It hasn't let up in days. And Tom's replacement is much better behaved. Thank you for whatever you did." I just smiled and closed the link. Dialed my favorite substitute uncle.

"Hello, Arie. I hope you are well." His smile would light up a room. He looked relaxed and like his usual calm self.

"Absolutely fine. Thanks for asking, Jessica. What can I do for you today?"

"I'm sending you two more for the cages, one female and one male. I'd appreciate it if the jet can come back to me here in Dublin?" He looked serious while he considered my request, then slowly nodded his head.'

"We can do that. Do you need anything sent back with it?" I shook my head.

"No, thanks, I've got your 104. They are special, all good here at the moment."

"Jessica, I've been reading your reports on Scotland. How long will you let that run?" I shook my head again.

"No idea, Arie. I've got Bob and his team in place. We're monitoring all their broadcasts. Bob has seen no evidence of mercenaries anywhere, and he doesn't sense a threat." Arie nodded acceptance of what I had said, not necessarily agreeing with it. I valued his experience as the preeminent spymaster for Israel, so I asked him the obvious question.

"Do you think we should wrap them up now?" I could feel his eyes penetrating all the way through to my backbone.

"No, I trust your judgment and that of Bob. If I have a worry, it's that you are stretched so thin. I can send you another team of the 104 if you need them."

"Keep them for when we move on Socotra. The 'Katrina' person came from there, before she joined the three from Scotland. I've got eyes on O'Cleary, she's with 'Katrina', and it's her partner-a 'Crissy'-who's holding the fort. I might be wrong, but I sense Socotra is some type of production plant, or even a laboratory. Scotland is an operational control point, and Killala is where they are currently operating, at what, we don't know. There is something very big happening here in Ireland, and we are working it as you know from our reports. There's something the terrorists want protected on Whiddy Island, don't know what, but we will find out. It's galling that the terrorists are winning by default, but I can't see any way around it." He smiled at me, in that wonderful grandfatherly way, and I felt the peace radiate from him.

"You're doing great. Keep your focus. Let me know when you need more resources."

"Thank you, Arie. I appreciate it." I looked at Anna. She gave me the same warmth Arie did, so I packed up and went out to eat. After all, even a condemned man gets a last meal!

DISCOVERY

Amira, dressed in a white pressure suit with orange gloves up to her elbows and a hooded head surrounding her face mask, looked like a person from another planet. When she walked, she towed a thick, corrugated air hose behind her, mounted on an overhead wire. She moved slowly and with purpose. On her bench, which was a glass-topped stainless steel monster, sat eleven small burgundy-colored sealed containers. A small white tag on the front of each one listed the contents. What she was determining now was what exactly one of the nanites contained in the vacuum jars was designed for.

She had confirmed the first three with simple tests she had designed years before at Harvey Mudd University.

The first nanite, the one she had invented and perfected, ate oil at the molecular level, turning the carbon in an oil spill into carbon three, a harmless byproduct that sank to the bottom of the ocean and started the organic growth cycle all over again. This had been proven in a live test on an oil spill.

The second, a further development of her original work by the terrorists, attacked oil and destroyed it, mutating and multiplying rapidly in its quest to destroy the very atomic essence of the mineral. A silver crud was left behind.

The third sample was similar, except it ate coal with a voracious appetite that took it all the way down to the organic beds where the coal originated.

The fourth example ate gas, also with a vengeance, so much so that no gas line, pipes, processing plants, or drilled wells had survived the nanite attack.

The really interesting thing about numbers two to four was that, for all intents and purposes, the nanites were the same, with very few atomic alterations. But she recognized genius when she saw it, and these minute developments were truly spectacular.

Then there was the version that attacked the carbon structure of specific plants, namely poppies, cocoa, and refined drugs such as cocaine, Ice, methamphetamine, and their derivatives. This nanite had other properties, in that it could be ingested by human beings and animals and then disposed of via the normal activity of the bowels. This had been achieved by 'coating' the nanite in a neutral fat that dissolved in direct light, allowing the nanites to attack the crops and drugs. This demonstrated a genius level a generation beyond where she had gone with the first nanite invention.

In every instance, the nanites had been trained to attack the specific carbon isotopes unique to their target and multiply in the process.

And now she faced the remaining samples: one that was reputed to convert organic mass into biofuel; one that could, literally, instantaneously boil water, or any liquid for that matter, creating a heat-work volume equal to that required to boil the liquid in a jug. The difference was that this was an instantaneous reaction. One second you had liquid, the next steam. This flash attribute she had studied under her electron microscope at its highest magnification, and the molecular reaction she had seen baffled her. She could see no immediate benefit from the reaction, but knowing the work of the terrorists, she knew it had a purpose. She had just yet to divine it.

The metal-dissolving nanite was simple to explain because the terrorists had used a derivation of it in creating the bimetallic shells. So in a sense, one version sealed the molecules of the metals, while the other simply removed their bonds at the atomic level.

The two nanites they had used in the conversion of sea water and sand into solar panels and power packs were both derivations of her original work, but in a sense reversed. She wasn't overly concerned with those. The proof of their efficacy was now out in the public sphere and being used every day to bring light back into a gloomy world. This was one of the terrorists victories that Jessica agonized over.

It was the eleventh nanite and the water boiler that gave her the most grief. She had discovered what the eleventh nanite did almost by accident, as she had spilled a drop on her counter top and looked on in amazement as the drop ate its way through the bench, dripped onto the floor, and ate through that, and as she raced down the fire stairs, she found that six stories down it was still going, this time through the concrete floor of the basement. When she looked up, she could see the light in her office shining brightly through the miniature holes.

How far down it had drilled into the earth was only discovered when she managed to get a thin enough weight attached to a nylon line, and the answer shocked her. The drop had penetrated the earth down to three hundred meters, plus the height of the six stories of the laboratory. And when she examined the holes, she found perfection in their shape and that once again all and any carbon in the bench, the floors, and the ground had been consumed.

When, days later, she managed to convince the lab team to uncover some of the hole in the ground, she found to her amazement that the entire three hundred-meter hole had been 'lined' with a glass-like substance, which, when tested, proved to be a rearranged carbon isotope. The net effect was that the sides of the hole had been fused closed by the molecular reaction to the nanite.

This was the same nanite Sandra had found by accident back at Whiddy Island, in the environmental plant. It had been labeled 'CD1' and had come with a data sheet describing how to prepare every type of substrate and photos of the same. Prepare for what? The instructions were specific and detailed.

And yet she still didn't have a single clue what the nanite was for.

CHAPTER FORTY

Rosie Hammond, having made her bones with Fay, albeit after a short and very sharp call from Tom, mentally forced herself into the low heather by the stone wall. She remembered a child's game where if you closed your eyes, put your hands over your face, and believed yourself to be invisible, the other children couldn't see you.

No such luck in the real world, and she pressed herself into the ground as far as she could. Not ten meters away, Katrina and two of the other women stood, surveying an empty house. They were about two kilometers from the beach and smack in the middle of the area north of Killara Fay, as Fay had predicted. She hardly breathed until they moved away, then relaxed a little as they moved into the house. One of her troopers, Fabio, had spotted the trio emerging from an electric vehicle behind the Fishing factory, where he reported they had disappeared into a shed at the back for over half an hour.

She pulled her mini out of her pocket, typed a text message for Fay, and copied her team.

'*Contact at bravo, photo to follow.*' And she primed herself to photograph the trio as they exited the house. They did eventually, then walked back the way they had come. She quickly texted Fabio. '*Trio back to you in ten.*' he responded with a thumbs-up emoji. She shook her head. The modern soldier had a lot to learn about battlefield discipline, and then she shook her head at her stupidity. This team had been in the thick of it on three continents and had taken fatal casualties, and it was she who had to modify her behavior, or she'd never fit into what had been Tom's team.

She remembered only too well Tom's admonishing of her just recently, reminding her his team had a solid core, was experienced, and was the best he had ever worked with. Her real problem was that she had been kicked from one squad to the next for the last three years before finally getting posted to Tom's as his replacement. She needed a home, and she needed to feel respected. But she would not have gotten Tom's team if the hierarchy didn't think she had the chops for it. She was learning quickly that working with Section Five required focus. And speed.

She remembered the chiding comment about her team wearing combat boots while they were in soft clothes, and she smiled. A simple mistake, but potentially a fatal one if the bad guys had seen them. As she watched the trio disappear into the trees, she promised herself to work harder and smarter. Her mini vibrated in her hands, and a text scrolled along the bottom. *'O'Cleary at council chambers, with an unidentified woman, advise?'* She texted back, *'Observe, then follow.'* She forwarded the texts to Fay and got an immediate response. *'Hold off on O'Cleary. Have a tail on her.'*

Rosie grimaced. This was what she had been afraid of— the two teams crossing each other's paths unknowingly. They were only five or six kilometers apart as the crow flies, but thirty kilometers apart by road. Fay had not sent any details on the O'Cleary woman. She had been picked up by accident by the soldier left on the foreshore just south of Killara. Another text swam across her small screen. *'No prior warning due to late development in their transportation. Apologies.'*

Rosie sent a text back, *'All good,'* and mentally relaxed, remembering the old adage that no battle plan survives the first shot. So now she had all five terrorists on her side of the Bay, with her people spread all over the countryside, not in a position to back each other up.

But Fay had not indicated any level of threat, so she levered herself slowly from her concealed position, took a good look around at the emerald-colored hills surrounding her, the pretty rogue flowers that insisted on fighting their way up towards the wan sky, the gray overcast reluctantly letting weak sunlight through in patches, and moved to the border of the house the terrorists had been interested in.

She pulled her mini out, pulled up the map from the council, and noted the house was on the far corner of the approved construction area. She made a note to check with Fay to see if a similar situation existed with the house the terrorists had been working in on the Inishcrone side. She sent a recall text to her team and slowly started to walk back to the village. Her mini buzzed.

"Rosie, they are on their way back from Killara, all clear. Have a look inside the shed they visited at the fish factory. We'll know what O'Cleary was up to in a while. We have an agent inside the Council office." Rosie nodded. Minute by minute, she was learning more and more about Fay, and she decided she really needed to sit down with her to get a solid brief.

"Fay, I need a proper brief." She realized she had blurted it out, almost put her hand over her mouth, and was half way to it when Fay answered.

"Are you secure? If you are, take a seat, and we'll chat now." Rosie looked around. The only company she had were a few black-headed sheep and a family of cows, who studiously ignored her, cropping at the brilliant green grass behind the low, mottled stone hedges. She slumped down against a moldy stone fence.

"Firstly, I've been with Interpol just two months, worked with them for three, and led a team of FBI agents out of Seattle. The Commander recruited me, I went back to school for specific training, and have been chasing the terrorists ever since with Section Five. O'Cleary was one of the terrorists we picked up on a satellite feed out of Afghanistan, which started us on the hunt for the nuclear shells. During that hunt, Ireland became of interest, and here we are."

"How did we find out about the other women with her?" Fay considered for a moment how much operational detail she should share and its relevance to their objective. Then she made a decision. You earned trust by giving it. Tom's team was first-class, well-seasoned, and experienced in hunting the terrorists, and for Rosie to be put in charge, the powers that be had to believe she was more than up to the task. In fact, Fay would expect her to be an exceptional leader.

"We intercepted transmissions from their controller some weeks ago, and we have followed them from Scotland, to Ireland, to Spain, to France, back to Scotland, then England, then back here. We don't know what they were doing, but in Europe they were doing it to shuttered nuclear power stations. We have Interpol teams on that as we speak."

"What do you think they are up to?" Fay gave the question considerable thought. It had been on her mind from day one, since they had learned of the 'test' that had been run over in Dundalk. Where they also had people on the ground but no new information. Or rather, no definitive information.

"To my mind, there have been distinctively different tranches of women terrorists. The latest group are very young, early twenties, and none of them seem to have been involved in the earlier attacks. O'Cleary is a link between two different groups-so is the Scottish team's handler, 'Freya'. This is all sup-position, but what I think we have here is 'Freya' linked her team of young women to 'Katrina", who we know came from Socotra, leaving a 'Crissy' behind. They went off and did a test here in Ireland, then played with the nuke plants.

"Then O'Cleary shows up, also via Socotra, and 'Freya' pulls her women off the nuke plants and sends them to Killara, spe-cifically to meet up with O'Cleary. Massive change of plans to my mind. Now if you want a brief on all this in detail, you'll find it in this folder. I've just sent it to you. Keep it close, please." Rosie nodded her head, which was reeling somewhat from the data dump, but she now had a better appreciation of why they were here.

"Was-or is-O'Cleary one of the original terrorists?"

"More than likely, she popped up just after the attacks, in league with a mercenary terrorist name of Malik Badawi. We took him down at an underground nuclear facility outside of Pollatomish. History suggests she was one of the first recruited by Trotsky or Mohammad bin Azaria's people. Her age fits, her profile fits, even for when her background went dark. Supposedly she is a nuclear scientist, genius level intelligence, and her role on the ship she was on with Badawi was to load nuclear material into the bimetallic shells, seal them, then supervise their use. She appears to have been well qualified for the role, because we have her on satellite imaging at the factory in Afghanistan where they made the nuclear-capable shells."

"Forgive me, I'm late to all this, but it appears this is a very convoluted activity on behalf of the terrorists. There seems to have been no damage done to any facility they visited, and you sense no threat here?" Fay looked at the English woman, her puffer jacket collar turned up, her woolen beanie pulled down over her ears, and her green mittens showing just at the edge of the screen.

Definitely not a military look, which was excellent. She thought about her options—what she could risk and what she could not. The trust equation again.

"As far as we know, including the takedown of seven terrorist locations so far, no woman terrorist has fired a shot at us. It's always been the mercenaries who pulled the trigger. The one exception is Maribelle Assiano, who was the captain of the gunboat we sunk in the Atlantic. Before she met her end, she shot down a coast guard helicopter, sunk a fishing boat, as well as a cruise ship with five thousand refugee children on board." Rosie sucked her breath in, the enormity of that hitting her smack in the middle of her gut. She started to ask a question, then realized there was no answer Fay could give her that would satisfy her.

"Rosie, you're on the ground, so it's your decision, but I would really like to know what's in the shed at the Fishing factory." Rosie nodded. Good, she needed to do something worthwhile other than just sit and watch. She was a highly trained warrior, and sitting on her arse, no matter how fine it might be, always made her uncomfortable.

"It will be my pleasure. Give me an hour." Fay nodded and disconnected. Rosie put a picture in her mind of where her people were and nodded to herself.

'Meet me foreshore outside the Fishing factory.' She waited until she got four thumbs-up, then started in, her bright pink rucksack slung over one long shoulder.

If they were facing an enemy who used their brains and not weapons, she would have to adapt her tactics. It was obvious from the little she had found out so far that the terrorists had superior technology, orders of magnitude beyond anything she had experienced. That didn't make her dumb. She was just behind the learning curve. And she'd always been a fast learner.

She rounded the bend in the dirt road and saw Luca kneeling at the corner of an old wooden structure, watching the beach.

"See anything?"

"No, ma'am. Very quiet. No workers in the factory. The women have driven off some time ago, and I can see two of our team sitting on the foreshore pretending to be tourists."

Good, leave them there. Let's see what's in the shed. She pulled out a tiny fiber-optic cable and ran it under the shed door. Immediately, she saw two cameras and a laser security system crisscrossing the floor. She took photos of what she could see via the miniature camera and noticed the rows of large cannisters, their color coding, and the stack of huge boxes off to one side. She pulled the rig back out, looked at the images on her mini, and shared them with Luca. He ran his fingers over the screen, humming to himself.

"You know what these are?" He looked directly at Rosie, whose furrowed brow suggested she didn't.

"These are the WMDs we've been chasing all over Europe." Rosie gave him a hard look, pulled at her recent briefing, and didn't remember anything about WMDs. She flicked the photo stream to Fay. The response was immediate.

"Retire to home plate. Good work. Call me when secure."

She packed her kit up, tapped Luca on the shoulder, and stood.

"Let's go back to our rooms, good work." And all the way back to their hotel, she worried about the WMDs, why she hadn't been told about them, and what they meant. And were they really WMDs?

Fay had a lot to tell her, and now she had a lot to tell Fay!

CHAPTER FORTY

The sound of crickets rippled across the empty road like firecrackers on Guy Fawkes Night. The warehouse sat inside a pair of wide metal gates, now wide open, and an old flatbed truck sat inside, connected to a charger. It had seen far better days but sat on a new set of tires. Sandra signaled to the Irish captain, who had willingly allowed her to take control of the attack, to move in. She had already sent half the squad of Irish soldiers around the back to flank the terrorists if, in fact, they were inside the shed.

They crept around the border of the long shed until the workers could be seen loading panels onto a forklift. In this case, the workers were an oldish-looking man with white hair fluffing out from under a battered blue cap and a gangly youth dressed in grubby overalls. Three military-looking men with rough faces and dirty clothes but unmistakable automatic weapons slung across their chests looked on, obviously bored with the lack of action. Sandra tapped Edwardo on the arm, pointed to the men, signaled 'three' with her fingers, then signaled to the captain.

He flattened his men into a crouch, and at 'three', Edwardo fired suppressed rounds, dropping the terrorists where they stood. The old man bent up, looked around in fear, then flew at the young youth and crushed him to the ground. The Irish troops arrived, standing tall and trying to look everywhere, and a rapid conversation ensued, none of which Sandra understood.

"Watch out for more." Edwardo moved forward, his barrel sweeping back and forth across the long, open side of the shed. A burst of gunfire rang out, and the captain and two of his soldiers crumbled to the ground. Edwardo and Sandra ran down the side, and before anyone else could react, she shot the terrorist with her H&K. She knelt beside the dead terrorist, sweeping the insides of the shed, with Edwardo moving away from her to extend their sight line.

"Clear!" He shouted. Sandra nodded but didn't lower her H&K. The captain, with a grunt, got to his knees, pulled his two soldiers over onto their backs, and then yelled at them in Irish. They responded by laboriously getting to their knees and pulling at their vests, which had stopped the terrorist's rounds. The ever-popular terrorist behavior of 'spray and pray' had missed the mark. They would all have heavy bruising but would live to tell the tale over a beer later in the day. If Sandra didn't shoot them first for their blatant stupidity.

"You"—and Sandra pointed to the old man, now lying prone across the youth—"are you hurt?" He looked around at the soldiers still crouching, guns weaving back and forth, then at the woman who had called to him, and then at the three soldiers now getting slowly to their feet, obviously in pain.

"No, ma'am, I'm fine, and young Sean here, I'm thinking he's fine too, but if you don't mind, can you point that bloody little buggar somewhere else?" The fact that he smiled caused Sandra to lower her barrel towards the ground, but her eyes never stopped moving.

"Who are you, and why are you here?" The three Irish soldiers regained their feet, and their team medic made a move to look at them. "Halt! Stay in your positions! You can get fixed up after we sort out this cluster fuck." The medic froze in place, and the captain straightened, trying to regain his dignity. He was being shouted at by a woman who had just gunned down the shooter who had shot him and his men, a shooter he had been responsible for but not seen.

"Captain, sweep the bloody shed, call your rearguard in, and get them to clear the rest of the area. Let me know when it's secured. And this time, keep your bloody eyes peeled!"

"Yes, ma'am."

"Edwardo, stay where you are until the good captain clears his area. Watch our backs." Edwardo just nodded silently. He had worked with Sandra on much harder missions than this one and was able to anticipate what she wanted almost before she spoke. And he knew by her tonality that she was pissed at the captain and his men for getting themselves shot. The simple fact was that they had been lax, not expecting another shooter, and should not have missed seeing him from their position before he opened fire.

The old man, fascinated with the byplay and sensing the beautiful woman with her deadly little gun wasn't going to shout at anyone else, pulled the youth to his feet and dusted him off.

"This here be my first son, Sean, as I said, and we be tasked with getting a load here of them there panels," and he pointed to the load being prepared, "and getting them back home today. And I be Patrick O'Connell, thanks for ya asking." Sandra looked him over, thin arms but tight muscles, wide hands, callused, and neatly dressed if not a little grubby, but his face was almost angelic, all sharp edges and planes, a high forehead, red cheeks, and the lovely creamy skin of the black Irish. She imagined he would have been quite a stud in his youth and could see the power and confidence that lurked behind his deep green eyes. Innate intelligence not to be underestimated or taken for granted. He had passed his excellent looks on to his son.

"Patrick, thank you, and where is home?" He held his son with an arm casually thrown over his shoulder—not so much possession but comfort, Sandra guessed. She was liking this old man more and more.

"We'll be heading back up to Dundalk in about three hours, that is, with ya permission, of course." Sandra matched him smile for smile.

"Of course. Captain, get two of your troops to help with the loading. Are we clear? Patrick, I'd be happy if you could get loaded and on your way as soon as practicable." He doffed his cap, still holding his son with his arm over his shoulder, now more than a little territorial, and moved back to the forklift.

"Ma'am, no sign of anyone else, you orders?" The captain looked nervous and sore, and Sandra felt no sympathy for him at all. Self-inflicted. Stupid even.

"See to your men, get these into body bags, leave four here to guard this site, with instructions to allow any truck that arrives for panels free and clear access, then you and the rest of your troop return to base."

"Yes, ma'am." He saluted, then shouted out orders to impose his will on his team, who were not at all sure of the pecking order at this point. Edwardo had moved over to the pile of panels and ran his hand over the sparkling surface. He hummed to himself. He had never seen anything quite like it. He could almost feel the power being generated by the miniscule sunlight that continued to fight its way through the overcast. Then he realized the panel was reacting to the solar radiation and not just the direct sunlight, and he briefly wondered how they could do that. Then he put two and two together. The panels had minute UVA reflectors or generators built into their substrate. That's what the sparkle was all about. He had read about experiments carried out back in the early two thousands, and he nodded to himself. These panels would be incredibly efficient.

Sandra had watched Edwardo as he fingered the panels, had his private conversation with himself, and arrived at a conclusion. She pointed to him, curled her fingers at him, and pointed to herself, still scanning the shed and its surroundings. He raised an eyebrow while sweeping the shed with his weapon.

"What's got your interest in these panels?" He looked at her to see if she was dressing him down, sensed a genuine question, and with his back to her as he covered the end of the yard, told her his theory.

"The shiny sparkles are due to UVA radiation being captured in some way. The panels don't just work in direct sunlight." Sandra looked at him over her shoulder.

"And you know this how?" she asked, just the mildest skepticism in her voice. She didn't know for a fact, but the thought that some pointy head somewhere or other hadn't worked out exactly how the panels worked before this seemed unlikely, particularly given the effect they had had in places like Helena and Roanoke.

"I was an electrical engineer before I joined up." He looked over as the forklift slid a batch of panels onto the flatbed. Sandra reviewed his comments and, keeping her H&K pointed at the deep, dark areas inside the shed, pulled her mini out.

"Jessica, the wonder boy here thinks he knows how the panels work. Are we interested?"

I looked at Sandra, one hand holding the mini, the other her weapon, which moved across the wide open side of the shed. The background showed the truck being loaded and some Irish soldiers bending to pick up panels. Four twisted bodies lay in uncomfortable positions on the ground, and the blood and abandoned weapons in the dirt told their own story.

"Anyone hurt?" She looked at me with what I could only call an evil grin.

"No one who didn't deserve it." I smiled at her bravado, happy to wait to hear the full details.

I thought of the comment that Brother Francis had made about how the power being used in Dundalk seemed to be more than could be accounted for by the roof panels he had been able to see, and I wondered if we had stumbled on a solution. Only one way to find out.

"Come up to Dublin, pick me up, then the three of us will go find out. I'll get Francis to meet us." Sandra just had time to nod before I cut the connection.

Things to do and places to be. I looked at Anna, presently sitting under a warm lamp reading some report or other, her feet crossed at the ankles, an empty coffee mug at her side. I walked over and tapped her on the shoulder.

"We're going on a little trip. You should change into daytime clothes; boots are essential; it might be muddy and wet.

You never know." She pulled her reading glasses off and looked at me with her deep blue eyes, the beginnings of a smile forming on her pretty lips.

"Have you read all these interviews Sandra did before I got to her?" I shook my head.

"No, haven't had the time." Anna stood, folding her glasses into her coat pocket.

"She's almost as good as you. She does the cold and hot switch as well as anyone I've watched, gets answers to questions she hasn't asked, and like you, she drills down to the guts of the matter, whether they want to talk or not."

"Good to know. Apparently she just engineered or survived a gun fight with at least four terrorists, so she's got sharp skills in that area as well." Anna just nodded. There had been a rumor going around Washington before she left about two female Interpol agents and a terrorist who had supposedly fallen off the side of an aircraft carrier at sea, and when the body had been retrieved by a trailing destroyer, it had two perfectly formed bullet holes in it, one in the head and one in the heart. When questioned, neither the Admiral nor the Captain of the aircraft carrier had any knowledge of the incident or of the terrorist.

"Do you want my people to come with us?" I had completely forgotten about the two FBI agents who had traveled with Anna. In fact, I didn't even know where they were at the moment. That confusion must have shown in my eyes, because Anna laughed and reached out and took my hand.

"They're downstairs with everyone else, keeping the peace." She stood, her perfectly cut black suit shimmering down her body, her bespoke jacket hiding her badge and weapon. If you didn't know her, you would see a pretty, well-boned female with a sense of style befitting any boardroom. Her short, cropped, light brown hair just reached her shoulders, and if you looked close, you could see the athleticism poised inside the suit. Millennials, or maybe Generation Z, would call her 'wired', and not be wrong.

"If you feel secure with just me, Sandra, Edwardo, and a couple of our studly Italians, then no, leave them here with the lieutenant." She nodded and moved off towards the accommodation side of the hotel. Two members of the 104 shadowed her, reminding me we were still, for all intents and purposes, in enemy territory. I started to walk downstairs, where only about half of the original spectators remained now that the President had left. Then I heard the unmistakable sound of an automatic weapon being cocked.

"Gun!" Just as the cry rang out, a hail of bullets smacked into the wall behind me, spraying bits of timber and plaster all over my face. I tasted the warm feel of blood running down my cheeks and lost my breath as my two Italian guards flattened me between them as they crashed me into the steps. Bits of wooden banister flew like missiles, and I saw one sliver rivet itself into the side of one guard before a piece of banister the size of Mars nearly took my head off. Then, like all firefights, the sudden silence was eerie, unnatural, and echoing, then filled with the moans and calls for help from downstairs.

I couldn't get up immediately, but I could just see the mess, where armed people swept around the room searching for anyone still standing. Then a bunch of medics ran in from the street side, and I finally managed to get to my feet. The guard who had been speared stood a little shaky, and I held him up as much as he held me. My second guard didn't get up. The one who had been between me and the banister, his white shirt had a neat line of red holes stitched across it, with blood starting to pool. I felt the edges of an adrenalin rush and stated to shake a little, but training took over and I steadied.

"Report!" I shouted, mainly to quell the miscellaneous noise from the milling survivors.

"Ma'am, four terrorists down, six civilians wounded, five dead. The area is now secure." I really hoped so. A big hotel in the middle of the Dublin CBD, civilians everywhere—why the fuck did the terrorists shoot, and what had they been aiming for? Then I looked down at the dead soldier at my feet, one with whom I had fought in four different countries, looked up at the wall that had been shot out, and put two and two together. My only real question now was whether or not it was about the bounty on my head or whether I had presented a target of opportunity. The lieutenant stepped down to me, followed by a squad of his men, and offered me a handkerchief for my bleeding face. He said nothing, but the look in his eyes told me all I needed to know.

"I have to be at the airport." I wiped my face. The handkerchief would not be enough to stem the blood. I watched in fascination as one of the 104 pulled the thin stake out of my guard, then applied a pressure bandage. The body at our feet might not be visible from downstairs.

"Lieutenant, have our man here taken upstairs, please." He nodded and motioned to two of his squad. The rest arranged themselves, cutting off any view from downstairs, where the chaos was starting to ease. I pulled my Interpol sticky patch off my sleeve and bent to lay it on the dead soldier. I stood, saluted him, and then looked at the Lieutenant.

"This one's on me, and I unreservedly apologize." He just grimaced and shook his head.

"No, Commander, we had the floor covered until the President left, then we got sloppy. Not on you, and thank you for the respect." He saluted, spoke rapidly in Hebrew to his men, and I found myself sandwiched by four really big Israelis and my remaining guard, who was pointedly shielding me from the crowd forming towards the door. His bandage was starting to fill, as was his anger, and the milling people must have sensed his fury because the way opened for us the way the water had parted for Moses. We made the armored vehicle and climbed inside. The 104 team remained on the footpath, and Anna rushed up, dressed in combat gear, with her two FBI agents, similarly dressed.

"Can't leave you for a minute before you go and get yourself shot!" Her anger was real. I could feel her vibrating from it across the seat.

"They shot Antonio." Her face sobered up as if hit with a bucket of ice. She reached across Marco and put a hand on my knee. She noticed the bloody bandage on Marco and reached for the first aid kit in its wall recess.

"Does it hurt?" she asked, pulling out a bigger pressure bandage.

"*Solo quando rido!*" We all laughed for him, sparing him any more pain and releasing some of the tension in the hold. I patted Marco on the leg and looked at him with a critical eye. He would not quit. It was not only his pride, but he had seen his partner shot in front of him, so now he was all steel and controlled temper. I secretly admired that. Anyone who could take a hit without blubbering had my respect. But operationally, I had a decision to make. The two FBI agents carried personal weapons as well as short-barreled automatic carbines, ideal for the close-quarters combat you would usually find in a built-up urban area. The black and white FBI labels on their kaki vests stood out, as did the multiple magazines stacked against their chests.

The airport came up without further drama, and we watched as Sandra's helicopter feathered down, engines screaming, rotor blades cutting the air like knives, the rear of the skids touching fractionally before the front. She leapt out and almost knocked me over, closely followed by Edwardo.

"How bad?"

"We lost Antonio, and I don't have the data on those killed or wounded on the floor." She grabbed me by both arms, looked at my bloody face, and looked at Marco, who was now glued to my side, trying to hide his bandage.

"We'll have to clean you both up. You'll scare the people we're going to meet half to death looking like that. Base medical, both of you." And she pointed to the long building at the end of the military hangar. We went where she pointed, and then, twenty minutes and ten stitches later, we climbed back into the helicopter. Edwardo and Marco sandwiched me in, with Anna and Sandra sitting opposite. The two FBI guys shared a bench seat behind them. No one looked happy. I thought I would poke the pity party bubble to make things easier.

"People, our job is to dig the terrorists out wherever they are, and we know they're around, as they've just proved. The fact that we have dead and wounded is part and parcel of the job."

"There's no rhyme or reason to it. The dickheads we found at the shed were guarding panels. From where they came, I've no idea, but by shooting at us, they gained nothing but a grisly death. What happened to you? We only got raw details over the intercom."

"Shooters in the crowd downstairs used the President's departure to get in and started firing when I started to leave for the airport. Antonio took what was intended for me, Marco and I got some splash-back, some civilians got caught in the cross fire, but the 104 and Italians downstairs cleaned it up very quickly." She looked at my face, now painted with orange anti-septic, covering a thin double red line of skin held together with stiches. The image I had seen in the mirror wasn't a whole lot better than the one I saw when I walked in. Any hope I had of joining Sandra on the catwalk was dead and gone! Sandra must have been reading my mind because she smiled.

"That scar will give you a really interesting look." If I could have reached her, I would have punched her, good and hard. Edwardo looked over at me and smiled.

"Vuoi che la schiaffeggi per te, Comandante?"

"Not worth the effort." I patted him on the shoulder. "But thanks for offering." We sat in relative silence for the next twenty minutes, then out of the low-lying scud a small town emerged, with some tall apartment buildings surrounded by an endless series of row houses, and we landed softly in a football field to be greeted by a wet and soggy Brother Francis and another priest wearing a black suit and hat, also soaked to the skin.

"Jessica, lovely it is to see you for sure. Meet Father Paul. He's after setting up a school for his order in these here parts. I remember you, Edwardo. We watched the earth rise up together, and Marco, good to see you again, my boy. What's that bandage I see you're sporting?" He moved from person to person after a mighty hug, stopped at Sandra, and held her by the elbows. "Sandra, my girl, have you grown a foot since the last time I saw you?" She laughed, returned the hug, and moved back to my side.

"Brother Francis, thank you for meeting us. We need to go look at the houses you have seen and maybe talk to some of the locals."

"Jessica, the good Moriah O'Sullivan has lent us her truck and has beds for you if you need them, and a hot meal straight away if you've time. She's letting me drive, which is a real thrill. I can't count the years since I was behind the wheel." I mentally shuddered at the thought of Francis driving but held my comments to myself. I had an operational decision to make, and I couldn't afford to get it wrong. I looked around at the different faces, the intensity in their eyes virtually shouting at me, and hoped I was making the right choice.

"Edwardo, leave your long guns, vest, and helmet here. FBI guys, stay with the helicopter. Marco, Father Paul, you too, please. All weapons to be concealed. Anna loses the FBI patches and the vest. We go in quiet, polite, and not looking for trouble. Have we got any wet weather gear?" The copilot reached back into the helicopter and pulled out a bunch of green ponchos. Not very civilian-looking, but given the conditions on the ground, practical.

"Thanks, they'll be fine. Francis, take us to the row houses, please. Our resident genius wants to look at how they're set up." The nominated team stripped down, covered up, then climbed into the cab of the truck. I noticed Sandra still had her carry bag, this time slung over her shoulder, outside her poncho. So we had firepower. I just hoped we wouldn't have to use it.

The cab had two long bench seats, a patched tear down one side, duct tape to the rescue, and a heater in the middle of what I presumed was the old transmission tunnel, which I hoped like hell would work. The short spell outside in the freezing drizzle had chilled my bones, and I suspected I was still just a little shocked from being shot at. Francis started the engine, which entailed a loud whine, then a crash and a shudder as he found the gear for drive. We juddered forward, then the ride smoothed out as we hit the sealed road.

On either side, we could see low buildings and houses, all with lights on in the windows, which tended to make the drizzle look like fairy drops.

"Francis, what's your take on these panels?" He looked at me in the rearview mirror, his large, bushy eyebrows highlighting his deep brown eyes. His perpetual smile was in place, and he looked like someone out on a Sunday drive.

I had never, in all my life, felt his innate calm, and I envied him.

"Well now, not being a bloody genius like most of you lot, I can only go by what I know. We have solar panels up in Belfast. In fact, they might well be the only thing holding up our roof, if the truth be known. But they only really work well in the sunlight, which we get precious little of most of the year, so we used to rely on power from the electric company. Then they stopped delivering, and we had to add in as many car batteries as we could scavenge to get us through the day. Even with all that, we mostly only have power for an hour or two at a time, sometimes not even."

I watched him think through what he was about to say and mentally thanked Stefarino for lending me one of his brightest and smartest monks.

"What we have here, I suspect, is a very different type of panel, one that is many times more efficient than those we have up home, and to be truthful, since I was last here a few weeks ago, they've got something else working for them, and not just the pretty batteries they're fitting to some houses. There's more, but I can't tell you what." The low row houses started to move past us with a vengeance, and the curve of the road made them look like the product of a cookie cutter. The panels on the rooftops sparkled in the rain, as if seeking attention, and if we weren't so focused on terrorists and WMDs, it would be a magical look.

"Go slower, please," Francis responded, taking his foot off the pedal and letting us coast down the shallow slope. There was pride and ownership here—little gardens with colorful flowers, pained low fences, cropped lawns—but the universality of it all made it look a little bland.

"Are there people living in these houses?"

"There are now. They're coming in from everywhere, they have power six hours a day, and there's work on offer in all sorts of places, and that's become a huge drawcard. And the most remarkable thing is that where Moriah, God bless her, was looking after the littles, those that lost their parents, many of the new homesteaders are taking in some of the children as if they were their own."

I nodded. This was a local version of the terrorists' plan for Helena, Roanoke, New Zealand, and the other seventeen countries where they had sent ecological plants before the attacks. I would have to meet Moriah. Way back, weeks ago, we had traced a broadcast from 'Freya', and while we hadn't pinpointed it at the time, someone in Dundalk had been the receiver. My money was on our mystery woman.

"Do any of the farms around here have power?" He looked at me in the rear vision mirror again, his smile crinkling his face.

"Good question, and yes, now they do, since the panels have been put on the houses nearest them, about two kilometers away." That gave me pause for thought, and I looked at Edwardo, who had been intently listening to our conversation.

"Well," he started, "it's all a question of watts and the size of the transmission cable." I held my hand up to stop him.

"Wait, Not a geek or an electrician. Speak English."

He laughed and bent his head. He pulled out his mini, drew on it, and held it up so we could all see it. "Imagine a garden hose being fed from a tank. The pressure in the hose would be equal to that in the tank, and as the water ran out, the pressure would lower, until you just had a dribble." We all nodded. So far, so good. "Now, the longer the hose, the lower the overall pressure. If the volume of the length of the hose equaled the volume in the tank, all you'd get at the end would be a drip." That made some sort of sense, so I waved him on.

'Now, imagine all these roof panels producing power and feeding into a power line. The same principle applies. Lots of sun, lots of power—all feeding into the line. The longer it gets, the lower the force or amount of power will be at the end. If this farm of yours is two kilometers away from the last house, I'd be very surprised if the power they are getting isn't being boosted in some way. In fact, it has to be." I could feel my brow furrow, pulling at my stitches, which were a bastard. Back to my bland face.

"How do you boost this power of yours?" He winced when I pulled a face and dabbed at the stiches with a medi pad. Thankfully, my facial gyrations hadn't loosened the stiches—just a little dribble of yellowed blood. He chose to look at Anna, who was also wincing.

"There has to be some other power source." As simple as that. So, where was it? What was it? How did it get here? And all the little pieces suddenly banged into the palace, and I could see by the light in her eyes that Sandra had arrived at the same conclusion as I did. I looked straight at her—a direct challenge. She accepted it without hesitation.

"You're thinking the Irish experiment the women conducted here set up some sort of power supply related to, but not part of, the roof panels?"

"Yes. And a bigger question is, have they done the same thing at the nuke plants?" She shook her head, drawing Anna's attention.

"The reports from HQ said we found nothing at any site apart from dusty footprints." I put my hand up again like a police traffic cop to prevent me from losing my concentration and to stop her from talking again. I dialed my favorite geek.

"Hi, Amira, you're looking lovely. Are you going somewhere?" Amira looked confused, flushed, and looked down at her dress, which was multicolored and flowed over her body as if sculptured, her hair in some sort of updo. She had also paid attention to her pretty face. Very formal. Very sexy. Very unlike the Amira I knew and loved.

"Hi, Jessica, Shami asked me out to dinner, and I borrowed this from one of my assistants." She ran one hand down her side, a nervous gesture I recognized. I hated to dress up probably as much as she did, and I always felt out of place when I did. In fact, I had never fitted into the dressed-up set, no matter where I was based. Dress 1A's suited me down to the ground: long striped pants, a fitted jacket, a military-style blue shirt, and a bow tie.

"Hey, you have to have a life. Go for it, girl. Just a quick question. Could the terrorists have been working on some sort of power supply at the nuke plants?"

Her face screwed up in thought. She tilted her head and looked straight into the camera.

"Possible, but nothing showed up in the reports."

"Okay, thanks. Have a lovely dinner."

I clicked off, wondering how to prove or disprove my theory.

"Francis, can you drive us to one of the farms, please?" He nodded and engaged the gear again, this time without shedding any of the drive components.

We could see it well before we reached it. It had massive outdoor flood lights burning through the drizzle without a care in the world. Then the buildings came into view and looked like Christmas decorations—lights all over, shining brightly, as welcoming as could be. I decided to gamble.

"Francis, let Anna, Sandra, Edwardo, and I out at that big building, please. The rest of you stay on your toes." Marco was about to protest when Sandra leaned over and patted her shoulder bag.

"You've got us covered. Relax, but stay sharp just in case." We climbed out into the drizzle to find a tall, well-dressed woman wearing a broad-brimmed hat, a long flowery dress, and a pair of thick rope gloves. Behind her, a horse cropped at a feed bag, and chickens ran squawking around her feet, totally ignored. A massive dog, about the size of a small elephant, sat at her side, its long tongue lolling out as it panted. Its eyes were dark brown and never left us as we walked towards her. If it was looking for a quick meal, I hoped Sandra could dissuade it.

"Hi, I'm Grace, and who might you be looking for then?" And she reached out one gloved hand towards Sandra.

"Grace, nice to meet you. I'm Inspector Thomas. This is SSSA Bernstein, and this is Commander Riley, our boss." She pointed to each of us in turn, and I watched the woman's face change when she saw mine.

"Oh, you poor dear, that must hurt something fierce." I shamelessly took a leaf out of Edwardo's book.

"Only when I laugh." She screwed up her brow, as if silently admonishing me for being flippant. I sensed no threat, not even from the elephant, who was now looking sideways at us, his tongue working overtime.

"We're new to the area and looking for some information, and I couldn't help but notice all your lights. Do you have a generator?" She looked amused, as if I had asked a dumb question.

"Well, yes, we have, but it stopped working months ago when we ran out of fuel." Her tone was almost dismissive, as if I lacked critical information or was stupid. I pointed up to the massive flood lights and put the most comfortable puzzled look on my face without managing a self-induced wince from pain.

"Then how do you power these monsters?" I tried to lighten my tone, but my restricted facial movement made me sound shallow. She waved her hands around, as if flustered.

"Aye, my apologies. You said you weren't local, so there's no way you could know. Moriah up at the apartments, she's come up with some scheme that linked us to the row houses and their solar panels, and now thanks to her and her littles, we have all the power we need to work the farm again."

"Have you got any panels up?"

"Oh, aye, we had a bunch of folks come over a week ago and cover every square inch of our roof surfaces. Gave us a battery as well, neat little thing. I can show it to you if you'd like." I nodded.

"Thank you. That would be lovely." She led us to a small shed in the next paddock, scattering the chickens as we moved, and opened the door. Inside sat a cylinder about a meter round and two meters tall, with the traditional electrical 'don't touch' signs and lightning flashes all over it. The way it was wired was interesting. A small screen indicated the power reserve in terms of percentage charge and had a red line marked 'recharge'. Edwardo gave it a close look, turned to the woman, and sought my eye for silent approval. I nodded, so he asked his question.

"Ma'am, forgive me for my ignorance, but what happens when you reach this recharge line?" She laughed, making the whole issue seem inconsequential.

"It just charges itself up again, all automatic. There's an alarm in the main house that will go off if something's not working as it should, but we just use the power as we have a mind to and let all this technical stuff take care of itself."

I looked at Edwardo. He was smiling and moving away from the door. We all followed him. He reached up and stroked a roof panel where it overhung the shed.

"I love the way the panels sparkle, even in poor light like we had today." She smiled back at him, nodding.

"Aye, it's a pretty thing for sure. I like to believe they're alive. You can feel the warmth all day long." I looked at him, he gave me a slight nod, and we were done, so I moved us all towards the truck.

"Thank you, Grace. This has been very informative, and we thank you for your help. I hope we'll see you again." I shook her hand, and we climbed back into the cab. If she saw Francis's well-patched Kāṣāya, she gave no indication.

I waited a few seconds until we were on our way and out of the glare of the flood lights. "Edwardo, give." I could see him literally trying to jump out of his clothes with excitement.

"Well, you could say we just saw a miracle, but then you'd smack me across the head." He laughed and pretended to dodge. "But believe me, Commander, what we just saw in there was generations beyond anything I have ever heard of, and I used to read everything I could get on the subject. It is an enduring passion of mine."

"Why? What's so special about the cannister?" He gave me a plaintive look, knowing I would react if he went all geek on me. His face settled, his eyes sparkled like the panels he just played with, and then he drew on his mini again.

"You know what a battery does?" We all nodded. He put a tick against the box he had drawn. Then his pencil, moving at a million miles an hour, crafted two bulky things with knobs and corrugated stems on top. It reminded me of the accumulators we had sitting on top of the telegraph poles back home. You know, the ones that blow up and shoot sparks all over every time it rains.

"Then you have your accumulator, which sort of works like a battery, but slightly different. But the magic is in the autotransformer here, the one with the knobs. It can take electricity at different wattages and amperages and sort them out—think a power generator producing four hundred and fifty volts, mixing with a solar panel producing just twelve volts. What that beautiful cylinder does, if I've guessed correctly, is take raw generated power—could be two twenty volts, maybe four fifty—and converts it all to two twenty volts for normal use. I looked at him with my most confused look, shook my head, and saw Sandra start to bounce up and down on her seat.

"I get it! If you just have the roof panels, you have to step up the twelve volts to two twenty, but you're saying that they are also getting raw two twenty as well from a separate source." He nodded and offered the biggest smile I had even seen on his young face.

"Exactly. You could turn the panels off or disconnect them and still have a full power load. The panels are being used as a backup, not the primary power source. It's the reverse of what we thought was going on."

"Why would they do that?" Anna asked, and then I saw the light go on in her eyes.

"Ahhhhh, the Irish test was setting up a power supply that feeds into the existing infrastructure, and the panels are being used as camouflage. Clever!"

"Yes, but then, clever is their default. Could it be that this is what they have done at the nuke plants?" Anna gave me a shrewd look, her eyes twinkling with excitement and humor.

"We had foot prints around the generators, but no evidence of anything being tampered with. What could their system possibly be?" No one answered, so I mentally added it to my ever-growing list of questions to be pursued and hoped that Moriah, whoever she was, could provide some of the answers.

The tall apartment buildings came up quickly, and even though the row houses surrounding them showed a multitude of lights, the apartments were somewhat muted in comparison, with dark hollows where windows resided but were unlit. Francis pulled up outside, and I noticed a group of young children run across the headlights, heading off down the street. Well dressed, good-looking, and full of energy, just like kids should be everywhere.

"There go the gang of ten, I call them, up to more mischief, I wouldn't be surprised; not one of them has parents. They're under Moriah's care."

"How many does she look after?" Francis turned to look at me over his shoulder.

"It used to be before the row houses got electricity, just shy of five hundred, I'm thinking, so it's down to possibly three hundred or so now. Getting the row houses electrified made all the difference, I'll tell you. People came from all over Ireland to claim one, and many of them took children in of their own free will."

"Where does she house those who don't get taken in?"

"The early ones, who turned up just after the attacks, she has got in the big tower over there, and the later ones in the other tower."

"How does she look after them?"

"The eldest of the children act as monitors, and an adult is assigned to every room to provide comfort, support, and look after anything they need. There's a basic school in the basement. Every child goes at least three times a week, and they have chores and responsibilities. Father Paul here is hoping to take over one of the abandoned buildings and set up a proper school, an 'Ed Shed' he calls it, something his Jesuit brothers came up with in Australia decades ago. He's already got five trained teachers from the new arrivals who have taken row houses, and Moriah's university up in Belfast will send down some more when he gets it going."

"This Moriah seems to be well organized." His face lit up, and as he stepped out of the cab, he grabbed me by my shoulders.

"Jessica, me love, she's a woman who'd have ya heart as quick as they look at ya, and as smart as can be. She was teaching up at the university when the terrorist struck, so she came straight home when they shuttered it, and has been looking after everyone around here since. There were more than two thousand people being looked after the last time I was here. The locals think of her as the unofficial mayor." And before I could fully absorb all this, the very subject of Francis's eulogy stepped out of the foyer. Once again, Sandra found herself in the lead and accepted Moriah's hand.

"I'm Moriah O'Sullivan, and how can I be helping you tonight?" In seconds, a group of teenagers, all well-dressed again, had swarmed behind her, making it obvious they were part of the conversation. Two of the boys were quite tall, and they managed to sandwich Moriah between them in a very casual manner that suggested they were far more than just interested. Francis let me go, turned to Moriah, and hugged her.

"Moriah, me love, I was just telling the good Commander all about you, and here you are. That'd be Inspector Thomas, whose hand ya shaking, and here's an FBI agent all the way from America, Anna Bernstein." The look on Moriah's face was classic. She went sheet white, then flushed, the enemy of all Irish women with flaming red hair and peach-smooth white skin. She was so flustered that she dropped Sandra's hand like it was a live grenade, latched her fingers together, and then simply let them sag until they were lying across her blue dress. Nothing fancy, but recently ironed by the knife-edged creases. She recovered very quickly. The color in her cheeks lessened, and a fierce determination came into her eyes.

"And, why, might I ask, would such important people as your good selves be interested in a small town like ours?" Her tone was almost haughty, and if anything, the children packed in behind her a little tighter. I held my hands with my palms out in the universal peace gesture, put on the warmest smile I could manage given my partly frozen face, and reached out my own hand.

"Ms. O'Sullivan, you've nothing to fear from us. We're in Ireland at the request of your government, to help ensure the terrorists who did so much damage to you and your country are gone once and for all. Our interest in you has come about only because you are collecting and using power panels that were stored down in Waterford. We simply wanted to see how the panels are being used." Her face didn't alter a fraction, and she seemed to pull into herself a little.

"How did you get to hear of them?" I watched her eyes. If she was going to lie, it would be now. To my surprise, she didn't, and if anything, her face hardened.

"Some friends of my professor came by to do some work, and they took us to get the first load." I released her hand, relaxed my posture, looked at Sandra, then at Francis, and watched Edwardo out of the corner of my eye.

"Might we bother you for a cup of coffee while we continue this conversation, please?" She reacted visibly, almost shocked, then turned to one side and pointed into the foyer.

"Forgive my poor manners. You took us all by surprise. Please accept my apologies." We followed her into the foyer, walking through the children, who stared at us with curiosity but no anger. The two boys stayed outside, watching us carefully. The lifts were closed off with yellow hazard tape, so we headed for the stairs. Twelve flights later, we turned into what looked like a big lounge room.

"Please take a seat. I'll make tea for us all." The lounge was sparsely furnished, the couches and chairs well-worn and patched colorfully here and there. Woolen throws hid most of the aged stains, and a flock of pillows strewn around added a warm female touch. One wall was covered with drawings and paintings obviously done by children, and I guessed probably the younger ones at that. On the short wall, a series of paintings that radiated passion and charm, painted by a more professional hand, added a contrast that was hard to miss. It was a rolling seascape that went from one frame to the next in a manner that suggested great calm, in spite of the boiling surf and screeching seagulls. You could almost feel the ocean slipping in and out between your toes and the warmth of the sun on your face.

"Who painted your seascape?" I asked, to break the silence that had descended like a cloud. She moved back into the room, holding a tray with odd mugs and a round yellow tea pot. She laid it on the table carefully, stood up, turned to look at the wall, and then, with the faintest of smiles, bent her head.

"I did, in better days, for sure, and I hardly remember a time now when I get the opportunity to paint anymore."

"They're beautiful and alive! You have a wonderful talent." She looked at me, pride fighting with professionalism and fear. But her eyes told me she had heard my compliment and taken it for what it was. Her hands shook a little as she poured the strong tea into the mugs. Anna leaned forward and helped her, offering sugar and milk, and as the strange tableau unfolded, I was struck by a thought—I could count on one finger the number of social occasions I had experienced in the past few months—and a weird sense of discombobulation came over me.

Had I lost the ability to be comfortable in a normal situation? Was I becoming a caricature of myself? Before I could wallow in more introspection, Sandra picked up where we had left off downstairs.

"Ms. O'Sullivan, these friends of your professor, do they have names?" She asked in a quiet voice, sitting back and holding her mug in both hands, a sure sign she sensed no danger to us.

"Well, the oldest one, that would be Katrina. She'd come from some faraway place, I'd be thinking, the way she talked about her journey. The other three came to us from Scotland, and a pretty group they were. The tall one, she'd be Lilian, wore the most fascinating tee shirts." At this, Moriah smiled, remembering the fun she had anticipating Lilian's daily message. "Then there was Else, she was the scientist, and very young for it, I'd be thinking, and her sister not much younger, Lily, her name was, a very charming young lady, if I do say so myself. She was a geologist, but heaven knows how the two of them got so far with their studies being so young."

"Do you know their last names?" Moriah turned her head to one side and smiled wistfully. She shook her head.

"No, it never occurred to me to ask. Katrina introduced them to us, and I don't recall her saying her surname either." Sandra nodded, as if it didn't really matter.

"What did they do while they were here?" Moriah looked up, interest in her eyes as she considered the question.

"Well, they asked to be driven around and down to a little shed on the water's edge, where they said someone had left some boxes of equipment for them. They were there for a day, then moved to the transformer station for another day or two. Then they packed up and left, not sure where they were going, but I think someone mentioned Europe." She put her mug down, looking a little concerned.

"They didn't do any harm. They were lovely and polite, and the children loved being around them. Why are they so important to you?" I decided to break the rhythm of the interrogation. I could only handle so much politeness in one sitting.

"Ms. O'Sullivan, you have access to a lot of electricity. Where does it come from?"

"Why, the panels, of course, and we've got recovered car batteries in our basement to store them for nighttime use."

"Yet you burn power like there's no limit, and you now have connected hundreds of row houses and even farms. Where is all this power coming from?" Her eyes had gone to slits, and she fisted her hands on her lap.

"I told you, the panels! And the ones that came up from down south are very efficient. When we changed the old ones on our roof, we doubled the amount of electricity we could get." I let that statement lie; she was telling the truth as she knew it, and while she might be an expert teacher in her field, I doubted it had anything to do with electrical engineering. Sandra cut across me before I could ask my next question.

"Did the women leave anything behind, something you could use to turn the power on or off?" Moriah looked surprised, then shot up out of her seat like a rocket.

"Come with me." The sound of mugs hitting the table provided the background for the sound of feet on the wooden boards as we followed her out to a large jut, fitted out as a kitchen. Very large catering-sized pots and utensils packed the benches, and the smell of lemon and herbs floated around like an invisible mist. She stopped at a black box plugged into a wall socket and pointed to it.

"I'm allowed to turn this on for four hours a day, adding to the time we allow the solar power to run. This gives us four hours of power in the morning and four hours in the afternoon. Now, initially the row houses weren't connected, but as their solar systems got connected, they get eight hours a day of power as well. Of course, many of the houses have those shiny batteries as well, so they are largely self-sufficient, and they use as much as they like, but we're thankful for the extra they provide for others."

The box was unremarkable other than for a knobbed switch. No dials, no indication as to what it did. I looked at Edwardo, and he shook his head.

"So, you believe the extra power comes from the row houses?" Sandra kept her voice low and warm, sympathetic, and encouraging, and I marveled at her ability to change her approach so significantly.

"Of course. Where else could it be coming from? The power station hasn't worked for months since the gas was turned off." She led us back to the lounge, where we all stood around unsure what to do.

"Ms. O'Sullivan, thank you. We'll trouble you no more. Do you have any questions for us?" She looked at me with hope in her eyes and concern all over her face.

"Is this all then? Are we free to go about our business?" I put my warmest smile on my face, nodded, and took her hand again.

"Yes, you certainly are. From what I see, you are doing a remarkable job, and I'll tell the President that personally. I understand the Jesuits are going to set up a school, and I wish you every success with that." I led our contingent back down the stairs, noticing my leg muscles were starting to complain, and I had another epiphany. I turned and ran back up through my people.

"Just wait here." Sandra turned and glued herself to my side. We caught Moriah with her hands full of mugs and the tea service.

"Ms. O'Sullivan, I wonder if you could do something for us, please?" She looked surprised but didn't drop anything from her tray.

"And what would that be, I'd be asking?"

"Just as an experiment, turn the lifts back on." She looked at me with a furrowed brow as she considered my request.

"That'll drain the batteries very fast, for sure, and why would you want to do that?" I just smiled at her, watching to see if she gave anything away. With a shrug, she went back into the kitchen, dropped the tray on the bench, and wiped her hands on a tea towel.

"I'll have to get one of the boys to climb up to the top floor and get into the control room to do that. Can you wait a minute or two, please?" I nodded. She went to the stairs, disappeared up a flight, knocked on a door we couldn't see, spoke rapidly to someone, then walked back down to us.

"I've asked young Jason to go on up. It's another 14 floors, but his young legs will manage. But I should warn you, the last time we tried to use the lifts with the solar, they drained the batteries so fast we had no light until the next afternoon."

"When was that?"

"Just after we set the batteries up, well over two months ago now." I just nodded. If my hunch was right, she'd never have to walk up the stairs again. We waited in silence, each lost in our own thoughts. I could tell Sandra had worked out what I was doing from the wicked curve of her smirk. Then we heard the sound of feet running down the stairs, and a young man dressed in jeans and a puffer jacked over a yellow t-shirt arrived, his face flushed from the exercise.

"Both banks are turned on, Moriah. The lifts are at ground level, so do you want me to summon them for you?" She was busy looking around the room at her lights, which had not dimmed or flickered in the slightest.

"Thank you, Jason." He dashed off down the corridor and hit both lift buttons. We all held out our breath, not realizing just how momentous this was. Lifts are working via an unknown power source in a tiny town in Ireland. The Boss had told me that some European cities that had good renewable power sources were allowing lifts to be used in government buildings and some hospitals, but never in apartment buildings or shopping centers.

With the predictable swish and clunk and the glow from the interior lights, a lift arrived, bathing Jason in a warm halo that had him dancing on the spot.

"It worked! Moriah, it worked!"

"Well, by my leave, the lights haven't even flickered."

"Come on back up," Sandra called to Anna, Francis, and Edwardo, and we led them to the lift. With not the slightest hesitancy, we all walked into it, Moriah pressed the 'G' button, and down we went.

When the doors opened, Moriah was mugged by the swarm of children, all shouting at the top of their voices. She looked at me over the top of their heads, more curious than anything else. I Just smiled at her, as big as I could manage.

"The row houses are giving back to you as you gave to them. Stay safe, and thank you for your hospitality." And I walked out through the crowd, got in the cab, waited until Francis had moved off, then sighed, deep and meaningfully, and poked Sandra in the ribs.

"What have you got to say for yourself?" She gave me a wicked smile and poked me back.

"A poster child for the good and righteous, Saint O'Sullivan, to be sure, for sure." We all laughed. In a sense, this was a victory for us, even though it was the terrorists technology that made it possible. But my mind had already moved on to what we would have to do next.

"Anna. Your reaction?" She looked at me with her serious FBI face, and I tensed waiting for her critique.

"Not a terrorist, not connected in any way with the attacks, but very much being used by them down stream. I think you'll find her professor is a little further up the command chain. We're going to find more like her, and we need to make sure they are protected." I nodded, something we all had to be aware of and make sure the forces outside our direct control respected our analysis. The economic survival of the entire world might depend on it.

"So, are the four women who set this all up terrorists or down streamers?" She looked at me, her serious face now holding a big question mark. I gave it some thought, then attacked the question in a roundabout fashion.

"Might be a mix of both. I'm thinking the age of the women will play into it. I can't dictate policy. The politicians will do that, but what I think we will have to do is draw the line in the sand— work out what constitutes being charged under the Terrorist Laws—and what doesn't. We now have at least two hard examples of downstream use—the President and his office, for that matter, the whole bloody Irish government—and now Saint O'Sullivan.

"We will have to make our case not just to the politicians, but to the World Court, the UN, UNHCR, and all the various players in this little game. The bottom line is the future of the children, and then of the other refugees in the camps. I can tell you now, some very powerful people will get their knickers in a knot over this, as they see their power base, their wealth, and position being eroded by the effects of the terrorism. And potentially, by the solutions the terrorists are providing. Effects that will see thousands, if not millions, of refugees migrate to countries willing to take them in exchange for a roof over their heads, and basically, power."

"And if what we just saw is any example, power without strings attached—no one will own it, no one will control it. Play the terrorist game, get as much power as you need. Don't, and you're on your own. And the economic benefits are strangely interesting." Sandra leant back in her seat, the helicopter filling the windscreen. It sat with its rotors bent towards the ground in a relaxed manner that suggested exhaustion from its previous flight. Father Paul, Marco, the pilots, and the FBI guys stood against the hull, looking a little forlorn. They moved towards us as we got out of the truck. I looked back at Sandra.

"Finish that thought."

"Well, you get power, you make things work, people get work, and maybe get paid as well. They spend their money, and around and around it goes again. The difference is the dickheads that controlled everything before now don't. How will that work out?" We all paused in our thinking, the import of what Sandra had just said sending chills up and down my spine. Something I had not given a single thought to and, quite frankly, didn't really know how to. The petrochemical barons, the financial dynasties, and the powerful families and companies that once ruled the world have been dethroned. Their assets turned into silver sludge because the one thing I had seen clearly here in Dundalk was the small scale but huge impact freely available power had on the people who needed it most.

I wondered if the terrorists had ever worked out that in saving millions of refugee children, they were sentencing millions of ordinary people to an economic hell and a very uncertain future.

CHAPTER FORTY ONE

The women had worked twenty hours every day and had done whatever it was they did in three houses so far, as well as converted the sewerage plant. Huge tankers now drove up to it each day and onloaded biofuel, clearly marked on the side of the tanks. Where the fuel ended up was not important to Fay or her teams. What was of interest was the work done inside the houses, and as they had watched from hidden positions as the massive boxes and packing crates were carried into each one, what they were doing was probably big. As Fay ran through all her options to get a look inside one of the houses, her mini buzzed in her pocket.

I looked at her. She looked a little peaked, obviously tired, but still had that amazing spark in her eyes that had drawn her to me in the first place.

"Fay, you're looking a little worn." She smiled at me, her background being a wooden bedhead, so at least she had planned on some rest.

"Just what a woman on the go wants to hear! Long hours, pretty cold here, and wet most of the time—it chills the bones." I nodded, glad it was her and not me being frozen to the bone. It had taken me hours to get warm again after our recent adventures.

"Where are you at?" I saw her look around the room, move to a work desk, put the mini on it, and use her hands to pull a hoodie over her head. She sat down, her smiling face filling the frame again.

"They have moved some large equipment into three houses so far, two on this side of the bay, one on the other, and converted the sewerage plant to produce biofuel. The fuel is being taken away in tankers. I don't know where to. They're working on another house as we speak. They're either working in shifts or very long days, because they are averaging a house every day and a half. I'm trying to work out how to get inside one of the houses."

"Hold that thought. We think we know what they are doing, just not how."

"Give." Fay's voice was almost pleading. I smiled back at her.

"Okay, take it easy. We only found out a few hours ago, and we're still testing our hypotheses with the geeks. They agree with our conclusions, but can't tell us the how of it either." I watched her face go wary, ready to challenge anything I said that didn't match what she had observed. After all, she had been a brilliant FBI agent before I recruited her, and her instincts were sharp and current.

"We believe—best guess, from hard data from Dundalk, which I have seen personally—that they are building some form of electrical generating power plant. We don't know how, but it is producing raw two twenty volts, which is integrated with power from their advanced solar panels by a large autotransformer. They are two meters tall, one meter in diameter, and the one we've seen was painted white, with all the caution signs and flashes." Fay nodded slowly to herself, brought up some pictures, and slid them to my mini. A large pile of packing crates and boxes littered the floor of wherever the photos had been taken, and the forklift was mid-sized, which suggested some weight in the boxes.

"These are the crates and boxes they are unpacking. There's one box that is almost four meters long and one and a half meters wide, and your autotransformer could be in one of these others." She highlighted a green, unmarked box of the approximate size I had given her. "My question would be, what for? What do they hope to power?"

"'Are the lights on where you are?"

"There's a little rationing, mostly during the day, but there is a sustainable grid using windfarms on the headlands for primary power. Plus, we're told there's a small peat-fueled power plant fifty kilometers up the road that feeds into the grid here, and more than half the houses and buildings are shuttered."

"The President told us that the county Killara Bay is in, Mayo, I think it was, had accepted the rezoning of two large areas, one on either side of the bay, on the basis of a fixed euro amount per block. We're talking fifteen to twenty thousand houses in total, so if they use the same model as they have in Helena, they'll build an environmental plant first, produce the panels, then build the houses."

"That's going to take years, at least."

"Well, we know the plant in Point Roberts experimented for the first eighteen months on the nanites, then went into full production on the panels and power packs a year before we got there. How many panels had they produced before we found them?"

"Thousands."

"And how fast did the houses go up in Helena?" I could see her thinking about it all. She had been on the front lines in both locations, and one of her former agents had volunteered to adopt two of the refugee children as part of the resettlement plan in Helena.

"From the time they started, the first house went up in about two weeks, then as more and more workers turned up, that got to around one hundred a week being finished by month three. The interiors were the holdup, finding furnishing and fittings as all industry on the west coast had stopped, as you know." She paused. Her face went very serious for a moment.

"There's one thing you need to know—Helena had all the infrastructure in place for waste management, sewerage, water, and power, due to the Westhall Trust. Do you remember that?" I nodded. The trust had prepared over one hundred thousand sites nearly five years before the terrorist attacks. No one really knew the original plan Westhall senior had in mind, but we suspected he was involved with the terrorist in some way, and this was an example of their superb forward planning. Other families had thrown their lot in with the terrorists. We just hadn't gotten them all yet.

"They had plenty of renewable power already, didn't they?"

"Yes, Helena virtually had its own grid. Of course, the panels and power packs the terrorists provided gave them a little extra." I nodded. The town council would have been happy with that. The fact that all the new houses for the refugee children would not impact the renewable power grid would have been a major selling factor. And the houses were pumping their excess back into the city grid at no cost.

"Did we ever establish how long it took to build the environmental plant?" She looked at me. We had both interviewed the major players, the CEO and the COO, and all the staff, but at the time we were only looking for advance knowledge of the terrorist attacks, which the senior people had. She brushed her hair back from her face and scratched behind her ear. She was restless. I could almost feel her body movements through the video connection.

"I believe it took them seven or eight months to get the plant up, including the hangar, loading bay, and all the buildings. They were producing panels after that, but I don't think we established where their power came from when they commenced building."

"Their starter nanites came from somewhere else?"

"Yes. But we're missing something. The Army engineers have already erected two additional plants next to the one in Point Roberts, and they did that from the crates supplied by Innomatchi."

"So, with the right equipment, one to two months?"

"Yes."

"Okay, I'll check that out for you. Can we do anything else?"

"When do you want to take the women?" It was my turn to think: what were we learning and what were we risking by letting them keep building things?

"Are you comfortable being able to take them without any civilian interference?" She smiled that little smile she used to disarm someone in interrogation, but I wasn't fooled for a second.

"What aren't you telling me?" She held her hands out defensively with open palms, but still didn't fool me.

"Well, they've kind of made it easy for us. They are all staying in a house less than four hundred meters from our hotel, and they all stay together on either side of the bay." I nodded. Now I understood the reason for her guile.

"So, they're working where now?"

"On the other side, Rosie's team has them covered." I nodded. The new leader for Tom's team was an English woman I hadn't had the pleasure of meeting to date. I hoped to rectify that as soon as possible.

"Let them finish the house they're working on. Where do you think they will build the environmental plant?"

"The plant is in crates stored at the back of the Fish factory. They are not hidden. The people working there know of their existence and show no interest. In fact, Rosie has a photo of three of the fisherfolk sitting on one of the crates smoking. And apart from going in the one time, the women have left them alone."

"Looking at an aerial map of Killara Bay, the ocean goes out a fair way at low tide. They need sea water and sand for their process. Where do you think they will set up?" She went into her thinking mode again, visualized both sides of the bay, and nodded to herself.

"There's good direct access four kilometers to the north of the Fish factory, lots of empty land. Given that the plant is pre-fabricated and the panels are already down on Whiddy Island, or stored somewhere close like they were in Waterford, with enough hands they could have it up and running in two months, start to finish. Do you want us to let them get that far?"

"I don't know. In the terrorist scheme of things, O'Cleary is of the most interest. The other four women seem to pose no threat, and the confusing thing is, if they really are planting some sort of power generator, why would we want to stop them?" She gave me a really curious look. Her eyes tightened as she focused on my face.

"You're not going soft, are you?" The challenge in her voice was obvious from her tonality. I smiled and shook my head.

"Not in the slightest. But the line in the sand has moved a little. The experience with the Irish President taught me that. Stay safe, keep sharp." And I disconnected, thinking about her question a lot more than I usually would. I still had major issues to resolve, not the least of which was what to do with Whiddy Island. Anna had listened in on the conversation from her chair next to mine, and now she looked at me over her coffee mug with a twinkle in her eye.

"Before you say a word, let me make a call." I dialed the agent we had left at Point Roberts.

"Hello Sam, how are you?" His background was deep and dark, so he was either in a cupboard or a shed. He pulled a cord near his ear, and the light flooded the camera, temporarily burning it out. As it resolved itself, the back of a massive empty space swam into view.

"Fine, thank you, commander. How can I help?"

"Quick question. How long does it take the engineers to build a plant?" He looked around where he was and turned the mini around so I could see some of the detail.

"This one took five weeks. You're looking at the storage hangar. Because it has a wooden frame and the panels snap together like Lego bricks, once the frame goes up, the rest follows very quickly. The machinery takes a little longer."

I expected that. Producing the most technologically brilliant materials from scratch would take skill and knowledge, and we had already locked up most of the terrorists who had demonstrated both.

"Have you started any production in the plants you have built?" He asked.

"Yes, we had the Israelis here last week to seed the nanite baths. That took two days, but it's all working fine at this point. Very low production rate, but we're using the people they had trained in the first plant who are teaching a new cadre of recruits as we speak."

"Thank you, Sam. Catch you later." I looked at Anna, and she smiled.

"We get weekly reports. If you need to see them, let me know." I nodded, remembering something else I had forgotten. I shook my head. I had to focus on our main objective.

'No, terrorists, where are they, what are they doing, and how can we clean them up?"

"Are you including your wandering minstrels over in Killara in those questions?"

"Don't know. O'Cleary for sure. The others I'm not committed to one way or the other at this point. How about you?" She smiled again, put her mug down, tilted her head to one side, and uncrossed her ankles.

"I see the bind you're in, and I sympathize. Initially we didn't know what we were up against. The attacks were fresh in our minds. They had used the nanites to build the nuclear-capable shells, we had Badawi and Abbas in full flight across Europe, the warning from the Irish website, then the FBI turns up Point Roberts, which leads to Helena, New Zealand, Roanoke, Innomatchi, and so it went. We had no choice but to sweep anyone even remotely associated up and lock them away.

"But since we cleaned up the nukes, sank Assiano's boat, and Abbas blew himself and half of the Gaza Strip up, the only terrorist activity of note has been the destruction of the drug crops, and, as you well know, no one is really pursuing that at this time. Then there's your mystery team of women planting power sources in Ireland, and maybe in shuttered nuke plants. I know we have listed the nanites as a WMD's, but I'm hard pressed to see that situation remaining once the pointy heads work out what's what."

"The nanites were used to create the bimetallic nuclear-capable shells. You can never get away from that. And our mandate, under the Terrorist Laws, is clear—any association, what-so-ever, no matter how removed or tenuous, is punishable by either a life sentence in a concrete cage or death." She looked at me with the sparkle gone out of her eyes and put her hand on my arm. I was getting worked up, and she could see it. "And don't forget the sixty million plus dead post-attack, the millions dispossessed around the world, and the sheer economic chaos we are all suffering from. The world we knew has been all but destroyed, turned on its head, and the ordinary person in the street has been left floundering, fighting just to survive. I can't let that go of that for any reason. I'm supposed to be the head of the pointy spear cleaning all this up, not the Mother Teresa applying calming balm."

"I know the ROE, I know the consequences, and I know you struggle with the line in the sand. You probably always will. Just don't let it bend you up."

"Without your expert reading of the President and the social worker, I would have arrested both and sent them to cages. Probably would have executed the President. I really didn't like him. I still feel like I should. How do I mitigate that? In fact, I'm tempted to do it anyway." I was starting to feel like my old self. The purge was doing my mental focus a lot of good.

"Look at it this way. We have a tranche of refugee women who have masterminded or implemented the attacks, all of whom we now have under lock and key—maybe one of two more around somewhere, but we have their number—and now we have a younger, new tranche who have applied their genius to solving some of the problems the attacks created. Are they equally guilty?" I looked at her to see if she was having me on, but all I saw was seriousness all over her pretty face. I stood, the better to vent my spleen, and tucked my hands into my pockets so they wouldn't fly around due to my anger.

"Absolutely. We wrote the Terrorist Laws to encompass anyone who had any knowledge at all, no matter how slight, and we did that for a reason. And it works. You know something, anything, even just a hint, you do nothing about it, we lock you up permanently. A concrete cage or a bullet. Why would I change that just because refugee children are being migrated into new homes around the world?" She stood, but obviously relaxed, and folded her arms across her chest.

"And another thing, what about the mercenary terrorists the women used to do their dirty work? Do we just let all the damage they did go as unintended consequences of the attacks? I don't think so. I really, really don't think so."

"Jessica, you're upset. I understand that. I've given you my opinion as to the culpability of the President and the social worker, and I stand by that. But if you want to incarcerate them, I'll back you up one hundred percent." I looked back at her. The truth in her eyes shone like a beacon. Here was the second-most powerful agent in the FBI telling me she would support my judgment unequivocally, in such warming tones that I was starting to feel relaxed! And then Sandra walked back in, three coffee mugs in her hands, her little carry bag banging at her hip. She looked at us both, then formed a grim smile.

"What have I missed?" Anna took a mug, inhaled the aroma, closed her eyes for a second, and let the caffeine do its work. She rolled her shoulders, something I was starting to see a lot in the people around me. We lived with tension. We created tension, and I needed to be more aware that we had to break it as often as we could. But for the moment, I was pissed, and what Anna said looking at Sandra made me even more so.

"Jessica's afraid she's going soft on the terrorists. The issue with the Irish President and the social worker is stuck in her craw." She looked at me over the top of her coffee mug, a twinkle in her eyes, and suddenly I sensed she was trying to send me a message. I stared back at her, then decided to play her game.

"Sandra, tell us how you feel about the Irish President, some of his people, and the social worker." I watched her for any immediate response and was reassured when she tilted her head and turned slightly to get both of us in her sightline. Her body language was anything but relaxed, and her physical projection of anger was palpable.

"Many of the government employees I interviewed had some knowledge of the timing of the attacks, we know they protected their IT infrastructure, they had a window to work with, and frankly, none of them were all that concerned with what happen to the rest of Europe, or the world, when it comes to that. They had a mission, and if you asked me what it was, it was to protect the revenue stream the refugees represent, and the economic possibilities for the country the entire million home scheme offers. They see Ireland rising out of the chaos in a position of great importance and power. And this mission has been sanctioned at the highest level of government-the President himself and his 'advisors', one of whom was the social worker.

"You ask me how I feel? After being shot, blown out of the air a couple of times, and attacked by drones, I feel as pissed off as I ever have, and frankly, if it wasn't for the overwhelming common sense you displayed, Anna, I'd have shot some of them and locked the rest up forever." I smiled. At least I had one supporter, but then Sandra had looked three terrorists, the absolute worst of the worst, in the eyes as she shot them point blank, standing at my side, whereas Anna had only been involved on the fringes, as it were. And she was an FBI agent at heart, living by an entirely different and more inflexible set of rules.

But Sandra's pointed and passionate response helped me make up my mind. We need to act, and act now. I pointed to her, smiled, nodded, and then toasted her with my mug.

"Spot on! And I'll add to that-the economics, the after party, sorting out all the social issues, that's under the purview of others, the pointy heads who love the lime light, take no risks, but take the credit for everything that works. Let them. Our task is to clean up the mess the terrorist have made, no holds barred. Sandra, put a team together, we're going to call on the President and his social worker, and rectify my mistake. Generate a list of the government employees we have to collect, work out with the lieutenant how to execute the warrants, I'll talk to Lyon. Wait here, please, while I make the call." I moved slightly away, dialed the Boss.

"I want to move onto the Irish President." He looked me straight in the eyes, didn't blink, and didn't so much as move a hair.

"What's your plan?" His eyes bore into mine, and I felt like I was being examined by an X-ray machine.

"Get a team together, get a Red Notice from you, deliver it personally, and take him in." He nodded, a thoughtful look coming over his face. He looked off to his left, then to his right, seemed satisfied about something, and then back at me.

"I have a better idea. How about I fly over and personally invite the president to join me in Lyon, so he can brief the UN?" If I looked astonished, it was because I was. Then the possibilities sank in, and I smiled.

"If your kind invitation ends up with him in a concrete cage, then yes, I can support that. Will you really let him talk to the UN?" His eyes became a little shuttered. Whether he was thinking about my caveat or something else, I couldn't tell.

"That will be up to Arie." The cunning bastard—no wonder I loved him to death—and suddenly I saw the way forward here in Ireland, with a whole lot less blood spilled and upset. I fired one last torpedo at him to see what I could hit.

"Any chance of taking the social worker with him, same end result?" He squinted and rubbed the side of his face with long fingers.

"You took his other advisor in, didn't you? And that's a very clever move, even for you."

"Yes." I momentarily glowed in the haze of his backhanded compliment, then watched as he nodded, opened his eyes wide, and set his face to smiling compassion, but I wasn't fooled a bit.

"Good. I can do that. In fact, on reflection, it makes it a stronger offer. What's your next move?"

"I'm going to let Sandra and the 104 collect a few people we think are involved at the government level, then we'll go and clean up Killara." He nodded, looked at his watch, and screwed his face up.

"I'm late for a meeting. Leave the President and his helper to me. Have the local office on standby to collect us from the airport. You go do what you have to do." I smiled, nodded, and cut the connection. If we timed it right, we could move on multiple targets simultaneously. I moved back in with Sandra and Anna.

"I've got a plan, but first, how many in the government do you want to sweep up?" Sandra broke out into a huge smile and patted me on the shoulder so hard that I bent with the force.

"Jessica, you make my day! Twenty-three hard cores will do it, nine from the IT department, six from a second, and the rest from the administrative support services for the President."

"Take the 104 plus any of our people you need, plan on simultaneous pickups, but you can't do it until I give you the go. Probably in twelve hours or so, no more than sixteen. Go plan your attack, contact Lyon for your red Notices, and when you finish that, work out a strategy to take down anyone of interest in Killara, using Fay as your pivot." She walked out as if on air boots, as happy as I had seen her.

"You've worked out how to take the President?" Anna asked. No frown, no concern, just genuine curiosity.

"Well, the Boss has, to give him credit where it's due. He'll issue an invitation, then fly here and take the President and his social worker to go to Lyon and present to the UN. No guards other than ceremonial, no arrest. Shelia will organize the invitations from our local office, and you and I will be noticeable by our absence. Which leads me to a question. Now that I've chosen to ignore all your good advice, do you still want to stay, or go back home?" She looked at me with a puzzled look on her face.

"You want to get rid of me?"

"Absolutely not. I'm just giving you the opportunity if our ignoring your advice is a problem for you." She almost laughed, then stood again.

"Jessica, you and I live in different worlds. Sometimes they coincide, sometimes, like this one, they clash. I support your decision, I understand what you are doing, and it's why Section Five was stood up in the first place." I nodded. The term 'full of grace' slipped into my mind from somewhere, and I saw it applied in spades to this dedicated FBI agent, one I was proud to call my friend and mentor.

"One last question before I get on with it. I intend to take Killara apart while Bob dismantles Freya's operation in Scotland. Would you like to come with me? It's unlikely we will get shot at, but you never know." I grinned to take the edge off the last part of my statement. I had put her in a position to get shot at a few times in the recent past, starting with our joint foray into the wilds of Montana a month or two ago. She just gave me that wonderful smile of hers, shrugged her shoulders, and opened her hands in fake supplication.

'A girl's gotta do what a girl's gotta do!" I smiled. My sentiments exactly!

CHAPTER FORTY TWO

The President of Ireland, resplendent in a fine blue Italian suit with creases so sharp they could have shaved cheese, sat opposite Liddy Cochran, his advisor responsible for arranging the movement of some five to six million refugee children. They both drank tea out of fine bone China, the office resembling a French Renaissance boudoir. The irony of the meaning of that word was lost on them both. The table was over three hundred years old and polished to within an inch of its life. Portraits of famous Irishmen, and women to a lesser extent, hung over pink and burgundy silk-clothed walls, their gilded frames accenting the masterful art, and the overarching atmosphere was not one of elegance so much as overpowering old, stale wealth.

"We've received an invitation from the UN to present our plans for migrating the children. It's an invitation from the Secretary General, and his office will supply transport, accommodation, and security. How much can we tell them?" He looked at his advisor, with whom he had worked now for over four years and trusted implicitly. The fact that her co-worker, Dr. Mary MacDonald, had been taken into custody by Interpol had upset them both, as she had been the technical expert helping the President navigate the logistics and the technology required to house the refugee children.

"Sir, our five-year project plan is sixty percent complete. Perhaps we start there with forward projections of how many we can take over what period of time? Before Mary was taken, she had updated the progress on the panels, the work being done up in Dundalk, and the preparatory work in Killara Bay. If we stick to just those two areas, we should be fine. The numbers are relatively low, and all are achievable this calendar year. Walk them through it in small stages, let them get comfortable with the idea and the process."

"We have to get the Whiddy Island plant back up and running as soon as we can." She nodded. That was a major obstacle to their plans being fulfilled. The President paused and looked at a note he had made just the day before. The protracted interview with the Interpol women still rankled, but he pushed that to the back of his mind.

"The report we've got from Helena is very encouraging. The blended family model is working, and the local community seems committed to the project."

"Yes, sir, the same in Roanoke and Dargaville. I'd have to say the New Zealanders are welcoming the children more enthusiastically than the East Coast Americans. They seem to have a more open mind to the refugees." He nodded, scooting his Montblanc pen across the report, ticking sections off as he went. A detail-oriented person, he moved from one thing to the next methodically.

"So, we'll go, but limit our presentation to the next six months, showing the success of the installation program in Dundalk, the willingness of Killara Bay to change their bylaws, and perhaps giving an estimate of how long that might take, but keeping it small and unthreatening." She nodded. From her perspective, she had all the processes required to move five million children over three years in place. She just needed the houses, schools, hospitals, supermarkets, and support infrastructure to cater for them. Dundalk would take a small number in the scheme of things, only around three to five thousand in total initially, as they needed to house the existing orphans first, which was well under way. Then she could prove her immigrant family model locally, and once she did, she expected the flood gates to open.

"I'll let the UN know we're happy to travel anytime from tomorrow, if that suits you." She nodded, the faster the better. She had things to do, people to organize, and five million refugee children to identify and prepare for the journey of their lifetime. The President, feeling quite smug, started on a list of demands, starting with the immediate release of Lady O'Brian Flattery, her assistant Patricia, and the other women taken by Interpol from Whiddy Island under the pretense they were some sort of terrorist. Hope was always a powerful motivator, but in this case, it would eventually prove to be nothing more than a bad pipe dream.

While the President was luxuriating in the illusion of his sudden worldly importance, Indigo reached the furthest point of Whiddy Island, having navigated the myriad of small Islands and sandbars in Bantry Bay in the good ship *'Scáthán'*. He could just see the Napoleonic-era fort on the northernmost tip, as well as across the bay to Ballylicky and its multitude of small grass plots just above the shale cliffs. His air alert sounded at the exact same time his mini screamed at him, so he hit the siren for battle quarters and looked at the small screen.

"Ito, good to see you, or maybe not. What have you got?" The diminutive Israeli navigator pointed to his own screen with his gloved finger, stained from the oil and grease of his equipment and more than a little personal sweat.

"Multiple drones, all headed your way, now at 40 miles, airspeed 220. knots. We still can't help you due to the possibility of civilian collateral damage, but I would advise you to use your long-range anti-drone systems ASAP." Indigo nodded, put his mini on the cockpit, and picked up the phone that connected him to his control room.

"Fire on all targets. Open up all antiair. Keep me posted." No sooner had he spoken than five missiles were launched, smoke billowing over the bow like a wraith. He felt rather than saw the electromagnetic drone killers fire. The air seemed to hold its breath as the electric blue bolts flashed out. He heard the gatling guns ramp up, their barrels spinning so fast they blurred, but they were not yet firing. The muffled voice of Ito cut through his concentration.

"Splash four bogies. Four more are on the way. They are very low to the ground, and you have two more coming at you from 30 miles east." Indigo didn't acknowledge, just put the targeting icon on the dots moving across his screen, mentally ducked as the anti-drone guns swiveled on their mounts, then felt the hair stand upon the back of his neck as they fired.

"Two east down, two still inbound, missiles fired, missiles fired!" Indigo selected the 'release' button for the CWIS, and the air was suddenly filled with the roar and scream of hundreds of twenty-millimeter rounds streaking through the air, closely followed by the booming impact and explosion of the missiles, one so close that bits and pieces fell into the sea just in front of the ship. The little splashes they made were in direct contrast to the size of the explosions of the drones and missiles, which now filled the air with a red-hot flame backed by ugly gray and black smoke as fireballs fell majestically on land and into the sea like silent blooming fireworks, sending up fountains of superhot steam.

One drone, so close to the ground it seemed to be skimming the verdant rolling cover, suddenly reared up like a spooked horse and exploded, showering the ship with burning pieces of metal and rubber and leaving its own dirty trail of destruction. The rubber thudded onto the deck, leaving a smear of soot and oily vapor, as if marking its territory. The sudden quiet was as deep as the booming explosions had been, and Indigo had to peer at his scope, wiping soot and minute material out of his eyes, to see if they were still under attack.

No blips, no incoming missiles, so he looked at his mini and saw it had been hit by a piece of something from the exploding missile and was now gently melting into the coming. He smiled a wan grin. He liked the mini better than one of the crew members, so he called for another mini and got reconnected to Ito.

"All clear at our end. What do you see?"

"We've marked where they all came from and are sending you the coordinates now. It looked like you got splashed?"

"Just debris, total casualties, one minicomputer, and probably my eyebrows." Ito laughed, glad that his team was okay but worried about the ferocity of the attack. He checked his gauges, saw they had three hours to bingo fuel, and instructed the pilots to orbit the drone field.

"We'll continue up here for the next couple of hours. Watch your back."

"*Apprezzato, e grazie.*"

"*Arrivederci, a dopo.*" Indigo closed the mini, thought about his next action, then opened it again to call Jessica.

I got Indigo's call just as I was heading across the hotel to check on the lieutenant and his troops. I listened as he outlined what had happened, asked him to forward the coordinates from the AWACS, and instantly changed my mind and agenda. I sent a group text to Sandra, Anna, my Italians, and the lieutenant, and copied his boss, the Sgan Aluf, Josephine Aria. My message was simple: camo battledress, ground attack, three hours, be ready to travel, and there might be some underground work required. I got responsive pings from everyone within seconds, then sent an FYI to my boss on the basis of the 'no surprise rule'.

In all probability, the President would get wind of our attack before he left for Europe, and I didn't want him spooked, so I counted on the Boss letting him know we had been attacked and were cleaning up the terrorists. No way he could object to that. It was what we had been chartered to do in the first place. I sent a further message to the Israelis on Whiddy Island, letting them know I would swing through to collect them on the way, and with the team I had with me in the hotel, I'd only need a squad as backup, even if the drone facility was deep underground.

"What's put a bug up your backside?" Sandra asked, looking around the floor as if we were being targeted. Her hand was actually inside her carry-on bag, so I put my hand on her arm and turned to look squarely at her.

"Stand down. There's no local threat I'm aware of. Indigo just got hammered by a squadron of drones. No casualties, but I've decided to go clean up the terrorist base on the way up to Killara."

"Good. About time you did something about O'Cleary. We need to change."

So we did, met everyone else at the vehicles, and headed for the airport. Anna was sitting across from me, her black-on-black FBI battledress with its big white lettering making its own statement. Back in the early days, she dressed in army combat fatigues, but now she obviously saw the need to be identified for what she was. Maybe that was a sign that we were moving into the political arena, like it or not.

"Do you need cover for what you are doing with us?" I gave her a steady look, and she just shook her head.

'No, the boys and girls and I are TDY'ed to Interpol formally, so we're covered. Roger wanted us in uniform because he sees an advantage in the visuals." I smiled, as there was simply no chance anything we did would end up on anyone's TV screen or the front page of any newspaper. What did I care about visuals?

"Just makes you a bigger target." And I let it go. I had more important things to think about. We boarded the helicopters and took off into a light drizzle. Does it always rain in Ireland? And headed cross-country. In just over an hour, we put down on a large paddock next to the house where the women terrorists had set up their headquarters. Now it was pouring, so we all stayed in the cabins, and the sodden members of the 104 team climbed into the spare seats. Josephine grabbed the seat next to Anna, turned to shake her hand, looked at me, water dripping from her helmet in small rivulets, until she shook her head like a dog, and gave us all a bath.

"Sorry about that. What's up? And what did you do to your face?"

"You saw the fracas up north?" I ignored her question about my stitches.

"Yes, we heard it as well. Colonel Kashasini and his crew were attacked, but he told us there were no injuries and asked if you would pick him up on your way through." I nodded, switched the headphones to intercom, and instructed the pilot accordingly.

"Chopper three has a seat, commander."

"Good. Get them to collect him. Can you give me access to all three aircraft when we're ready?"

"Yes, ma'am, just let me know when." We hovered over the stern of the ship while Indigo was collected from the roof of the top deck, and from the air you could see the impact marks on the decks of the debris from the missiles. The boat looked as though it had been pelted with burning garbage by someone in a fit of temper. As we all lifted back off and up into the scud, losing any visibility of the ground, I made my connection.

"Indigo, Josephine, welcome. Nice to have you both on board. Indigo, take over your team. Josephine, you take the 104. Sandra, Anna, and I will form a control team. More to follow on the ground, eleven minutes to run." I switched off, bringing up the military map of the area we were going to attack. Our drone airport was in the lee of Shelby Mountain, at 546 meters. I wondered at the term 'mountain', but the good news was that the terrain around was stripped mostly bare, with low-lying grass, dirt roads, and precious few houses. The greatest danger to us looked like the massive wind turbines that were scattered over the area in some sort of random pattern.

"Land us on the downside of the mountain, below the start of the target area."

"WILCO." I dialed Ito, somewhere high over our heads, flying in circles.

"Any signs of underground work?"

"Affirmative, commander, I'm sending you a graphic now."

"Got it. Maintain a watch. We will not execute until last light. Let's say 1930 hours local for a hack mark. At that time I want you to jam everything on every frequency, and hold that until I give the all-clear."

"Can do. For information only, your strength, please?"

"Col. Moschin, 9th Assault Parachute Regiment, twelve plus one; your 104 commandos, twelve plus two; Section Five, four good guys plus four. Copy?"

"Copy. Good luck. See you on the other side." And my extra surprise package in the Section Five team was Tom, who had inserted himself into the ground force in a heartbeat. I looked at his grimy face squeezed in next to the Sgan Aluf and felt a warm flood of comfort wash over me. Here was an ex-SEAL team leader, one who had worked with the Boss for years and was now my personal official quartermaster/weapons specialist. I smiled at him, then reached up to hold on as we slammed into the ground, buckets of water thrashing against the rotos like a car wash gone mad. I could see the other two helicopters through the scud, made the 'cut' signal to our pilot, and we all sat in anticipation as the rotos wound down, until the click-clack of the metal bits cooling down was the only sound louder than the torrential rain slapping at our canopy.

"Okay, listen up, I'm going to brief team leaders first, then they will brief you, then we'll all have a chat. Chopper one, 104. Two, Col Moschin. Three, and that's me, all team leaders. Move." And water and mud flew through the air, saturating the fabric seats as bodies climbed out, then back in, as we rearranged ourselves. I found myself looking at Anna, the Sgan Aluf, her lieutenant, Indigo, Tom, Sandra, and Anna, with our four Italian studs sitting behind. I pointed to each of them, then at Anna.

"Two of you shadow Agent Bernstein, two shadow inspector Thomas, and me. Tom, I'll leave you to take care of all of us. We'll go in as if we did a HALO, we'll tab it from here, Josephine, you'll take the drone track, mine it, but don't blow it. Then set up a ringfence at the base of the facility. Indigo, I want you and your team on my shoulder, we'll go in the front door, and work our way in. We don't have schematics, we're going in blind, and I'm designating the entire area hostile based on their recent attacks, so we will move with firepower forward. Anyone has a problem with that?"

"You expect them to erupt from hidden exits?" Josephine looked at the drawing we had on her mini, no doubt working out how far she needed to position herself to avoid getting encircled. I nodded, looked at my own drawing, and looked at Tom.

"Past behavior isn't relevant here. These people have been attacking us on and off for weeks, with no rhythm or reason, and to be honest, at this point in the operation, I'm not particularly interested in the why." Josephine gave me a very hard look.

"If any of you come up above ground unexpectedly, you'll be in our direct line of fire." I nodded again, something I had also thought of.

"Position a long gun and a spotter in a position so they can identify us if we should, but I'll also give you a heads up if I can." Her turn to nod, which she did. I looked at Indigo. He had no issues. He had run down dark tunnels under fire with me before and lived to tell the tale. So had Sandra and Tom, but Anna in her black-and-white advertisement for the FBI was a different matter. I needn't have worried. She stripped off her bulky FBI labels and slipped a khaki jacket on, now looking like a two-tone popsicle. I just grinned. People willing to get shot at with me have always won my heart. I dialed the Boss, waited until his head moved into the frame, waited again as he single-fingered me with a waggle, and finally his face came into focus.

"I've just sent you the coordinates of a confirmed drone facility. I need a Red Notice to support our attack."

"You've got it, broad enough to cover most eventualities. I'll cover off the President. He's agreed to a pickup tomorrow. Hopefully you'll be finished by then?" I nodded, thinking through the timing.

"I hope to be in Killara Bay early AM. I want that over and done with that before you grab him if I can." He just looked at me as if I asked for the sun, stars, and moon.

"Jessica, you greedy girl, if I have him on a plane while you do your nefarious best, he won't know for the next four hours at least, and we can kill his phone if we need to." Why hadn't I thought of that? I shook my head as if to get rid of the cobwebs and grimaced.

"Sorry, I've got a bit going on at present. I mentally ticked him off when I passed him to you. I'm going to sweep Scotland at the same time as Killara." He nodded, his hair blowing freely in the wind. I momentarily envied him his position, not having to chase terrorists all over the globe and back, then shook my head again.

"That will just leave Socotra."

"Yes. I hope someone in Killara will tell us what that is all about, then we'll work out what to do."

"Watch your six," he said as he disconnected. I pushed my mini into my pants pocket, looked around the cabin, and saw everyone focused on me.

"Go to your teams, brief them, have everyone in position by 1900, and wait for my signal." I was left with Sandra, Anna, and Tom, all of whom looked at me expectantly.

"Tom, we don't know the ground, we don't know the numbers we face, and we don't know their weaponry. I need you and our team to work out how to take the cavern. I have some ideas, but I'd like yours first." He nodded and pulled his mini out.

"Let's assume it's like their other three bases—a ramp, a downgrade, and an opening into a large work area. They have to store the drones and missiles somewhere. That suggests a large space. Do we know how they launch them?" I pulled my mini out and dialed my favorite navigator.

"Ito, did you see a launch?"

"Affirmative, we captured one on the long lens, sending it to you now. I watched as a drone suddenly appeared from under the ground, then shot off the rails. I marked where it had appeared from and swiped it to Josephine, who called me immediately.

"We'll sit on that. Do you want it blown as well?"

"If they make a run for it, they may use that lift if they don't take it down with the ramp."

"WILCO." Anna tapped me on the leg to get my attention.

"That suggests a level of sophistication we haven't seen before." I nodded, my thoughts exactly. What else did we face? I signaled for Tom to continue.

"How many tangos escaped from Whiddy Island?" I thought for a minute, then recalled the report on the first attack on the old fort and the estimate that between ten and twenty people had been at that site. The other two forts had weapons and supplies for tens of more terrorists, so I just waved my hands around a lot and guessed.

"Anywhere from ten to fifty." He looked down at his notes and tilted his head to one side.

"Allowing for a team for the drones, let's say five or six, given the rate of fire they used on the *'Scáthán',* allow for thirty bad guys, the real issue is we don't know the real estate. But we know the area, because we have it mapped by Ito and his friends. I would hypothesize the drones are in this corner, below the elevator, and the missiles are probably stored on the other side for safety, which means the living quarters will be in the middle." I looked at his hand-drawn map. It made sense to me, but the terrorists had rarely shown much common sense, for reasons that escaped me.

'How do we neutralize an area this size quickly?"

"I'd put a GGM (ground-to-ground missile) down into each corner, advance behind them with squad weapons, and electronically blind them, crash their power, and literally turn off all their lights."

"Advantage us."

"Advantage us."

"Do we have GGMs on board? And the ability to blind them in every wavelength?" He just smiled that little smile of his, the one he used to disarm the toughest terrorists right before he killed them.

"The admiral let me have my head, so yes, we do, and by coincidence, the four brutes we have sitting behind us are qualified on them." One of the Italian brutes he referred to reached between the seats and punched him on the shoulder, her hair swirling around her pretty face like a small hurricane. A second fist shot out at his other shoulder, and not without some force.

"Attento a come parli, soldato, o te lo pulisco io!" We all laughed. The idea of the five-foot-four Bianca leveling the six-foot-three Tom is a sight we would all pay to see.

"Bianca, sto scherzando, ma tu sei un bruto!" Tom ducked as another fist shot out at him, laughing so hard he folded in half.

"So, notwithstanding the lack of decorum, we have the weapons, and we have the ability to use them. Now all we have to do is find the way in." He nodded, rubbing his shoulder, then looked back over it to make sure Bianca wasn't lining him up again. She threatened him with a curled fist and a sneer, her fellow commandos egging her on.

"Now, now, Bianca, you know I love you." She broke into a grin, waved her fists, and jabbed her partner in the ribs.

"Not a brute, pretty girl, Tom, remember that!" The laughter subsided, the tension from the briefing completely dissipated, and the wall of rain storming outside our cabin created the illusion we were cut off from the world. But there was serious stuff afoot because I could see both Anna and Tom meshing their thoughts like metronomes on a piano.

"What?" It came out a little sharper than I would have liked, but the stitches on my face were pulling, and it made me twitchy. Anna leaned forward, her short hair spilling over her eyes. She brushed it away, her painted nails standing out in the filtered light.

"Jessica, with all that firepower, do we need to go down the tunnel?" Was this a search and destroy mission, or a seek, find, then destroy? Did I have to know what was in the underground hangar when we had proof that drones had operated from the rails? Did I need prisoners to interrogate? I looked at Tom, then at Anna, and I saw them mentally running through the same questions. I dialed my team leaders.

"I've got a question. Think before you answer. There is no wrong one. Do we need to go down the tunnel if we can destroy it and the contents from above ground?" Tom's face remained neutral. Anna's was a little withdrawn, Indigo's showed curiosity, Josephine's was puzzled, and her lieutenant was mildly amused, as if I had asked a rhetorical question. Josephine broke the stalemate.

"Who do you have to prove what to?" In a nutshell, and from a hardened warrior.

"Thank you. Stand by for a change of plan. Josephine, take your positions as briefed. Anyone you see in the target area is a designated tango, so handle them accordingly."

"Anna, never let me doubt your combat smarts ever again. Tom, work out how to crash the tunnel and the hangar from the front stoop. We don't go in unless we fail to collapse the hangar. Clear?" He nodded, looked back down at his plan, then back up at me.

"I want Indigo and four of his team plus the brutes behind me. We have enough ammunition to salvo downstream twice, and if we get the timing right, at two seconds apart, times four, there shouldn't be much left. Their fuel and ammunition might also blow. That's a bonus, and we'll be able to see that in any case." I nodded my approval. Tom called Indigo and made the arrangements. The four brutes and Tom climbed out, and ignoring the sheeting rain, which had a definite chill in it, they sloshed over to the helicopter next to us and started to unload the GGMs. I dialed Ito again.

"Commander, all quiet on your front. How can we help?"

"Just a heads up, time mark 1930 hours. We will use GGM's in salvos. Watch for any inground detonations. Will you have enough fuel?"

"Negative, if we bug out now, we can refuel and be back over the top in 45 minutes. We'll refuel in Cork."

"Do it. Stay safe." I dialed everyone on our net.

"Heads up, we are losing air cover for 45 minutes. If the tangos are going to try something, they will try it now."

"Can we engage if we see a drone?"

"Affirmative. If you can jam the elevator, so much the better; Tom, get your missileers in position, watch for movement;

Indigo, send the rest of your team to me." We jumped out into the muck and started to slog towards the point where we believed the entrance would be. Indigo's commandos slogged towards us, singing some strange Italian opera—weird at the best of times, but in the heavy downpour and the tension of a possible explosive combat encounter, perhaps not so much.

Anna ran beside me, her helmet streaming water, her poncho doing its best to keep it off her but failing at every step. We reached our mark; I signaled for everyone to spread out, half facing downrange, the others outwards, and Tom and his toys slipped between us and to where we thought the door might be. One blackened figure started crawling across the grass, using a box-like detector, and when she suddenly stopped and pumped her fist three times, we had our way in.

"Going to be a ramp, opening upwards, but wide enough for a small vehicle towing a drone. Wings off at this point, but that still gives us six to ten feet." I held my hand up, watched the snooper, and saw she was now on her belly, sticking yellow pegs in the ground as she crawled. Tom was right—about ten feet from edge to edge. I called Josephine on our little handheld talkies.

"Can you map the drone lift?"

"Already done."

"How wide?"

"Thirty feet by fifteen." I stopped to think it all through. We could blow open the smaller entrance or the drone elevator. Either way, we could then expect tangos to pop up in a nasty mood. I checked the time. Aircover wouldn't be back for another 20 minutes, but in truth, they were there for morale purposes, as they would not shoot no matter what because of the risk of civilian collateral damage. And there were a few houses and farms within eyesight of our position. Chances were, whatever we did would attract some interest from the locals.

I pulled my mini out and dialed Indigo, Tom, Josephine, and Anna, pulling the little computer in close to me to keep it dry.

"Question, does anyone have any objections to blowing the door and the ramp simultaneously?" Silence reigned supreme as my leadership team considered the risks to their people and what we might gain. Then Tom's measured voice cut across the empty air.

'I'd want a couple of GGMs at the lift, but otherwise no negatives from my side."

"Agreed. Send me two, two rounds each, and give me a mark for synchronization." Josephine's voice was edged with her Israeli accent, very dry and pedantic, just like her humor. But her steely determination warmed my chilled bones.

"Travelling. Commander, time hack?" My time to break the silence.

"Blow at 1930 as originally planned; launch missiles as soon as you can after that mark. Be very ready for return fire, and avoid blowback." A series of clicks acknowledged my instructions, so I lay in the sheeting rain, forming my own personal lake, and watched as two of Tom's missileers crawled off, towing a pair of GGM's in their green canisters. There was perhaps one hundred yards between our two positions, so by the time they got to Josephine, I was betting they would be saturated. Interestingly, one of the crawling figures was our not-a-brute pretty girl, Bianca!

"Mark, in three, two, one, mark!" We were synchronized; there was nothing to do now but wait. I felt rather than saw one of Tom's people rigging the electronics that would effectively blind the terrorists, and then, as they say in the movies, 'all was quiet on the western front.' Except we were in the middle of Ireland, but I let that factoid go in favor of the rhythm of the expression. Like everyone else, I huddled down, finding warmth where I could and protecting my weapon from the worst of the storm. Then on the horizon, a magical thing occurred: the streaming rain and low flying scud cleared, letting the faintest of waning sunlight filter through and creating parallel shafts of light that moved slowly over the low hills. I shook my head. Irish magic could be a distraction at the best of times, and this was not that.

It seemed like forever, but finally Ito's voice floated over the communicators.

"Back on station, overhead you in five. Report?"

"There will be no change-mark at 1930, but for information, both entrances will be blown simultaneously. We will not breach physically unless necessary."

"Roger that, we will have you on camera from hack minus two. Luck." And the silence filled the target area again, even the rain slowing down to a mere drizzle as the patch of light from the hills moved towards us.

At exactly 1930, the call out 'fire in the hole' resonated across the target area, and then two massive explosions killed the fading light as masses of dirt, rock, and bent steel rose up only to rain back down, hitting the ground like miniature bombs. Before the shock of the first blasts wound down, a litany of small explosions rang across the grass, seemingly in stereo. And then the entire target area rose up ten feet in the air, releasing fire and smoke with the ferocity of which I had never seen before in combat. Sandra, who was pressing into my side for her own survival, turned her muddy face to mine.

"That would be their weapons and fuel." I just grunted, not having the breath to talk. The constant thud of dirt and muck hitting us kept us with our hands over our heads and our bodies tucked tight. Then the unexpected happened.

"Contact, four hundred meters to your north, force of twenty, on foot, emerging from a dirt mound." Ito's voice had gone tight with tension, and as I turned around with Sandra, I felt Tom's team close up on us.

"Spread out, go wide, stay low. Anna, on me. Indigo, watch our backs; Josephine, keep cover on the target area." Clicks across the net, and black and brown mud-covered bodies started swarming on their bellies to defensive positions. We couldn't see squat from where we were, so Ito would have to be our eyes.

"Josephine, does your long gunner have targets?"

"Affirmative."

"Hold fire until they are within two hundred meters of our front. Targets of opportunity, you are weapons free." Click. Click.

"Sandra, your little toy won't be much good at this range. Get something bigger from Tom." Click. I looked sideways as far as I could, saw Anna moving through the mud and slush like the trooper she was, and was pleased to see her pushing a long gun out in front of her. We reached a small rise, kept our heads below the ridge line, and I lifted my mini up and pointed the camera to where Ito had indicated enemy movement. Sandra linked hers to mine and shared the screen with Anna and me. They advanced in a ragged line, making no attempt at cover or concealment, all dressed like the terrorists we had rounded up in other locations—dirty combat uniforms, an unkempt physical look, and all looking really pissed. Can't say that I blamed them. But if there was one hidden underground tunnel where troops could hide, there well might be another, so I quickly thought through my options and then decided I had dispersed my teams as best as possible.

Then the unmistakable crack of the fifty-caliber Barrett sniper rifle snapped its way over our heads, quickly followed by a second, then a third, then a fourth.

"They've gone to ground." They had all but disappeared back into the short grass, which was now looking like a huge black mat in the partial moonlight. I fitted my night vision gear, Sandra changed the sensitivity on the mini and set it for infrared, and the heat-generating mounds of human flesh just two hundred meters away pulsed in the green-filtered light.

The sniper kept up his cadence, one shot every three seconds, and one by one, the bodies sank from sight. I lined my weapon up on the mound closest to me, fired three rounds, and had the pleasure of seeing the mound disappear. Beside me, Anna and Sandra stopped playing with the mini and joined in the turkey shoot.

There was no pleasure or joy in this. The lack of professionalism the terrorists displayed added to their demise. I could think of ten dozen ways they could have avoided us and lived for another day.

"Whoever hired this lot should get a refund." Sandra's disgust filtered through the sounds of selective fire, and then silence filled the void as suddenly as the sharp sound of gunfire had.

"Tangos down, no movement." The call came from Josephine's spotter, the Israeli accent providing a warming human touch to a grim nightmare.

"Cover us." Tom led a team of three in a low crouch towards where the last of the terrorists had gone to ground, and while no Olympic records were broken for the two hundred meter dash, the swerving, bobbing, rocking figures made hard targets, but no one seemed interested in trying to shoot them.

Then from one flank, a massive burst of machine gun fire erupted, cutting Tom's team down where they ran, and the fifty caliber started its high velocity singing again, and then the machine gun nest disappeared in a haze of small explosions. I jumped up from my crouch, felt Sandra on my shoulder and the Italians just behind me, and raced to our fallen troops. Halfway there, I suddenly saw a flash of light on my right. I just had time to shout "down!" when the air split with red-hot metal so close I could feel the burn on the back of my neck as I dived for the ground. To say I hugged the earth is an understatement of some magnitude. I forcibly pushed myself three inches into it at least, before my heart stopped racing. And then another three inches as more screaming hot metal flew overhead, this time from a massive explosion, the pressure wave of which helped me with my burrowing. Our Israeli sniper was earning his keep.

The whine and pinging noises ricocheted across the field, and we now had two large burning pyres on either side to light the way. I stayed exactly where I was, waiting for information on what we were facing. We had been ambushed in a classic flanking cross-fire set-up, and only our Israeli shooters and their massive long guns had saved our proverbial arses.

"Both tango nests neutralized!" Josephine's call sounded a little tinny, my hearing having been blown away by the proximity of the gunfire. I cautiously looked up, then started to belly crawl towards where I had seen Tom go down. It took some time—stop, start, stop, start, waiting for the next terrorist nest to open up on us. They didn't, and we got to Tom to find him lying over one of his teammates, bleeding profusely from a bullet wound. His shell-shocked face turned to mine, and he shook his head and rolled off onto his back.

"Didn't see the bastards, caught us in the open, got my team on a zig." His three team members were dead, having multiple bullet holes in them, and the rounds had been armor-piercing judging from the way they had chewed up their protective vests. Tom had a hole through and through in the mid-thigh, which Sandra slapped a field dressing on. Anna just lay facing the line the terrorists had taken, waiting to see who shot at us next. I waved to the Italians and Anna and motioned for them to stay down with Tom.

"Sandra, with me." And I started to crawl towards the line of the mercenaries, halting when I got to the first one. It was dead as a door nail. Its torso was shattered in several places, with its arms and legs hanging loosely at odd angles. I crawled to the next one, with a similar result. We had been effectively sandbagged. The line of terrorists was no more than a line of mechanical range dummies and androids. The machine gun nests were the real threat, and we had run and crawled right into their field of fire. I mentally took back all the insults I had heaped on the terrorists. This had the hallmarks of some smart thinking—not smart enough, as it turned out, but deadly none-the-less.

"Josephine, any movement on your end?"

"Negative."

"Indigo?"

"Negative."

"Anna?"

"Negative."

"Ito, did you get the location of those nests, and can you identify any others from their signatures?"

"Clear identification once they opened fire. Nothing until then."

"You think there are still some tangos around?" Sandra spun around on her belly, facing towards the nest on our flank.

"Yes. This set-up was designed for a frontal attack on the drone hangar."

"We came in from the side." She nodded, seeing the same tactical plan that I did. "They're set up somewhere else."

"Yes. How else would you attack this site?" Even in the gloom, with the light from the fire where the nest had been, I could see Sandra shake her head.

"We drop down from a HALO jump. We land by helicopter. But both those require us to know where the entry and exits are for the hangar."

"So where did the tangos run from the fort?" She looked at me over her shoulder, her face screwed up in concentration.

"No idea. The Irish *Sciathán Fianóglach* made contact with the first group. They disappeared out to sea somewhere." I thought about that, then shook my head. Didn't matter now. I tapped her on the shoulder and started to crawl towards the nest. It had been shredded by the fifty caliber, and the five bodies that lay strewn amongst the shattered machinegun were undoubtedly human and equally shattered.

"Indigo, check out the nest on your side. Body count." Click. I stood up. If there was another nest, it would be now or never. Sandra looked up at me from her belly position, grinned, then stood herself, shaking mud and debris off her uniform like a dog shaking water off after a bath. I had to admit that my skin crawled, and I mentally tightened the muscles in my backside, waiting for the impact of a bullet, but I rolled my shoulders to dissipate some tension when it didn't come.

"Five tangos, two squad weapons totaled." Indigo's use of English spoke volumes for his temperament. He was pissed but kept it between us. But that made ten dead terrorists, so I wondered how many more we still had to deal with. While we had seen none at two of the forts, it had only been eight or ten who had escaped from the first one.

"Help Tom recover his team. I'll call a chopper in. See if they get shot at." Click. I sent a text to the pilots, warning them they were flying into a potential hot zone, asked the second to pick up Josephine's team, and moved back to Tom. By the time we got there, Anna, filthy from head to foot, was directing traffic and getting everyone ready to evacuate. She studied me when I stopped. Sandra was dripping mud and slime.

"You two look like you had a bath in a pool of crap." Sandra punched her in the arm, flicked her hand between her helmet and her ear, and slung her long gun over her back. Whatever she was about to say was stalled by the throbbing sound of the helicopter smothering us with a torrential downwash and rotor noise as it skidded to a stop. The crew helped with the bodies, and the rest of Tom's team mounted the helicopter. I pulled Anna, Sandra, and Indigo into a huddle.

"We need to get to Killara. We have two teams there. Unless you have other ideas, I'll send Josephine and her teams back to Whiddy Island. Tom needs professional treatment, so either Cork or Dublin. Comments?"

"Do you expect any hostile reaction in Killara Bay?" Anna looked as dirty as I did, and in a weird way, that made me feel good. I would never win the fashion stakes with Sandra, Fay, and Anna looking like catwalk models, but when you covered everyone with mud and slime, we all looked as crappy as each other. I shook my head. Sad way to think of three beautiful women who just happened to be first-class warriors as well as good-looking. And, my friends, wasn't that a kick in the backside?

"Fay senses none. The women are working as a tight team, moving from house to house, in Inishcrone and Killara. My plan would be to take them when they get back to their house in Inishcrone. Get Fay to organize transport, land far enough away so no one knows we were there. So small team, do we take the boys and girls or just go ourselves?" Sandra looked at Indigo and saw him shake his head minutely. Turned to look me straight in the eyes.

"We've just lost three good soldiers, so in the interests of not losing any more, I vote we take our Italians." Both Indigo and Anna nodded in agreement.

"Okay, mount up. I'll brief the helicopter crews." I sent a text to Josephine and instructions to Tom's pilot, then moved out of the rotor wash far enough away to be able to talk on the mini. The Boss's face swam into focus. This time, his background was the plush interior of a corporate jet.

"Good to see you're not blowing the budget on luxuries." My sarcasm went over his head, or he just ignored it, smiled at me, and shook his head.

"You need a wash. I can smell you from here."

"Thanks for that. We lost three of Tom's team. He got shot as well. You can tell the President we accounted for ten of his terrorists, and we're still looking for more." His face moved into a grimace, and I saw the pain run across his eyes.

"Nothing we could do. We were ambushed. They used android training drones to sucker us in, then caught us in an effective crossfire." He sucked his breath in, looked at me with hard, deep black eyes, and I answered before he could ask the question.

"Tom can give you a detailed report. On scene, they played a better game than us. I take full responsibility." His face became a hard mask, the intensity of his eyes now like lasers.

"Bullshit. I know Tom, and I know you. And the only thing you are responsible for is getting the job done. And you demean yourself and Tom when you take that stance. Get over it." I felt annoyed, but he had the truth of it: we reacted exactly as we trained. We had covered everything we could think of, but got caught out by superior tactics. But I still felt responsible, so I just shut my mouth and looked back at him. Old interrogation tactic: the first person to speak loses the high ground. He shook his head at me and looked down at his watch.

"We're picking the President up in fifty minutes. What's your next move?"

"Killara Bay, O'Cleary, and her playmates." He just waved a hand at the screen, as if shooing flies away.

"Stay safe." And he disconnected. If I felt his boot on my ass and a prickle of resentment, it had been my plan, so I was responsible, but given that we had air cover and mitigated the perceived risk as far as possible, all I really had was the fact that war plans never survive the first shot. I walked back to the helicopter, climbed into the cabin, and waved at the pilot. I had two and a half hours to get my grin back, so I rested my head on the door frame and closed my eyes.

CHAN EIL DUINE DHACHAIGH

The approach to the three-story house, with its retail shops on the ground floor, was textbook. A member of the local Police Scotland, resplendent in his dark blue woolen uniform and bright yellow jacket, knocked on the door, repeated the process when there was no answer, tried for a third time calling out 'police, please open your door' in a brogue so heavy with accent only locals would understand it, then stood back as one of his companions moved to the door with a portable battering ram. Two solid hits had the door swinging back on its hinges. When both policemen stood back and allowed the entry of Bob and three of his team, weapons pushed forward, bright lights attached to the barrels poking the dark gloom away.

They cleared every room, floor by floor, only to find every window shuttered, every room empty except for furniture, and a layer of dust suggesting human occupants had not been in residence for some considerable time. Bob moved back to the massive room with wall-to-wall electronic equipment, all of which was plugged in and working. While he had some idea of what he was looking at, he really didn't understand the totality of it, so he called for his technical expert, who had waited outside with the rest of the breech team. He was skinny at six feet four, had short blond hair, a wicked smile that attracted women like moths to a flame, and deep-set, rich, dark blue eyes that never stopped moving.

His name was Laurance—just Laurance, as he proudly told everyone—and being picked for the Presidential detail back in Washington seemed to be the highlight of his army career.

Then his team had been seconded to Interpol, first as a guard on the Presidential train that had been provided for them to cross America in search of terrorists, then sent around Europe chasing terrorists with nuclear-capable shells, and now to Scotland, where he had helped stake out a suspect terrorist headquarters in the rolling hills around the tiny town of Aberfoyle. He had never had so much fun in his life!

And now, ever the energetic geek, he was being asked his opinion of walls and walls of super-high tech, all in working order, a miracle in itself. He walked around the room slowly, touching something that caught his eye, then moving on until he ended up back facing Bob. With two sons of his own, Bob understood the passionate, vacant look in Laurance's eyes—one of love and desire for all things electronic.

"Well?" The two Police Scotland constables stood to one side, in awe of the electronics. Like the rest of the world, they had lost their computers, phones, and internet during the original terrorist attacks, and seeing all this equipment

up and working left them breathless. The fact that it had existed for months right under their noses left them angry. Laurance looked around the room again, then down at Bob, who was a full head shorter.

"Sir, this equipment is being operated remotely, that bank of servers over there is being used to generate identification documents for someone. These screens show you the names and data, and whoever is doing the work is experienced with a keyboard. They may be using AI. The server bank on the other side is being used for communications. We know they receive and send microwave transmissions, that shows on this screen here," he pointed to a screen with green gibberish on it, "and it outputs to this box here," and he walked and pointed to a small termination device, "which is connected to a dark fiber cable that exits here." He pointed to a thick cable that terminated in the corner, securely concreted into floor. Bob walked over to it, gave it a poke with one booted foot, then grimaced.

"Can you track the cable?" Laurance looked a little dubious and walked to the side wall where the windows had sturdy wooden shutters over them. He cautiously opened them and peered outside.

"If we had a GPR (ground penetrating radar) scanner, yes, sir, we could track the cable." Bob thought for a minute, then rolled his shoulders.

"Like the ones we used in Montana and the Middle East?"

"Yes, sir. Exactly."

"Hold that thought." He reached for his mini and dialed Jessica.

CHAPTER FORTY THREE

I came out of my sleep to the incessant buzzing of my mini, snapped it open so hard the top almost departed of its own accord, then sat upright in my seat. Outside visibility was zero, and my pink girlie watch told me we still had ten minutes or so to run. Bob's stern face was backlit by a huge wall of flashing lights attached to what I presumed were electronics.

"Commander, sorry to interrupt, but the nest is empty, except for these electronics. We need to track a dark fiber cable."

"Can you get a GPR locally?"

"Stand by one." Bob turned to face the two policemen, who were watching in amazement at Bob's casual use of the mini.

"Sergeant, do you know where we can get a ground-penetrating radar scanner from close by?" The sergeant scratched his head, pushing his hat to one side, revealing an unruly thatch of gray black hair.

"Aye, I'd be thinking we might get one down in Glasgow. I don't have much use for them up here." Tom weighed his options. This was still a terrorist hunt, and letting the local police take the lead did not seem like the sensible thing to do.

"Commander, it's possible, but it would involve the locals." He hoped what he said was not interpreted by the police as a slight. Neither policeman reacted, so he breathed a silent sigh of relief. Battered egos were the last thing he needed at the moment.

"I'll have one sent to you soonest. Report?"

"No one here, but they left all their electronics behind. Our tech guy says they are producing IDs for unknown persons using an advanced AI program. All their data comes in and out via a Dark Fiber cable. I want to track it to its source."

"Understood. Be very careful. We just got caught in an ambush. Tom lost three. The attack on us showed some smarts. Stay safe." And I disconnected, to see Sandra looking directly at me from her curled-up position across two seats.

"Scotland?" I nodded. I sent a text to our office in Glasgow, asking them to contact the local police, get a GPR, and then take it to Tom as fast as they could. I copied Tom into the message so he'd have both the details and the contact address for our agent, whom I did not know. That meant that we would probably not have an outcome in Scotland for a day or two, depending on how far away the mysterious Freya was actually located.

"Have you checked on Tom?" I asked, getting my head into the game again. She nodded.

"He wants to join us. I told him you'd think about it. He gave me a look that suggested he wouldn't take no for an answer." I nodded. Typical Tom, worked too long with the boss and picked up all his bad habits.

"No way. We should start thinking about the bigger issue." She sat up, stretched, rolled her shoulders, then crossed her ankles. Her carry bag was sitting in the middle of her stomach, and her long gun was standing on the floor at her side. I wondered if she regretted leaving the Chicago office, where her life had been far simpler and much safer. All she had to do on a regular basis was outsmart a bunch of SWAT dudes and a few FBI ringers.

"Is the bigger issue you're alluding to anything to do with politicians?" I grimaced. She had hit it in one.

"We're going to get pressure on how we manage the ecological plants and anything else the women have created. The world is hurting in so many ways that I can't see a solution without maximizing the use of their technology."

"So they win?"

"On one front, yes, the economics of the children migrating are self-evident, and I can't see any country holding out for long. And as far as the politicians will see, about the length of their arms, all the damage has been done. Now it's just a recovery effort, and the technology the women have employed will help with that recovery. In fact, it may well be critical. And to be absolutely honest, the factories and the technology are not really in our purview. Once we have accounted for the terrorists, the issue is who takes over the managing of the plants and the factories?"

"If only it was that simple. A lot of this will fall on Amira's shoulders, won't it?"

"Not if I can help it, I'll isolate her from the solutions as far as I can. What was developed from her original work is well and truly after the fact. We've already positioned the Israelis as the nano experts. No one can start a plant or keep one going without their direct help, but the one thing that worries me is Innomatchi. They were producing some weird stuff according to Amira, and maybe, just maybe, what the women are doing in Killara Bay is related. We'll soon see."

"Can we assume that the Japanese government will take over running Innomatchi? And if it were a perfect world, how would you organize the whole environmental plant thing anyway?" It was a question that had been running through my mind since I had first set foot on Point Roberts and then seen the outcome in Helena. Economics, power, greed, selfishness, politics, vested interests, and sheer disgusting human behavior had driven the old world, but then it all came crashing down due to the terrorist attacks. The new world was stalled without electric power, fossil fuels, or communications. No power, no work, no money, no economy, and no peddling influence. And no internet to bitch about it on. And a whole lot of countries that had been power brokers in more ways than one were on their economic knees, having lost their ability to hold the world to ransom on a whim.

Their biggest issue now was how to house and feed their people while escaping the natural wrath of a previously disenfranchised population. A gold Rolls Royce, even if it was electric-powered, held no sway in the new world and was just as likely to be stripped for parts as its owner was to be savagely beaten to death on the spot. OPEC no longer existed. The Gods of commerce had forever changed in favor of renewables, and even that stranglehold was being eroded by the terrorists provision of free power—at least if the model demonstrated in Dundalk was anything to go by.

So, in effect, the terrorists were offering financial gain and free renewable power to any of the nineteen countries they had selected as targets for the refugee children. And one of those countries was the United States of America. The littlest, it could be argued, was New Zealand. And the biggest single beneficiary of the entire plan looked like it would be Ireland, with its five or six million refugee children and billions and billions of euros to support them. What of Russia and China? Or Australia, or any of the other one hundred and seventy-six countries in the world? How long would they let the nineteen countries reap the benefits of playing the terrorist's game and profit from the experience?

Russia has gone to war recently. Look at Ukraine.

At this point, like so many countries in Europe and Asia, they were on their own. Which raised the question in my mind: what were the mysterious powerplants—if that was what they were—being created in Scotland, England, Spain, and France in shuttered nuclear facilities for? What role were those countries supposed to play in the future?

My mind went back to their genius clinical psychologist, Rena Niele, the bedmate of the notorious Maribelle Assiano, who had sunk a ship holding over five thousand refugee children in the Atlantic Ocean before being literally blown to atoms in a nuclear explosion that had sunk her boat and killed her crew. Rena had used a supercomputer for years to model the predictive behavior that could be expected after the initial terrorist attacks, and we assumed the same behavior would be expected in the recovery phase. As social experiments go, it was on a grand scale, making the worldwide pandemic five years earlier look like a kindergarten picnic.

And I felt sure they had gotten it wrong. No way would they have predicted sixty to seventy million deaths due to social unrest. In direct terms, the women had perhaps killed less than twenty to thirty thousand people in their attacks and had actually spared the crew of the International Space Station. And the only shots fired at us in all the months we had been chasing them around the globe had come from hired mercenaries, the last of whom, with luck, we had now accounted for. And then I had an epiphany. Yes, another one!

Who did I trust most in the world as it now was? Who had the ability to stand tall and stand firm against political pressure, greed, avarice, vested interests, power brokers, and, in a real sense, all comers. I looked at Sandra and Anna, thinking I might just be going to make one person's day and disrupt anothers. Dialed my mini, bringing them into a group call, including Indigo, Fay, Arie, and the Boss. Watched as the fabulously lined but perpetually calm face of Stefarino swam into focus. He was in his cavern, reading a book, of all things.

"Jessica, what a pleasure to see you. What happened to your face?" I unconsciously reached up and stroked my stiches with a big smile on my face.

"Stefarino, lovely to see you too. It's just a scratch. I have a question for you, and if you need time to consider your answer, I'll call you back. You can see we have General Anthony, General Rosenberg, Colonel Kashasini, Inspectors Remer, Thomas, and Richards on this call. They are not aware of my intent, and any discussion we have after this call will not influence my question in any manner." He looked at me, his warm, smiling deep gray eyes looking deep into my soul, and I could actually feel him radiating peace and tranquility across the link.

"What is your question?" He had the look of a fatherly confessor, which I guess he was.

"Some background—as you would be aware, we have requested the Israelis take over authority and control of the development and supply of the nanites, as they invented the first tranche." He nodded, his eyes crinkling slightly at the corners as he engaged his huge mind.

"And the assumption is that every country with an environmental plant will manage its outcomes in favor of the refugee children and the funding they bring with them, at least initially, and then we expect they will divert their energies to benefiting their individual countries." He nodded again, the creases deepening slightly as he tried to anticipate my question.

"We have a reason to hypothesize that the women have another technologically advanced power source, which we hope to uncover in an hour or two, which will only add to the recovery of the world's economy. What it is and how it works is not yet clear, but we know it does work, as I've seen it in action for myself." A third nod and a little loosening of the creases.

"My question is this: Innomatchi is the sole provider of the technology and machinery for creating the environmental plants, the nanites, and the new technology, whatever it is. Would you, and your order, consider taking control of Innomatchi and any other production facility we might uncover, and thus prevent any one country or political influence from being able to dominate the supply of the hardware and technology they produce?" The silence that followed my question was absolute, not even an indrawn breath. Then Sandra broke the informal covenant with a wicked grin and a muttered, 'brilliant!' I chose to ignore her. She had asked the question, and I had answered it—maybe not in a conventional manner, but never-the-less, in definitive terms.

"Jessica, if the good Generals and your team agree, this is something we can do. It will take some time for us to prepare our people, but we will take that responsibility as you request."

"Stefarino, *assolutamente!*" Indigo's call rolled across Sandra's muttered endorsement, and the Boss was nodding, as were Fay and Anna.

"Thank you, Stefarino. Let's leave it there, and I'll get back to you in the next day or two." He nodded, smiled, made the sign of the cross, and disconnected.

"Very ballsy. What brought this on?" The Boss's craggy face filled the frame, his expression inscrutable.

"Sandra asked me a question." He smiled and shook his head.

"Perfect timing. I'm running into more and more roadblocks here in Lyon and Geneva, as the powers of old are trying for a resurrection. Russia and China, as you'd expect, are really pissed at being left out of the party and are making demands and waving swords. Promises are being made and alliances formed, so it will be interesting to see how your little idea pans out. Thanks for the heads up." His sarcasm was heavy and directed, but for once it rolled off me like mercury across a tin plate. We could only control what others let us control. The very least we could do now was protect the future for everyone, not just some greedy ex-superpower or industrial robber baron. And I was absolutely not a politician, as was pointed out to me at every opportunity.

I was soon left with Sandra, Anna, and Indigo, all of whom looked at me as if I had spouted three heads. We landed with a thud, and I suddenly realized we had arrived. I looked outside, and to my surprise, I saw a beautiful, lush green field with small trees and stone walls forming rectangles as far as I could see. I climbed out, followed by the others, all of whom formed a protective circle around me as we moved out of the rotor wash.

Fay stood beside a small electric vehicle, her poncho and knitted hat making her look more like a civilian than a soldier, which I respected, as that had been her brief.

"Fay, how's it going?" Sandra asked, moving in for a hug.

"Anna, great to see you again." Hug, hug, in the way of women everywhere, Indigo and I left to our own devices. I waved to get their attention.

"Where are the women? Where are we?" Fay looked at me and grinned, then brushed some stray hair back behind her ear. Short, brownish, and unruly.

"According to the good warrant officer, they're on their way back to this side of the Bay. We're about a mile from their base, to the east. What are you going to do with your helicopters?" I looked at the choppers, rotors winding down, looking like bug-eyed green and black alien bugs about to snack on the pasture. Only the heavy machine guns drooping from the open doorways spoiled the image.

"Do you have a tag on them?"

"Yes. Powered bicycle, very common around here."

"Okay, good. What's your plan?" She looked at me suspiciously, as if she expected me to take over.

"Ah, you want O'Cleary taken into custody. What about the other four?"

"Well, my instinct is to sweep them all up at once, then sort them out in interrogation." She nodded. Looked at her tactical watch.

"They should be here in half an hour." I nodded. As far as I could see, there were some houses near us in the next paddock, but no movement of people or vehicles.

"Is it always this quiet?"

"Yes, we learned that over sixty percent of the population has left in the last three years. The pandemic killed the tourist business, as it did worldwide, and the fisher folk can't create more work than they have, as transport has been effected by the lack of petroleum products. Like many parts of Ireland, they're in a holding pattern, waiting for the next big opportunity."

"And according to the President, migrating refugee children will fill the economic holes all over the country."

She nodded, looking at her watch again. Suddenly, her mini buzzed. She opened it, looked, and listened, a scowl forming on her face. She snapped it shut.

"The women are taking a detour. They're driving into Ballina, maybe replenishing their supplies. I've told our eyes to wait at the bridge." Makes sense. Then I put a mental map of the area in my mind's eye and remembered how one of them had gotten here in the first place.

"How far is the airport from the township?"

"Less than three kilometers." I looked over at the helicopters, now sitting somewhat forlornly, rotors drooping towards the ground, cockpits dripping from the drizzle. It would take at least five minutes to get one airborne, then another twelve minutes flat out to get over the airport. The women were less than two kilometers away. They would beat us by at least ten minutes if they were in a hurry, but I hadn't come all this way to lose them now. I made the 'wind up' signal to the aircrew, grabbed Sandra, Fay, Indigo, and our four brutes, and ran to the chopper. The unmistakable whine of the turbines and the stutter of the rotors trying to turn cut the air. We scrambled in, then the whine increased, as did the wop-wop-wop of the blades, and with a lurch, we were airborne.

We achieved transitional lift about ten feet off the deck, and nose down, we ripped over the small village of Inishcrone with a few feet to spare. The pilot, whose blue hair flowed out from under her helmet, had a grimace on her face that spoke of determination. We flashed over the rectangles of lush green, the sleet starting to occlude our vision, and the pilot suddenly pulled the aircraft up into a steep climb.

"Apologies, commander, we're too low in this weather. I need at least eight hundred feet not to hit anything." Before I could answer, Sandra reached across me and pointed to the door gun, which was unmanned and had the classic 'I'm not loved' look as it tilted down towards the ground, vibrating in its mount. I shook my head. The last thing I wanted was an aerial gunfight in full view of civilian airspace. If we had to fight, we would have to be clever about it.

The unmistakable shape of the row houses outside Killara swept beneath us, little puffs of stratus cloud creating a peek-a-boo feeling. We were flying between layers of clouds, the upper ones boiling and dirty gray, the lower ones fluffy white. In a way, it was surreal. Killara township proper raced by on our starboard side, and the pilot took us down through a hole in the clouds. We could see the outline of the long, slick tarmac in the distance and the unmistakable shape of a midsized jet at one end. A vehicle was parked next to the jet.

We landed with some force, the skids hitting the rear ends, then the nose thumping down with a vengeance. We all but leapt out, only to see our favorite terrorist standing beside the vehicle as the jet accelerated down the runway with a mighty roar. She turned to look at us and stood calmly with her hands tucked in her pants pockets and a shallow smile on her face. She looked like her photos: long blond hair, chiseled face, great figure, dressed in puffy, warm clothes with a woolen hat pulled down to her eyebrows. We stood facing each other, as if we each needed some time to let our emotions settle. Here was the woman we believed had invented the nuclear-capable bimetallic shells. Here was a woman who, in company with a notorious mercenary by the name of Malik Badawi, we had chased all over Europe and the Middle East. A mercenary that Sandra and I had unceremoniously dispatched with a bullet in the head and one in the heart before allowing the body to fall into the Atlantic Ocean.

"Siobhan O'Cleary, I'm arresting you for violation of the Terrorist Laws as modified in 2022, on a string of charges including, but not limited to, the manufacture of nuclear-capable shells, the procurement of nuclear material, the association with a known mercenary terrorist, and other sundry crimes that will be specified at your trial. Do you understand the charges against you?" She looked me in the eye, almost smiled, then grimaced when Sandra pulled her hands behind her back and cuffed her. The roar of the jet engines filled the void, and the white shape disappeared into the clouds. She turned her face to look at it and muttered something under her breath.

"What did you say?" Sandra demanded.

"Slán a dheirfiracha, is beannaithe iad."

"Goodbye, my sisters. Blessed be."

"Yes, you speak Galic?"

"A little. Come." I motioned to the helicopter, and O'Cleary, now with Fay on one side and Sandra on the other, was shuffled awkwardly into the back seat, her manacled hands making it difficult for her to get settled. The pilot turned to look at me. I simply pointed back the way we had come, and like an elevator, we lifted back up into the low-flying scud. I dialed Ito, somewhere high overhead.

"Commander, good to see you. You're airborne?"

"Yes, I'm flying back to Inishcrone. I need you to put a marker on the jet that just left our position and track it, please."

"WILCO. Marker ID as Bogie One. It's climbing through 15,000 feet, directly towards Europe, heading one-four-zero. In one hundred nauticals, we'll have to pass it off to the monks." I thought about that. It was incredible to think that the most reliable satellite tracking system in the world was run by an ancient brotherhood of monks headquartered in a massive underground dungeon in Venice. Such was the new world.

"Good, thanks, Ito. How long will you stay on station?"

"As long as you need us."

"Let me know when you plan to refuel and where. I'll have a passenger or two for you to take back home with you."

"WILCO." I shut my mini and watched O'Cleary watch me. She seemed very relaxed for someone facing, at best, life in a concrete cage, but maybe that reality hadn't set in yet. I ran over everything I knew about her, going all the way back to picking her face up off a satellite photo taken over a terrorist camp in Afghanistan. Massive bio, genius-level qualifications, nuclear science, engineering, physics, and double doctorates before she was twenty-five. There was no attempt to hide her background. They used it to scare us into believing they had the capability to build, load, and fire nuclear missiles at us. It had worked. Big time.

For reasons we still did not understand. On the surface, the nuclear option seems to go directly against what the women were trying to achieve with the terrorist attacks. I shook my head. Well, now I would have the chance to ask her why she did what she had done.

"Fay, have Rosie ready to inspect the houses they were working in on the Killara side. Indigo, we'll drop you off with the

W/O. We'll have a chat with Miss O'Cleary here, then we'll examine the houses on the Inishcrone side. Anna, Fay, Sandra, I'll need your help before we do that. Questions?" Everyone shook their heads. I relayed the change in destination to the pilot, who promptly turned the helicopter on its side and headed across the Bay. We dropped Indigo next to the fish factory, then took off back across the bay directly towards Inishcrone.

We landed without further excitement, the rotors wound down, and we moved to the vehicle Fay had parked. A short drive later, we were at the hotel. We moved straight to an area that looked like a ballroom and noticed it had been cleared except for a table in the middle and six chairs. I motioned to Fay, who removed the handcuffs from the prisoner. Our four grunts took up posts at each doorway, locked them, and then stood at ease facing us. Sandra and Fay sat on one side. Anna was next to the prisoner, leaving me at the head of the table. I put my mini in sight, bent it backwards, sat it in front of me, and turned on the record function.

"Miss O'Cleary, we are being recorded. Is there anything you need explained to you?" She worked a very thin smile across her lips. Her stunning green eyes had a sparkle, and for someone in her position, she looked remarkably calm.

"May I have your names, please?" Her voice was laced with a broad Irish accent, something that under more normal circumstances I would find charming. A member of the hotel staff walked in, escorted by one of the grunts, and placed a lager tray on the table. I smelled the coffee, held my hand up to stop any further conversation, motioned to Sandra to pour, and waited until we had all settled again. I pointed to each member of my team in turn.

"That's Inspector Remer and Inspector Thomas, Interpol. Sitting next to you is SSSA Bernstein, FBI. I'm Commander Riley, also of Interpol." She nodded, seemed to be thinking about her next question, then pulled the mug that had been placed in front of her and sipped it with a wishful look on her face. She carefully placed the mug back down, turned to look at Anna, then across at Sandra and Fay, and lastly at me.

"I'm sure you have a lot of questions for me. Why not start there?"

"What were you doing here in Killara Bay?" Sandra's voice was calm and modulated, with no apparent threat. She had obviously decided to play nice, at least for the present. But her little, pretty handbag was within easy reach.

"I came here after getting way from Badawi. It was what I had been promised for giving up over a year of my life to live with that scum. I was promised thirty thousand refugee children, once I had the buildings and support infrastructure in place. What I was doing here with the girls was getting things started so we could build." I continued to look directly in her eyes. She didn't prevaricate. She wasn't trying to hide anything; if anything, she was unnaturally relaxed. And telling the truth. Almost.

"You came here from a small Island in the Arabian Sea called Socotra." Her eyes opened wide in surprise, then she just nodded to herself.

"Yes, I did. I fled there after the crash, to get away from Badawi, to regain my sisters and a sense of normalcy and purpose again." I decided to let that sit. Socotra was a target for another day. I wanted the biggest question we'd all had for months answered.

"Why were you sailing around the Mediterranean Sea ready to fire nukes at targets of opportunity?" She gave me a look that only a super smart person can give someone much dumber than them, but I wasn't insulted in the least. She was the one soon to be incarcerated, and I was the one holding the chains.

"I wasn't firing nukes at anyone. I was alongside Badawi to make sure the so-called nukes could never go off. I gave a year or more of my life to get close enough to him to be able to completely control the technology, which I successfully did." The bitterness and hurt in her voice were unmistakable. She was speaking the truth as she knew it. I decided to draw her out a little to see where she would go.

"The bimetallic shells you manufactured were genius, as was the use of nanites to both open and close them. Our specialists determined the shells could never be exploded once loaded and sealed. Were they correct?" She looked at me as if I had two heads.

"Why on earth would we let a bunch of crazy mercenaries loose with nuclear weapons?" Now her voice had gone up in pitch, as if she were insulted.

"The very question we were asking ourselves: Why did you get involved with the crazies?" This time she looked a little lost, as if the memory of what she had done was painful. She shook her head, went very still, then seemed to make a decision.

"If you guarantee me that you will let this project in Ireland develop to its full potential and leave the four girls alone to continue their work, I'll tell you everything." We don't negotiate with terrorists, and sitting here in front of us was, to some minds, the worst terrorist we had faced since the initial attacks. How do we balance this all out? Anna gave me a doorway.

"If the girls you refer to had no knowledge of the attacks beforehand, and if they are now involved in work that will benefit everyone, then I believe we can convince the authorities to let them be. We know that they have been working at nuclear power plants as well as houses here in Killara Bay, and at some point you will have to explain that to us. Right, Commander?" Anna very cleverly had put me back at point, seemingly deferring to my authority. So I used it.

"We have already arrested the CEO and COO of Whiddy Island; all the women associated with the drone operation; incarcerated the President and his two 'advisors', and have arrested a number of civil servants we believe knew of the attacks in advance. At this point, if we chose to, we can shut down the entire refugee plan you have for Ireland in a heartbeat. And I can do it now." Her face went a pasty white as all the color drained out. She held her hands out to me.

"You can't do that! Millions of children will die if you do that!" I fixed a serious look on my face and looked across at Sandra, Anna, and Fay, who were now emulating me, looking stern and determined. We were a small club, but a very talented one, and one that was expert in interrogation techniques.

"I can do that, and I will. Now, first cab off the rank, why did you get involved with nuclear missiles?" And for the next two hours, we unpicked the grand plan the woman 'Helen'—Natasha Trotsky—and Al Hemish al-bin Mohammad Karesish, also known as Mohammad bin Azaria, had come up with over the past thirty-five years. Helped by a bunch of innocent child gamers and two not-so-innocent geniuses, the two adopted refugee sisters, Reve and Nazreen Anaisha, whose mother owned and ran Innomatchi, the technology company that made all the hardware and software that the terrorists had created to support their program.

I called for a break, leaving O'Cleary to go to the rest room under guard while we decompressed in a small anteroom Fay had requisitioned.

'It's a lot to process," Anna offered, slumping in her chair. Sandra was rubbing at her ears, looking very unhappy.

"What's up?" She looked at me, her expression one of frustration.

'I'm having trouble rationalizing all the good with all the bad. You said earlier something about the length of a politician's arm and their attention span, and I can see where all this could go to the crapper in a heartbeat if we don't keep the lid on." I pointed at her and nodded.

"Right now, it's we three and the grunts, and we can count on them keeping stum."

"And O'Cleary."

"And O'Cleary. But we know what she wants."

"But can we give it to her?" I looked off into space. Here was the question for the ages: If we did little more than close down Scotland and investigate Socotra, let the 'girls' as O'Cleary had called them, go about their business unheeded, and worked out how to control Innomatchi (done but not dusted) and the nanites (done and dusted), we could be seen to have done what was asked of us by our member countries immediately after the first of the terrorist attacks.

If.

But what was the alternative?

I decided I needed guidance, so I asked the team to give me ten minutes and walked until I found a quiet spot. I dialed Stefarino, Arie, and the Boss.

"Gentlemen, although that's probably a stretch for you, general, I need your advice." Three very somber faces stared at me unflinchingly. "And I was talking about PJ, not you, Arie." With little smiles, they knew me contacting them without my team meant something important was up.

I gave them a detailed report, summarizing everything in the equivalent of dot points; it still took fifteen minutes, during which time no one butted in or talked over me. I wound down with a relatively weak implied question.

"Normally, I would do what we have been chartered to do on behalf of our member countries without hesitation, but my sense is the political mood is changing, as the Boss has pointed out, and we need to do what we can to see that every advantage the terrorists have given us, overtly or covertly, is taken advantage of. And if you go down that path, I have no option but to let the four 'girls' on their way to France keep going, and let Ireland ramp up their environmental plant, and get on with the rest of their plan."

"But you'll incarcerate O'Cleary?" I nodded.

"Yes, I have no option given what those shells led to. But no rush; I may have a need for her in the short term."

"Scotland?" I nodded again.

"Now knowing what Scotland is all about and that they are providing guidance and direction for the 'girls', perhaps we'll let that run. My team is tracking them as we speak."

"The Island? Socotra?" Now I took a breath, after what we had learned about the Island from O'Cleary had both terrified me and given me hope.

"I think I'll plan a visit, but I'd want to take Amira at least with me, but there's no rush from what we've gathered." They held their silence, giving nothing away by their facial expressions, good poker players all. Then the Boss leaned forward, and his craggy and scared face filled the screen.

"I back your judgment one hundred percent, and I trust your instincts. Wrap this all up the best way you think gives us the maximum advantage with the politicians. I'll have your back here. You can count on that." I smiled inwardly. He was responding to my instincts and my natural desire to provide security and stability to a world fraught with tension, civil unrest, and a number of political power kegs with short fuses. But I still desperately wanted to kick some arse.

It was what we did in Section Five. The Boss sat back, and the screen was filled with the calm face of Stefarino.

"Jessica, I sense this is a hard moment for you, given what you are charged with doing. There are some very angry countries rattling their swords, and the potential for a world-wide war is great. I believe you need to keep the technology and the machinery as far away as possible from everyone else, for as long as you can. There are nineteen countries that have access to the technology so far, and over one hundred and fifty members of the UN who do not. If you now count Scotland, England, Spain, and France as players, you still have some very powerful people who will array themselves against you to gain an advantage. It is my belief that we need a massive ramp up of the production of the environmental plants, and spread them out as far and as fast as possible. Like you, I abhor politics, but countries are fighting for their very survival. And with over sixty five million people dead now due to the social unrest, the problem is only getting worse." My guts shrank at his impassioned speech, my worst fears realized in his simple words. And the death count had gone up rapidly in the last few days.

Save the children, kill the planet. Or save the children and the planet?

His warm face was replaced with Arie's, a very solemn look that caused his eyes to partially close as if he were squinting.

"Jessica, these political issues are for General Anthony and others to fight. My advice is to go about your business as you think best and minimize the release of information as best as you can. Whatever you do, you have our unqualified support." And his lined face faded back into a small square at the bottom of my screen.

"Have you secured the Irish President and his advisor?"

"Yes, they are safely tucked away," Which left my immediate team and the three I had just spoken with as the only ones who knew the potential of what the four 'girls' were doing, except for the control team in Scotland and whomever was running Socotra. I closed my mini and walked back into the conference room to see everyone seated at the table, looking relaxed, including our prisoner. There was a fresh jug of coffee in the center, so I helped myself.

"How well did you disguise what your 'girls' did in Dundalk?" O'Cleary gave me a strange look, as if I'd asked a stupid question. Her face contracted with curiosity.

"Why do you ask?"

"Miss O'Cleary, remember where you are and answer my question." I snapped at her. I couldn't help myself. Visions of the world at war and the planet burning fill my mind. It was perhaps an unintended consequence of what the women terrorists had done, but it was now quite possibly our future if we didn't control things. I noticed Anna giving me a considered look right before she nodded silently to herself. Sandra actually perked up at my hard tone, grinning like someone who had just won the lottery.

"Well, the design was to put an autotransformer every few houses or so, which makes it almost impossible for anyone to detect the additional raw current. Unless you go looking for it, you would not detect it."

"And what have you planted here in Killara Bay?"

"Until they are connected to the grid, they are undetectable, and even then the plan was to have panels and autotransformers in the line to disguise the system." Sandra was giving me a hard look as she tried to divine my line of questioning. Fay, true to her training as an FBI agent, was sitting absolutely still, absorbing everything that was being said. The lights were on in her eyes, and I suspected she was honing in on what I was getting at. She didn't let me down. She stood, called for the door, motioned to the grunts, and watched as O'Cleary was escorted out of the room again.

"You're trying to ascertain how much of what the terrorists have done might be, or might get, out into the public eye. Why?" She sat down, her body showing she was braced for a fight. Who it was with, I didn't know, but it wasn't with me. Her tone was inquisitive, not interrogative.

"Yes." She looked at me, turned to look at Sandra, looked at Anna, then back at me.

"Buggar me dead. I never thought I'd see the day when I turned into a white knight!" It was very unlike Fay to swear, very un-ladylike, but she made her point. Sandra picked it up, connected the dots, and then slumped back in her seat.

"Who are we supposed to save and from what this time around?" she asked, shaking her head from side to side. I let the silence develop for a few seconds, then I smiled, looked around at my team, and pushed the grin a little harder.

"Everyone, and from a world war!"

"So, nothing us smart girls can't do?" And she raised her eyebrows in a challenge, which caused us all to break out into tension-breaking laughter.

"Somewhere in a refugee camp one child under 10 years of age dies every eight minutes"

READ ABOUT HOW IT ALL BEGAN

The Tears of Hope - Book 1 of the trilogy

The Mentor

"We had a plan, a good plan, but like all plans, once we war-gamed it, we discovered it would not have survived the first few minutes of battle. So now we have created several plans and strategies; you might call them one for each force element. You will be self-tasked on your timetable under your command and control. You will have just one primary target, with a secondary only if the primary becomes compromised. You will be expected to work from our data and fit into our overall timing schedule. Still, the logistics, personnel, weapons, delivery systems, and exit strategy are for you to create. And only for you to know. It's your backside, and we trust you to keep it in one piece out of self-preservation if nothing else." The two people, one at the penultimate stage of a brilliant career, the other still radiating the bloom of the fast-tracked youth, sat opposite each other, the late afternoon sun creating exciting shadows across their faces.

"Imagine you committed an atrocity—an act of terrorism so vile that literally, half the world would be trying to either kill you on sight or incarcerate you forever in a deep hole, you would never see natural light again. Imagine that others, like you, committed this heinous act in parallel to you another five or even six times in the same seventy-two-hour period. Thousands, possibly tens of thousands, dead or worse, broken, maimed, or damaged and mentally scarred for the rest of their lives. Predominantly collateral damage, civilians, real innocents of the finest type, with a small mix of real targets, but sadly in the minority. Where would you hide, for the rest of your days, assuming that you were still alive at the end of it all. Where?" The general's piercing green eyes bored into the young woman, looking for the faintest sign of discomfort. The woman smiled back, completely at ease, confident and comfortable with the concepts being discussed. After all, war was just politics and the projection of power by other means, however and wherever politicians might apply it.

Their cause was possibly the most just cause ever underpinning a warlike action.

And the woman was a warrior.

Trained from an early age to instinctively follow the Code of the Warrior to the point of death.

"Sir, the only place that would be safe."

"And where would that be?" the general asked, somewhat amused by the sense of calm that seemed to exist between the two of them, given the nature of the discussion and the difference in their experience, rank, and age. The woman smiled again, twisting a small gold band over and over between one thumb and forefinger.

"Sir, the only place where people like us could survive. In plain sight."

READ THE NEXT EXCITING BOOK IN THE TEARS OF HOPE TRILOGY (BOOK 2)

The Tears of Wonder

by

Peter A. Hubbard

Flashback

The Boss stood; everyone else in the conference room ringed outside by Israeli soldiers in full combat gear sat, mostly uncomfortable on the small metal chairs. They formed a circle, so everyone could see everyone else without turning their heads, and for once, there wasn't a single presence of electronic equipment in evidence. On the contrary, a massive sign on one wall said, "מישרוממיינורטקלאמיירישכמניא !הרהזא, חטבואמומטאןקתמוהז שוע." I wondered how many years of jail time I would serve if I breached the no electronics rule, then forgot about it as the Boss started to talk.

"Firstly, thank you, Colonel, for your excellent performance in bringing down Shetani and his mercenaries and for your support in getting Mohammad bin Azaria and his henchmen." The Israeli Sgen Aluf, head of the Shayete 104 commando troop, looked anything else but happy, the stoic look on his face giving nothing away. "Colonel, Tom, I'm asking you both to leave at this point and pass out thanks to your men and women for excellent work." Tom, who Pete had forewarned that this would happen, stood, smiled, looked directly at the Boss, and saluted.

He walked out behind the Israeli commando, whose body language was anything but compliant.

"We now enter a difficult phase of our investigation, and I'm going to hand over to Captain Riley to summarize where we are and what we will do next." And he sat down in the seat vacated by Tom and looked expectantly at me. I looked around the faces I was now so familiar with, Indigo with his little smile, as if all was right with the world; Anna, a little grim-faced, probably still lagged from her flight back across the Atlantic; Pete, relaxed, although anyone who knew him would easily spot his eyes casually scanning every inch of the room. Arie, looking all his years, the past weeks had taken a heavy toll on him, yet the sparkle in his gray eyes was encouragement in itself. General Bridget Saunders, now dressed in mufti, looks like someone's mother but is not able to disguise her military bearing. She had flown over with Anna, an afterthought by the president, who was feeling distinctly not in control of her country or the events that were unraveling at such a frantic rate.

The room we were in had been organized by the local Interpol office in Tel Aviv, and in recognition of this, Senior Agent Beth Arezzo was also sitting in. As I had had the pleasure of briefing her just an hour ago, I was again impressed by the caliber of agents Interpol attracted.

At just thirty-two, she ran one of the busiest offices in the area and worked under the same duress as every other Israeli citizen from the constant rocket attacks on the city.

She was married, had a child, and dressed like a fashion model, currently wearing a tight red sheath with a purple-and-gold scarf dropping between her arms. A lightweight cotton jacket in peach completed the ensemble, no doubt concealing her weapon and credentials. She also spoke five languages like a native. I stood up, breathed in deeply, held my hands loosely in front, and relaxed as far as I could.

"We have Mohammad bin Azaria and his lawyer secured and under guard; we have left the Jesuit priest to his own devices, but we have asked him to remain to be debriefed sometime tomorrow. The electronics and intelligence we recovered from both successful attacks are now being examined, and we expect the first summary within the next hour. This meeting aims to determine exactly what we will do from here on and who will be responsible for each activity.

"While we have used paramilitary tactics against the terrorists and the mercenaries, this is, still, essentially a police action. Interpol has been commissioned by several countries as well as those represented here to discover and bring to justice the persons responsible for the attacks that were initiated last month in Italy, Jerusalem, Abu Dhabi, the United States, and, more recently, the international consortia that controlled the International Space Station.

"Our investigations uncovered the mercenaries led by Shetani, who was responsible for at least two mass bombings, the destruction of the Arabia oil field, and the destruction of some three hundred and fifty oil and gas pipelines and fracking sites. Needless to say, every country impacted by these attacks has requested us to add their support to our mandate, which we have accepted on the condition that all political interference be withheld until a satisfactory outcome has been achieved."

"And what, exactly, do you think a 'satisfactory outcome' looks like?" asked the general in a tone more suited to the parade ground than a meeting of the minds. I turned slightly to look at her and sensed the Boss flexing his shoulders, a sure sign he was going to jump in, so I paused in my reply to let him do so.

He didn't.

I continued.

"For some days, we have been working closely with one of the refugees who was groomed to participate in the developing the technology weapons used in the attacks. She quit and ran, years before the attacks were launched.

"Apart from helping us to uncover the internet destruction, she had records of her time with some of the other participants, who we are now identifying and tracking.

"When you look at the possibility of combining what the Jesuit priest can tell us, what your secretary of state can tell us, the intelligence we are now unraveling, we may well get a better understanding of how to find the refugees who did participate in the attacks."

"You'll have to go through the president to get to the Secretary," the General barked, "and you'll have to go through me to get to the president."

"We understand the circumstances. We have been briefed by both Roger and Julius." The general seemed to be thinking about something; she nodded to herself and tilted her head to one side. She looked directly at me with an intensity I felt in my bones. She held up one manicured hand, her perfect nails showing just a hint of clear polish, and ticked off her fingers, one by one.

"So, firstly, you have identified and taken out of play a mercenary terrorist crew in Canada responsible for shutting off the oil and gas pipelines as well as destroying the fracking sites across northern America and Canada. Secondly," as another finger flicked up, "you seemed to have solved the UAV attacks on the sports arenas, at least in the US." I held her eyes, determined to hear everything she had to say before I acknowledged anything.

"Then you have masterminded an attack on Arabia, forcing the third regime change in two weeks, destroying the mercenary terrorist leader Shetani in the process." She watched me for any reaction and saw none; I played poker with people so hard to read you had to actually rely on the cards you were dealt! A wan smile crossed her eyes, her thin lips struggling to follow.

"Fourthly, you have identified, located, and captured the banker and prime suspect in the organization of all the attacks and currently have him here somewhere under guard." I held her eyes as hard as I could, not giving any sign of acknowledgment. The silence in the room was deafening; I could almost hear everyone breathing. She wasn't exactly attacking us, but her tonality suggested she was after something, but I wasn't sure what it might be. I nodded, just once, to see what she would say next. Her hand opened up so all fingers could be seen as she ticked off the last on her list.

"The problem I'm having is seeing exactly where a military action starts and stops, and a police one takes over." The tension in the room ratcheted up a notch, and I saw Pete stiffen out of the corner of my eye and Indigo visibly lean forward as if to pounce on the general. Before I could answer, the Boss stood up again, rolled his shoulders as if preparing for a physical fight, and motioned for me to take my seat.

"General, as you would know, my unit within Interpol is authorized to engage and utilize military forces as and when we see fit. As you know, our standing guard is made up of US Special Forces on loan to us from the Pentagon.

"The two attacks in the desert were led by an Israeli Colonel supported by Israeli commandos, whom you have been introduced to, and Interpol simply provided an observer in each of those two attacks. And before you point it out, yes, we had more boots on the ground when we took down bin Azaria; the situation was judged to warrant it. And don't forget the Canadians and all the other countries who have used lethal force in attacking the various arms of Shetani's network of mercenaries, including your very own, on several occasions, all without any Interpol presence." The look he gave the general was anything but contrite; the edges of his face would have cut glass. If there was one thing the Boss hated, it was Monday morning quarterbacking. The general, to her credit, immediately sat back as far as her little metal chair would allow and shook her head.

"Colonel, I apologize if it seemed I was attacking your tactics. I fully realize we would not be as far down the comeback road as we are without the excellent efforts of Interpol and your team. I was just trying to see where the line in the sand was; please put it down to bad manners and bloody-mindedness." The Boss visibly relaxed, and with one simple gesture, the tension drifted out of the room. Pete sat back, Indigo relaxed, and even I felt some existential crisis had been avoided. But I still did not know what was behind her verbal attack.

"General, we're all a little wound up, and I suspect if you have had as little sleep as my people, more than just a little tired. The fact remains, and I freely admit it, we have used national troops for various parts of our investigation, with the overt approval and under the direct control of each country involved. In the case of the mercenaries, we provided intelligence to some sixteen countries, and each country then dealt with them as they saw fit—the US is one of those countries. All within our mandate. And I took the measure of checking in with the director of your FBI, NSA, and CIA, and even yourself and the president, as warranted before we initiated any direct action." He flexed his shoulders again, looked down at his scuffed boots, raised his eyes in surprise, then looked up back at the group. Maybe he had meant to clean them?

"So as for a satisfactory outcome, while we have involved the politicians at every step so far, what we do next will be determined by what evidence and data we can analyze and which direction it suggests we move in. And to answer your unasked question, no, we may not collaborate with anyone nation-state at that point. The next moves will be an Interpol police action, full stop."

"You suspect a nation-state of masterminding the attacks, or at least covert support of the banker?" she asked.

"We have from the very start. The fact that the earliest attack on the computer systems in the US and Europe took place on the back of the Y2K debacle, now over twenty-five years ago, which would make the women we are chasing just out of nappies at that time, means that someone was setting all this up well before the use of the refugees was even thought of. Or, at the very least, concurrently. We have a statement from the Jesuit priest that the discussion regarding taking the children occurred around twenty years ago; we can't be definite, but we might get closer to the actual date once we chat with him tomorrow.

LOOK FOR BOOK THREE OF THE TEARS OF HOPE TRILOGY

The Tears of Joy

We had chased terrorists together from continent to continent. We had escaped certain death together more than once.

And then we had personally executed unarmed, confined prisoners together, shot them in the head and in the heart, and left their bodies to rot in a three hundred year old subterranean prison underneath a beautiful Island in Venice, where thousands of tourists once walked in the evanescent sunshine.

But the world had changed, thanks to a cadre of women terrorists who had started their lives as abandoned, parentless refugees on the worlds' scrapheap. No oil, no gas, no coal, but unlimited power from the sun, had literally changed the face of the Earth in less than six months.

No internet, few computers, or anything electronic that worked, changed the way we communicated, reminiscent of what we did as a species back in the 1950s and '60s.

Local, very much not global, except for certain military and private networks that had been protected at the time of the worldwide hack.

And millions upon millions of innocent people were killed by panic, chaos, and home grown militia that forced migration around the world on a scale never before seen.

But thanks to the invention of a nanomachine by a brilliant young Israeli genius, herself a refugee, the world was slowly regaining hope as devices able to convert the sun's power more efficiently than ever thought possible popped up around the country.

That was the good news.

The better news was that Sandra 'just call me Sally', my partner in crime and the bubbliest person I had ever had the privilege to be around, and I were now enjoying the tropical sun together, sipping cold drinks in long glasses with little umbrellas in them, the images of the executions and what followed now just a dim memory.

"Did you get the banks to release the funds from the terrorists' accounts?" The Boss, lying flat on his stomach, his lounge chair buckling from his weight, squeaked as he moved his head to look at me. Behind him, Pete, recovering from three bad bullet wounds, was asleep on his back, snoring slightly, while his inamorata, a world-class cellist, slept beside him. If you didn't know, you would only see a group of friends relaxing around the pool without a care in the world.

If you tried to come over and be our friends, large well-dressed people would politely stop you, throw a million words at you in Italian so fast your head would ring, then turn you around to where you had started. If there was one thing other than his monstrous espresso machine that Indigo guarded with his life was us, which was stupendous because it allowed us to act like normal people when we were anything but.

"Yes. We had to threaten them with Red Notices, but Sandra got the last of the funds early this morning, and the monks now have several billion to play with. I have given them a list of what we need funds for and requested another fifty minicomputers. Stefarino was very happy, a lot of his private funding dried up because of the terrorist attacks, and he is linking our Italian headquarters to his cavern. He sends his regards and wants to have a conversation with you at some time." I received a grunt for my trouble and decided to drink more of the wonderful green thing that sloshed around in my glass. It tasted like a tropical fruit bomb but had a sensitive kick on the palate that was unmistakably a high-quality rum base of some sort.

I looked up as Indigo returned, accompanied by a beautiful woman, who I recognized as Fay Remer, our latest recruit from the FBI. Like Sandra, she was positively glowing, having just completed the Interpol boot camp, which had the driest international legal subject matter in the known universe. She had then completed the physical training for attachment to Section Five, and that was obviously what had put the color in her cheeks. The fact that she was dressed in the skimpiest bikini with a flowing silk thing over her shoulders didn't fool me for a second.

"Commander, great to see you. At last, thanks for the invite." A guard hastily set up another sun lounge, and she plopped a handbag big enough to hold a child, a towel, a smaller bag which I assumed held her weapon and credentials, then a huge floppy straw hat.

"Intend on staying long?" Sandra asked, mumbling over her drink, as she shielded her face from the sun with one delicate hand as she looked up at Fay. Fay just laughed, plonked down on the lounge, and pointed to my drink.

'I'll have one of those, thanks, Indigo." He beamed at her. I promise you, his whole face lit up.

"Sarà un piacere per me, e scusa questo maleducato qui, la farò rimuovere se lo desideri!"

"Yeah, you can try!" Sandra didn't exactly mumble, but the humor came through, and obviously, Indigo's invitation to throw her out of the pool area hadn't concerned her in the least. Indigo took the cowards way out when faced with determined women and left to organize Fay's drink.

"How was the training?"

"Excellent. The HALO (High Altitude, Low Opening) jumps were the best, and the one we did in daylight was over Sardinia, and that's a sight I won't forget in a hurry."

"What about the weapons training? Learn anything new?" Sandra was getting into the swing of it now, sitting up next to Fay, looking like a supermodel in her multi-colored top, baseball cap, and aviator glasses. Between her and Fay, I would forever look like the ugly sister.

"Yes. How much the modern squad weapons weigh, and how loud a flash-bang is without ear protection!" They both laughed. In my day, the big event was surviving the gas chamber without a mask, but that test now seemed old school.

I let them bubble on and turned back to the Boss.

"Have you spoken to Roger lately?" Roger was the head of the FBI and a lifelong friend of the Boss's, and had been one of the instigators in involving Interpol in solving the terrorist attacks. He looked at me with one eye open, the other shut, and it squeezed his face into an even more distorted look than his usual scarred appearance.

"Earlier today. All good on his end, they have three plants up and running, and they are happy to maintain the status quo for the time being." I gave him my hardest look over the top of my sunglasses, but half-naked, with a silly drink in my hand, it was difficult to pull off bad arse. He just closed his open eye and shrugged, causing the lounge to squeak again.

"What do you mean 'for the time being'?"

"You don't goad the bear in his own cave and expect to come out unscratched." I settled back. To a certain extent, I had anticipated what the Americans might do by placing the UN in charge of the international distribution and installation of the ecological plants that had been designed and built by the terrorists. And left the nanomachines firmly in the hands of Israel and Amira, who was now one of our agents attached to the Israeli Security Service. Or, in truth, was an Israeli agent attached to Interpol.

"I had hoped that they would at least play the gracious savior for a while longer." He turned to face me, both eyes open this time, his serious look anchored between his scars.

"They took a huge hit-the Catholic and Jewish, and for that matter, Muslim communities in the States are quite large, West Point was an attack on their very militaristic soul, and the smart way the terrorists pushed the immigration of thousands of refugees on them still rankles." I nodded, put my drink aside, and considered my next move. I pulled my towel off my lap and dived into the pool.

The water was crystal clear, comfortably cool, and invigorating. I lazily swam a few laps, letting my muscles warm up, testing my recovering shoulder a little, wishing this quiet time could last a little longer. But the Boss had been pulling in information from all over the world, and all his nefarious contacts in the deepest and darkest places on the planet said the same thing.

In the vacuum created by the terrorist attacks, the lack of fuel, water, and food, and an almost complete lack of international will, was driving the creation of a whole new subset of bad behaviors.

And there was a new actor on the block with the resources and the skills to cause several of our supporting member countries to become very nervous.

I smelt a hard stop to our little vacation down the road.

And in countries where camels, horses, and donkeys were viewed as state-of-the-art transportation, and hard men and women made their living off the land, the balance of power had once again shifted away from technology and civilization to campfires and word of mouth. And no intelligence agency in the world had ever been particularly good at intercepting the spoken word, often in dialects unknown outside of tribal boundaries, without their agents literally losing their heads in the process.

Afghanistan was the center of it all. In the half-decade since the American withdrawal, it seemed that an endless series of new versions of ISIS had erupted, spewed their venom and hatred on anyone in their sights, mostly unarmed and innocent civilians, then self-destructed like one of their suicide bombers. But there were rumors emerging of a newly formed group, disciplined, as yet unnamed, and unidentified, working with some sophisticated weaponry. Didn't know what that was all about and didn't want to until it was on our radar.

We had just spent shy of two months fighting to save the planet, literally, and we needed to decompress, heal our wounds, find our centers as people, not puppets, and regain our balance. When you killed a person one-on-one, no matter the circumstances or how righteous that kill was, it affected you deeply, and you couldn't just shrug it off and pretend nothing had changed.

Unless you were a narcist and a sociopath. And if you were, you would not be working for the world's preeminent anticriminal and antiterrorist organization, Interpol.

I let the water flow over me like a liquid blanket, upped my tempo, pleased with the lack of any twinges or discomfort in my shoulder. The doctors had done a good job, and the physiotherapist that had been assigned to me, straight out of an East German gulag, I swear, had worked me to the bone, cheerfully destroying any excuse I came up with to evade her massive hands. The only good thing I had to hang onto was Pete telling me his recovery from his wounds had been worse than mine. But he didn't have that haunted look he had just a month ago, so he must be close to fully recovered.

The next thing I knew, I was sinking to the bottom of the pool, the sound of crashing water filled my ears, and the rolled-up body of Pete was sitting on my back. We both bobbed back up to the surface, spluttering and laughing like loons, most unladylike, and certainly not the done thing in a prestigious military organization. I funneled water into my hands and pushed it into his face, having the time of my life. His laughter lifted my spirits. I had been worried about him, he had been shot three times while protecting me, and while I was not the cause, I always felt I was the root. Being around me could be a very hazardous occupation.

"Children, children, play fair. No hurting each other unless you mean it!" Pete ignored the Boss, and reached over and dunked me again. Now I had options. I could punch him in his manhood, pull him under and drown him, or just let him have his way with me.

Seeing his live-in partner of some fifteen years looking at us over her blue-tinted glasses, with a smirk on her face, lying back and talking, it seemed the best option. He let me up, still laughing like a loon but staring to look like the shooter I had entrusted my life to on more than one occasion. The new scars were only obvious from the old ones because they still looked like painted-on pale, puckered healing holes on his otherwise suntanned skin, and his ropy chest muscles flexed and rippled in a very nice manner.

It was hard to believe that it was less than a month ago that I had helped load him onto an Israeli C-17 with blood running freely down his chest from three bullet holes that clustered just below his collarbone. And I had been shot as well, but that seemed trivial at the time. And for the life of me, I couldn't remember why.

I drifted to the side of the pool, completely relaxed for the first time in days.

"You look relaxed."

"I am. How're the wounds?"

"Getting me plenty of sympathy, Jenny and I are off back home tomorrow. The Boss has made it clear I'm off calling for at least the next six weeks."

"You'll go stark raving mad," I said, climbing out of the pool. He grabbed the side of the pool and levered himself up and out with a nimble twist of his lean body that had more scares than I remembered. But then, I hadn't seen him naked for quite a while.

"Has Jenny got any concerts planned?" He looked over at his life partner, smiled when she grinned at him and turned back to look at me.

"Yes, one in New Zealand, a benefit for their recovery program. They have resettled nearly two thousand children in the site they built on the Wairoa River at Dargaville. The New Zealand government has approved the construction of ten more townships spread across the country, and that means that another twenty thousand girls will be taken in. There are families putting their hands up from as far away as Samoa."

"Chalk one up to Mohammad bin Azaria and 'Helen.'" I didn't let the bitterness creep into my voice, but it took all my effort not to. He gave me a hard look, but I suspect he saw what was under my less-than-warm response. He just nodded and walked back to Jenny. I reached for a towel and sat back on my couch. The Boss had one eye open again, a sure sign I was going to get blitzed.

Not quite.

"One thing I picked up from Arie this morning, you might find interesting. Just as the French promised the world that they would remove the radioactivity from the Arabian oil fields, persons unknown clagged up the wellheads all the way across the desert and shut it down permanently." I sat up, this was news, and it might mean that we had missed one of the mercenary terrorist groups.

"Do we know who did it?"

"No. And the French, as you can imagine, are seriously pissed about it."

"Why? Surely the radioactivity was enough. Those fields were out of action for thousands of years."

"Seems like the tech heads got it wrong. They changed their forecast to less than thirty years, and within a week of that being made public, the well heads and pipelines were attacked with the nanomachines, and that ended that."

"Who had that capacity? That would have taken five or six simultaneous attacks across different countries, those fields were the biggest in the world."

"Maybe, but out of play since yesterday. Think about who had the nano technology-the canisters from Canada, the ones we collected. Amira estimates that it only needed around four to do the job. And no, before you ask, she hasn't been cooking up nano bugs out the back of Mossad, and she assures me that the nanomachines in use in the plants would have a different effect on raw oil. No, this was someone left over from the original attacks, someone we missed, being very selective and very, very fast." I thought about it and couldn't see how it could have been done without state-level resources and, most of all, a supply of nanomachines. Who? How? Did it matter? There weren't any oil or gas pipes or coal fields anywhere as far as I knew that hadn't already been attacked, so was this a once-off?

For all the books and information go to https://linktr.ee/peterahubbard